Memory

A Tale of Pride and Prejudice
Volume 1: Lasting Impressions

Linda Wells

Memory: Volume 1, Lasting Impressions, A Tale of Pride and Prejudice
Copyright © 2010 Linda Wells

Cover Images © Dmitry Mikhaylov (front), Roger Asbury (back), David Kay (front Vol. 2): Dreamstime.com

ISBN: 1453698388
EAN-13: 9781453698389

lindawellsbooknut@gmail.com

To

**Catherine and Tania
Bill and Rick**

And to all of the readers at the Meryton Literary Society and Austen Underground, thank you for your exceptional support.

Main Cast of Characters Volume 1

Darcy
George d. 25 September 1807
Fitzwilliam b. 2 October 1784
Georgiana b. April 1796
Lady Anne d. 1796
Four deceased siblings

Fitzwilliam
Lord (Henry) & Lady (Helen) of
Matlock married 1774
Stephen (Viscount Layton) b. 1776
married 1806 to Alicia
Richard b. 1783
Audrey b. 1785 m. Robert
Singleton

Bennet
Thomas and Francine
Jane b. 1789
Elizabeth b. 16 August 1791
Mary b. August 1793
Catherine b. August 1794
Lydia b. June 1796

Gardiner
Edward and Marianne
Benjamin b. 1804
Amy b. 1807
Paul b. 1808

Bingley
Louisa b. 1785 married to Gerald
Hurst 1805
Caroline b. 1787
Charles b. 1788

De Bourgh
Lady Catherine
Anne b. 1786

Others
George Wickham
Lord and Lady Creary
Victoria Gannon
William Collins

Lucas
Sir William Lucas and Lady Lucas
Charlotte b. 1785
Robert b. 1786
Maria b. 1793
Two other brothers

Friends of the families
Jeffrey Harwick (wife died mid-late
April 1807)
Evangeline Harwick Carter b. 1784
widowed 1806
Lord and Lady Moreland (Stewart)
Daniel Stewart b. 1784
Laura Stewart b. 1788
Mr. and Mrs. Robert Henley
Julia Henley

Servants
Mrs. Somers (Nanny Kate)
Mr. Foster (butler, Darcy House)
Mrs. Mercer (housekeeper, Darcy
House)
Mrs. Reynolds (Housekeeper
Pemberley)
Mr. Nichols (Steward, Pemberley)
Adams (Darcy's Valet)
Millie (Elizabeth's maid)

Chapter 1

"Fitzwilliam! Welcome home!" George Darcy stood from the chair behind his desk in the study of Darcy House in London and greeted his son with a warm embrace. Still holding his shoulders he stepped back and beamed. "I missed you, Son!"

Darcy smiled and laughed. "Thank you Father, I missed you as well. It is so good to be home."

"Well, sit down, sit down, I want to hear all about it!" Mr. Darcy settled back into the chair and rested his folded hands over his ample belly.

Darcy took a seat, and although he had just arrived after nine months of travel on his Grand Tour and dearly wished to relax in a bath, he could not deny his father's request. "Where shall I begin? You received my letters?"

"Of course, I imagine that I will continue to receive them for weeks now that you are home."

"That is very likely." He stopped and knit his brow, slowly realizing that his father's belly had not been nearly so large when he left, and looking closely at his face, he saw that his skin and eyes had a yellowish cast. "Father, are you well?"

The great smile faded and was replaced with resignation. "I had hoped you would not notice so soon. I believe that Georgiana remains ignorant, probably because she sees me every day." He sighed. "I did not want you to return and have to face this."

"What is wrong?" Darcy said urgently and sat forward.

Never one to varnish the truth, Mr. Darcy simply delivered the news. "I am dying, Fitzwilliam. It began about a month ago, and now . . . now I am this bilious shade of yellow. My liver, the physician tells me."

"Surely something can be done!" Darcy cried.

"No Son, I will not survive this. I am resigned to that and in many ways I welcome it. At last I will be with my dear Anne again." He smiled back at a portrait of himself with his wife then sat up and grasped Darcy's arm as he saw the myriad of emotions fly over his face. Denial. Anger. Fear. They were all there. "I accept that my time approaches, and I am grateful that you are so prepared to take my place."

"I am not at all prepared! How can I fill your place?"

"You know everything, Son. You just have not had to draw upon your knowledge. When you have need of it, all will come to mind. I wish to die at Pemberley."

"You will not die!!" Darcy said desperately.

"Yes, I will." Mr. Darcy said calmly. "I want to make the journey in two days. I want to teach you everything that I can before the end."

"Father . . ."

"Tomorrow our solicitor will come to go over the will and legal papers with you. Your uncle and Fitzwilliam will come as well. I have decided to give guardianship of Georgiana to both of you boys, not because I do not trust you or believe in you, but just to give you some more support. Of course, you will be the primary guardian. She will remain with you."

"I do not want to hear this." Darcy whispered, staring at his twisting hands.

Mr. Darcy ploughed on. "Son, there is more. Your Aunt Catherine has already come to me, suggesting that it will be best for you to be married; to give Georgiana a sister to guide her since you will be so busy learning your new role. She is demanding that you marry Anne, and claims it was a wish of your mother's."

Darcy's head snapped up. "NO!"

"I told her in no uncertain terms that I will not put such a choice to you. Your mother never wished for an alliance, so when I am gone and Catherine undoubtedly brings this up, *Know* that no agreement was ever reached on this subject. Of course, you are free to marry her if that is your wish."

"NO!"

"Very well Son, I understand." He laughed.

"How can you feel such levity?" Darcy said angrily.

"Son . . ."

"No . . . I cannot . . ." Darcy stared at his hands again, he felt powerless.

Mr. Darcy stood and placed his hand on his son's shoulder. "I need to lie down, and I think that you need some time alone." He squeezed and Darcy's hand came up to grasp his father's, and let go. He heard the door close, and knew not how long he sat there, staring down at the floor. A knock finally tore him from the thoughts that filled his numb mind. He wiped his face and straightened. "Come."

"Sir, these letters came for you in your absence."

Darcy looked at the butler blankly and murmured, "Thank you, Foster." He sat down behind the desk in his father's chair and drew the pile forward. There were letters from friends, letters of little consequence, invitations, news, nothing truly important. His eyes passed over to the letters lying on the desk, his father's letters. Letters of business, letters affecting the lives of hundreds of people, potentially thousands; the reach of Pemberley was enormous. It went so far beyond the livelihood of the servants and tenants. He swallowed and read an open letter, then picked up his father's half-written reply and whispered, "I am not prepared for this."

Raising his eyes, their gaze rested on a beautiful landscape hanging across the room. It depicted Pemberley on a summer day. He had always looked at this painting with pride. It was home. Suddenly it was something more. It was responsibility; it was his future, his ancestors' work, his children's security. His gaze passed again to the desk where a miniature of his mother and another of his sister sat. The weight of what was to come fell upon his shoulders. "My God, what am I to do?"

He wiped his eyes again and slowly rose. At least Georgiana was busy with her governess. He would not have to assume a happy countenance for her yet. It was still early in the afternoon, and it was sunny, he needed to walk. Physical activity had always helped him to calm. It was invaluable when he lost his mother, and it seemed as though exercise would again aid him through the loss of his father. Donning his hat he found his way deep into Hyde Park, wandering blindly, just allowing the movement to keep the jumbled thoughts of fear and inadequacy at bay for a time.

Darcy finally stopped his pointless walking and sank onto a bench, dully watching the people pass. The sound of a feminine laugh cut through the fog that surrounded him and he looked up to notice a lovely blonde girl with a gentle smile gracing her lips standing directly across from him. He was struck by her resemblance to his sister and watched her, wanting to hear that warm laughter again.

"Lizzy, not everyone is as good a walker as you, please; can we not return now?" The blonde girl pleaded, exasperation was evident in her voice.

"Oh Jane, we have been in London for weeks, and you wish to deny me this taste of freedom? I have not been able to enjoy nature since we arrived!"

"You have walked the park in Gracechurch Street every day!" She reminded her sister.

"That is nothing to this glorious place." Elizabeth opened her arms, hugging the park with her gesture, and a wide smile appeared.

"You will never be a city girl, Lizzy." Jane laughed softly.

The sound of her laughter disconcerted Darcy, and he turned his head away from the first girl to take in her companion, a slightly younger girl, and so different. Her hair was dark and her eyes were warm, dancing with joy and sparkling with amusement. She laughed again and his heart skipped, *this* was the source of the musical sound.

"Come Lizzy, we should return to Aunt Gardiner, she will not be happy with us wandering off like this. London is not Hertfordshire."

"I know; I just miss home so much." Elizabeth said with a sigh. "All that I like of London are the bookshops." Darcy smiled, he felt the same way.

"Do you miss Longbourn so much?" Jane asked.

"I suppose that I miss my solitude, well, that is, the solitude I achieve on my walks. I am enjoying meeting new people, but I truly miss just wandering off with a book and becoming lost in the words." Elizabeth looked around and smiled at the beautiful setting, then noticed the handsome young man. She walked closer to Jane. "That gentleman is watching us." She whispered.

"What gentleman?" Jane whispered back.

"The one there, in the blue coat." Elizabeth, thinking that she would disconcert that man from his staring, locked her eyes with his. Suddenly she could not look away from their penetrating blue. *He looks so sad!*

Darcy swallowed. *She must be so young, but she is not dressed as a child, so she must be out, but she seems so young . . .* He was never good with approaching strangers, but he wanted to speak to her, very much. She had said many intriguing things.

"Fitzwilliam!" He started and looked up, tearing his gaze from Elizabeth. Georgiana Darcy ran up and he stood to wrap his arms around her. "Oh, Brother! You have come home! I missed you so!"

"I missed you as well, Georgiana. How much you have grown! How did you find me?"

"Mr. Foster said that you were in the park and I asked Nanny Kate if we could look for you!" She said excitedly.

A breathless older woman finally appeared. "Forgive us Mr. Darcy; there was no holding her back once she knew you had arrived."

"It is quite all right, Mrs. Somers. I left unexpectedly." He smiled down at his sister, then looked back to Elizabeth. The two girls were walking away, and looking down he closed his eyes for a moment then lifted them back up. Elizabeth had turned, and was watching him. She gave him a warm smile, and he found himself returning it. He watched her turn away and followed her as she and her sister disappeared from view. Georgiana's chatter recalled his attention, and he allowed her to guide him back to the house.

After finally ridding himself of his travel clothes and bathing, Darcy returned to his father's study where he found the man bent over his desk, answering the abandoned correspondence. He noticed that his own letters remained, but were neatly piled in a corner. He quietly took a seat and watched. Mr. Darcy nodded and smiled, and returned to his work, steadily scratching out his response. Darcy had a sudden vision that soon he would be the one with the burden to carry, and wondered for the seemingly millionth time that day if he was capable.

Finishing the letter, Mr. Darcy set down his pen. "Son, you see before you the last piece of business correspondence I will answer. From this moment on, you will take over this task."

"I?" Darcy said with a startled expression. "But, I would not have the first idea how to . . ."

"Would you prefer to learn this suddenly, after I am gone? No Son, I want you to begin to take on my duties while I am here to correct and guide you. From now on you will read the letters, and tell me what your reply would be, and I will tell you what I would have said. Then you will write the letter. I want our contacts to know that you are the one to rely upon now."

"Father, I . . ." Darcy saw his father's steely gaze, and knew that he would brook no opposition. "Yes, sir."

"Very well." He sat back and regarded his son. Already he could see him feeling the weight of all that he was about to inherit. "How was your walk? I understand that Georgiana ferreted you out?"

Darcy laughed softly. "There was no stopping her. I will have to give her the presents I had packed away after dinner."

"Oh yes, she will be relentless in their pursuit, as any woman is." He smiled, and tilted his head. "Did the solitude help?"

"No. I find this so difficult to comprehend; I cannot accept this news so easily. I thought it would be years, decades before I would . . ." He stopped, as he felt the emotion rising, and suppressed it. He closed his eyes and the sound of a warm laugh filled his head. "Father, do you know a family named Gardiner?"

"Gardiner?" He said, surprised. "No, I cannot say that I do. Why do you ask?"

"Do you know Gracechurch Street?" Darcy continued.

"Yes, it is in Cheapside, by the river. That is where all of the warehouses are. I know that the tradesmen live in that area, convenient to their businesses." He watched Darcy's face fall.

"A tradesman could have a relative that is a gentleman, could he not?" He said softly.

"Of course, you know how marriages work, the first son would get the estate and the second is left to find his way, army, church, law, the same would work for any other family." He leaned forward. "What are these questions about?"

"Father, you mentioned Aunt Catherine's desire that I marry Anne, and you know my reply, and I am grateful for your support." He paused. "I know that I am expected to marry and produce an heir to secure Pemberley . . ."

"Certainly, but it must not be done tomorrow. Are you hoping to find someone before I die, to gain my blessing? I assure you that is not necessary. You know what you are raised to do, Fitzwilliam. You will choose from among the brightest jewels of society, and I have no doubt that you will find a fine mistress for Pemberley. I do hope, very much, that you will have the supreme joy of loving your wife, as I did your mother. That is my greatest hope for you."

"But what is more important to you, that I find a woman to love or one who is considered suitable for society?"

"You know as well as I do the demands that will be placed on any woman you marry. She must be one who will be able to fulfil her role successfully." He wrinkled his brow and watched Darcy's hands slowly twisting together. "Have you made an acquaintance in your brief hours home from your travels? Or is this someone you have pined for while away? And, I cannot help but wonder if this lady is not of our circle for you to ask such unusual questions."

Darcy did not answer and his father watched him carefully. "Son." He waited until Darcy finally looked up. "I trust you to make the correct decision in this."

"But what is the correct decision?" He searched his father's eyes.

"You have been raised a certain way, with certain expectations. But remember, you must always be prepared for the unexpected to arise."

"What does that mean?" He looked at his father anxiously.

"It means allow room for your heart, as well as your head." Mr. Darcy smiled sadly, seeing his son did not understand, and hearing Georgiana in the hallway, he stood. "Come, enough of this speculation, let us go eat this welcome home feast the staff has planned for you, and regale me and your sister with your adventures." Darcy stood and his father placed his arm around his shoulder for a slight embrace, and together they left the room.

ELIZABETH SAT WITH her aunt and held her infant cousin Amy in her arms. She smiled down at her. "She is so perfect."

"She is a good girl." Mrs. Gardiner smiled. "I could not ask for a better behaved child, well maybe I have earned it after her elder brother was born." She laughed and looked over at her three-year-old son Benjamin. "He is unusually quiet today."

"I think that he is feeling bad for making Jane cry." Elizabeth whispered. "When he pulled her hair during their game he seemed quite taken aback when she yelped."

"He will like to tease his sister, I think."

"I imagine he will be a fierce protector of his siblings." Elizabeth said thoughtfully. "Did you notice how he stood in front of Amy with his hand on her blanket when you presented the children to those visitors the other day?" She sighed. "I wish I had an elder brother, or any brother for that matter."

"I wonder if your wishing has anything to do with your mother's determination to marry you and Jane off as soon as possible?" Mrs. Gardiner said gently.

Elizabeth rolled her eyes. "I felt terrible for Jane when that man was writing her sonnets two years ago, but now that I am fifteen and out, I suppose that I am to be in the same situation. I am just grateful that Papa roused himself from his bookroom long enough to notice what was happening and put his foot down. Poor Jane would have been married at fifteen and likely have a little one in her arms right now if he had not. She would have just gone silently along with Mama's scheme."

Mrs. Gardiner studied her niece; she was very observant of her parents' marriage and far wiser than most girls her age. Her mind belied the fact that she was still a child, but Mrs. Gardiner chose to address her as an adult. "She feels her duty to her family, and your mother feels the fear of losing Longbourn to the entailment if your father passes prematurely. What would become of you all is a serious concern."

"But why should that force Jane; or me for that matter, to marry simply for security?" She lifted her chin. "I will only marry for love. Nobody will force me to accept the inevitable simply because it is."

"I doubt that anyone could force you to do anything you did not already have a mind to do, Lizzy." Mrs. Gardiner laughed. "However, I also feel that it will be some time before you have to face such a decision. Your father is quite healthy."

"Besides nobody would want me anyway." She said softly, but not enough that her words were not heard.

"Why do you say that?"

"It is nothing." She looked down at the baby's face; her own clouded over with the memory of her mother's unending pronouncements of her lack of beauty and refinement. Mrs. Gardiner watched as her lively niece's face reflected her insecurity and youth, and guessing her trouble, now addressed the child.

"You are very young yet Lizzy, soon you will blossom just as Jane has. Your mother should have waited another two years for you to be out. This should be Jane's first season, but clearly worry over her and your family's security is what has driven her to push you both out so soon."

"I will be sixteen in a month." She stated softly and saw her aunt's nod. "Well, at least I am permitted to wear some pretty dresses now." She sighed and looked down at the cotton gown. "That is something, I suppose."

"That it is, my dear." Mrs. Gardiner tilted her head. "I heard you and Jane whispering in the carriage. Did you attract a young man's eye in the park?"

Elizabeth blushed. "I think so, but he did not have a chance to speak to us, it seemed that his sister arrived before he could and they left."

"It would not have been proper for him to speak to you without an introduction." Mrs. Gardiner saw her resigned nod and continued, "But it proves that you are not so displeasing to look upon; does it not?"

Her chin lifted, and she smiled. "I suppose not! Thank you, Aunt!" Amy awoke and started squirming, and Mrs. Gardiner took her back. Elizabeth stood. "I will be upstairs if you need me."

She started to run then checked herself, *a lady walks,* and entered the small bedchamber she had been assigned for her visit. Sitting down at the writing desk, she opened up the journal her father had given her for Christmas, and filling a quill with ink, bit her lip and began a new page.

25 June 1807

Today Jane, Aunt Gardiner, and I went to shop on Bond Street. It was such an adventure to look in the windows of those fashionable shops, but I loved the bookshop the most. I could have spent the day there very happily, but Jane and Aunt forced me to go after only a half-hour. We had tea then finally I got to see Hyde Park. What a beautiful place! I think that I loved it almost as much as the bookshop! But the best part of today was when I received my first attention from a man. He was very tall, and so handsome, with black hair that he wore down to touch his collar, and such lovely blue eyes that just seemed to see right through me! At first I thought what an arrogant man he was to stare at me so blatantly, but when I looked closer he seemed so sad. I wondered what was wrong and I was working up my courage to speak to him when a girl arrived. I think she was Lydia's age. She called him Fitzwilliam. What a funny name. I thought it was his surname, but then a woman approached and called him Mr. Darcy, so it must be his Christian name. And the girl was Georgiana. She was his sister, I am sure. He is much older than me, I think, or maybe it only seemed that way because he had the weight of the world on his shoulders. I hope he is well. I did smile at him. I should like to make him laugh, maybe someday I will. I will never forget his smile. It was all for me.

Elizabeth put down her pen and reading over her entry, giggled. "He did smile just for me! Men always smile at Jane, she is so beautiful, how can they not? But this man is the first one to look only at me!" She sighed happily. "Thank you, Fitzwilliam!"

AFTER THE EVENING meal, Darcy sat with his father and sister and handed out his gifts. He enjoyed seeing Georgiana's happiness with the dolls he had purchased in Italy; and her worry over the sheet music he had found. She was only starting to play well, and the music he had chosen was not easy, which was of course done purposely. "I look forward to hearing this played for my birthday gift, Georgiana. That is just over three months from now, so it gives you plenty of time to learn it."

"That is a good thing Fitzwilliam, because I do not know how to even approach this!" She looked up at him with worry. "This is so difficult!"

"Perhaps we can find you a music master to work with you when we return to Pemberley." He smiled and looked at his father. "I wonder if Mrs. Hopkins still gives lessons."

Mr. Darcy chuckled. "I wonder if she does, you were certainly a challenging student."

"I was determined."

"You were stubborn as a mule. It is a wonder she stuck with you."

"I wanted to please Mother. She said that she hoped I would learn." Darcy said very softly, but Mr. Darcy heard and smiled.

"And so you did." Their eyes met and Darcy looked away.

"It has been an exhausting day, if you will excuse me, I think I will retire." He stood and kissed Georgiana's cheek. "Good night dear, it is so good to be home with you again." He turned to his father and bowed. "Good night, Father."

"Good night, Son." Mr. Darcy watched him go, and saw his shoulders slump as he left the room, and wondered over how he could ease the burdens to come for him.

Darcy entered his chambers, the ones he had taken after leaving the nursery, and after his valet finished preparing him for the night, stood and leaned on the window frame, staring out at the dark street. Eventually the sound of his sister and father retiring broke him from his silent reverie and he walked over to his writing desk, opened his journal, and pausing to gather his thoughts, began to write.

25 June 1807

Today I returned home from my Grand Tour only to learn that my brief time of frivolity as a gentleman is now over. I have reached the age of two and twenty and at this moment I feel that I am closer to the age of two and eighty. My father has told me he is dying, and I am to take over Pemberley immediately. God help me.

I can barely comprehend this news. Yesterday afternoon I stepped onto the docks after nine months away, full of the wonders that I had seen. I knew that my return to London meant that I must at last take my place in society, and I had been steeling myself for the attention I knew I would draw as father's heir. I have both dreaded and anticipated this time, but I thought that I would have my father with me as my guide. I pray that his physician is wrong, and the malady is just a passing event. I have never recovered from Mother's passing, what will I do if Father leaves me as well? What will I be for Georgiana? Will I destroy Pemberley with my poor management?

I walked today in Hyde Park and tried to clear my head from the overwhelming news. I saw nothing of the beauty, and felt only the fear that I would fail. And then I heard a sound that broke through my pain. A laugh, so warm, so musical, it lifted my eyes from my boots and I saw before me a girl, smiling and laughing, and looking at me. Her name is Lizzy, which must be for Elizabeth. She is from Hertfordshire and an estate called Longbourn. She has relatives in London named Gardiner who live in Gracechurch Street. She loves walking and books. She is very young. And she smiled at me today. I hope that someday I might return the gift.

Darcy set down his pen and read over the entry. He wiped his eyes as they blurred over and felt the familiar ache in his heart that he had known for ten years, ever since his mother had died, and now he was to lose his beloved father as well. His hand clenched and the quill broke in half. Closing his eyes again he concentrated, and heard Lizzy's laugh, and remembering her smile, felt better.

Chapter 2

"Darcy, welcome back!" Captain Richard Fitzwilliam declared upon entering the front door of Darcy House and shook his cousin's hand happily. "So, how was it? Did you enjoy the adventure? You were away far longer than I expected with the war on."

"It was quite a memorable trip, Richard. I understand now your enthusiasm for travel." The two men entered Mr. Darcy's study and sat down, waiting for their fathers' arrival.

"Ah, but my experience with the army was likely not nearly as comfortable as yours, eh?" He winked. "Were you sleeping in a tent with a group of filthy men?"

"Admittedly not." Darcy smiled. "But I did have to hike over the Alps."

"Poor suffering bastard." Fitzwilliam chuckled. "You were not carrying the luggage were you?" He burst out in laughter to see the look of horror on his cousin's face. "Soft man! You are soft!"

Darcy flushed with embarrassment. As the second son, Fitzwilliam had few choices but to find a career; and the army is what he chose. Darcy, by fortune of his birth, would always live a life of luxury and his cousin's comments were not lost on him. "I imagine you are off to war soon." He said softly.

Fitzwilliam sobered. "I imagine I am. There is an ill-wind blowing from the direction of France, but who knows what that miniature despot will move our generals to do. I have heard rumours of Sweden and Portugal. I could be anywhere in a few months' time." He sighed. "Well, it is a soldier's lot."

"I do not understand why you could not simply buy a commission that would assure your stay here. A militia officer would remain . . ."

"That is not honourable, Darcy. Would you shirk your duty if it were you? It would be like you abandoning Pemberley and Georgiana to run off with an actress. She would be attractive for awhile, but the guilt would get to you eventually." Fitzwilliam raised his brows to smile at his younger cousin and saw him smile and nod. Duty and honour were his bywords. "I choose to do this properly, which is why I began with the captain's commission. I want to earn the rest."

"I expect to see you are a major at least upon your return." Darcy clapped his back.

"And I expect you to raise Pemberley's profits to an all-time high." Fitzwilliam laughed.

Darcy shook his head. "What if I fail?"

"You will not." Fitzwilliam met his eye and tried to encourage him. "You feel overwhelmed now, but what is it Aunt Catherine is fond of saying? Oh yes, *breeding will win out.* That Darcy blood will prevail and you will be outstanding. I know that Uncle George wants me to share this guardianship of Georgiana with you, but truly Darcy, the job is yours. You cannot count on me being with you, not as long as the little devil is free to spread his poison. I will support you as much as I am able, but it is truly on you. This is the making of you."

"So it is." Darcy looked up to the landscape of Pemberley and resolved to do just as his cousin demanded. He would do his duty.

The sound of footsteps and low voices were heard and into the study stepped Mr. Darcy and Lord Matlock. His uncle smiled and offered his hand. "It is good to see you home safely, Darcy. Your aunt was worried over you."

"She had nothing to fear. My guides knew their business, and kept our group well away from any danger. We had to go a little out of our way a few times, but for the most part it was the normal route. Probably the same as you took yourself." Darcy smiled a little and resumed his seat. "How is Aunt Helen? Well, I hope?"

"Of course, fully in the thick of the Season, you know her, she never stops. The Derby and Ascot are over, so she will be happy to enjoy the cricket matches and a few more dinners and balls before we head home to Matlock. She was all set to introduce you to a number of young ladies, but it seems you are off to Pemberley in a day or so." He dropped the jovial attitude and looked at him soberly. "Whatever you need, you know that you can turn to me."

Darcy nodded. "Thank you, sir. I cannot say that I am sorry to be missing out on Aunt Helen's plans."

"You never were one to enjoy a good party were you, Darcy? Next Season she will demand your attendance, you know. She is determined to marry you off young since she has failed so terribly with Richard, and it took Stephen until he was thirty to find Alicia. After Audrey's wedding last year, she is itching to begin the hunt again. You will be very popular and quite the catch." He smiled and looked to Mr. Darcy; obviously the two men had discussed getting Darcy out in society. "Well, I suppose all we need is the solicitor."

"Yes, before he comes, I want to say a few things." Mr. Darcy moved uncomfortably, and grimaced for a moment, then immediately hid the pain behind a slight smile. "I realize that you have had little time to digest this news Son, but as your uncle said, he will gladly lend you his expertise to help you manage the estate. We have a very capable steward in Mr. Nichols, and our staff is well-trained and loyal. It is perfectly reasonable for you to leave the work to him and simply supervise from afar, as most landowners do."

"That is not what I was raised to do, Father."

Mr. Darcy smiled at him proudly. "No, it is not. However, at the beginning it will not be shameful for you to accept that perhaps you may rely on them more heavily than you would wish."

"I . . .will keep that in mind, sir." Darcy swallowed and looked at his hands. A knock at the door made the men look up and Foster announced the solicitor's arrival. They gathered around a large round table and studied the will and the documents giving over Pemberley to Darcy, as well as the details of Georgiana's guardianship and dowry. With the discussion and questions, it took hours. When at last the meeting ended, and a meal was consumed, Darcy found himself alone again with his father.

"Do you have any private questions?" Mr. Darcy asked him quietly.

Darcy hesitated then spoke just as softly. "Wickham."

"You disapprove of the living and bequest I leave him?" Mr. Darcy said with a raised brow. "It is a very generous gift I know, but it does come with the stipulation that he take holy orders."

"Sir, it is not my place to question your decisions . . ." He saw his father's unrelenting stare. "However, I wonder if this is . . . not wise. You do not know him as I do."

"I thought that you were great friends." Darcy's face flushed with anger. "No? Well, you have hidden your disdain well. Why is that?"

"You seemed to take pleasure in his company, and I was pleased to see that you took pleasure in anything after Mother . . . well, you know that I was not the most entertaining boy after . . ." He sighed. "I did not wish to get in the way of your happiness."

Mr. Darcy smiled. "I appreciate your care Son, and yes, I understand why my shy boy became even more reticent after his mother died." Darcy looked away. "What has Wickham done that has disappointed you? I was sure that you were friends."

Darcy's head snapped up. "Sir, he is a profligate, a gambler, a brawler and drunk. He stole from me in school, he cheated on exams. He did no work and slid through. I could go on but it would be more of the same." His face was flushed. "I never understood the favour he received from you, sir."

"You sound jealous."

"This goes beyond jealousy of a son for a father's attention. I see Wickham as a dangerous man who has no business leading any congregation. Would you wish such a man as your pastor? Now? At this time in your life?" Darcy stood up and paced. "Was not the gift of a gentleman's education enough? I cannot stress enough my objections, sir!"

"Enough Fitzwilliam."

Darcy stopped his movement and turned to face his father. "Wickham's father was my steward for fifteen years before his death. He took me in hand when my father died, and I was grateful for his loyalty and hard work. When his son was born, I vowed to pay back my steward's loyalty by giving his son the benefit of my favour. Certainly I know that he is a charmer and that he used his wiles upon me, but I did not give him anything that I felt would not return him a real benefit. I wish that I had been aware of his true nature from your perspective, I would have made my displeasure known." Mr. Darcy watched his son's angry visage. "He was a thorn in your side?"

"To say the least, Father."

"When did this change occur?"

"When you sent him to Cambridge with me." Darcy chose not to mention the instances of baiting that Wickham inflicted upon him as they grew up. He had ignored the events then in favour of keeping a friend.

"And he was assumed to be more than he was and drafted off of your success." Mr. Darcy mulled and saw his son nod. "He pretended he was the heir?"

"He used my name on occasion and I cleaned up his . . . errors to save my reputation and . . .yours as he was your ward." Darcy looked down but his father saw his disgust.

"Do you think that he will accept the living?"

"Why must it be in the will at all?"

"I promised his father that I would provide for his future. If he chooses to refuse the living, then offer him a cash equivalent along with the other bequest, and I will deem my promise discharged. You are unhappy with this decision, and I am unhappy to learn of his behaviour, but . . . I will not back out of my promise." Mr. Darcy regarded his son. "I am sorry."

"It is your decision, sir, and I respect your will." Darcy said stiffly.

"Is there anything else? Any other questions?"

"Too many." Darcy pinched the bridge of his nose to hold off the headache that was blooming. "However I believe that actually doing the work will be far more beneficial than simply discussing it incessantly." He looked up to meet his father's eyes. "When do we depart?"

"Early tomorrow. I have already directed Mrs. Mercer to have our luggage packed, the carriages are inspected, and arrangements for exchanging horses and the inns have been made. I will go over how to accomplish those tasks with you as we ride tomorrow; there is no need to discuss that now. I suggest that you spend the rest of the day addressing any other business you have in town, if you would like, visit with friends or shops . . ."

"Because I will not be back for some time." He nodded. "I . . . I think that I will not be home for dinner tonight."

"Of course." Mr. Darcy smiled, and thought to admonish his son to be prudent and thought better of it. "Enjoy your evening." Darcy stood and left for his rooms, dressed for the evening, then went out. When he returned near dawn of the new day he was exhausted, barely sober, stank of cigars and perfume, and felt no better.

"AH, SENSE HAS RETURNED to Longbourn." Mr. Bennet embraced Elizabeth and Jane, and happily received their hugs. "You were away far too long."

"Papa, it was only six weeks!" Elizabeth laughed.

"Weeks of misery for your old father." He complained. "You have no compassion for my poor nerves!"

"Oh, where have we heard that before?" She looked at Jane.

"Well you know where I have heard it!" He smiled. "And what did you learn from your trip to town? Are you pleased or disappointed to return to the country?"

"I am happy to come home, Papa." Jane said softly. "I missed my family."

"Well said, and you Lizzy, did you miss us?"

"I missed a great many things in Hertfordshire." She said with a grin.

"Ah, a diplomat, my child, well done!" He laughed and shooed them from the bookroom. "Go and entertain your sisters, they are awaiting their gifts."

The two girls looked at each other with wide eyes. "Did you?"

"No, did you?"

"Oh dear." Elizabeth giggled and led the way out the door. "Well, have you any wool to stuff in your ears?"

The front door banged open. "There you are, girls! Well tell me all about town! Did you meet any gentlemen?" Mrs. Bennet arrived in the hallway, out of breath and fresh from visiting her sister Philips in Meryton. A maid hurried forward to take her shawl and packages. "Where did my sister Gardiner take you? Did you attend many parties?"

"Mama, you know that Aunt and Uncle Gardiner do not go out to parties!"

"Surely they must have taken you somewhere! You did not go to London to visit, you went to meet gentlemen! Oh, I knew that I should have gone with you! I told your father this! But did he listen?" She huffed and followed them up the stairs. "Now, stop teasing me, what did you do?"

Elizabeth began, "We wrote to you . . ."

"You know I have no time to read letters!" Mrs. Bennet admonished her.

"We . . .did attend the theatre one night, Mama." Jane said softly. "We went to Covent Garden."

"You DID?" She cried in delight. "AND?"

"We saw *As You Like It*." Elizabeth saw the blank look on her mother's face and sighed. "Shakespeare?" Nothing. She sighed again and chose a subject her mother would like. "We bought new dresses for the evening."

"Oh, let me see them!" Mrs. Bennet brightened and the girls opened their trunks to pull out their new frocks and showed them off to their mother. Mary looked around the corner and saw the fuss over the brightly coloured dresses.

"Come in Mary, would you like to see our gowns? Soon it will be your turn to be out, and you will receive new clothes." Jane smiled at her.

"No, oh no, it is not right to think of such things. A girl must be modest." She blushed and disappeared.

Mrs. Bennet sighed in frustration. "I do not know what put these ideas in her head! How is she to catch a man if she is dressed in mourning all the time!"

"Mama, she is dressed as any girl of her age, and she is only thirteen!" Elizabeth tried to explain. "She is simply remembering what we have learned in church, after all."

"Well, she is the only girl of thirteen I know who wishes to bury herself in sermons! You always have your nose in a book as well, Miss Lizzy, but at least it is occasionally a sonnet or two." She shook her head. "Although why you want to read at all is something I cannot fathom. Reading books is for men, your father treating you as a boy with these debates over books is foolish. You should be studying the fashion magazines and improving your needlework."

"Oh Mama, that is so silly! Every gentlewoman should read! They should attend school as well to become well-rounded and accomplished in many areas." Elizabeth hinted.

"What nonsense! I did not attend school, and I turned out just fine, my mother taught me all that I needed to know." She humphed and conveniently forgot that she was not born a gentlewoman. "I have given you precisely the education you require to find yourselves husbands. No man is going to care if you read some silly book. You can write a letter and do your household accounts; that is enough. Your mind is not what will interest him." She saw the looks of confusion on their faces and stopped herself from saying more on that subject. Instead she changed her tone. "Now you, dear Jane should have no trouble at all, every man should see immediately how beautiful you are." She patted her face. "Why your aunt did not put you in the way of men in London . . . well, I shall write to her and see what she was thinking. However, next time you go to town, I expect you to return with a man on your arm."

"Is that all that matters?" Elizabeth said angrily. "Marriage?"

Mrs. Bennet spun to face her. "Yes, it is! And it will be a miracle if any man gives you a second look. You are hardly pretty, but if they do look, one evening of listening to you will surely chase them away."

Elizabeth threw the gown she was holding onto the bed and left the room in tears. She grabbed her bonnet from a peg by the door and ran outside. Seeing her sisters Kitty and Lydia making wreathes from flowers and giggling, she glared at them in fury. "They are exactly the kind of girls who need an education! What will become of them? Mama does not care of anything but men, and Papa does not care of anything but his books! If it was not for Jane and me teaching them, I wonder if they would have learned to read at all! Why must we rely on ourselves to be educated?"

She strode through the garden, barely realizing where she was going, until she found herself climbing Oakham Mount and sat upon the hill, staring out over the land. Her hurt had dissipated through the long walk, and now she looked out at the scenery and allowed the beauty of nature that she had been deprived in the foggy smelly city to calm her further. She was old enough now to see her parents' marriage with open eyes and after spending the past six weeks in the Gardiner home, which displayed a marriage of respect and love, the return to Longbourn made the deficiencies of her parents' union painfully clear. She began to resolve that when she married, if she married, her goal would be to emulate her relatives.

Her thoughts turned again to her mother's cutting words and her determination to see the girls settled. Elizabeth was no fool; she knew that her options for survival after her father died were very limited and bleak unless she made a good match. Her aunt's words of gentle admonition were not lost on her; she just did not understand why her mother never seemed to like her. Some movement in the distance caught her eye and she watched the tenants tending the fields surrounding Netherfield Park, and pleasant thoughts of a man who *did* look at her came to mind. She wondered if he would prefer a girl who had improved her mind with reading or wished only for an ornament for his arm.

"VERY WELL DONE, dear, very well done!" Mr. Darcy clapped and Georgiana hopped up from the pianoforte to curtsey prettily. He laughed and she ran over to join him on the sofa. "Your brother will be very pleased with the progress you have made on his birthday song."

Georgiana curled up next to him and hugged his chest. "I hope so, Papa. It would be nice to see him happy." She paused then peeked up to her father's face. "He is changed since he returned from his trip. I wonder if it was not as enjoyable as he describes. I do not think that I will ever wish to travel if it leaves one so unhappy."

Mr. Darcy closed his eyes and gave her shoulders a squeeze. "No, no dear, you brother is not unhappy with his tour, he is simply taking on a great many burdens a little sooner than he expected. We must be patient and supportive to him as he adjusts."

"What burdens?"

"Well, he is a man now. He has completed his education and now he must think of his future. For Fitzwilliam, that means being the master of Pemberley and caring for all of the people within its reach. It is a very important occupation, and he is feeling the weight as it settles on his shoulders." He smiled at her confused expression. "Do you have a question?"

"Yes, Papa, why would Fitzwilliam need to take on all of these duties now? Is this not your duty? What are you to do?"

"Have I not earned a rest?" He laughed and she smiled. Mr. Darcy kissed her brow and ruffled her hair. "I would not be a good father if I did not prepare my heir properly to do his duty. I have given it all over to him to learn well while I am here to guide him."

"Are you going somewhere?" She teased. "I think that you already had your Grand Tour, Papa."

"Ah, many, many years ago, dear." He looked at his little girl, so innocent and trusting. A pain clenched his gut and he knew that it was time to tell her the truth. He played with her curls then kissed her forehead and hugged her tightly to him. "Georgiana, I have been keeping a secret from you."

"A secret?" She whispered. "Is it about Fitzwilliam?"

"It is about all of us." He swallowed. "Fitzwilliam is learning my duties so that he is prepared to take over Pemberley when I die."

"Papa, do not speak of such things!" She said worriedly.

"No dear, I have managed to hide the truth from you long enough and you know how much I despise disguise of any kind. I was waiting for your brother's return before I spoke of this to you. I am ill and . . .I will die soon."

"NO!" Georgiana tried to wrench herself from his arms and he held her tightly as she began to sob.

"Yes dear, I do not know when, but it will come sooner than later. Fitzwilliam will be your guardian as will your cousin Richard. I considered sending you to live with your Aunt Helen and Uncle Henry, but decided that you and your brother should not be separated. He will need you as much as you will need him."

"Papa, please do not die." She whispered and hugged him tighter.

"I do not wish to my dear child, but I cannot question God's will. He wants me to return to your mother's side. She has been lonely for me," he smiled as the tears rolled down his cheeks and dripped into Georgiana's hair, "and I have been lonely for her, so you see, it will be well. You will have your brother who loves you dearly and all of our family will look after you."

"I do not care about me, Papa."

"Well, that is a very selfless thing to say, and it makes me proud of you. Now, will you do something for me?"

"Anything, Papa."

"Will you look after your brother? He is going to need you to make him smile, so that will be your duty. Do not give him any trouble, just take care of him. Can you do that for me?" He looked down and wiped her face.

"Yes, Papa." She whispered.

"Good girl." He hugged her again and closed his eyes.

4 SEPTEMBER 1807

The harvest is in. I have always enjoyed this time of year, the activity; watching the skies for any sign of rain and seeing the workers rush to get the wheat and barley in dry. The threshing will wait for another time, but at least the crops are safely in their barns. There is so much left to do, so much that I hardly noticed as a mere resident of this estate, but now that Father and Mr. Nichols are looking to me to give the orders, I am intimately aware of the details and the great planning that was involved months ago that made this whirlwind of activity a success. I am indebted to them both for their patience. I am not blind to all of the mistakes I am making and how I have been corrected.

Georgiana has changed. I noticed that she had become withdrawn and clings more than ever to Father. When I spoke to him about it, he informed me that she knew the truth now. It is good that she does know. I remember clearly losing Mother, but that was so sudden, only days after Georgiana's birth. Perhaps that is why I never have accepted it. At least Georgiana will have the opportunity to prepare herself, and when the time at last comes, she will be grateful for his release from pain. At least that is what I am telling myself.

Darcy set his pen down and closed the journal, too overcome with emotion to continue. He stood and went to lean on the window frame and looked out at the trees and remembered. The devastation he felt with the loss of his mother was never relieved. He did his best to cheer his father, but he remembered seeing him walk along the corridors, stopping to lean on a wall and gasp back his sorrow before moving off to his study to hide and work. Georgiana was left to the care of her wet nurse and nanny. Darcy was soon sent off to Matlock and then Eton. He understood now that his father did not want his son to witness his mourning. That was when Darcy turned his emotions inward, not letting anyone see what he felt inside. As time passed and his father resembled his old self again, at least to his children, Darcy was able to be open with his emotions, smiling and laughing along with his cousins and friends at school. He was forever shy and serious, but had his moments of liveliness as well. But now, he felt his old talent of masking his emotions reasserting itself. It was as if some cold fingers were stealing over his heart.

"May I join you, Son?"

Darcy startled and turned to see his father in the doorway. "Of course, please come in, Father." He hurried to help him walk into the room, and lent him his strength as he lowered slowly onto a chair. "May I get something for your comfort? Some wine?"

He chuckled. "No, no, I am well, please sit down. Now, tell me what is to be done next."

"The extra labourers have been let go, the corn is being put up in ricks, and soon the fields will be ploughed for the spring wheat." Darcy recited. "Then the threshing will begin and the extra cattle and sheep will be driven to market."

"You are forgetting something important." Mr. Darcy tilted his head. "You must take care of your tenants and workers and thank them for their labours. When will you hold the Harvest Home celebration?"

"Oh, I forgot . . .I suppose that I am not thinking of celebrating, sir." Darcy looked down.

"It is important to not only be a good landlord but also an appreciative one. This celebration is more than a reason to drink and be merry; it will cement the good will of your people in your favour, especially this year, when you are taking charge. Do you understand me?"

"Yes, sir." Darcy bent his head and twisted his hands. "I know that you are suffering, sir, but I would want you to be with me."

"I will be by your side as long as I am able, Son."

"WHAT IS THAT supposed to be?" Lydia bit into an apple and leaned over the table where Kitty was sketching.

"A cat!" She looked up and glared at her. "It is perfectly obvious."

"It looks like an orange pillow." She took another bite and wiped the juice running down her chin with the back of her hand. "Why do you want to waste your time playing with crayons?"

"I enjoy it." She said defensively.

Mrs. Bennet entered the room and looked over the drawing. "Do not mark up the table, Kitty."

"I was not going to, Mama, I am careful."

"Well, see to it that you are." She tilted her head. "Are you drawing a cushion?"

"That is what I thought it was!" Lydia declared.

"What a clever girl you are, my dear Lydia! And so pretty!" Mrs. Bennet touched her hair and patted her face.

"It is a cat." Kitty said quietly.

"Mama, will you show me how to retrim my bonnet? I think it should be in autumn colours now."

"Oh yes, my dear, it is very important to know how to dress properly!" The two left the room laughing and discussing ribbons.

Kitty looked down at her drawing and back to the empty doorway, then putting her crayons in the box; she balled up her drawing and threw it in the grate. "Wait for me!" She called and ran after them.

Mary looked up from her chair in the corner where she had remained unnoticed, and turned the page of the book she had just found in her father's library that morning, containing Doctor Fordyce's sermons. Quietly she stood and walked to the table, closing the art book that lay open there. Elizabeth had given it to Kitty the day before, encouraging her to read it and study the techniques for drawing that it described. She had laughingly admitted her utter incompetence in the exercise but assured Kitty that with practice she would do well, just as she hoped to do someday with her piano playing. Kitty glowed with the attention of her elder sister and sat right down to work. Mary had watched her from the corner, and every time Lydia ran through the room Kitty would look up with a wistful expression. Now Mary could hear her mother and her sisters laughing in another part of the house, and uninvited, she returned to her sermons.

In the drawing room, Elizabeth bent over her journal.

4 September 1807

I have tried again to interest Kitty in some occupation beyond ribbons and given her an art book to study. How such an instructional tome found its way into Papa's bookroom is a mystery. I suspect that it was part of the collection he bought when the Porter family was forced to sell their belongings to pay off their creditors. She seemed genuinely pleased to receive some praise. I worry over her; she is so influenced by Lydia. I think that she is as I was at that age, hoping for some attention from Mama and imitating Lydia because she always gets it. Jane always had Mama's eye then, especially when she had just turned fifteen. I wonder if Jane has ever heard a cross word from Mama, no wonder she is so serene! Now that Mama's only words to me seem to be criticism or invocations to marry, I believe that I will spend more time walking than seeking her out.

Elizabeth heard the gaiety and rolled her eyes at Jane. "I give up."

"You can never do that, Lizzy. There is hope for all of us." She smiled and went back to her needlework. "Now play me that new tune you have been practicing."

"You are too good, Jane. Have you ever had a vindictive thought for anyone?"

"mmm, no." Jane laughed and Elizabeth shook her head. "Come on now; impress me with your skill. Pretend that I am Mr. Darcy." She giggled to see the warm smile that appeared on her sister's face. "Ah, so that is the secret, just mention your sweetheart and all is right with the world."

"He is hardly my sweetheart do not tease me, Jane! I will never see him again and if Mama heard any of this conversation she would be wringing her hands and lamenting how I did not catch him, and what a failure I am again." Elizabeth whispered furiously.

"I am sorry Lizzy; I did not mean to make you unhappy." Jane patted her shoulder. "No more talk of men, now play for me."

"It is awful, I warn you." She said honestly and set out the sheets.

"That is why you are practicing." Jane laughed, and listened as the tune was slowly played, and clapped loudly as it finished. "It is better."

"I would rather be outdoors." Elizabeth turned to her. "Why do you think that Mr. Darcy's eyes were so sad?"

"I do not know, Lizzy."

She stood up and leaned on the window frame and stared pensively out at the fading garden. "I hope that he is well."

DARCY SAT UPON his jet black stallion at the top of the hillside and looked down into the valley. Below him was Pemberley House, its stone edifice blending perfectly and naturally with the background of trees behind it. The lake, formed long ago by another Darcy damning a stream sparkled in the bright sunshine. He took a deep breath of the clean fresh air and relaxed. He always found peace here on this precipice. His mount shifted and he unconsciously moved with the animal, readjusting his weight and not once breaking his gaze over what he knew would soon be his land. He sighed and then turned when another horse whinnied behind him.

"Father!"

Mr. Darcy smiled slightly, and slowly guided his horse to his son's side. His colour was terrible, his body, simultaneously wasted and swollen, was slumped, and his breathing very laboured, but his eyes retained a look of fierce determination to make this, obviously final, ride over his land. "I thought we should share this view together." He said then squeezed his eyes shut, and reaching for the flask containing the pain killer the apothecary supplied, swallowed a dose. Darcy noted that what had once been an occasional drink had, over the past three months, become a nearly constant companion. His father grimaced. "Terrible taste, even wine does nothing to mask what it is." He coughed and clutched his stomach, then drawing a deep breath straightened, and met Darcy's worried gaze. "It will not be long."

"Please do not say that, Father."

"No Son, I pray for it now." He smiled. "I am ready, as are you." He held up his hand to stop the inevitable protest. "You have learned well. I was correct; you did already know everything; you have observed me for years. I have no doubt over your abilities to carry on. It will be difficult for a little while, but you will do well. Be proud of your name, Fitzwilliam! Remember, you are a Darcy! For hundreds of years our family has owned and tended and coaxed this land to bear its fruit. We made this land what it is. We are not titled, but we are great, and any who hear our name respect it, as they should. You must treat it with care, Son. Protect it, and when you have your family, teach your sons to be proud of it as well. Carry on the tradition as I have, make this land rich for generations to come."

Darcy's chest swelled to hear his father's speech. "I will Father, I will not let you down."

He nodded and coughed again. "Look after your sister, I trust her to you."

"She will be cared for Father, I promise." He said softly.

"And do not forget what I said of your choice for a wife." Darcy looked at him in confusion, trying to remember his words. Mr. Darcy coughed harder and gasped. "Take me home, Son."

Darcy grabbed the reins and turning the horses, he slowly guided them back to the stables. Within an hour, Mr. Darcy lay in his bed. Georgiana was brought to his side and sobbing, received a last kiss and pat on her cheek. Her governess led her away, leaving Darcy alone to sit by his father's bedside, grasping his hand and listening to his laboured breathing and the ticking of the clock. He knew not how long he waited, wishing to ask so many questions and realizing that the time for that had passed. The curtains were drawn, and the room was shadowed. He felt his father's hand grow increasingly cold and he tried to stop his own from trembling as he felt the life ebb away. Finally the time came when the pounding of his heart was louder than the sound of the rare breaths, and then that was all that remained. He waited and listened, there was nothing. The clock ticked, but time stood still. George Darcy was dead, and Fitzwilliam was alone.

2 OCTOBER 1807
We attended the assembly last night, and had such a good time! I danced five times with boys of the neighbourhood. They were nice enough but did not have much to say. I liked Mr. Hugus the best, but Mama said that he was not good enough for any of her girls and shooed him away. I asked Papa why she would discourage him, and he explained that since he was a tradesman, a marriage to a gentlewoman, even one with little dowry, would be a great step upwards for him. That is when I realized that his smiles for me were not those of admiration, but of opportunity. It seems that love is a notion for novels and poets, and a business for everyone else. I suppose that is why Mama married Papa, I cannot think of any other reason.
Poor Charlotte only danced twice. She is very discouraged, but she is only two and twenty, and has plenty of time to find a husband. I felt so terribly when Mama spoke of her as plain to Aunt Philips! I wish she would keep her views to herself, or at least learn to whisper more softly!
Jane danced every set, of course. Dear Jane, she will be sure to marry soon. I hope that she finds a man as good and kind as she is. Lydia and Kitty were sorely disappointed that they were not allowed to attend, but after seeing the frivolity of the evening, I am glad that they were not there, I cannot imagine what sort of mischief they would have found! Mary was glad to remain at home. I am sure that she spent her time playing every ponderous song she knew on the pianoforte since Mama was not here to chastise her!

Elizabeth smiled at the thought of Mary delighting in her chance to play in peace, then closed her journal and sighed, and looked out the window at the falling leaves. She suddenly felt melancholy and was not sure why.

At the same moment, Darcy stopped his pensive leaning on the window frame and looked down at the black armband he wore, then sat down in the chair behind the great mahogany desk in his father's, now his, study. He looked upon the miniatures of his mother and sister, then up to see a portrait of Guillaume d'Arcy, the ancestor who had come with the Normans and William the Conqueror from France and was the father of Darcys in Britain. He drew a deep breath and fought back the emotion he felt, hearing his father's words in his mind that last day, only a week ago. "Remember, you are a Darcy!" He opened his journal and began to write.

2 October 1807
The week of public mourning is over, and at last Pemberley is free of visitors. The distraction of people was good for a time, but I am happier now to be alone with my thoughts. Georgiana is lost and only seems to stop her weeping when Aunt Helen holds her. I was so grateful that Aunt Catherine did not come; I believe that she would have upset her more. I only learned yesterday that Aunt Catherine had written to Georgiana saying that she would take her away to live at Rosings. I would

never allow that, but I am afraid that it has frightened her terribly. I will write to our aunt to ask her to desist. I am certain that she will; she wishes to curry my favour. Uncle Henry said that he had received an express from her already asking when I would wed Anne. The thought of marriage is hardly uppermost in my mind, least of all to Anne.

Darcy sat back in the chair and set down the pen. He had been stoic and strong over the past days. George Darcy was an exceptional man; no further proof was needed than the scores of men who came to bid their last respects. Numbly Darcy shook countless hands, putting faces to names he had previously known only through letters. Each one had an anecdote, speaking of a time when his father had aided them or given advice. And others came with stories of his mother. For some reason those were even more painful to hear. It was the child who lost his mother and never understood why she left him so suddenly who received them. It had taken every bit of his willpower to stand and listen without emotion. Like a man. And now he was alone in the silent house, Georgiana gone away with their aunt and uncle, and still he could not grieve, he was a Darcy, he must be strong.

Slowly he turned back the pages of his journal, reading his thoughts over the past three months, until he found the entry for that first day, when he had learned the news. He read it over and felt that first wave of shock flow over him again, then read of the girl, and heard her laugh, and closed his eyes, remembering the warmth in hers. *What are you doing now, Lizzy of Longbourn?*

A knock startled him from his thoughts. "Come."

"Mr. Wickham is waiting to speak to you, sir. I was not sure if you were receiving visitors . . ." Mrs. Reynolds paused, she knew of the men's animosity towards each other, having witnessed or heard of Wickham's cruelty to the young Mr. Darcy enough times over the years.

"Send him in, Mrs. Reynolds." He said tersely. Watching her go he sat up in his chair, and remained seated when his beaming *friend* entered the room. He glanced at the extended hand and kept his fingers laced. "What brings you here, Wickham?"

"Well well, only a week and your new power has quite gone to your head, Darcy!" Wickham smirked and took a seat across from him. "I have come for my inheritance."

"My father is barely cold and you come here demanding . . ."

"No more than any creditor does to a widow the moment they hear their pigeon has died." He laughed at Darcy's frown. "Come now, I know that I have been left something, what is it?"

"A thousand pounds," he ignored the sound of disappointment from the ungrateful leech, "And when the living at Kympton Parish becomes available, and *If* you take holy orders, you will receive that position."

"The church?" Wickham said in surprise. "*When* it comes available? When might that be?"

Darcy shrugged. "I have not heard any news of the pastor wishing to retire. I cannot remove him from the position without cause and he has served competently for years. You may have years to wait."

"Here now Darcy, I will not wait around for years to get my due!" Wickham grew infuriated with the impenetrable mask that had slipped over Darcy's face. "What is your game?"

"There is no game; this is the condition of the will. The thousand pounds should last quite some time if you are prudent."

"You do not want me to have this living. I am sure of it." Wickham rubbed his jaw and regarded him closely, trying to see a crack in the visage and failed. "Look, I do not wish to be a pastor any more than you want me to be a pastor. I want to study law. What do you say if you give me the value of the living now, and I will relinquish any further claim."

Darcy contained his satisfaction. "And the value?"

"Ten thousand."

"Are you insane?" He laughed. "I will offer you three, not a pound more. And you will sign papers certifying that you have relinquished it."

"Five."

"My, what a precipitous drop. Three. Do not attempt to claim more." The men's eyes locked, and Wickham was the one who looked away.

"It seems that I have no reason to complain of such an arrangement. Very well then, agreed."

Darcy leaned forward and drove his finger into the desktop, "After this transaction is completed, I never want to see you on my property again. Is that clear, Wickham?"

Wickham's eyes narrowed. "Perfectly clear, old friend."

Chapter 3

25 December 1807
It is Christmas Day and precisely three months ago our father died. This was never a day of great celebration in the past, and I told our family that there was no reason to make the trip now. They protested, but I remained firm. We will have a dinner and perhaps Georgiana will play for me. I wonder if I am doing enough for her. I was not blind to how Father doted on her and I am sure that she misses his attention. I am so overwhelmed with work. I do not remember Father being forever at his desk, but then, I was a child when he became the master of Pemberley. I am taking this quiet time of the year to immerse myself in the details. The quarterly rents are due soon, so I will be marking the ledgers and paying the bills. I am fortunate that I have such excellent housekeepers in Mrs. Reynolds and Mrs. Mercer. I only have to give them the funds and they care for the homes. I know that I need to learn all of that detail as well but I will concentrate on the estate for now. Perhaps I will marry and my wife can take over that duty before I have a need to take it on.

Darcy paused in his writing and shook his head. "Marry." Entering the fray for finding a wife was so far down on his list of things to accomplish. "I know that it must be done, but I dread the exercise." He looked at his mother's miniature. "How did you manage it, Father? You married by duty, it was practically an arranged affair, and yet you loved each other deeply. How did you come to be so very fortunate? To marry with affection . . ." He sighed wistfully and turned back through the journal to find a worn page. "Lizzy. How tempted I am to try and locate this place of yours, this Longbourn. But if I find you, what am I to do? Torment myself by seeing you, knowing of you, and realizing that I cannot have you and also perform my duty? Father told me that I must marry well, did he not? I must find a woman who will do well in society, a place where I already know you do not live. What is this connection that I feel for you?" His eyes closed and he heard the laugh and voice, then saw the smile that had kept him company and drawn him from his darkest moments in the past months. "This is so unfair." He whispered, then looked up to see his sister in the doorway.

"Brother, are you well?" She asked in a small voice, stepping forward and holding out a handkerchief.

Darcy blinked and realized his cheeks were damp. He drew up his shoulders and took out his own cloth and wiped his face. "I am fine, dear."

She tucked her handkerchief back in her sleeve. "I . . . I thought that maybe you could read to me. Do you remember Papa used to read to me?"

"You were a little girl then." He smiled then saw her face fall. "Of course, I will read to you. Just let me finish my work and I will come to you. Will you be in the music room?"

"Yes, and I will play for you if you wish."

"I would like that very much, thank you. I must order you a new instrument now that you are making such excellent progress and new sheet music as well. Perhaps you would like to try the harp next?" He smiled as she left the room, and then it fell away. *I wonder if Father was correct to leave Georgiana in my care? A man does not shed tears! How can I care for her if I cannot control my emotions!* He felt ashamed that she had seen him behaving so weakly and vowed it would not happen again, then a thought entered his mind. *Would a woman I court be unhappy that I have a young sister to care for? Would that make me unattractive? Would Lizzy care?* Shaking Elizabeth out of his head he closed his journal and went back to work until an hour later when Mrs. Reynolds appeared at the doorway, her lips pursed tightly.

"Sir, the staff is enjoying its day of feasting and would like to thank you for allowing them the time to themselves and their families." She added pointedly, "I have sent tea in to the music room for you and Miss Darcy."

He set down his pen and he smiled at this mother hen. "Yes, I have been too long in joining her. Thank you, Mrs. Reynolds." Rising, he walked down the hallway, and hearing Georgiana playing his birthday song, walked a little faster. She had mastered it months ago, and would be an exceptional performer one day.

Darcy clapped and smiled when she finished. "Excellent dear, truly excellent!" She stood and he opened his arms to give her a hug. "Please forgive my tardiness."

"You work too hard." She said softly into his waistcoat. "Why do you work all of the time? Even today? Reverend Repair would be unhappy with you."

"He would at that." He smiled and ruffled her hair. They sat down and he watched as she very carefully poured out the tea, obviously this was a recent lesson. "I am only trying to fulfil our father's request of me."

"What did he ask you to do?"

"He asked me to remember that I am a Darcy." He saw her confusion. "We must be very proud of our family, Georgiana. Our family has been here for nearly eight hundred years, which is as good as royalty." He lifted his chin. "You and I have a great deal of history on our shoulders. Our ancestors are watching us to make sure that we do not bring shame to our name. So my position is to work hard and yours is . . ."

"To become very accomplished?"

He nodded and regarded her seriously. "Yes. We must both do our duty. Now, shall I read to you?"

She looked at him doubtfully. "Will it be something happy or will it be a history book?"

Darcy smiled a little. "Very well, I hear you. No more history tonight. I will read whatever you like." She jumped up and laughed, running to get her book and he called after her, "but Georgiana, please, no novels!"

"COME IN MY DEAR, come in." Mr. Bennet put down his paper and smiled to see Elizabeth peeking in the doorway. "What tears you away from the merry making?" He noticed her journal in her hand and guessed that she had taken a moment to chronicle the events of Christmas Day.

"Oh Papa, there is only so much noise one can take in an evening." She smiled and he chuckled as she settled down in her favourite chair to keep him company.

"I understand entirely hence my seclusion here, but why would you wish to miss this time with your aunt and uncle? You seem to enjoy your visits with them." He raised his brows and stirred from his desk chair to sit across from her, and waved to begin their nightly chess match.

Elizabeth moved and he quickly countered, sitting back to watch as she deliberated. "I do enjoy my visits with them, very much. It is educational." She glanced up and moved her bishop.

He responded and relaxed. "Educational? Interesting term to choose. And what can you learn in London that you do not see here? People are people wherever they are. They may have different homes or clothes or occupations, but the personalities are the same."

Elizabeth moved and he took her queen almost instantly. She glared at him and he shrugged. "But are not those people influenced by their circumstances, giving us an endless variety to examine?"

"I suppose that is true." He chuckled to see her hopeless attempt to anticipate his strike and looked at her with a raised brow. "Check."

"I give up." She sat back and sighed.

"No dear Lizzy, you must never give up. Tenacity is an excellent quality to possess."

"Mama would call it stubbornness and label it unattractive."

"Your mother does not appreciate the subtle difference. You should."

"Mama says that I will never catch a man if I do not stop speaking my mind." She met his eye and said hesitantly. "She says I am too much like a boy."

"ah." He said softly. "That is a barb sent to me. Sometimes your mother is not quite so silly."

"What do you mean, Papa?" Elizabeth leaned forward to try and read his face, but he gave her no clues. "Papa?"

"Enough of this child; go out and join the family. Expand your education by observing the difference between town and country, and try to decide which you prefer." He saw her concerned expression. "Do not allow my musings to upset you."

"Yes, Papa, but I wish you would join us, your company is missed." She stood and kissed his forehead and left the room, closing the door behind her, and returning to the chaos of the Bennet household.

"Lizzy! There you are; it is time for you to exhibit!" Mrs. Bennet pushed her forward.

"Oh Mama, my playing is so poor, I would not wish to subject our guests to it." She smiled at the gathered crowd. "Surely Charlotte would perform very well . . ."

"I would much prefer to hear you, Eliza." Charlotte smiled as Elizabeth shot her a look. "You must sing as well." She added and pressed her lips together to contain her laughter.

"Is there anything else you would like while I am at it? Shall I dance a jig?"

"Miss Lizzy, do as you are told!" Mrs. Bennet shrilled. Elizabeth turned to respond when her aunt touched her arm.

"Lizzy." Mrs. Gardiner said softly. "You are out, and when asked to exhibit, must do so graciously. This is what a lady does."

Immediately she blushed. "Forgive me, Aunt. I was not upset with the request for a performance so much as the way it was presented to me."

Mrs. Gardiner smiled. "I understand, but the goal in both circumstances is the same. The audience requests to hear your talent; and you must take advantage of the opportunity to display it."

"But everyone here knows me, they will see nothing new."

"Someday you may be in a situation before strangers and will need to show yourself to your best advantage. Would not this experience before friends now give you the confidence you will need then?" She nodded and sat back down.

Elizabeth could not dispute the sense in that, and walked forward to sit at the bench. Jane offered to turn the pages and she played first the piece she had been struggling to learn for months, and receiving the warm applause of her family and friends, relaxed and imagined herself in a drawing room in a fine home, and the eyes of a remembered gentleman upon her. She smiled and her voice lifted in song. When she finished she was rewarded with cheers and encouraged, broke into playing a jig to satisfy the young people, who jumped up to dance.

Mr. Gardiner looked to his wife and squeezed her hand as he spoke softly. "That is her talent, her voice. Perhaps we might find her a master the next time she comes to visit."

"Will you ask Thomas?"

"I know that I should, but I hesitate. He is so odd about their education. You cannot care for your children and their futures if you never leave your study." Mr. Gardiner added fiercely, "Marianne, if you ever catch me doing such a thing to our children . . ."

"You never would, Edward. You are already a caring father and pay them more attention than any man I know. But what of your sister, why do you have such good views on education and she does not?"

"Francine is lively and I think she is bright, but our mother never challenged her or Margaret. We had no governess, and Mother taught them the best as she could, but she certainly had no education. They were left to find their futures by being personable and pretty, not by wit or talent. Lizzy will have all of those things, imagine what she could do if she was given the proper guidance, she has such potential. Her father sees it, but keeps it to himself."

Mrs. Gardiner watched as the girls danced with each other and the Lucas boys. "That is what concerns me.

"If Thomas does nothing to educate his girls; surely Francine should know that the more accomplishments they have, the more attractive they would be to suitors. They cannot win them with their dowry, should they not be given every other tool? I know how worried she is about the future, but surely she should understand this."

"She won a gentleman with her looks, as far as she is concerned that is all her girls need." He smiled sadly at his wife. "I grew up with her, I know." He looked over to Jane, smiling placidly as Robert Lucas spoke to her. "I believe that Jane will suffer for her serenity."

"Jane?" Mrs. Gardiner said with surprise. "Surely you jest!"

"Well, what are her accomplishments? She is good with a needle and behaves as a lady. She is not witty or well-read, nor talented with music or art. She is kind and well-behaved, but truly Marianne, do not tell me that she will not sacrifice herself to the first man who offers her a home and security for her family. She will not speak up for herself and her desires."

"Lizzy said something like that this summer." Mrs. Gardiner said softly.

"She is no fool, dear." He smiled. "I hope that our girls take after her."

"Oh, and not after their mother?" She raised her brow and received a kiss on her cheek. "That is better." He chuckled. "Well, I will invite both girls to come to us again this summer for a time, and we will see what we can contribute to their improvement. The other girls, however . . ." She met her husband's eye and smiled. "Well, they are still young."

28 MARCH 1808
At last I believe that Spring is truly on its way! I have seen evidence of buds swelling on the apple trees and the happy activity in the animals as I take my walks. It feels so good to have these occasional days of bright sunshine breaking up the days of incessant rain.

Elizabeth paused from her writing to look out the window and spied Lydia and Kitty setting off down the lane, probably to visit Maria Lucas, and smiled to see a bird alighting upon a tree branch, its beak filled with bits of dried grass for its nest. A thought came to mind and she turned to pick up the book of poetry that lay by her side.

Spring, the sweet spring, is the year's pleasant king,
Then blooms each thing, then maids dance in a ring,
Cold doth not sting, the pretty birds do sing:
Cuckoo, jug-jug, pu-we, to-witta-woo!
The palm and May make country houses gay,
Lambs frisk and play, the shepherds pipe all day,
And we hear aye birds tune this merry lay:
Cuckoo, jug-jug, pu-we, to-witta-woo!
The fields breathe sweet, the daisies kiss our feet,
Young lovers meet, old wives a-sunning sit,
In every street these tunes our ears do greet:
Cuckoo, jug-jug, pu-we, to witta-woo![1]

Giggling she closed the book. "Cuckoo, jug-jug, pu-we, to witta-woo!" She smiled. "What a silly man to try and interpret what a bird would say! I wonder at any man being so silly to try and write that down!" She returned to her journal, writing of her latest endeavours to study the atlas her father had recently acquired and hoped to determine a way to interest her other sisters in places beyond their garden.

Darcy closed his book and slipped it into his saddlebag, then continued his solitary ride over the estate, humming to himself, "cukoo, jug-jug, pu-we, to witta-woo!" Stopping again he looked down over the fields where the sheep had been herded for the night, leaving their manure for the coming planting, and saw the frolicking lambs dancing near their mothers. It was a very successful spring in that respect, but he made a mental note that he must mark his calendar for several foxhunts beginning in autumn to control the vermin and protect his flocks. His father's death had cancelled such seemingly frivolous activity at the estate last year and he was now concerned that his newborn lambs might be targeted soon. It was an error of judgment to not allow the hunts, and he had ignored his steward's advice. It would not happen again. The man knew his business, and where his steward could not speak to him, his uncle could, and did. Darcy simply had not been up for hosting guests, and did not feel he could while in mourning. He watched with satisfaction as his shepherds trained a group of new dogs to look after the animals. One item checked off of his list, he rode away to speak with Mr. Nichols. He would leave for London in two days, and had to make sure that everything was in order at Pemberley before his departure. He had no doubt that the estate would be left in good hands.

"The post has arrived, sir." Mrs. Reynolds informed him as a maid took his coat late that afternoon. Darcy smiled slightly and adjusted the black armband.

---

[1] Thomas Nashe *Spring the Sweet Spring,* Summer's Last Will and Testament

"Thank you Mrs. Reynolds. Is there anything that I must address for the household before we leave? I do not intend to stay in town for the entire Season, but it will be several months before I return." He walked into the study and she followed him.

"No sir, I believe that all is well. I have hired six new maids and four footmen, all are relatives of our former servants, so I do not expect any trouble from them."

His brow creased. "I suppose that I should know this but . . .is it common to lose so much staff in the Spring? Were they unhappy? Is there a need amongst the staff that I should know?"

Mrs. Reynolds regarded her master with approval of his concern. "Oh no sir, we have a turn-over every few years of the lower staff. It is not that Pemberley is unpleasant, but you know, these young people think that London is where their future lies." She shook her head. "And then I hear how so many become ill there and die. Nasty air. I hope you return to Pemberley soon, sir. I would not want you to take ill as well."

Darcy smiled at this old protector. "I think that I am immune to whatever lurks in the air by now, Mrs. Reynolds." He noticed her doubtful expression and appreciated her care. "We will come home more than ready to enjoy the fresh air here. Now, the accounts are in order?"

"Yes sir, don't you worry about a thing. I hope that you enjoy visiting your family." She smiled and left the room. Darcy sighed and looked down at the pile of letters on his desk, seeing one from his uncle and another from Lady Catherine.

"Enjoy, hmm, interesting word." He opened his uncle's letter first.

Dear Darcy,

I expect to see you in town in the next fortnight. Your aunt wishes you to inform us of your arrival, and be warned, she has great plans for you. Now, I know what you will say, you remain in mourning, however, six months have passed and you are now free to socialize a bit, so you cannot use that as a complete excuse. You can visit family for dinners and if some friends and neighbours happen to be present it will certainly not be your fault! Helen has been to Almack's and has studied the new crop of ladies for the year and has found a number of beauties for your perusal. I must say you are the envy of the men, so young and such a fortune available. I assure you that you will be quite the popular fellow! The ladies all know that you are to arrive soon, and they are already forming their battle plans! You should have quite the delightful time enjoying their smiles and whispers. Ah, to be young again! Well, do not let your aunt hear that, but I am looking forward to seeing the pretty birds showing their feathers for you! Enjoy it, Son!

I have received a letter from Richard, he is well as of three weeks ago, and has been promoted to Major. From the rumours I have heard around the House of Lords, I believe that he is part of the forces who will support Sweden. Of course he provides no details, only assurances of his health. It is very trying on us to wait and wonder; more so as you know the members of our society seem to prefer to ignore anything that occurs outside of ballrooms, so there are few friends with whom to commiserate. Well, I digress. We hope that he will return soon, his mother in particular.

Be warned that my sister is greatly anticipating your arrival at Rosings. I am certain that you know why and have devised your defences. Give our love to Georgiana, and we look forward to your arrival.

Sincerely,
Matlock

Darcy refolded the letter and stared at it for a few moments. His uncle's confession of worry over Richard was remarkable, but this was the first time that his second son was truly in harm's way. His previous trips had been relatively brief and uneventful. This time it was bloody and there were no guarantees of return. Darcy's worry over Richard had been constant, but like his uncle, he had no one in whom to confide his feelings. He thought to look into purchasing a small estate to hold for a second son. He did not want to face the possibility of his child dying in war simply by order of birth. He wondered if he would have chosen the path of the military and decided that had he been forced to make a decision, he would have followed the law as his career. Opening the letter from Rosings, he braced himself for his aunt's demands.

Dear Darcy,

I expect your arrival on the 15th. Easter Sunday we will enjoy the company of our pastor and his wife. Anne is excited by your visit and has spoken of little else for weeks. You will be well-pleased with her; a bloom comes to her cheeks when I speak of your pending betrothal. Your mother would be so proud to see this come to pass, she told me often how she wished for you and Anne to join the estates, and of course, how could you deny the wish of your dear mother? I spoke of it often to your father as well.

Darcy closed his eyes. "Yes, and my father assured me that neither he nor Mother supported your scheme. Bloom in Anne's cheeks, indeed!" He snorted. "Perhaps from a fever brought on by your insistence that she sit as close to the fire as possible!" Sighing he read the rest of the letter, but it was the same as ever, assumptions over his marriage to Anne and directions for Georgiana's upbringing. Folding it he turned and tossed the paper into the fire and watched as it was consumed. "Marriage to Anne would be a last resort, and according to my uncle," he closed his eyes, "the ladies of town will not allow that to occur." He glanced down at his journal and read the day's entry.

28 March 1808

I am preparing for my return to society. I suspect that I will take little enjoyment of it. I might take frequent walks in the park and find better companionship there.

"DID YOU SEE that Netherfield Park was let again?" Charlotte Lucas said as she and Elizabeth waited their turns at bowls. The two families had gathered at Lucas Lodge for a picnic on the sunny day.

Jane tossed her ball and they watched it roll to a stop near the pins. "I heard from Mama that it is a Naval officer and his family. She was vastly disappointed." Elizabeth grinned at Charlotte and took her turn. "I imagine Lady Lucas was as well?"

"Yes, to say the least. She was hoping for some boys of marriageable age, not ones still riding their stick ponies on the lawn." She smiled and shrugged. "Well, someone will come along eventually."

"Someone to love." Elizabeth said determinedly.

"Eliza, you really have to rethink this philosophy of yours!" Charlotte clapped as Maria's ball travelled to strike down the pins successfully. "Marriage is for security, not love. If love occurs it is a fortunate bonus, but surely not necessary."

"Your heart is hardening Charlotte."

"Not at all, my heart is the same as it ever was. I am simply older now and feeling the concern of my family that I find my own home." She smiled sadly. "It will not be long before Jane feels the same, I am sure."

"Lydia!" Jane cried.

"What?" Lydia quickly stopped her attempts to rearrange the pins into an advantageous configuration for her ball.

"Stop that!" Elizabeth admonished. "You may not change the rules to suit your desires!"

"Oh Lizzy, who wants to play by silly rules? I want to make up my own game!" With that she began grabbing balls, rolling one after the other down the length the course, merrily whacking the pins every which way. Kitty giggled and joined in the fun. Jane and Elizabeth looked at each other helplessly as Mrs. Bennet laughed and applauded their antics.

"I am sorry, Charlotte." Elizabeth said quietly.

"It is fine, Eliza." She smiled slightly and they walked out to retrieve the balls before they were lost forever in the grass. Mr. Bennet looked up from the book he was reading and took in the chaotic scene, then returned to his page.

"Such wonderful lively girls they are!" Mrs. Bennet cried. "Do you not agree, Mr. Bennet?"

"Lively indeed, they will undoubtedly attract the best of men one day, and they will be as pleased with their marriage as I." He said tonelessly.

"Oh Mr. Bennet, how you make me blush, still!" Mrs. Bennet gushed and waved her fan vigorously. Lady Lucas looked between her and Mr. Bennet then raised her brows to her daughter.

Charlotte pursed her lips and saw Elizabeth and Jane flushed with embarrassment. "I heard that you are to visit London, Eliza."

Elizabeth looked up. "Oh, yes my aunt Gardiner asked for me to come in

May. She is expecting again and would like some help with the children. Jane will go in autumn for her confinement."

"And see to it that you look out for some gentlemen this time, Lizzy!" Mrs. Bennet called. "Mr. Bennet, we must order some new gowns for her before she goes, Lord knows that she needs something to make her more attractive!"

"Mama! I want some new gowns, too!" Lydia whined. "Why can I not have new things?"

"Me, too! I want to wear pretty dresses, not this silly smock!" Kitty cried.

"You are not out! You can not suggest that you are available to men by your dress!" Mary admonished.

"Oh what do you care? You will never look at a man! Besides, what do I care of men? I just want new things." Lydia stuck her tongue out at her sister. "Please Mama; let us go to the dress shop now!" She turned to her father. "Please Papa, please? I want a new dress and bonnet and gloves, and oh a parasol! I am tired of wearing Lizzy and Jane's old things!" She jumped up and down eagerly and began pulling on his arm, making his book bounce.

Annoyed he shook her off. "Fine then, go and buy whatever you wish, just leave me to my book."

The girls squealed and Elizabeth looked at Jane and whispered. "The expense!"

"I know." She said softly. "But it makes them happy."

"Yes, and it leaves us with no dowry." Elizabeth shook her head and looked at her sisters dancing around her mother and then saw Lady Lucas staring at her with a satisfied smile. "Why is she so pleased, I wonder?"

"I suspect that she thinks the same as we, Lizzy." Jane said softly.

"Charlotte's dowry is as small as ours."

"And that makes us equal in our hunt for husbands."

"We are still a gentleman's daughters, Jane." Elizabeth looked at her with a small smile. "We do have that."

"I HOPE THAT your visit to Rosings was not too objectionable." Lord Matlock laughed as he saw Darcy's eyes roll. "She was lying in wait for you?"

"She sounded like one of the parrots, *Marry Anne, Marry Anne, Marry Anne.* If I was as weak-minded as her pastor I would have given in simply to escape her voice." He sighed while Lord Matlock chuckled. "And then there were the demands for Georgiana. I know that I am not the most prepared parent in the world, but the thought of subjecting her to Aunt Catherine as her example is impossible."

"No, I believe that your aunt would have put a stop to such a scheme before that could happen." He paused and looked at Darcy speculatively. "Would you prefer to have Georgiana come to live with us?"

Darcy hesitated and then shook his head. "No, no, Father entrusted her to me. I will not give her up. Besides, she is all that I have." He smiled sadly for a moment, revealing the man he used to be, then replaced his emotion with a smooth mask.

Lord Matlock noticed that he had nearly perfected the ability to hide every expression behind this new talent, and wondered if it was a good thing. His nephew had changed since his father's death. "Well, you cannot hide here in the corner all night."

"I cannot dance, Uncle."

"You can smile and greet the ladies, though." He gave him a push. "I know how you do not enjoy the exercise, but next Season you will have no excuse. Now get out there." Darcy unhappily ventured forth into the crowded drawing room where several men stepped forward to introduce him to their daughters. Darcy bore it all with seeming equanimity. The compliments, the smiles, every comment he made was met with laughter and cries of delight. He was not fooled. The conversation was dull, stilted, and uncomfortable, certainly not something that should inspire such excitement. He turned away from another eager debutante and heard her high-pitched giggling in the background, and slowly made his way back into his corner to hide.

Were none of them taught that to laugh with false amusement is unattractive? Just one of them I would like to see greet me with a genuine smile. I cannot remember the last time . . . He stopped his musings as the image of a girl suddenly appeared in his mind. *Lizzy.* A soft smile came to his lips and his eyes warmed. He remembered a musical laugh. *Where are you now?* He wondered and tried to recall the name of her estate. *L . . . it began with an L, I am sure . . .* He had almost sounded it out when a woman approached and greeted him in French. Startled he turned and focused on her, forced to pay attention to translate the conversation. The woman slipped into Italian. He smiled, she was displaying her education. When he returned the conversation to English and began to ask her of poetry, she hesitated. He frowned, and soon she was gone, only to be replaced by another girl and her mother. It was a long evening, and when it was over, the expression in his eyes and set of his lips clearly communicated his displeasure with the experience.

"Darcy, you really must improve your manners. What has become of you?" Lady Matlock said as the last of the guests departed. "You have lost your smile."

"Surely you cannot be surprised Aunt Helen, nobody likes to be hunted."

She laughed and patted his face. "Until you are caught nephew, I suggest that you become accustomed to it." His frown deepened. "I know that you cannot attend any balls, but we will host another dinner in a fortnight, your cousins will be present for it and both look forward to seeing you."

"No, I will attend to business, take Georgiana to a few sights, then we will return to Pemberley. I am no good mood for courting." He smiled slightly. "Perhaps next year."

She sighed. "Perhaps."

25 MAY 1808
I visited my club today and I wonder if I should end my membership. If it were
not for the fact that Darcys have been members since its inception I would have left
immediately. Allowing in tradesmen is insufferable. I have voiced my displeasure,
but I do not know what good it will do. Someone sponsors them, and they have the
money. But surely there must be some sort of requirement that your money be more
than a step away from the till box! No matter, what is done is done. They are there,
and we must put up with them. But if this fool that I met today is an example of what
is to come, I am sure that I will go to my chess club or fence instead. Bingley,
Charles Bingley. That was the boy's name. Not a day over twenty and in cotton so I
heard. Smiling and laughing at everything. How can anyone be so agreeable?
Surely it must be an act to ingratiate himself with his betters. Bingley, a name
known to no peer. I would like to see him receive the attention I have from the
ladies!

Darcy finished his entry with a flourish and dropped his pen back in the tray
with a satisfied nod. "Yes, will any lady want *your* favour Mr. Bingley?" He
demanded of the page, then sat back and smiled, remembering his cold
reception and the approving nods he garnered from the old members gathered
nearby. Then he thought again of how Bingley seemed to take no notice of his
cut, if anything he seemed to be grateful for the conversation and endeavoured
to be . . .very pleasant. "Listen to me speaking of the ladies as if there were a
competition for them! Take them all Bingley, not one of them interests me."
Darcy thought it over some more, and remembered actually feeling a twinge of
pity for the young man, as friends and acquaintances seemed to join together in
small conspiracies, telling him of initiation rituals he must endure to truly
become a member of the club's upper circles, and how Bingley eagerly lapped
up the information. "You are in for a rough time." Darcy said softly, reverting
to his old self, and felt ashamed that he did nothing to step in. He would have
been listened to, a Darcy of Pemberley was important; a Bingley of nowhere
was not.

A knock at the door was quickly acknowledged and pulled him from his
thoughts. "Georgiana, you look very pretty!" He said a little more
enthusiastically than was his wont of late.

She blushed with pleasure and looked down at her striped gown. "Thank
you, Fitzwilliam; at least it is no longer all black. I am ready to go if you are."

"Yes, yes, come, I understand that the exhibition is quite breathtaking." He
jumped up, offering her his arm, and led her from his study and out to the
carriage where they were quickly on their way to the Royal Academy of Art. He
smiled warmly at her. "Tell me of your studies, what has Mrs. Somers set you
to learn this week?"

"Oh, we are discussing Donne and Blake, and then tomorrow we will begin
studying the new globe that you purchased for me."

"Excellent!" He smiled. "You will be a very accomplished lady one day, and will add admirably to any conversation."

"I hope so, Brother." She whispered. "I want you to be proud of me."

"I will be, dear." He smiled. "I already am. Father would be so pleased with you."

She smiled shyly in return and they arrived at the exhibition. "There seems to be quite a crowd today."

"Yes." He frowned at the varied dress of the visitors. "It seems that anybody is able to visit." Shrugging, he stepped out of the coach and offered his hand. "Well, we shall enjoy it despite the company." They entered and joined the slow-moving queue as they wound their way about the exhibition. Darcy took the opportunity to point out his favourite artists and encouraged Georgiana to speak and comment on hers. Coming behind a man and two ladies, they waited their turn to step closer to one painting. He listened to the intelligent comments of the gentleman, nodding in approval, then startled when he heard a soft, musical laugh, followed by an equally warm voice from the young woman as she made her observations. Her companions laughed with her and he attempted to see around the brim of her bonnet to no avail. The group moved on, and as much as he wished to follow her, he was forced to remain with Georgiana to look at the painting. But instead of his original opinion that had formed as he waited, he thought over the remarks of the young woman and smiled, seeing exactly her points, and even chuckling softly.

Georgiana looked up to him. "What amuses you so?"

"I am not sure; I suppose that I am delighting in the comments of someone with great insight." He smiled warmly and she responded happily. Squeezing her hand they moved on, and he searched the crowd for the mysterious woman, his smile falling away as he found no success. The laugh had struck him, he was sure that he knew it.

From across the hall, Elizabeth stood by her uncle and watched as Darcy scanned the room. He seemed to be searching for someone and she noticed his furrowed brow and disappointed expression. *Who do you search for, Mr. Darcy?* She wondered. He was instantly recognizable to her; that was a face she could never forget. Her heart beat faster just to be in the same room with him, but to approach with no introduction was impossible. She considered walking by to see if he noticed her, and bit her lip.

At that moment Darcy's searching eyes found hers. Once again she was speared by their sad blue, but this time there was more, he was examining her. *Am I so changed from a year ago? Remember me!* She urged. Question appeared in his expression and she gathered her wits and smiled, softly, warmly, kindly. She saw him tilt his head and draw a breath, then his lips lifted, and the breath was let go. The sadness was replaced with hope. The girl at his side, undoubtedly his sister, spoke to him and he bent his head to answer her question.

Darcy looked back up again but only saw the crowd. His brow furrowed. *Lizzy? Where are you?*

25 MAY 1808

He saw me! I cannot believe that he remembered me but he did! And he smiled! He has the sweetest smile; I could look at it all day. The corners of his mouth just start to tug upwards and his eyes light up. I sound silly but nobody will read this besides me so I really do not care. Mr. Fitzwilliam Darcy smiled at me!

I wish that Uncle had not pulled me away, but I guess that I was standing there gaping like a fish and Aunt must have nudged him. They asked what had interested me, and of course I could not say that I was staring at the most beautiful and handsome man in the world; could I? But I was!

His sister was with him again, she has grown since last year. I wonder if she will be as tall as her brother? He still looks so sad, and I believe that I know why now. He wore a black armband and his sister was dressed in half-mourning. I am afraid to know who they might have lost. I wish that I could offer my condolences; they both seemed in need of a friend.

I hope that I do not have to wait another year to meet him again, and maybe next time I will speak to him. I would just die to hear him say something to me!

Elizabeth giggled and set down her pen. Mrs. Gardiner stood in the doorway and watched her niece and smiled at her happiness. "What has pleased you so, Lizzy?"

Instantly Elizabeth closed her journal and stood. Mrs. Gardiner's brows rose. "Oh, nothing, I was just thinking about what we saw at the exhibition. It was very pleasing." She blushed and hurried past. "I should go and find Benjamin, I am certain that he is ready to play." Her aunt watched her go and looked back at the journal, shook her head and left to see to her duties.

When the three adults gathered for dinner that evening Mr. Gardiner watched Elizabeth pick at her meal and stare dreamily off into the distance. He raised his brows and silently asked his wife what was occupying their niece. She smiled. "Lizzy, I do not recall you ever looking so happy, and that is saying quite a great deal since you are nearly always that way. I enjoyed the exhibition; however I do not feel a need to be pulled from the clouds."

"Oh, I just enjoyed seeing so many things, Aunt. It was nice to see beauty in person rather than trying to imagine it." She bit her lip and blushed. Mr. Gardiner chuckled. "Well then Lizzy, do you think that you will enjoy viewing something a little less educational? I thought that you might like to attend the Derby at Epsom Downs this weekend."

"A horserace?" Elizabeth's eyes opened wide and she looked to her aunt. "Really? Oh yes, I would love that!"

"It is not Ascot but yes, it is quite a horserace." He chuckled at her. "Good, we never miss it, well, except when your aunt is with child." He smiled at his wife. "I thought that you and I could go together. What do you say?"

"Yes!" She laughed. "Oh it will be so hard to return to Longbourn after this trip. I am afraid you may have a new resident here."

"Thank you dear, you are forever welcome, but I am sure that before long you will want to return to your walks and your books." He smiled. "It becomes a dull place here when the Season ends and all the gentry leave for their sport in the country. The rest of us are left to endure the quiet of our simple lives."

"I had not really thought of that. I have never visited in autumn or winter. I suppose everyone leaves." She said thoughtfully. "I do not know why I am surprised, though. They all seem to appear in the countryside!"

"Yes, except they are brandishing guns when they come to your home." Mr. Gardiner laughed.

"May we visit Hyde Park one day before I return home?" Elizabeth turned to her aunt. "I enjoyed it last year."

"Of course, Lizzy, I knew that you would ask. Perhaps you will show me that path that drew your particular attention."

"I hope to Aunt, I do."

"WELL THEN IT IS settled, we travel to the Derby this weekend." Lord Matlock took a sip of wine and reached for the snuff. "Whose carriage will we take?"

"Mine is largest, so it should be comfortable for the four of us." Darcy offered.

"Nobody likes a braggart, Darcy." His cousin Viscount Layton smiled, and Darcy frowned. "I was joking, where has your humour gone?"

"Forgive me Stephen, I find very little to be humorous of late." He picked up his glass and took a sip. "I am not good company. I probably should not even be attending the race."

"You need to be with people, Darcy. You have shut yourself up in this house for too long. It is affecting you."

"I went to my club yesterday." He said defensively.

"Oh, I heard about that, you were all over that puppy from Scarborough, what was his name? Bingley?" Robert Singleton sat forward and laughed. "I heard that you cut him as skilfully with your tongue as you could with your blade. Well done!"

"Did you?" Lord Matlock's brow drew together. "I wonder what your father would think of that."

Darcy met his eye. "I was thinking of my father when I did it, sir." The earl's brows rose and Darcy flushed, remembering his discomfort with his behaviour.

"Pride goeth before the fall." Singleton said with a twitch to his lips.

Layton grinned. "I see that my sister has been successful in her quest to take you to church."

"Not at all, I am merely responding automatically in fear of having my knuckles rapped if I do not speak up." The men laughed, except Darcy, who was staring pensively into his glass.

"Come on, man, we are simply having a joke!" Singleton looked at his brother and father-in-law. "Darcy!"

He startled. "Forgive me, I was thinking of something else."

"Obviously. Who was she?" Layton winked and nudged his father. Darcy startled and looked up at him with wide eyes. "Damn, do you mean I was correct? Well, who is she?"

A knock on the door was heard and Darcy called to allow entry. "Pardon me, sir, but the ladies request that the gentlemen join them in the drawing room." He bowed and left.

Darcy was instantly on his feet. "Shall we?"

"Smooth, Darcy, but we will return to this conversation." Layton smiled and saw that his cousin had once again slipped away behind the mask. He met his father's gaze and they shook their heads.

"I AM AFRAID that you will not be able to see a great deal, Lizzy." Mr. Gardiner said apologetically. "I tried to get seats in the grandstands, but they were snapped up by the gentry instantly."

"Oh Uncle, I do not mind at all standing here with the rabble." Elizabeth laughed. Her eyes were bright; taking in the crowd, the holiday atmosphere was infectious. "There are so many people here to study, I am sure that even if I cannot see above their hats, I will still have a very entertaining time. I suppose that we can still place a bet?"

He chuckled. "Of course. Which horse do you choose?"

Elizabeth scanned the names on the list printed in the morning paper and bit her lip. "Pan." She nodded.

"And why is that?"

"Is he not the Greek god of the forests and nature? What more appropriate choice for a girl who likes to roam the woods?"

Mr. Gardiner chuckled, "Well, yes that is some of his history." He stood close to her, keeping her safe from the rowdy crowd, and they moved as far forward as they could. Elizabeth drank in the sights. Her eye was drawn to a handsome young man, smiling and speaking rapidly. Then her brow creased, noticing that the young man was the subject of a great deal of attention from his neighbours. She recognized their thinly veiled disdain and his oblivion. From behind she heard men's voices, and turned her head to see them. The voices were cultured, and more significantly, she heard a name.

"We should have left sooner."

"Well if you had not been so drunk on Darcy's wine . . ."

"It was not his wine; it was the ball we attended afterwards."

"I cannot stand being left to watch from here. Come now Father, an Earl with the public? You know it will be frowned upon if anyone hears."

"There are plenty of people being turned away from the grandstands. Ever since that fool tried to attack a horse three years ago, attendance has grown. I should have known, the public loves to see blood."

"Darcy, look there, is that your new friend, Bingley?"

"He is not my friend, Stephen, and I wish that you would desist." Elizabeth's breath caught to hear his voice and she rose up on her toes to try and see his face. A man moved and as his head turned she saw him "Oh." She whispered. Darcy's eyes were fixed ahead. She followed his gaze and saw that he was watching the young man and his tormentors. She heard some laughter from the group, then watched as the man withdrew a large handful of notes from his coat and was counting it out, looking up to the ringleader, almost as if he were asking if the tribute he was paying was sufficient. Clearly he was being hoodwinked and it made her angry. She glared at the scene

"He seems to be laying down a bet or two." Singleton observed with a knowing wink to his brother. "He had better be careful or he will be through his money before he even comes of age."

"What do you mean?"

"His father died a year or so ago. There is a board of directors running his factories so he really does not do anything at all. Good thing for the business since he is still in school."

"His father died." Darcy said softly, and looked at him with a different eye. "And his mother?"

"I do not know. Why do you care?" Layton asked.

Darcy turned his head to respond and saw Elizabeth. His breath caught and he stared at her, recognizing the man from the exhibition at her side. He studied her face and saw that her eyes were flashing in anger, and following her gaze, realized that she was watching the same scene, and knew it was not right. Raising his chin, Darcy strode forward into the group.

"What is this, gentlemen?" He spoke quietly

"Darcy!" One man grinned and held up the cash. "Bingley here did not realize that there was a fee to stand here and watch the races, but as a member of the governing board, I offered to accept it from him now and let the incident go." He chuckled and winked.

"Bosworth, return the funds to Mr. Bingley."

"Darcy, you know that . . ."

"I know that this race is free to all who wish to observe from this area, and you are no more a board member here than you are of the club. You are taking advantage of Mr. Bingley's ignorance and I find it distasteful." Darcy stared at him. "Return the funds."

"See here, who are you to say anything, you cut him just as much as the rest of us did at the club!"

"And I was mistaken to do so." Darcy turned to Bingley. "Please forgive my behaviour, I regret it. Would you care to join my party for the race?"

Bingley smiled and nodded eagerly. "Yes, that would be excellent, thank you, Mr. Darcy." Darcy nodded and led the way back to his dumbfounded family, introducing Bingley to them all. When he had a chance he glanced over to Elizabeth who was smiling warmly and approvingly at him. He smiled and returned her look, his chest puffing with the gift of her admiration. He began to move towards her when his arm was caught.

Lord Matlock spoke softly. "Your father would be proud of you."

"Thank you, sir." Darcy looked down then back to just spot Elizabeth's small figure as she continued to look to him. He smiled and started to move towards her again when the first race began. The crowd surged forward to the rail, and he lost sight of her just as his uncle grabbed his arm again.

"Come, seats in the grandstands have opened up, bring your friend along." Darcy stared at Lord Matlock in confusion. "Bingley."

"Oh . . .oh yes, Bingley." He looked back to where Elizabeth had stood and once again he realized he had lost her to a crowd. *Lizzy . . .will you please stay still?* Searching behind him, he tried to locate her even as Bingley spoke in his ear. He heard nothing of the conversation, and wanted nothing more than to return to his former location, but now as Bingley's host, he had no choice but to stay with him. Frustrated was hardly a strong enough word for his feelings, but he sighed and resigned himself to his new friend. *I have seen her twice, it is reasonable that we will meet again, is it not?* He assured himself of that and hoped that her companion, a man that he hoped was a guardian and nothing more, was keeping her safe, and turned his attention to his new companion.

"I cannot thank you enough for intervening as you did. I rather suspected that they were having some fun with me, but I thought it would be best to just play along."

"Why on earth would you think that?" Darcy asked in amazement. "You have enough going against you in this society, being labelled an easy mark does not help your reputation."

Bingley glanced at the earl and viscount and whispered. "I know, I . . .you see, Mr. Darcy, I do not have a great deal of direction. I am the first of my family to be . . .well, raised a gentleman. Father had no idea what to do besides sending me off to school. I am the first at Cambridge, and he died before he could find an estate to purchase; my children will be the first to be born as gentry. Mother died three years ago and my sisters and I do not have much in the way of guidance."

Darcy sighed, then looked him over. "No estate?"

"No sir, but Father saved nearly one hundred thousand pounds to purchase one."

"Hmm, that is admirable. Your family is still in trade?"

"Yes sir, but when the estate is purchased . . ."

"Yes." Darcy looked at him speculatively, thinking over how Lizzy had clearly disliked how Bingley was treated and how much she approved of his rescue. She would like him taking this boy under his wing, and for some reason he knew that his father also would. Maybe it would do him some good as well. "I will guide you."

"Sir?"

"Well, I have essentially given you my blessing by publicly, very publicly, defending you today, so that is a major coup for you. You may be unaware but the Darcys are . . ."

"Oh, sir, I know all about your family, I asked about you after we met at the club."

"You did?"

"Well sir, you may find it amusing but if one is to be cut, it is good to know that it came from one of the richest families in England. A mark of distinction." Bingley grinned.

Darcy laughed outright, causing his family to stare. "Well, if that is something that makes you proud Bingley, I will not say anything. However, I suggest that your goals in the future address receiving the *approving* notice of the richest families instead."

"I will keep that in mind, sir." Bingley winked.

"Darcy." He held out his hand.

"Darcy it is." Bingley smiled. "I am in your hands."

Chapter 4

"*S*ay what is on your mind or desist from staring at me." Darcy glanced up from where he had been looking intently out of the carriage window as they joined the parade of day trippers returning to London from Epsom. He had seen the eyes of the men alternating from looking at him to each other in the glass's reflection.

"I just cannot in any way understand what has come over you to accept someone so low . . ." Singleton began.

"So it is wrong to give a man a leg up?" Darcy murmured to the scenery. "A connection to greater things is such a sin?"

"It is shocking when only a day or so before you had openly disparaged him before your true peers."

"I had not taken the time to know his circumstances then."

"So knowing that he is an orphan makes him more acceptable?" Layton scoffed.

Darcy turned slowly to meet his eyes with cold fury. "Do not even attempt to pretend to understand this situation. Even if my aunt and uncle, forgive me sir," He nodded to Lord Matlock, "were to die tomorrow, you are two and thirty years old. If you do not fully appreciate your duties and role now, it is the fault of a lazy student, not youth. You cannot judge my desire to help him." He returned to the window. "I am hopeful that it might do me some good."

With that statement hanging in the air the others remained silent. Lord Matlock crossed his arms and studied his nephew. "So by teaching Bingley the ways of society, you might find your path through yourself?"

"It will certainly clarify that which I do not already comprehend." He said softly.

"You are a very intelligent man, Darcy. I admire your plan and approve. Please consider Bingley welcome to whatever affairs we might hold in the future, he is perhaps a little excitable, but I am sure that is youth as opposed to bad manners. No doubt you will correct him in your own particular style." He chuckled and Darcy turned to look at him, his lips rising in a slight smile.

"I appreciate your confidence, sir."

"And you two will leave him alone." Lord Matlock looked at them pointedly. "I rather look forward to seeing what you make of this young man."

"I do as well." Darcy returned to staring out the window, his thoughts now turning to the long line of carriages, and wondering where in the convoy Lizzy was. *She must be returning to Gracechurch Street, that man had to be her uncle . . .what was the name? Something from the outdoors, she likes to walk, she likes the park, Gardiner, yes, that is it.* He closed his eyes and remembered the scent of her perfume as they stood so near to each other at the exhibition. *I could have touched her. The lilac was so sweet, so delicate, so perfect for her. Why did I let her go today? You idiot! Dare I go to her relatives' home and seek her out?*

"Darcy . . . Darcy!" Lord Matlock called and Layton kicked him. Darcy turned to face them. "When do you return to Pemberley?"

The weight of duty fell upon him. "In four days. I will take care of some business and then we will depart. I hope that you will come to enjoy some shooting with us this autumn, and yes Uncle, I will be scheduling hunts all winter for the vermin." He smiled slightly. "I have learned my lesson."

"Good man." Lord Matlock chuckled. "You will be fine, Son."

"SO, HOW WAS THE RACE?" Mrs. Gardiner looked between her husband and niece. He chortled and nudged her.

"Go ahead Lizzy, gloat away."

"I won twenty pounds!" She giggled.

"Lizzy!" Mrs. Gardiner clapped. "However did you do that?"

"She chose the winner, and I laid out the funds. I promised to split our winnings. Pan won." Mr. Gardiner grinned. "So our trip was free from my end and our niece made a tidy profit."

"Well dear, what will you do with such a handsome fortune?" She led the way into the drawing room where tea was waiting.

"Oh, I . . .I think that I will save it." Elizabeth blushed. "It would be foolish to waste such a sum. If it was less . . .much less, I might buy a book or two, but this much, I cannot bear to waste."

The Gardiners exchanged approving glances and smiled. "I think that is very admirable, Lizzy."

"I want to change out of these things, I will return soon." She practically ran from the room and Mrs. Gardiner handed her husband a cup then poured her own.

"What else happened?" She asked knowingly.

"She was staring again, as she did at the exhibition. I could not tell who it was, but undoubtedly it was the same young man who caught her eye there." He smiled as he took a sip. "Our little girl is grown."

"I hope that she is prepared to be disappointed when this man does not return her looks."

"But that is just it, I think that he does. Why else would she be smiling so? It is not a smile of one who admires; it is one of a woman communicating a message to an active participant." Mrs. Gardiner's brow knit. "She was not flirting, Marianne. This was different, a connection was formed. I only wish that I knew who it was."

"I suppose that asking her would be unwise."

"She likely has no idea who he is. Just leave it be; no harm was done." Mr. Gardiner smiled. "I wonder at her need to go upstairs, she already spent the last three hours staring dreamily out the carriage window, I suppose she needs to dream a little more." The couple laughed and glanced up at the ceiling.

4 June 1808

I saw Mr. Darcy today at Epsom Downs. He came to the aid of a young man who was obviously in great need of a strong arm to rescue him from his own good nature. I am young, but I hope I am not as naive as this gentleman appeared to be! Mr. Darcy saw that he was in trouble and strode right into the fray; gave the instigators a look that would melt steel and set things right. He even retrieved the gentleman's money. And then he turned and saw me. Well of course I smiled at him! I was so proud of his behaviour. Such a good man he must be! He looked as if he wished to come and speak to me. My heart was racing so! But an older man kept stopping him from coming my way, and then the races started, and I lost him again in the crowd. Why cannot this man just stay in one place? It is so frustrating! And Papa wants me at home next week. I hope that when we walk in Hyde Park tomorrow Mr. Darcy will be there. It is such a miniscule chance, but oh how I wish to see him again! Even for just a moment.

Elizabeth read her note and sat back. Receiving Mr. Darcy's attention this time was different from the last. He recognized her instantly, and sought her out twice. This was more than just noticing a girl; this was a gentleman looking at a lady. She felt somehow different with that realization. When she stood up from her writing desk she moved with grace, and when she entered the drawing room to join her aunt and uncle, she sat down quietly and smiled warmly at them. Mr. Gardiner tilted his head. "I believe that a woman has entered this room." He stood and bowed. "Miss Elizabeth Bennet, I am very pleased to meet you."

DARCY CLOSED HIS JOURNAL and closed his eyes at the same time. His fingers were itching to turn back and look at that worn page again, but . . .that journal was from the year before and resided on the bookshelf behind his desk at Pemberley. Instead he imagined the page with her name and address, and pictured her person, and then remembered the warm approving smile she gave him. His heart began to race with the thought of seeing that smile before him, inches instead of yards away, and then closer . . .he panted as he imagined what the feel of his lips caressing that smile would be like, and then to hear her sigh with his touch. *How does your kiss taste, Lizzy?*

"Mr. Darcy?"

He startled and stared at the open door, then gathering himself together cleared his throat. "Yes, Foster?"

"Sir, there is a gentleman here, I was not sure if you were at home." He stepped forward and handed him a card.

"Bingley, oh yes, please show him in." Darcy cleared his throat again and straightened his neck cloth, pulled at his topcoat, nervously looked down to his breeches, and took a deep calming breath. Bingley appeared cautiously, and he stood. "Mr. Bingley, please come in." He stepped from behind the desk and extended his hand. "Did you have any trouble finding the house?"

Bingley laughed. "Hardly. My sister pointed it out to me some time ago." Darcy's brow creased, and he shrugged. "She is greatly enamoured of status."

"Is she married?"

"No."

"ah." Darcy settled down in his chair and Bingley took one. "Well, I hope she is successful in finding what she desires."

"I am as well." Bingley winked. "Are you in the market . . ."

"Bingley."

"I had to ask!" He laughed and Darcy relaxed. "You were saying yesterday that you are returning to your estate, which should have answered my marriage question."

"I am also still in mourning."

"Yes." Bingley smiled with understanding. "It is a long year."

"I feel that it will be a lifetime. Do you not miss your parents?"

"Honestly, no I do not. We were never particularly close. Mother was busy climbing society's ladders, and left us children to the governess. Then I left for school, Eton, so when she died, I was really only seeing her for a few months of the year. Father, well, he was determined that I be a gentleman, so he taught me next to nothing of the business. We rarely spent time together, and when we did, it was to listen eagerly of the experiences I had. He liked to hear of the people I would meet . . .it sounds cold I suppose, but I do not miss them since I barely knew them. I guess that what I miss is having a base, a family, even if it is in name only. I have relatives in the north, and my sisters of course, but that is all."

"Forgive me Bingley, but that sounds even sadder than me missing my parents who I loved so well."

"Ah, well, love was not a word that was tossed around in our household." He shrugged. "You cannot miss what you have never known, can you?"

"I suppose not." Darcy inexplicably felt great sadness for this young man. "Well, your sisters, they are both unmarried?"

"No, my eldest sister, Louisa, married Gerald Hurst about two years ago. He is heir to a small estate near Bath. My other sister, Caroline, is the one on the hunt. She is one and twenty."

"How is she handling the Season? I suppose that the Hursts are sponsoring her?"

"Yes, but they both hope for greater connections to give them entré to the higher circles." He looked at him apologetically. "They will be very interested in my meeting you."

"Must they know?"

"Well, I suppose not." He smiled. "You mentioned a sister?"

"Yes, she will be twelve soon." Darcy's face clouded over. "Georgiana is a great challenge for me. I am trying to . . . give her more than simply a governess, but I admit to not being very sure of myself, and greatly employed with the duties of the estate. At what age did your sister Miss Bingley, come out?"

"Well, unfortunately Father died so she had to wait for last year, this is her second Season. She has a substantial dowry and attended a fine finishing school, but there are no takers yet. I am not sure what the problem is."

"How substantial is the dowry?"

"Twenty thousand." Darcy's brows rose. "So you understand my concern."

"Quite." Darcy bit his lip, already suspecting that either Miss Bingley possessed no beauty or no personality. That was quite a dowry to leave untaken after two Seasons.

"Well, I return home to Pemberley in a few days. You are welcome to visit if you are so inclined before the next term begins. This will be your senior year?" Bingley nodded. "And will you go on your tour?"

"I suppose that depends on Napoleon." He smiled and Darcy laughed.

"Fitzwilliam . . . oh, forgive me, I did not know that you had company." Georgiana blushed.

"Come in, dear." Darcy and Bingley stood. "Mr. Bingley, this is my sister, Miss Georgiana Darcy."

He gave her a dazzling smile and bowed. "This is an enormous pleasure, Miss Darcy."

She stared at the dashing man with wide eyes and whispered. "Oh." Darcy fixed his gaze upon her and she caught his look. "It is a pleasure to meet you, sir." She cleared her throat. "I . . . I only wanted to ask my brother a question about our travel. It can wait for later. Please excuse me." She fled the room and Bingley turned to see Darcy looking after her.

"She is charming." He smiled and Darcy relaxed.

"Thank you."

"Well, I have trespassed on your time long enough. If we do not meet again before you depart, I wish you a safe journey home. I will write to you and see if I can work in a trip to Derbyshire before I return to school."

"You will be welcome. My uncle and cousins will be visiting for the grouse season in August." They walked to the door and out to the hallway. A footman handed Bingley his hat and gloves, and he smiled up at the steps. Darcy turned and caught Georgiana peering at them. Bingley shook his head and then Darcy's hand.

"She is sweet; do not be hard on her." He winked and left the house. Darcy turned to see that Georgiana had disappeared. He swallowed the chastisement that was on his lips and instead asked for his hat and walking stick, and set off across the street and into the park.

"LIZZY SLOW DOWN." Mrs. Gardiner said quietly. "Whatever you seek will still be here ten minutes from now."

"I am sorry Aunt." Elizabeth slowed and resumed the stroll that the other visitors to the park seemed to be practicing. "I am not seeking anything; I guess that I am just anxious to see everything."

"That is a very contradictory statement."

Elizabeth laughed. "I suppose it is. Papa would have enjoyed skewering me with it."

"Do you look forward to going home?"

She sighed and studied her gloves as they walked. "Would it be wrong to say no?"

"If that is your opinion, it would be dishonest to say otherwise." Mrs. Gardiner smiled and looped her arm with her niece's. "Tell me what troubles you."

"It is not one thing alone. Mama does not like me. Why? She seems particularly anxious to see me married and gone. I cannot for the life of me understand what I ever did wrong?" She looked up to her aunt who was nodding.

"I had a friend that I knew from childhood. He was born when his father was away from home on business. His father never forgave him for that and treated him harshly all his life until he was old enough to become apprenticed to an attorney. He gladly left home, and his family never saw him again."

"How ridiculous! It was not the boy's fault when he was born!"

"No it was not, and it is not your fault that you were not born a boy as your mother had determined you would be. And it is not your fault that you are bright and that your father showers what attention he does give upon you instead of his wife and other daughters. None of it is your fault, but the result is that your mother unreasonably resents you."

"So I am not pretty, but I must find a husband with my charms and save the family from starvation when father dies because he is . . ."

"Yes." Mrs. Gardiner squeezed her arm. "Although I imagine that your mother would be happy with any of you girls marrying. She is very anxious to push you all out of the door to find husbands and secure her future."

"What if our husbands do not care for the way she treats us and do not provide for her." Elizabeth said with a hint of bitterness in her voice.

"Lizzy, that is unkind."

"Oh please Aunt, do not sound like Jane!" She saw the raised brows and sighed. "I am sorry."

"I understand."

"She will have nothing good to say of you when I arrive home since I am not engaged." She smiled.

Mrs. Gardiner laughed. "Oh, I expect a letter soon describing how I have failed you and at the same time begging me to invite you girls back for a second chance. She does not realize that we ask you here, not only for the pleasure of your company and to educate you a bit more, but also to relieve you of her pushing. You are too young to marry. However, Jane is now at the proper age to begin looking, and we will not discourage any men who might seem interested. I do not expect her to meet any when she comes for my confinement, though. We will be busy." She winked.

"Will she be present at the birth?"

"No, of course not, but she will look after the children and perhaps calm your uncle." She smiled. "It is not proper for an unmarried woman to see such things."

Elizabeth nodded and brought up a delicate subject. "Aunt . . .will you teach me . . .about being a wife?" She looked up at her and blushed then looked away. "I have witnessed the animals . . .but . . ." She spoke nervously. "I have listened to Mama's friends . . .it sounds terrible and they wish to avoid it . . ."

"Lizzy, I will gladly be the one to tell you of the duties of a wife, and no it is not terrible or something to fear. Whatever your mother tells you should be taken with the knowledge that she is unhappy with . . .well, just do not listen with both ears if she speaks of it." She patted her arm. "When you are engaged dear, we will have a good long talk. Until then, just be assured that it is nothing to worry over and perhaps if you find a good caring man, something you will enjoy with him."

"Thank you." She whispered.

"Now, your uncle tells me that you smiled at a young man yesterday?" Mrs. Gardiner saw her blush even brighter and bite her lip. "And did he smile back?"

"Yes."

"Do you think that you will see him again before you leave?"

Elizabeth looked up the path and searched the park. "I dearly hope so."

Darcy slowed from his brisk stroll and stood near the Serpentine, staring out over the water. *Of course she is not here, it is not as if she lives in Grosvenor Square, is it?* He picked up a rock from the ground, studied its shape and with skill learned from childhood, skipped it across the surface, and stared in surprise when after one hop, it sank. He heard feminine laughter and looked up only to be disappointed, but not before the ladies stopped and smiled at him expectantly. He nodded stiffly and looked back to the water, hearing the giggles and discussion of his look as they strolled away. *I suppose that I should simply become used to this. There will be no excuse next Season. I may cling to the sight of Lizzy, but she is not the one I will marry someday. That would not be fulfilling my duty.* He picked up another stone and attempted to skip it across the water, and again failed. *I need to stop thinking of her. I must put her out of my mind. I cannot let the ghost of her memory prevent me from looking honestly at all of the women who are suitable for me and Georgiana.*

Elizabeth and her aunt approached the Serpentine, and stopped to gaze upon the water. She looked up to see the back of a tall man standing by the edge, his dark hair touching the collar of his fine coat. She drew in a sharp breath and stepping forward purposefully, decided that this time, no matter how improper, she was going to speak to him.

"Lizzy, what are you doing?" Mrs. Gardiner asked.

Ignoring her, Elizabeth moved quickly and approached the man. "Pardon me . . ."

He turned and looked at her face, then took in her clothes from head to toe, his face wrinkling in a look of disdain. Elizabeth gasped and blushed. "Forgive me, sir, I mistook you for someone else!" She turned and fled. Mrs. Gardiner met the man's eye who was regarding her with equal disgust for the display of impertinence. She curtseyed and followed Elizabeth who had rounded a corner and was sobbing into her handkerchief.

"I . . .I thought it was him!" She gasped. "Oh what a fool I am! Wanting to come here and perhaps see him, and instead I behave so badly. I am so sorry for embarrassing you!" She cried and covered her mouth. "He looked at me as if I were lint!"

"Yes dear, he is rich and clearly we are not."

"You are not poor, Aunt." She drew her shoulders back. "I will go tell him that!"

"Lizzy you will do no such thing! The incident is over! Keep your opinion to yourself!" Mrs. Gardiner whispered. "He had every right to feel offended."

"And I have no right to be here." She sniffed again. "I belong back at home with the mud and the sheep."

Darcy walked back along the banks of the water and came upon Lord Reginald Creary. He nodded at him and saw his expression. "Is something amiss, Creary?"

"Indeed Darcy, some little guttersnipe just walked up to me and had the impertinence to presume we were acquainted. Well, one look from me and she and her companion scurried away. I looked at her dress; it was not what the Queen would call fashionable. Women of that sort should not be allowed to walk here. They should have been stopped at the gate!" He sniffed and noticed the black armband. "Sorry to hear of your father, good man."

Darcy's brow furrowed as he listened. "Thank you. This woman you described, what was her age?"

"How should I know, seventeen perhaps?"

"Dark hair?"

"Yes, has she tried to talk you up, as well? Not that I am averse to a bit of fluff now and again, it does not belong here in the daylight!" He tilted his head, "but if you would care to meet up with her, she went up around the bend."

Darcy glared at him. "I am not interested, but thank you for the concern." He walked away and up the path. Far off in the distance he could see a small young woman walking with another and his pace picked up. He instinctively knew it was Lizzy, then the words of Creary returned to his mind and he slowed. "If someone like he thinks that she does not belong in our circles, without even knowing her, how could I ever subject her to them by pursuing her? It would be unfair to her . . . and disappointing to my father." He stopped and watched the women disappear. His voice caught and he felt his heart clench, but still he murmured. "Goodbye, Lizzy."

Chapter 5

11 August 1808
Uncle Henry wrote to me and has confirmed our fears, Richard is on his way to Portugal, and may even be there now. This will be a real battle, not the little skirmishes he experienced in Norway. He once said that my taking over Pemberley would be the making of me. I fear that it is nothing to the man my cousin will be when he returns. He must return! Uncle says that Aunt Helen is beside herself with worry, and his guilt for not convincing him to study law instead of joining the army is weighing him down. I pray that Richard survives; I fear that his would not be the only life that would be forfeited.

Darcy stopped writing and dropped his pen, and ran his hand through his hair. Biting his lip he worked hard to control his emotions, but then a glance at the black armband for his father sent him up and out of his chair. He began pacing the room. "God, please do not make this piece of cloth a permanent part of my attire. Please keep him safe." He stopped to stare out of his window. There was nowhere to go, nobody to talk to about his fear for his cousin and friend, and deep down he knew that it was more than Richard that was overwhelming him. Since his return to Pemberley, the duties and decisions had rained down on him hard. It was his first harvest alone. Of course Nichols and his staff were keeping watch but it was he who was truly in charge. That was how Pemberley was always run. The master hired the best, but retained command. Darcy looked down at his hands and willed them to stop shaking. "Stop this, now! Take control, you can do this!" He looked to his mother's miniature and received some comfort, then his eyes drifted to the bookshelf where his journals were kept. Without thinking his steps led him there and before he knew it the page was open and he was reading her name. He swallowed hard, closed his eyes, breathed and relaxed, then put the book away.

A knock roused him. "Sir? An express has arrived for you." A footman held out the silver salver and he took the letter, staring at the heavily blotched envelope curiously.

"Whoever penned this must have had a faulty nib." He opened it and squinted and stared, turning the paper in several directions until he finally made out the script. A small smile came to his lips. "Obviously penmanship was not a subject chosen for study by Mr. Bingley for his son." He rang the bell and the footman reappeared. "Please inform Mrs. Reynolds that Mr. Bingley will be arriving this afternoon."

"Yes sir." He bowed and left the room.

He relaxed further. It would be good to have company, and good to distract Georgiana with some ladies about the house when the party from Matlock arrived. Darcy sat down and began reading his correspondence and spent the next several hours at work, there was no point going out on the estate when he had a guest coming. Late that afternoon he received notice that a carriage had entered the park. He stood and walked through the house, stopping in the library where Georgiana was seated with her governess and practicing her French. "Mr. Bingley will be here soon, dear. Shall you join me in greeting him?" He smiled and raised his brow.

"Oh, yes I would like that." Georgiana jumped up and Mrs. Somers gave her a look. She blushed and walked slowly to the door. Darcy nodded with approval to see her behaving as a lady, and she smiled to see his pleasure. "You would have made Mother very proud to see what a fine mistress you are becoming."

"I am hardly the mistress, Brother."

"Nonsense, you are the only Darcy woman in the house, are you not? Therefore the position is yours." He tilted his head. "Someday if I ever host a ball, you will be the one at my side greeting our guests."

"That will be a very long time!" She cried. "I cannot even attend a ball let alone host it until I am out. Why, to hear Mrs. Somers talk, I should not even be eating meals outside of the nursery!"

"Well that would make meals very dull for both of us. I appreciate your company." She held his arm and they walked to the front door, stepping outside to await the carriage.

"I visited Papa today."

Darcy turned and looked at her with surprise. "You did? I wish I had known; I would have joined you. This was your first time, was it not?"

"Yes, I wanted to go alone and apologize to him for not coming sooner." She looked up at his sad eyes. "Do you think he minded? I just could not visit before; really it was my first time visiting the cemetery at all. Papa never took me there."

"So I think that he would understand."

"I visited Mama, too."

"Yes." He said softly.

"Fitzwilliam, there were four other little graves."

"Our siblings. You knew about them, Georgiana. The girls were both stillborn; the two boys were lost to fevers when they were infants."

"Did you know them?"

"No, not that I remember, I was a baby myself when the boys died, only five, and the girls, well I remember Mother's pregnancies, and the sadness when they seemed to just end, but nothing was ever said to me. She and Father were sad for awhile, then all returned to normal, I suppose. Until she had you." He smiled and patted her hand. "You were a gift."

"But Mama died because of me."

"Mother died because she had an infection. That was not your doing." He attempted a smile for her then looked up at the sun to blink hard. "Now, how can we dispense with these sad thoughts? We have a guest to entertain. Will you play for him?"

"Oh no, please!"

"Very well dear, I was just teasing." She looked at him doubtfully.

"Truly, I was."

"It is difficult to tell sometimes."

"Have I become so sombre?" His brow creased with the thought and then he looked up to see Bingley's carriage arriving. The door opened and the young man jumped out.

"Darcy!" He held out his hand and they shook vigorously, then he bowed to Georgiana. "Miss Darcy, such a pleasure to meet you again."

She giggled and he grinned, then looked back to Darcy. "I did not know at all what to expect when we emerged from the trees up above, but . . .this place is magnificent. I have never seen the like!"

"Thank you Bingley, we are very proud of it. Welcome to Pemberley." The servants had rushed to gather the luggage, and the group moved inside. Darcy gave Georgiana a look and she curtseyed and excused herself. Bingley watched her go. "She is a sweet girl, I hope that she will join us and not be shuttered away in a school room the entire time I am here."

Darcy laughed. "So should I presume by your statement that you miss your sister's company and wish to replace it with mine?"

Charles chuckled. "No, no, perhaps it is the comparison between the two . . .well, you have not met Caroline so I should not colour your opinion with mine. I am afraid that she discovered my destination and was quite put out that the invitation was not extended to her."

"Really?" Darcy's opinion of Miss Bingley dropped a notch. "That is rather presumptuous of her, particularly when we have not been introduced."

"Ah, yes, well, just wait until you are." Charles laughed to see his friend's brow knit and then nearly gasped when he finally noticed the atmosphere. "Good Lord." He whispered, looking around at the grand hallway and taking in the artwork, furnishings and splendour. "Um, how long has your family been here?"

Darcy was inwardly enjoying the expression of awe on Bingley's face. "We have been on this land for nearly eight hundred years, but the house itself has burned twice and naturally been rebuilt and added to over the generations."

"So, just as a curiosity, my father's savings for an estate would purchase me . . ."

"The guest wing."

Bingley's eyes widened with shock. "So little?"

"I see that my sense of humour is definitely poor." Darcy shook his head. "You can afford a fair-sized estate with that, perhaps something a third or with luck even half the size of Pemberley, but certainly that can wait until after you finish your schooling."

Relief was evident and Bingley relaxed. "You do know how to frighten a man!" He shook his head and grinned, the clapped his hands and rubbed them together. "Well, I am here to learn, what does a gentleman of leisure do to occupy his time?"

Darcy smiled and chuckled. "Well, if you are this man, you work."

"COME ON JANE, WALK WITH ME!" Elizabeth urged. "After tomorrow, you know that it will not be safe with the men out shooting. I wish Papa would take me along."

"Lizzy!"

"All they have talked about for weeks is the coming grouse season; it is as bad as listening to Mama and her lace theory!"

"She has a theory over lace?" Jane smiled and added some more roses to her basket. They were outdoors escaping the stifling heat of the house and gathering flowers for making into scented water.

"Surely you know it by now; the lace on your décolletage draws a gentleman's eye to your best assets!" Elizabeth recited as Jane groaned. "She says that I need all of the help I can get because my assets are so limited." Elizabeth looked down at her dress. "Am I truly so poorly formed?"

"Lizzy, I am not even going to dignify that query with a response." Jane snipped some more roses and turned away.

"Very well, I will stop. I just wanted to see you react." Elizabeth looked back at herself and covered up her concern with a smile. "If you will not walk with me, then I will go alone."

"If you do not wish to hear another speech from Mama, you will stay at home." Jane shook her shears at her.

"I miss London." Elizabeth said softly, thinking of Mr. Darcy.

Jane looked at her sister's sad eyes and thought she was remembering the town. "Maybe Aunt Gardiner will ask you back again next Season."

"I am certain that she will." She heard a gun fire and looked to see her father and Sir William shooting targets. "I imagine all the gentlemen are in the country now."

"The ones with estates are." Jane smiled.

"And the ones without are begging to stay with those who do!" Elizabeth laughed and smiled, recovering her humour. "Well, I am off then, if Mama is hunting for me, tell her I am searching for a husband in the lanes."

"Lizzy!"

Elizabeth laughed and giving Jane's hand a squeeze, set off on her walk, finally climbing up an old apple tree, and reclining within its branches. There in her privacy, she allowed the tears that she kept to herself to fall again. "You are being ridiculous, Lizzy." She chastised herself. "Even if you had met him again in the park, what did you truly expect to have happened? Aunt Gardiner was correct when she told me that a gentleman must think very carefully when he chooses his wife. He must consider his duty to his family and estate even more so than his heart. Even if Mr. Darcy had feelings for me . . ." She choked and sobbed. "He could never act on them. I have no dowry, nothing to offer him. Nothing." She stifled her sadness in her handkerchief. It was not just the loss of her dreams of Mr. Darcy and his smiles, but the cut from the other gentleman that hurt her. "It is clear that I must look elsewhere for . . . love." Taking a shaking breath she let it out. "I will never forget you, Mr. Darcy. I will think of your smiles with pleasure, and . . . try to forget the rest."

She wiped her eyes and settled herself, remembering how kind her aunt had been, listening to her confession of her imaginary love affair. Elizabeth had not told his name, but almost everything else was blurted out. Never could she have spoken to her mother of such things, or even Jane. And she thought, after behaving so foolishly, she would probably never admit to her aunt if she let her heart be touched like that again. Her thoughts returned to her mother and she laughed. "If she had known I was receiving the smiles of a gentleman, she would have tracked him down and thrown me on his step!" One more deep breath and she let the sadness go again until next time. Opening up her journal, she took out a pencil that was tucked inside.

11 August 1808
This morning Papa asked me to visit some of our tenants. He had heard a story from Mr. Grassel that they were in need of aid and hinted that it was of a female nature. Mama, of course, would not go and Jane was forbidden, but she did not seem to mind at all that I was willing, although she said it was unseemly for a gentleman's daughter to be traipsing around alone after tenants, so Papa asked if our steward was good enough company and she agreed. Mr. Grassel and I took a gig and set off together. I think that Aunt Gardiner would have had a fit of nerves to equal Mama's if she had known that I was alone with a man like that! Well, we visited two homes, and the ladies were both very grateful to see me. I listened to their concerns, although it made me very nervous. They were both with child and were worried that the midwife who had served our area had moved away, and they were concerned about what would happen when their time came. I can understand why Papa wanted to avoid this conversation, but to send an unmarried girl to solve the problem was, well I hardly know the word, but inappropriate comes to mind amongst others. I asked Mr. Grassel to take me to the apothecary and then said that I would walk home. I spoke to Mr. Jones and he said that he was sending out word that a midwife was needed in our part of the county and assured me that he would keep us informed if he heard anything. I walked home wondering of so many things, and I realized that if I ever marry and become mistress of an estate I will be sure to visit the tenants, and not travel there alone with a man!

Elizabeth closed the book and closed her eyes, knowing that her trip that morning had been an error, even if it did do some good. "If I did not realize that Mama truly did not see the impropriety, I would say that she was purposely setting out to see me compromised. But to a steward?" She put the back of her hand to her forehead and laughed. "Oh the flutterings of my poor heart!"

"AH, I JUST LOVE A COUNTRY DANCE!" Bingley smiled. "Come Darcy, I must have you dance; you cannot stand about in this stupid manner!"

"Bingley, I am the master of Pemberley, I do not dance with my tenants." Darcy looked at him sternly. "I sponsor this Harvest Home; I make my appearance, drink a tankard of ale, then leave."

"Well where is the pleasure in that?" Bingley's eyes scanned the room. "There are many pretty girls here . . ."

"Tenants, labourers, townsfolk. Not your peers, man. Have I taught you nothing over the past two months?" Darcy sighed. "Very well, dance, but in two days when you depart for school, do not whine to me about leaving your love behind, she is not in this room."

Bingley laughed. "Well wherever she is, she will have to wait another year before I come of age and can even consider the notion of marriage. Until then . . ." He walked over to a blushing girl and bowed, then looked up at Darcy and winked.

"Bingley certainly has a great deal of enthusiasm." Layton drawled. "Have you had your fill of doing good for the less fortunate?"

"You still dislike him?"

"It is not a matter of like or dislike; he is not one of us."

"So he could never rise in your esteem, no matter the fortune he possesses." Darcy studied his cousin. "What does your father have to say about your attitude?"

"He would prefer that your friend at least own an estate, however . . . he has said nothing derogatory other than noticing his youth."

"Ah." Darcy turned back to face the crowd.

"What would your father say of this friendship?"

Darcy automatically looked down his sleeve for the black armband and remembered that it had been retired that morning, a year and a day after his father's death. "I think that he would be glad that I had a friend, but would hope he would find an estate." He smiled slightly to hear his cousin's laugh. "I am not blind to the favour I am doing for him."

"hmmph." Layton regarded him and decided to take him unaware. "So tell me of this lady who has captured your imagination."

Darcy startled. "Lady? There is no lady."

"Then why are you flushed and clenching your fists?" He laughed. "Come on, Darcy, Richard is not here to interrogate you properly so it goes to me to discover who she is. I have witnessed you looking out of windows and not seeing the scenery far too many times during our visit." He chortled with the thought and noticed how his cousin's face had set into a smooth expressionless mask. "What did I say?"

"Nothing at all." He looked towards the dance, the set had ended. "It is time to leave. I will collect Bingley."

Layton watched him walk away and crossed his arms. Darcy made his way through the crowd, visibly relaxing as he walked through his people and spoke to the tenants, stopping to hear their thanks and their concerns, and clearly making a point to remember what was said. Layton realized that his cousin actually knew their names. It was certainly not something that he could claim to do for Matlock, and wondered if his father could. Thoughts of his fitness to be master took over his musings, and replaced the desire to tease his cousin.

"MAY I INTRODUCE YOU TO MR. STEWART?" Sir William beamed. "He is a cousin to Captain Carver and is staying at Netherfield for the shooting." He turned to Stewart. "This is Miss Jane Bennet, and Miss Elizabeth Bennet. I believe that you have met their father already?"

"Yes, we have taken many birds together in the past few weeks." He smiled warmly at them both, his eyes passing from one sister to the next, first stopping to consider Jane, then alighting on Elizabeth. "I am delighted to meet such lovely ladies, and I hope that I might request a set from each of you this evening."

Jane smiled serenely and looked down. "It would be my pleasure, sir."

Elizabeth studied his soft brown eyes and expectantly raised brow. "I believe that I may have a set available, sir."

His eyes crinkled with amusement. "I would surmise that to be so as you are not presently dancing, Miss Elizabeth. Perhaps our set might be first?"

Unembarrassed she nodded. "If you insist, I shall remain available for the next, and refuse all others."

Chuckling he bowed and walked away. Jane grabbed her arm. "Lizzy! What has gotten into you? How can you speak so impertinently?"

"He asked for a dance, Jane, not a courtship!"

"He will never ask for more if you do not curb your tongue!" She chastised.

"Then I will leave him to you." Elizabeth smiled and the sisters linked arms, walking around the room and speaking to neighbours and friends until the music ended and Elizabeth found herself suddenly staring into Mr. Stewart's striped waistcoat. "I see that you have remembered our set, sir." She took the offered arm and they walked to the line.

"I am not so old to have forgotten so quickly, Miss Elizabeth." He smiled and the music began. The couples on either side moved and they remained staring at each other until it was their turn. "Tell me, why are you so defensive?"

"Am I?"

"There it is again."

Elizabeth flushed. "Forgive me, I . . . I . . ."

"You are very pretty; otherwise I would not have asked you to dance. There, is that better?" He smiled to see her face brighten. "I think it is."

"It does not hurt to hear a compliment, sir." Elizabeth relaxed and they moved through the pattern. "So sir, you are the cousin of our illustrious Captain."

He chuckled. "Illustrious? That is hardly the term I would assign, but then I am family. Yes, I am. I live mostly in town."

"Oh, and how do you occupy your time?"

"I am the second son, so I studied law. My cousin urged me to the sea, but that is not for me. And with this war raging on, I am glad to be free of it. I am also glad to come and keep my cousin's family company while he is away."

"Mrs. Carver must be desperately worried." Elizabeth said softly as they passed each other. Stewart smiled at the compassion he saw in her expression.

"She is indeed. I read the papers and give her any news I can glean, but it is a long wait. We are not entirely sure where he is at this point."

"Will you stay in the neighbourhood long?" She met his smiling eyes then looked down.

"I will be here until November when court resumes, then return in December until court again resumes in January. Beyond that, I have no fixed plans. Will you and your family be here during this time?"

"We will, however my sister Jane, Miss Bennet, will be leaving for town tomorrow to attend to our aunt in London." She looked up and saw that he seemed only slightly disappointed with the news. The music came to an end and he bowed.

"I hope that I will have the opportunity to call on your father during my stay." He smiled at her and she blushed. "Would he object, do you think?"

"No sir, I think that he might be pleased with the honour." Elizabeth returned the smile. He nodded and offered his arm, returning her to Jane who took his other arm and followed him out to the floor. Mrs. Bennet slid up next to Elizabeth as she looked after him curiously.

"Oh, that was nicely done, Lizzy! I know that he is but a second son, but his father is an Earl, so that makes him quite suitable for you. He is a gentleman. Now then, keep smiling and remind him that you are there. You must not miss this opportunity!" She reached up and began pinching her cheeks.

"Mama, please stop!" Elizabeth whispered furiously.

"Miss Lizzy, you have failed to secure a man in town, and that is because I was not present. Your aunt clearly does not know what she is about, so it is up to me to make sure that this attachment takes its proper course!"

"Attachment? We had one dance together! I do not know him! How can you . . ." Elizabeth closed her eyes and reopened them only to see her father across the hall, laughing at her discomfort with her mother. She flushed again and tore away from Mrs. Bennet and headed outside to get some air. Charlotte followed her.

"Are you well, Eliza?"

"No." She wiped her eyes with her hand. "Why must Mama ruin everything?"

"She is only seeing an opportunity. My mother would be doing the same if he had asked me to dance."

"He did dance with you." Elizabeth looked up in confusion.

"But he did not ask. Papa pushed me onto him and he was too polite to say no." Charlotte smiled sadly and squeezed Elizabeth's hand. "Do not wait to secure him."

"Charlotte! You are as bad as Mama!" Elizabeth stared and began to laugh.

"I only see what is clearly before me." She shook her head at her young friend and they re-entered the hall. The rest of the evening passed pleasantly, however by the time that they arrived home, Mrs. Bennet was loudly expressing her anger with Mr. Stewart for not asking for second dances and rounded on her daughter.

"What did you say to him, Lizzy?"

She sighed. "Nothing, Mama. He simply did not ask again. I notice that he did not dance twice with anyone besides Mrs. Carver." She turned to her father. "He did wonder if you would accept his visit, Papa."

Mrs. Bennet's ears perked up and she purred. "Oh, did he? Well, that is fine." She patted Elizabeth's shoulder, approving of her again. "And you will of course accept him, Mr. Bennet."

"I will. I like him. I enjoy speaking to a person with sense and have enjoyed the hours I have spent in his company this past month." He smiled and saw Elizabeth flush and Jane bow her head. "I would find him a suitable mate for either of you girls."

"Papa!"

He shrugged. "I will not demand that you marry anyone if you are not so inclined. I am simply saying that if you wish to pursue this avenue, I will not stand in your way."

"Thank you for the blessing, Papa, as unnecessary as it is." Elizabeth said dryly. He chuckled and watched as the girls went upstairs to retire.

Jane dressed in her nightclothes and crawled under the covers while Elizabeth plaited her hair and sat staring at herself in the mirror on their dressing table. "He liked you, Lizzy. Do you return the admiration?"

"I hardly know. I do not feel . . . fluttering in my chest when I look upon him as I did with . . ." She stopped and blushed.

"With?"

"Nobody." Elizabeth sat up and blinked away the blurriness in her eyes. *At least you have spoken to Mr. Stewart, and danced with him. What have you done with Mr. Darcy besides smile?* She turned to Jane and smiled. "Just someone I imagined."

"That is all of those novels you read." Jane sank down under the covers. "This is real life, and we must think of our futures."

"You do not wish to marry for love anymore?"

"Of course I do. Can you love Mr. Stewart?"

"I just met him!" Elizabeth stood up and blew out the candle. "Do you seriously think that he is wondering if he could love me? Besides, he may be just as interested in you or any other girl of the neighbourhood." She climbed into the bed and drew the covers around her. "Good night, Jane."

"Good night." She whispered.

Stewart poured himself a glass of port and settled into his chair in the Netherfield library, and looked at the crackling flames in the fireplace. "Well, you have finally met the famous Bennet sisters, renowned as the beauties of Hertfordshire. Miss Bennet is a beauty without a doubt, and by watching her tonight, I am sure that she would make a pleasant and compliant wife, if a bit dull. However, Miss Elizabeth, you are a rose about to come into full bloom, with a personality that is a mix of impertinence and compassion which is very appealing." He smiled at the memory of her insecurity. "You do not know how beautiful you will soon be, and what a lucky man I would be to capture that beauty before any others have the opportunity." He rubbed his glass on his chin while he thought, then lifting it to his lips, swallowed the burning liquid. "Well, we shall see."

"MAY I TOP OFF YOUR GLASS, STEWART?" Mr. Bennet asked.

"No sir, I have had enough. I am not in the habit of beginning so early in the day." Stewart smiled.

"Ah well, marriage can do that to you." He chuckled. "It is one of my indulgences." He waved his hand at the shelves weighted with books. "This is my other."

"It is impressive. My father is fond of his library as well. This is a familiar atmosphere."

"Your father is an Earl, I understand?"

"Yes, the Earl of Moreland, in Nottingham. He encouraged me to study the law and I see much of him in London when I am in court."

"A barrister."

"Yes."

"So do you spend your time hanging about the court looking indispensible and hoping to impress potential clients by your supposed industry?" Mr. Bennet's lips twitched, "Or do you follow the circuit judges around the countryside?"

Stewart held back the retort he wished to throw at Mr. Bennet for his insult, and found it difficult to believe that this man would consider laughing at the position of a potential suitor. "Sir, I wonder, are you familiar with the steps involved in becoming a King's Counsel? Like any goal, it is a long process to earn my place. All men of law must endure their time at the bottom, and work their way up."

"So you have been called to the bar already?"

"I have." He said stiffly.

"Well done." Mr. Bennet saw the ire in the man's eyes, and did not push further. "I must thank you for not listening to my wife's invitation to take all of our birds from our coveys."

Stewart relaxed a little. "I assumed that she was simply being very hospitable."

"No, after nearly twenty years of marriage, she still has not grasped that to take all of the birds in this season's shooting will leave no birds for the table in the next." He smiled and laughed at Stewart's astonishment. "My wife was not raised on an estate. Her meals came from the butcher or the chickens her mother raised. I doubt that her father ever set foot in a field to hunt. Of course, he was merely a solicitor and had not the leisure time to wander the countryside."

"I see." Stewart stared down into his glass uncomfortably. With each new visit to Mr. Bennet, it became increasingly difficult to ignore the qualities that were wanting in this family. He thought of his father and tried to convince himself that the bright jewel that was Elizabeth would overcome all of the Earl's objections to her family. It would be a difficult. He focussed on his hopes instead. "Miss Elizabeth seems to be very well-read. She must have made good use of this room."

"She has. I have spent many hours with her, debating books and challenging her thoughts. It has been a joy to see her grow in understanding and confidence. She is worthy opponent." He smiled fondly out the window where Elizabeth and Mary could be seen gathering the last of the lavender before the hard frost arrived.

"I have been on the receiving end of her opinions, sir. She delivers her views very charmingly." He looked out to her. "She is unique."

"That she is. I will be sorry to see her leave me."

"My father felt the same of my sisters. He delayed their presentation as long as possible." He smiled at the memory.

Mr. Bennet snorted. "My wife pushed them out at the first possible opportunity." Stewart's brow rose. "The entail has her concerned."

"Well, of course, but surely her settlement will care for her?"

"Of course." Mr. Bennet looked away and Stewart understood what was not being said. The girls were being pushed to marry, and the lucky son-in-law would inherit the other girls and their mother to support as well. It was a very expensive prospect for a second son.

"Sir, I think that I have trespassed on your time long enough for today, and will greet Miss Elizabeth and Miss Mary then return to Netherfield." He stood up and Mr. Bennet did as well. "Thank you for your hospitality."

"You are always welcome. It is pleasant to have a male to speak with for a change." Mr. Bennet bowed and Stewart escaped the bookroom. In another part of the house he could hear the shrill notes of Mrs. Bennet's voice as she berated Kitty for some offence. He slipped outside unseen and stood for a moment in the sunshine, watching the two girls at work. It was a pretty sight.

"Good afternoon ladies, I am pleased to have not missed you today." Stewart said as he approached.

The girls curtseyed and Elizabeth smiled. "I am pleased to have not missed you as well, sir. I was just considering a stroll in the garden."

"May I join you?" He bowed and looked to Mary. "Both of you?"

"Oh, I would rather read, you go ahead, Lizzy." Mary smiled a little and Elizabeth nodded her thanks. Stewart offered his arm and they began to stroll the paths, well in sight of the house.

"I hope that you enjoyed your talk with Papa." She looked up at him and bit her lip.

Stewart smiled. "It was informative and challenging all at once. Although after three visits, I think that I am becoming familiar with his style."

"You are too kind. I know how difficult he can be." Elizabeth said quietly. "I appreciate your patience."

"Well, I suppose that patience comes when one spends their time waiting." He laughed. "Actually my father can be rather irascible as well. He was definitely born for politics."

"Does he win his point often?"

"He does more often than not. He knows the value of exploiting his connections." He smiled and saw a frown form. "Miss Elizabeth?"

"It is nothing." She smiled back up at him and he studied her soft gaze.

"I was just telling your father how much I have come to admire your education." She shook her head and he laughed. "Come now, you can easily best me in so many topics."

"There is no need to build up my good opinion of myself sir; however, your statement does help to build my good opinion of you." They both laughed and Stewart squeezed her hand. "I understand that barristers often move from the courts to government service."

"Yes or become a judge, but ultimately that is my goal, to win one of those lucrative and well-funded positions. My father will intervene if needed, but I am attempting to earn my way there on my own."

"I respect that, but cannot look down my nose at your father's help if necessary. Are there many young men hoping to achieve the same?"

"Certainly."

A thought struck her. "When you began, did anyone outside of your family ever come to your aid, give you a helping hand?"

"No, I never needed any help; my name was useful, which in all honesty was good because there are few who are generous enough to offer any assistance." He smiled. "You are very much out for yourself."

"I see."

"Is that wrong?"

"No, it only makes he who does offer help to those who do not have the useful family name that much more valuable." She said thoughtfully then noticing his gaze, laughed. "Forgive me, did I offend you?"

"Not at all, Miss Elizabeth, if anything I admire you more."

"Mr. Stewart, you make me blush with such kind words." Their eyes met and she looked down. "You are fortunate to have such a caring father."

"He is a very great man, and very proud of our family. My brother is well-versed on the legacy he must continue."

"As are you, no doubt."

"Yes." He said softly as their eyes met, and Elizabeth looked away.

Chapter 6

*F*our weeks after the Meryton Assembly, Stewart determinedly paid his first official call on Elizabeth. On his previous calls with Mr. Bennet, he had unwittingly witnessed the household's functions as he entered and left, and had become increasingly discouraged. However, his pleasant strolls around the garden with Elizabeth at the conclusion of each visit gave him the impetus to return again and enjoy her company. No stroll would occur this day, the weather was poor, and a call to a daughter required a drawing room and tea with her mother and all four sisters. As the lone man in the room, he should have enjoyed the attention, instead, he felt increasingly trapped.

"Show Mr. Stewart the cushion you embroidered, Lizzy." Mrs. Bennet ordered. She turned to her guest to smile and simper. "It really is not the best quality, but she does well enough with the mending."

"I am certain that she does." Stewart murmured and looked up to see Elizabeth's mortified expression. "My sisters were not particularly fond of their needlework, as I recall. They excelled in other areas."

"No doubt that they did! Why they must have had the best of everything! Our girls have made do with the education that I have provided, but some lessons they simply refused to learn. Now, Lizzy for example, she was always asking to be sent to school, but I said what can a school teach that your own mother cannot? Do I not know how to run a household? Well, my girls are well-acquainted with the important areas of study, sir. Do not doubt that! Lydia, show Mr. Stewart the bonnet you redecorated this morning!"

Lydia jumped up and ran from the room and moments later a bonnet was thrust in his hands and he found a little girl of twelve hanging over him and whispering in his ear. "Is it not pretty?" He looked at her with his mouth agape and saw her batting eyelashes.

"It is . . .very nice, Miss Lydia." He pushed it back in her hands and Mary spoke up.

"What do you feel is the proper age for a girl to marry, and what sort of attentions should a suitor bestow upon her to make his interest known while preserving her modesty?"

He stared and stammered. "I believe that the young lady should be out and he should follow the rules of propriety . . ." Lydia chose that moment to start an argument with Kitty, fighting over the bonnet with a tug of war. Mrs. Bennet ignored the two and smiled invitingly to Stewart.

"More tea?"

Mr. Bennet appeared in the doorway, and bellowed. "What is all of this noise? A man cannot think!" Stewart looked at him, hoping he would take control of his household and was dismayed to see him turn and leave, then heard his bookroom door slam shut. He turned to find Jane staring at her needlework, working industriously and attempting to blend into the furniture, then looked to Elizabeth who met his eye. He saw the pain in her expression and wished to relieve it, but before he could, Mrs. Bennet leaned in again. "I understand that a man in your position brings home a good income?"

"I am comfortable, madam." He bristled. "I am a barrister, not in trade."

"I did not mean to imply that, sir! Not at all! No, I know that your wife may be presented at court!"

"Mr. Stewart, the day is fine; perhaps you would enjoy a stroll in the garden?" Elizabeth finally spoke. Stewart glanced out of the window at the grey day and nodded. "I would enjoy that Miss Elizabeth."

She stood and went to the hallway for her coat and bonnet, Jane appointed herself as chaperone, and Stewart followed after enduring a litany of compliments. Elizabeth looked at Jane and bit her lip. They stepped outside and Jane remained on the porch while Mr. Stewart offered his arm and tried to keep his hat in place in the strong breeze.

"Yes, the weather is fine today, Miss Elizabeth." He laughed a little and looked down to her.

Elizabeth stared at her feet. "Sir, I would like to apologize for my family's behaviour; it was . . ."

"No, stop there." He paused and looked down at her. "Miss Elizabeth, I have enjoyed meeting you and your sister, Jane. You are both very lovely and . . ."

"Sir, please." She looked up. "I have been made aware once before of my unsuitability to aspire to a higher social circle. I felt at the time that I could write it off as the behaviour of an arrogant man who did not know me, but I cannot use that excuse for you, since we have enjoyed each other's company."

"It is not you, Miss Elizabeth."

"It is my family."

"I am afraid so. I wish it could be otherwise, but I am a second son and I must have a very good reason for choosing without consideration of fortune, and unfortunately my family . . ."

"Would not support accepting a dowerless girl who has nothing to offer but herself, at least one with a family such as mine." She said dully.

"I am very sorry for having raised your expectations, Miss Elizabeth." He said sincerely.

She shook her head, then raised her chin. "No sir, I never had any." Letting go of his arm she stepped back, and held in the tears. "I thank you for your honesty, sir."

"Miss Elizabeth . . ."

"Please go." She whispered.

Stewart squeezed her hand then walked over to where his horse was tethered and mounted. He took a long look at her lonely figure and with great regret for what might have been, rode off. Jane stepped off of the porch and hugged Elizabeth while she sobbed. "He did not love you Lizzy, or he would have stayed."

"He would not be allowed to love me, Jane, even if he did."

"Mama scared him away."

"It was all of them, Jane. I once thought highly of myself. Papa told me how intelligent I was. You have been told how beautiful you are." She lifted her face from where it rested on Jane's shoulder. "But now it has been made abundantly clear that no man of quality will want us because wit and beauty are not enough to overcome small fortunes and poor relations."

"Lizzy, do not give up yet, surely there are men for us."

"If there are we will have to meet them in London." Elizabeth hugged her tightly. "When you go again, remember, that will be where our future lies. We must introduce any suitors to those relations before they meet the Bennets."

"Would that be dishonest, Lizzy?" Jane murmured.

"No Jane, that would be prudent." She sniffed, and patted Jane's face. "Do not feel sad Jane. I did not love him either, but I did enjoy being liked." They slowly made their way back into the house to face the disappointment of their mother.

THE HUNTING PARTY RETURNED to Pemberley full of conversation over their victorious ride against the fox. The dogs were braying loudly, and the temperamental hunters danced as their riders attempted to control their mounts. Darcy felt surprisingly good, the hard ride, and the freedom he experienced after each jump was exhilarating and eased some of the burden that he carried. Lord Matlock came up beside him and grinned. "That was excellent, Darcy. I enjoy the hunt at Pemberley far more than at Matlock."

Darcy chuckled. "And why is that Uncle? Your park is just as beautiful as mine."

"Ah, I should not say this as my ancestors will likely come to attack me in my dreams tonight, but that is not true. I have been envious of this estate since I first laid eyes on it, when I visited the Christmas that your mother was engaged to your father."

"That was some time ago." Darcy smiled. "Five and twenty years?"

"About that, you were definitely a honeymoon baby." He laughed to see Darcy's flush. "Speaking of which, it is time to get you out and looking at the ladies."

"Yes, I know. Aunt Helen made that abundantly clear last night."

"She will do so again tonight, be warned." He raised his brows and Darcy closed his eyes. "Come on, Son. You do not have to marry this year, but you must admit that having a woman about the house would do you and Georgiana some good."

"I am doing my best with her." He said stiffly.

"I am not criticizing."

"I know." He shook his head. "I am performing my duty."

"Hmm. Well, be that as it may, you are not a monk, and should not live as one. I want you to enjoy the Season, and be open to the advances of the ladies. Their mamas will be pushing, their papas will be encouraging, the girls will be charming . . .so you simply have to decide to play the game."

"I find it all rather distasteful."

"It is a market to be sure." Lord Matlock rubbed at his chin thoughtfully with his gloved hand. "Just do not allow some social climber to catch you before you have had a good look at all that is on offer."

"So I should not fall in love on the first day? I assure you, that will not be a problem." He looked down and watched the horse's breath freeze in the winter air.

"Layton tells me that someone got under your skin this summer."

"I do not wish to speak of it, Uncle."

"Very well." He looked at him carefully. "Do you remember what your father told you of marriage?"

"Sir, please, I do not wish to speak of it. I know my duty." Darcy's face was unreadable and he stared fiercely ahead. Lord Matlock dropped the subject and the two men rode into the Pemberley stables. The rest of the guests dismounted and followed them to the house for refreshments before leaving for their homes. Darcy saw them off, made sure that his houseguests were comfortable and after changing clothes went into his study, and closed the door.

21 December 1808

I hosted my first hunt today, and it was a great success, I think. At least everyone said so. I asked over my neighbours, the Henleys, and of course the family was here. Uncle Henry asked his friend the Earl of Moreland to come along. It was so good to see him and my old classmate Daniel Stewart. It was a small hunt, but as it was my first attempt, I was happy to keep it that way. Perhaps we will try again in January. I hoped that Richard might have returned by now, a hunt with a cavalryman is exceptional to behold and since it is considered army training for him, he does not rein in his mount. I pray that he is safe.

I had a curious conversation with Stewart. He seemed heartbroken. I suppose that I recognized the face he presented to me, although I really have no right to even claim such an emotion since I never had the opportunity to give my heart away. He said he had spent several months in Hertfordshire, and had come under the spell of a beautiful girl. The way he described her was so familiar, which made it painful to hear. I asked what had happened and he said she had no fortune and questionable family, but that the girl herself would have been a joy to court. I asked her name and he would only say Miss Elizabeth, and that he regretted leaving her behind. I asked if he had indeed loved her, and he said not then, but now that he had abandoned her, he was full of regret. I understand the feeling. I know a Miss Elizabeth in Hertfordshire as well. If it is the same, I will selfishly say that I am glad she remains at home. Wherever that is.

"You sir, are an idiot." He shook his head, remembering once again how he let her walk away in the park that day. "You gave her up, and left her to be snatched up by another." Closing his eyes he thought of his uncle's attempt to speak of his father's words on marriage. "Do your duty." Darcy said softly. "Well, in another month or so Father, I shall begin."

21 DECEMBER 1808
The Gardiners arrived today for Christmas, thank heaven. At last I will have a buffer between me and Mama, who has not stopped her shrill accusations of my ungrateful behaviour since the afternoon that Mr. Stewart rode from our drive. Even if I were to tell her the truth of the matter, that it was she and our family's behaviour that caused him to flee, she would find a way to twist it and place it back on my shoulders. I did not love him; I know that for certain now. I do not regret him so much as I regret the sure knowledge that I am not good enough for any gentleman.

A soft knock at the door made her look up and Mrs. Gardiner smiled and entered, closing it behind her. "Writing in your journal, I see. Does it help?"

"It keeps me from blurting out the worst of my feelings." Elizabeth smiled and closed the book. "When may I come to London again?"

"It is truly impossible for you here." She took a seat on the bed and patted it, inviting Elizabeth to sit beside her.

"Aunt you have been here but one day, but I assure you, Mama's voice is not going to stop declaring my worthlessness anytime soon." Elizabeth's eyes pricked with tears. "Papa does nothing to check her. He allows me to come into his bookroom for a little while since I cannot escape so often on my walks but . . .Oh Aunt, it is not my fault!" She fell into Mrs. Gardiner's open arms and they embraced while Elizabeth sobbed and her aunt stroked her hair. "I suppose it would have been worse if I had loved him."

"Then thank the Lord that you did not." She whispered.

"May I come home with you?" Elizabeth pled.

"That is up to your father, and I think that he is inclined to keep you here. He has no outdoors to escape your mother either, and he sees you as *his* buffer during the winter."

She sat up. "That is ridiculous! He has a houseful of daughters!"

"They are not you." Mrs. Gardiner stroked back her hair.

"Yes, and by receiving his favour I am deemed unsuitable for all men." Elizabeth said bitterly.

"Did Mr. Stewart say anything of your accomplishments being wanting?"

"No."

"Then do not regret the favour your father gave you by the education you did receive." Mrs. Gardiner laughed at her disbelief. "I know, you do not feel quite so charitable, but it is a gift, and one day a truly special man will recognize that and revel in what you may give to him."

"Oh how do you always know what to say?" Elizabeth smiled a little. "Well, if nothing else, I am not quite as naive as I was with courtship."

"That is very true, so when the next young man comes along, you will be able to assess him with open eyes."

"And perhaps I will be the one to send him away first!" She declared and laughed. "Oh imagine me finding a gentleman wanting for a change!"

"It will be glorious, I am sure." Mrs. Gardiner stood. "Come now dear; are you ready to meet the family again?"

She sighed. "I suppose, but keep the escape route clear!"

"THANK YOU." Darcy nodded to the maid who left the tea tray and turned to smile at Georgiana. "What shall we do today?"

"Do?"

"Why yes, I am certainly tired of bookkeeping, it is too cold to ride, and with the family here for Christmas and New Year's we did not have much opportunity to spend time together. Of course if you would prefer lessons I will be happy to ring for Mrs. Somers . . ."

"No!" She said quickly and he raised his brows. "I mean, no, I would rather spend time with you. Soon it will be March and we will be back in London and you will be busy with the Season."

"Excellent, so what shall we do for the next month?"

"Will you teach me billiards?"

"Georgiana!"

"I knew you would say that!" She giggled, and he smiled. "Well, I suppose that there are any number of games we could play . . ." She laughed again at his wrinkled nose. "I know, you dislike cards. Well, what do you suggest? And nothing educational!"

Darcy closed his mouth and swallowed his suggestion. He looked at her speculatively. "Have you ever seen the Darcy jewels?"

Georgiana's eyes grew wide. "No." She whispered. Darcy's face broke out in a wide grin.

"Well, come on then." He stood up and held out his hand. Georgiana followed him to the study where she watched him open up the hidden door behind a bookshelf. He disappeared for several minutes and returned carrying two cases.

"This case," he touched the larger one, "contains the jewels that will always remain with the mistress of Pemberley, so they will go to my wife one day." He met her eyes to make sure that she understood and was therefore not jealous when she saw what it contained, then touched the second box. "This case contains the jewels that Father set aside for you alone when you are out. There is one heirloom from the Darcy collection, most of the jewellery that he purchased for Mother, and some things that he selected just for you, to be given at specific moments in your life. I will not show those to you now. He selected them when he first learned of his illness and showed them to me when we arrived home."

Opening up the case with the Darcy jewels, he began removing velvet bags and boxes. There was a mirror in a corner and Georgiana was up and down time after time, trying on each piece and running to see how she looked. She determined that sapphires were her favourites with diamonds close behind. Darcy laughed and delighted in seeing her excitement. Finally when the last piece was properly stored, he opened the second case. Georgiana was practically trembling with anticipation. He took out three boxes and set them aside, and chuckled to see her eyeing them speculatively, imagining what was inside. Then he began opening her jewel cases.

"Oh, Fitzwilliam! These are all sapphires and diamonds!"

"And pearls." He smiled. "These jewels all looked very well on Mother, so they are sure to be lovely on you."

"Mama wore these." She stood before the mirror and touched them. "Do you remember her wearing them?"

"Oh yes."

Georgiana looked back to him and saw his sad face. "Stop, this is a happy time." She walked over and sat beside him. "Papa told me that my duty was to take care of you. How can I make you happy?"

"Is that what he told you?" Darcy laughed softly. "Well you make me happy everyday with your music and your company. I am happy watching you grow up."

"And I am happy to see you smile." She whispered. "Please do it more often, I miss it so."

"I am sorry to have become so serious, dear. I think that I am at last becoming confident with my duties, well at least a little, and perhaps with that I will relax a little more. Bear with me." He hugged her. "I am trying."

"Will you find a wife this Season?"

"Do you wish for a sister?"

"Sometimes." Darcy tilted his head and raised his brows. "I would like a sister to talk to and spend time with, but then I do not want to share you with anyone either." He chuckled. "And I am afraid of who you might choose." She said softly.

"Why is that?"

"I have seen the ladies of society, Fitzwilliam. I may be young, but I have eyes. Please find someone kind who will take care of you when I am gone someday."

Darcy closed his eyes and hugged her tightly. "I promise; I will do my best. That is what I hope for, too." A knock sounded. "Come." He called.

Mrs. Reynolds entered, and did not look twice at the fortune in jewels spread before her. "Sir this just arrived from Matlock. The messenger will wait for your reply."

"Thank you." He took the letter and standing, ripped it open and walked to the window to read. He let out a long breath. "Thank God."

"What is it?"

"Richard, he has returned." Georgiana jumped up. "He is exhausted and ill, but he landed in Portsmouth four days ago, and found a carriage to London. He is in Matlock House. Our Aunt and Uncle are departing tomorrow for town and will simply remain there for the Season. Stephen and Alicia will remain at Matlock to continue the preparations for the spring then come to town in a month. Uncle asks if we will come early. He said that Richard specifically asks for our company." Darcy licked his lips and began thinking. "I still have some things to accomplish before I can go." He walked to his desk and paged through his calendar, then looked through the stack of papers. "A fortnight, that should be sufficient." He turned to see Georgiana standing with tears rolling down her cheeks. He held out his arms and she fell into his embrace. "It is a month sooner than I expected, but I think it is a worthy reason to go, do you not?"

"I do, Brother." She sniffed and pulled away, taking off the jewels and carefully packing up the cases. "We will just put these things away for another day."

Darcy stayed her hand and kept out a delicate chain holding a pendent containing a single large pearl set in diamonds. He placed it around her neck and adjusted the chain. "I think our cousin would like to see you wearing this."

She looked down and touched it, then back up at him. "Why?"

Darcy laughed. "Because when he was a boy of five, he broke a strand of pearls Mother was wearing and they scattered all over the grass. This was the only pearl that was retrieved, and Mother named it Richard in his honour." Georgiana giggled. "He also received a scolding from his mother that I think he still hears in his sleep."

"The pearls were never found?" She said wide-eyed.

"Well, not exactly." Darcy opened up the case with the heirloom jewels and held out a velvet bag. Georgiana opened it and he poured the contents into her hands. "I found them all, and never told him."

"Fitzwilliam!"

He chuckled and took them back. "I gave them to Father. But to this day, Richard will go out in the grass to that spot and casually hunt around for them."

"I thought that you dislike disguise of any sort!" Georgiana placed her hands on her hips and pursed her lips, looking so much like her mother that he nearly gasped.

"Oh, I will tell him someday. Besides, Father knew."

"So you are innocent."

"Precisely." Darcy grinned.

"Please do not lose that smile!" Georgiana hugged him and ran from the room. Darcy picked up the rest of the jewels and returned them all to the lockbox. He felt the best he had since the day he returned from his tour. *Maybe this is the beginning of the good times again.*

"I AM NEVER MOVING FROM THIS SPOT." Fitzwilliam muttered happily. "Never."

"Sir, your bath is ready."

He lifted his head from the pillow where his face was buried and looked at his new batman. "Well, so much for keeping promises to myself. I will never turn down a chance to bathe again." He rolled out of the bed and stood on wobbly legs. The lance-corporal was right by his side and ready to help him to walk. "No, no, I am fine, Sanders. Well, relatively." Shuffling into the bathroom he sank down into the warm water and groaned. "My God, this feels so good." A glass containing brandy was offered and he lifted a brow and grinned. "I think that we will get along very nicely."

"Yes, colonel."

"Well, from what I understand I will not be leaving these shores again for quite some time, if ever, so you have been assigned a safe post. My last man was not so fortunate." Fitzwilliam raised his glass. "To Corporal Hargrove." He took a sip.

"May I ask sir, the fighting, I only read the accounts in the *Times* . . ."

"It was hell on earth, on a frozen battleground. Any romantic notions any man there had of war were dispelled when the screams of dying men and horses filled the air." He sighed. "But the 15th served well. God bless the Hussars, God bless Sir John Moore!" He raised his glass again, then set it down. "I am ill."

"I was inclined to ask for a physician, sir."

"He would just want to bleed me. I have seen enough of blood." He closed his eyes. "No, what I need is sleep, good food, and quiet. I think that my father's house will serve me well. I expect that they will arrive soon." He opened one eye. "Look out for Mother."

"Sir?"

"You will see." Slowly he sank down below the water and blew bubbles as he exhaled, then rose back up. "Ahhhhh."

A knock sounded. Sanders answered and held a whispered conversation. He turned around. "Sir, a message was just delivered; your parents will arrive tomorrow afternoon."

He chuckled. "That was faster than I expected." He arose from the water and let Sanders steady him as he stepped out and into his robe. "Well, I am going to dry off and go back to sleep. Wake me when they arrive."

"Tomorrow, sir?" Sanders asked in disbelief, and Fitzwilliam met his eye.

"Tomorrow."

"MMMMM."

Lord Matlock smiled and waved the piece of bacon under his son's nose again. "Come on, Son. You know you are hungry."

Fitzwilliam's eyes opened to see his father smiling and blinking back tears. "Father." He sat up and the men embraced.

"You had us worried, Son." He held him tight. "Forgive me. Forgive me for making you choose this life. Forgive me for not providing you an estate."

Fitzwilliam hugged him back just as hard. "Stop Father, you are correct, I chose this life."

"You had romantic ideas of the cavalry."

"I wanted to serve my country, and I have. I will not be going back out, Father. I have been promoted to colonel and will be training men for now on." He drew back and wiped his eyes. "I am safe, sir."

Lord Matlock nodded. "Very well. But if you get the fool notion of fighting again, be assured that your mother will take you down before you mount your horse."

Fitzwilliam chuckled and then it grew into a loud laugh. "Mother would probably succeed. She was always the disciplinarian."

"Really?"

"Oh come on Father, you were the soft touch." He smiled and saw his father's sheepish grin.

"Your brother and sister would beg to disagree, I think. I was easy only with you, Son. You were special." He hugged him again. "I love you, Richard."

"I love you, Father." Fitzwilliam blinked back the tears, and his father sat back.

"Now eat. Be prepared for your mother to arrive at any moment so I suggest that you at least don a robe." He smiled and stood up. "Darcy will be here in about ten days."

"How is he?"

"Better in some ways, and worse in others. Perhaps you can help each other to heal." He smiled and paused at the door. Suddenly it was thrown open.

"Richard!" Lady Matlock swooped into the room and sat on the bed to embrace her son.

"Mother, I am not clothed!"

"Oh, I have seen you unclothed before!" She kissed his face and held it in her hands. "You hold no surprises for me!"

"MOTHER!" He pushed her off of the bed and pulled the covers up to his chin. "Father could you do something about her?"

"Come Helen; let the man eat in peace." He took his wife's hand and led her from the room. "I will give you one hour, Son, then you are on your own." He chuckled and closed the door behind him.

Fitzwilliam lowered the blanket with a sigh. "It is good to be home."

Chapter 7

"*Y*ou have changed." Fitzwilliam said as he took in Darcy's face. They were sitting before the fire in leather wingback chairs, each holding a glass of port, and with their feet propped up on hassocks.

"As have you." He retorted.

"Ah, but my change is that of experience and wisdom." He laughed to see Darcy's eyes roll. "Well, alright, my change is due to a hellish experience, but it is also over forever. I will have to live with the memory, but I also know that it is unlikely that I will have to experience it again; the wounds took care of that. You however, carry a burden that will never be relieved and it shows."

"How so?" Darcy looked down into his glass.

"Your smile does not reach your eyes anymore, Cousin." Fitzwilliam set his feet on the floor and leaned forward. "Georgiana walks around you with caution and seems to cry for attention. Father worries over your sheltering yourself from living. Mother is determined to find you a wife to draw you from yourself."

"I have not been a hermit!" Darcy insisted. "And I have made a concerted effort to smile and be pleasant for Georgiana!"

Fitzwilliam laughed and sat back again. "You cannot force happiness."

"She is taking Father's charge to take care of me too seriously." Darcy muttered.

"Perhaps it is you taking your duties too seriously that is the problem."

"Oh, and I suppose that your performance on the battlefield would have been so much better if you had been lax in your duties? Or should I be toasting your short life right now instead of looking at your ugly face?"

"tsk tsk. I am not the Adonis that you present, but I am hardly homely." He smiled and sat back. "Very well, point taken. I will not question your dedication to duty and honour and all that. However, you do need to let go a little. I can see how tightly wound you are; and I have no doubt that is what Georgiana senses."

"I have missed you, Richard." Darcy said softly and looked up at him. "There has been nobody to talk to."

Fitzwilliam nodded to let him know that he was heard, and said quietly, "Father is more than willing to aid you."

"It is not the same." Darcy shrugged and smiled a little.

"I hear that you have adopted a puppy." A crooked smile crossed his lips. "Named Bingley."

Darcy laughed with genuine happiness. "So I have. He is a good man, and I am enjoying teaching him how to be a gentleman and how to move in society. I admit that he frustrates me at times and he is entirely too easy with those below him, but he is learning."

"He is from trade, I understand."

"Yes, it is unfortunate." Darcy took a sip of his drink. "However he graduates from Cambridge soon, and I will sponsor him at his levee, and that will get him accepted into the higher circles. Your father has graciously offered him invitations to events at Matlock House."

"Your offer of sponsorship is exceptional, and my father's offer, well you are correct, it is gracious and very unusual. I wonder what my brother thinks of that."

"He is not pleased, and your father likely only offered because he saw me in need of a friend." Darcy shrugged. "You see, it is all your fault. If you had been home. . ."

"Do not blame your poor choices of companionship on me, Cousin." Richard laughed. "You were struck by some flash of altruism. I sincerely doubt though that it will be extended to every level of society. Or am I incorrect, will you next invite your valet to the theatre or perhaps offer for a milk maid?"

"Now you are being ridiculous."

"Ah, but it is time for you to consider marriage, and me as well, I suppose." He mused and took a sip of his drink. "Well, if you are to charm the ladies when the Season begins, we must lift this dour visage of yours. I propose that we spend the next few weeks kicking up our heels about town. We will take in the theatre, meet a few actresses, visit the clubs, see a fight, all of the activities of men with time and deep pockets . . ."

"I assume that I am paying." Darcy said with a small smile.

"Of course!" Fitzwilliam laughed. "Then we will go to Rosings, have a good dose of cold water thrown over our boyish high spirits, and return for the Season and the serious business of choosing our mates. What say you?"

"I will try Richard, but I doubt very much that I will be the companion you desire."

"As long as you give it a try, Darcy, I will be satisfied."

"PLEASE, PAPA." Elizabeth sat in her customary chair and leaned forward. "Please let me go."

Mr. Bennet set down the letter from Mr. Gardiner, inviting Elizabeth once again to visit London, and suggesting that she stay for the entire Season. "Is it really so terrible here that you must appeal to your relatives for relief?"

"Papa, you live here, Mama has not let up from her wailings over Mr. Stewart for four months! I can bear it no longer."

He studied her before answering. "I apologize for letting her go on so long, Lizzy. I was selfishly sparing myself from hearing her speeches by letting her focus on you."

"Why could you not simply tell her to stop?" Elizabeth tried to control her tears. "I cannot stand to hear the constant complaints anymore. I can only imagine how much worse it would have been if I had felt anything beyond liking him. I would have been dealing with my heartbreak along with her criticism of him for leaving, and me for being a bad daughter."

"It seems that I have allowed my desire for peace to supersede my duties as father." He looked at Elizabeth's pleading eyes. "Very well, you may go and stay as long as you feel is necessary, or until they grow weary of you."

"Thank you, Papa!" She cried and jumped up to hug him.

Mr. Bennet embraced her lightly and pushed her away. "I shall miss you, Daughter, you are my one joy in this house."

Elizabeth took his hands and stared into his eyes. "You have a houseful of daughters; please give them your attention. It is not too late to educate them as you have me. I worry for my younger sisters, what will become of them?"

"They are too silly to teach." He shook his head. "Mary cares only of sermons."

"But she reads, Papa! She is thirsting for direction, take away her sermons and thrust a history in her hands!" Elizabeth urged. "Kitty is not a reader, but she loves to draw. It is only Mama's criticism that prevents her from trying. Ask her to sketch Longbourn for you and hang it in here. Make her feel that you care for her!"

"And Lydia? How shall I parent her?" He asked with a little twitch to his lips.

Elizabeth sighed. "I fear that she is in need of a strong hand. Perhaps less indulgence would help."

"Less of your mother." He smiled. "And what of sweet Jane?"

"May she come to London with me?" Elizabeth said hopefully. "Truly Papa, we would both benefit from the experience; and Aunt promises to take me to dances and dinners in their circle. Perhaps if she comes, we might both find husbands there?" She tilted her head and he chuckled. "That argument would work for Mama."

"It would." He smiled. "Well, perhaps she might come later in the Season. She has not been invited yet. You may go and we can always send her to town later."

"Would it not be more economical to send us both now?" Elizabeth suggested.

"You are wearing me down!" Mr. Bennet closed his eyes. "You are determined to remove all sense from this house."

"Then perhaps you will be inspired to replace it with my other sisters." Elizabeth looked down at her hands and he opened his eyes to study her. He could not chastise her for insubordination when he was the one who had encouraged it.

"Very well, Lizzy. Go tell Jane that she may travel with you, and I will write to your uncle and inform him of the plans." She jumped up and smiled happily for seemingly the first time in months, and he saw the difference. "Go on."

"Thank you, Papa!"

Mr. Bennet watched her go and sadly pulled forward a sheet of paper and sharpened his pen.

14 March 1809
Longbourn

Dear Gardiner,
I hereby entrust you with my daughters. I am not a fool. I realize that it is you and your good wife who truly own the prestige of having made them into the ladies they are. I have just now received a gentle but pointed remonstration from Lizzy as to my poor parenting. I will endeavour to correct my failings with my younger girls, however, I trust you to care for the eldest. As much as I will regret them marrying and leaving home, I can no longer ignore the seriousness of their situation, and I will trust you to act as their guardians. I will accept your decisions should any gentlemen come to call. Yes Gardiner, I know what you are thinking, once again I am abdicating my role of parent. We will send them to you as proposed.
Sincerely,
Bennet

Mr. Gardiner read the letter and walked into the drawing room where his wife was reading to their son. He handed her the letter while the little boy clambered up into his lap and he hugged him tightly. Mrs. Gardiner read and shook her head.

"Abdicate his parenting. Well who did not know that!"

"Are you getting your dander up, Marianne?" Mr. Gardiner chuckled. "Well, it seems that our brother has charged us with finding husbands for our nieces. Are you up for the challenge, my dear?"

"Of course I am!" She tilted her head. "You know this is what we have been hoping for."

"I do." He kissed his son and set him down. "I will go and consult my bank balance so that you ladies can go shopping." He winked. "Before you use your feminine wiles to convince me."

She shrugged and picked up the book. "Well if you do not want to be convinced . . ." Her statement was stopped with a sound kiss on her lips. "Edward!" He chuckled and winked and walked out of the door. Mrs. Gardiner smiled at her son. "Did you see that? Your Papa will have to teach you how to do that!"

FITZWILLIAM GROANED. "WE HAVE ARRIVED."

Darcy smiled grimly. "So we have." The carriage began the turn onto the drive for Rosings and was just about to roll through the gates when he nudged his cousin with his foot. "Look, the Reverend Mousely is at his post."

"It seems he has a new companion to bow and scrape at us." They noticed a small wide-eyed man eagerly bobbing at the reverend's side. "Who could that be?"

"I understand that he is studying to take Holy Orders with Mousely, the man is practically blind and his hands so gnarled he cannot turn the pages of his bible. This man will assist as curate and get the living when he retires."

"Retires?"

"Well, Aunt Catherine cannot dismiss him."

"She might urge him out of the door, though." Fitzwilliam chuckled and sighed as the carriage pulled to a stop. "Are you prepared for this? Have you your shield and armour at hand?"

"I suppose."

"Well, just use that damned mask you have been wearing for the past month and you will be fine."

"Forgive me for not being the most entertaining companion, Richard." Darcy's lips lifted a little.

"You had a few moments." Fitzwilliam winked. "I got you loosened up quite admirably a few times." Darcy groaned with the memories. "Well, escape this visit unmarried and we will really have some fun this Season!"

They descended onto the drive and Darcy looked back at him. "Should you not be returning to duty or something?"

"In another month or so. I seem to recall some mention of you missing me." He chortled at Darcy's closing eyes. "I will enjoy seeing you dance."

"I will not dance."

"Not if Mother has anything to say about it." Fitzwilliam clapped his back and looked up at the steps. "En garde!"

The men were shown directly to the sitting room where Lady Catherine awaited them. "Darcy, Fitzwilliam! Do not stand at the door, come in here!" They exchanged glances and entered, bowing to her. Darcy kissed her proffered hand.

"You look well, Aunt."

"And you have become a fine-looking man." She nodded in approval then turned to Fitzwilliam. "And you nephew, a colonel now!"

"Yes, Aunt." He bent and kissed her hand.

"But Napoleon lives on!"

"If he had been in my sights, I would have gladly taken the shot, Aunt."

"Still vulgar I see, Fitzwilliam." She sniffed and waved them to their seats. "I suppose that life with the army brings that out in a man."

"I suppose it does." He rolled his eyes. "May I ask where our cousin is? I hope that she is well?"

Lady Catherine's lips pursed, disliking that it was not Darcy who inquired after her. "She is resting, but will be with us for dinner." She smiled at Darcy. "Anne wishes to look her best for you."

"I am certain that she would look well despite the company." He said without emotion.

Her eyes narrowed. "Where is your sister?"

"Georgiana remained in town at Matlock House. She is studying with a music master and did not wish to interrupt her lessons by leaving."

"That is admirable, I suppose. One must practice to achieve perfection. If I had ever learnt . . ."

"Madam," A footman interrupted. "Pardon me, Miss de Bourgh sends you a message." He handed her a note and she took it from him with a scowl. Opening it she smiled. "Darcy, Anne saw you arrive through her window and sends her greetings." She looked at Fitzwilliam. "To you as well."

The men nodded, and seeing they would say nothing else, she continued. "What are you doing for Georgiana's education?"

"She has a governess; however I am considering sending her to a girls' school. I think that the companionship of girls her age would be good for her, and she would form friendships, such as I did at Eton and Cambridge."

"Yes, I can see where that would be useful." Lady Catherine considered. "And with her out of the house, you would be free to concentrate on your marriage."

"I am not married, Aunt."

"Your courtship, perhaps?" Fitzwilliam offered and Darcy glared at him.

"Precisely." Lady Catherine looked at him with approval. "Anne will take up all of your time."

"Aunt, I have made no offer to my cousin." Darcy said tersely. "I am not in search of a wife; my responsibilities for Pemberley are very consuming. When I feel confident with my duties, I will begin to consider marriage."

"And Anne will be ready for you then." Lady Catherine nodded. "You were formed for each other."

Darcy closed his eyes and clenched his fists. Fitzwilliam stood. "Aunt, will you excuse me, I would like to change from these clothes, and Darcy perhaps you would like to do the same? After the last battle I find that I cannot abide a soiled uniform for long."

Their aunt was displeased but agreed. "Oh, well yes, proper attire is necessary. We will see you at dinner." Darcy rose and they bowed, slipping up the stairs as quickly as possible.

"I am sorry about the courtship comment, I could not resist." Fitzwilliam muttered.

"It did not help the situation."

"I got you out of the room did I not?" He chuckled and they stopped outside of their traditional rooms. "It is only a week, Cousin."

"I pray that we survive without spilling blood." Darcy said under his breath and entered his chamber with his cousin's laughter ringing in his ears.

31 MARCH 1809
Jane and I arrived in Gracechurch Street yesterday afternoon. Oh it is so good to be back! The children have grown, and it was wonderful to meet my baby cousin Paul. He is the image of his father. Aunt said that after Easter, they have been invited to several small affairs and we will join them. Today we went to the warehouses and purchased a few gowns for the occasions. It is a terrible expense, and I am certain that Uncle is footing the bill, but they would hear nothing of our protests. It is noisy here in the city, but the lack of Mama's voice makes the din of the carts outside of the window sound like birdsong to me. I will miss my walks but I cannot express enough how grateful I am to be here. Perhaps this will be a chance to find my future.

Elizabeth closed up her journal and gazed out at the busy street, wondering who she might meet in the coming months. Mr. Darcy immediately sprung to mind, but she shook him away. *No, stop it now! He is an impossible dream.* Perhaps a tradesman like her uncle would like her. She sighed then straightening her shoulders, stood and went down the stairs to join the family.

"Lizzy, I just received an invitation to a dance Monday night with some friends of ours. I will ask her if you and Jane may come, and I am certain that she will be delighted to include you."

"Who are these friends, Aunt?"

"This is the Hendersons. They are fabric exporters, and work closely with the cotton mills in the North. I know that several of their clients will be guests."

"So this is not just a friendly dance, but business as well?" Elizabeth asked.

"I am afraid that most dinners or balls have an element of business about them, dear." She laughed. "A little bit of relaxation makes for a good atmosphere for negotiations. Your uncle has done very well in the studies while we ladies strike deals of another nature in the drawing rooms."

Jane smiled. "You strike deals, Aunt?"

"Of course! Discussions of marriage are always popular and finding suitable husbands for girls is a favourite subject, however we have also been known to discuss our husband's business and hear things to whisper in their ears."

"Aunt, really?"

"There is no more powerful persuader than a woman who knows her business." She smiled and nodded. Elizabeth laughed with delight and Jane looked on with horror.

"But, it is not the woman's place . . ."

"If it has anything to do with caring for her family, it is her place." Mrs. Gardiner said firmly.

"Oh." Jane whispered.

"So, I suppose that Jane and I are to be part of these negotiations for husbands now?" Elizabeth asked.

"I will do my best for you, if you wish it." She smiled. "I want you to be happy with your husband, whoever he may be."

"DARCY, COME ATTEND YOUR COUSIN!" Lady Catherine barked.

He closed his eyes and stood, then walked over to Anne. "Forgive my tardiness, Cousin."

She placed her thin hand on his arm. "It is well, Darcy. You will come to me eventually." Darcy shot her a look. Her implication was clearly about more than escorting her to dinner. She said nothing more and he moved to sit across from her. He glanced at Fitzwilliam who raised his brow in inquiry. Darcy looked back at Anne who was staring at him.

"Does she not look well, Darcy?"

"Yes, quite well."

"Anne's doctors assure me that she is growing healthier by the day. Of course the glow in her eyes is new to this day." Lady Catherine smiled at her with satisfaction. "It will be good to see her established in her own home, and overseeing her staff as she has been taught."

"I look forward to the happy day when she finds her home and will be glad to know the fortunate man who will be her husband and, of course, the master of Rosings one day." Darcy murmured. Anne's eyes widened and she raised her brow. Lady Catherine's eyes narrowed as he continued, "The mistresses of Pemberley and Rosings will undoubtedly become good friends."

"There is no mistress of Pemberley."

Darcy turned his head and smiled slightly. "No, Aunt, not as yet, but then I have yet to speak to her."

"We will have this discussion later, Darcy."

"There is nothing to discuss, Madam."

"You know your mother's wishes!"

He looked her straight on. "I do, because my father told them to me. I know his desires, and I will follow them without fail."

Anne made an odd noise with her throat and Lady Catherine turned to her. "Look, look what you have done, you have upset her!" She waved at a footman. "Help her upstairs, Mrs. Jenkinson, do not just sit there, move!"

The companion who had sat silently by Anne's side jumped up and led her from the room. Anne paused at the door, looking back at Darcy for a moment and stared at him unblinkingly then disappeared. Darcy glanced at Fitzwilliam who cleared his throat. "Does that happen often, Aunt?"

"What?" She said angrily.

"Anne having such an emotional fit."

Darcy's eyes closed and he shook his head, then lifted it to see his angry relative huffing at him. "Aunt, I should have said this last year, but I will say it now. I will not marry Anne. No matter the reasons or circumstances. I will not marry her. Please stop making your pronouncements, please stop encouraging her to think it might happen. If she is truly healthy enough to marry, then by all means, take her to London for the Season and see what comes of it. My father told me that no scheme existed between my mother and you for a marriage and has instructed me on his expectations. I do not wish to address this topic again with you." He spoke quietly and firmly. "Do I make myself clear?"

"How dare you speak to me this way!"

"I am the master of my house; you are suggesting who should be its mistress. I have every right to say what I feel on the subject. I ask again, madam, am I clear?"

"Yes." She barked.

"Do you wish for Fitzwilliam and me to remove ourselves from Rosings?"

"No, that will not be necessary." She said tersely.

"Very well, then." Darcy said softly in his quiet steady voice. "May I compliment you on the meal?"

"I am unhappy with my cook."

"Of course you are," muttered Fitzwilliam under his breath. Darcy glared at him and he lifted his shoulders and smiled. The rest of the meal proceeded in silence, with only the sound of cutlery on the plates breaking the oppressive atmosphere. When at last she rose from her chair, the men quickly stood.

"I will retire now. There is port available. I expect to see both of you ready for breakfast at nine and you will meet my pastor." She looked from one man to another and without a word, left the room.

Fitzwilliam collapsed back into his chair. "That was exhausting. What made you do it? Confronting her with her delusion? I was betting you would go on year after year, dancing around the subject and never saying anything to keep the peace."

"That actually was my original plan." Darcy sank back down in his chair and thanked the servant who poured him a glass of port. "You know me well."

"So what moved you?"

"Anne." He shook his head. "She whispered that she expected me to eventually come to her. It was . . . unnerving."

"I bet." Fitzwilliam laughed. "The stuff of nightmares."

Darcy closed his eyes. "Well, let us survive Easter and spend the next few days looking over the estate with her steward and return to town."

"She will probably never forgive you for this."

"It is a relief; believe me, to have cleared the air." Darcy took a deep breath. "Now I can court with a clear conscious."

"You owed neither of them anything." Fitzwilliam poured a new glass of port and automatically filled his. "So, you have yet to speak to your future bride." Darcy's head shot up and his cousin smiled knowingly. "Clever, Darcy."

"I WISH THAT JANE COULD HAVE COME." Elizabeth looked around the crowded ballroom nervously. "She is so good at these things."

"Oh, I find it hard to believe that you are not." Mrs. Gardiner patted her arm. "Unfortunately Jane's headache will not be relieved for several days." She smiled at Elizabeth and she rolled her eyes. "So what exactly does your sister do that helps you at dances?"

"She is beautiful and attracts men to dance with her. I invariably get asked for at least a few sets." She shrugged. "At least I dance."

"You really need to stop thinking of yourself as unattractive, Lizzy. I know that you are sensitive to your mother's pronouncements, but please remember the source and her motivation." She gave her a hug. "You will do well tonight, I am certain."

"Thank you, Aunt." Elizabeth smiled.

"Well, I will ask you here and now for the second set." Mr. Gardiner smiled. "My wife of course has the first." He bowed gallantly and offered his arm. Mrs. Gardiner laughed and they walked off to line up with the rest of the dancers and Elizabeth stood on the side looking over the room. She had never attended a ball in London before, and had already noticed how different it was from the country dances she knew from Meryton. Beyond the dress of the participants, their behaviour and speech was much more formal and made for a fascinating study. She was startled from her observations by the appearance of a tall blonde man before her.

"Pardon me." He bowed. "I know that I should wait for an introduction, but the music is about to begin, and frankly, I do not wish to miss this dance. May I have this set?" He smiled warmly and his eyes twinkled at her. "I promise not to step on your toes."

Elizabeth laughed and curtseyed. "Well with such an incentive how can I say no?" She took his arm and they walked to the line. "May I know the name of my partner?"

"Ah, I knew that I forgot something! Charles Bingley, Miss . . . and my partner is?"

"Bennet, Elizabeth Bennet."

"Miss Bennet." He stood opposite her and bowed again. "A pleasure." The music began and they danced reasonably well together. She thought of him as an enthusiastic puppy, whose feet were too big for the rest of him, but he smiled and laughed, and did not give her one moment of doubt over her performance or appearance. She thoroughly enjoyed herself. When the dance finished he offered her his arm and they walked to the side. "May I fetch you some punch, Miss Bennet?"

"Oh I would like that; however my uncle will be claiming me soon for the next set. Perhaps we could just talk until it begins?"

"Of course!" He said with bright eyes. "What shall we discuss? What brings you to town?"

"How do you know that I am visiting?" She asked curiously.

"Ah, a guess, but you were looking about the room with wonder. I could only suppose that this was new to you." She blushed and he grinned. "Do not worry; it is new to me as well. I recognized myself in your eyes."

Elizabeth laughed. "So you are not a Londoner?"

"No, well, yes. I am staying in my brother's townhouse, but I suppose that technically I am . . . well, newly a resident. You see I have only just graduated from Cambridge so everything is in a bit of a muddle for me now."

"Oh, and what are your plans? Will you take a tour of the continent?"

"My advisor has recommended waiting for the hostilities to settle down."

Elizabeth laughed. "Your advisor, that sounds quite serious. Is he a wizened old man?"

Bingley laughed at the thought. "No, no, he is quite young. He is, I believe, four and twenty. He will be sponsoring me at court in a week. I am very grateful for his kindness. I am still somewhat surprised that such an important man would welcome someone of my background as a friend."

"He must be very good. He is taking you under his wing, I gather."

"Indeed, showing me the ropes." He added with in a whisper, "I am new to this gentleman business."

"I will not tell." She whispered back.

"Everyone already knows, I am afraid." He laughed. "And you?"

"I am not a gentleman."

"Miss Bennet!" He smiled. "That is not what I asked."

"I know, sir, but you made it too easy." Elizabeth smiled at his warm eyes. "I am a gentleman's daughter, from Hertfordshire."

"Aha! I was correct. You are new to town. Well then I am pleased with myself for puzzling it out." She tilted her head and studied him. He was sweet and kind, obviously not a scholar, and she liked him.

"Lizzy, I have come to claim my dance, but perhaps you would prefer to continue with your companion?" Mr. Gardiner said with a smile.

"Oh, Uncle, this is Mr. Bingley of, lately of London." She smiled as he chuckled. "Mr. Bingley, this is my uncle, Mr. Edward Gardiner and his wife."

"Sir, it has been a pleasure to speak with your niece. I am sorry but I seem to have lost my sisters or else I would introduce . . . oh wait there they are. Caroline!" He called.

A tall thin woman with sharp eyes and superior air approached. "Mr. and Mrs. Gardiner, Miss Bennet, may I present my sister, Miss Caroline Bingley, and my other sister Louisa Hurst and her husband."

"It is a pleasure Miss Bingley, Mr. and Mrs. Hurst." Mr. Gardiner said affably as they nodded. "I hope that you are enjoying yourselves this evening."

Caroline sighed and looked around. "It is tolerable, I suppose."

Elizabeth's brow shot up, and she turned back to her far more amiable brother. "I am sorry that I cannot introduce you to my elder sister tonight, Mr. Bingley, but perhaps we will meet again some other time."

"She remains at home at your estate?" Instantly Caroline and Louisa turned to regard Elizabeth closely.

"No, she is in town, but was unable to attend tonight." She smiled. "But we will be here for the Season."

"You have an estate?" Caroline smiled. "May I ask where?"

"In Hertfordshire, near the village of Meryton. Do you know the area?"

"No, I am afraid not." She looked Elizabeth over carefully, judging her clothes and her lack of jewellery. "A small estate?"

"I suppose it is how you look at it." Elizabeth picked up on her immediately, and saw that in this Bingley's eyes, she was unsuitable for her brother. Although she already instinctively knew that Mr. Bingley was not the one, the familiar feelings of unworthiness stole over her.

Charles noticed that Elizabeth's smile had disappeared and looked at his sister then to Mrs. Gardiner, who was watching the sisters closely. He had no idea what had happened. Mrs. Gardiner did, however, and smiled. "And what trade does your family practice?"

Caroline flushed and looked at Louisa. "Our father manufactured cloth from cotton, however he has passed and my brother is hoping to purchase an estate."

"Hoping to? Well, I hope that you are successful, sir. Someday your descendents will be able to state as our Lizzy does today that her family has owned its estate for well over one hundred years." She turned and took Elizabeth's hand and gave it a squeeze. "We are very proud to be relatives of hers."

"Thank you, Aunt." Elizabeth smiled at her.

Mr. Gardiner nodded and met Bingley's eye. "Congratulations sir, I suppose all of us men of trade harbour the hope that our children will join the gentry."

"Well, it was my father's dream and I hope to fulfil it." He smiled at Elizabeth. "With the help of my advisor, of course."

Chapter 8

"Well?" Jane asked when they returned from the dance. "How was it?"

Elizabeth sat down on the bed while she took down her hair. "It was very nice, but so different from the dances in Meryton, and so many more people to watch. I am glad to have visited London before, for if I only had my country manners to rely upon, I am afraid that I may have felt even more nervous."

"I am sure that Aunt and Uncle would have made the experience easy no matter the situation, you had nothing to be nervous about." Jane tilted her head. "Lizzy, you are smiling."

"Is that so terrible?" She laughed and stood up to remove her gown.

"No, of course not, but truly it has been so long since I have noticed it being genuine. What has changed?"

"Oh, I do not know precisely. Escaping Mama has a lot to do with it, I am certain, and . . .I met a young gentleman who was very kind to me." She laughed to see Jane throw off her covers and stand to hug her. "No Jane, I am not in love!"

"Tell me about him!" She pulled Elizabeth back down onto the bed.

"His name is Charles Bingley, and he is just graduated from Cambridge and is the first of his family to live as a gentleman. His parents are passed and he is hoping to buy an estate. It did not occur to me at the time, but Aunt said how surprising it was that he would reveal so much to a stranger, particularly when it was information that was not complimentary. His ties to trade, I mean." She mused, "I suppose that if we had been in a different circle he would have moderated his confessions."

"He must be very amiable to have inspired such a smile from you. Is he handsome?"

Elizabeth returned from her thoughts and smiled again. "Oh yes, very. He is tall and lanky with straw blonde hair, and pretty green eyes. And he laughs quite a lot at himself and, well everything to be honest. I wonder at him having a serious bone in his body. He made me feel very special, but I imagine that he does that with anyone he meets."

"He sounds wonderful." Jane sighed. "Did you dance?"

"Yes, one set; the first actually." Elizabeth blushed as Jane's eyes widened. "I honestly do not believe that he understood the implication of that, Jane. On the way home Aunt Gardiner gave me a gentle chastisement for accepting him without first being introduced. The rules for proper behaviour are more strictly observed here, but I think that he simply spotted me and saw someone just as unfamiliar with the atmosphere and approached."

"Oh."

"He said that he has an advisor who was helping him to learn how to be a gentleman. I have a feeling that this advisor will have his hands full." Elizabeth's eyes crinkled as she smiled. "His advisor sounds very intriguing."

Jane laughed. "Why is that?"

"I do not know, but from what I could glean, he is a young man, but seems to be very important and from the highest circles. I can only imagine what an honour it is for Mr. Bingley to even be noticed by such a man, which tells me of his inherent goodness." She noticed Jane's stare and squeezed her hand reassuringly. "Oh Jane, you think that I am falling in love with a phantom!"

"I think that you should concentrate on Mr. Bingley." She said seriously.

"No, as amiable and sweet as he is, I could not marry him. I am afraid that he is . . .too amiable."

"That is ridiculous!"

"No, I know now that I want a husband whom I can respect and admire; someone to care for and hopefully hold with some affection, and I hope likes me for myself. If I am destined not to find love and must marry for security, I at least will not give up those qualities. Our parents' and our aunt and uncle's examples have determined what I want. I understood Mr. Bingley's character within minutes. He would make a wonderful friend or brother, but not a husband, not for me. I hereby give him to you." Elizabeth held out her hands.

Jane smiled at the gesture then bit her lip. "Will he call, do you think?"

"I did not give him the address, but I hope that we will meet again sometime. His sisters have higher aspirations for him than me, though." She shook her head. "He is familiar. I cannot quite put my finger on it, but I am certain that I have seen him before . . ."

Hours later, as dawn was breaking and the city was coming alive, Elizabeth sat bolt upright in her bed and her hands flew up to her face as she gasped, "Mr. Darcy!"

"AN ANGEL." Darcy said dryly and sighed at the beaming smile on Bingley's face.

"You should have seen her, Darcy! Raven black hair, dancing eyes, and a laugh that would lift the spirits of the most miserable man, even yours I would wager." He laughed to see Darcy's grimace. "Ah, Miss Bennet was a delight!"

"And where did you meet this Miss Bennet?"

"Oh, some family friends of ours held a dance and my sisters and brother attended. With you gone I had to occupy my time somehow." He said defensively.

"These were tradesmen?"

"Yes . . .and I know that you do not wish me to associate with my old circle, but I cannot gain admittance to yours without your presence, and they did know my father . . ."

Darcy held up his hand. "I understand, but you really should not allow it to happen again. Your brother's circle is acceptable, but tradesmen are not. You aspire to be better than that."

"But my income is still from trade, Darcy. Until I have an estate, I must rely upon that and the interest from father's savings. Is it wrong to cut my ties completely?" Bingley watched Darcy closely.

He rubbed his hand over his face, considering the notion. "It does you no favour to be seen with them. You may do business, but do not socialize." He saw Bingley's disappointment. "I am afraid that this eliminates your angel from your circle of acquaintances, as well. No tradesmen's daughters are acceptable."

"Yes, my sisters have made that clear, and they said that Miss Elizabeth Bennet was not good enough for me." Darcy looked up at hearing the Christian name then fell into a thoughtful consideration of a raven-haired Elizabeth with a joyful laugh and beguiling smile, one he had tried and failed to forget. Bingley continued, "I thought that with her being a gentleman's daughter they would like her, but I suppose her father's small estate in Hertfordshire is not good enough for them." Bingley was staring at his hands and did not notice Darcy's head jerk up or his stare. "I do not think she was interested in more from me in any case. She has a quick wit, and I am afraid that she discovered fairly quickly that I do not." He laughed, "But she did seem to be very interested in you."

"In me?" Darcy sat up and leaned towards him. "Miss Bennet knew me?"

"Oh, I did not mention your name but I spoke of my advisor. She seemed to admire how a man of your stature would be willing to aid me in society." Bingley suddenly noticed the intensity of his friend's look. "Darcy, I say, have I said something wrong? Should I not speak of her?"

He waved impatiently, "No, no . . . She is a gentleman's daughter?"

"Yes, my sister Caroline was drawn to that until she determined that the estate was small, then I gather that she said something disparaging to Miss Bennet," Darcy's eyes narrowed, "And then her aunt, Mrs. Gardiner, spoke of Miss Bennet's family owning the estate for one hundred years and how she hoped that someday my family could declare the same." Darcy's eyes widened again in surprise, and Bingley laughed. "I admit that I did not understand what the lady had said to my sister until much later. Miss Bennet seemed to be very pleased with the exchange. I had the impression that she was working very hard to rein in her response and was happy that her aunt took the shot."

Darcy smiled; there was no doubt that this was indeed his Lizzy. He remembered her flashing eyes at the Derby . . . *The Derby!* "Bingley, did Miss Bennet seem to recognize you at all?"

"No." He wrinkled his brow. "No, I cannot say, but then I suppose that my powers of observation are not that keen."

"Did you promise to call on her?"

"Well, no, I did not, we danced the first set, and talked, but then my sisters encouraged me to visit the rest of the room."

"The first set." Darcy said softly.

Bingley looked at him worriedly. "Was that an error? I saw her and thought she was pretty and just walked up and introduced myself."

"Just like that? You just. . ." Darcy closed his eyes, the behaviour was entirely wrong and he would have to correct Bingley, but he could not deny the fact that he should have done the same, so many times. "Did she dance well?" He asked, again very softly.

"Yes, she was very graceful." He smiled then puzzled over the wistful expression that appeared in his friend's eyes.

"She lives in Gracechurch Street."

"I . . . I do not know." Bingley stammered, "How do you know?"

"Oh, I . . . I just surmised. Her uncle is a tradesman and many live there." Darcy bit his lip and leaned forward. "Bingley if you should happen to meet her again . . ." He faltered. *What, do what exactly?* He glanced up at his parent's portraits and his shoulders fell along with his hopes. Duty, honour . . . *Remember, you are a Darcy!*

"Yes?"

"I would like to hear about it."

"Of course." Bingley tilted his head and could not miss the disappointment in his friend's eyes, despite the frozen features of his face. "Are you well, Darcy?"

"I am." He sighed. "I have to be."

"DARCY, I WOULD LIKE YOU TO MEET MISS PATTERSON." Lady Matlock took his arm and planted him in front of a young woman. "Miss Patterson, this is my nephew, Mr. Darcy." She nudged him and he smiled slightly and bowed.

"It is a pleasure, miss."

She spoke breathlessly, "Oh, sir, the pleasure is mine. I have heard so many wonderful things about you!"

"Have you, I hope that they are true and not the result of someone's imagination?" He glanced at the girl's mother hovering nearby.

"Why no, unless I am incorrect about your estate, I understand that nothing compares to Pemberley in all of England." She gushed.

Darcy attempted not to roll his eyes. "That is kind; however, I am sure that any number of men, some in this room, would undoubtedly disagree. I am certain that our monarch would." Lady Matlock audibly sighed beside him. Darcy bowed and moved away. A woman with a confident smile approached him.

"She is so young Mr. Darcy, was it really necessary to cut her like that?"

He raised his brow at the handsome woman beside him. "Mrs. Webster, I did not cut her, I simply stated a fact."

"Rather baldly, I thought." She looped her hands over his forearm. "No matter, she probably did not catch it in any case. Look, see how her mama is scolding her for failing with you?" She smiled up at him. "You are quite the man to catch this Season."

He attempted to remove her hand from his arm but she was not giving him up. "I am aware of the attention, madam and do not welcome it."

"Not from naive little girls, but perhaps from a woman of experience?" She raised her brow. "Perhaps, you could show me some of the books in your uncle's library? I imagine it is quite private there?" Her gaze was direct and she brushed her breasts against his arm. There was no question what the widow was offering.

Darcy clamped down on the visceral reaction that betrayed his body, but not before she noticed, and smiled in welcome. "It would be rude to leave my aunt's dinner prematurely madam; however you are certainly welcome to go peruse the shelves alone." He detached the clutching hand and moved swiftly away, heading for the balcony and the cool night breeze. Closing his eyes he held onto the railing.

"Not interested, Cousin?" Fitzwilliam followed him outside and leaning against the railing, folded his arms and looked back into the crowded room. "She certainly has a great deal to offer. Widowed at two and twenty, how very sad, and a tidy bit of money will come with her. Perhaps I'll have a go at her." He chuckled and nudged Darcy, whose head was hanging down. "What is it?"

"I know her name."

"Mrs. Webster? It is Marion, I believe."

"No. Lizzy."

Fitzwilliam turned sharply. "Lizzy? Lizzy of the park, Lizzy of the races, Lizzy of the museum, Lizzy of Stewart? *That* Lizzy?"

"Yes. Elizabeth Bennet. That is her name. She is in town, and . . .she danced with Bingley a week ago." Darcy looked up at him. "What am I to do?"

"Do? About what? She is a daydream, a fantasy. You cannot have her. Damn it man, you let her go!"

He shook his head. "No, I fooled myself into thinking that."

"You have never spoken to her! For all you know, she is . . ." Fitzwilliam waved his arms at the crowded room, and at the young women peering out at them. "She could be worse than all of these women combined!"

"No, Richard." He looked at him. "Stewart fell for her, Bingley calls her an angel, I . . .I have seen her, heard her . . ."

"So, do you have the courage to go against society and call on her? Stewart caved in to reality." Darcy looked up at him and Fitzwilliam saw the torment in his eyes. "All right, here is what I propose. Before you make such a spectacular move as appearing on her doorstep; and possibly unwanted by the way, you need to make damn sure that none of those ladies of society who are so eager to meet you are what you want."

"Must I meet them all?" Darcy said angrily. "I am already aware of what they are!"

"You have met only a few. We have only been back here eight days! It is only the beginning of April! Give the Season a chance. Surely there is a woman . . ."

"Better, more appropriate, with a dowry and a pedigree to match." Darcy said dully.

"I am not saying that Miss Bennet is not the woman for you, but I want you to know with your mind and your heart this decision, and not simply react with your loins."

"Take that back, Richard!" He growled.

"You are a man, Darcy. It is not a subject that is far away from any of our minds, and you would be a hypocrite to say so." He hung his head again, remembering his automatic response to Mrs. Webster's unwelcome suggestions. Fitzwilliam sighed. "Look, Father would demand the same if he knew of this."

His head snapped up. "You will not tell him!"

"No, I will keep your confidence. But I do want you to be sure of your decision."

"And what if in the meantime, some man comes along and takes her away?" Darcy met his eyes.

"Then you will move on." Richard grasped his shoulder. "Come on, let us return, you have work to do."

"CHARLES, WHEN WILL WE MEET MR. DARCY?" Caroline asked and followed her brother into the study. "I think that it is only proper that we meet the man who is guiding your entrance into society."

Bingley sighed. "I told you that I invited him here for dinner after my levee."

"But should we not be acquainted before then? I propose some other social event, perhaps we could meet for tea tomorrow."

"Caroline, Darcy is a very busy man; he generously gives me his time. I will not ask for more of it."

"I was only thinking that we could be more comfortable with each other at dinner if we had already met for tea. And perhaps we could advance my friendship with him as well! Would it not be a fine match for your sister?" She smiled and tilted her chin.

"It would be exceptional; however I will not suggest it." He braced himself for the reaction.

Her eyes flashed and she screeched. "NO? Do you think that I am not good enough for him? He is obviously looking for a wife."

"Caroline, he is simply meeting the requirements of the Season with his socializing. I will not press him on this subject. He receives enough demands from his family."

"What does his family want from him?"

"The same as ours, I suspect. He now owns the estate, and they want it to be secured with its heir." He sighed and took her hands in his. "The business of being a gentleman addresses a variety of requirements. Once I have been presented and begin attending the functions in his circle, I have no doubt that I will learn of a great many areas where I am woefully deficient. No, Caroline, I will not promote you to him. If he meets you and expresses interest; that is a different story."

Caroline did not like what she heard but thought it was best not to push her brother further. "Will you at least ask him to include your family in his invitations to the first circles?" She smiled and raised her brow. "If I am not to press Mr. Darcy, perhaps there is a gentleman of his level in want of a wife."

"Perhaps." Bingley considered her for a moment. "Have you had any callers? I have not checked the cards lately."

"Of course I have had callers!" She huffed.

"Gentlemen?" He asked with raised brows, and saw her flush. "None?"

"Not precisely, Mr. Rycroft paid a called yesterday."

"He is that gentleman with a small estate in Buckingham?"

"Yes."

"And?"

"Charles, really! He is lesser even than Mr. Hurst! Surely you want more for me?"

"Of course I do Caroline. I only fear that your aspiration to find a husband in the first circles is unlikely."

"It is unlikely if you do nothing to promote me!"

Bingley shook his head, arguing with his sister was always a losing proposition and he would rather just walk away. "Caroline, I cannot help you if you refuse to accept the attentions of gentlemen who genuinely express interest. Now I must be off. Have a pleasant afternoon." He kissed her cheek and gratefully escaped the room. *I must ask Darcy for advice on finding her a suitor.*

18 APRIL 1809

I am without words. No, that is incorrect, I have words but I choose not to use them. Bingley's boundless enthusiasm and joy left me ill-prepared for meeting his sisters tonight. Thinking back, I should have been. His little anecdotes of Miss Bingley certainly never impressed me, and obviously her behaviour towards Lizzy gave me no reason to like her. However, I left St. James's after his levee, feeling very proud of his accomplishment and ready to share the joy of the day with what had to be a very happy family, to be almost instantly smothered with attention from Miss Bingley.

Her manners were impeccable, but I could not help to notice how the servants jumped at her voice or grimaced with her orders. It was eerily similar to the servants' behaviour at Rosings. But worst of all was from the moment I walked into the parlour Miss Bingley was by my side, offering refreshments, complimenting my townhouse, my estate, my carriage, my sister, my suit, boots, the way I sipped my tea, my choice of dessert, my God I could go on and on. And even that was not so intolerable, annoying, but certainly familiar after these past months in town, certainly every woman I meet wishes to stroke my self-opinion, but then she began the comments on the members of society.

She has never met these people and yet she was full of knowledge, intimate details, whether true or imagined I have no idea, but the woman gossiped with an annoying superiority and disturbing familiarity that I found distasteful and oddly fascinating. She was an expert at all things, and almost desperate to cling to me and show off what she considered to be her assets. I could not leave fast enough. I understand now why there have been no gentlemen clamouring for her dowry, although I am certainly aware of men as shallow as she who would be willing to meet her. The problem I fear is that she fancies herself above them and would reject them out of hand. Her sights are set for the first circles and nothing less will do. I must be careful around her and be sure not to encourage her in any way.

Her sister Mrs. Hurst is a gossip of the first order as well, but at least she had the sense to marry appropriately. Hurst is an indolent lout from what I could see, nonetheless, he is a gentleman and a step up for their family. When his father dies, I hope that he employs a good steward or the estate will quickly fall to ruin. I cannot say that I have not met people of their ilk in my level of society; however, it is certainly clear that the Bingley family has a great deal of work to do before being accepted there. If it were not for my friendship with Bingley, I would never dream of associating with such people. Unfortunately they come as a part of the bargain of knowing him, so on Sunday I will take Georgiana and meet them at Kensington Gardens. I can only imagine what fawning my poor sister will receive from the ambitious Miss Bingley.

Darcy closed his journal and blew out the candles on his desk, then wearily walked up the stairs, Caroline's overwhelming attention still causing his mind to wonder. How can three children come from the same parents and turn out to be such polar opposites? Perhaps that was the difference between raising boys and girls. He mused to himself and thought of Georgiana, they were alike but different, but he had the benefit of a loving mother for nearly eleven years and she did not, and she would be shaped by the loss of her father as well. No wonder she clung to him so tightly. At last he let his mind wander to Elizabeth. *You would not be like Miss Bingley, would you, Lizzy?*

23 APRIL 1809
Uncle took us to Kensington Gardens today after church, they are adjacent to Hyde Park and the entire way there I was hoping that somehow we would be refused admittance and I would then propose to walk in the park instead. It was silly and

foolish of me to think of such a thing. I know that both Jane and Aunt looked at me with great concern so I obviously displayed my anxiety.

Upon arriving though we were naturally admitted to the gardens and they were everything that I had hoped to see. We wandered the paths, admiring the landscaping and admittedly watching in wonder the very finely dressed people strolling with us. Aunt had insisted that we wear one of our new gowns for the occasion, and after my memory of that man who looked at me from head to toe with disdain last year, I did not protest the suggestion at all.

We walked for nearly an hour when I noticed a tall man walking with a group of people, two other men, two women, and a girl. I just knew that it was Mr. Darcy. It was difficult to remain where I was. I was certain that the smaller man speaking animatedly to the girl was Mr. Bingley, and as we are acquainted, I could reasonably greet the party, but just as I considered doing so, one of the women stepped beside Mr. Darcy and took his arm. She looked up at him and he down at her, she held him in such a familiar way. Then I realized that the woman was Miss Bingley. How natural it would be for Mr. Darcy to fall in love with his friend's sister? It would have lowered my opinion of him to be taken in by such a wretched woman, but I supposed it was understandable. Just as my dream burst as all dreams do upon a rude awakening, I saw Mr. Darcy firmly remove Miss Bingley's hand from his arm, then step over to his sister to claim hers. I laughed out loud and I know that my family thought me odd, but I do not care. My good opinion of Mr. Darcy remains. He showed himself to be a man of good sense. The path they took was different from ours, and I lost them in the trees, but I felt good for seeing him once more.

"How am I ever to forget you?" Elizabeth blew out her candle and climbed into her bed.

MR. GARDINER AND JANE led the way and Elizabeth followed slowly as they window shopped in the fashionable part of town. They were in search of a birthday gift for Mrs. Gardiner. Elizabeth had seen nothing of the items on display. Instead she was lost in thought about the events of the past week. Two nights she had joined her family at dinners. There had been a few unmarried men, but as usual, Jane drew them like flies while she was left to smile and laugh, and attempted to attract them with her conversation. More often than not, she found that the men's eyes glazed over when she spoke of anything more challenging than the weather. *I do not know the topics that interest these men. Perhaps I should ask Aunt for ideas. I just do not understand. I can speak to Uncle about so many subjects, and he does not seem to mind. Does that make him unusual? Mr. Stewart did not mind my conversation, if anything he seemed to enjoy it. Maybe tradesmen wish to talk of different things than gentlemen. What is wrong with me? I do not seem to fit in anywhere!* She blinked back tears that pricked her eyes. *What would Mr. Darcy be like? Would he like me as Mr. Stewart did or walk away as these others do?* She shook her head and chastised herself. "You really must stop dreaming of him. It is impossible."

"What is impossible, Lizzy?" Mr. Gardiner smiled and looked over to her.

"Nothing, Uncle." She blushed and noticed a bookshop. "May we stop in here?"

"Certainly!" He called ahead to Jane, "Lizzy wishes to look at the books."

"Oh of course she does!" Jane smiled. "I think that we should just leave her here and go to a tea shop; she will take no notice of our absence."

"I am not that terrible!"

"Lizzy, when your nose is in a book, you are deaf and blind to the world!" Jane laughed.

"That is true." Mr. Gardiner nudged her and Elizabeth shrugged and smiled. They entered and immediately Elizabeth paused and breathed in the scent of parchment and leather. "I believe that we have lost her already!"

She wandered off to the back of the shop where the poetry was kept and Mr. Gardiner and Jane stayed in the front, examining a display of books meant to catch a lady's eye. She slowly strolled past the shelves, looking up at the titles and nearly tripped over a man kneeling on the floor. "Oh, pardon me, sir!"

"No, no, it is my fault." He stood and turned to smile. "Miss Bennet!"

"Mr. Bingley, what a pleasant surprise!" Elizabeth smiled warmly at him. "Are you in search of something in particular to drive you to the floor?"

Grinning widely he shook his head in mock despair. "Oh, Miss Bennet, I have no idea what to purchase. I am not a reader, but I must purchase a gift for my advisor. He sponsored me at court and he is so self-effacing, he will not hear of my thanking him incessantly as I wish." He laughed. "Neither would he hear of me apologizing for nearly destroying his carriage's cushions with that sword I had to wear."

"He seems to be a very supportive man." Elizabeth said softly.

"He is very serious, and very busy, but Darcy is a friend of the like I have never hoped to have before." Bingley smiled and tilted his head. He did not miss the quick intake of breath from his companion; or the expression of . . . something . . . that appeared in her eyes when he spoke. "Miss Bennet?"

She blinked and focussed on him. "I am very happy for you, Mr. Bingley, congratulations on your presentation. Now you say that you are not a great reader, yet you wish to choose a book of poetry for Mr. Darcy?"

"Yes, well, he has a library that would put any great collection to shame, not just in town but at his estate Pemberley in Derbyshire. I was sure that a book would be the gift he could not refuse." He lifted his chin to the shelves. "The problem is that I have no idea what to purchase, and he likely has it already."

"May I make a suggestion?"

"I was hoping that you would, I had a feeling that you enjoyed reading."

Elizabeth reached to a shelf and pulled out a pocket-sized copy of Shakespeare's Sonnets. "This is small, but it is also something that he can easily carry with him. You can never go wrong with the classics."

Bingley took it from her and paged through with a smile. "Excellent idea!" He grinned. "Thank you so much!"

"I hope that he enjoys it."

"Lizzy?" Elizabeth heard her name called and she turned.

"Oh, my uncle is calling for me, I should go."

"Mr. Gardiner, well I should go and greet him." He offered his arm and Elizabeth smiled and took it. They appeared from the shelves and Mr. Gardiner's brows rose as he bowed. "Good afternoon, Mr. Gardiner. Imagine my surprise to meet Miss Elizabeth here. It is such a pleasure to see you again!"

"Likewise, Mr. Bingley. I hope that you and your family are well?"

"Indeed we are." He looked up and saw Jane standing silently nearby. Mr. Gardiner noticed and stepped back to her side.

"Mr. Bingley, this is my niece Miss Jane Bennet."

"Miss Bennet. It is a pleasure." He stared at her, and Elizabeth watched Jane blushing and staring back.

"The pleasure is mine, sir." She said softly. Bingley looked at Elizabeth who had tilted her head, then back at Jane.

"I hope that you found a book to your liking."

"I . . . no, I am afraid that this shop was my sister's choice." She smiled and he smiled back.

"How fortunate that she chose it then. She has aided me in finding two beautiful things today." He bowed and looking to Elizabeth who raised her brow at him as he winked. "Perhaps we will meet again sometime?"

"Anything is possible, Mr. Bingley." Elizabeth smiled.

"You are welcome to our home in Gracechurch Street, sir." Mr. Gardiner offered.

"I will remember that, sir." The group departed and Bingley watched them walking down the sidewalk, and noticed Jane looking back at him through the glass. He sighed.

"An angel."

"GEORGIANA, I HAVE TO LEAVE."

"You are never home!" She cried. "Why can you not be here?"

"I know that this is difficult for you to be here alone every evening. I do not enjoy the constant dinners and balls either. I only enjoy the theatre performances to be honest with you. But I must go!"

"Why?"

"Georgiana, you know full well why. I have to do my duty. I have to find a wife. Would you prefer that I just select the first woman who smiles at me tonight and then you will have her as your sister? You asked me to find someone who will care for me when you left home, did you not? Well finding that person takes time."

"I am sorry, Fitzwilliam." Georgiana sighed and hugged him. "I was being selfish. I miss you."

"I miss you, too. We are both more accustomed to evenings at home together. Father certainly was rarely out and when I was home from school I played with you. We are both learning our responsibilities."

"Must you stay out so late? I hear you return then you sleep until nearly noon, then you work and go out again. Perhaps if you returned earlier we could see each other a little more."

Darcy sighed with frustration. "You are exaggerating, Georgiana, I could not sleep until noon unless I was medicated. These events do not start until nearly ten, you know what town hours are like! This is not Pemberley!" He saw her pleading expression and sighed again. "I will try, dear." He kissed her forehead and a footman knocked.

"Sir, Mr. Bingley is here." Darcy felt Georgiana startle and straighten up, and look eagerly to the door. He suspected his sister had developed a little crush on his friend and smiled.

"Would you like to greet him, Georgiana?"

"Oh yes!" They walked out to the front hallway where Bingley stood studying the bowl of calling cards. He turned at their entrance and grinned.

"Good afternoon! Miss Darcy, how pretty you look!"

She blushed bright red and whispered. "Thank you, Mr. Bingley!" She opened her mouth to speak again and looked at her brother for help. Darcy smiled.

"I think that Mrs. Somers is waiting for you in the Library, is she not?"

"Oh, oh yes, she is. Excuse me." She smiled shyly at Bingley and he returned it with a huge smile of his own.

"It was a pleasure to see you again." The men exchanged amused glances as she floated down the hall and went to take seats in Darcy's study. "She is getting prettier by the day."

"She is rather fond of you, I think. You charm every lady you see, it is an interesting talent. In the hands of a scoundrel it could be quite disturbing."

"Well then luckily I am no scoundrel!" He laughed and settled into his chair. "Funny that you should mention charming ladies though, I met the loveliest angel today . . ."

"Another angel, Bingley? Do you make a habit of falling in and out of love?" Darcy smiled at his friend.

"Hmmm, well I am certainly fond of ladies." He shrugged. "I am in no position to offer marriage to any woman yet. So for now I will admire the beauty that surrounds me."

"Poetry is not your strong point." He chuckled.

"Ah, speaking of which, this is for you." He handed Darcy the parcel from the shop. "It is a small token of thanks for all you have done for me."

"I do not require gifts. I value your friendship." Their eyes met and Darcy looked back down immediately. "Well, it seems to be a book. Let me guess, the history of horse racing in Britain."

"No, try again!"

He opened the paper and smiled. "Sonnets! Why this is a very handsome volume Bingley, thank you!"

"You are welcome, but I merely purchased it. The book was chosen by another." Darcy's brows rose in inquiry. "Miss Elizabeth Bennet found it for me. She thought that you would like something that was portable and what did she say? Oh, *you can never go wrong with the classics*." He watched the same expression appear on Darcy's face as had been on hers.

"You . . .you saw her in the bookshop?"

"Yes, and I actually did say your name this time and she fairly gasped."

Immediately Darcy's mind began to race, how did she know his name? It hit him like a bolt; he could see Georgiana running to him in the park calling his name, followed by Mrs. Somers doing the same. *She wanted to remember me!*

"Darcy?" Bingley smiled and laughed. "Come on man, wake up!" Darcy was enveloping the small book within his hands and staring at it as he unconsciously caressed the cover. "Darcy?" Bingley said quietly.

"I . . .I thank you for this gift, Bingley." He looked up and held his gaze this time. "I will treasure it."

"You are very welcome." He paused and took a stab at his theory. "She looked very well."

"I am glad of it." Darcy's eyes dropped down to the book.

"Her uncle invited me to visit their home, you were correct, it is in Gracechurch Street." Bingley watched and waited for some sort of a response, a remonstration not to mix socially with tradesmen, perhaps even a request to accompany him, but Darcy remained silent and held the book. When the silence became uncomfortable, Bingley moved on.

"You are still going to the Whitcomb's tonight?"

"Yes, unfortunately." Darcy sighed and rubbed one hand over his face. "I cannot understand how people do this for months. I am exhausted."

"Well, that is not surprising; you have been out nearly every night but Sundays for over a month. I enjoy socializing, but even I am growing weary of the Season. Forgive me Darcy, but when I have attended these events with you, I cannot help but notice your lack of enjoyment."

Darcy sat back in his chair, still holding the book. "It is my duty."

"To be miserable?" Bingley laughed. "Truly Darcy, you present the most forbidding countenance, it is a wonder that any woman smiles in welcome at you."

"They smile because of what they see as their reward for marrying me." He glanced around the finely appointed room. "They know the prestige of being Mrs. Darcy."

"Surely some of them actually might like you, if you let down that frown of yours." Darcy shrugged. "Do not tell me that not one lady has caught your eye or had something interesting to say?"

"Of course there were, Bingley. I am not such an egoist that I reject every woman in London."

"That is not what I see." Darcy glared at him. "Look, if you hate it so much, why go?"

"Because I am the head of this family, and I am responsible for its legacy and its continuity. I have been charged with doing my duty and that means marrying well. You are in the same position, might I add."

"Yes, but I like the ladies!" Bingley laughed. "I am sorry, I only wish for you to be happy. I also overheard your aunt speaking with your uncle."

Darcy's brow creased. "What was said?"

"They worry that you are retreating deeper into yourself. I do not know you from the time before your father died, but from their conversation, I would say that the change has been marked. You do not impress me as ever being an outgoing individual . . ." He saw Darcy close his eyes and shake his head. "Well I suspected as much, but it seems that your relatives considered you to be more amiable."

"It seems that I need to speak to my uncle." Darcy smiled a little. "So have you become my advisor, now?"

Bingley stood. "I am hardly qualified to give advice on any subject; I simply want my friend to be happy. I will see you this evening." Darcy walked him to the door. "By the way, Caroline is determined to win you."

"And you wonder why I frown at the ladies." Bingley laughed and departed. Darcy returned to his study and sat back down, taking the book in his hands and feeling the leather, imagining Lizzy touching it as well. A knock on the door startled him and he looked up. "Come."   The door opened.   "Mrs. Somers, what can I do for you?"

An hour later Darcy was sitting in his uncle's study in Matlock house. "What should I do?"

"When does Mrs. Somers wish to leave?"

"By August." Darcy ran his hand through his hair. "She has been with Georgiana since she was eight, she helped her through Father's death, taught her . . .I have relied on her care more than I can say. I cannot blame her wish to aid her father and return to her family, in fact, she indicated to me several months ago that this may happen. I cannot be everything to Georgiana that she is."

"Why not hire a new governess?"

He sighed. "Well, Richard and I have discussed sending her to a finishing school. I thought that the exposure to other girls would be good for her."

Lord Matlock nodded. "There is merit in that. Audrey attended for a year, but she was a little older than Georgiana is now."

"Well she is far too young to have an establishment formed for her. She needs more than simply a companion at this point, and honestly, I think that she would learn little from another governess."

"Have you spoken to her about this?"

"No, she will do as she is told, of course."

"Of course she will." He considered his nephew, not agreeing with his decision, and saw the worry etched in his face. "We would still be willing to let her live with us."

"I am afraid that she would see that as more objectionable than me sending her away to school. That would seem like a personal rejection."

"Hmm, possibly, but I believe that she already feels rejected by your being out every night."

"What exactly am I supposed to do, Uncle? I must be her brother, but find a wife. I must care for Pemberley, but also play the game of society. Father doted on her so she expects a great deal more attention than most children receive from their parents. I cannot live up to his example and fulfil everything else at once! I am just barely feeling confident in my duties now!" Darcy stood and began pacing the room. "Her behaviour of late has been increasingly upsetting to me as well. I know that she is unhappy with my town hours and socializing. I have hardly been happy with it either, but she does not understand that. She does not understand the pressure . . .I am doing my best Uncle, but I should not be taken to task by a barely thirteen-year-old girl!"

"I agree, but are you correcting her behaviour or just letting it go? Do your feelings of guilt for her losing your father and your fear of not measuring up to him translate into anything more than the gifts you constantly purchase for her? Indulgence is not the way to correct her. She needs parenting."

"I am not her father!"

"Yes you are."

Darcy hung his head and shook it. "Then she will go to school. She will be safe, she will learn, she will make friends. I think that is what she needs above everything. She is going to have to learn how to get along with ladies, and that can only be learned with girls of her own age." He stopped and nodded. "Yes, I have made my decision. Is Richard at home?"

"No, but I will speak to him when he returns. When will you speak to Georgiana?"

"I must attend this damn ball at the Whitcomb's tonight, tomorrow I have no engagements. It will be as good a time as any to tell her the news."

Lord Matlock nodded and studied his nephew's strained expression. "I hope that you manage to repair your humour before you go to the ball, and for once go with an open mind. A wife would be good for you and your sister. Perhaps the pressure you speak of would be relieved."

Darcy's hand slipped into his pocket and touched the book of sonnets, then slowly withdrew. "I know what I must do.

Chapter 9

"Richard, please join your mother and me in the study." Lord Matlock sent him a pointed look. Fitzwilliam handed his hat to the servant, and straightening his uniform, walked curiously into the room. "Shut the door." He did as he was told and stood before his seated mother and pacing father.

"I did not break it, whatever it was." He smiled.

"This is not a moment for levity." His father barked.

"Then please inform me of my offence."

"It is not an offence, dear." Lady Matlock said then glanced at her husband. "It is Darcy."

"Darcy."

"What the devil is wrong with him?" Lord Matlock exclaimed. "Do you know that he intends to ship Georgiana off to school?"

"We had discussed it. What is the problem? Many girls start school at ages younger than Georgiana. Aunt Catherine thought it was a sound idea."

"And when exactly did you start listening to her?"

"You disagree with your sister's pronouncements?" Richard laughed and saw his father's glare. "Forgive me; I just do not understand the problem. My sister attended school until she was sixteen and you formed an establishment for her, why should Georgiana be any different?"

"Your sister had not just lost her father. We are concerned that sending her away will make her feel even more alone at a time when she needs her family."

"Uncle George died over a year and a half ago. I think that if we continue to mollycoddle her, it will do more damage than good." He saw his parents exchange glances with his harsh words and he sighed with frustration. "Well what do you suggest Father? I assume that Mrs. Somers has informed Darcy of her departure date?" He saw the nod and continued. "I see. Well, what do you expect of the man? Can you not see how utterly overwhelmed he is? He is working so hard to satisfy the requirements that have been showered on him to operate Pemberley and the townhouse, he has Georgiana, and on top of that he has you two pushing him out in the marriage mart every night! He is so concerned about doing his duty that he is not taking time to consider the consequences of the methods he uses, and on top of that, he is so afraid of making a mistake. Everywhere he turns it is another person demanding his attention, no wonder he chose Bingley as a friend."

"What do you mean?"

"Bingley is grateful for his help and makes it clear. He is guileless and undemanding. Darcy is willing to overlook his ties to trade and from what I hear, an abominable family, just for the safe harbour of his friendship. And then when it comes to marriage . . ." Richard stopped. He would not betray Darcy's fascination with Miss Bennet.

"Yes?" Lady Matlock pressed. "Richard, he has been absolutely unwelcoming to every woman . . ."

"Every woman you have pushed at him." Fitzwilliam laughed. "He is clearly not interested in the game; he has too much on his plate. I asked him to look carefully at the ladies, but I am relieved he has not made some rash move to achieve peace."

"A wife would solve his problems with Georgiana."

"You would expect his wife to teach her?" Richard sat down and crossed his legs. "I would like to see a woman's reaction to that idea. A lady of the *ton* would not be marrying Darcy to become a governess. If anything, the future Mrs. Darcy would expect a whirlwind of activity, glittering social engagements and appearances with her prize on her arm." He shook his head. "Darcy hates his life now; I cannot imagine how dour his visage will become after marriage. I pity the man."

Lord Matlock looked at his wife who had closed her eyes. "Perhaps we have been pushing too hard."

Lady Matlock nodded. "I have. I just see him as so alone, Richard. I know that a wife would relieve his burdens."

"Not the ladies I have seen you thrusting at him. Really Mother, what would some little girl do for him? Or the widows or even the older women who are not taken yet. Leave him alone; take this pressure away from him for awhile. He is so changed from what he was before Uncle died, I fear what might happen if this pace is allowed to continue. I fear that he will start believing all of the people petting his ego. He will grow disgusted with it, but it cannot help but influence him."

"Yes, he is clearly a changed man. I cannot remember the last time he had a genuine smile on his face, and his father specifically told me that he hoped Darcy would be happy." Lord Matlock looked at his wife. "Do not press him tonight and I will tell him that if he is finished with the Season, we will understand."

"He would appreciate that, I think." Fitzwilliam agreed. "What of Georgiana?"

"I would be happy to have her come here for a visit, and give him a reprieve. If we are not marrying him off, then perhaps we can give her some attention while he relaxes. And then we can speak about school for her." Lady Matlock suggested.

"Fine, I will suggest that to him tomorrow when I see him. I will be out tonight with members of my regiment. I need to catch up with the news before

I return to duty." He stood and paused. "If you leave Darcy alone, he just might find precisely the woman he needs on his own." Fitzwilliam smiled at their confused faces and left the room before they could ask for more.

BINGLEY STEPPED OUT OF HIS CARRIAGE and looked at the Gardiner's townhouse, and chuckled to himself. "If this was any other tradesman's house, Darcy would be dressing me down, but since this is the home of Miss Elizabeth . . ." He smiled; there was no doubt in his mind that his powerful friend was smitten with her. How it had happened was a mystery, but he was determined to further it along. It was the least he could do to repay Darcy's kindness to him. He handed his card to the housekeeper and while waiting, he briefly entertained the idea that Darcy would not appreciate his interference, and brushed it aside, remembering how his face shone with hope when Miss Elizabeth was mentioned. Soon he was shown into a drawing room. "Good morning, ladies!"

"Mr. Bingley, this is a pleasant surprise!" Mrs. Gardiner showed him to a chair between the girls. "My nieces told me of their meeting you in the bookshop."

"It was a fortuitous event, Mrs. Gardiner. I am rarely in bookshops and I desperately needed aid, and there like an angel was Miss Elizabeth to rescue me." He laughed and she smiled.

"To trip over you, I think is the correct story, sir." Elizabeth tilted her head and he shook his.

"You make it sound so dull that way."

"Very well then, I shall revert to your version, I was a ray of hope during your search." She laughed and he joined her.

"Indeed, and the gift was received very well, so your assistance was most successful."

"Your advisor liked it?" She said softly.

"Indeed he did, and he was particularly pleased knowing that it was chosen by a person who was so knowledgeable of books. He said he would treasure it, and it remained tightly gripped in his hands for the remainder of my visit."

"oh." Elizabeth whispered and looked into Bingley's warm and sincere gaze, while he smiled and nodded. A small smile lit her face, and she fell into her own thoughts. Bingley felt completely satisfied with the message he had delivered for his friend.

Mrs. Gardiner watched the exchange and sent a curious glance to Jane who shrugged. "Mr. Bingley, may I offer you some tea?"

He startled back and smiled widely. "Oh madam, I would not wish to put you out, I am afraid that I have already nearly overstayed my fifteen minutes."

"We have no other visitors, sir; you are welcome to remain as long as you are able." She smiled and he laughed.

"Well then, prepare for a siege! I have nowhere to be for another hour." He turned to Jane. "Miss Bennet, was your shopping trip a success?"

"Yes sir, my aunt is wearing the result." She indicated the broach on her dress.

"Ah, jewellery, always a favourite of my sisters'."

"How do they enjoy the Season?" Mrs. Gardiner asked as she poured out the tea and nudged Elizabeth to hand around the biscuits.

"Well enough, I suppose. There is certainly plenty of activity to occupy them. We enjoyed a stroll in Kensington Gardens recently, if you have the opportunity you must go."

"Oh we did, sir, Sunday last."

"Really? That is when we were there! It is a pity that we did not meet." He looked to Elizabeth and she was smiling warmly at him. "Or did you happen to spot us?"

"I did, sir, I recognized everyone in your party, and would have approached to greet you, but you were too far away."

"That is a shame, Miss Elizabeth. I believe that everyone would have been delighted to meet you." Their eyes held and he saw hers light up with the confirmation of Darcy's admiration.

"Well then, the next time I spot you, I will not hesitate."

"Please do not." He turned back to the other ladies. "Do you have plans to attend any other events?"

"My husband is trying to secure tickets for a performance, and we have a dinner to attend tomorrow night."

"Hmm, do you grow weary of all of the activity? I confess it is rather overwhelming at times. Miss Bennet, do you enjoy the theatre or prefer balls?" He raised his brow and studied her beautiful face.

"I think that I enjoy them equally, sir." She smiled at him and he smiled back. It was a safe answer.

He returned to Elizabeth. "And you, Miss Elizabeth?"

"There is merit in them both. I enjoy the theatre because it is an opportunity to see something that I have read and imagined come to life, but I enjoy balls because there are so many people to meet and observe, and what lady does not enjoy a dance with a skilled gentleman?"

"I hope that I qualify as skilled in your mind?"

"You did as you promised sir, my toes remained intact."

Bingley laughed at her dancing eyes and looked back to see Jane's demurely cast down, and tilted his head. "Well, I really should be on my way if I mean to appear at my appointment on time." He stood up and the ladies did as well. "I thank you for your hospitality, Mrs. Gardiner."

"It was my pleasure, Mr. Bingley. Lizzy, would you see him to the door?" She raised her brows and Elizabeth smiled at her aunt the matchmaker. They walked down the hallway and the maid handed him his gloves and hat.

"Mr. Bingley, I must thank you so very much for telling me of Mr. Darcy, I must ask, he knows me? He knows my name?"

"Yes, Miss Elizabeth. I do not know how he did, it seemed to hit him like a thunderbolt when I told him of meeting you at the dance, and he became as flustered as a schoolboy, and when I told him that you had chosen the book, the expression on his face would melt your heart. May I ask how you met?"

"We have not ever met, sir. We have never spoken. My sight of him at Kensington Gardens was the first in nearly a year, and I do not believe that he has seen me in that time either. We seem to be dwelling on the memories of each other equally, though." She saw his astonishment and smiled. "I thank you for that gift, sir. I cannot say how dearly I appreciate it."

"May I tell him of this conversation?" He touched her arm. "He is so unhappy; I would like to see him smile."

"What troubles him?"

Bingley shook his head. "He is an important man with heavy burdens. May I tell him of you?"

"If I can ease his burden . . ."

"You would, I am sure of it." He bowed and smiled. "Good day, Miss Elizabeth. Please give my compliments to your aunt and sister."

Elizabeth closed the door after him and returning to the ladies, slowly took her seat. "Mr. Bingley seems to be very interested in you, Lizzy." Mrs. Gardiner observed. "I would say that he called specifically to see you."

"Oh that is silly, Aunt. Mr. Bingley is not attracted to me."

"He did not centre his attention on me." Jane said.

Must every man in London look only at you? Elizabeth held her tongue. "Mr. Bingley is an amiable and kind man who does not really have the rules for drawing room discourse figured as yet. He has improved though, do you not agree, Aunt?"

Mrs Gardiner studied her niece and nodded her head slowly. "He has indeed. Perhaps his advisor's work is at last paying dividends."

"I have no doubt of his skill." Elizabeth smiled. "None at all."

BINGLEY STOOD AT THE EDGE of the dance floor and watched closely as Darcy moved with his partner. The young woman looked oddly familiar, and it took him a few moments, but when he saw Darcy actually smile slightly at her, the realization hit him. This woman resembled Miss Elizabeth. "You poor fool." He whispered. The dance ended and Darcy bowed to the lady, and escorted her from the floor. A flurry of conversation followed the couple. Darcy had danced only rarely that Season and for this girl to have won a dance, one where he seemed to enjoy himself, was remarkable. He lingered with her for a few moments then bowed and walked away, spotting Bingley when he waved.

"You danced, Darcy." He observed curiously. "Who is she?"

"Miss Victoria Gannon." He said and glanced back at her. She was surrounded by women who were all looking at him. "She is satisfactory."

Bingley began to laugh and Darcy frowned. "Such a compliment! Tell me about her?"

"She is friendly, her laugh was not grating, her conversation was intelligent, in fact I could find nothing at all wrong with her. She is certainly a handsome woman." His brow creased when he saw his friend's shaking head. "What is it, Bingley? I have finally discovered a woman of my circle who I do not find intolerable."

"I paid a call to the Gardiner home today." Bingley heard Darcy's quick intake of breath and saw how his eyes focussed on him. "I sat next to Miss Elizabeth, as close as you and I stand together now."

"Bingley . . ."

"It is remarkable how closely she resembles Miss Gannon." He tilted his head as Darcy's eyes closed and his shoulders slumped. "I told her of your reaction to the book. She was . . . delighted is not the proper word, happy, relieved, it is difficult to describe, but her eyes glowed to know that it made you happy. I asked how you met and she confessed that you never have." Darcy's head shook. "She saw you at Kensington."

"She did?" He whispered.

"She said it was the first time she had seen you in nearly a year." He nodded. "She said that the two of you seem to be dwelling on memories of each other." Darcy met his eyes, and Bingley could not mistake the hopeful expression. "Listen to your heart Darcy. She is beautiful, delightful, witty, and cares for you. You have been carrying this attraction for so long, there must be something to it!"

Darcy looked back at Miss Gannon. There truly was absolutely nothing wrong with her. She was the daughter of a landowner similar to himself. She had an enormous dowry, the proper connections, was educated, and he had no doubt she was very accomplished. She could surely serve as Pemberley's mistress without hesitation and take on her duties quickly. And she was healthy and could provide his heir. She smiled at him and he returned it, then glancing at his reflection in the mirrored walls of the room, he saw that the smile did not reach his eyes and barely lifted his lips. He turned back to Bingley. "I think that I will return home now."

Bingley nodded and clasped his shoulder. "I hope that you sleep well. I will be happy to accompany you anywhere, should you decide to go."

"Thank you, Bingley." Darcy straightened and left the room and was soon on his way home. Bingley listened to the speculation by the ladies over what made him depart so early and laughed quietly to himself. "If they only knew."

"YOU CAME HOME EARLY." Georgiana said when Darcy applauded from the doorway to the music room.

"You say that almost like an accusation." He smiled a little and entered.

"I am sorry, it is just unusual, and you did not come down for breakfast. I was afraid that you were ill." She stood up and hugged him. "You are well, are you not?"

"Yes, dear. I was up very late. I had a great deal on my mind." He sat down on a sofa and invited her to join him. "I have a great many decisions to make and some of them concern you."

"Me?"

Darcy nodded and bit his lip, then plunged in. "Mrs. Somers is leaving us in August."

"What?" Georgiana's eyes grew wide and she began to cry. "No! What did she do wrong? Brother, please do not dismiss her!"

"No, no, this is her choice. Her father's health is failing and she wishes to care for him. I will present her with a gift of funds for her retirement so she will be able to keep her father's home after he passes."

"But . . .what will become of me?" Georgiana said through her tears. "I . . . I need her."

"Richard and I have talked it over, and we have decided that it was time that you attended a school." Georgiana sat up and stared at him. "We think that you would benefit from spending time with other girls your age, and establish friendships that will last the rest of your life. And undoubtedly the school will teach you things that Mrs. Somers never could, particularly about how to move in society."

"NO!"

"Georgiana, it is for the best, and it is proper for you to be educated." He said calmly.

"You just want to be rid of me!"

"That is not true."

"You want to go to your parties and balls and do not want me in the way!"

Darcy held on to his anger with her accusations. "No, I want you to become an accomplished woman. Your cousin Audrey went to a school, I went away when I was twelve. I would hire a new governess, but even Mrs. Somers said that she is at the limit of what she can teach. I doubt that any other woman could do more. You need what a school could provide to help you understand the society you will be entering."

"I do not want any more!" She cried. "You cannot make decisions for me!"

At last reaching the end of his patience, he stood and glared. "I am your brother and your guardian; yes I can and will make decisions for you. I will do the same with my wife and my children one day, just as I do for every person whose life touches Pemberley or Darcy House." Georgiana jumped up and ran from the room. "Georgiana, come back here!" He watched her run towards the front door and ordered, "Georgiana! Stop!"

She kept running. "No! I will not go to school!"

Fast on her heels flew Darcy. His mouth was set in an unforgiving frown. "Georgiana, enough of this display! Return immediately!"

"No! You cannot make me!"

Darcy saw that the servants had disappeared. He was at a loss, and had no idea what to do. Glancing up he saw Mrs. Somers at the top of the stairs. Summoning all of his will he took control of his anger and said in a tense even voice. "Go to your chambers. I will speak to you when you have calmed and can listen like a lady." He looked at Mrs. Somers. "Please take your charge."

"Come along Miss Darcy." Mrs. Somers came down halfway and called. Georgiana wiped her face and walked quickly past her brother and up the stairs. Darcy stared after them, then seizing his hat, placed it haphazardly on his head and strode out of the house and across to the park. He walked quickly, attempting to dissipate his anger and frustration.

Now what do I do? How am I supposed to make things better? I am no good at this . . .this fatherhood, mothering, I do not know! Dropping onto a bench, he stared unseeing at the trees and whispered, "I am so tired." He had spent the entire night before awake, tossing in his bed, struggling with his desires, his duty, his family. He did not realize when he bowed to Miss Gannon the night before and asked her to dance that it was a futile attempt to find a twin of Elizabeth. "Thank God for you Bingley!" He said fervently under his breath. "But what do I do now? Father what would you want me to do?" A couple walking nearby looked at him quizzically and embarrassed, he rose to his feet and began walking again. His thoughts drifted to another walk he had made, almost two years earlier in this same place, only that time he was trying to walk off the news of his father's pending death.

The conversation of that day washed over him, and he began to hear his father's voice once again. He arrived on the path above the Serpentine, and stood staring out at the water. The sound of Elizabeth's laughter seemed to come to his ear, just as it had that day. It comforted him once again. His eyes closed and he drew a deep breath, imagining the scent of her perfume from the gallery. He imagined her eyes, smiling at him in approval when he rescued Bingley. *Bingley.* This man saved him from Miss Gannon the night before with his story of Elizabeth. She remembers him, she was so happy to hear of his reception of the book. Instantly the struggles of the night reasserted themselves. "Father help me! What should I do?" He looked back down at the water, once more remembering that terrible afternoon when he let her walk away from him in that very park. A wave of despair flooded throughout his body.

NO! Do not let her go! He screamed at himself, then his father's voice once more filled his mind. *"Remember who you are!"* He must always honour his name, he must do his duty. Was that not what his father had said? The charge had tortured him from the moment he returned from the ball, he had thought of his duty, and reached no conclusion. His mind raced over that last conversation with his father. They were looking out over Pemberley . . .honour our name . . .*By caring for the land! NOT by being a social snob, he meant the land, our people, our family, our ancestor's accomplishments!* Darcy's suddenly opened eyes stared at the sparkling lake. His father had told him something else about marriage, what was it? Once again that day he was at a loss, and desperately fought to remember his father's words.

Suddenly a gust of wind came up and toppled his badly placed hat, and it flew, hitting the ground and began to roll, picking up speed as it found a slope leading down to the lake where it at last came to rest at the feet of a young woman with ebony curls peeking from beneath her bonnet. The sound of her laughter moved Darcy from his petrified state, and he was drawn to her like a siren. She retrieved the errant hat and turned with a triumphant smile to locate the owner. Her eyes were sparkling. She brushed off some dirt and met him. "Here you are, sir." She at last found his eyes, and she gasped, nearly dropping the hat as her hand came to her mouth, and her eyes were bright with the sudden wash of tears, "Mr. Darcy!"

He saw so many emotions passing over her face, the first and clearest was fear. Elizabeth stood frozen and studied him, carefully trying to read his expression for any trace of disgust. Darcy remained staring at her, returning the examination and trying to understand what was wrong. *Please, whatever it is, do not fear me!* He thought urgently and tried to put his assurance in his look. The moment seemed to last for hours, but at last he saw her relax, and a smile appeared.

Her smile warmed him as nothing he had ever known before. "Thank you, Miss Bennet. I am deeply in your debt." He smiled at her, the happiness reaching his eyes and shining into hers. Elizabeth felt the power of his admiration and responded in kind, their easiness with each other was instantaneous.

"Oh dear, that is serious!" The laugh returned, bubbling, happy. "No, sir, I am honoured to rescue your hat from its certain fate of joining the armada in the lake, although I am sure that it would have been the sturdiest craft there!"

Darcy noticed a group of boys and their makeshift navy on the water. "I am quite certain that you are correct. If I may not be in your debt, may I at least thank you properly?" He smiled again.

"And what would you consider to be a proper thank you, sir?" Elizabeth's lips twitched, but she raised her eyebrow with mild chastisement.

He laughed softly and the thought of a kiss to those lips came to mind at once. He blushed and did not meet her eye for a moment but when he looked up again, he saw that she was blushing and studying her gloves. Obviously the identical thought had come to her. He smiled with delight. "Miss Bennet, forgive me, I seem to have disconcerted you somehow. I am forgetting my manners at an alarming rate. I am calling you by name and yet we have not ever been properly introduced."

"I am afraid that my companions will not be of help in that endeavour, sir. They do not know you either." She laughed and he sighed.

"Well then shall we pretend that we have indeed been formerly acquainted? May I also know your companions, Miss Bennet? I am glad to know that you are not in the park alone." He held out his arm and tilted his head.

"Miss Elizabeth, sir. You see, I am the second sister." She took his arm and they began to stroll slowly. Darcy looked down at her hand resting on his forearm, it felt so right. "My aunt and sister are here with my little cousins. They are just over the rise, you see." She pointed and he saw a group of women nearby. "I wished to look at the water and . . . remember." She looked up at him then back down.

Darcy stopped his movement and spoke quietly, "Miss Elizabeth, I am afraid that I must end this charade. We share memories of each other, and our first impressions were clearly equally powerful to have lasted so long. I know of your reactions to the mention of my name, and that you know of mine to yours. Our mutual friend Bingley has made sure of that. For the past two years I have always thought of you as Lizzy. Your appearance has changed, but I have never forgotten you." He smiled to see her happiness. "I heard your name spoken by, I believe, your sister. I heard of your love of reading and unhappiness with the city. Will you tell me all of your loves?"

"That is a rather impertinent question, sir." She raised that brow again. He was enchanted.

"It seems that I will be continually apologizing to you, Miss Elizabeth."

She smiled and studied his suddenly flushed face, then became concerned. "Are you well, sir?"

His brow creased. "Why do you ask?"

"Your eyes try to smile, but I see such sadness there." She studied him and he fell into the gaze, he would never tire of those eyes, he knew it.

"I fear that I will say something that will drive you away from me. Now that we have at last met, I cannot bear to see it end. Your laugh and smile have teased me for far too long." He said softly. "Why did you become fearful just now? What did I do wrong?"

Elizabeth looked to her shoes. "I . . . I thought that you might reject me. I . . . I have been . . .I know how it feels and I . . .wished to leave before I heard you say it. I believe that I could bear it from anyone else, but not you."

"I am no orator, Elizabeth . . . Miss Elizabeth." His fears eased when he saw her blush. "I was thinking of how beautiful you have become, not of rejecting you. Please believe me."

Elizabeth continued to observe his unwavering gaze and knew that she would forever remember that shade of blue, that soulful warmth. She felt a desire to touch his face and managed to stop herself before her hand rose too far. "I think that you should know that I am weary of observing you from afar as well. You should also know that your smiles have brought me so much happiness. I have compared every other man I have known to the memory of you."

Feeling a wave of emotion come over him, he shook his head. "You cannot know how the memory of you has carried me through so many moments of despair."

Elizabeth drew in a sharp breath, his feelings were palpable. "I hope that you might be happy to accept my friendship now, one of a more corporeal nature than a memory." She smiled, and he felt his mouth rising in return.

"I am very happy to have the honour of your friendship, Miss Elizabeth, and hope you will accept mine." She nodded and his smile grew. They both took deep breaths and laughed with relief. "Thank God that is over."

"What on earth does that mean?" She laughed and squeezed his arm. "Was that such a trial?"

"Yes, and do not tell me it was not." He placed his right hand over her left. "We both have thought of this moment, I am sure."

"Yes." She said and sighed. "I do not know why, but now that it has happened, I . . .feel as if we have been friends for years."

"We have."

They gazed at each other for a long silent moment and she swallowed. "What brought you to me, today? Do you often roam the park?"

He chuckled and pointed behind them. "I live just over there, on Park Lane. I come here to walk when I am troubled."

"Like you did the day we did not meet." She tilted her head to see his eyes cast down. "What troubles you today?

"My sister." He said softly.

"She is the girl I saw you with here and at the gallery?"

"Yes, Georgiana. She is thirteen." Darcy opened up to her without hesitation. "We just had a terrible row. Her governess is leaving and I proposed continuing her education at a girls' school that had been recommended to me. I think that she dislikes the idea of being away from home, although I am not sure if her reasons are fear or if she would miss me. I remember hating to leave home when I was her age, but attending Eton was expected of me and well . . ." He caught himself before he blurted the truth that he was overwhelmed with responsibilities. "I lost my temper when she began behaving very poorly. First I demanded that she return to speak with me, and when she ran further away, I sent her to her chambers with her governess and told her that I expected her to behave as a lady and speak with me later; and I came out here to walk and think."

"Pardon me sir, but that will not work."

"Why not?"

"Threats will not work on a petulant child. I have three younger sisters and I recognize her behaviour quite readily." She tilted her head and raised her brow to him, her lips twisted into a gentle smile.

Fascinated he looked at her, the sparkle in her eyes momentarily making him forget the problem of his sister. His brow creased, "What do you suggest, then?"

"Simply ignore her, sir." Her smile widened and her eyes danced with humour.

"Ignore her? But I cannot just let it go!" He noticed her shaking her head, gently disagreeing. "I have to maintain my authority!" He insisted.

"Sir, I assure you, this young lady wants attention and does not concern herself with what method she uses to achieve it. I am willing to wager that even now, she is sitting at a window staring out at the park to see what has become of you. She will come to you when she realizes you will not chase after her." She observed the disbelief on his face, "She does not wish to leave home, that tells me that she is missing something." Before he could respond, he heard a woman's voice calling. Elizabeth turned and waved to the women she had indicated before. She noticed his attention and smiled gently. "Your parents have much to discuss with Miss Darcy."

"Our parents have passed. I am afraid that I am quite alone in this." His expression hardened as he controlled the emotion that his parent's loss always inspired.

"Forgive me sir, I did not mean to offend you!" Elizabeth blushed, and looked to her shoes with embarrassment, and wondered if a parent is who they had mourned a year ago.

"Miss Elizabeth," he said softly. "There is no way that you could have known." He found her movement from confidence to shyness endearing.

Elizabeth looked bashfully up at him, then glanced to the woman she had acknowledged before. "My aunt tells me I am far too outspoken and it will lead me into trouble one day." Then returning to good humour she continued, "But one is only young once!" She laughed.

He gladly laughed with her. "And just how young is that, Miss Elizabeth?"

She raised her brows at the direct question but smiled and tilted her head. "Nearly eighteen sir; but rapidly aging."

Lizzy, Lizzy, Lizzy . . . eyes, laughter, smiles, joy . . . my Lizzy, my Elizabeth is a beautiful woman! He was captivated when she blushed with his words, "I believe that you shall be forever young. Please accept my sincere appreciation for my lesson today."

"In the proper handling of petulant young girls?" She laughed, and his face lit up as he laughed with her, delighting again in the welcome notes, and feeling a lightness he had never experienced before.

"Yes, that is it precisely. You should perhaps pen a book on the subject." He suggested, biting his lip and trying his hand in the very unfamiliar territory of flirtation.

"Sir, a woman writing? Scandalous!"

"I prefer poetry, and am especially fond of Shakespeare."

"Oh." Elizabeth bit her lip as well and looked up to see his warm gaze. "I am so very glad."

"Fitzwilliam!" They both startled to see Georgiana approaching with Mrs. Somers. She could not help noticing the young woman on his arm, or the way that her brother's hand was clasped over hers. "Forgive me, I . . .I wished to apologize and . . .I will go back home and wait for you."

Darcy looked at his sister then to the raised brow of his companion and shook his head at Elizabeth and smiled. "No dear, we will speak later but first," He drew a deep breath, and spoke warmly; using a tone that Georgiana had not heard since their father had died, "Miss Elizabeth Bennet, may I introduce you to my sister, Miss Georgiana Darcy?"

Elizabeth curtseyed and smiled. "I am pleased to meet you, Miss Darcy."

"I . . .I am pleased to meet you as well, Miss Bennet."

"Miss Elizabeth." Darcy and Elizabeth said simultaneously and smiled at each other. Georgiana blushed and they all looked up upon Mrs. Gardiner's approach. Darcy glanced at Mrs. Somers and she nodded, and left to return to the house.

Elizabeth noticed her aunt's eyes on Darcy's arm and reluctantly let him go. "Aunt, this is Mr. Fitzwilliam Darcy of Pemberley in Derbyshire. Sir, this is my aunt, Mrs. Edward Gardiner."

"It is a pleasure, madam. I am grateful for Miss Elizabeth's assistance today." He smiled first at her then back down to Elizabeth, and looked at her hand, wishing it was back on his arm.

Mrs. Gardiner watched his gaze with appreciation and nodded. "Well, I suppose that it was destiny, sir. Lizzy has wanted to walk here for weeks, and finally I acquiesced after her insistence this morning. She has been quite determined to come here, as she is every time she comes to town." Darcy looked to Elizabeth quickly and saw her blush. His heart beat faster, knowing instinctively that it was he that she sought. Mrs. Gardiner continued, "I am afraid that she misses the freedom she has at home at her father's estate."

"You often walk in Hertfordshire, Miss Elizabeth?" He smiled again at her, already knowing the answer.

Her brow creased, not recalling mentioning her county to him, but then laughed. "Oh yes, I know that it is not fashionable, but I much prefer nature to sewing."

Darcy nodded to Georgiana. "I believe that my sister would agree with you. She prefers nearly anything to sewing."

"We would get along famously then!" Elizabeth tilted her head to catch Georgiana's eye and saw her peek up at her and nod.

Realizing that the shy girl would say no more, Mrs. Gardiner wanted to pursue her own line of inquiry. "Mr. Darcy, I hope that you do not mind my asking, but my niece said that you are from Pemberley?"

He looked at her with surprise. "Yes, madam, do you know it?"

"Indeed, I grew up in Lambton, but have not been back for several years. Have there been many changes in the area?"

"Lambton! No, I would say other than a few new roofs it is as it has been since I was a child, a pleasant market town. I will pass through there when I return home."

"Someday I hope to return, London has much to offer, but I am sure you agree sir, there is no scenery like the Peaks." Mrs. Gardiner nodded and he smiled.

"I see that I have met someone who shares my enthusiasm, yes I agree, if it were not for business, I would never leave. I have not been home for months, and it will be good to see it again."

"You have been in London all of that time?" Elizabeth asked.

"No, I spent some time in Kent, visiting our aunt." He looked to Georgiana who stared down at her feet. "It was a short journey, unlike the day that we first spied each other. I had only that afternoon returned home from my Grand Tour."

"Oh, how wonderful that you had such an opportunity to experience the world! What did you see?" Her eyes were bright and clearly her imagination was working. "Surely you could not have gone through France. If not, then how ever did you cross the Alps? Did you take your carriage apart? Did you walk or did they carry you?" Darcy started to answer and laughed to see her still thinking out loud. "What a memorable experience you must have had to visit Italy and see the artwork, and actually practice your languages!"

Darcy grinned widely and laughed. "It seems that you are quite a student, Miss Elizabeth!"

"My niece is curious of many things, sir. She is a voracious learner." Mrs. Gardiner smiled at her burst of girlish behaviour.

"That is very admirable and refreshing to see, Miss Elizabeth. I hope that my sister will emulate you." He looked at Georgiana who had been watching Elizabeth's guileless enthusiasm with awe.

"Forgive me; I am afraid that I let my excitement run away with me, sir." She said apologetically. "I have only been able to glean a little from books; it is rare that I actually meet someone who can give me the details of what I have only imagined before."

"Hopefully the true tales do not prove to be disappointing in comparison."

"I suppose that we will have to find that out." Her eyes danced and he drank in the sight.

Darcy glanced at Mrs. Gardiner, who was watching her children becoming increasingly restive with the maid. He did not want to leave, he wanted to sit with Elizabeth and regale her with stories of his trip, then listen to her questions and hope to entertain her, and . . . He wanted so many other things, but clearly it was time to go. "Well, we should return to our home. It was a pleasure to meet all of you." He looked at Elizabeth and she locked her eyes with his.

They both seemed to be making a new memory of the other's face. "I especially enjoyed meeting you at last, Miss Elizabeth. I hope that you might accept a call from me?"

Elizabeth blushed. "I would enjoy that, Mr. Darcy." He nodded and started to step away then turned.

"Mrs. Gardiner, would your husband have any objections to my calling? I imagine that he is Miss Elizabeth's guardian while she is in town."

"Yes sir, he is, and please be assured of your welcome in our home." She smiled and met his happy eyes. "We look forward to seeing you."

"Thank you." He bowed, first to Mrs. Gardiner, then a slow bow to Elizabeth who laughed at his solemnity. He rose and found a smile on his lips. "Until we meet again." He turned with Georgiana and walked back down the path and towards their home.

"Lizzy, you certainly charmed Mr. Darcy." Mrs. Gardiner said speculatively, at last she knew the source of her niece's smiles, and remembered her confessions of the unnamed man from the summer before.

"I believe that he has charmed me." She laughed at her aunt's raised brows and watched his tall retreating figure, then gasped when he stopped and turned, looking back at her. He raised his hand and bowed again. Elizabeth raised her hand and could just see the smile that formed on his lips, then she turned and walked away.

"She is quite pretty and young." Georgiana smiled up at her brother, hoping to tease him a little.

"She is almost eighteen." He said, still watching. She disappeared from his view and realizing he did not know her exact address, began walking, taking long strides, seeking her out again.

Georgiana started to hurry, trying to keep up. "Where are we going?" She asked and saw his focus was back on Elizabeth. "Perhaps we could ask Miss Elizabeth for tea! Oh it would be wonderful to have someone nearer my age to talk to!"

Darcy glanced at her, still striding. "You do not like talking with me? You hardly spoke just now."

"Oh you know what I mean, alone with a girl!"

"You will have a whole school full of girls to talk to, Georgiana." He briefly met her eye. "You are going."

"I know, Brother." She said softly. "I wish that I could stay at home though." She peeked up at him.

He glanced down at her. "We will discuss this later, Georgiana."

Arriving on the other side of the park, he finally caught sight of Elizabeth, and was struck by the scene. She was holding the hand of a little boy, perhaps about five years old, and a little girl of about three was clutching her skirts. She was laughing and talking to Mrs. Gardiner, and he noticed that a tall blonde girl had joined them, a sleeping baby in her arms. He let out a breath and slowed his ground-eating pace, and knew for certain that he could happily spend the rest of his life hearing this woman laugh.

Then he saw to his dismay Elizabeth help the children into a waiting carriage. He stood still and watched as she turned her head to look out of the window in time to catch sight of him, and smiled. They gazed at each other as the carriage quickly departed. Darcy sighed, and he kicked himself for not asking her address sooner. "Gracechurch Street." Bingley would know the house, all was well. "Come Georgiana, let us return home."

THE ENTIRE WAY BACK TO GRACECHURCH STREET Elizabeth was silent. All she could do was wonder at the extraordinary sight of Fitzwilliam Darcy standing outside of her carriage. *Why did he return? Perhaps he just wanted to see me once more!* She thought over the first time that she had seen him, and realized that was when he heard her mention Hertfordshire. She gasped when she realized that he had remembered every second of that day, just as she had, he wanted her all that time!

Mrs. Gardiner observed the myriad of emotions playing over Elizabeth's face. "Lizzy, is Mr. Darcy the gentleman you have noticed on your other visits to town?"

She nodded and looked down. "I have thought of Fitzwilliam often."

"Lizzy!" She chastised her with the use of his Christian name and stopped. "You knew who he was?"

"Yes, only his name. I realized recently that he was Mr. Bingley's advisor, and have learned more of him. For two years I knew only what I have observed . . .and imagined." She looked back up to see her aunt's small smile and Jane's astonishment. "I suppose if I had told you his name you would have been able to fill in some details?"

"A few." She nodded. "But if he does call on you, he can do that himself."

Elizabeth smiled and looked back down at her hands. "I hope it is soon."

Chapter 10

arcy and Georgiana returned to the house and as much as he wanted to relive every second of his meeting with Elizabeth, he knew that he had to address his sister's behaviour first. "Georgiana, please come with me to my study."

She followed with her hands clasped and her eyes cast down, and passed before him to wait in front of his desk as he shut the door, jumping slightly as it clicked shut. He stood for a few moments, gathering his thoughts, and inexplicably wishing that Elizabeth was there to help him. He crossed the room and stood beside her. "Georgiana, my disappointment in your behaviour today is indescribable. Never could I have thought that my sister would put on such a display! What excuse do you have for imitating the most uneducated urchin this city possesses? Obviously Mrs. Somers has failed in her schooling. If she were not already planning to leave us, I would be forced to dismiss her."

Georgiana's eyes shot up. "No! Nanny Kate is not at fault! It was me, she has been so kind to me, she has been with me for as long as I can remember, she is the closest thing I have to a mother!" She began to sob and hid her face in her hands while Darcy closed his eyes, and felt the guilt and pain that he understood too well. "I am so sorry, Fitzwilliam! I know that I have been just awful to you of late, but you have been out nearly every night and I cannot bear to see her go . . .I thought that if I was bad, you would convince her to stay or you would stay home more often. If you send me to school, I . . .I will lose you, too . . .and . . ."

"And I am the closest thing you have to a father." He said quietly. Georgiana looked up and only saw him towering above her and frowning.

"I am behaving stupidly; a Darcy does not do this." She sniffed and pulled herself together. "I have shamed you and our family."

He sat on the edge of the desk, and indicated that she take a seat. "So you have attained your goal. You have my attention. It is just you and me. Please tell me how I have failed you."

"Oh Brother, you have not, truly." She stammered. "I . . . I sometimes wonder if I can live up to the expectations you have of me. You speak so often of what it is to be a Darcy and I have tried to become accomplished in all of my areas of study, but I wonder if it will ever be good enough. I . . . I wonder sometimes what it would have been like if . . ." Her voice trailed off.

"If Father had lived?" He studied her. "So do I. To say that the past two years have been easy would be a lie. But to wish that things were different will serve neither of us well. I do not want to be both your brother and father, but I am. So I must make decisions on your behalf, and you must trust that I am doing what is best for you."

"I understand." She looked down.

"I will take your objections to the school into consideration and will consult with Richard, but you certainly should know that school is a normal and expected step for a girl of our society. It would only be until you were fifteen, then we would form an establishment for you and find you a companion. You would have masters to teach you and you would benefit from more exposure to the world outside of the sheltered home I have given you." He saw her dejection and added softly. "I do not wish to send you away because I do not love you, Georgiana. I do this because I do love you, and want the best for you."

"I understand."

"Do you?" Darcy bent his head to see her nod and held her hands when she stood. "We will discuss this again when we are both a little calmer, however, I never want to experience an episode again as I just did. You must suffer some consequences for it, and for that reason I will not allow you to practice your pianoforte for a week, and with the time you now have available," He walked over to a bookshelf and pulled out a heavy tome, "I want you to read this cover to cover."

She read the title. "Our family history?"

"It is only complete up to our grandfather, but it should give you a good idea of just what it truly means to be a Darcy." He paused and then added. "Being a Darcy is not about status." He saw her frown and remaining stern-faced, watched her turn and leave.

The door clicked shut and he sighed. "I am certain I botched that. This is why Georgiana needs a sister, and why I need a wife, well one of the reasons I need a wife." He looked up to see the Pemberley landscape. "I need an heir, and I need . . ." His thoughts returned to Elizabeth Bennet. "Elizabeth." He whispered. "How many times have I thought of the girl who laughed and smiled on that day, and knew she was never to be mine, could never be mine, not if I listen to my father, not if I am to hold up the name of Darcy? She has been so near, so many times, growing lovelier with each year. And now I understand that all of the pride that I have carried for my name was misplaced, it was not pride of station at all. Father, now I understand." He spoke softly and thought of Elizabeth, her face looking through the coach's glass, and how dearly he needed to reach inside and pull her out and into his embrace. "Where are you now, Elizabeth?"

The question caused him to turn back to the bookshelves and look for his journals. "Pemberley, that is where they are." He cursed and closed his eyes, imaging the worn page that he stared at countless times, describing his first sight of her. He recalled speaking to his father, knowing that her family was below his; and his father telling him he must marry well, but that he . . .what? The last ride he took with him at Pemberley, the day he died, George Darcy urged him to remember those words. "What did you tell me, Father?" He shook his head, it was lost in the pain of those two significant days, and he did not know how to get it back.

Darcy turned to stare up at the portrait behind him. It showed his parents dressed in the fashion of twenty years past. His mother was seated, and wore a warm smile, her blue eyes sparkled. Mr. Darcy stood behind her, a hand placed on her shoulder, a gentle smile on his face. His parents had loved each other deeply. He so wanted to marry and experience that same love, but how could he and uphold his promise to care for the Darcy name? *Stop thinking like that you idiot; you know it is not about status anymore! What did you want me to do, Father? I need to know if this is right, before I take this relationship as far as I dearly wish.*

He sighed again and stared down at some papers lying on his desk. He wondered if he had met Miss Elizabeth a week earlier if he would have allowed the pressure to make him consider, let alone act upon, such a desperate idea, and was grateful that only he knew what a fool he had been.

Fitzwilliam stood in the doorway unnoticed and watched his cousin wrestle with himself. "What have you there, Darcy?"

He startled and looked up. "Richard, when did you arrive? I did not hear the door open."

"Never mind that. You have been staring at those papers with an expression of mourning I have never before witnessed, not even on your miserable countenance." He walked to join his cousin behind the desk and picked up the papers. "A settlement?" He read them with a concerned brow. "Who are these for, Darcy?"

"Someone . . . I decided that . . . I may as well make the family happy; and that I should just make a choice and marry." His voice was sad and resigned.

Fitzwilliam, keeping the settlement in his hands, walked away and sat in a chair opposite the desk. "Talk to me Darcy. You keep things bottled up. Have you spoken to anyone? You must not have said anything to my parents, and they surely would have told me. Talk to me. What is wrong?"

Darcy looked into the eyes of his cousin and friend and confessed. "No, I have not spoken to anyone. I had these papers drafted after a particularly difficult day with Georgiana last week; not that today was any better. I realize now that I did this in a moment of insanity and as you witnessed, I have not moved to make anyone my offer. I decided to listen to your parents' demands and made a concerted effort to identify a potential wife last night, and fortunately Bingley stopped me before I advanced the meeting beyond one dance."

"Thank God for that, choosing a wife should not be done in a hurry." Fitzwilliam said with heartfelt relief. "Now, what is behind all of this? Why the sudden desire to wed, and for God's sake, tell me why you wish to give in to my parents' demands?"

Darcy looked down at his hands, twisting together. "Georgiana's behaviour tells me that she needs a sister."

"Yes, I agree, that still does not explain your sudden choice."

"Richard, I have been exposed to hundreds of candidates for my wife, peer's daughters, heiresses, titled ladies. I have attended the balls; I have visited Almack's. I hated every moment of being under inspection and despised the machinations of the ladies and their parents to catch my eye or force my hand. None of them, not one, has ever attracted me for longer than a moment of pleasure, well until last night when I discovered that the woman who I thought was acceptable was one who resembled Miss Elizabeth." He looked down and back up to his cousin's suddenly understanding eyes. Darcy continued, "Georgiana needs someone, a woman, to guide her through her coming out."

"Well, we just agreed to put her in school . . ." He looked up to see Darcy's shaking head. "She objects, am I correct? And in a particularly poorly displayed manner?" He chuckled, earning a glare from his cousin. "Forgive me, but she *is* a Darcy, would you not expect her to express her objections with some level of spirit?" He smiled to see the surprise on Darcy's face and nodded. "Well, what of the other ideas we tossed around? Form an establishment for her. My only concern there is that Georgiana is probably a bit young for that step. I would prefer to stick with the schedule we had discussed. I spoke to Father and Mother about this. They would like to take her for the rest of the Season to give you a reprieve and have promised to stop pushing you to marry. They also see the sense in school for Georgiana." Darcy's eyes closed in relief and Richard looked down at the settlement. "But what I do not understand is why you suddenly need to be married?"

"Perhaps I do not have the desire to look anymore." Darcy said quietly.

Trying to read his inscrutable mask, Fitzwilliam studied him. "I think that the pressure of all that is on your shoulders drove you to this; and that some lady of the *ton* is not your real choice, but by marrying one you would be forced to forget the woman who is." He saw Darcy blush and smiled, sitting back in his chair. He waved the settlement papers at him. "I wager you have someone entirely different in mind for these papers, and her name is Miss Elizabeth Bennet. Darcy, I know that my parents have been pushing you, and I demanded that you look over the ladies of society and be sure, and you have been absolutely miserable. Clearly your decision was made long ago. So what are you waiting for? Do not tell me she is attached, or married? Is that what drove you to look elsewhere?" He sat up, suddenly struck with the thought.

"No, she is not."

"Ah ha! So, go to her!" He grinned. "What is the delay?"

Darcy closed his eyes and sighed. "You know that she is not of our social sphere, Richard." He was suddenly struck with a vision of Elizabeth's face and how afraid she had been of his rejection. He closed his eyes again, and instead tried to remember her laughter and smiles. He whispered. "How can I walk away from her now? I cannot bear to hurt her."

Fitzwilliam leaned forward. "You have seen her?" Darcy nodded. "What happened?"

A small smile appeared. "You know that I have spotted her in several locations over the past two years, we have exchanged looks, and I have felt her ire and her approval." He laughed softly. "She was there and gone so quickly I sometimes thought it was an apparition. She has grown into an exceptionally beautiful woman." His smile continued to grow, reaching to his eyes. "Georgiana argued with me today, and I stormed off to the park to calm, and there was Elizabeth, waiting for me, caring for me. We talked, we laughed, we even confessed some of our fears, and when I asked to call on her, she happily accepted me." His head dropped down and the smile disappeared. "And when I returned here I wondered if Father would allow me this choice."

Fitzwilliam looked at his cousin and understood his hesitation. "Are you letting her social status dictate your decision? Because quite honestly Darcy, if I had your money, I would not let that stand in my way. As the second son, I must take dowry and status into consideration. You do not." Darcy let out a deep breath, and Fitzwilliam decided to test his feelings. "I spoke to Stewart at the club last week."

"Why?" Darcy demanded.

"Why not?" He laughed. "We second sons share a camaraderie of sorts." He watched Darcy attempting to control his jealousy and leaned forward. "He is obviously unhappy, he is not the same man he was, and after some cajoling and port he admitted to regret for abandoning a wonderful woman because of her circumstances. Is that what you want, Darcy? Do you want to live with a lifetime of regret? You clearly have feelings for her that you do not hold for any other person."

"After I first saw her, well, the next day we went over the will, then we left for Pemberley, and you know what happened then." He looked away to the window. "She was so young, I realize now that she was just fifteen, close to Georgiana's age . . .the thoughts I had of her then, my God, if I knew of any man thinking such things of Georgiana I would kill him!" Fitzwilliam smiled and nodded. "I did not realize . . . well, I also knew then that she was not of our circle and . . . asked Father about it."

"About marrying below yourself?"

He nodded. "Yes, he said . . ." His speech slowed and he looked back to the portrait. "He said to be prepared for the unexpected to arise. He said . . ." Darcy stood and stared into his Father's eyes. "He said to allow room for my heart as well as my head!"

"What has come over you?" Fitzwilliam demanded.

"I have been trying to remember that for years! He told me that practically on his deathbed, *Remember what I said to you.* That is what it was! I remember at the time that I did not understand what he meant, I only heard him saying that I have been raised with certain expectations. Richard! He was giving me permission to love . . . anyone!" Darcy spun around to face his cousin. "I remember! She is in Gracechurch Street right now!"

"So tell me Cousin, why are you not there now as well?"

"I have only just remembered, and . . ." He sobered. "What if I do see her, what would such an alliance do to Georgiana's prospects?" He looked down at his desk as his soaring heart suddenly slowed. "Perhaps Father was not telling me I could marry so far below my station."

"Do you seriously think that a girl with a dowry of thirty thousand pounds will find herself shunned by society if you marry with your heart instead of your pocketbook in mind?" Fitzwilliam lifted his brow. "You could dye her skin purple with grape juice and there would still be a line of suitors waiting at your door. Besides, Georgiana is at least five years from marriage, whatever you do now will be long forgotten by then."

"Do you really think so? I could not bear to hurt her in any way, she is all I have." Darcy's voice shook as he looked for his cousin's reassurance. "I know that I must find a wife, but also the support that Georgiana truly needs."

"So your solution is to marry without feeling? Surely you can do better than that!" Fitzwilliam waved the settlement papers at him. "I have not met this woman, I know nothing of her, but she has animated you in a way that I could never fathom you achieving, and this is all after only two, no really one, conversation. What could happen if you actually paid her a call?" Darcy looked up with a small smile and met his grinning cousin's eyes. "So tell me, why exactly are you looking to marry anyone else?" He again waved the papers at Darcy.

Darcy stood and grabbed the settlement from Fitzwilliam, threw it into the grate of the fireplace, and quickly set them ablaze. "What are you talking about, Richard? I never said that I wanted to marry anyone!"

They laughed, and Darcy walked over and shook Fitzwilliam's hand. "Thank you. I almost made a terrible mistake. I think that I heard too many times the drumbeat of "duty and honour" pounded into my head, and forgot that there is more to it than just marrying a rich woman, and failed to understand and remember the most important lesson my father ever tried to teach me." He looked gratefully at his cousin.

"I am looking forward to meeting this lady who captured you so quickly!" He grinned. "Now, you have an assignment. It is not too late to pay a call; shall I ask for your carriage to be prepared while you run upstairs and change into some courting attire?"

Feeling better than he had in years, Darcy smiled widely. "I believe my green coat will look very well on me." He took off up the stairs and Fitzwilliam rang for a footman to give the orders for the coach. He walked over to pick up a crystal decanter and poured a healthy glass of port, and raising it to his lips, paused and toasted George and Anne Darcy.

"To new memories."

DARCY PEERED OUT at the neighbourhood as his coachman paused and called to a passing tradesman. "Do you know the Gardiner House?" He did not hear the reply but the coachman obviously did as they began moving again, not too far, when they came to a stop before a modest townhouse. A maid was on her knees outside, scrubbing the front steps clean. He drew a breath, straightened his cravat, and stepped out when the door opened.

"I am not sure how long I will be John, but I suspect it will be brief."

"Yes sir, I'll just wait here, then." He closed the door and jumped back up on the coach, and he and the footman watched surreptitiously as their master handed his card to the maid who bobbed a curtsey and ushered him inside the door. "What brings Mr. Darcy to this part of town?" He asked his partner.

"I dunno, but he looks nervous."

"How can you tell? I never know what he's thinking."

"Didn't you see the way he was chewing his lip?" Robbie chuckled. "Something special is afoot, I'd wager."

Darcy waited in the hallway and took in the decoration. Like the outside, the house appeared modest but well-kept. There was nothing at all wanting, clearly Mr. Gardiner was successful in his business. The maid returned, followed by an older woman who was obviously the housekeeper. "Mr. Gardiner will be pleased to speak to you, sir. Please follow me." He walked through the home, looking, listening, pleased to smell the scents of a meal cooking and wax from the floors and furniture. A well-run home indeed, it spoke volumes of Mrs. Gardiner. "Mr. Darcy, sir." The housekeeper moved from the doorway to a study and Darcy stepped in, hearing the door close behind him. He was greeted by a man of about forty years, his face was good humoured, but his eyes were shrewd and curious. Darcy liked the combination and did not feel at all offended by the close inspection he was receiving.

"Mr. Darcy, I am pleased to welcome you to my home, I am Edward Gardiner."

"Sir, it is a pleasure, please forgive my late call." He took the indicated chair and watched the man settle behind his desk.

"I must admit that the note on the back of your card intrigued me, as well as your identity." He smiled to see Darcy's brows rise. "My wife lived in Lambton for a time. The praises of Pemberley have been sung here many times, and she did happen to mention meeting you this afternoon."

"Ah, well then, the element of surprise has been thoroughly eliminated from my visit."

"I assure you, sir, welcoming a gentleman of your eminence into my home is quite surprising, even without the notation on your card." He picked it up and read aloud. "I wish to speak with you on a matter of some importance regarding Miss Elizabeth Bennet." Setting it down, he rested his hands on the desk and looked Darcy in the eye. "You can understand my curiosity."

"Yes, I can." He smiled slightly and plunged in. "Perhaps I may begin by saying that I first saw Miss Bennet in Hyde Park two years ago. She made a very strong impression on me, an unforgettable one, although at the time I realized she was too young to approach, and circumstances in my life prevented me from pursuing a friendship with her." Mr. Gardiner nodded and waved him on. "I did not speak to her, but as I said, I was gifted with a display of her . . ." He struggled for words.

"Unique personality?"

"Indeed." Darcy flashed a warm smile for a moment. "I thought of her often, but as my father had just died and I had my sister to care for, I am afraid that I felt that the memory of my encounter would remain just that until this afternoon when we met again. I . . .have had the pleasure of spotting her from afar on several occasions through the years, at the Royal Art Exhibition, at the Derby last summer."

He saw Mr. Gardiner nod, and arriving at the events of that day felt the importance of impressing him. Darcy began confidently but by the end his anxiety showed as he rushed through the story. "I realized that she was just as strongly affected by our reunion as I. I . . .well, she gave me advice for my sister and we . . .enjoyed our conversation, and she said that she would welcome my call, but she left before I could confirm her address. My friend Charles Bingley has called here, but he was not available to consult immediately, and I . . .came here now to make sure that another two years does not pass before I speak to her again."

Mr. Gardiner listened in fascination. He could well-imagine how Lizzy might impress such a powerful man, but he had to ask the important questions. "What is your interest in my niece, Mr. Darcy? I am very aware of your place. Are you aware of my niece's?"

"She is the daughter of a gentleman with a small estate in Hertfordshire named Longbourn."

"Yes. She has very little to offer besides herself."

"If my intuition is correct sir; that would be a treasure indeed." Darcy said and met his eye sincerely. "You ask my intentions? I have hopes for many things, but my first is to be given an opportunity to meet her properly and ascertain if she truly desires my attentions."

"Mr. Darcy, I doubt that there are four hundred families in England that possess your wealth, why would you . . ."

"I have found them wanting." He said simply. "I assure you sir; I am not a man in search of a mistress if that is your fear. My intentions are honourable. If she is willing, I wish to begin courting her. Will you grant my request, sir?"

"I would be a fool not to, and I believe that my sister would never speak to me again if I did not." He chuckled and stood. Darcy sighed with relief and rose. "By the way, Lizzy is no fool, and will not hesitate to put you in your place, but she also has the kindest heart I have ever known beyond my dear wife. Show her the respect she deserves."

Darcy smiled at the description. "I will sir. I grew up watching an excellent marriage, and hope for the same someday."

"Very good. I am sorry to say that we are going to attend a dinner this evening and the ladies are upstairs preparing. I will ask Lizzy to come down to greet you, if you do not mind waiting for a few minutes?"

"No sir, in fact I would be willing to leave and return at a more convenient time."

"Now Mr. Darcy, you know that is not true." Mr. Gardiner laughed. "Make yourself comfortable."

He left the room and Darcy blew out the breath he had been holding. The interview had gone very well, and he realized that it was due in no small part to the skill of his host. "Perhaps I need to rethink my opinions of all men in trade, not just Bingley." He mused and wandered the room, scanning the bookshelves and appreciating the collection that was there.

"Oh." Elizabeth had flown down the stairs and came to a sudden stop in the doorway. Darcy turned at the sound and they stood frozen for a moment, then he advanced to stand before her. "Mr. Darcy."

"Miss Elizabeth." He bowed and took her hand, and lifted it to brush his lips softly over her warm skin. Darcy closed his eyes and breathed in the scent of the perfume that clung to her fingers. Slowly he straightened and looked down into her face, and delighted in the dreamlike expression. "I returned home and realized that I had forgotten to ask you a question."

"A question?"

"Yes, an important one." His eyes twinkled and his mouth lifted in a small smile.

Elizabeth relaxed and smiled in return. "Then do not delay a moment longer, sir."

He removed the volume of sonnets from his pocket and held it out to her. "I did not learn your favourite. Bingley purchased this for me, but I am afraid that I have always thought of it as a gift from you, and . . . I confess that I am never without it."

She blushed with pleasure and her eyes shone. "That is quite a confession to make to a girl you have just met."

"You are not a girl, Miss Elizabeth, and you are hardly a new acquaintance. Will you please tell me which you love?"

"That is a private matter, sir." She teased.

Darcy shook his head and squeezed the hand he still held in his grasp. "What must I do to convince you to reveal your opinion?"

"Tell me yours." He smiled and slowly shook his head. Elizabeth laughed at his refusal and tried to withdraw her hand from his. "Sir, you must let go, I hear my uncle's descent."

"Only if you promise to walk with me tomorrow."

"Where?"

"Anywhere you like."

"When?"

"You know my answer, Miss Elizabeth." He raised her hand to his lips again and she closed her eyes as he closed his and murmured. "Please."

"Yes."

"I will come at one o'clock."

"I will be waiting."

"Thank you." Darcy's eyes opened to find Elizabeth looking at her hand enveloped in his. "They look well together, do they not?"

"I always thought they would." Their eyes met and looking down to her parted lips leaned forward, then checking himself, stepped back and let go of her hand.

"I told your uncle that my intentions are honourable, Miss Elizabeth. I want you to be confident that I am serious."

Elizabeth drew up to her full height and he smiled, appreciating that she only came to his chin, but her expression was fierce. "I would accept nothing less, Mr. Darcy."

Mr. Gardiner arrived and was satisfied with what he saw, he had only left them for five minutes but the necessary words had clearly been exchanged. "I am sorry sir, but we will be departing very soon."

Darcy slipped the book back in his pocket and nodded. "I understand. I hope that you enjoy your evening."

"Let me see you to the door, Mr. Darcy." Elizabeth offered. She wrapped her hands around his forearm and they walked from the room to stand before the front door.

He looked down into her gently dancing eyes. "Do not let any of the gentlemen steal you away from me tonight."

Elizabeth laughed and he raised his brows. "Sir, I assure you, I am the most unappealing woman in London. Nobody ever looks at me."

"Well they are fools, but I will not attempt to correct them." He squeezed her hand and stepped away. "I will see you tomorrow. Good night."

She watched him walk out to his carriage and board. He waved to her as they departed and she waved back and leaned on the doorframe. "Good night, Fitzwilliam."

Mr. Gardiner waited and watched her then looked up to the top of the stairs where Mrs. Gardiner stood with Jane. He stepped forward and touched Elizabeth's shoulder and when she turned, he saw that her face was covered in tears. "Lizzy!"

She fell into his arms and sobbed. Mrs. Gardiner came down and took over, leading her into the drawing room and holding her, rocking her back and forth. "These are tears of happiness, dear?" Elizabeth nodded. "You never thought that this would ever happen?"

"How could I, Aunt? Even before Mr. Stewart rejected me, I knew how unworthy I was for any gentleman, and that all of my dreams for Mr. Darcy were just that." She sniffed and looked up. "He said that he was serious. He told Uncle that he wants to court me, and is coming tomorrow to walk with me."

Mrs. Gardiner kissed her forehead and whispered in her ear. "I was going to talk to you about all of the liberties you took today, speaking to him alone, holding his arm in the park, even being a little too forward in your talk, but I can see that Mr. Darcy clearly appreciated everything that you did, and has been hoping to meet you again, too." She smiled and looked into her eyes. "He obviously needs a girl like you to bring some liveliness into his days."

"I am so afraid of disappointing him." She whispered and dabbed at her face with her handkerchief.

"I guarantee he feels the same way about you." Mrs. Gardiner laughed. "Now, let us go to this dinner, and then we will discuss this walk the two of you are taking tomorrow."

5 MAY 1809
My hands are shaking. This is a page that I know I will reread forever, and my hands are shaking so hard that I can barely put my thoughts down. Today I finally touched my Elizabeth. When my lips met her skin, it was all I could do not to allow them to continue up her wrist and ultimately to her beautiful smiling mouth. I will marry this woman. I realize that we need time to know each other, and I know that we both have so much to learn, but I also know that she is the only woman I have ever wanted. As much as I despised the Season, and fought against the charms of all of those women who I met, I must thank Richard for forcing me to go through the exercise. I can say for certain that I know there is not one woman who matched my Elizabeth. I am nervous and worried about somehow making a mistake that would drive her away, but I am also aware that she is as well. That knowledge alone gives me confidence. Father gave me his blessing to marry as I wish. That is what I intend to do. I cannot wait until tomorrow!

Darcy closed his eyes and relived the kisses to her hand and remembered the sweet subtle scent of her perfume. "What a day this has been."

"Brother?" Georgiana peeked nervously into his study. He looked up and smiled.

"Come in." She slipped inside and took the chair before his desk. "What can I do for you?"

"I wanted to apologize again for this morning, and I wanted you to know that I trust your decisions for me, and if you feel that I should go to school, I will without protest." She sat back and watched him anxiously.

Darcy tilted his head and studied her. "I accept your apology and thank you for your trust. What brought this about?"

"Richard spoke to me about my behaviour."

"And was it helpful?"

"He helped me to understand your responsibilities. I am so sorry, I was just thinking of myself."

"That is a hazard of your age, I think." Darcy smiled and she relaxed with his ease. "Did he speak to you of staying at Matlock House for the rest of the Season?" She nodded. "And what is your opinion?"

"I would like to go. Aunt Helen can do things with me that you cannot."

"That is very true." Darcy smiled again. "I think that it will do us both a bit of good to have the separation. But please know that I think it will be a good experience, and not that I wish you away because I am angry."

"I know that, I do." She tilted her head. "What will you do with yourself without me here?"

Darcy laughed and held up his hand. "I apologize, that was rude."

"You are happy!"

"I am very happy."

Georgiana gasped. "Miss Elizabeth, does she have something to do with your smiles?"

"Do you like her?"

"Yes, very much. I thought that she would be a wonderful friend."

"Well then, you should know that I have asked her uncle for permission to court her, and tomorrow we will begin." He smiled and leaned back. "What do you think of that?"

"Really?" He nodded and the smile remained on his face. "Will Aunt and Uncle approve of her?"

"Probably not, and Aunt Catherine will hate her. She is not of our circle Georgiana, but she is a gentlewoman and I have no doubt in my mind that she will win them over. And I will do everything I can to help her."

"Well if she makes you smile then I will do everything I can to help, too!" She jumped up and came around the desk to hug him. "I am so happy for you!"

Darcy blinked hard and hugged her tight. "Thank you, dear."

ELIZABETH CLOSED HER JOURNAL and laughed softly. "What a day this has been! I at last meet my Fitzwilliam and am so happy that I say nothing at dinner, and I am suddenly surrounded by interested men!" She looked up into the mirror on the dressing table at her exultant face. "Well, now I know what was wrong with me, it was not what I said in my conversation; it was that I spoke at all! Oh how wonderful that Fitzwilliam likes me for myself!" She stood up and spun around the room, landing with a thud on the bed and immediately hugging her pillow. "What can I say to him tomorrow? I must hear his laugh again!"

There was a knock at the door and Jane spoke. "Lizzy, may I come in?"

She sat up and moved aside, patting the bed. "Of course!"

"You are just brimming with joy." Jane smiled.

"Oh Jane, it is as if an albatross of failure has been lifted from my shoulders. I did not realize how deeply hurt I was from Mr. Stewart's rejection and well, everything, until Mr. Darcy accepted me. I have dreamed of him for so long." She smiled and saw Jane's creased brow. "What is it?"

"You loved Mr. Stewart?"

"No, I did not, but naturally it hurt to have a man who you know is good and kind reject you because of your poverty and poor relations. And Mama's disappointment only drove home to me how unlikely it was that I would ever be wanted by a good man again."

"Do you love Mr. Darcy?"

"Jane . . . My feelings for him are so difficult to describe, until now this was a courtship of our imaginations." She smiled and squeezed her hands. "We begin courting in truth tomorrow."

"It seems that all of the men care for you. Tonight they all seemed to look at you."

Elizabeth tilted her head. "That is because I did not behave as myself. If you think about it, I was behaving like you."

"What is that supposed to mean?" She snapped.

Elizabeth dropped her hands. "Jane, what is wrong? Ever since we came to town, every man we met has been interested in you and barely acknowledged me. Do you begrudge me a little attention on one night?"

"No, no. I am sorry Lizzy, it is just . . . I suppose that I am a little jealous of you." She looked up and smiled. "But you have been waiting for Mr. Darcy for a long time. I only remember speaking of him a little some time ago. I did not know that you had harboured these dreams."

"Does it hurt you to know that I did?"

"It should not."

"I am sorry, Jane. I barely let myself think of them." Elizabeth smiled. "But now I will let my imagination run wild!"

"He is a very handsome man." Jane acknowledged.

"I did not tell Aunt, but he kissed my hands twice and we held hands the entire time that we spoke."

"Lizzy!" Jane cried then whispered, "What was it like?"

"Absolutely wonderful!" She sighed. "I hope that it happens again."

"I have no doubt that you will encourage him."

"Jane!" Elizabeth protested, then smiled. "Well, I will not discourage him!" The girls laughed and Jane stood.

"Good night, Lizzy. Get some sleep. I think that tomorrow is the beginning of your future."

"No, that was today. Tomorrow I will embrace it with both arms." Elizabeth saw the door close and blew out her candle, then settled into the bed. "Goodnight Fitzwilliam."

Chapter 11

ingley entered Darcy's study with a smile. "Good morning!" Darcy looked up and back down at his letter, and said nothing. Bingley settled into a chair across from the desk and peered at him. "I say Darcy, are you well?"

He slammed the letter down and glared. "I would like to know Bingley, by what authority you were moved to discuss my feelings with Miss Elizabeth Bennet? Or even to presume to know them? If I wanted her to know my feelings I would have told them to her myself!" Darcy growled and watched as Bingley shifted uncomfortably in his chair. "Now you have given this woman the expectation of my addresses! If word of this gets around, I will be labelled a cad for raising her hopes and abandoning her, or worse, I might be seen as some rich gentleman wishing to take advantage of a poor girl as a mistress!"

"Darcy, I am sorry, I was not thinking of that I , I , I only saw that two of my friends cared . . . seemed to care for each other . . . and you have been so miserable, well not miserable, um, but I thought you could use a smile, and then I saw you dancing with that woman who resembled Miss Elizabeth . . ."

"Ah yes, and what of her? Do you know how many women I have danced with this Season?"

"No." Bingley whispered.

"Three."

"Oh."

"Can you imagine how disappointed her mother was with her to lose a suitor like me?" Darcy was satisfied to see Bingley staring at his hands, and biting back the smile that was threatening to appear, schooled his features. "Well, I am afraid that this is very grave, Bingley. And I have two words to say to you."

"Begone forever?" He said to his boots.

"Bingley." Darcy said sternly and waited for his friend to finally look up. "Thank you. Thank you for being my invaluable interfering friend. You urged me from that ballroom before I made a terrible mistake, and yesterday . . . .yesterday I met Miss Elizabeth in the park, and today . . ." Darcy sighed and beamed. "Today we begin our courtship."

"What?!" Bingley stared and jumped up when Darcy came around the desk and placed one hand on his shoulder and shook the other. "You are courting Miss Elizabeth?"

"I am, Bingley. I am. I spoke to her uncle yesterday." Darcy laughed. "I am meeting her today for a walk."

"Good Lord! I was sure that you were about to call me out. Do not ever frighten me like that again!" Darcy laughed and Bingley stared at him in disbelief. "How did this happen?" He dropped down into his chair and smiled incredulously.

Darcy leaned on his desk and folded his arms. "Georgiana and I argued and I took to the park to walk off my frustration. Elizabeth, Miss Elizabeth was there, seemingly just waiting for me." He sighed. "I am forever in your debt."

"I did nothing; you found her and must have said something."

"Yes, but you gave us both hope, and pointed out the obvious to me. Thank you, Charles." Darcy smiled. "Thank you."

"I still do not believe that I deserve your thanks, but after all you have done for me . . ." He smiled to see Darcy turn away from hearing praise and resume his seat. "Well, so you are paying a call."

"Yes." Darcy smiled ruefully. "I have no idea what to do."

"Well that is simple. Miss Elizabeth is the easiest girl in the world to talk with. The difficulty is keeping up with her, but I daresay she will draw you out." He saw his friend's worry and laughed. "Where are you walking?"

"I would like to take her home. I know that she will love it there." He looked up then back down to his hands.

"Hmm, a wonderful idea but seeing as Pemberley is three days away . . .perhaps the park in Gracechurch Street?"

"I suppose." Darcy smiled a little.

"You will have a chaperone. Probably Miss Bennet."

Darcy's smile fell away. "I had not thought of that."

"Would you like me to come along, keep Miss Bennet distracted while you court Miss Elizabeth?"

"Would that give Miss Bennet the wrong impression of your feelings, Bingley? You are in no position to be courting."

"I will make that clear." Bingley smiled. "I find her beautiful, but she is not the girl for me. When do we leave?"

"An hour, are you hungry?"

"Absolutely!"

ELIZABETH BATTED AWAY JANE AND HER AUNT. "Will you two please stop fussing over me? It is just a walk!"

"It is not just a walk, Lizzy! You must look your best!" Jane held her hair up and debated the arrangement of her curls.

"Jane, if you do not stop acting like Mama I will pinch you!" She hissed.

"Pardon me, madam. Mr. Darcy and Mr. Bingley are here. I put them in the front sitting room." The housekeeper announced.

Elizabeth froze and looked at the clock. "He is early!"

"Five minutes." Mrs. Gardiner laughed. "Come along girls."

Darcy paced nervously in the small sitting room, wiped his hands on his breeches, cleared his throat, pulled on his neck cloth, then paused to lean against the window frame. "Relax man!" Bingley laughed.

"I am." He said unconvincingly. They both looked up when the ladies arrived and Darcy's focus was immediately on Elizabeth. He bowed and watched her approach. "Good morning, Miss Elizabeth."

"Good morning Mr. Darcy." She took a calming breath then smiled to see that he had been struck dumb and clearly had no desire to look anywhere else in the room. Bingley nudged him and he startled, and bowed to Mrs. Gardiner, then looked inquiringly at Jane.

Elizabeth touched her arm. "Mr. Darcy, this is my sister, Miss Jane Bennet."

He smiled slightly. "I am happy to meet you Miss Bennet. I remember seeing you in Hyde Park the day that I first noticed your sister."

Jane looked down as she realized that he had not ever taken notice of her. "Oh, yes I remember you as well, sir."

Bingley stepped forward and smiled. "Ladies, it is a pleasure to see you all today. I happened to be visiting Darcy this morning, and invited myself along for this stroll in the park."

Elizabeth laughed, bringing a smile to Darcy's face, and turned to Bingley. "How thoughtful of you to impose yourself upon us."

He chuckled. "Ah Miss Elizabeth, I am merely doing my friend a service in providing a proper chaperone."

"Do you imply that Mr. Darcy and I are incapable of behaving properly? I am offended, sir!"

"Now, now, Miss Elizabeth, I am certain that your aunt would agree." Bingley nodded to Mrs. Gardiner.

"But would Mr. Darcy?" Elizabeth turned to him and saw that his brow had creased. Darcy had grown uncomfortable watching the easy conversation between Elizabeth and Bingley. "Sir?" She asked softly, not quite understanding his expression.

He read her worried eyes and jumped. "Oh, forgive me, of course I know that your aunt has no reason to fear my behaviour, but I will bend to her desires, I know what is proper." Darcy bowed his head to her.

Mrs. Gardiner bowed her head in return. "Well, I am afraid that I must insist upon it. Jane was to walk along."

"Splendid! Then Miss Bennet and I will serve as spies!" Bingley proclaimed and stepping to her side, winked. "We will keep the couple in line."

"We will attempt to, sir. However I know my sister; and it might be a challenge." She smiled and Bingley smiled back.

"Now I *am* offended." Elizabeth laughed. "I think that we should depart immediately and challenge these preconceived notions of our behaviour. Where is our destination, Mr. Darcy?" Elizabeth looked up to him and he happily took his place beside her.

"You know that I will gladly take you wherever you wish, but I did think of your local park. It would achieve our goal sooner."

"Then we shall go there, sir." The two couples set out, and the instant they were outside, Darcy offered Elizabeth his arm and contentedly felt her hands wrap around it, and thrilled to hear her satisfied sigh. They walked in companionable silence down the street until they entered the park gate. Elizabeth looked up to his face, his eyes were soft, and there was a trace of a smile on his lips. "Shall we have some conversation sir, besides the one you are obviously holding with yourself? Would you care to share your thoughts with me?"

"Forgive me; you may as well know now that conversation is not my forté." He glanced back at Bingley talking animatedly to Jane. "Unlike my friend. I fear that you are much easier with him than with me."

"That is simply because we have known each other longer. I observed no trouble with your speech yesterday, Mr. Darcy."

Shaking his head, he smiled. "I was behaving in spectacularly uncharacteristic ways yesterday, Miss Elizabeth."

She raised her brow and regarded him speculatively. "So I have accepted your courtship under false pretences? You have misrepresented yourself to me?"

"You are putting words in my mouth."

"Somebody has to."

Their eyes met and they both laughed. Darcy visibly relaxed and lifted his hand to cover hers on his arm. "Thank you."

"I did nothing, sir, but I am pleased to hear your laugh again. It is a very warm sound." Darcy blushed with the praise and looked down. "Have you known Mr. Bingley for long?"

"You witnessed the moment our friendship was formed. In fact, you are the reason it exists at all. Your anger at his treatment at the Derby spurred me to act in his defence." He laughed to see her astonishment. "Yes, Miss Elizabeth, I was trying win your approval." He squeezed her fingers. "In the process I gained a friend who I value highly, and who has helped me to find you."

She blushed with the affirmation of his admiration and squeezed his arm in response. "I was impressed with you, and I . . . I hoped that you would speak to me then. It looked as if you were trying to come over to me?"

"Yes, but my uncle kept interfering."

"He did not wish for you to speak to someone like me." She looked down at her feet.

"No, no Miss Elizabeth, he had no knowledge of you. He was speaking of Bingley. It is a very unusual choice of friend for me, you must understand. My uncle was expressing his approval and although it was welcome, I only wished for yours. And then before I could come to you, the crowd moved and once again you were gone." Their eyes met and she saw his sincerity, and relaxed.

"Yes. I was angry that you never stay still." She laughed and he joined her.

"I thought the same of you." They smiled into each other's eyes and walked slowly along. "My aunt and uncle will be hosting a ball in their home a week from now. May I hope for your company? I have no desire to attend without you."

"Mr. Darcy, I would love to go!" Darcy beamed then grew uneasy when her eyes cast back down to the ground. "Would they want me? I imagine that they are like you."

"Like me?"

"I . . . I have been . . . I am acquainted with how unsuitable I am for a gentleman of your status, sir."

Darcy knew she was speaking of Stewart, and he swallowed down his jealousy to address the woman on *his* arm. "Miss Elizabeth, I cannot say how my aunt and uncle will respond to you. I hope that they will welcome you because they care for me and have been hoping to find me a wife; actually they have been very insistent that I go out this Season to socialize and become attached to a woman. Only yesterday I learned that they have decided to leave me alone because I was so miserable." Elizabeth looked up to him and he squeezed her hand again. "I was miserable because I wanted you."

"oh."

"I am sorry that you have experienced rejection at the hands of a gentleman. I can only imagine the hurt you felt, but . . .it did leave you available for me, and I am grateful for that man's foolish decision. I know that there will be those who will not accept you and will make their opinions heard, but I will not be influenced by them, and I will defend my choice vigorously. You, Miss Elizabeth, are stuck with me."

Elizabeth's laugh make his heart soar and he wanted nothing more at that moment then to wrap her in his arms and kiss her senseless. His head dipped down to claim her mouth when Bingley's cough stopped him. Darcy and Elizabeth both blushed. "Forgive me." He whispered, "I do not know what came over me."

"When you find out sir, please be sure to remember it for another time." Elizabeth whispered but kept her gaze down to her shoes. She heard no response and peeked back up to find his focussed gaze waiting for her.

"I will."

"Mr. Darcy, I am not as forward as I sound."

"Miss Elizabeth, I am not as confident as I sound."

"I am stubborn."

"So am I."

"I love to laugh."

"I love to listen to you."

"I am very afraid of doing something wrong." She looked back up to him. Darcy tilted his head and regarded her with a creased brow. "Oh please, tell me what you are thinking!"

He entwined his fingers with hers on his arm and said quietly. "I am marvelling over the incredible good fortune that brought us together."

"DARCY I AM DELIGHTED to see you smiling!" Lady Matlock exclaimed when he arrived at Matlock House. "What has come over you?"

"I had a good day." She laughed with delight when he kissed her cheek. "Is Uncle at home?"

"Yes, he is in his study with Layton."

"Richard?"

"He is in his rooms." He smiled and bowed. "Darcy, are you sure that everything is well?"

"Yes, Aunt." He walked upstairs to his cousin's chambers and knocked. "What is this, still abed? The day is nearly over!"

"Ha, I am just filling my reserves for the night!" Richard sat up and stretched his stiff legs. "By the grin on your face I would say that your little stroll today was a resounding success?"

"It was. My instincts were correct; she is everything my imagination created. I cannot wait to discover more."

"Smitten." Fitzwilliam laughed and stood up. "What is next?"

"I will visit her tomorrow, her family invited me for dinner, and I was thinking that I might bring Georgiana along another time so that I could introduce them properly." He bit his lip. "I invited her to accompany me to your parents' ball."

"Uh-oh."

"I know; I was going to speak to your father but not with Layton in the room."

"No, definitely not." Richard leaned against a wall. "She cannot come alone with you."

"Her aunt and uncle . . ."

"A tradesman in Matlock House? As an equal? Are you out of your mind?"

"Her sister?"

He shook his head. "She is unmarried and under thirty. This is a problem, Darcy."

"Perhaps Bingley could chaperone her?" Darcy thought desperately and looked up to see his cousin's incredulous stare. "What other choice is there? I will not come without her!"

Fitzwilliam donned his coat. "Come on, we will ambush them."

"I hope that you truly are healed Cousin, because you may need to keep me back from strangling your brother."

"Why would I stop you? I would be the Viscount then!" Fitzwilliam laughed and clapped his back, and they made their way downstairs. "What happened during the walk?"

"We talked, it was actually becoming a serious conversation and I believe that we both had a great desire to talk about ourselves, but unfortunately just as we were about to begin, Elizabeth's sister inexplicably walked up to join us. Bingley followed naturally, and the four of us continued on. I cannot help but think that she was jealous of her sister."

"She is the elder?"

"Yes. Very beautiful, in a classic sense."

"hmm." Fitzwilliam contemplated that fact and knocked on the study door. They entered and after the greetings were completed, took their seats. "Father, Darcy needs your advice."

"Do you? Well I am happy to help. Estate business?"

"No, not precisely."

"Love?" Layton laughed and saw his cousin's glare. "Well, based on recent conversations in this house, I imagine that it concerns Georgiana, so I will remove myself from the room." Fitzwilliam held up his hand to stop Darcy from correcting him. Lord Matlock observed the two men curiously and when the door clicked shut, Darcy drew breath and looked to see Fitzwilliam urging him onward. "I would like to bring a friend with me to your ball."

"Bingley? Well of course, he is invited already."

"No, not Bingley, sir." He closed his eyes and then met his uncle's. "I have begun a courtship with a young lady."

"What?" Lord Matlock stared. "Who?"

"Her name is Miss Elizabeth Bennet. Her father's estate is in Hertfordshire. I am very serious about her."

"Serious? I have seen you with nobody! You have spoken to her father?" Lord Matlock demanded. "I have heard nothing of this girl, and believe me; I have heard the names of every debutante in London over the past months."

"I have spoken to her uncle who is her guardian in town. He has granted my request and she has as well. She is nearly eighteen. I would like her to attend the ball with me, and would like to know if I may invite her relatives to be her chaperones for the evening."

"Well yes, of course." Lord Matlock studied him curiously. "How did this come about, Darcy?"

"I first came to know of her two years ago. She made an indelible impression on me, and when we met again, I knew that she was the woman I had been waiting for." Darcy's expression was fierce. "I will not be dissuaded."

"Why would you think that we would object to her?"

"She is not of our circle." Darcy said and Fitzwilliam groaned. "She is the daughter of a gentleman with a small estate. Her relatives in town are in trade."

"You really need to rethink your opinions on honesty." Fitzwilliam muttered.

Lord Matlock's mouth dropped open. "What are you thinking? Courtship to a . . . Tell me what dowry does she bring with her?"

"I do not know the exact figure, and it does not matter. I do not need it.

"Do not need it? Why of course you do! What wiles has this girl used to charm you? I know you are not yourself Darcy, but to entertain such a notion! Is not Bingley enough of a charity for you? Must you marry a poor girl, too? I can hear my sister now, *the pollution of Pemberley is nigh*! I do not even wish to think about what my wife will say about this!" He shook his head, "I cannot fathom you taking such a step! What about Miss Gannon?"

Darcy jumped to his feet. "One dance is not a marriage proposal, and if I had been thinking clearly I would have approached Miss Elizabeth the moment I knew she was in town and not lived through this torturous Season that you have demanded me to experience!"

"Calm down!" Lord Matlock bellowed. "What have you told this girl?"

"I told her that my intentions were honourable and that I would not be persuaded otherwise. She was concerned how my family would receive her."

"Not well, obviously." Fitzwilliam muttered.

"Quiet!" Lord Matlock glared at him. "You implied marriage already?" Darcy met his eyes and nodded. "What would your father say?"

"I told him about her, Uncle. He gave me his blessing."

"He did no such thing!"

"Yes, he did. He knew her status, he knew her family's connections, and he told me to think with my heart as well as my head. That is what I am doing. Now, if you do not wish for the woman I am courting and her chaperones to appear in your home, I will understand and remove myself as well. And Georgiana will remain with me." He bowed. "Good day."

"Darcy stop. You are not going anywhere." Lord Matlock took a calming breath. "Your father did speak to me of an unusual conversation the two of you had regarding marriage, and he did tell me exactly what he said to you, and that he wanted you to find love. I did not expect this choice to come from someone so far below . . . In any case, I cannot invite a man of trade to my home, I would be a laughingstock."

"If I were married . . ."

"That would be family. You are barely courting her, not even engaged. I will make a suggestion. Could she come along in Bingley's party? Perhaps her aunt could escort her?"

"And her elder sister?"

"No, I understand that Bingley is escorting his sister, we cannot have the man arriving with three unmarried women." He looked at Darcy sharply, "The manners of these people Darcy, they will not embarrass your aunt?"

"No more than any of her other guests will, sir." Darcy said stiffly. "I do not see why Miss Elizabeth cannot arrive with me if her Aunt is in attendance."

"Because to do that would raise a great deal of speculation, of a nature that I do not think your young relationship can endure. Doing it this way will give your aunt . . .and me, an opportunity to observe this young woman. Your aunt could meet her without prejudice and I could meet her without spending the evening placating my wife. She would be seen as a friend of Bingley's sister, perhaps."

"I have no intention of hiding my attachment, sir."

"I ask you to behave prudently." Darcy's stare told him his opinion of that statement. Lord Matlock stood and came to him. "Are you sure of this? Once you appear in public everyone will know. Your honour will be engaged."

"It already is, sir." Darcy shook his head. "Sir, I intend to dance with Miss Elizabeth, I will not leave her side the entire evening. Arriving alone and allowing Bingley to be her escort will imply his attachment to her, and that is unacceptable. I will not tolerate disguise in this most important subject. If you do not wish for Mr. Gardiner to enter this house, I will bow to your will, but I want my . . . Miss Elizabeth on my arm, as well as her aunt and elder sister. Arriving any other way will only delay what will be perfectly obvious the moment we are together."

"There is nothing that I can say that will make you change your approach?"

"No sir." Darcy stared him down.

"You always were stubborn as a mule." Lord Matlock mused. "Very well, have it your way, but I will say nothing to your aunt about this. I suggest that you caution Georgiana . . .I assume that she knows?" Darcy nodded. "Well, tell her not to speak of it. I am not looking forward to this."

"I, on the other hand sir, am." Darcy flashed a sudden smile, stunning his uncle. "Good afternoon."

"I AM SORRY LIZZY, TRULY!" Jane followed Elizabeth around the house as she paced. "It looked as if you and Mr. Darcy were becoming too intimate."

"I have been waiting for two years to speak to Mr. Darcy! How could you interrupt us like that! We have so much to say to each other; of course we were talking intimately!"

"Girls!" Mrs. Gardiner walked from the nursery and shut the door. She looked from the angry niece to the distressed one and motioned them into the sitting room attached to her bedchamber and pointed to two chairs. "What is the problem?"

"Mr. Darcy and I were finally relaxing and starting to talk about ourselves, when Jane decides that we were flaunting propriety and joins us. I thought the role of a chaperone is to provide company from a distance!" Elizabeth glared.

"I said that I was sorry!"

"Why did you interrupt their conversation, Jane?"

"I . . .did not want Lizzy to . . .Mr. Darcy leaned his head down to her, and . . .I felt that I should do something. Mr. Bingley coughed loudly once, so I thought that he saw something before that was improper, and I decided that when Mr. Darcy leaned towards her, I should interrupt . . ."

"For *that*?" Elizabeth stared. "Mr. Darcy is a head taller than me! He was trying to hear! How can you . . ." Elizabeth stood and paced for a moment. "No, I am leaving before I say something I will regret. Excuse me." She opened the door and closed it behind her, leaving Jane alone with her aunt.

"So, you are jealous of your sister."

"No, I am very happy for her! I was afraid that Mr. Darcy would forget himself!" She insisted.

"Jane, I understand that as the oldest daughter, you expect to be the one to be married first, and you probably feel that Elizabeth had her chance with Mr. Stewart. Do you understand why Mr. Stewart abandoned her?"

"Our family and our fortune."

"Yes, and Mr. Darcy seems to be willing to overlook those things, although admittedly he may not appreciate the truth of your family yet, he has shown a great deal of tolerance for continuing with Elizabeth knowing her connections to a tradesman and her lack of dowry. It speaks enormously of him. Why would you deny her such a man, one who she has hoped for long before meeting Mr. Stewart?" Jane was silent and Mrs. Gardiner shook her head. "You have always been a favoured child by your mother, Jane. You have not endured the misery that Lizzy has. Your begrudging her happiness is not attractive."

Jane said softly, "He never noticed me in the park, he only saw Lizzy."

Mrs. Gardiner sighed and took her hand. "And when you find your suitor, he will only see you."

"I thought that maybe Mr. Bingley would like me."

"You should realize that Mr. Bingley is barely of age and is in no position to be courting. It is admirable that he knows that." She leaned and gave her a hug. "Your time will come."

Mrs. Gardiner left Jane to her thoughts and went downstairs to find Elizabeth in her uncle's study reading a volume of Shakespeare's sonnets. "Are you well?"

She looked up and shrugged. "It will do me no good not to be, and I will not let my sister's jealousy put wrinkles on my brow."

"No, let your husband do that." Mrs. Gardiner laughed and Elizabeth smiled. "So you recognize Jane's behaviour as jealousy?"

"Of course I do. She has men buzzing around her at balls and dinners but none come to call. That made sense at home, they would know our circumstances there, but I am not sure why it is so here? She smiles at everyone."

"Perhaps they wish for more than a smile."

"That does not follow, I talked and it got me nowhere."

"You speak on a level that surpasses their intelligence, dear. What man wants to feel inferior to a woman?" Mrs. Gardiner settled into a chair and looked over to her. "Jane needs to learn how to smile and talk at the same time."

"And I?" Elizabeth tilted her head.

"I think that Mr. Darcy is very pleased with the challenge that you present, and you would not settle for a man you could not respect."

"That is true." Elizabeth glanced at the sonnet she was reading and closed the book. "A note arrived from him while you were with Jane. It is for Uncle." She looked over to the desk and to her aunt. "Could we peek at it?"

"What do you think it concerns?"

"He invited me to a ball at his uncle's home next week." Mrs. Gardiner's brow rose and she looked at the note, sealed with wax and impressed with the Darcy crest. "Please!"

"Your uncle will be home soon." She said while walking over to touch the envelope. The sound of the front door opening and Mr. Gardiner's voice in the hallway made them jump. He entered the study and found the note thrust into his hands and two pairs of eyes boring into him.

"No welcome home?" He chuckled, and broke the seal to read. His brows furrowed and he nodded with understanding. "Well Lizzy, you are to attend a ball at Matlock House, home of Lord Henry Fitzwilliam, the Earl of Matlock, Tuesday next. Marianne, you will accompany her as chaperone, and Jane is invited as well. You will be under Mr. Darcy's care. He apologizes that he cannot invite me. He also cautions that his uncle is not entirely pleased and that Lady Matlock will not take news of this courtship well."

"An Earl's home." Mrs. Gardiner said softly. "Why are you not invited?"

Mr. Gardiner raised his brows and smiled. "It is an Earl's home, dear."

"He is ashamed of my connections?" Elizabeth's eyes welled up with tears, once again imagining him abandoning her.

"Lizzy, I swore last night that if this man makes you cry I will call him out, but in this case, as unhappy as it makes me to agree, he is correct. I am not offended, and neither should you be. If it helps you to be accepted sooner, then I believe that you should agree to the terms and have a wonderful time." He kissed her forehead and sat down at his desk to dramatically take out his bank book. "Now, I suppose that we need to purchase some gowns?"

"But we have new gowns." Elizabeth sniffed and dabbed at her eyes.

"No, not good enough for this occasion." He consulted the note. "Mr. Darcy has arranged for you to visit Madame Dupree's shop at eleven tomorrow and she has promised to have three gowns ready in time for the ball."

"He is dressing us?" Elizabeth cried. "That is rather . . ."

"Prudent." Mrs. Gardiner said softly. "I imagine that your funds will not be required, Edward."

He smiled and put the book away. "Well I never could fool you."

"But why?"

"Because my dear, you are entering his world, and you must look the part." Mrs. Gardiner hugged her shoulders. "Come on, let us go and tell Jane."

8 MAY 1809

What a whirlwind my life has become! Two days ago I met my Fitzwilliam, yesterday I spent in the shop of a very expensive modiste, and tonight he came to dinner. He was so reserved, if I did not know that he cared for me, I would have been afraid he found my company unappealing and worried that I was doing something wrong. He was quiet and his movements at the table were measured. I did not notice it when we first met or on our walk, but I know now that he seems to take into consideration everything before he speaks, or even lifts up his glass! It is as if life is a chess board and he wants to determine the effect of his move on future events. Oh that sounds silly, but I suppose that it comes with the weight of responsibility he carries. Aunt's description of Pemberley is frightening, and I cannot imagine Fitzwilliam taking his duties as lightly as Papa does. We had the opportunity to talk a little, but not privately. I think that frustrates him as much as it does me. He is impatient with these rules for courtship. He whispered to me that he would like so much to pull me into his carriage and take me away somewhere so that we could just speak together openly. I asked Aunt about that freedom and she said that is what comes with marriage. I think that it is terribly silly to keep two people from communicating just for the sake of appearances. Perhaps tomorrow we will work out some time together. We are to visit his home and meet Miss Darcy. I hope that it goes well; I know how important this is.

"Lost in thought?" Jane asked when Elizabeth closed her journal and stared off into the distance.

"Hmm? Oh, yes. I was just . . . Jane, when we visit Mr. Darcy's home tomorrow, do you think that you could manage to distract Aunt for a little while?"

"Distract her? Why?"

"So that Mr. Darcy and I can speak privately."

"Lizzy, you know that is not proper!"

"I am well-aware of that, but it does not curb my desire to do so. Please Jane! It is only fair; you owe me after breaking up our conversation in the park!"

"I said that I was sorry!"

"Yes, but that does not change the fact that the moment was lost and we have had no opportunity to resume since then." Elizabeth watched her considering. "We are not in public! It is his home!"

"What exactly do you have in mind?"

"I do not know, but . . .if an opportunity comes about, if we can, I do not know, if he offers to show me some special object or something, give your attention to Miss Darcy and ask Aunt for her opinion. You know I would do the same for you!"

Jane sighed, and felt the guilt for her behaviour. "I know, very well, I will do what I can, just . . .be careful, Lizzy."

8 May 1809

"I give you leave to smile, Mr. Darcy." That is what she said to me at dinner, sitting by my side, smelling of lilac and those beautiful enticing curls spilling down and dancing around her neck. What I would give to see her hair unbound! I must have looked so stern, but it was all I could do to remain still beside her. She cannot possibly understand how my fingers itched to take her hand. Each laugh deserved, no required, an answering kiss.

The business of courtship is meant to drive a man to distraction, I am certain! The proximity but unavailability of his object must be what drives them to propose and fix the wedding date. We need time together, without a roomful of relatives. I want to talk to her. I feel so much better now with her in my life, but she is still just barely there, on the periphery. What will it be like when I have the privilege of her being with me every day! Tomorrow she comes to Darcy House. I hope she is pleased, and I must steal a moment with her alone!

"Mr. Darcy, do you have any other directions for your guests tomorrow?" Mrs. Mercer said loudly for the fourth time.

He startled and looked up. "I am sorry, I . . .I was not attending. My guests, no, I just want the house to look its very best, one guest is particularly important."

"Yes sir, will you be showing the entire house? Are there any rooms in particular that should be aired?" She raised her brow but maintained her smooth expression. A small smile appeared on Darcy's lips.

"As much as I would like to answer in the affirmative, Mrs. Mercer, I think that particular tour must wait for a future visit, but hopefully it will not be long." He saw a pleased crinkle appear in her eyes as she nodded.

"I will wait for your direction then, sir."

Mrs. Mercer left the room and he chuckled quietly. "Well the staff is on alert now, poor Elizabeth, she will be scrutinized from every corner." He stood and walked around the study, wondering how he could steal a few precious moments alone with her. "I need to talk with her. I know that she will listen, and I can see how much she wishes to share with me. If only her sister had not interrupted!" He glanced up to his parents' portrait, remembering coming upon them time and again, holding hands and walking in the garden, and laughing together, or finding them in the library before the fire, with books in their laps but discussing goodness knows what. It was comforting for him; it was something he imagined for himself someday.

"Well Cousin, how goes the courtship?" Fitzwilliam asked from the doorway.

"You have an annoying habit of simply appearing without warning." Darcy glared.

He laughed and dropped into a chair. "Perhaps I should be a spy! He rubbed the leg that had been shot through, and then touched the scar from the bayonet that had found a home first in his batman before continuing through to his abdomen. "Well, not now." He smiled ruefully. "I am set to return to duty."

"You are healed?"

"Enough. The infection is gone, and I seem to have most of my strength back. I came to propose a ride in the park, test my new mount."

"Ah, she has arrived!" Darcy smiled. "Do you have a name?"

"I considered Elizabeth." He pursed his lips and saw Darcy's instant glare then laughed. "Just testing you, Cousin. I wanted to see if the bloom had worn off now that you have spent some time with her. I have never known you to tolerate a woman any longer than it takes to . . ."

"Richard."

"I know, I was exaggerating." He cocked his head. "How long has it been?"

"It is none of your business." Darcy stared down at his hands.

"That long?" Fitzwilliam sat back and laced his fingers. "Well, well. She is visiting tomorrow, Georgiana tells me"

"You spoke to her? How long have you been wandering my hallways?"

Laughing, he sat forward. "I saw you scribbling in that journal of yours with a smile. I did not care to interrupt until you had finished. So I went in search of my ward. She is excited and apprehensive."

"I know, but they have met already. I wanted this meeting to take place before she leaves for your parents' home next week." He laughed, "Although it might be useful to keep her here, it provides a ready reason for Miss Elizabeth to visit often."

"That it does, well, there is no reason why the two cannot meet here regularly, since it may not be welcome at Matlock House." Fitzwilliam saw the worry appear in Darcy's eyes. "Father is not happy, but he did speak to me of Uncle George's desire that you find love. I hope that your Miss Elizabeth is up for the challenge that faces her Tuesday. You had better warn her, and her relatives. It will not be easy, not when Mother has no idea you will be arriving with three women on your arms."

"Should I speak to her?"

"No, the surprise will be in your favour, she cannot behave badly in front of her guests, so be prepared for the morning call on Wednesday!" He stood. "Enough, I see that you are beginning to worry, we need some exercise!"

"I will go change." Darcy stood to go upstairs and saw him heading to the decanter. "Do try to leave me some port."

"You can afford it." Fitzwilliam laughed and poured.

"AND THIS IS THE MUSIC ROOM." Georgiana said proudly.

"Oh what a beautiful pianoforte!" Elizabeth exclaimed and walked up to it, drawing her hand over the intricately carved wood. "Your brother tells me that you are very accomplished with your playing."

"Well, I am improved from when I began."

"Hopefully we can all declare that." Elizabeth laughed and looked up to see Darcy watching her with an expression of warmth that made her heart beat faster. "I am afraid that my playing is poor. My sister Mary is always at the instrument, so my time to practice is limited."

"May I hear you? I am sure that Fitzwilliam would like it, would you not, Brother?" Georgiana looked at him hopefully and his smile widened.

"I would indeed Miss Elizabeth, if you would care to oblige us?"

Elizabeth shook her head, then glanced at Mrs. Gardiner who was looking at her with raised brows. The moment to perform graciously for the man she had imagined had arrived. "Very well, sir. But I make no promises for pleasure in the performance."

"I can bear a missed note or two." He smiled and taking her hand settled her at the bench, and spoke softly in her ear. "Shall I turn pages for you?"

"If you like, but I know this piece by heart." She added softly. "I do not know why, but I think of you when I play it." Their eyes met and he took his seat beside her.

The other ladies took their places and waited expectantly. Elizabeth closed her eyes, breathing in the intoxicating scent of Darcy's cologne as he moved, and leaned unconsciously against his solid form, his thigh and calf touching hers. His sharp intake of breath brought her back to the present and they looked at each other, then she began to play.

Across the room, Georgiana gasped. "Fitzwilliam, it is your birthday song!" Elizabeth looked up to see a delighted smile, and his head nodding in agreement.

"So it is." He leaned down to Elizabeth as she played. "I gave this to Georgiana when I returned from my tour, with a request that she learn how to play it for my birthday."

"I purchased this to learn two years ago, after my visit to town." She looked up from the keys to meet his intense gaze, and her playing faltered.

"Elizabeth." He breathed.

"Will you sing for us, Lizzy?" Mrs. Gardiner called out.

The couple startled and both blushed. "Oh, yes." She cleared her throat and clasped her shaking hands nervously. "Do you have a request?"

"Anything you do will make me smile, Miss Elizabeth." She laughed and his smile grew. "Especially if you laugh, I so enjoy your laughter." Tilting her head, she raised her brow, and looking at him with sparkling eyes, began to sing:

"When the green woods laugh with the voice of joy,
And the dimpling stream runs laughing by,
When the air does laugh with our merry wit,
And the green hill laughs with the noise of it.

When the meadows laugh with lively green,
And the grasshopper laughs in the merry scene,
When Mary and Susan and Emily,
With their sweet mouths sing, Ha Ha He.

When the painted birds laugh in the shade,
Where our table with cherries and nuts is spread,
Come live and be merry and join with me,
To sing the sweet chorus of Ha Ha He.[2]

Darcy burst into laughter and the rest of the room followed. "That was wonderful! William Blake?"

"Yes, *The Laughing Song*." She giggled and gasped to feel his hand slip around her waist to draw her into a brief embrace. She looked up to see nothing but joy in his face. "You like my silliness?"

"I do, I need your liveliness more than I can say."

Mrs. Gardiner turned to Georgiana, "Would you play for us, Miss Darcy?"

She immediately stopped smiling. "Oh, no, I am not ready for performing."

She patted her arm reassuringly, "That is fine; there is time enough for that in the future."

"I do not recall you giving me such an easy pass when I declined, Aunt."

"You were not thirteen." She pointed out and Elizabeth rolled her eyes. Darcy looked to Jane.

"Miss Bennet, may we hear you?"

Jane blushed. "No sir, I am afraid that my accomplishments do not include the pianoforte."

"You sing, Jane." Elizabeth prompted her. "I have heard you when you think you are alone."

"Lizzy!"

"Well you do not have the excuse of youth, come now, sing for us! You have a lovely voice." Jane shook her head and Elizabeth sighed. Darcy leaned to her. "Is something wrong?"

---

[2] *The Laughing Song*, Songs of Innocence, William Blake, 1789.

"No . . .I guess . . ." She looked to see his genuine concern and spoke softly. "I worry for her future."

"I understand; her singing could help to win attention from a gentleman?"

"We have so little to offer." She looked down to her hands in her lap.

With the piano serving as cover, he slipped his hand over hers and squeezed. "I am discovering with every meeting the wealth that you possess, Elizabeth. I will be richer than Midas someday. I hope." He entwined their fingers briefly then let go when Mrs. Mercer arrived to announce that refreshments were ready. The party rose together, and he lingered behind, letting Georgiana lead the way. He bent to Elizabeth's flushing cheek. "Finish your tea quickly; I would like to show you something privately." She nodded and swallowed, and took his offered arm to follow the women.

Entering the sitting room she gasped. "What a magnificent display!" A table had been set with platters of strawberries and pastries, sliced meats and delicacies she could not identify, all on beautiful gleaming silver platters. "Sir, were you expecting more guests?"

Darcy laughed and Georgiana piped in. "He told Cook to be prepared for special guests today."

"Is that so?" Elizabeth smiled at his blush then looked at Georgiana. "It seems that your brother is not comfortable with teasing."

"No man is, dear." Mrs. Gardiner winked. "Only amongst themselves; or inflicting it upon others."

"Ah, like Papa." Elizabeth smiled at Jane. "We know that all too well."

"Your father has a sharp wit?" Georgiana asked.

"That is the source of my sister's humour, I think." Jane smiled.

"I look forward to meeting him." Darcy spoke and took a cup of tea while the ladies filled their plates. "I understand that Hertfordshire is only a two-hour ride, and I should probably go and speak to him in person about our courtship." He smiled at Elizabeth and creased his brow when she looked away. "Is something wrong?" Jane gripped her hand as Elizabeth's eyes welled up with tears.

"Mr. Darcy, Mr. Bennet has given my husband complete authority as Elizabeth's guardian. There is truly no reason to make such a lengthy journey at this time." Mrs. Gardiner met his eye and he tried to understand what she was communicating. The memory of Stewart came to his mind, and his explanation that Elizabeth's family was unsuitable. He nodded slowly.

"Well then, I will meet him in the future. Thank you for saving me the journey." He looked to Elizabeth and smiled reassuringly. He noticed that the others had taken their seats and were laden with plates and teacups. "Miss Elizabeth, I see that you are not hungry. I would like to show you a rendering of Pemberley in my study, if you would care to come with me? If that is acceptable to you, Mrs. Gardiner?"

Mrs. Gardiner looked between her niece and her concerned suitor and nodded. "I am sure that it will be a brief exhibition?"

"Yes, madam." He nodded and offering Elizabeth his arm, they walked down the hallway to his study where he moved the door, but did not push it shut. They stood for a moment looking at each other, her eyes still filled with tears. He took her hand and led her to stand before the landscape of Pemberley. "This is home."

"Oh." Elizabeth took a breath and examined the picture. "Is this accurate or an artist's fancy?"

He chuckled and without thinking moved to stand behind her and wrap his arms around her waist; she naturally leaned back against him, sinking against his chest. Darcy brushed his lips on her ear and she trembled. "This is very true to life. The house was built and burned twice, and now what you see has been added to many times."

"It is enormous. You must rattle around in there all alone."

"I do." She looked back and up to see his mouth so close to hers, and his eyes focussed on her lips. Darcy swallowed. "Why did you cry, Elizabeth? Do you not want me to meet your family?"

"Mr. Darcy," He sighed, "Fitzwilliam." Darcy looked up and smiled, "You do not want my uncle to come to the ball, and you know him to be a good and admirable man. My family . . ."

"*My* uncle is the one who did not invite Mr. Gardiner, not I. I fought for him. I fought to be allowed to escort you and your sister and aunt. My uncle wished for Bingley to bring you as his guests. I informed him that even if that was done, the moment you entered the ballroom it would be perfectly obvious that you were attached to me. I intend to display my preference for you very clearly. You are a gentleman's daughter; I am not ashamed of you."

Elizabeth choked and started to cry again and he turned her around in his arms. Darcy rested his cheek in her hair and rubbed her back, closing his eyes and impressing the feel of her body on his memory. As she calmed, she looked up to see tears in his eyes. She reached up to wipe his face. "Why do you cry?"

Darcy kissed her fingers and letting go of the embrace, took her hand and led her to the portrait of his parents. "This is my mother and father. They loved each other deeply." Again he stood behind her, his arms around her waist, and his hands clasped over hers. "My father wanted me to have a marriage like his. He told me twice to be prepared to find my future in an unexpected way, and to allow my heart to make the choice. I know that you fear my rejection; I know that you fear me meeting all of your family. I know of the entailment, I know there is no heir; I know that all I gain by an alliance with you is the woman I hold in my arms right now." He turned her around to look sincerely into her eyes, and lifting her chin, he gently caressed her cheek with his thumb. "And that, my Elizabeth, is enough."

Chapter 12

"**M**r. Bennet! You received a letter from my brother, what news is there?" Mrs. Bennet stood in the doorway of the bookroom, clutching a handkerchief.

Mr. Bennet glanced up from the letter and regarded his wife. "It seems that our daughter has done her duty. A gentleman has asked Gardiner for permission to court."

"Oh Mr. Bennet! We are saved! I knew our dear Jane would catch a man's eye in London! Such a good girl! But how could it not be? She is so beautiful!"

"Yes, yes, Mrs. Bennet, Jane is beautiful, but it is not she who is being courted."

Mrs. Bennet's fluttering stopped. "Not Jane?"

"No. It is Lizzy who will save you." He watched as her face fell.

"Oh no, no it cannot be! Lizzy will fail! She drove away Mr. Stewart! Surely this man, whoever he is, will discover quickly how undesirable she is and will run from her as soon as may be! Oh why does Lizzy always ruin everything for Jane!"

"I hardly believe that Lizzy set out purposely to steal away this gentleman from Jane, and perhaps Mr. Stewart left the area for other reasons."

"Do not be ridiculous Mr. Bennet! Of course it was Lizzy's fault!" Mrs. Bennet sat down sadly. "Well, when this ends, perhaps Jane will have her chance at him. I must go to London and do what I can!"

"You will do nothing of the kind." Mr. Bennet looked at her sternly.

Mrs. Bennet sulked. "Well, what do you know of the man?"

He consulted the letter. "He is a gentleman of some means. Our sister knows of his family and confirms that he is all that he claims."

"His income?"

"It is not mentioned, but he does own an estate in Derbyshire."

"Derbyshire? I do not wish to live in Derbyshire! Why could she not find a man here?" Mrs. Bennet fretted while her husband stared at her in disbelief. "Well it will come to nothing I am certain." She stood and nodded as she pointed her handkerchief at him. "Mark my words; Lizzy will ruin it for us all."

"Well that is just as well Mrs. Bennet, then you will not have to worry about living in Derbyshire when I die and you are left to live in the hedgerows." He chuckled as his wife screeched and ran from the room.

Mr. Bennet looked back down at the letter and read it again. "Mr. Fitzwilliam Darcy of Pemberley, ten thousand a year, a house in town . . .why would you want my Lizzy?" He read on to see Gardiner's assurances of Darcy's good intentions and genuine care for Elizabeth, and hinted at the long-standing attraction to her. "How long have you harboured thoughts of my daughter!" Mr. Bennet demanded, then sinking back down into complacency he relaxed. "Mrs. Bennet is probably correct, nothing will come of it. She will be crossed in love and will enjoy the experience." He chuckled to himself. "And I will tease her about it!"

"Brother?"

"Come in Georgiana." Darcy looked up from his correspondence and smiled to see her carrying a heavy book. "Have you finished the family history already or do you have a question?"

"Both." She smiled shyly. "I did not realize how much time I spend playing!"

"Yes, I admit that I rather miss the house being filled with music, but I think that the punishment was effective." He raised his brow and saw her look down and nod. "Well, two more days, and you may play again."

"Oh."

"You thought I would give you a reprieve?" He shook his head and laughed. "No."

Georgiana's face expressed her disappointment. "Well, at least you are smiling. It has been a very long time since I have seen you so happy."

"I am. I am very, very, happy." He sighed and reached forward to touch the book. "What have you learned from our history?"

"I believe that I have learned that our family has worked very hard to become what it is now, and that when some members failed to perform their duties, the succeeding generations had to work twice as hard to regain what was lost. It is important for the younger generation to understand its history and to maintain and grow what has been left for them."

"And what of our status?"

"It seems to be a happy consequence of our longevity, but it is more important to see what good we do with it as opposed to flaunting it carelessly." She looked up and was pleased to see his approving nod.

"I am glad that you have learned this lesson now, Georgiana. I only understood it properly a week ago, and if I had not, I am certain that I would not be smiling as I am today."

"Father did not teach this to you?"

"He did, but I was not listening well enough, and after he died, too many others were whispering in my ear, and drowned out the memory of his lessons." He smiled and tapped the book. "Someday you will marry, and it is your husband's history that you must carry forward, but you will take the principals of the Darcys with you."

Georgiana nodded and said softly, "Miss Elizabeth will not be well-received, will she?"

Darcy's smile faded and a look of determination replaced it. "I will do my best to see that she is."

"Does she have a proper gown for the ball?" She saw his brow crease and added hurriedly. "Forgive me Brother, but I could not help but notice on the two occasions we have met that her dresses are not . . . not like mine."

"It is so obvious?" He mused softly.

"No, not that bad, really, I . . . I have visited the modiste with Aunt Helen and Cousin Audrey, and I have seen . . ."

"Yes, I suppose that I was just surprised that you would care about fashion at your age."

"I *am* thirteen, Fitzwilliam." Georgiana huffed.

He chuckled. "Of course you are, how silly of me to forget. Well, I did have her go to Madame Dupree and have a ball gown made. I do not know what to do beyond that, though. It was rather presumptuous of me to suggest that purchase." He rubbed his jaw and thought of speaking to Mr. Gardiner.

"What of her jewellery?"

"Um."

"She cannot go to the ball without some sort of jewels." Georgiana said positively. "May I lend her some of mine?"

"Oh, well, certainly. I would lend her the mistresses' jewels but they are at Pemberley." He watched her jump up and run from the room, and heard her ascending the stairs. Five minutes later she flew back in and handed him a velvet bag.

She gasped for breath. "She may wear this, it is my prettiest necklace."

Darcy opened the bag and peeked in, and began to laugh. "Very well then, I will present it to her today, unless you would like to do the honours and come with me?"

"Oh no, Fitzwilliam, after I interrupted you two in here when she visited, I know that you do not wish for my company!" His mouth dropped open and she giggled. "Maybe you will get to kiss her this time!" She ran from the room again before he could chastise her.

"It seems that I have to have a talk with my sister about proper behaviour." He sighed with the prospect and shaking his head he picked up the necklace, looking at the single pearl surrounded by diamonds. "However, the next time I have an opportunity to kiss you, Elizabeth, I am locking the door."

"It is beautiful." Elizabeth said softly as she looked at herself in the mirror. The fine fabric in a rich shade of emerald green draped over her body, exposing a shape she hardly knew she possessed. The modiste walked around her, tugging here and there, then dipped her hand down the front of the gown to lift Elizabeth's breasts. Jane stared at her and gasped. Madame Dupree took no notice and nodded. "You have the perfect figure for a man, Miss Elizabeth." She ran her hands down her flat stomach and over her hips. "A man likes curves." She tugged again at the neckline. "And such plump breasts. You will have every eye on you."

Elizabeth was blushing furiously. "I think that you must be mistaken, I have a very unfortunate figure. All of the magazines . . ."

"The magazines prefer a figure like Miss Bennet's." She turned to her. "Tall, willowy, fabric drapes well without fuss. Men like this." She turned back to Elizabeth. "But you have the figure that appeals to a certain man, a passionate man." She nodded and stood back. "Yes, I will enjoy dressing you."

"I . . . I hope that I will be able to come again sometime." An assistant had jumped when the modiste nodded and began to remove the gown from Elizabeth.

"I am the best, and for Mr. Darcy, there is nothing but the best." She raised her chin and looked over the simple gown that Elizabeth was slipping on and eyed it unhappily. "Perhaps we could make you a few other things now?"

Mrs. Gardiner interjected, "We will return soon. I must thank you for performing this miracle for us."

"It is nothing madam, but I thank you for the kindness."

Madame Dupree left the room and Elizabeth's gown was packed in a box. The three ladies followed a man out to the carriage, where their dresses were stored on a seat, and began the journey back to Cheapside. Elizabeth was silent as they travelled. Their carriage passed near fashionable neighbourhoods, containing homes similar in size to Darcy House. She observed the people in their fine clothes strolling by and glanced at the boxes across from her. Gradually the neighbourhoods changed. The streets were still crowded, but it was a different population. Not the enormous crested carriages of Mayfair, but the carts of the peddlers hawking their wares. People were dressed simpler as well, and the sight of a woman in a fine gown meant that it was bought from a ragman or given as a cast-off from the mistress. *What does he want with a girl like me? I am going to an Earl's home, dressed like a doll, and pretending to be something I am not. And when the evening is over, I will return to this world, put away my pretty gown, and will have nothing suitable to wear anywhere that he belongs. They will hate me!*

"Lizzy?" Mrs. Gardiner touched her hand. "Are you well?"

"No."

"Tell me what is wrong."

She said nothing, and only stared at her hands. Mrs. Gardiner exchanged worried looks with Jane and rubbed her shoulders until they arrived home. Outside of the house, Darcy's carriage waited. Elizabeth saw it and choked back a cry, then ran into the house and up the stairs. Ten minutes later, a soft knock on her door went unnoticed, and slowly it opened. Mr. Gardiner looked in to see her sobbing on the bed. "Lizzy?"

"Is he still here?"

"Yes, he is very worried about you. I had to use threats to keep him from tearing up the stairs after you."

She sniffed. "What did you say?"

"I said that I would never allow you two a second alone again." He smiled to see her shake her head. "I know how frustrated you both are. You have so much to say to each other. I think that this difference in your circles is something that is troubling you both."

"He regrets me? Well . . .fine, let him end it now. I am used to being rejected!

"Hush, Lizzy enough of that! He does not think anything of the sort! He wants to help you into his world and has no intention of leaving you. We just had a long talk about this. After this ball, he will be escorting you all over town. He wishes to take you to the theatre, to other balls, even to the Derby."

Elizabeth looked up to see his smile. "That is a special place for you, I gather."

"I can go nowhere, Uncle. Our Father cannot afford the dresses."

"Mr. Darcy has offered to purchase whatever you need. Your father did send some funds for purchases in town, but I will write to him for more. This is his duty to you."

"Mr. Darcy is buying me." She said dully.

"Mr. Darcy is showing you his feelings." He hugged her. "Do you think that Mr. Darcy would offer all of this to someone he did not care for? He has no doubt whatsoever that you will shine in his world. It will not be easy for either of you, but he is positive that it will be well. Just remember, he is a very young man who is barely confident in the role he has as master of an estate, guardian of his sister, and, he hopes, husband." Elizabeth looked up to her uncle's kind eyes. "He desperately needs you, nobody else will do."

"Why has he not said this to me?"

Mr. Gardiner laughed. "Because your aunt and I have not let him." He hugged her again. "I think that we will loosen our restrictions a bit. We will allow you to occupy an empty room, with the door open, so that you may visit in some privacy." He stood and held out his hands. "Beginning now."

"I must look horrible!"

"You look lovely." Elizabeth followed him down the stairs; and into the parlour where Darcy was staring out of the window pensively. "Mr. Darcy."

He spun around. "Elizabeth! I . . .Miss Elizabeth, are you well?"

Mr. Gardiner left the room and Darcy took her hands. "What is wrong? Did I do anything . . .?"

"No, no. Forgive me, I . . . I left the modiste and she made me feel . . .so terrible."

"What did she do?" Darcy said sharply.

"Nothing . . . I realized that in her eyes I was unsuitable for you; she hinted rather baldly that my clothes were poor. And then I began to think of your family. Your uncle is an Earl! What are you doing with me?"

He shook his head and disregarding the open door pulled her into his embrace. "Dearest Elizabeth, you are perfect for me."

"How do you know?" She whispered into his waistcoat. Darcy sighed and felt her arms tightening around his back and the fierceness of her hold. She clearly did not want them to end, she simply needed his reassurance.

"How do you know that I am the man for you?"

"That is not fair, answering my question with a question."

"I believe that we have similar answers." He smiled and looked down to her teary eyes. "I need you, and nobody I have ever known has touched me as you do. Nobody speaks to me as you do, nobody makes me laugh and smile, or pine the way you do. How do I know? I just do." Darcy leaned down and brushed his lips over hers then moved away to read her expression.

"Was that . . .a kiss?"

"A little kiss, yes. Have you never been kissed?"

Elizabeth shook her head, and Darcy beamed. He would be the first and only man to ever kiss her. "Would you like another?" She nodded, and this time his lips pressed to hers, lingering then stroking lightly before he moved away, and looked down to see the light of passion kindling in her eyes. He took a shaking breath. "I dare not do more, but . . .oh how I wish to kiss you again!"

"There is more?" Her voice trembled.

"Oh, so much more." Darcy rested his cheek in her hair, and forced away the temptation of her soft inviting lips. "I am a doomed man now."

Elizabeth laughed softly and nestled into his protective arms. "How is that? What crime have you committed?"

"I have tasted forbidden fruit, and now I will be satisfied with nothing else." He whispered and held her possessively. "Are you frightened, Elizabeth?"

"Yes."

"So am I." She looked up to him. "Not for anything that you may or may not do. I fear that I will need to kill every man who dares to have a dishonourable thought about you."

She giggled. "I find that highly improbable."

"Me killing or men thinking of you?"

"Both."

"Hmm." He let go as he felt her relax. "Georgiana sent you a gift, well a loan." He reached into his pocket to draw out the velvet bag. "She wanted you to wear something special with your gown. I recently gave her this from the Darcy jewels." He placed the pendant around her neck and noted how it just touched the swell of her breasts. He looked up to find her staring at the diamonds in stunned silence. "This is Richard."

"Who?"

"The pearl is named Richard." He chuckled and hugged her. "I will let its namesake explain it to you tomorrow night."

"Is it a sordid tale?"

"As sordid as a five-year-old boy can be." He moved a curl from her brow. "Are you better now?"

"Yes, thank you for bearing with me."

"I am counting on you to bear with me tomorrow. I am terrible in crowds, especially ones that expect me to perform. I will need you to assure my good humour."

"How may I do that?" He shrugged and smiled while she cocked her head and considered him. "Fitzwilliam." He closed his eyes and sighed. Elizabeth rose up on her toes and brushed her lips to his. Darcy's eyes flew open. "I think that I found a way."

Mr. Gardiner's throat clearing loudly in the hallway forced them apart hurriedly. "Well, are you ready to join the rest of the household?" He looked from one flushed face to the other and bit back his laugh. "Come along children. Back to propriety."

LORD MATLOCK WALKED slowly down the steps, fiddling with the emerald stickpin nestled in the folds of his neck cloth, and paused at the bottom to observe the frenzied activity of the servants. Fitzwilliam appeared from one of the supper rooms, a piece of ham in his fingers. His father raised his brow and his son shrugged. "Why wait? There will be crumbs left by the time the supper dance comes around." He finished the morsel and wiped his fingers on his handkerchief. "Now I am thirsty."

Walking over to a table, Lord Matlock poured them both glasses of port. "I can use this."

"Not looking forward to the evening, Father?" Fitzwilliam's eyes moved to watch his mother, brother, and sister-in-law descending the stairs. "I cannot wait to meet Darcy's Miss Elizabeth and better yet, see him with her. It is an exceptionally important night for him."

"I hope that this love affair of his survives it. I do not want to see that boy hurt."

"What of his lady?"

Lord Matlock shrugged. "I hope that she is what he claims. I have to meet her first. My concern is with family, and she is not family."

"Yet." The men exchanged glances and set down their empty glasses.

"Henry, what are you doing? That is for our guests!" Lady Matlock looked over the trays and the punch bowl, then hurried off to check the card rooms and the ballroom.

"She is in her element here." Layton laughed and turned to his wife. "Did she let you do anything at all?"

Alicia shook her head. "I was permitted to check the responses to the invitations and review the menu."

Fitzwilliam grinned. "Well that is an improvement over last year when all you were allowed to do was show Lord Hancock your wedding ring."

They all laughed except for Layton, and his wife patted his arm. "Never mind Stephen, he is not invited this year."

Lady Matlock bustled up to them. "Well we are as prepared as we will ever be."

"It will be a glittering affair and a crush, Mother." Fitzwilliam kissed her cheek as the first guests arrived. The family lined up to receive them, and gradually the house filled with the cream of London society. Each time the door opened, Fitzwilliam and Lord Matlock looked up expectantly.

"Hmm, Miss Gannon looks excited." Fitzwilliam murmured to his father. Mrs. Gannon and her husband shook hands and smiled, pausing to exchange whispered words with Lady Matlock. Miss Gannon looked around the hallway, searching for someone. Fitzwilliam greeted her. "Do you seek anyone in particular, Miss Gannon? Perhaps I can tell you if the person has arrived?"

"Oh yes, Colonel, I was hoping that Mr. Darcy was here?"

"I am sorry, but he has yet to arrive. I am certain that you will notice him when he enters, he will be the tall man, likely in black." He smiled and she nodded eagerly and bent her head with her mother as they moved into the home. Fitzwilliam met his father's eye. "She is on a mission."

"He danced with her; she thinks she is the one."

"She is in for a rude awakening."

Lord Matlock felt a hand on his arm and looked up to see his friend. "Moreland!" The Earls shook hands, and he bowed to his wife. "I am delighted to see you. Are any of your brood joining us tonight?"

"Just Stewart." Moreland bent down. "I hope that you invited some interesting girls, he is still moping about someone who got away."

Lord Matlock looked around to see Stewart standing and quietly listening to Layton tell a story, his expression was neutral. "Poor bastard." He heard Richard whisper. The family moved on and he turned to his son with raised brows. "He fell in love but rejected her, felt he could not marry a poor girl." Richard looked at his father significantly. "She left quite an impression."

"What are you saying, Richard?"

"Ah, there is Bingley." He straightened and said under his breath. "Here we go."

"Is it too late for another drink?" Lord Matlock muttered.

Bingley approached, smiling and greeting his hosts affably. On his left arm was a beautiful blonde woman, a soft serene smile on her face. Beside her walked an older woman, dressed very fashionably in a blue gown and speaking to the girl quietly. Lady Matlock was polite but brushed them along, rolling her eyes at her husband then turning to the door, and did not notice when Bingley stopped and turned to the door as well. Her mouth dropped open when into her house stepped Darcy, whose focus was entirely on the lovely dark-haired woman holding his left arm. He was leaning down and speaking softly in her ear. Lady Matlock saw her smile and look up at him. Her expression said everything and his matched it exactly. Darcy approached, stood next to Bingley, and bowed. "Lady Matlock, Lord Matlock, Viscount Layton, Lady Layton, Colonel Fitzwilliam, may I present Mrs. Edward Gardiner and her nieces, Miss Jane Bennet and," He smiled down at Elizabeth, "Miss Elizabeth Bennet."

The women all curtseyed and looked expectantly at their hosts. Richard met Darcy's gaze and stepped forward. "Mrs. Gardiner, Miss Bennet, it is a pleasure. Miss Elizabeth, it is a delight to meet you at last!" Lady Matlock turned to stare at him. He took Elizabeth's hand and bowed. "May I ask for a dance before the rest of the room steals them all?"

Darcy felt her hand clutch his arm and saw her take a breath before speaking. "Oh, yes of course Colonel, I look forward to it. I . . . I believe that I am available for the third set."

He held her eyes and smiled reassuringly. "The third? Who has stolen you already?"

Elizabeth relaxed then looked up to her escort with a smile. "Well, Mr. Darcy owns the first."

"I have anticipated this for a very long time." He raised her hand to his lips. Lady Matlock gasped.

Elizabeth blushed and turned back to Fitzwilliam. "And Mr. Bingley asked for the second, so you see sir; you are my only other partner."

"Hmm, well I suppose that I can wait." He paused and tilted his head. "Miss Elizabeth, is it my imagination, or are you wearing . . ."

"Your namesake? Yes, Colonel, I am. Miss Darcy insisted that I borrow it, and Mr. Darcy promised me you would tell the tale behind its creation." Her eyes danced and he grinned in delight to see the woman Darcy described come to life.

"I promise to give it to you in excruciating detail." He bowed lingeringly over her hand, only to rise and see Darcy's glare. He laughed. "Ah, I believe this will be a fascinating evening." He turned to Jane. "Miss Bennet, has your first dance been requested?"

"No, sir."

"Well then, I must claim it if Mr. Bingley has no objections?"

"Not at all, sir. It was my error not to ask before. I would like to request the third, however." He smiled and Jane nodded. "Excellent!"

Richard held out his arm to Jane. "Shall we go into the ballroom now? I believe the arrivals are petering out, and I hear the musicians preparing to play. We can be in place immediately."

"Thank you, sir. I look forward to our dance." The couple moved away and Mrs. Gardiner looked speculatively between them and Darcy, and deciding that

Elizabeth needed her presence more than Jane, stood off to the side to watch her reception. As soon as Richard departed, Lady Matlock spoke quietly.

"Darcy, I should like to speak to you privately."

"I have no doubt of the topic Aunt; however, this is no time for discussion. I intend to dance this evening." He bowed and smiled slightly; and looking back down to Elizabeth, placed his free hand over hers. "Shall we, Miss Elizabeth?"

"I am in your hands, sir." She laughed when he lifted his chin proudly. They began to walk off when Layton awoke from his stupor.

"Ah, Miss Elizabeth, may I have your fourth set?" She glanced at Darcy who nodded slightly and smiled.

"Of course sir, I look forward to knowing another of Mr. Darcy's cousins." They moved away and into the ballroom, and instantly Lady Matlock rounded on her silent husband.

"Who is she?" Lady Matlock demanded. "Why have I heard nothing of her? And this sister of hers? Who are they? How did she meet Darcy? What has happened?"

"Dear, we are neglecting our duties." He nodded to people waiting in line to greet them, and whispered. "Finish here and we will speak." He caught her glare and he looked over to his heir.

"She is stunning, Father, as is her sister. I have no memory of either of them this Season," He turned to his wife, "Do you?"

"No, I would have remembered them, particularly Miss Bennet, she is beautiful. Miss Elizabeth has clearly captured Darcy's attention."

Lord Matlock held his tongue and greeted the final arrivals. "Come, we must begin the dancing." He took Lady Matlock's arm and guided her into the ballroom. As they walked he whispered to his wife. "Darcy has cared for Miss Elizabeth for two years but knew that she was too young to pursue. They just recently met again, and their . . .attraction was mutual and re-established all of their previous feelings."

"He has longed for this girl?" Lady Matlock watched as the couple took their places for the opening quadrille.

"From what he told me, he has thought of her steadily, and thrilled with each glimpse over the years." Lord Matlock saw his wife's eyes softening at the thought of this delayed romance. "Now I understand why he was so resistant to our efforts."

They took their places and the music began. Lady Matlock came to meet him in the centre of the floor. "How long have you known of this, Henry?"

"One week."

"And why did you not tell me?"

"I wished for you to be surprised." Lord Matlock smiled weakly and his wife of five and thirty years read him instantly.

"What are you hiding, Henry?"

"Look Helen, see how Darcy smiles!" He distracted her and they looked to see that indeed, Darcy was smiling.

"How are you; Elizabeth?" He whispered as they passed each other, then came around to link arms.

"Frightened out of my mind. And you?"

"Shaking in my boots." He smiled to hear her laugh. "You are so beautiful." Elizabeth blushed and he bent down as they let go and moved apart again. "I can think of what will relieve my fear."

Elizabeth considered him as they stood still, waiting for their turn to move again. When at last it arrived she held out her hands to him. "Perhaps a reassuring sermon?"

Darcy chuckled. "No, I believe that my thoughts do not belong in a church."

"Oh, then a calming game of Whist, I saw the card rooms set up as we walked to the ballroom." Elizabeth lifted her brow and he shook his head emphatically. "You do not like cards? Oh Mr. Darcy, that is a problem, I cannot abide a man who does not play. I find him wanting."

"Do you? Well I find a woman who purposely avoids the topic to be . . ."

"Yes, Fitzwilliam?" She whispered as she drifted by.

"Intoxicating." He whispered on her return and heard her giggle. They turned again and his eyes bore into hers. "Will you hear me?"

Elizabeth was about to reply when the music ended and they came to a stop. She smiled warmly at him and called across the floor. "Perhaps another time, sir."

"Infuriating woman." He growled. They stood gazing at each other as they waited for the second song in the set to begin.

"*WHO IS SHE?*" Miss Gannon whispered furiously to her mother. "This is supposed to be MY night! He danced with me!"

"He is dancing the first with *her!*" A helpful friend leaned in and smirked. "Perhaps he was just practicing with you. Remember, he left the ball immediately after your dance."

"Quiet Emily! He left because he did not want to bestow his attention on any other woman." She lifted her chin and glared at Elizabeth. "See how she resembles me? He must have been fooled by that!"

"She is small with dark hair, that is true, but where you have no figure, hers is prominently displayed." Emily looked over Elizabeth's gown with admiration. "I wonder who her modiste is, that is gorgeous!"

"Whose friend are you?" Miss Gannon demanded. "Help me find out who she is!"

Emily sighed. "He cannot dance every set with her. Go stand nearby and remind him of you, and see if he asks you to dance. That will tell the tale." She nodded over to Darcy as they began to move again with the next tune. "But by that rare smile he is wearing, I would say you are fighting a losing battle."

Mrs. Gannon piped in. "She has not lost. Now be a friend and circulate, find out the news on this girl!" Mother and daughter glared at the crowd, and other interested mothers drifted by to lend their advice.

On the dance floor a lively jig had begun, the dancers were weaving far down the line and back up to their partners. Elizabeth came back to take Darcy's hand and smile up to his twinkling eyes and danced away again, taking the hands of another man only to look up with a wide smile then gasp. "Mr. Stewart!" He stared at her in stunned silence, and gripped her hands tightly.

"Miss Elizabeth! What brings you here?" The steps changed and she returned down the line to Darcy. He immediately saw the change in her demeanour.

"What is wrong?" He whispered urgently.

"Oh . . .oh nothing, I . . .I thought that I misstepped." She looked distressed and he read her face then looked back down the line to see Stewart staring at her. His face set into its mask. The requirements of the dance forced them apart, and she looked back at Darcy, not knowing this stone-faced man who was now going through the motions. Elizabeth found herself again holding Stewart's hands and looked up to his eyes.

"Miss Elizabeth, please I must speak to you. May I have your next?"

"I am occupied until the fifth set, sir."

"Then may I have it?" Elizabeth moved away without answering. To refuse would keep her from dancing the fifth and the sixth, and that was the supper set, and promised to Darcy. Instead she came back to clutch his arm. "I was asked to dance the fifth."

"By Stewart?" Darcy growled.

"Do you know him?" She looked up in surprise. "Of course you would, he is a friend of your relatives'." She looked away as tears filled her eyes, this particular friend of Darcy's would tell him everything of her unsuitable family, and he would be sure to tell Darcy to end their relationship immediately.

"Did you agree?" He broke into her thoughts. He was still staring down the line at Stewart. She moved away to the man at her side and he, unseeing, swung the woman by his. They came back together as his eyes returned to hers, his glare disappeared. "Elizabeth, are you well?

"No." Immediately he led her from the floor and they walked from the room to the refreshment table, where he found her a cup of negus. The powerful wine punch made her gasp.

"I can see that Richard has had some influence here." He took the cup away and grasped her hands. "Are you better?"

"I should not have come here." Darcy started to speak when he was interrupted.

"Lizzy?" Mrs. Gardiner approached. "Do you need anything?"

"Oh Aunt . . .I . . ."

"Well Miss Elizabeth, it is our turn!" Bingley appeared and offered his arm. "Shall we?" He smiled warmly and Elizabeth gratefully attached herself to him and he led her away. Darcy stared after her and looked back at Mrs. Gardiner.

"I did nothing, I swear." He said to the woman whose eyes had narrowed. "She was asked to dance by Mr. Stewart."

"Oh." Mrs. Gardiner's stance relaxed. "I see. Mr. Darcy, are you acquainted with Mr. Stewart?"

"Yes, we are good friends." He added quietly, "We seem to share the same taste in women."

"Mr. Darcy!" Mrs. Gardiner spoke. "Do you know of . . ."

"Mr. Stewart's rejection of Miss Elizabeth? Yes, I do." He looked back to the ballroom where Elizabeth danced with Bingley. His infectious smile had restored hers somewhat. "He spoke of it to me last December. He did not say her name, other than to call her Elizabeth and describe her and her location. I . . . I puzzled out who his friend was. I knew it was my . . . Miss Elizabeth." He said softly. "I heard his regret, and his reasons, and I . . . rejoiced in her remaining free. I could not act on it at that time, but I . . . selfishly was glad for her hurt because . . . it allowed my impossible dream to remain . . . possible."

"Have you told her of your knowledge?"

"No, when she referred obliquely to her unsuitability for me and her awareness that her family did not measure up, I knew she meant Stewart's rejection. I thought it would embarrass her to have me confess my knowledge, instead I assured her of my constancy." He looked back to his companion. "Was that wrong?"

"No, not as long as you did not meet him. But I daresay Elizabeth is afraid that you and your friend are going to exchange information now, and you will abandon her once you have certain knowledge of her family."

"I will never leave her." He said fiercely.

She saw Stewart standing on the side of the dance, watching Elizabeth and Bingley. "I think that your friend is re-evaluating his decision. Seeing her here might make her more acceptable."

"Over my dead body." Darcy bowed an excused himself. He approached and addressed his friend. "Stewart."

"Darcy!" He startled and tore his eyes from Elizabeth. "I was surprised to see you dance tonight, and the first."

"Indeed?" Darcy folded his arms and watched Elizabeth as well. "I had a great incentive."

"Miss Elizabeth is a beautiful woman. I imagine that you snatched her up as soon as you arrived."

"No indeed, she arrived with me, so our arrangement was made long ago."

"You . . .escorted her here?"

"I did."

"How . . .how do you know her?" Stewart said and looked at Darcy intently.

"I noticed her two years ago." Darcy saw the astonishment, and continued. "I knew she was too young then, and was very pleased to meet her again in town this Season."

"I have not seen you with any woman!"

"It was a very recent reunion." Darcy met his eye. "I have asked for a courtship, and she has accepted me. I find nothing wanting in her. She is a treasure, and I will rejoice in her company all of my days."

Stewart realized then that Darcy knew that Elizabeth was the woman he rejected, and was about to respond when Layton arrived and whispered furiously. "Are you out of your mind, Darcy? A girl with no dowry and a houseful of sisters to marry off? How can you be such a fool? Pemberley will be overrun by spinsters, or you will have to use your funds to pay men to take them!" He laughed and snorted then gestured at Stewart. "Stewart here would not consider such a ridiculous alliance!"

"Where did you hear these things?" Darcy demanded.

"Why her sister told me. She was not dancing so I went over and asked a few questions. She was only too glad to provide the answers. It was almost sad, really. A great many men are looking her way, but once the word of her having no dowry gets around . . ."

"And why must it?"

Layton laughed. "What do you care, they are not of our circle, they are barely above that dimwit puppy Bingley you ferry about with you!"

"How dare you disparage these people, they have done nothing to you!"

"Oh, and as if you have never done the same." Layton smirked. "You forget yourself, what is it, he who is without sin should cast the first stone?"

Stewart stepped forward, "Then why are you?"

"Because I can." Layton began to walk away and Darcy grabbed his shoulder. "If you ruin this night for Miss Elizabeth and Miss Bennet, I will cut off all ties with you. Do not forget that you are nothing until your father's death, but a Darcy surpasses you forever."

"You are threatening me?"

"Do you feel threatened?" Darcy glared at the older man. Lord Matlock walked up and stood between them.

"What the devil is going on? You are drawing attention to yourselves!"

"Darcy's lover is nothing but a poor gentleman's daughter." He tattled to his father. "She and her sister are fortune hunters."

"She is not!" Darcy and Stewart cried together. Father and son gaped as Darcy and Stewart exchanged glances.

"No, she is not." Lord Matlock recovered and turned to his son. "I am aware of Miss Elizabeth's and her sister's origins. Darcy told me when he asked for permission to bring her here tonight. You will stop interfering or I will send you packing to Matlock at first light."

"Father!"

"If I hear one rumour circulating, I swear I will settle the estate on Richard." Layton's eyes grew wide and he bowed, then hurried away. Lord Matlock sighed. "Now, what about you two?"

Darcy looked back into the ballroom. Elizabeth was standing with Bingley and Jane, but looking worriedly at the arrangement of Darcy, Stewart, and Lord Matlock.

"What is wrong?" Jane asked her and took her hand.

"Oh Jane, look, Mr. Stewart is surely telling them of us!" She fought her emotion. "See how Mr. Darcy looks over here?"

Bingley turned his head from where he had been observing Miss Gannon staring at Darcy and chuckled, then saw the whispering sisters looking at him as well. "Well, Darcy is certainly enjoying a great deal of attention from the ladies tonight." The sisters stopped their talk and looked at him. "See that woman over there, Miss Elizabeth? Does she bear a touch of a resemblance to anyone you know?"

The girls looked over Miss Gannon and Jane mused. "You know Lizzy; she looks a little like you."

"No . . ." Elizabeth gasped and turned to Bingley. "Is this the woman he danced with?"

He smiled, "Ah, I see that he confessed that to you. Good man." He shook his head. "Miss Gannon has been plotting all night to get another dance from him; of course, he has not cooperated. I believe that she was sure he was going to offer for her. Silly girl, he is besotted with another woman entirely." He smiled and saw Elizabeth's blush. The music began and Richard arrived with a grin.

"Well, it is my turn, Miss Elizabeth!" He took her off to the dance floor and Bingley followed with Jane. "How do you enjoy your evening thus far?"

"I do not know, sir. It began well, but I fear that it is bound to end sadly." Elizabeth looked back over to the men. Richard saw her distress and followed her gaze, noticing the group for the first time.

"Hmm, that is interesting."

"Sir?"

"A bit of a cockfight. That must be gratifying for you?"

"I do not understand your meaning; Colonel." Elizabeth's eyes searched his and he moved away from her then returned. He recognized fear in her expression.

"Have you never told him of Stewart?"

"*You* know?"

"Yes, and more importantly, *he* knows. Has for some time."

"What?" Elizabeth's mouth dropped open and Richard smiled, seeing the fear turn to ire.

"Now, now, Miss Elizabeth, you cannot be angry for something he did not confess when you did not confess yourself. Can you?"

"What does he know?"

"Stewart courted you and walked away."

"Did he . . . tell . . ."

"I am a second son, just as Stewart is. I must marry with a dowry in mind. So must he." Richard smiled to see her relief. "So you see, no matter the delights of the woman, the reality of our situation requires us to be prudent, no matter how much we wish to overlook them."

"He did not love me." Elizabeth said. "And I did not love him."

Richard watched her expression. There was love in her eyes, but it was directed at Darcy. Stewart's feelings were discovered after he had left her. He nodded. "What are your feelings for my cousin?"

"That is private, sir."

"It is, however, I will be interrogated by my family tonight after you leave. I am Darcy's closest friend, and I want to represent his case the best way possible. You do not have to tell me any feelings that you have yet to express to him. But please assure me that you love more than his wealth."

"I am not a wealthy girl, sir. I would not know what to do with a King's ransom if I tripped over it. All I want is . . ." She looked over to see Darcy looking intently at her, a question in his eyes. She smiled at him and his stiff posture relaxed, and a slight smile appeared on his lips.

Richard watched the exchange and nodded. "You do not need to continue. I know my way now." He cleared his throat. "Now then, would you like to hear the amusing tale of my pearl?" He grinned and she turned her eyes back to his, and gratefully saw acceptance there.

"I hear that it is one for the ages, sir." Elizabeth cocked her head and he chuckled, then let go of her hands to move to the side as the song ended.

He called over to her while they waited for the next to begin. "There were no pirates, but the earth did swallow up the bounty."

"Davy Jones' locker come to land?" She laughed and he grinned as they came together again.

"I never thought of that. I had imagined a group of very industrious ants, but then, I was five!" Elizabeth's musical laugh carried across the dance floor and both Darcy and Stewart drank in the sound.

Lord Matlock cleared his throat. "Gentlemen, you both cannot be in love with her."

"I have asked her for a dance." Stewart declared.

"I have asked her for a courtship." Darcy growled.

"And the lady has said yes to both, I presume?" Lord Matlock looked between the two, the men continued to look at each other unhappily. "Darcy, allow him his dance."

"Why?"

"So that I will forever see the mistake I made." Stewart said softly. He looked back up to see Elizabeth's bright smile as she listened to Fitzwilliam's nonsense. "Have you met her family yet, Darcy? I mean the other sisters and her parents?"

"No."

Stewart turned back to him. "You have a reputation of intolerance for those below you. If you continue with Miss Elizabeth, you should prepare her for your display of disdain. I have seen it growing over the past few years, you can be quite cruel."

Darcy started. "I . . .I have changed."

"Well if ever there was a test of that, meeting her family will do." He sighed. "I was a fool."

"So her connections would not dissuade you, why should they bother me?"

Stewart laughed. "I am not the master of Pemberley. I am a barrister who hopes for a government position or maybe a seat on the bench someday. I could have borne it. But someone as proud as you?" He shook his head. "I wonder. If you abandon her, I will beg her to take me back."

"That will not be necessary." Darcy strode away and stood watching as Elizabeth now danced with Layton. The cousins' eyes met and Layton remained silent through the set, only bowing at the end and delivering her to Darcy before walking away.

"Your cousin seemed to be bursting with questions but never uttered a word." Elizabeth watched him go. "It was strange."

"Do not mind him; he is . . . not a favourite of mine." He placed her arm on his. "Are you better now?

"I think that you and I need to speak."

Stewart arrived and bowed. "Miss Elizabeth, this set is ours."

She smiled softly and took his arm, looking back at Darcy as she left. Distress and jealousy were apparent in his eyes. He felt a movement by his side and he noticed Miss Gannon standing there. Inwardly he groaned, and turned his gaze forward, steadfastly ignoring her. The music began and Elizabeth and Stewart danced. He watched them talking, saw Stewart's eyes glowing as he drank in her smile. Darcy's heart clenched when she laughed and he did not miss Stewart's appreciative smile when he watched her move away from him. That gown that had enticed Darcy was doing the same for Stewart. There was no question that his eyes were drawn to the pearl and its location over Elizabeth's bosom. A soft growl and muttered curse fell from Darcy's lips. Miss Gannon glanced up to see his set jaw and eyes clearly on Elizabeth. He did not notice when she sighed and slipped away from his side.

At last the supper set arrived and he had her back. The grip on her hand told her of his relief. "What did you talk about?" He asked insistently.

"Memories of our past."

"I do not like that at all."

"That I remember?"

"Yes."

"But if I did not remember, I would not have continued to dream of you." Elizabeth drifted past him and he reached out to take her hand back, then walked her from the dance floor. "Fitzwilliam?"

"Come."

He took her arm, placed it safely on his and guided her out of the ballroom, nodding to Mrs. Gardiner as they exited. He led her past the crowded rooms, and took her down a back hallway then through a side door to a small walled garden. He closed the door and turned. Elizabeth stood with her hands clasped before her, and her eyes cast down. Darcy walked forward and lifted her chin gently. "I cannot pretend that I am courting you anymore, Elizabeth. I cannot do anything but say the truth. I love you. I fell in love with you the first time I saw you, I only had to wait for you to grow up and for me to become a man. I do not want to wait anymore. There is nothing more that I need to discover. You are the woman of my dreams and now of my reality. Please Elizabeth, be my wife, and never part from me again."

"Oh."

"Please."

"I . . .I cannot say yes."

"Why?" Darcy gripped her shoulders. "Why? What have I done to dissuade you?"

"No, it is I who am unworthy, not you!" Elizabeth cried and turned away from him. Darcy sighed and wrapped his arms around her waist, and leaned his head on hers.

"Dearest, I confess, I know about Stewart. I know that he loved you and left."

"He loved me?" She whispered.

Darcy stiffened. "Yes, he confessed it to me when he spoke of his abandoning you. He told me this in December."

"Because of my lack of fortune."

"Yes."

"But he did not tell you of my family. Mr. Darcy, I could not accept you without you knowing how unsuitable my family is, if your friend felt that he must reject me then you . . ."

"I do not care."

"But you have not met them!"

"I know." He turned her around and wiped the tears that flowed down her cheeks. "But twice tonight I was told what an intolerant man I have become, even without realizing it, I allowed my pride to rule my opinions of those lower than me. Then I witnessed a trusted friend confess that it was his intolerance that kept him from loving the most beautiful, kind, intelligent and fascinating woman he had ever known, and informed me that when I allow my prejudice to rule my decisions, that he would be waiting to beg you for your hand. I cannot bear the thought of any other man holding you as I am now. Whatever your family is, I will not let it stand in my way, our way. Please dearest Elizabeth. Say yes."

"Are you sure?" Elizabeth searched his eyes and he smiled and nodded, then she watched as her fingers were raised to his lips.

"Please, I am so alone without you."

"And if my family is intolerable?"

"We will live in Derbyshire, far away." He smiled and she laughed.

"Thank heaven for that!"

Darcy laughed and tilted his head. "Well?"

Elizabeth sighed. "I love you, Fitzwilliam, I have from the moment you stopped and looked at me in the park. I have dreamed of you and written of you, and now it seems that I am to marry you. Yes, my love, yes."

"My love." He whispered and drawing her back into his embrace, lifted her chin and kissed her softly. Elizabeth sighed and before she was through, his mouth fell upon hers again, stroking slowly, tracing his tongue over her lips. Her embrace tightened and he could feel her heart pounding against his chest. "More, dearest?" He did not wait for her reply and instead resumed his kiss, stroking until her lips parted and his tongue searched for and found the sweet taste of hers. She began trembling in his arms, encouraging him to caress with increasing ardour. His hands moved, one wound into her hair, the other to her back, and drew her body securely to his. His kisses became more passionate and he felt the joy of her response, no longer passively receiving, but tentatively expressing her love. Their tongues touched, and slowly his withdrew, and he felt the extraordinary pleasure of hers following to enter his mouth, exploring his taste, and her lips savouring his. Elizabeth moaned, a soft satisfying sound, and he moved away to kiss her throat and breathe in her ear. "You will dearest Elizabeth; you promise you will marry me?"

"I do, I promise."

"You will not leave me again? You will not fear that I will leave you?"

"Never again, Fitzwilliam." Elizabeth moved from his overwhelming embrace to caress his face. "Neither of us will be lonely again."

Chapter 13

"**R**ichard, have you seen Darcy?" Lord Matlock asked quietly.
"He was dancing with Miss Elizabeth." He looked up and around. "Perhaps they went to the supper rooms early, you have to admit, they have much to talk about, and this is probably their only opportunity tonight. That aunt is watching like a hawk." The men glanced over to Mrs. Gardiner who was standing near the door, alternating her gaze between Jane dancing with a young man, and down the hallway. "See, she must know where they are."

Lord Matlock sighed and nodded. "Very well. If there ever was a man who followed the rules of propriety, it would be Darcy."

"What are you trying to say, Father?" Fitzwilliam grinned as his father cleared his throat.

"Son, I wish I had your *joie de vivre*."

"Oh come, you do, you simply have not had it challenged as I." Fitzwilliam's smile faded as his father's eyes saddened. "I am here by your side, Father, not on a bloody battleground."

"If you are ever to be sent back, I will stop you. Let me find you a living, or the law, something!"

"I am too old." Fitzwilliam shook his head. "My course has long been set."

"You are six and twenty, Son. You are not old."

"I just feel that way." He smiled slightly and looked back to the crowded ballroom. "What do you think of Miss Bennet?"

"She smiles a great deal." Lord Matlock tilted his head. "You danced with her, what is your opinion? How does she compare to her sister?"

"She does not." Fitzwilliam watched Jane dance perfectly, then cast her eyes down demurely when her partner escorted her from the dance floor and towards the supper rooms. "I know that girls are taught the rules of non-engagement," he saw his father's smile, "I peeked at the etiquette book that Audrey had once. No wonder men never have any idea if they are making headway in a courtship! No encouragement from the woman until she is convinced of his intentions? Well why should he make his feelings known if she acts indifferently? And then once you are engaged, no time alone, no touching, not even a little peck of a kiss!" He shook his head and laughed. "Sometimes I think that all of this overzealous protection of virtue creates nothing but lifeless marriages. Well, seeing how Darcy stares at Miss Elizabeth, he will have a difficult time limiting his attentions to a kiss on the hand. At least he knows by her looks that she cares for him."

"So you see Miss Bennet as the model of virtue?"

"I wonder what she is thinking beneath that smile." He mused. "She is certainly attracting a great deal of attention from the gentlemen. I think she has danced nearly every set. If she had a dowry I have no doubt that any one of them would be calling tomorrow. Just wait, by the end of the night someone will be approaching Mrs. Gardiner or even Darcy for information and then what will come of it? Threatening my brother not to spread his knowledge was amusing Father, but it is only effective until someone here decides to pursue her, then the truth will be out, and both she and Miss Elizabeth will be the objects of scorn."

"I doubt that Darcy is prepared for this." Lord Matlock observed. "I should have insisted that Miss Bennet stay away this night." He shrugged and looked at his son. "What did you think of Miss Elizabeth?"

"She is witty, intelligent, and utterly charming, and so afraid of losing him. She is young, and I believe that she has no idea how bewitchingly lovely she is." He noticed his father's raised brow. "Yes Father, I danced with a woman who I would have seriously pursued. There is something about her that would attract men like Stewart and Darcy, is it not possible that I can be affected as well?"

"Son, this is going to be difficult enough, please do not make it worse by entering the fray."

"No, no, I have been listening to Darcy pine for her for months, they have been together for merely a week, but truly, they have been connected for much longer. I welcome back the cousin I lost." He turned to see his father's thoughtful look. "Will you support him?" Lord Matlock did not answer.

IN THE QUIET OF THE GARDEN the newly engaged couple listened to the muffled sounds of the ball permeating the walls. "Do you have any idea how many rules of propriety we have broken?" Elizabeth whispered from the safe cocoon of Darcy's embrace. "My sister Mary would be waving her copy of Fordyce's sermons and preaching loudly if she could see this."

"I know this is wrong. Part of me is screaming to lead you immediately back to your aunt and step far away, never to touch or be alone with you until our wedding day, but . . ." Darcy lifted his cheek from where it rested in her hair. "The other part wants to stay rooted to this spot until the end of time."

"What happens now?"

"We should return before we are missed, I doubt that it has been a quarter hour." Reluctantly he let go and stepped back, but took her hands in his. "I do not think that we should announce our news, I need to speak to your uncle first."

Elizabeth looked down to see how his hands enveloped hers. "I do not think your family will be happy."

Darcy nodded and pursed his lips. "Will yours?"

She started to answer quickly then stopped and looked up to him. "I . . .I honestly do not know." She saw his surprise and smiled. "Of course my aunt and uncle will be happy, and I am certain that once my mother believes it is true she will be ecstatic, but my father and my sisters, I do not know. I hope that they are pleased for me, and do not expect . . ."

He caressed her cheek and pushed a curl from her forehead. "What do you think they will want?"

"I do not know." She paused and drew up her courage. "Truly Fitzwilliam, we have only courted for a week, even if we have felt linked in our hearts for years. Why did you propose tonight? Was it Mr. Stewart who drove you?"

"You think that I proposed without thinking?" He searched her eyes.

"This is a very serious step, if . . . if you have second thoughts . . ."

Darcy let go of her hands. "It seems that you are the one having those, did you not just promise never to leave me again?"

"Yes." She looked down and stepped back.

"Then what is it?" He demanded.

Elizabeth lifted her gaze to his. "I want to be sure that your proposal is not to win a prize over your friend. I . . .I want to be sure that the man I marry is . . .the one I hope you are."

Darcy closed his eyes, but felt hers boring into him. He knew then that the woman he was marrying may be young, but she was no fool, and not weak. She would challenge him just as strongly as she enticed and amused him. She was no mindless beauty to fill his bed. She was everything he hoped for and she was waiting for his honesty. He opened his eyes to see that she had not shrunk away from his silence, if anything, she looked stronger.

He nodded. "Very well, yes, Stewart's presence drove me to propose tonight. I have imagined proposing to you countless times for years. I knew that there was a chance that some lucky man might find you before I did and I would never have that opportunity. Perhaps I am more confident in my feelings for you because through Stewart and Bingley, I am assured of who you are by two trusted friends. Because Stewart clearly has thoughts of winning you back, I could not take the risk of him succeeding, and no, I am not questioning your commitment to me by supposing that he could. This is my personal fear of losing the woman I love. Proposing to you tonight prevents that possibility. It is exceptionally soon, I know Elizabeth, but I swear; it was always intended. I am a good man. I know that over the past two years I have changed, and not for the better, but I hope that you will set me back to who I was. I already am beginning to return to myself; ask Georgiana if you do not believe me. If you wish for a long engagement to be sure of me, I will not object, but . . .I am already sure of you."

Elizabeth listened to all that he said, then slipped her hands back into his. "Thank you for your honesty, thank you for listening to me and treating me with respect and not as a silly woman, and thank you for not laughing at my concerns. You have just proven to me that you are who I always knew you would be."

Darcy lifted one hand to caress her jaw. "Do you torture all of your suitors this way?"

Elizabeth laughed. "I did not have an abundance of gentleman paying calls. Perhaps this engagement *is* too hasty, perhaps I should try a few more gentlemen?" She began to move away from him and he quickly pulled her into his arms.

"Do not tease me, Elizabeth." He said quietly. "I cannot bear it."

She looked up to him and he bent to first softly caress her lips, and then to kiss her cheek, along her jaw, down her throat, and finally to kiss the bare shoulders that had begged for his touch all that long evening. Her silky skin was scented and sweet, and he brushed his lips down to gently nudge away the pearl and at last taste the suggestion of the soft valley that peeked from her bodice. Elizabeth's moan and her hands in his hair brought his lips back to hers and again they melted into each other. A door opened somewhere and the clear sounds of the ball spilled out into the night. Darcy forced himself away and straightened. "Dearest Elizabeth, can you forgive me?"

"Forgive?" She whispered and her hand lifted to rest over her pounding heart.

Darcy smiled and shook his head, and again lifted his hand to gently caress her face. "We must return."

"Yes." Elizabeth said shakily and righted her dress, blushing when she noticed Darcy watching her fingers readjusting the placement of the pendant.

Offering his arm he smiled, appreciating the glow in her eyes and the lovely flush in her cheeks. "Do not worry, nothing is amiss."

"There is nothing to be done if it were." She smiled and he chuckled. "Fitzwilliam, I know that outwardly I appear very calm and relaxed, but inside my heart is racing and I am bursting with happiness. If we were able, I would be . . ."

"Like me and wishing to be proclaiming our news from the rooftops?"

"You feel the same excitement? You hide it so well."

He flushed and looked down. "It is a habit." Elizabeth took his hand and squeezed, and he lifted it up to his lips.

She stared at his mouth and visibly sighed; Darcy could not help but appreciate the effect his touch had on her. "I . . . I suppose that it would be prudent to be as formal as possible with each other when in public."

"Very prudent." He opened the door and glanced inside to make sure they would not be seen entering. They stepped in and just as they were about to emerge back into the swirling frenzy of the ball he leaned to whisper to her. "I love you, my Elizabeth."

"Ah there you are Darcy!" Bingley smiled and joined them. "I lost you in this crush!"

"Yes, the supper rooms are hopelessly jammed." Darcy plastered a look of annoyance on his face. "I am afraid that we have had nothing and I am certain there is not a morsel left. Leaving the dance floor early was a useless exercise. Forgive me Miss Elizabeth for the attempt to beat the crowd."

"Now I understand why my aunt insisted that we eat before leaving." Elizabeth pursed her lips to see his hauteur and caught the hint of a twinkle in his eye.

"Ah, that is where you two went: tongues were wagging when you disappeared." Bingley did not notice the glance between the couple. Instead he pulled at his neck cloth. "Blasted warm in here as well!" He observed then started. "Oh, forgive my language Miss Elizabeth; I merely noticed that you must be feeling the heat." Her eyes grew wide. "Put my foot in it again." He sighed. "If my sister were here I would never hear the end of it."

"Where is Miss Bingley? I am sorry that I did not think to ask when you and Mr. Darcy arrived to collect us." Elizabeth said quickly and peeked up to see that Darcy was smiling appreciatively at her blushing face.

"She managed to acquire a cold." Bingley laughed. "She was dressed and ready to come tonight, but after the tenth sneeze I refused to let her out of the house. I do not think that our hostess would have appreciated her presence."

"I can assure you of that." Darcy said dryly.

"So I am free to mingle!"

"And have you found anyone to your liking, sir?" Elizabeth smiled and he shook his head.

"Ah there is much to like, but I am afraid that I am still too new to be desired." He sighed and looked around. "Perhaps next year."

"Darcy, may I have a word?" Lord Matlock appeared and bowed to Elizabeth.

"Certainly." He looked to her then to Bingley. "Could you . . ."

"Of course!" Bingley offered his arm and Elizabeth gratefully held on. He looked down and smiled. "How are you holding out tonight?"

"This is overwhelming." She glanced around at all of the people and felt the eyes examining her closely. "Now I understand the term *a fish out of water.*"

"Well at least you are not gasping for air." He chuckled and led her into one of the less crowded supper rooms. "Are you hungry?"

"No, I am far too nervous to eat."

"A drink, perhaps?" Elizabeth smiled up to him and nodded. He asked for two glasses of wine and brought them over. "There, now we can both drown our nerves."

"Are you as frightened of all of this as I am? You look so comfortable."

"I was thinking the same of you. In fact, if I am not mistaken I would call you glowing." He lifted his glass in a toast and smiled. "We are well-matched."

"Mr. Bingley." She said softly and he laughed louder.

"Did I do it again? Forgive me, Miss Elizabeth. I know my role is that of trusted friend." He saw her blush, and took her glass and set it down. "Let us go and find your sister and aunt."

She laughed and took his arm. "I am so ridiculous tonight. I do not know what is wrong with me!"

"I understand, Miss Elizabeth." He patted her hand and they walked through the crowd. Elizabeth saw the eyes of guests trained on her and she clung to Bingley's arm, trying to smile and meet the gazes bravely. "Ah, there they are."

"Lizzy! Where did you go? Were you ill?" Mrs. Gardiner demanded and peered into her eyes. "You are very flushed!"

"Mr. Darcy thought that I needed to move to a cooler location, Aunt."

"He should have spoken to me, I had no idea where you had gone, and the commentary that I heard was quite outrageous. I know that you are courting dear, but you must keep in mind your reputation, even in a crowded room. You are an interloper in this world."

"Yes Aunt, I am very much aware of that fact." Elizabeth sighed then noticed that she remained an object of curiosity. "Jane, how is your evening? I am sorry but I have been too busy with my partners to speak to you. I noticed that you have been dancing a great deal."

Jane smiled. "Yes, it has been very pleasant. The gentlemen are so different from those of my experience at home."

"Really? How so?"

"They are very curious of home and family. I suppose that in Hertfordshire everyone knows us, so those questions are not necessary." Jane looked around the room then back to see Elizabeth's astonishment. "What is it, Lizzy?"

"Jane, what have you been saying?"

"Nothing, I said that Longbourn is in Hertfordshire and that I am one of five sisters." She looked from Elizabeth to Mrs. Gardiner. "It is not an untruth."

"So everyone knows that we have no heir." Elizabeth sighed.

"Yes, I suppose they do. I still do not understand the problem, Lizzy?"

"Jane, no heir, a small estate, and five daughters, have you forgotten that those were all very key reasons for Mr. Stewart's rejection? We walked in here as unknown ladies, and now I am very much afraid that the whispers behind the fans are about the two fortune hunters who have entered their midst."

Mrs. Gardiner nodded. "I was afraid of this, but it is inevitable."

"But why did it have to happen tonight!" Elizabeth cried. She felt a presence beside her and looked up to see Stewart.

"Miss Elizabeth, may I speak to you?" He looked to Mrs. Gardiner who raised her brows to Elizabeth. She looked around for Darcy, and he was nowhere to be seen.

She sighed and nodded. "Yes, Mr. Stewart."

They walked away and he spoke softly so the ever present eavesdroppers could not hear. "Miss Elizabeth, I have heard the talk in the house, I do not know how the rumour was spread, but the news of your . . ."

"Poverty, undesirability, mercenary scheming . . ."

"Please stop." He said sincerely

"Forgive me, sir. My sister apparently has a loose tongue." Elizabeth spoke with bitterness. "But no doubt they would know soon enough. Have you added the news of my family to the litany against us?"

"I know that I deserve that, but I want you to know that I regretted you the moment I walked away."

Elizabeth met his eye and said without emotion. "I was told that you loved me."

Stewart flushed with her direct statement. "I discovered this after I was gone. Darcy told you?"

"Yes."

"I realize that you are courting him, and I understand that you have had a friendship for years . . .but it must not have been that strong for you to have accepted my attentions last autumn. I do not believe you capable of playing with two men's hearts. You are not mercenary."

"I thank you for that, sir." Elizabeth shook her head and sighed. "I had no connection to Mr. Darcy when we met."

"Then if I had not been such a prejudiced fool, we could have been married by now."

She closed her eyes. "Sir, do not torture yourself."

He reached out and touched her arm. "I cannot help it."

Elizabeth's newfound confidence born of her engagement drove her to speak plainly. "Mr. Stewart, if you came to know your feelings as far back as December, why did you never act upon them? Why was I left at Longbourn to feel the pain of rejection and the unending rebuke of my mother? If you cared so deeply, you should have returned. Was seeing me tonight in your world convincing enough to make me acceptable, especially away from my family?"

He was struck by the thought. "I . . . I . . . suppose that it was."

"But sir, the only reason that I am here is because Mr. Darcy, who did know of my family and poverty through you, brought me here. If it were not for him, I would still be alone and rejected, and you would remain in your regret because you did not have the courage to come and bring me here yourself." Stewart stared at her as the truth sank in. "Mr. Stewart, are you certain that you loved me?"

"I was." He looked down to his hands and shook his head. "I feel such confusion, I do not know myself."

"Sir, I believe that if circumstances were different, we might have made a very comfortable and happy couple, but my heart was taken by a dream, and yours was not allowed to care more for someone you could only dream about. I think that you are a very good and kind man, but please do not wish for me any longer. Allow your guilt for rejecting me to go. I am happy, truly."

Stewart smiled softly. "We met at the wrong time and the wrong place."

"We will never know, will we?" She smiled. "I want you to be happy."

"Thank you for this. But if you ever need me . . ."

"Miss Elizabeth." They both started to see Darcy looking unhappily at Stewart. "Are you well?"

Elizabeth slipped her hand onto his arm and felt the tension in his muscle. "Yes Mr. Darcy, I am."

He moved his eyes from hers and they rested on Stewart. The two men remained silent for several long moments until Darcy spoke very quietly. "The only man that Miss Elizabeth will ever need to rely upon is me, Stewart. Do I make myself clear?"

"Yes, Darcy. I want to assure you that Miss Elizabeth made that perfectly understood before you arrived. If you had heard our entire conversation you would have realized that she has managed to chastise me for my behaviour most effectively, but in the kindest way possible. I hope that we three may remain friends."

Elizabeth squeezed Darcy's arm, and he looked down to her. "You have nothing to fear, believe me."

He studied her for several moments, and feeling the reassurance of her touch, turned back to Stewart. "I would hate to lose your friendship." Stewart nodded and they both looked to Elizabeth who had startled by the approach of a determined couple. Seeing that it was family, Stewart moved away.

"Darcy, I say man, when were you going to introduce us to your friend? We have been waiting all night!" Singleton appeared with his wife Audrey on his arm. Darcy stiffened and Elizabeth took the cue to be on her guard.

"The opportunity simply has not arisen. Miss Elizabeth Bennet, this is my cousin Audrey Singleton and her husband Mr. Jeffery Singleton. Audrey is Colonel Fitzwilliam's sister."

"It is a pleasure." Elizabeth smiled and curtseyed.

"Well then, it is indeed." Singleton looked her over then offered his arm. "Come, let us dance."

"Oh, I . . ."

"No, the best way to know you is by dancing, I insist." Elizabeth looked to Darcy and he nodded, but clearly did not like the arrangement. Tension radiated from him. Audrey watched them leave and raised her brows.

"No offer to dance with your cousin?"

"Do you mind if I do not, Audrey?"

"I suppose that you can observe better from the side." She laughed and he looked at her quickly then away to watch Elizabeth. "The room is swirling with rumours, Darcy."

"I have been informed of them by your father."

"Mama is furious."

"Over what aspect?"

"That you could be taken in by a fortune hunter." Audrey saw his eyes grow dark with anger. "By your expression I suppose that the rumours that she is your mistress are also false?"

Darcy spun to stare and she was instantly taken aback by the fury and hurt that was expressed in his look. "Who dares to say such things?"

"I am sorry, clearly it is incorrect, but it is the only logical explanation for you accepting one so different. Mama has introduced you to countless women this Season and you have had no interest in any. To walk in here with someone of her status is an insult to all of the ladies you rejected, and their justification is that if you were not ready for marriage, you chose a mistress instead."

"Miss Elizabeth is *NOT* my mistress. What man brings a mistress in the company of her sister and chaperoning aunt? If these women are disappointed in my disinterest perhaps they should ask what I found wanting in them!" He fought back the need to announce their engagement. "I am courting her. Your father and brother are aware of this. I am sure that by now your mother is as well."

"I have heard nothing of it." Audrey saw him return his gaze to Elizabeth, and his feelings were transparent. "My goodness Darcy, you are in love with her!" He looked down to his cousin and nodded shortly and swallowed hard, then returned to watch Elizabeth dance. Audrey observed his unwavering attention, and could not ever recall her husband looking at her in such a way. "Oh cousin, you are lost. How does Miss Elizabeth feel about you? Do you know?"

"I do." He said softly. "We are in harmony."

"I am so very happy for you." Audrey touched his arm and he turned to her, and she saw the gratitude for her support. She nodded her head. "I will speak to Mama, and perhaps if Alicia is willing, she and I can help Miss Elizabeth."

"How?"

"We can teach her what she needs to know in our society, I am sure that she is adrift here tonight."

"I would be forever grateful Audrey, thank you." Darcy paused, and biting his lip asked softly, "Why would you wish to help her?"

She smiled and shrugged. "I was not permitted a love match, but I would rejoice to see yours."

He grew concerned. "Are you unhappy?"

"No, I am fond of my husband, despite his penchant for gossip." She watched him dancing and clearly interviewing Elizabeth. "It was an arranged marriage Darcy; you know that, just as my brother's was. Richard will likely find the same someday. It would be so good to see one of us marry for love."

"Who is she, Stewart?" Lord Moreland asked his silent son. "You have been staring at her all evening. I hear rumours that are frankly disturbing. Has Darcy really taken a mistress?"

"What?" Stewart rounded on his father. "Who dares suggest that Miss Elizabeth is anything but a proper young woman?"

"You are being unusually defensive of this girl." His father said sharply.

"I know her well." Stewart turned back to see her dancing with Singleton. "I met her in Hertfordshire; her father's estate is adjacent to Netherfield."

"You know her?"

"She is a witty, kind, and intelligent woman. Darcy is courting her, and I know that he will marry her." Stewart looked to see Darcy reacting to his cousin's words. "I think that he has just been informed of the same rumours you bring me." Stewart turned back to his father. "When did it become a crime to be a gentlewoman from a small estate? Why is being one of five daughters mark you as undesirable?"

"Son, what are you about? Did you . . . my God, this is the woman you have been mooning over all these months!"

Stewart looked away and back to her. "She is a lovely girl, but I feared pursuing her."

"Why?"

He laughed shortly. "Why? Look at the reaction of this place to her! Granted that is jealousy by a roomful of the wealthy with nothing better to do but gossip about a supremely eligible man, but what would you have said? You would have told me the truth; I could not afford to have her."

"I am sorry, Son." Lord Moreland stared at his son's angry visage. "You turned away from this woman because . . ."

"I am a second son, someday I will have an admirable income and it might be possible, but right now when she is free . . ." He looked up to see his father's reaction and let down his defences. "It is my fault Father. I had my opportunity, and Darcy has snapped up the treasure. And I'll be damned if I will see either of them suffer for the amusement of these people!"

Lady Moreland approached and touched his arm then looked to her husband. "What is wrong?"

"I hope that if you do not listen to me, then you will speak to Lord Matlock. He knows the truth." Stewart watched as Singleton returned Elizabeth to Darcy's side. Immediately he took her hand and kissed it, and placed it on his arm, then covered her hand with his free one. The gesture was clear enough, but then Darcy gazed directly into her eyes. The smile; and her happy smile in return expanded the story. All around him tongues began wagging, new speculation about the relationship blossomed. Behind him he heard two women burst into conversation.

"Besotted!"

"Could it be true, Mr. Darcy is in love with her?"

Stewart saw his opportunity and turned, and leaning down, spoke in a conspiratorial whisper, "Ladies, I know without a doubt that Mr. Darcy is courting Miss Elizabeth Bennet, and his intentions are honourable."

"Sir, are you certain?" One woman asked eagerly.

"Indeed, I am. She is restoring his good humour after his father's sad death. Is it not a blessing?" The women nodded and put their heads together. Satisfied, he watched as they began moving around the crowd. Soon gasps, pointing, and whispered conversations began. Stewart moved to the couple and walking to Darcy's side leaned to his ear and spoke quietly. Darcy glanced up quickly and nodded. "Come, Miss Elizabeth." He bowed to his cousins and they began moving through the crowd.

"Where are we going?" She asked worriedly.

Darcy squeezed her hand and gave her a small smile. "We are striking while the iron is hot."

"You are speaking in riddles! Please tell me what is happening?" They approached his goal, Lord and Lady Matlock were standing together, and Fitzwilliam was nearby. Both men were speaking to her and she was listening with a doubtful expression on her face.

Darcy whispered to her. "Dearest, if ever there was a moment to be charming, it has arrived."

"What are you asking me to do?" Elizabeth came to a stop and demanded.

"I am asking you to be yourself, follow my lead, and trust me." He spoke softly. "Please."

She nodded and the couple approached his family. Fitzwilliam nudged his father and Lord and Lady Matlock stopped speaking to see what they had to say. "Uncle, Aunt, I have heard some outrageous rumours spreading throughout your home tonight regarding my friendship with Miss Elizabeth. I wish to correct them immediately."

"Yes?"

"I have to speak to Miss Elizabeth's uncle, but I wish you to know that tonight I proposed marriage to Miss Elizabeth, and she has accepted me." He turned and gave her a beaming smile. "She has made me the happiest of men."

"Darcy."

"I am my own man, Aunt, so I hope you will not attempt to dissuade me. I know my mind. I also suggest that you protect your family by accepting the inevitable, and show this crowd of hawks that you welcome her to our family."

"A rift would not do, Helen." Lord Matlock bent to her. "All eyes are upon us."

Lady Matlock looked between her nephew and the woman by his side. Darcy's face was lit up with happiness, an expression that she despaired ever seeing again. Elizabeth's head was tilted and shaking, her lips were pursed and her eyes were sparkling at him. "Miss Elizabeth, my nephew is clearly very pleased with his announcement. I wonder at your reaction."

Without looking away from Darcy's gaze Elizabeth spoke softly. "Lady Matlock, forgive me if I do not appear to be excited enough for you, but please consider the wide variety of emotions I have been subjected to this evening. I anticipated coming here in this exquisite gown in the company of the man I have dreamed about for two years. I was nervous and frightened to meet his family and to be under the examination of his peers. I felt the extraordinary pleasure of our first dance, and the fear of losing him when rumours of my origins began to circulate, and then experienced the joyous overwhelming surprise of Mr. Darcy's heartfelt and sincere proposal of marriage. This night I have dropped to the depths of despair and achieved the highest pinnacle of joy so many times that I am rather proud to be standing here now with some semblance of sanity and my equilibrium intact."

Darcy began to chuckle, as did Fitzwilliam and Lord Matlock. "I warned you that this would be a challenging experience."

"You did not warn me that I would need a program to understand each act of this operatic evening!" Elizabeth laughed.

"And how do you feel about the conclusion, Miss Elizabeth?" Darcy said softly.

"Have we arrived, at last?" She smiled and he nodded. "It was emotionally exhausting, but worth every moment." Elizabeth looked to Lady Matlock. "I suspect that I will not find sleep easily tonight, nor will I believe it is all real when I finally wake in the morning, but I assure you, I care very deeply for your nephew and I hope to keep that expression of happiness you are witnessing now upon his face for the remainder of our days."

Darcy again raised her hand to his lips as Elizabeth blushed and looked down. "I feel the same."

"I expect you to come here tomorrow afternoon Darcy, and explain how this came about." Lady Matlock regarded Elizabeth. "And I expect you to come along, Miss Elizabeth. You display many promising qualities, not the least of which is you charming my frustrating nephew. I will reserve my opinion until I know you better."

"That is fair, Lady Matlock. I hope that you will find me worthy and . . .I hope that I might ask for your help. I am afraid that I have nobody to guide me in this world that I have entered."

"You ask for my help?" She studied the sincere expression of the suddenly young girl.

"I have no desire to embarrass those who will be my family one day, and particularly Mr. Darcy."

"Well . . ." Lady Matlock's expression softened and she let down her angry stance.

Darcy saw the opportunity and jumped in. "Audrey has already spoken to me of her willingness to guide Miss Elizabeth Aunt, and she promised to recruit Alicia as well. If you were to lend your expertise . . ."

"You may stop your flattery, nephew." Lady Matlock looked Elizabeth over from head to toe and nodded. "Come here tomorrow at three o'clock." She looked to Darcy and he smiled triumphantly. "Very well." Turning back to Elizabeth, she held out her hand. "It seems that I must welcome you to our family."

Elizabeth took it and they clasped briefly. Behind her she could hear a wave of whispers, and understood the significance of the gesture. "Thank you madam, I will never do anything to cause your regret."

Darcy leaned forward and kissed his aunt's cheek, and she patted his face. "What a mother will do for her child."

He whispered softly, "You will love her as I do."

Straightening he saw Lord Matlock patting Elizabeth's hand and smiling, then Fitzwilliam bowing to her with a grin. "When do we announce the news?"

"Keep quiet, Richard. I must speak to her uncle." He reclaimed Elizabeth's arm. "Have you had enough for one night?"

"More than enough." Elizabeth laughed. "Please assure me that they are not all like this!"

The group laughed and he shook his head. "No, but it was memorable, was it not?"

"One for my journal, that is certain!" His eyes lit up with her words. "Mr. Darcy?"

"You keep a journal?" He saw her nod and smiled. "I do as well. Perhaps I may read yours sometime?"

"Why?" She asked suspiciously.

"If yours is as mine, I suspect there are many references to me in there. I would love to know your thoughts over the years."

"Will you share?"

Darcy paused as if struck by a thought and spoke in a low serious voice. "What is mine is yours." He placed her hand back on his arm. "Come, let us collect our friends and take you home." When they did not immediately move, Elizabeth noticed that he had raised his free hand, and that he was tenderly tracing her bare fingers.

"Fitzwilliam." Elizabeth whispered. When his brightened eyes met hers she smiled. "You are holding all that is mine. And it is yours."

Chapter 14

"Do you mind if I . . ." Mr. Gardiner indicated the decanter of brandy sitting behind his desk.

"No sir, not at all." Darcy watched as a small amount was poured and nodded when he raised his brows. The two men settled into their chairs and sipped. "This is exceptional, sir."

"Hmm? Oh, tradesmen do have their uses; that is when their taint is not ruining the chances of their nieces to marry." Mr. Gardiner closed his eyes, then met Darcy's steady gaze. "It is a very good thing that you have proposed, sir. After hearing of Lizzy's defamation, I would have demanded it to restore her reputation. I am glad that you have taken what I otherwise would have seen as a very premature step."

"Yes sir, although when I made my proposal, I had no knowledge of the whispers that were travelling the room."

"No, no, you were acting as a jealous suitor and making damned sure nobody would ever threaten your desire. I suppose that you are quite used to getting what you want?"

Darcy bit back the retort that was on his lips. "You do not paint a favourable picture of me."

Mr. Gardiner shrugged. "I do not have to. I have the upper hand to deny or approve your request."

"But you also just said that you would have demanded it had I not already proposed, did you not?" Darcy raised his brows and Mr. Gardiner smiled. "Sir, you were already well aware of my intentions. I told Miss Elizabeth that I would bear a long engagement if she wished."

"Does she?"

"We have hardly had the opportunity to speak, sir."

"No, that is true." He set down his glass. "How did the rumours begin?"

"I spent some time going over it in my mind last night, and the only logical source could be Miss Bennet." He saw Mr. Gardiner's eyes close again. "Was she aware of how damaging that information could be? Surely she understood that her value would rise considerably after Miss Elizabeth and I marry? The connection, I am not ashamed to say, is significant."

"You are a proud man, sir." Darcy stared at him unblinkingly. "I cannot fathom her thinking, but I do know that she is feeling the shame of never having attracted a single suitor, when for her entire life her mother has showered her with praise for her beauty and informed her that said trait is what will save the family from certain poverty when her father dies."

"She does not strike me as conceited."

"No, she is not, but she does move along in blissful serenity since she has never had to struggle for praise. Her father loved her as his first child; her mother loved her for that and her beauty. When she was born all was still well in their marriage and a girl first was not a problem. She had the benefit of attentive parents."

"And Miss Elizabeth?"

"Was not a boy." He smiled to see Darcy's face darken. "And not pretty."

"She is beautiful!" Darcy cried.

"She is, but she never heard that from her mother. Criticism followed her through every awkward stage of her childhood. She will likely never believe it when you tell her she is beautiful, but be sure that you do. It will be appreciated a thousand fold."

"By your words, may I hope that we have your blessing?"

"You are a very focussed man, Mr. Darcy. I like that very much. I have no doubt that you will do great things with your estate." He sighed and nodded. "Yes, of course you have my blessing. However, I also want this engagement to be of some significant length. You need time together."

"I must return to Pemberley at the end of July for the harvest."

"That is merely two months, sir."

"Then when?"

"When will you be free to leave your estate?"

"Not until Michaelmas." Darcy said unhappily. "Four months, and that would give me two months without Miss Elizabeth's company. What good does that do either of us to be forced to separate that long?"

"But you will be free to correspond." Mr. Gardiner laughed to see Darcy's despondency. "I know, it is no substitute."

"Perhaps she could visit Pemberley?" He looked up hopefully.

"Will your sister be there? I remember Lizzy mentioning something of school for her."

"If it meant the difference between Miss Elizabeth coming to Pemberley or not, I would hire a new governess and have masters come to teach her." Darcy sat forward. "Georgiana can attend school next year."

"I will consider it; however your sister's presence is hardly enough. You will require a proper chaperone. My wife would love the opportunity to return to her old home, but I cannot see her leaving her children for so long. My sister is wholly unsuitable. Perhaps one of the married ladies from your family?" Darcy's brow creased as he thought. "Would you truly wish to change your plans for your sister's education simply to be with Lizzy?"

"I allowed my wish to be with Miss Elizabeth to overtake my responsibilities, sir." Darcy admitted. "May I ask, Mr. Bennet, does he take no interest in his daughters? I feel that I should at least visit the man. After all, he will be the one to sign the settlement, is he not?"

"I can well understand your confusion, Mr. Darcy. Let me say this. My brother is very intelligent, and I think, easily bored. He is not interested in his estate, and the only member of his household who holds his attention with any regularity is Lizzy. She is equally intelligent, but it does not stop him from making sport of her just as much as he does with his other children and wife. I suggest that you draw up your settlement and I will sign it. You may then pay a courtesy call upon Mr. Bennet. I am afraid that he may just provoke you to anger, and he just might refuse Lizzy's hand to you, simply to watch the reaction."

"That is cruel!" Darcy said in disbelief.

"Indeed it is, but possible." A soft knock came to the door and Mr. Gardiner called to enter. It opened and there stood Elizabeth. Darcy was instantly on his feet and across the room. He bowed low and she laughed.

"I thought I heard your voice!"

"I have been here marking time until I could hear yours." He took her hand and kissed it. Elizabeth blushed and he smiled. "You are lovely, Miss Elizabeth."

She looked down. "Thank you." Darcy glanced at Mr. Gardiner, who shrugged and smiled.

"We were just discussing your engagement, Lizzy. Why not take a seat; we would like your opinion."

"Just marking time?" She asked with a smile as he guided her to a chair and sat beside her.

"Yes, time away from you is wasted as far as I am concerned." He moved his chair a little closer and touched his boot to the pink slipper that peeked from beneath her dress.

An eyebrow lifted and her eyes danced. "You are full of pretty words this morning."

"Be prepared for a lifetime of them. I am afraid that my normal reticence has been abandoned this morning." Darcy smiled and chuckled to see her blush again. The couple looked up to see Mr. Gardiner shaking his head.

"Very well, children. Shall we make some decisions? I would like to have some answers prepared before we inform the family of this unexpected news." He saw Darcy watching Elizabeth and the way his fingers were stretching towards hers and smiled. "Well Lizzy, I proposed a wedding date in four months. Mr. Darcy must return to his estate at the end of July, and cannot leave again until October."

"We would be apart all of that time?" She looked first to her uncle then turned to see Darcy watching her.

"I feel just as distressed about it. Therefore I proposed that you come to Pemberley to visit, perhaps Miss Bennet could come as well?"

"Would you allow that, Uncle?" Elizabeth looked at him hopefully.

"Ahem, I told Mr. Darcy that I would consider it. More than your sister's company will be required." He looked at him sternly.

Darcy smiled then became serious. "I wish to meet your family." Elizabeth's face fell, and he continued. "Every time I hear someone speak of your family, whether it be you, your uncle, or even Stewart, I hear nothing admirable, however when I marry you, they will be my family as well. I take my heritage very seriously, and am teaching my sister to respect it as well so she will take that with her when she marries someday. I hardly expect my wife to forget her origins. I also understand that someday I could very well be responsible for your mother and unmarried sisters."

"Please Fitzwilliam . . ."

"Lizzy!"

"Please . . ."

Darcy shook his head and took her hand in his. "No, Elizabeth. I must go, and I believe that it should be soon. You questioned me last night about my proposal and I admitted that I made it in reaction to Stewart's desire to renew his addresses. He proceeded despite all of the obstacles that prevented him from proposing to you before. He clearly knew that you were worth bearing whatever came with you. Supporting your family is not an issue for me, not really. But it was their behaviour that was a factor in his thinking as well. I know, he told me. He made an effort to know them and still abandoned you. I must meet them." He gripped her hand as it trembled in his. "We do not have to announce our engagement to them. I could just be paying a courtesy call as your suitor."

"I . . . I will go with you."

"It is not necessary."

"No . . . I will, and then when . . . when they drive you away, I will remain there." Elizabeth's eyes became bright with tears.

"Do you doubt me so much?" He asked quietly.

"No, I simply know them."

Mr. Gardiner watched the exchange closely and could understand the emotions on both sides. "Lizzy, I think that you should recognize that this is an enormous gesture on Mr. Darcy's part. I gave him leave not to visit until the settlement was signed. His willingness to go assures me that he loves you, whatever comes."

Darcy's fingers entwined with hers. "I thought that you could visit Madame Dupree and order some new things tomorrow, and then we could drive out to Longbourn on Friday morning, stay for the day and return here that afternoon. Then when your order is ready we can begin this engagement on the right foot. The air will be clear, you will have no fear of losing me, and you and I will be free to . . ."

"Love each other?" She whispered, and he smiled and nodded, then wiped her cheeks with his handkerchief. "Do not say that I did not warn you, sir."

He laughed and Elizabeth took his handkerchief, and kept it in her hand. "I believe that I am thoroughly on my guard. Will you come with us, sir?"

"Yes, I will. I will send a letter to my brother today, and tell him of our plans." Mr. Gardiner stood and walked to the door. "I believe that breakfast will be ready very soon." He looked at the couple, still holding hands, and left the room.

Darcy stood and closed the door enough so no curious eyes could see inside then turned to find Elizabeth beside him and leaning into his arms. "Dearest." He whispered before he claimed her lips for a kiss that communicated reassurance and love. It was soft and slow, but still all too brief. They remained in the embrace, holding each other in a comfortable, already familiar way.

"Fitzwilliam, during this visit, I do not want to hear a single complaint from you."

"I promise."

"If I am in the carriage riding back to London . . ." Her voice was suddenly stopped by an insistent, possessive kiss that left her gasping for breath. ". . . I give you leave to complain until your face is blue." Darcy chuckled softly and tightened his hug.

"When do you wish to marry?"

"Is two months too soon?"

"Is four too long?" He countered. They heard a throat clearing loudly in the hallway and reluctantly drew apart. "We do not need to decide today."

"I fear that if I come to visit you at Pemberley . . ."

"You may as well stay forever?" He laughed and she smiled as the door opened to reveal Mr. Gardiner looking at them expectantly.

"Are you on the cusp of a decision?"

"No Uncle. I think that we need to discuss this more, and I would feel better doing that after Mr. Darcy meets the family." She wrapped her hand around his waiting arm. "It would not be fair to you to do otherwise."

"I am committed to you now."

"I am still giving you a reason to change your mind without penalty."

Darcy shook his head at her stubbornness. "Do you not see how that gesture tells me of your devotion? I assure you, no woman of the *ton* would accept a broken engagement without demanding compensation."

Elizabeth raised her brows. "Which proves again how I do not belong in your circle."

He let out a frustrated groan. "Why do you keep trying to discourage me? You do realize that it makes me more determined than ever?"

"Perhaps you have realized my gambit, Mr. Darcy." Her eyes danced and he broke into a wide smile.

Mr. Gardiner laughed and led the way to the dining room. Mrs. Gardiner and Jane looked up in surprise to see their guest, and especially to see Elizabeth holding his arm and looking up to his happy face. Clearing his throat, Mr.

Gardiner announced, "Ladies, I am surprised but pleased to announce that Mr. Darcy came to me this morning to ask for Elizabeth's hand. After assuring myself of his sincerity and her acceptance, I have given my permission to marry. Congratulations to our happy couple."

"What?" Mrs. Gardiner stared between them and Jane's hand went to her mouth. "When did you propose?" She demanded.

"When we disappeared during the supper dance." Elizabeth admitted.

"No wonder you were flushed when you returned." Jane said softly.

"Is nobody happy for us?" Elizabeth looked between the two and they both jumped up to hug her and shake Darcy's hand. They all sat down at the table and after a moment of silence, Darcy looked to Elizabeth and raised his brows. She laughed and he smiled, then she turned to face her aunt. "Go ahead, begin your inquisition."

"I SWEAR FATHER; it was not I who spread the rumours." Layton paced in his father's study and ran his hand through his hair. "But you cannot deny that I was correct!"

"About what, that she is without dowry or connection? Yes, I will give you that, but that young woman displayed an exceptional amount of poise last night, despite the drama that was swirling around her. I am very impressed with Darcy's choice."

"I am ashamed!"

Lord Matlock watched his heir's movement. "Well I suppose that you will have to come to grips with that because they are engaged, and I am sure that Darcy is at this hour receiving her uncle's consent. It will be in the papers within days. It will not change. Your wife, by the way, has already met with your mother to discuss how to introduce Miss Elizabeth to our circle."

"I will forbid it."

"Oh, yes, that will go over well. How did you become such an insufferable snob?"

"I learned at my father's feet." He snapped.

"Do not blame this on me, Layton." He shook his head and sat back in his chair. "Sometimes I think that you would have been better as the second son."

Layton spat. "Oh yes, precious Richard should be the heir!"

"That is not what I said. As the second son you would not have been idle, you would have an occupation. Right now your occupation is waiting, and in the meantime, you fill your time with drink and dissipation." He laughed. "You have become an old woman with your fondness for gossip!"

"Are you finished?" He stopped and glared.

"You will never win an argument with Father this way, Stephen." Richard closed the door behind him. "So, what have I missed?"

"Nothing of note." Lord Matlock sat back and closed his eyes. "Your mother is unhappy but resigned."

"I thought that she was pleased with Miss Elizabeth? That is what I gathered when the guests were at last gone. I also noticed that the tide had turned back in her favour. At least the whole mistress debate was quashed as quickly as it appeared; now they are only talking about him foolishly being sought by a fortune hunter, which if you think about it, defines just about every woman."

"Or every man." Lord Matlock said with a twitch to his lips.

"Touché. Who will accompany them, I wonder." Richard mused.

"Mr. Gardiner, I believe." Lord Matlock saw Richard's amused smile. "Yes, I appreciate the irony, Son. The man I refused entry to my home as a tradesman is now welcomed as future family."

"I hope that he appreciates humour." Richard settled into a chair and looked to his brother. "Are you well?"

"I am fine." He said sourly. "What will you say to Darcy?"

"He is the head of his household, I can only give advice. His father gave him permission to wed as he liked, and to allow for sentiment in his choice." Lord Matlock tilted his head and regarded his son. "Is this perhaps what angers you? That you did not marry for love, but rather for benefit?"

"I thought that you are happy with Alicia?" Richard asked. "She is a lovely woman."

"We are happy and comfortable." Layton said quietly. Richard and Lord Matlock exchanged glances and let the subject drop.

"My Lord, Mr. Harwick is here to see Viscount Layton."

"Bring him in here." Layton sat up. "Harwick was here last night; I wonder what this could be about?" The three men stood to receive their guest and shook hands before resuming their seats.

"I was not expecting to see you again so soon, Harwick, what brings you back?" Layton offered him some port and he accepted.

"Perhaps I could not stand to stay away?" He smiled and the others chuckled. "I came to inquire after one of your guests last night. Miss Bennet."

"Miss Elizabeth?" Lord Matlock asked cautiously.

"No, the elder sister, Miss Jane Bennet."

"Oh, well, what would you like to know?" The men all turned to look at him and he stared down at his hands.

"As you know, I lost my beautiful wife Ellen five and twenty months ago when she gave birth to our daughter, Ellie." He paused to stop the welling emotion and took a breath. "I . . . I have completed the public mourning, however I know that I will never recover from her loss." He paused again and Richard refilled his glass. He took a sip and set it down. "If it were not for the fact that my daughters deserve a mother figure and that I need an heir for my estate, I would not consider remarrying. However, I realize that I must do my duty. Miss Bennet seems to be a pleasant woman, and is certainly beautiful. She is not of the *ton* so she likely would not miss the society that I have no desire to explore anymore without Ellen. She is a gentleman's daughter and from what I heard last night, she is unlikely to find a partner who is willing to take her on. Ellen's dowry now belongs to my daughters, but I have enough funds to give Miss Bennet an attractive settlement." He stopped and looked back up to Layton. "I ask you, your cousin Darcy is courting her sister, I respect him, and know that he would never make such a move without his family's approval, would you agree that Miss Bennet is a worthy candidate for my wife?"

Layton let out a breath and looked to his father. "It would be without a doubt a loveless union?"

"Yes. Perhaps we could grow fond of each other over the years."

"Forgive me Harwick, but that is a very dismal prospect. Would you not prefer a chance to find love again?" Richard asked curiously.

"There will never be anyone to replace my Ellen. Never." He looked up and swallowed. "I am doing my duty."

"And she is the best that you can find?"

"I have no desire to spend a Season sampling the possibilities. I would like to conclude this transaction as quickly as possible and return home." He shook his head. "That sounds so cold, even to my ears. Look, you know me, I am happiest at home, I am not mean. I am a decent man. I know what has to be done and I am offering a future to a girl who likely does not have one without a great deal of luck."

"Well." Layton looked helplessly at his father who had an understanding expression on his face.

"You remind me of Darcy's father. He was deeply in love with my sister and when she died after having their daughter, he was devastated. Fortunately he had his son already and never had to contemplate remarrying. Darcy and Miss Elizabeth will be here within the hour. Would you care to stay and speak to her? Darcy might be able to answer a few questions, but obviously her sister would be of great help."

Harwick nodded. "If it would not be an imposition?"

"No, we do have some family business to address, but it can wait a little time. I believe that Mr. Gardiner, the Misses Bennets' uncle and guardian, will accompany them, and you may apply to him for permission to call."

"Thank you." Harwick let out a deep breath and sat back in his chair. "I have been dwelling on this all night."

"May I ask you a question?" Richard saw his nod and continued. "If you had it to do over again, would you have married for love, or would you have preferred a marriage of convenience?"

"And not face the heartache that I do now?" Harwick sipped his port and shook his head and sighed. "I suppose there are ways to argue both sides; personally, I would not give up the memory of my Ellen for anything." He smiled sadly.

"Is it fair to Miss Bennet to have to live with a ghost?"

"Would it be better to wind up a spinster aunt living with her sisters or make a match to a man who would not treat her well, or become a governess or companion? I suppose that she could conceivably marry better by being sister to Darcy, but unless he is willing to give her a dowry, her circumstances really will not change with that union. Perhaps a rich man like Darcy who does not need to worry about such things might come along, but all of us know how unlikely that is."

"These are all valid discussions." Lord Matlock said softly and watched as Layton remained silent, clearly thinking over the situation. "Well, until they arrive, shall we retire for some billiards?"

"HOW DO I LOOK?" Elizabeth asked Jane nervously. She was wearing one of her new gowns, but now it seemed shabby in comparison to the magnificent creation from Madame Dupree.

"It is beautiful, Lizzy." Jane stood and hugged her. "I am happy for you."

"Thank you, Jane. I am so nervous!"

"You will do well. After all you have already conquered the biggest obstacle; you have captured Mr. Darcy's heart." She paused and thought for a moment. "Do you truly love him?"

"I know that it seems strange to declare love for someone you barely know, but yes I do." She picked up her journal and flipped through the pages. "I reread this last night. It covers the past two years. I read every entry about Mr. Darcy and Mr. Stewart with clear eyes. My feelings were always there for him." She sat down and took Jane's hands. "He has always, from that first moment, made me feel unconditionally special. Nobody has ever done that for me, except Papa. But then when I was old enough to realize that Papa was using me as a buffer between him and Mama, I did not feel quite so special anymore. Mr. Darcy, every time that he saw me, communicated his love."

"But he did not try to find you."

"No, but Aunt said something to me when he asked for my courtship. Neither of us were ready before. I was too young, and he was so burdened with the death of his father. While I may have dreamed and wished for him, he was mature enough to know that neither of us was ready. The moment he realized that he was, he came to me."

"You met by chance."

"Yes, but I know that he would have found me wherever I was."

"And his hat blew away." Jane smiled.

"And I grew up."

"Will I find a good man? Nobody called today, not one man that I danced with last night." Jane said softly. "What is wrong with me?"

"Nothing Jane."

"I am ready to settle for security, not love." Jane said and met Elizabeth's eyes. "I can see now how rare that truly is."

"Please do not turn into Charlotte! You are but twenty!"

"But I would be happy being a good wife for a decent man, Lizzy. That would be more than most women achieve. I was raised to marry and save the family when Papa dies. That is what Mama told me. That is my duty."

"But my marrying Mr. Darcy . . ."

"He should not have to carry the burden for all of us. If I find a man willing to take me, I will say yes." Jane stood and smiled. "No more fanciful dreams, Lizzy. We have been here for months, and nobody has called. Beauty seems to win dances but money wins suitors." She kissed Elizabeth's cheek. "You will have to have the love match for both of us."

"FOR HEAVEN'S SAKE CAROLINE, enough with the inquisition!" Bingley said tiredly.

"If you had let me go with you, I would not be asking you these questions." Caroline huffed and sneezed into her handkerchief. She moaned and Louisa poured her new cup of tea. "What did Mr. Darcy's relatives think of the chit?"

"Caroline, please do not refer to Miss Elizabeth that way. She is a wonderful girl and I am pleased that she is my friend."

"Oh Charles, you have not fallen for her, have you?" Caroline moaned.

"If he had, then Mr. Darcy would be free." Louisa suggested and raised her brows.

"That is true."

"Caroline, enough. Miss Elizabeth and Darcy are courting, and I have no doubt that it will lead to marriage one day. Leave my feelings for her out of it."

"You have feelings for her?" Caroline pounced.

"Friendship, Caroline, only friendship." Charles stood. "I think that you should be concentrating on your marriage prospects, not mine or Darcy's. Who has called lately?" Caroline became silent and Bingley nodded. "There, I made my point." He nodded to Louisa and left the room.

"He is insufferable." Caroline pouted.

"He is correct, though. The Season is half over. You were supposed to be married this year, as I recall."

"I set my sights on Mr. Darcy."

"Well obviously that ship is sailing." Louisa laughed. "I suggest that you lower your expectations."

"And marry as you did? I do not think so."

"At least I am not a spinster." Caroline shot her sister a venomous look.

"There must be something. Perhaps if I suggest to Mr. Darcy that Miss Elizabeth loves my brother . . . but then when will I ever be in Mr. Darcy's company again?"

"I do not think it matters, Caroline, Miss Elizabeth will surely be present. Your thoughts of taking advantage of Charles's friendship with him were reasonable at first, but surely you should recognize that he never entertained thoughts of you in return." She cocked her head at her glowering sister. "Mr. Hurst does not seem so terrible now, does he?"

ELIZABETH SAT ON A LOVESEAT in the blue sitting room of Matlock House. She looked around surreptitiously, and was glad that Darcy House was decorated with quiet elegance instead of this ostentatious display of wealth. "It is such a lovely room, Lady Matlock."

"Thank you. It is in desperate need of redecoration, though." She glanced around. "I did this when my husband became the Earl." She shook her head. "I was flaunting the title, I think."

Elizabeth's surprise showed and she smiled. "I see that you agree?"

"I would never say so, madam."

"I realize that Miss Elizabeth, and I appreciate your discretion. It is a worthy accomplishment. Now, tell me of your others."

"I sing, and play the pianoforte." Lady Matlock nodded and lifted her brows. "I read a great deal."

"That is useful in conversation . . .not novels, I hope?"

"Occasionally, but mostly poetry and histories."

"Excellent. Have you attended the theatre?"

"Not often."

"Then I suppose you have not attended many balls?"

"Assemblies mostly, and a few balls with my aunt and uncle, but nothing like last night before."

"And what did you think of last night?"

"It was . . .exhausting."

Lady Matlock's lips twitched but she did not smile. "Why?"

"You were aware of the gossip, Lady Matlock."

"But you were not."

"No, but I was aware that I was the object of interest."

"And how did you react?"

"I tried to give them nothing to gawk at." Again Lady Matlock's smile threatened to appear.

"Do you have any idea what is entailed with becoming Mrs. Darcy?"

"Besides giving him a home that he prefers above all other places? No madam, I do not." Elizabeth lifted her chin and raised her brow. At last Lady Matlock smiled. "I hope that you will be willing to teach me. My aunt has done her best, but of course she is not from this circle."

"You are visiting Madame Dupree tomorrow?"

"Yes."

She handed her a folded paper. "This is a list of items to purchase. These are not your wedding clothes. That will be a far more extensive list. This will take you through the remainder of the Season. Until they are complete, you may borrow from my closet, we seem to have a similar build. I do not want you to be out of society for the weeks required to prepare this order. You will come here Friday and we will choose your wardrobe."

"Mr. Darcy and I are visiting my family on Friday." Elizabeth cast her eyes down but Lady Matlock saw the fear there.

"Miss Elizabeth." She looked back up. "My nephew will not run away from you. Not now. He has been a lost soul since his mother died, and his father's passing devastated him. I have not seen him smile so easily since he was a child. This, above everything, is why I am accepting you."

"Then I will endeavour to impress you with my other abilities." Lady Matlock's brows rose. "I hope that one day your acceptance will be based on my merits as Mrs. Fitzwilliam Darcy."

"I hope so as well." She cleared her throat and smiled. "Perhaps my daughters will accompany you to the modiste." She tilted her head, considering the idea. "Hmm, well we shall definitely meet Saturday, and now, let us join the gentlemen." She stood and led the way to her husband's study. "This is my husband's private room. I generally leave him alone in here, after all the rest of the home is mine, but I like to drop in from time to time."

Elizabeth smiled to hear this little story of their domestic life, and considered what she might do with Fitzwilliam someday. The men stood with their entrance and Darcy was immediately at her side. "Are you well?"

"I survived." She smiled and he relaxed. "And you?"

"We have yet to begin." He nodded to Harwick. "Your sister has a suitor, and he would like to meet you. Miss Elizabeth Bennet, this is Mr. Jeffrey Harwick."

She contained her surprise and turned to the man who came up to bow over her hand. "Miss Elizabeth, it is a pleasure to meet you. I hope that we will become better acquainted during the remainder of the Season."

"I do as well, Mr. Harwick." Darcy took her to a chair and the rest of the Fitzwilliam family exited. Lady Matlock was giving her husband the eye and he smiled and ushered her along. "I understand that you are interested in my sister Jane?"

"Yes. I . . ." He looked at Mr. Gardiner for help.

"Lizzy, Mr. Harwick is a widower with an estate near Leicester."

"Which is about thirty miles from Pemberley." Darcy interjected.

"He has two daughters, ages three and two. He is hoping to find a lady to become his wife and their mother, and hopefully bear him a son." Elizabeth's face clouded. "He is interested in Jane."

"A marriage of convenience." Elizabeth said softly.

"It would be very advantageous. She would receive a settlement of fifteen thousand pounds; she would want for nothing, my income is seven thousand a year, and the estate is profitable. Viscount Layton attended school with me, I assure you, I am . . . I would treat her well."

"But you will not love her."

"I hope to grow fond of her." He said honestly.

"And if she does not produce this son that you desire? Will she be forgotten?" Elizabeth looked up to him. "Will she be made to feel the guilt for her failure daily? Will she have to fear for her future when the estate is given away to some distant male heir? Will she become a silly, thoughtless wreck as a result of your disdain?" Elizabeth stood and walked away to stand by a window. The men all stared at each other. Darcy was up on his feet, and stood by her side, wishing to reassure her with his touch. "Jane told me today that she does not expect to marry for love anymore, that the best she hopes for is security and some happiness. She may have given up, sir, but I have not. You may not ever fall in love with my sister, but I hope that if this marriage takes place, that you treat her with the respect you gave to the wife you did love. She deserves it for giving up her dreams." Elizabeth looked up to Darcy and caught her breath. "Excuse me." She hurried from the room and Darcy paused for a moment and looked to Harwick.

"She is speaking from the heart, sir. I hope that you listened." He turned and went after her.

Mr. Gardiner closed his eyes as he listened to the description of his sister, then moved on with his job as guardian. "Mr. Harwick, it seems that my niece Jane will be receptive to your advances. Do you wish to continue?"

Harwick sat back and stared out the open door. "Is Miss Bennet like her sister?"

"No sir, not at all."

He nodded and continued to look out at the empty hallway, then recalling himself, he nodded. "Yes, I would like to continue. When shall I call?"

"ELIZABETH?" Darcy found her back in the blue sitting room and standing alone by the window. He closed the door part way and advanced to her side. "Dearest, are you well?"

"Forgive me Fitzwilliam." She swallowed and wiped her eyes with his purloined handkerchief. "I should not have spoken so frankly to him. He has probably left by now."

"No, he truly is interested in her. He knows how cold it sounds." Darcy stood behind her and embraced her waist, then kissed her hair. "My uncle said that he reminded him of my father after Mother died. Sometimes I wished that he had remarried. A mother for both me and Georgiana would have been good for us, and a wife, even one that he did not love deeply, would have been good for him."

"Do you know him?"

"Not well, he is about eight years older than I, but he has a good reputation. Jane could do so much worse, I am sorry to say. Layton vouches for him."

"Forgive me, Fitzwilliam, but that does not reassure me." Darcy laughed softly and she turned her head to look at him. "What is amusing?"

"Layton." He turned her around to face him and loosely held her in his arms. "He began the day bound and determined to fight our engagement, and this afternoon he was our cheerleader."

"Why?"

"Because he had no love match and was jealous, and after seeing Harwick's misery over his ending, Layton feels very good about his marriage of convenience."

"So he hopes that your love match ends in tragedy?" Elizabeth stared as he chuckled. "Forgive me Fitzwilliam, but that hardly recommends him to me!"

"No, he is an odd duck, my cousin." He looked down to her mouth and gently brushed his lips over hers and sighed. "Whatever his reasoning for support, I will accept. My uncle is very fit. I am afraid my cousin will have a very long wait before his ascension. In the meantime he has nothing else to do but meddle in others' affairs."

"He is a gossip."

"He is."

"What else is he?"

Darcy shrugged. "He is typical of his class, Elizabeth. He does what is normal for his circle. His wife understands that. As long as he treats you civilly, I will have no quarrel with him."

Elizabeth looked down to his waistcoat and back up to his eyes. "Are you typical of your class, Fitzwilliam?"

He smiled a little and caressed her cheek. "No, I am not."

Elizabeth sighed then looked back up to him. "Your aunt is lending me some of her gowns so that we may begin appearing in public."

"Really?" He stared in disbelief. "She likes you!"

"So she says." Elizabeth bit her lip and smiled. "I did well, I think."

"I am so proud of you!" He kissed her soundly and she laughed. "Where shall we go first?"

"Surprise me."

Fitzwilliam left the room where he and his family had retreated to give the others some privacy. The thoughts that had filled his mind while listening to Harwick's description of his lost wife and his reluctant realization that he must remarry continued to confuse him. His parents had an arranged marriage, as did his brother and sister. There was no doubt that his parents did care deeply for each other now, but he knew that the marriage had not begun that way. It had grown from friendship to some semblance of love over the years and shared life. He expected that someday he would find the same. A girl that he liked, enjoyed her company, desired, and that they would marry and at least be comfortable friends. His brother had a wonderful wife, but they had not advanced much beyond the fondness that they had when they began, perhaps with children . . . And then his sister, she was much like himself, and hoped that someday the man that her parents had chosen for her would come home from his clubs, and focus on her. There was certainly a wide variety of marriages to observe around him.

Making his way down the hallway Fitzwilliam heard Elizabeth's laugh, and like a magnet he was drawn to the doorway where he watched as Darcy cupped her upturned face and kissed her. He leaned in the doorway, smiling to see his cousin so relaxed and happy. He was unconcerned with propriety, not when the couple was engaged and so clearly in love. Elizabeth's hands rested on Darcy's shoulders while he kissed her gently; then drew her to his chest for a warm embrace. Fitzwilliam chuckled to himself, knowing the condition his cousin was likely in, and how that embrace was satisfying a physical need just as much as it was comforting the woman in his arms. *Poor fool, you will be in a bad way until you are married.*

Seeing that they were relaxing he cleared his throat, and laughed when they jumped apart. "Richard!" Darcy growled.

"You really should have closed the door, you know." He walked in and smiled at Elizabeth, who was burning with embarrassment. "I am not shocked or offended, Miss Elizabeth. If anything I am deeply envious."

"I . . . I . . . I should go apologize to Mr. Harwick. Excuse me." Elizabeth slipped through door and returned to the study. Fitzwilliam stopped Darcy before he could follow.

"You must be careful, Cousin. My catching you is not a problem, Father would probably give you a stern look, but Mother would not mince words. From the look of Miss Elizabeth's response, this was not the first time this has happened."

Darcy coloured and looked away. "No, it is not."

"Have you considered all of the risks you take with her reputation? Your behaviour at the ball was selfish. Miss Elizabeth was following your lead."

"I know that. Mr. Gardiner has spoken to me about it many times today."

"And yet you continue to kiss her so openly?"

"Could you resist, Richard?" He noticed Fitzwilliam regarding him thoughtfully.

"I doubt it. This is more than a physical need, I suspect." Fitzwilliam clapped his back and they walked from the room. "I have been given a great deal to contemplate about marriage today."

"And I have been given even more to anticipate." Darcy smiled to see his cousin's cocked brow. "Miss Elizabeth is a passionate woman, and that goes far beyond her embrace."

"I look forward to seeing what she makes of you."

Chapter 15

lizabeth held Jane's hand; she had joined her in the sitting room after Mr. Gardiner explained Mr. Harwick's proposition and left the women alone. "What are you thinking?"

"I am not quite certain." She looked up and then over to her aunt. "I have been wishing for so long to be courted and . . . Now that it is about to happen, I am not sure how to feel. When Uncle told me of Mr. Harwick's interest in securing me as his wife, I was overwhelmed, especially with the detached nature of his presentation. Somehow I thought that marriage would not be quite so dispassionate."

"I believe that you should feel flattered." Mrs. Gardiner said with an encouraging smile. "Mr. Harwick is hardly a minor suitor, and I am sure that he is sought by many women. He has a significant estate, and is clearly not at all put off by your circumstances."

"Yes." She turned to Elizabeth. "I am so sorry my thoughtless prattling about our home and family caused so much trouble for you at the ball, Lizzy. Aunt talked to me a great deal while you were gone. It just never occurred to me that I could damage your chances by speaking the truth. I know that I have been jealous of you and Mr. Darcy, but I truly did not mean to hurt you. I was trying to make conversation while dancing. Mama always told me that it was rude to remain silent during a set."

Elizabeth held back her opinion of her mother's ideas on what was rude. "I think that we both have suffered from loose tongues. Our mother was not raised a gentlewoman, she did not learn to restrain herself, and she did not teach us to do so either. I am afraid that I was rather angry with Mr. Harwick when he spoke to me today, and I had to return to him and apologize for my behaviour. It was embarrassing, but he seemed to understand. That was more likely due to Uncle's work than my apology."

Jane began to feel uneasy. Could her only suitor be lost to her sister's interference? Elizabeth had her father's sharp expression when riled. "Lizzy! How could you speak against our mother! Why our parents have always done their best for us! What did you say to him?"

Surprised by Jane's reaction, Elizabeth rapidly explained, "He spoke of his desire to marry to give his girls a mother and to produce his heir. He spoke of hoping for fondness for you. I could not help but think of our parents' marriage, and told him that I hoped he would treat you well even if you did not bear him a son."

"Lizzy!" Mrs. Gardiner admonished as Jane's hand flew up to her mouth, then she sighed, and nodded her head. "I suspect that you did not express it quite so calmly at the time?"

"No." She noted Jane's horrified expression. "Uncle said that Mr. Harwick asked if you were like me, and he assured him that you were not. Mr. Harwick seemed to take a great deal of comfort in that." Jane smiled a little and met Elizabeth's eye.

"Well, it seems that Mama was correct then, a worthy gentleman prefers girls who smile and do not challenge. That is good to know." Elizabeth caught her aunt's warning look and held back her response to her sister's insult upon Mr. Darcy and herself, deciding that she deserved the jab. Jane missed the exchange and sighed. "I enjoyed dancing with him. He was very kind and we seemed to get along nicely. It is gratifying to know that he spent the night thinking of me."

"He will call tomorrow afternoon. Lizzy, you will be at the modiste then?"

"Yes, Mrs. Singleton will come here to collect me and help with Madame Dupree."

"Good, and Jane and I will meet Mr. Harwick." She smiled and held her hand. "It would be a wonderful match, dear, an excellent opportunity. Your uncle was impressed with him."

"Well, I hope that I can at last fulfil my duty to my family." She lifted her chin and smiled. "Mama will be so pleased!"

"Jane . . . Mr. Darcy said something that made me think. He said that he sometimes wished that his father had remarried, and that it would have been good for him and Miss Darcy, and his father, even if he had not fallen in love with the woman. She would have brought their broken family together again. Maybe . . . maybe that is what you will do for Mr. Harwick and his baby girls. You will save them from certain loneliness. I know how deeply sad Mr. Darcy is from his losses, and his care for me has helped him. I think that you will do the same for Mr. Harwick."

Jane hugged Elizabeth and started to cry. "Thank you." She whispered. Elizabeth looked up to see Mrs. Gardiner wiping her eyes and nodding. Elizabeth hugged Jane tight and prayed that she was correct.

"MADAME SINGLETON, WHAT MAY WE DO FOR YOU TODAY?" The assistant to Madame Dupree asked immediately.

"Miss Bennet has an appointment with Madame." The girl looked at Elizabeth standing quietly by her side and remembered her from the week previous. Speculation in the shop was that Mr. Darcy was dressing his mistress, but now she was visiting with his family member, which had entirely different connotations.

"Ah *oui*, Madame, I will fetch her right away." She curtseyed and hurried to the back room, whispering the information to the modiste and seeing that her employer had the same opinion as she. Madame Dupree swept into the room.

"Mademoiselle Bennet, you have returned to me so soon, I hope that your gown was received well?"

"Oh yes, Madame, it was admired by so many. I . . . I will be requiring a few more items for the rest of the Season and I hope that you might be able to accommodate me?"

"*Mais bien sur*, Mademoiselle!" Madame Dupree noticed that at the mention of Elizabeth's name, the heads of several women examining fabrics were lifted and eyes were turned her way. "Is there anything in particular that you require?"

Audrey also noticed the attention and spoke quickly. "Why yes, Miss Bennet needs to augment the wardrobe she brought to town for the Season with one or two more gowns. Imagine her surprise and delight to be asked for a courtship by my cousin, Mr. Darcy? Naturally she wishes to look her absolute best for him. It is quite an accomplishment to win his approval." She smiled warmly at Elizabeth and nodded. "We are delighted with the match."

Elizabeth did not miss the gasps from around the room and saw Audrey looking at her meaningfully. She lifted her chin and smiled. "I am delighted to be so warmly welcomed. It would not do at all to look anything less than perfect when I have the honour of holding Mr. Darcy's arm. That is why when Lady Matlock recommended returning to you Madame, there was no question that I had to agree."

Madame Dupree preened. "Lady Matlock is a woman of excellent taste, and a favourite customer. Come, we will retire to a private room and discuss precisely what you need." Elizabeth and Audrey followed her, walking through a small contingent of watchful women in the process. They entered the room, and when the door closed, Elizabeth let out the breath she had been holding.

Audrey laughed. "I am sorry for walking over you, but I was afraid that you were going to give Madame your list in front of everybody. It is one thing for your modiste to know you do not have a thing to wear, but it would not do for those gossips out there to know."

"Well they certainly know that I am being courted by Mr. Darcy, now." Elizabeth smiled. "Oh, and thank you for the ringing endorsement of the family. I wonder if they agree with you."

She shrugged. "They will in public." Turning to Madame Dupree she took the list from Elizabeth's hand. "My mother wants all of these items made for Miss Bennet within the next fortnight. She also wants a seamstress at Matlock House Saturday afternoon to adjust any gowns that Miss Bennet will borrow until this order is prepared."

"Yes, of course." Madame looked over the list and nodded. "Well then ladies, I will bring out the pattern books and we may begin. Would you like some tea?"

Audrey settled onto a sofa and nodded. "Yes, it will be a long afternoon." She smiled at Elizabeth and patted the seat. "It will be far worse when you marry him."

She settled beside her. "I can hardly believe that might happen someday."

"Believe it. I have never seen him so happy." Audrey smiled and took her hands. "You are living the dream that we all had when we were little girls, to marry with love."

"Forgive me but, you do not love your husband?" Elizabeth whispered.

"Love is a luxury, marriage is a necessity. Mr. Singleton and I are friends. Perhaps that will grow in time to more. It did for my parents, so I hope for the same someday." She smiled a little. "Surely you know how rare it is to be loved and actually able to act upon that desire? I loved a young man very much, but of course I knew that I was not permitted to consider him so I kept my feelings hidden."

"Why was he unsuitable?"

"He was a second son." Audrey said softly. "Just like Richard. He has become a barrister, but that was not good enough. I did as I was told."

"My sister has been approached by a man."

"Mr. Harwick, yes I heard. That is an excellent match for her. She could not have found a better place. He is a very kind man, do not worry for her. He will not lose himself in his club or disappear with his mistress. He cares about his estate, and his daughters." Audrey smiled tightly then seeing Elizabeth's brow crease relaxed again. "What is wrong? Do not worry for her. She will be well; they may even love each other someday when she gives him a child.

"Yes, that occurred to me, too." Elizabeth would have liked to explore the subject of clubs and mistresses, but thought that would be far too intimate of a conversation for this fledgling friendship. Madame Dupree reappeared with pattern books and assistants bearing bolts of fabric. By the time that Elizabeth's new wardrobe was ordered, three hours had passed. There were new women in the shop, so they were able to exit without notice. When Audrey waved goodbye to her on the steps of the Gardiner home, Elizabeth's thoughts returned to her sister.

MR. GARDINER LOOKED UP from his book to see Darcy staring across the carriage at Elizabeth, and she in turn staring out the window. He cleared his throat and she looked at him then back to the scenery. "Have you spoken with Jane, Lizzy?"

"Yes."

"What did she think of her visit with Mr. Harwick?"

"She finds him pleasant and kind. She enjoyed dancing with him at the ball, and had no idea that she had impressed him so much then." Elizabeth finally turned to meet her uncle's gaze. "She feels confident that they will get along."

"You sound doubtful."

"I seem to be feeling more emotion than she." She looked down to her gloved hands. "She says that at least she will have two little girls to love, and since they have no memory of their mother, they will hopefully readily accept her. Mr. Harwick was glowing in his descriptions of the children and that reassured her of his kind heart."

Darcy spoke softly. "Layton did assure us of his excellent reputation, Miss Elizabeth. I am sorry that I cannot add my direct knowledge of him, but I have never heard anything that would cause alarm. I joined society just as he left it. Richard knew a little more than I, and he seems convinced of his sincerity."

"It is a fate that all of my sisters face, sir. I am increasingly cognizant of how fortunate I am, and how foolish were my girlish dreams."

"I hope that you have not given them up."

Elizabeth looked back up to see his concern, and his clear desire to reach across the coach to her. "No, Mr. Darcy, I intend to live them out daily." His mouth lifted in a small smile and he nodded, keeping his eyes fixed on hers. "I find it odd now, all this fuss over our sudden engagement when Jane and Mr. Harwick know even less of each other. But it seems that an immediate engagement and marriage for them is unremarkable. What is the difference, I wonder? Is it because we dare to care for each other and theirs is a business transaction?"

"That is a very valid question Miss Elizabeth. I think that the difference is that this is our first marriage, I am young and noted to be very eligible, and the disparity in our situations also comes into play. Although Mr. Harwick and I are similar in that we do not particularly care to participate in the activities of the *ton*, he has already been down the road of courtship, marriage, and children. Miss Bennet is . . ."

"Simply a new member of his staff." She closed her eyes and clasped her hands tightly. "Forgive me; that was entirely uncalled for. Mr. Harwick is no ogre. He is offering Jane a sound future."

Darcy's brow furrowed as he tried to understand the root of Elizabeth's unmistakable discomfort. "I was going to say that she would not undergo the scrutiny that a first wife would. However, keep in mind that Mr. Harwick's eligibility was noted, and many women had marked him as a potential husband. His reappearance in town is very recent. Have no doubt that your sister will be envied by those who missed this opportunity to charm him. Mr. Harwick is a veteran of the marriage mart, and knew that he had no desire to wed one of those women. That is what caught his attention when he looked at her. First he saw beauty, then he saw possibility."

"And I nearly ruined everything by lashing out at him," Elizabeth sighed and looked at her uncle, "as you told me in no uncertain terms. I conveniently forgot that marriage for duty is the normal course of events, not the exception." Darcy looked between niece and uncle and realized that he had taken her to task for her outburst at Matlock House.

"Lizzy, I think that you are taking this much too hard. We have discussed your behaviour with Mr. Harwick, and he was kind enough to listen to my explanation that you were thinking of the marriage you grew up witnessing at Longbourn. He was actually grateful for the information, realizing that it undoubtedly would affect his relationship with Jane, although admittedly it will probably manifest itself differently with her. I am just grateful that none of the residents of that house witnessed your outburst and prejudiced them further against you." He noticed her embarrassment. "Enough, we have been through this already. Please remember that this is a very advantageous offer for Jane, and I believe that she recognizes it." Mr. Gardiner closed his book and glanced at Darcy.

Elizabeth smiled ruefully and blinked back the tears that had begun to fall. "I know that Uncle. You will forgive my pensiveness today. I am afraid that I am allowing my thoughts of Jane to occupy me rather than dwell on more personal concerns."

"What may I do to convince you of my dedication, Miss Elizabeth?" Darcy sat forward and touched her hand. She shook her head and turned to the window. Darcy looked at her helplessly then at Mr. Gardiner.

He glanced out of the window. "We are here, this is Meryton."

Elizabeth sat up and found Darcy's handkerchief being held out for her. She took it and wiped her eyes, and handed it back. In the process they entwined their fingers for a few moments before resuming their places. She took a deep breath and looked around. "We are drawing attention with this magnificent coach."

"I am certain that my sister will be gossiping about it in moments, especially if she spots us in the windows." Mr. Gardiner smiled. "Ah look, there she is." He lifted a hand and Mrs. Philips' jaw dropped. He chuckled and looked at Elizabeth who had turned to Darcy. "That is my aunt Philips. She married the man who was clerk to my grandfather, who was a solicitor. Uncle Philips took over the business."

"You did not wish to pursue your father's trade, sir?"

"No, I am afraid that the law never really caught my fancy." He smiled and looked around the town. "I had dreams of London, so became apprenticed to an importer friend of my father's there, and built my business after leaving his."

"I suppose that I would have followed the path that Stewart has if that was my destiny." Darcy mused. "I have an uncle who is a judge."

"I cannot see you in a wig, sir." Elizabeth teased.

He smiled to see her spirit appear. "No, that fashion has happily gone by the wayside for the rest of society, although I suppose it has its merits for the winter months." They looked at each other and took deep breaths, and Elizabeth turned back to the window.

"There it is." She said softly.

Into a gate the coach rumbled and they slowed to a stop by the entrance. The footman jumped down and opened the door. Mr. Gardiner descended first, followed by Darcy who held out his hand for Elizabeth. "I love you, nothing will change that." He said as she clutched his hand and moved past him. She looked up and he smiled. The front door flew open and there he received his first brush with Elizabeth's fear.

"OH WHAT A BEAUTIFUL CARRIAGE!" Darcy recoiled instantly and he felt Elizabeth stiffen by his side. He recovered, and taking her hand placed it firmly on his arm. "We were wondering when you would arrive. Mr. Bennet only told us this morning that we were to have company. I thought that you would have told us sooner, Brother!" Mrs. Bennet received his kiss on the cheek and turned to see Elizabeth with her hand on Darcy's arm. She beamed up at him. "And who is this?" Darcy's brow creased, realizing that she was not going to greet her daughter. Mr. Gardiner cleared his throat.

"Mr. Darcy, this is my sister, Francine Bennet. Sister, I am sure that you are aware, Mr. Darcy is courting Lizzy."

"Yes, of course, Mr. Darcy. You could have knocked me over with a feather when I heard that news! Now, come in and meet the rest of the family. I am sure that my husband will be along soon. He has disappeared this morning, so vexing, he is always here in that bookroom of his, but for some reason he took it in his head to go out today." She led the way indoors without pausing for breath. "You must tell me all about yourself, sir. Mr. Bennet has kept all of the news to himself." She entered the drawing room. "Girls, girls, come greet your uncle and our guest. Mary! Put that book away at once!" She turned and waved. "Mr. Darcy, these are my daughters, Mary, Kitty, and Lydia."

"I am happy to meet you all." He said quietly and bowed.

They curtseyed and swarmed Elizabeth. Mary kissed her cheek and Kitty hugged her. Lydia naturally asked for any presents and Elizabeth hugged them all, assuring them that she and Jane were well, and promising that the next time she saw them she would definitely come bearing gifts. When the noise of the greetings died back she peeked at Darcy, who was standing silently by Mr. Gardiner and watching the reunion with a slight smile. The girls broke apart and his attention was taken by Mrs. Bennet's cloying voice.

"I am certain that you would like some refreshment after that long ride! Please, sit here next to Lydia." She urged him to a love seat where Lydia sat perched and studying him. He swallowed and saw that Elizabeth had taken a seat across the room on another sofa, and he quickly moved to her side. Mrs. Bennet frowned for a moment and then brightened. "Some tea, Mr. Darcy?"

"No thank you, madam." Darcy smiled slightly and watched as the teapot was replaced on the table then leaned away when a plate of biscuits was thrust forward. "I will await the meal, madam, I am certain it will be delicious."

"Well, I had no idea of your favourite dishes, but it is two courses, I am sure that for a fine man such as yourself it will be simple fare. You must have four French chefs at your disposal!"

"No madam, I have a cook in town, and another at Pemberley. I do not entertain often."

"Well that is something that will certainly change with marriage, will it not, sir? Have you met Jane?"

Darcy glanced to where Elizabeth sat silently looking down to her clasped hands. "I have met Miss Bennet. She is a very pleasant young woman."

"Do you not agree that she is beautiful? I wonder why she has not been snapped up by now. I fear that my brother has kept her quite hidden away. Of course you managed to meet Lizzy; no doubt she was running about somewhere when you did. I never could keep her in the house, she was always outside behaving as a boy, wandering the fields and forests like some wild creature. Were the girls together when you met?"

He lifted his chin. "As a matter of fact, Mrs. Bennet, they were. I noticed Miss Bennet, but once I glimpsed Miss Elizabeth, I could not look away." He looked directly at Elizabeth and she lifted her eyes to meet his steady gaze. "I find her to be everything lovely."

"Oh." Mrs. Bennet noticed him staring at her blushing daughter. "Well, I understand that you live in Derbyshire, sir?"

"Yes madam."

"I have heard no mention of your income . . ."

"I do very well, madam." He said stiffly.

"Well of course you do. Why you must have four carriages at least!" She looked at him hopefully and he closed his eyes then reopened them to see that she was still staring at him eagerly. "I have several."

"Mr. Darcy, do you have any siblings?" He turned gratefully to see Mary looking his way.

"Yes, I have a sister. She is thirteen."

"I am almost thirteen." Lydia declared. "Do you know any soldiers?"

"My cousin is a colonel."

"ohhhhhh. Does he wear a red coat?"

"Yes he does. He will soon be returning to duty."

"Why did he stop?"

"He was wounded in battle in Portugal."

"Where is that?" Lydia asked. "That is near Paris is it not?"

"Portugal is a country, Miss Lydia. It is located adjacent to Spain." He frowned.

"Oh." She turned to Kitty and they started giggling and whispering. Darcy had no doubt that it was about him and looked back to Elizabeth. She was making no attempt to chastise or interfere; he realized very quickly that she had made a conscious decision to let him see her family in their full glory. He glanced at Mr. Gardiner and he lifted his shoulders slightly.

"I am certain that my brother will return soon, Mr. Darcy." He looked to Mrs. Bennet. "He told you this morning that we were coming?"

"Oh, yes, and he said that he was looking forward to seeing what Lizzy's suitor was made of!"

Mr. Gardiner shook his head. "Perhaps Sister, we could take this opportunity to refresh ourselves from our journey before he arrives."

"Certainly, you know the way." She turned to Elizabeth. "Show Mr. Darcy where to go, Lizzy. If you are to be a wife you must know how to behave to your guests!"

"Yes, Mama." She stood and he followed. "This way, sir." Darcy waited until they left the room to speak, but just as he was about to he heard Mrs. Bennet in the background directing her other daughters. He waited for the shrill voice to quiet and bent to her.

"Are you well, Elizabeth? I expected your mother to be happy to see you attached."

"So did I. I thought that she would be ecstatic, but I suppose that she remembers that I failed before." She indicated that he follow her uncle. "I should remain here. My uncle can show you where to go." She looked up to him and met his eye before turning away. Darcy looked after her then proceeded upstairs, finally taking in the decor of the old house. It was clean, certainly not of the most fashionable style, but seemed adequate. Mr. Gardiner took the opportunity of their privacy to apologize for his sister's display and his brother's absence, which was certainly intentional. When they descended, Elizabeth was standing at the foot of the stairs.

"My father is home, please come with me." She led them to the bookroom. "Papa." He glanced up from his book and stood. "Mr. Darcy, this is my father, Mr. Thomas Bennet." Mr. Bennet raised his brows and bowed slightly.

"Sir, it is an honour to meet Miss Elizabeth's father." Darcy bowed in return.

"It is an honour to meet someone of such eminence." He nodded to the door. "Please leave us, Lizzy." She looked at Darcy, holding his gaze for a moment and left the room, the click of the latch startlingly loud against the strained silence within. "Well, take a seat." Mr. Bennet sat down. "Forgive me for not being home when you arrived. I expected you to come later."

"I told you of our plans, Brother."

"Yes." He turned to Darcy. "So you are courting my Lizzy. What could draw such a man as you to my daughter?"

He raised his brow at such an abrupt beginning. "Do you find her wanting in some way, sir? I find her appeal to be obvious. She is as fascinating as she is beautiful."

Seeing that he would not rise to the bait, Mr. Bennet tried a different provocation. "I suppose that you are used to getting whatever you want."

"I am accustomed to having my way, yes. However, that applies to my estate and my amusements, not to my family. I am certain that you are aware sir, one cannot control free will, only direct it to be expressed properly."

Mr. Bennet heard the criticism of his household, but moved on. "Your intentions for my Lizzy?"

"I hope to make her my wife."

"And she would live . . ."

"At my estate, Pemberley in Derbyshire, and of course in town. I would hope to travel with her as well. I notice that she has great curiosity for the world. I would like to show her as much as I can." He saw Mr. Bennet's attention drifting to his own thoughts. "I would make a very generous settlement upon her. She would never have any worries for her or our children's future."

Mr. Bennet's eyes narrowed. "Is that directed at me, sir?"

"It is a simple statement of fact."

"My wife feels that you should have chosen my eldest daughter, Jane. I cannot help but agree that she should have the honour of marrying first, it is her right. Lizzy may have to wait for that to take place." Mr. Bennet watched for Darcy to anger and make demands, but was disappointed to see him remain calm.

"Regardless of Miss Bennet's prospects, which are through no fault of her own admittedly poor, why would you risk the chance to secure the future of Miss Elizabeth, and potentially the rest of your family? You have acknowledged my wealth; surely you know that unlike some other suitor, I am capable of assuring your family a home following your demise. I have enquired of Mr. Gardiner what sort of income your wife would receive and it is unfortunate indeed. You would wish to see your family struggle by the loss of such a promising suitor out of some misguided sense of . . . fairness for the order of marriage? I find that irresponsible, sir."

Mr. Gardiner cleared his throat and Darcy ignored him, sat back, folded his hands in his lap, and stared at Mr. Bennet steadily.

"I believe that I shall reserve my blessing of this proposed union until Jane is clearly attached."

"So you say that Jane must find a suitor before Elizabeth may marry?" Mr. Gardiner said quickly.

"Yes." Mr. Bennet smiled. "That should teach this haughty man that he cannot have everything that he wants."

"I am happy to report then that Jane does indeed have a suitor, a very serious one." Mr. Gardiner contained the smirk that was attempting to appear. Darcy's face remained blank but he stood and bowed.

"I thank you for your blessing, sir. I will go immediately and inform Miss Elizabeth. She will be very pleased. I proposed just three days ago, and she has accepted me. I am sure that her mother will want to begin to plan for the wedding immediately." He nodded to Mr. Gardiner. "I know that you have a great deal to discuss with Mr. Bennet regarding Miss Bennet, so I will leave you to your privacy." He turned and left the room quickly.

Mr. Bennet stared at the closing door then at Mr. Gardiner. "He hoodwinked me!"

"He did, and very neatly, too. He is not a fool; your provocation was not effective."

"Apparently not." He let out a long breath and sat back in his chair. "What on earth does Lizzy see in him?"

"He is a very good man, Bennet. She is exceptionally fortunate to love him."

"Love? It is a love affair?" Mr. Gardiner nodded and Mr. Bennet shook his head. "And this arrogant man loves her?"

"He does, deeply, and for years, as has she."

"Years?"

"Yes."

"But what of Stewart?"

"Friendship, not love." Mr. Gardiner shook his head. "If you had stopped teasing Lizzy and listened to her, you would have known that."

"I suppose I would." He sighed. "Well, the family is saved and with no trouble to me. What of this love affair of Jane's?"

"Not love, security. May I add Brother, that her suitor is not a young man passionately in love? He is a man of experience, has loved and lost his first wife, has two children, and is willing to save Jane from a sad fate caused by your indolence and my sister's poor decision to promote her beauty over her ability. Mr. Harwick will not tolerate this game you are playing with Mr. Darcy today, and may very well choose to remove his wife from her family's influence to protect his own." Mr. Bennet stared at his brother in disbelief and Mr. Gardiner leaned forward and began to go over the details of Jane's potential future.

DARCY WALKED INTO THE HALLWAY to find Elizabeth seated on a small chair with her head down and hands folded. He knelt beside her and encasing them in his warm grasp whispered, "We are to be married, my love."

Her head flew up. "He said yes?"

He smiled, "Well, he did not know that he was; he thought that he was saying no, but it worked in our favour." He stood and pulled her with him.

"Come, show me your garden. I feel a need to celebrate our future before your mother hears the news."

"What happened?" She demanded as they walked outside, arm in arm.

"He insisted that Jane be attached before you could accept me."

"What?"

"I felt that he was toying with me, so I let him go on. Your uncle delivered the coup de grace and I departed before he knew what had happened." He chuckled to see her incredulous stare and looked around. "Is there somewhere secluded we could go?"

"Why?"

He leaned down and whispered. "Because, my love, I at last see the sparkle back in your eyes, and I must admit that I want to take advantage."

"Mr. Darcy, what are you implying?"

"I intend to . . ." He drew her into a stand of trees, then pressing her against a tall oak, ran his hands down her shoulders and arms to rest on her hips. He looked up slowly, taking in her form, pausing to watch her bosom rise and fall as she breathed unsteadily, then up to look into her eyes and finally, focussed on her mouth. He spoke to her lips, leaning closer with each word until his body weight pressed her tight against the tree. "I love you, my dearest, beautiful, Elizabeth." His mouth brushed hers, and in a moment Elizabeth's arms were around his neck and his were wound around her body. They began slowly, with soft open caresses. Darcy tried to hold back, but the strokes rapidly escalated as he gave over to his hunger for her kiss and the emotion of the moment, possessing her mouth as never before. His eyes flicked open to see hers closed, and he watched her face as he ran his hand firmly up her waist to pass over the side of her breast. Her eyes flew open to stare into his. Darcy slowed his kisses, now using his hips to press her against the tree, and he watched as slowly both of his hands travelled upwards from her waist to cup and caress her bosom. Elizabeth's eyes closed again and she gasped, then moaned. He kissed her vulnerable open mouth then moved his lips to her throat, breathing in her ear as his fingers continued the slow torture. "Fitzwilliam." She whispered with a catch in her voice as he gently suckled. "Ohhhhhhhhh." She swallowed and her hands moved to clutch his lapels. As he pressed against her, an ache of mysterious longing spread from where he slowly rubbed her body. His mouth returned to love hers again, his arms wound once again around her back, and his movement ceased. All that remained was the kiss, slow, gentle, and intensely loving. Darcy stopped, and drawing her to his chest, he moved them away from the tree, intentionally leaving them both at the brink of discovery.

"Why did you stop?" She whispered as her heart pounded.

Darcy kissed her forehead, and whispered in her hair. "Do you think there should be more, my love?"

"There must be more, you said there was so much more than just a kiss, I remember."

"There is dearest, there is. And there is much more than what we have done together now." He drew away and smiled. "I want you to anticipate our marriage, not fear it. Did you like what you felt?"

"Yes, so much." Elizabeth sighed.

"That makes me so happy." Darcy kissed her softly and then brushed back some loose hair. He moulded her back against his chest. She was so soft and willing, and . . .innocent. The thought struck him hard. "Oh Elizabeth, I am so sorry." He whispered. "I . . . I never should have kissed you like this, not yet, I should not even be holding you like this . . . I am taking advantage of your naivety and satisfying my desire. I did not mean to, truly dearest, I am just so happy to . . ."

"Fitzwilliam stop." Elizabeth looked up and he could not meet her eyes. "I needed your kisses."

"But I was carried away."

"So was I." She looked back down. "I know that we should not touch each other like this, even if we are engaged, I am wanton for not stopping you, but . . .I truly needed your kisses. I have been worried for so long."

"But you do not know what is to come, what these touches will lead to . . ."

"If you are hoping to frighten me of marriage you are doing a very good job." Elizabeth smiled softly and stroked his face, but could not smooth away the distress that was clearly displayed.

He spoke quietly. "We should go tell your mother our news."

"I want to stay here. You are not yourself."

"Do not tempt me. You cannot possibly know how difficult it is for me to walk away from here, and how very guilty I feel for leading you here at all. I have so little control around you." He kissed her hand and removed it from his cheek. "Now do you understand the insistence for chaperones?"

She leaned into him. "I do, and I also understand the reason for short engagements."

"Indeed." He closed his eyes, she could not know how deeply he needed her embrace.

"I love you Fitzwilliam."

"Those words are as sweet as your kiss." They emerged from the trees and back into the garden. Mary stood with her back to them, her hands on her hips and clearly looking vexed.

"Mary." Elizabeth called and she turned. "Are you looking for us?"

"Where did you go? Mama sent me to find you; Papa has some announcement to make at dinner." They caught up to her and she wrinkled her brow. "What happened to your mouth? Are you wearing paint?"

"Of course not." Elizabeth glanced up at Darcy.

He bit his lips and whispered another apology. "They are just a little red."

"How little?"

He tilted his head to study her mouth, and did not answer. Elizabeth pinched his arm. "Ow!" He rubbed the spot and furrowed his brow at her. "I think that my mouth is probably in the same condition as yours." Her hand went up to her lips and he could not resist smiling. "Do not rub, it will become worse!"

Mary turned before they entered the house. "Why did you not call me, Lizzy? I should have chaperoned you. Remember, I did that when Mr. Stewart came to court you. I liked him a great deal; he was everything that Dr. Fordyce said a suitor should be." She glanced at Darcy whose smile had left his face, then at Elizabeth who was looking at the porch floor. She let go of Darcy's arm when she felt him stiffen, but he caught her hand before she could retreat inside.

"Elizabeth, Miss Elizabeth." His face showed his distress. "Forgive me. I should never have taken such liberties with you. I promise I will not do so again. Please stop me if I . . ."

"I did not love him, Mr. Darcy. You are the only man I have ever wanted to . . . take liberties." She met his gaze then stood up on her toes to brush his lips with hers, then entered the house. Darcy closed his eyes and stood alone for a few moments. Her gesture with that slight kiss was far more enticing than everything they experienced in the woods. The effect of her innocent kiss and Mary's insightful reference to Stewart, who had blessedly *never* touched Elizabeth improperly, made his self-reproach roar back with a vengeance. He took some time to restore his equilibrium, then taking a deep breath, crossed the threshold.

"Are you well?" Darcy nodded curtly and she led the way to the dining room. Elizabeth took her place at her father's right and Darcy was given the seat by her side. Mr. Bennet looked them over, his gaze moving from one mouth to the other. He looked at Mr. Gardiner and, although he was not surprised, did send a pointed look at Darcy, who nodded.

"Ahem." Mr. Bennet cleared his throat. "Well, it seems that we have some news to impart. Mr. Darcy has asked for Lizzy's hand and apparently I have given my blessing." Mrs. Bennet screeched. "I also have the news that Jane has been approached for a courtship by another gentleman. It seems that Longbourn will have to grow used to losing all of its sensible women permanently."

He sat down and listened to the noise begin. "Mr. Bennet!! Jane is to marry?"

"She is courting, but I believe that the gentleman is most anxious to conclude the contract rapidly. Am I correct, Brother?"

"Yes, Mr. Harwick wishes to return to his estate soon. He has two young daughters and misses them greatly."

"He is a widower?" Mrs. Bennet paused in her joy.

"He is. Jane will be a mother as well as a wife upon her marriage."

"Well! That will not do. No, that will not do at all! My Jane should not have to mother children that she did not bear! Her husband will never care for her children! And what of the estate? Would it not go to the first family? I do not like this at all, Mr. Bennet."

"Jane will be a mother! What a joke!" Lydia laughed. "She will have the misery of the children without the pleasure of getting them!"

"LYDIA!" Elizabeth exclaimed.

"Well at least she did not have to birth them." Lydia pouted.

"What do you know of such things?" Kitty asked and chewed on a roll. "I think that you are just making things up."

"I am not! I heard Mama's friends talking about their duties."

"It is a woman's duty to submit to her husband and bear his children." Mary informed the table. Mr. Gardiner looked from Elizabeth's furious face to Darcy's set jaw to Mr. Bennet's amusement and Mrs. Bennet's oblivion and decided he would take control.

"Lydia, Kitty, and Mary. You do not discuss such topics in mixed company, and furthermore, you should not discuss them at all until you are engaged."

"It is discussed in the Bible." Mary said stubbornly.

Mr. Gardiner addressed her sternly. "That may be so, but that is for private contemplation, not for public discourse."

Darcy could not hold back his affront. "I am accustomed to children spending meals with their governess. They should not be with the adults."

Looking to his brother, Mr. Gardiner waved his hand over the table. "I hope that you take note of this, and address the girls' behaviour. Lizzy and Jane have suffered enough with this family's indiscretions."

"How?" Mr. Bennet nodded to Elizabeth and Darcy. "She has caught herself a rich man, and from what you tell me of Mr. Harwick, he is rich as well."

"He is rich?" Mrs. Bennet perked up.

"Papa said he had an estate, Mama." Kitty pointed out. "Is it bigger than Mr. Darcy's?"

"No." Elizabeth met her eye. "It is not."

"Elizabeth." Darcy said softly and looked to her. She took his meaning and removed herself from the fray again. The first course arrived and the family began eating in silence, but it did not last long.

"So tell me Mr. Darcy, what drew you to my daughter at the tender age of fifteen?" Mr. Gardiner closed his eyes. His brother had not listened to a thing he had said in the bookroom.

Darcy considered Mr. Bennet and spoke quietly. "I did not know that she was fifteen at the time. I was very surprised when I learned that news; I could hardly be blamed for that mistake. I am not familiar with girls being out at that age." Mr. Bennet coloured and he continued. "Regardless, the day that I first saw her was the day I learned that my father was dying. Miss Elizabeth's presence in the park was very comforting to me." He looked up and smiled a little at her and she rested her hand in his under the table.

"Thank you." She whispered.

"Your father has died?" Mrs. Bennet asked.

"Yes madam, it will be two years this October."

"So you are the master of your estate?" Darcy sighed, realizing that it was not concern or compassion that drove her question.

"Yes madam."

"He has ten thousand a year." Mr. Bennet said with a smile.

"TEN THOUSAND?" Mrs. Bennet turned to Elizabeth. "Oh my, what riches, what pin money! Oh Lizzy, you have at last done your duty! We are saved! Even if we must move to Derbyshire, we will be living in luxury, your estate sir, it is very large?"

Darcy's eyes grew wide at the thought of this woman and her brood moving into Pemberley. "It is comfortable, but should your family need to leave Longbourn, I will provide a suitable home for you on the grounds, or perhaps you would prefer to stay here amongst your friends. Hopefully this will be a subject that will not need to be addressed for many years." He nodded to Mr. Bennet.

"Nonsense, we will live in your home!" Mrs. Bennet declared.

He closed his eyes and balled his hands into fists, fighting back the vitriol that was dancing on his tongue. Mr. Gardiner saw the danger and took charge. "Sister, when the time comes, I am sure that Mr. Darcy will take care of you and any unmarried daughters. Until that time we will not discuss this further, and you will not presume to impose your desires upon Mr. Darcy's hospitality."

"Well, at least you no longer need to fear starvation, my dear." Mr. Bennet smiled and bowed his head to Darcy. "Thank you for your care, sir."

Darcy's patience had reached its limit. He looked at his future father and said quietly so that only Elizabeth and Mr. Gardiner heard, "It is fortunate that someone will be anticipating their disposition, sir."

"I do not like your tone, sir.

"And I do not care for your baiting. I would appreciate that you desist before I lose all respect for the father of my betrothed."

"I can rescind my consent."

"And leave your wife to the hedgerows? Shall we tell her now? I am certain that she will not hesitate to express her opinion." He turned his head to address Mrs. Bennet.

"Mr. Darcy." Mr. Bennet said quietly. "Twice today you have used my words against me."

"Perhaps you should rethink your strategy." Their eyes met and held. "Sir, if you choose to rescind your consent, I will simply take Miss Elizabeth to Gretna Green. It would be a scandal, but it would be bearable to have her as my wife. She will receive the same settlement regardless of how or when we marry. The difference will be when or if we will continue to acknowledge her family." Darcy felt Elizabeth's hand grip his and he squeezed back, but he did not break his gaze.

Mr. Bennet looked to Elizabeth and saw that her eyes were focussed on her future husband. He nodded and deflated. "It seems that you do not have a sense of humour for wordplay, sir."

"No, I have no patience for unnecessary posturing and taunting. I find nothing amusing in discussing the fate of my family."

"Perhaps you might accept it as the weak attempt of an old man to keep his children by his side as long as possible."

Darcy inclined his head. "As you wish."

The servants came around with dessert and it was quickly consumed. The men declined to separate and the party moved to the sitting room. Mrs. Bennet spent the time making wedding plans out loud while Elizabeth remained silent, realizing that anything she said would not be heard. The entire time Darcy's hand remained tightly gripped around hers. He whispered to her his regret for publicly losing his temper with her father and she whispered to him that she had barely restrained her own reaction. Suddenly the last unaddressed subject was broached by Mrs. Bennet.

"Mr. Darcy, when is the wedding to take place?" He looked at Elizabeth and raised his brows.

Mr. Bennet spoke first. "Jane should have the honour as she is the eldest." He noted the disappointment in Elizabeth's face.

She looked to Darcy, who was valiantly holding his tongue. Instead he lifted her hand and kissed it, disregarding the self-loathing he had felt since their kiss in the woods, and inciting gasps and giggles from the women and a tender smile from his bride-to-be. Mr. Bennet cleared his throat.

"Lizzy, I would like to speak to you in my bookroom."

"Yes, Papa." She stood and followed him, exchanging glances with Darcy and her uncle as she departed. Once inside of the room, she assumed her accustomed chair and waited for her father to begin.

"You seem displeased with me, daughter."

"It is not my place to disagree with you, Papa."

"That is quite a change. When have we not had lively conversations? Your association with Mr. Darcy has changed you."

"Yes, it has, I am happy to say. Aunt and Uncle have exposed me to greater society as much as they can in their limited circle, but I have now seen what the first circles expect in the way of behaviour, and I have confirmation of how wanting my education has been. I have to think through my conversation before I open my mouth. I witnessed how Jane's innocent talk of our family's circumstances quickly spiralled to condemnation of my character. A houseful of people speculated about my machinations towards Mr. Darcy, and questioned his intentions towards me. I realize that some of it was simple disappointment that such an eligible catch would be lost to someone of my status, but the lesson was not lost on me. You have taught me the art of argument and creative conversation, but nobody taught me how to curb my thoughts before they reached my tongue. I am doing my best, and I hope to always make my husband proud of me."

"You no longer wish to make your father proud?"

"You gave that power over to Uncle, sir." She said softly, and looked up to see his stricken expression. "Why did you treat Mr. Darcy so poorly? Why would you attempt to frighten away such an incomparable suitor? He feels remorse for losing his temper at dinner, but I cannot blame him for it, not when I know that you purposely pushed him to do so."

"I was simply taking my enjoyment from the man who dares to take my favourite child away forever. You denied me that pleasure by conducting this courtship away from home." He saw Elizabeth's eyes flash but she did not respond, waiting for a better explanation. "He did not rise to the bait."

At last she spoke. "You mean that he did not become angry and flustered, and did not allow you to enjoy watching him dangle, while pleading for your blessing."

"It sounds very weak when you put it that way, Daughter."

"If Mr. Darcy was a weaker man, he would have left me here and departed for London a quarter hour after he arrived. Do you not see how our family's poor behaviour has done none of us any favours? Mr. Stewart was driven away because if it. My poor dowry and the family he would have to support forced him to reject any thought of an alliance."

"Would you have preferred him?"

"No, I was already in love with Mr. Darcy, even though there was no hope of ever marrying him. I might have accepted Mr. Stewart, and we would have been friends. But I love Mr. Darcy."

"Then perhaps in this case, our family's poor behaviour did you a favour."

Finally losing her temper she cried out, "Can you not see that Mr. Darcy loves me so much that he will bear anything to my husband?" Elizabeth contained her anger and spoke in a controlled voice. "Why does Jane have the right to marry first? She has only just met Mr. Harwick."

"I want to hold onto Elizabeth Bennet a little longer." He said simply.

Elizabeth felt frustrated with his weak answer, then saw his sad expression. "Papa, I will still be your daughter, even when my name is Darcy. Please do not keep us apart any longer than necessary."

He nodded and sighed. "I could never deny you anything, Lizzy. Forgive me for today. Mr. Darcy is everything that I could hope for in your husband, I suppose that I wish that I was the one who gave you these things. You are no longer the Lizzy Bennet I knew. Mr. Darcy has influenced you."

"For the better, Papa." She stood and kissed his cheek. "Thank you."

He patted her cheek. "It is not too late for my sisters, Papa. Please think about schooling them. I am afraid that they do not have the desire to learn by themselves as I did. It is so important. Jane may marry a good man purely by chance. Beauty clearly is not the only accomplishment a girl requires."

"I will think about it. Now, I imagine that your young man would like to return to town before the hour grows any later."

Elizabeth turned to go. "Are you not coming?"

Mr. Bennet shook his head. "No, have a safe journey."

She returned to the sitting room and was speared by Darcy's concerned gaze. She took a seat beside him and leaned to his ear. "Papa apologizes for his behaviour and has given us leave to marry whenever we wish."

Darcy closed his eyes and took a deep breath then opened them to find Elizabeth smiling warmly at him. He wanted nothing more than to kiss her then. Instead he squeezed her hand. "I believe that we should begin our journey home."

"Together."

"I never expected to go any other way."

25 MAY, 1809

Mr. Darcy accepted my family today. They did everything possible to drive him away, and he was steadfast and determined. He bore it all, the insults, the behaviour, the prospect of them coming to live with us, everything, and it was all for me. He loves me, he truly loves me, and oh how I dearly love him! I cannot wait to make my life with him. Something put us together in the park that day when we first spotted each other. God knew that we were two lost souls who needed each other. I promise you my Fitzwilliam, I will always love you.

Elizabeth blew out her candle and climbed into the small bed. She lay on her side hugging her pillow, remembering the feel of Darcy's body pressed to hers, and imagined what he meant when he said there was so much more for them to experience. She shivered with the thought and closed her eyes, wishing for the day when they would at last be together.

25 MAY 1809

This was the most frustrating, horrifying, and joyous day of my life. I now understand Elizabeth's fears about my meeting her family, and thoroughly understand Stewart's departure from the vicinity with alacrity. Never have I met such a rude, ill-mannered, poorly managed, and uncontrolled family! Where Mr. Bennet attempted to, I suppose, test me with his baiting, Mrs. Bennet appalled me with her almost complete disregard of Elizabeth! I believe that she was attempting to match me with Miss Bennet, or even Miss Lydia! Elizabeth only seemed to win her approval when the wedding, no, when my income was announced. The sisters, I cannot describe the sisters. Miss Lydia is frightening, spouting off comments about subjects that I pray she is parroting from eavesdropping on her mother's friends.

Miss Kitty giggles incessantly; and Miss Mary has a propensity for ill-applied propriety that can only lead her to a life as a spinster. Perhaps I can help them, educate them. I will be willing to send them to school if Mr. Bennet will allow it. I cannot imagine foisting his children into the world and expecting them to find husbands without some sort of help.

I am overwhelmed that somehow from this home emerged my glorious Elizabeth and Miss Bennet. That clearly is the result of the Gardiner's influence. I bless my parents for being loving, attentive, and caring. I see clearly the effect of indifference on a family. Elizabeth suffered a cruel upbringing. I am determined to care for our children and Georgiana as my parents did. I will protect them and provide for them. They will know they are valued and loved.

But at the end of the day, I am engaged to Elizabeth. She sat across from me in the carriage, her embarrassment and anger when we departed was clear, but the farther we moved from Longbourn, the more she changed. Her eyes sparkled, her smile was warm, and her laugh filled the space with joy. I have never had a happier journey. I at last have convinced her of my dedication, and for that I will be rewarded with her love for the rest of my days. For that I will bear anything. May God bless you, my dearest Elizabeth.

Darcy blew out the candle on his desk and walked out of his sitting room and into his bedchamber. Taking off his robe he looked at the empty bed then walked on to open the door to the Mistresses' chambers. He leaned on the doorframe and looked into the dark space, smelling the beeswax from the recent cleaning and wondering if Elizabeth would prefer to live there or if she would allow him to sleep with her. He thought of their kisses in the woods, and remembered her desire to experience more. "Oh Elizabeth," he breathed, "come home."

Chapter 16

"I tell you Bingley, it was appalling. I have thought it over countless times, and I still cannot reconcile Mr. Bennet's behaviour. To what purpose would he intentionally try to drive away a suitor? Did he realize what he was doing? I have been told that he is intelligent, but surely that is eclipsed by his thoughtlessness." Darcy placed his hands on the arms of his chair and pushed back from the desk. "My admiration for Miss Elizabeth has grown immensely. I admit that I was frustrated with her determination not to believe my dedication to her, but now . . . I understand her fear and I am overwhelmed by her effort to educate herself. I am committed to providing a sound education for my sister, and giving her every advantage. She will marry well, without the struggle that Miss Elizabeth and Miss Bennet experienced. I will do the same for our children. I have been given a clear lesson on what can go terribly wrong when the parents of a child practice neglect."

Bingley listened thoughtfully and nodded. "I believe that I am the product of neglect or in my case it should be called ambition; however as a boy I was sent to schools that took me away from that atmosphere."

"Your sisters were also schooled." Darcy pointed out. "The Bennet girls did not have that, they were left to find their way, and I have witnessed the result."

"That is true, and although Louisa used her instruction to her advantage, I am afraid that Caroline has fancied herself suitable for a marriage far above herself. Of course she had her sights firmly set on you." Bingley smiled and Darcy's eyes rolled.

"That is why I have politely declined most invitations that include her company, Bingley. Perhaps now that I am engaged I will be more inclined to be in her presence."

"I understand, and I would appreciate that. Perhaps appearing in your company, with Miss Elizabeth of course, she might attract more interest. After all, her dowry is not a pittance. Miss Bennet has an excellent suitor, even given her poor background, so there is no reason that Caroline cannot find the same. Do you know of anyone . . .?"

"To match with your sister? I do not like that position, Bingley. If a match takes place and it is a failure, I do not want to be held responsible."

"An introduction is hardly a marriage ceremony, Darcy."

Darcy studied his friend for a few moments and let down his stance. "You are becoming desperate?"

"I do not see my chances of finding a bride happening easily with Caroline at home." He laughed and shrugged. "She is far more ambitious than I."

"I wonder if you would have done well with Miss Bennet." Darcy mused and rubbed his jaw. "Of course you must marry a gentlewoman, and it would be best to find one who can augment your status as well as your estate."

"Hmm? Oh perhaps Miss Bennet would have been a good choice. She is beautiful, and likely easy to live with, but . . . I wonder if I would have eventually become, I do not know, bored?" Bingley smiled and Darcy's brow rose. "I am aware of my fickle nature."

"Yes, so am I. Are there any new angels in the heavens for you?"

Bingley laughed. "Ah, I wish there were. No, I have been listening to you, Darcy. I am not ready for an estate, let alone marriage. I cannot seem to stop tripping over my tongue, and have so much to learn. I think that the only young lady who would be willing to tolerate me is Miss Elizabeth."

Darcy's smile disappeared and he focussed his steely gaze on his friend. "I hope that there are no thoughts of that nature in your mind."

"Darcy, put down your sword. I am not going to steal her away from you. Good God man, you cannot be serious?"

"Forgive me." He said quietly.

He laughed and crossed his legs. "You are as bad as Caroline! I make a passing reference to Miss Elizabeth and she sees it as an opportunity to match me with her!"

Darcy's eyes became cold again. "What was this reference?"

"That we were friends, Darcy." Bingley's smile faded. "I am not pursuing her. Surely her response to you should make that clear. We are simply two people who share common worries about our fitness for this society we have entered. We are friends." Bingley looked down to his hands. "Perhaps I should leave."

"No, no." Darcy sighed. "Forgive me, Bingley. I . . . I am jealous of any man who might catch her eye. I suppose I will always be cognizant of how many times I almost lost her. It is not you, it is fear."

Bingley looked back up and saw Darcy's sincerity. "I understand. I suppose I would feel the same after waiting so long. Well, what are your plans?"

"In keeping with my determination to care well for my sister, I will deliver her to Matlock House to stay for awhile. She will be exposed to my aunt, and be able to learn and observe how a mistress runs her household. I see the great influence that Mrs. Gardiner had upon Miss Elizabeth, so I can only expect that Georgiana will absorb a great deal from our aunt."

"When would you like to attend the theatre?"

"I propose that we go to see *Rozelle and Rosa* next Wednesday. That should give the modiste enough time to make a new gown for Elizabeth, and I imagine that Miss Bennet will be purchasing some things as well. Then, of course, I must take Miss Elizabeth to the Derby."

"She likes horse races?" Bingley smiled.

"She was there when I approached you last year, Bingley." Darcy smiled at his astonishment. "She was yards away, and I wanted so much to speak to her."

"And I was prattling on, and keeping you from her?" Bingley smiled sheepishly and Darcy shrugged.

"It was not yet time for us."

Bingley stood. "Well, I will not keep you any longer. Enjoy your engagement, Darcy. I am delighted for both of you."

Darcy stood and shook his hand. "Thank you." He saw him to the door and returned to his study to read over the letter on his desk. He wrote one more note and called for the butler. "Mr. Foster, please have one of the boys deliver this letter to the *Times*, this to my solicitor, and then post these two express." The butler departed and he lifted his eyes to look at Pemberley, and imagined taking Elizabeth to that very spot to view her new home. *I wonder if she will kiss me there?* He closed his eyes and sighed to himself.

"Brother?" Georgiana said softly. "Are you awake?"

"Yes dear, just daydreaming." Darcy sat up and smiled. "Are you prepared for your visit?"

"Yes, I am really looking forward to it. Miss Elizabeth will be visiting frequently?" She watched as he stood up and came around the desk.

"I think that she will, but I will not let our aunt take all of her time. I claim most of it for myself." He laughed at her pursed lips. "What did I say?"

"She is to be *my* sister; I want my share of time as well! Especially if I am to go to school."

"So you will try to make me feel guilty for this decision? It will not work, Georgiana. After meeting Miss Elizabeth's sisters, my decision is set. You will go and have every advantage. I spoke to Miss Elizabeth about this, and she said that she begged her parents to allow her the privilege of an education. She wholeheartedly supports my stance."

"I understand, but somehow it does not bother me so much now. With you marrying, I know that you will not be alone without me. Miss Elizabeth will be there to take care of you, and when I come home, we will be a family." Georgiana hugged him and he kissed her forehead. She whispered quietly as he hugged her in return. "I promised Papa I would look after you, but now you do not need me anymore."

"I will always need you, Georgiana." He looked down and smiled. "I promise."

"Mr. Darcy, you have a caller." Foster announced. "Mr. Harwick."

"Oh. Well show him in." Darcy gave a look to Georgiana and she quickly left the room. Harwick entered and the men shook hands. "I expected to see you at the Gardiner's home this evening, this is a surprise."

"I wished to speak with you privately." He glanced around the handsome room and spotted the painting of Pemberley. "This is your estate?"

They walked over to examine the landscape. "Yes, I am immensely proud of it. I look forward to returning."

"I understand; I am anxious to return home as well." He smiled slightly and glanced at his companion as they took their seats. "How are you holding up from the transition from son to master?"

Darcy laughed softly. "You have done the same not so long ago. My father taught me well, and prepared me for everything, but the reality of the responsibility was almost crushing at first. I feel that the weight is slightly relieved after two years. At least my steward is nodding readily in agreement now instead of placating me with murmurs of assent."

Harwick laughed. "Yes, you are earning the man's respect. Interesting how easy it is to forget how important those people who run your estate are, and how lost we would be without them."

"That is one lesson that my father drove home to me. Pride in our land and family's accomplishments is better than pride of place."

"A wise man."

"Indeed."

"I come to you today to speak of another estate owner." Harwick watched Darcy closely. "Mr. Bennet. I understand that you visited him yesterday."

"Yes, it was . . ." Darcy searched for words and then gave up. "Horrifying."

"So Miss Elizabeth's outburst was wholly justified."

He spoke quickly. "She regrets it deeply. She feels the weight for having jeopardized her sister's chances by behaving so . . ."

Harwick held up his hand. "Stop there, Darcy. I was not offended."

"That is not the impression I received. I must say that she is a very passionate woman and feels emotion deeply. She is very protective of her family and only wants her sister to be happy."

"I understand. Her behaviour, while it would not be smiled upon by the likes of your family, I am sure, was honest. It was clear that it was so when her uncle hurried to defend his niece but did not attempt to refute the implication of her parents' poor marriage. Even you have confirmed it to me. No, Miss Elizabeth did not offend, not at all." He saw Darcy's creased brow and lifted his chin. "You are deeply in love with her."

Darcy flushed and looked down to his hands. "It is so obvious?"

"To one who has also experienced such an emotion, yes it is. You would overlook anything for her, not that she has done wrong. I imagine the only others who would be able to read your emotion are those who are very close to you. You are excellent at hiding your feelings." Harwick continued softly. "Miss Elizabeth reminds me very much of my Ellen."

His head shot up. "She does?"

"Oh yes, her manner, her smile, her passion, even her look is reminiscent of my wife. When she departed from the study at your uncle's house, I was taken with the memory of so many passionate conversations with my wife, especially when she was with child and perhaps a little more susceptible to emotion. To see you run after her . . .it was like watching a scene from my life being played out before me." His mouth lifted in a sad smile. "I can well imagine what happened when you caught up with her."

"Harwick."

He held up his hand. "No, I did not mean to question any violations of propriety by either of you."

Darcy recovered from his embarrassment and then examined his companion. "Then, may I ask, why are you interested in Miss Bennet for your wife? She is as dissimilar from Miss Elizabeth as night is from day. She is fair, quiet, docile . . .I am afraid that I do not understand."

"I hope that you never do. Do you not grasp it, man? I can never replace my Ellen, and to try to do so with her twin would be an insult to her memory. I am purposely choosing someone unlike her."

Understanding Harwick's reasoning he nodded. "You have no expectation of love."

"None. I hope that we get along tolerably. I realized quickly that Miss Bennet does not belong in society and would be better off at home, she is beautiful, she will provide me with pleasant company, and most importantly care for my girls and hopefully give me an heir. It is all that I want. If we become friends, I will be happy, and she will be treated well." He leaned forward and said slowly. "I had my love, and I am cognizant that my actions will save Miss Bennet from a certain poor fate by marrying her and hopefully solving the disposition of my estate that I cannot ignore. However, her family is a problem. If it is truly as bad as it seems, I may at the least rethink choosing Miss Bennet, and if we marry, I will not allow her relations, aside from Miss Elizabeth and the Gardiners, to come to my home and influence my children. I will not visit their home either. I will not ban my wife from visiting or writing, but I will not allow them my sanction. The remaining sisters, they are . . ."

"Uneducated and rather frightening in their ignorance of proper behaviour and discourse."

"Does their father have any plans for them?"

"I was considering offering to school them."

"Are you out of your mind?" Harwick cried. "Why should you clean up another man's mistakes?"

"Why should his children suffer for them?" Darcy said angrily. "I witnessed the girls embracing Elizabeth where her mother barely acknowledged her presence. Their behaviour was horrendous, but they showed Elizabeth affection. They were the only people in that household who did, in my opinion."

"They may be too old, you know." Harwick sat back and said thoughtfully. "The damage could be too ingrained."

Darcy sighed and nodded. "Yes, that has occurred to me, but I would feel worse for not attempting to help, at least."

Harwick looked at him sternly. "I maintain that this is not your business, it is their father's."

"He has been wholly indifferent up to now. Our Misses Bennet are the product of attention to a first child and the determination of the second, as well as the intervention of the Gardiners."

"Mr. Bennet, how did he treat you?"

Darcy's face expressed his growing irritation. "It was odd, he baited me, seeking to laugh at my discomfort and even tried to deny my request for Miss Elizabeth's hand. It was ridiculous and perplexing."

"And you tolerated it because you are in love with her." Harwick smiled to see Darcy's assenting nod. "I do not have that salient fact to keep me from walking away. If I were so treated, I would have abandoned the notion and departed, leaving her behind. There is no sentiment blinding me."

"Will you visit Longbourn?

"I must meet the man eventually." Harwick rubbed his jaw.

Darcy looked off to stare at the Pemberley landscape as he thought. "Perhaps . . .You truly do not want to meet Mrs. Bennet or the girls, it would harden you irrevocably from Miss Bennet, I promise you. If Mr. Bennet was brought here to London, off of his own turf, he might be more reasonable. You could conduct your business with him, and ignore the rest if that is your desire."

Harwick smiled grimly and glanced around. "You mean show him what his behaviour nearly lost Miss Elizabeth? Intimidate the man?"

"Yes. Perhaps show him your home or," Darcy laughed softly, "introduce him to my uncle the Earl."

"Ah, that just might do it as well. I like this idea of yours, Darcy. Would he be willing to come?"

"As much as I dislike the thought of spending any time with Mr. Bennet, I will make the invitation and the arrangements, and tender the offer to educate the girls, and pay for it."

"I will aid you with that if you have determined that he will not pay himself."

Darcy's head shook emphatically. "No, no, I will take it on. You have two daughters to educate."

Harwick sighed at his stubborn companion. "You have a sister, and future children."

"I will not give in to this, sir." Darcy said quietly.

Harwick smiled and reached out to shake his hand. "Fine then, I will do my part by intimidating the fool. I imagine that your Miss Elizabeth will be very grateful for your offer."

"I do not wish for her gratitude."

"Spoken like a man in love." Harwick said approvingly. "Well done."

DARCY'S CARRIAGE ARRIVED at the Gardiner home and he saw Elizabeth disappear from the front window. By the time he had exited and was approaching the steps, the front door was open and she was waiting, a smile of welcome lit her face and she fairly bounced with anticipation to reach out for him. He laughed when she finally touched his sleeve and hugged his arm to her bosom. "I believe that you missed me!"

"Terribly." She sighed dramatically. "Where have you been all day?"

He touched the long curls resting on her neck, and whispered affectionately, "I did have some business to address, my impatient love."

"What could possibly be more important than me?" She raised her brows and he laughed to see her eyes dance. "I am sorely disappointed in you!"

Darcy marvelled at her ease. "You are a woman transformed today; you are brimming with confidence and good humour. It is breathtaking and makes me feel so happy. "

"It is only that I am finally permitting myself to enjoy the happiness that you bring to me, sir." She said softly.

"Please do not call me sir." He whispered against her ear. "Nobody calls me by name, and I love how it sounds on your lips.

"But . . .it is not proper. I should call you Mr. Darcy, at least in public."

"When we are private then." He whispered. "And I hope that we have that opportunity before I depart. I need to kiss you again. I promise to be circumspect." Elizabeth blushed and rested her head on his shoulder for a moment. Darcy brushed his lips over her hair. "You smell so sweet, dearest."

"I think that you missed me just as much as I missed you."

"To know that your feelings are as deep as mine is gratifying indeed." Again his lips brushed her hair. "Dearest, would you gift me with one of your curls?" He bent his head to see her blush deepening. "I wish to carry you with me."

"If I may have the same from you." She caught his delighted smile and nestled back against his shoulder.

"Mr. Darcy, may I take your hat?" The housekeeper appeared and he straightened, handing her his things then turned to Elizabeth to find her smiling at him shyly. Claiming his hand, she led him back to the sitting room with the rest of the family. They made their greetings and he took a seat next to Elizabeth and the couple simply sat and smiled at each other until Mrs. Gardiner and Jane could not hold back their amusement. "Oh what a picture you make! If I had my crayons, I would like to capture those smiles for posterity!"

"I make no apologies, Aunt, I feel such elation, and I have no intention of hiding it." She turned to face Darcy and tilted her head. "Now, tell me what kept you from my side today. What was this so important business of yours?"

"Ah, I can see that I will never be able to keep secrets from you." He laughed softly to see her nod emphatically and continued. "You know one of the reasons already; I delivered Georgiana to Matlock House and of course informed my aunt and uncle of your father's blessing. Prior to that Bingley visited; and I told him our news, and he wishes us great joy. I also had important letters to write. One to my solicitor to prepare your settlement," he noted her looking down and biting her lip. "Then one to the *Times* to announce our engagement to the world," he smiled to see her smile to her clasped hands. "Another to Mrs. Reynolds, our housekeeper at Pemberley, to announce our news and orders to begin preparing the house for its new mistress," here her smile was replaced with her teeth biting hard down on her lip, and he touched her hands to reassure her. "And finally a letter to my Aunt Catherine and Cousin Anne, to announce our happiness."

"Will they be happy with our happiness?" Elizabeth asked softly.

"No, Miss Elizabeth they will not. My aunt filled my cousin's head with the delusion that I would one day marry her and join her estate to mine. I informed her quite strongly that it was never to be, and she seemingly accepted that, but it will not prevent her from feeling the disappointment when our engagement is presented as incontrovertible fact."

"I see."

"Lizzy, not everyone is going to accept you, it is to be expected. You will simply have to learn to behave more civilly than they when in their presence, and to avoid the possibility of public confrontation as much as possible." Mrs. Gardiner turned to Darcy. "Are you in your aunt and cousin's company often, sir?"

"No, I rarely see them. I visit every Easter. My cousin has a weak constitution and my aunt prefers to keep her at their estate in Kent." He smiled and gave Elizabeth's hand a squeeze. "Aunt Catherine's vitriol will come in letters. I have never known her to rouse herself to actually make an appearance. I wonder though, it could be interesting to see the two of you clash."

"You are encouraging me to argue with your aunt?" Elizabeth stared.

"No, of course not, but you are both stubborn women. I can see a battle of the titans brewing someday." He smiled at her surprised expression. "Well, I see how formidable you are, even if you do not."

"Mr. Darcy, I have been attempting to rein in my tongue and here you are actually encouraging me?"

Darcy cleared his throat to distract himself from the enticing flash of passion that had appeared in her eyes and spotted a pair of tiny scissors lying next to Jane's embroidery hoop. "Miss Bennet, may I borrow your scissors for a moment? And perhaps a bit of silk?"

"Of course, Mr. Darcy." She snipped a length of blue silk and handed it to him along with the scissors and gave her aunt a look of confusion. Mrs. Gardiner was smiling at Elizabeth, who was again blushing. Darcy touched her curls, looking for just the one he wanted, and chose a shiny ebony tress that rested on her shoulder, carefully tied the silk around it, then snipped. He tenderly wrapped it in his handkerchief.

"Thank you." He said softly and smiled when Elizabeth held out her hand expectantly. He gave over the scissors and bent his head to her, closing his eyes as her fingers gently searched for the perfect curl. Elizabeth laughed and he lifted his head to see her happily admiring the sunlight on his hair. "What are your plans for that, Miss Elizabeth?"

"I have a locket upstairs. I think that I should place this within before I lose it. Excuse me." She left the room and Darcy noticed Mrs. Gardiner watching him.

"What are your plans for your treasure, sir?"

"I will have a ring made from it." He saw Jane looking at him contemplatively. "I have noticed men wearing such things and I have hoped to have such a token of Miss Elizabeth for some time. Now that we are engaged . . ."

"It is entirely proper." Mrs. Gardiner nodded and looked up to see Elizabeth returning with a small locket in her hand. "Does it not fit, dear?"

"No." She said sadly. "I will have to think of something else."

"I will purchase you a new locket; perhaps that is something we could do tomorrow?" Darcy offered and smiled to see her surprise. "Well I was chastised for being away from you too much today, was I not? Perhaps Georgiana would like to come along. I know that she wishes for more time with you."

"That would be wonderful! Thank you!" She looked to see Jane's attention then back to Darcy.

He noticed it as well and smiled to her. "Mr. Harwick paid me a call this morning; he is looking forward to dinner with you this evening. He has accepted my invitation to the theatre next week, and he made a suggestion for an excursion for us all, one that I have managed to avoid taking for all of my adult life." He glanced around the room and sighed. "Mr. Harwick suggested that we visit Vauxhall Gardens one evening."

"OH!!" Elizabeth cried and turned eagerly to Jane. "I always wished to go there!"

"Mr. Harwick suspected that you would enjoy the spectacle, Miss Elizabeth. I see that he was correct." Darcy shook his head, and looked at Jane. "He thought that you would enjoy the music, Miss Bennet."

"Mr. Harwick is very thoughtful." Jane said appreciatively. "May I ask why you have avoided the pleasure gardens?"

"I am not fond of crowds, but I know of no particular entertainment that is scheduled so hopefully we will have a pleasant evening that is not a crush." He looked to Elizabeth. "And please, do not wear anything that might be attractive to a thief."

"Really?" She smiled widely and he started to chuckle in disbelief. "What else might we see?"

"I will let you interrogate our host for the evening. Mrs. Gardiner, my cousins Mr. and Mrs. Singleton will be coming with us to serve as our chaperones." He saw her raised brow and was relieved to see her nod.

"Very well sir, they are married, and more likely to enjoy the experience than Mr. Gardiner and myself."

"Thank you madam." He bowed his head and turned back to see Elizabeth's dancing eyes. "May I have a word with you privately, Miss Elizabeth? I would like to discuss our wedding date, now that the engagement is about to be announced, we should make a choice."

"Aunt?"

"You may use Mr. Gardiner's study; he has a calendar on his desk for you to consult." Mrs. Gardiner looked at Darcy pointedly. "I expect this will not be a protracted decision."

"We will not be long away, madam." He stood and offered Elizabeth his hand to rise. They walked tranquilly down the hallway and into the study. Darcy followed her in, closing the door almost completely then turned to find her waiting for him. "Dearest Elizabeth." He slipped his arms around her waist as she did the same to him. She looked up as he bent down to tenderly touch her lips, and drew away to see her eyes closed and her mouth parted, waiting for more. He closed his eyes, remembering his resolve to behave, then felt Elizabeth's lips gently caress his. He drew a shaking breath, and drowned in the pleasure of her tongue tentatively entering his mouth. With a moan, he took control and deepened the kiss. Darcy's arms embraced her waist and shoulders, so that the entire length of her body was bound to his. Even through the restrictions of their clothing they could imagine and feel what lay beneath. The ardent kiss gradually slowed, and transformed into passion of a different nature. Their embrace was not so tight, their hands moved freely to express love through caresses, and their kisses became a soft endless exchange, filled with so much promise for long nights safe within each other's arms. Finally they parted, and gazing into each other's eyes, smiled between kisses. "I have failed again." Darcy whispered huskily.

"I am glad of it."

Darcy laughed quietly and touched her hair. "I think that the only solution to this problem is to marry, so that I may kiss you without guilt."

"Do you still feel guilt, Fitzwilliam?"

"Well, not quite as much as before . . ."

Elizabeth's laugh filled him with contentment and he could not hold back from kissing her in response. "When shall we marry?"

"Would seven weeks suit you? Shall we say the eighteenth of July? That would be time enough to order your wedding clothes, and then we could leave for Pemberley at the end of July as a married couple. I do not wish to wait for

Michaelmas as your uncle suggested. I see no reason to wait for anything at all."

"Neither do I." Elizabeth settled her head on his chest and listened to his heart. "Where?"

"I leave that choice to you, my love. Do you wish to be married from Longbourn?"

"No." She whispered. "I do not, and I think that I would prefer something very simple and private. To marry at home would mean my mother putting her stamp on the ceremony, and . . . It would be an incentive for her to crow over you and claim that she was the reason we married. Nothing could be further from the truth. I . . . I want to be happy on my wedding day, not mortified."

"I understand." He said softly and kissed her hair, deciding that now was not the time to speak of his plans for her father. "We will marry from London, in my church or your uncle's church, or even in the parlour at Darcy House." She nodded and he whispered in her ear. "It does not matter as long as we marry. I want to take you home."

"Your home frightens me."

"Our home, and may I tell you a secret? It frightens me, too." He saw her surprise and he shrugged. "I have left it all to Mrs. Reynolds and concentrated on the estate. I was planning to begin learning the ins and outs of the household this winter."

"How convenient for you to marry and therefore avoid the task altogether." She laughed and he kissed her nose.

"You found me out!" Darcy hugged her to his chest and did not notice the door opening.

"Children, Mr. Harwick has arrived. Shall we join the party?" They straightened to see Mr. Gardiner had come home and was watching them expectantly.

They passed him silently and once again, Darcy and Mr. Gardiner exchanged glances. This time Darcy did not feel abashed. He had just set his wedding date; kissing Elizabeth was mandatory. Entering the sitting room they found Jane sitting next to Harwick, holding a nosegay of purple violets and smiling happily.

"Oh Jane how lovely!" Elizabeth exclaimed and beamed at Harwick. "What a thoughtful gift, sir. I suppose that Jane has already confessed her love of violets to you?"

Harwick turned to her and smiled. "No, Miss Bennet did not share her secret. Will you tell me your other favourites so that I might surprise you with them sometime?"

"I believe that I would be happy with any gift, sir." Jane smiled kindly.

"You are forcing me to conspire with your sister, Miss Bennet." He looked to Elizabeth to see her nodding. "And it seems that she will not hesitate to speak."

"There is no doubt of that." Darcy whispered and Elizabeth turned to see his eyes twinkling at her.

"Mr. Darcy, are you baiting me?"

"I am, I own."

"And you presume to know me so well as to think that I would . . ."

"Meddle in your sister's affairs?" He raised his brow and pursed his lips. "I do."

"I am offended!"

"I see you applying your skills to the care of our tenants and their concerns." He tilted his head. "I know them all, but I can believe that they will be delighted to have an interested mistress again."

"Oh."

"Well done, Darcy." Harwick turned to Jane and smiled. "I know that the tenants of Meadowbrook would appreciate a compassionate mistress as well."

"Is that the name of your estate?" Jane smiled to him and he nodded. "It sounds lovely. I hope that it is a place that brings you peace." Harwick's head tilted as he studied her face. There was no pretence in her expression, simply kindness. He had not seen that from a woman in a very long time.

Darcy felt Elizabeth's hand steal into his and he looked to see her watching her sister and her suitor. He saw her hope that this might someday be a marriage of some affection. He squeezed her hand and felt her squeeze in return. Her hope spurred him to speak. "Mr. Gardiner, after dinner, I would appreciate hearing your opinion on a matter of some importance." Harwick raised his brow and Darcy nodded to him.

Mr. Gardiner caught the exchange and nodded. "Of course Mr. Darcy, whatever I can do to help."

"I WONDER WHAT THEY ARE TALKING ABOUT." Elizabeth mused while the ladies waited in the sitting room for the men to return after dinner. "I noticed that Mr. Harwick seemed to know the topic."

"You did?" Jane asked. "When did you notice Mr. Harwick?"

"Why when Mr. Darcy spoke to Uncle, they seemed to exchange glances." She shrugged and took a sip of tea. "I suppose I would have missed it but I was looking Mr. Darcy's way."

Mrs. Gardiner laughed softly. "Yes, I think that staring is the proper description." Elizabeth blushed. "However I notice that he spends quite enough time doing the same in your direction."

"He is rather sweet." She bit her lip and touched the tiny locket that barely contained his lock of hair. Noticing Jane's eyes on her fingers she smiled. "Mr. Harwick seems to be very kind, Jane. I am so glad to see that. He is obviously a devoted father from the way he speaks of his girls."

"Did he speak of them? I could not hear; his head seemed to be turned away from me."

Mrs. Gardiner's heard the hint of jealousy in her voice. "I believe that he was addressing the entire table, Jane. It would be impolite to limit his conversation to just one person."

Jane blushed. "I suppose that is so."

"You are only just beginning to know him. Keep in mind that Lizzy and Mr. Darcy have years between them, you have barely a week. They are also just engaged, they have every right to be particularly pleased to gaze upon each other." She raised her brows to her niece and Jane nodded.

Elizabeth tried to encourage her. "Mr. Harwick seems to be very gentlemanly, Jane. He reminds me in some ways of Mr. Stewart in his manner."

Lifting her shoulders, Jane smiled happily. "That is true; he does behave differently than Mr. Darcy, does he not? He is anxious to follow the proper rules of courtship and will not give away any indication of fondness before it is time. Mama told me never to express my feelings before the gentleman does himself, and of course I never have done that with any gentleman."

Elizabeth's brow furrowed. *Did Jane just insult Fitzwilliam? Did she call him ungentlemanly? Because he had kissed her and spoken to her, because they danced and sat alone together?* Elizabeth's affront on his behalf began to rise, but unsure of Jane's meaning she chose a different target and spoke incredulously, "Mama taught you to behave demurely?"

"Yes, you know that, I am sure that she must have said the same to you. I remember her telling me that someone with my beauty did not need to put on a show for a gentleman. All I needed to do is smile and they would come to me. As you see, she was correct." She turned to Mrs. Gardiner. "Do you agree, Aunt?"

Mrs. Gardiner spoke slowly, thinking of the months, and even years where Jane had not a single suitor. "Your mother certainly had formed great expectations for your beauty to capture a man's attention, but it certainly was a risk to place all of her hopes on your looks alone. You are fortunate to have gained Mr. Harwick's court without ever having to exhibit."

"But that just proves that Mama was correct." Jane lifted her chin. "I have succeeded without compromising myself."

"Are you implying that I have?" Elizabeth said in disbelief.

"Have I said something wrong, Lizzy?" Jane looked at her in surprise. "I did not mean to. Of course I do not mean to imply anything of you compromising yourself. Please forgive me if I have offended you! I was just speaking of Mama's teaching."

"I am sorry if I misunderstood you. We received very different educations from our mother. I was told that I had no hope of attracting a man, especially with my beauty."

"I am sorry, Lizzy." Jane said softly.

Elizabeth sighed and nodded, then embraced Jane. "It is well. Regardless of how we found them, it is good to know that we both have a chance for secure and hopefully happy futures now."

The sound of boots in the hallway ended the ladies' conversation and soon the gentlemen arrived. Darcy instantly sought out Elizabeth's presence after the tense conversation with Mr. Gardiner. He kissed her fingers and studied her face as she worked to regain her good humour. Without thinking he caressed his fingers along her brow, and saw her tension melt away with his touch. She smiled at him. "Did you complete your mission?"

Darcy relaxed and smiled back. "You make it sound so mysterious."

"You left my imagination free to roam." She laughed to see his shaking head. "What are you plotting?"

"May we leave it until tomorrow? We can speak privately."

"When are we ever able to really speak privately?" She demanded. "Please tell me or I will imagine so many horrible possibilities."

Harwick had been watching the whispered exchange with a gentle smile on his face. "Darcy, I recommend that you give in."

"No . . ." Darcy laughed to see Elizabeth's eyes flash and he felt his desire rise. "I want to see just how imaginative you are Miss Elizabeth."

"You are sure to see how stubborn I am, sir."

"Sir?" He said quietly.

"SIR." Elizabeth said emphatically.

Darcy sighed and looked to Mr. Gardiner. "Could we send a servant to have my carriage brought around?" He turned back to Elizabeth. "You are not the only stubborn person in this conversation." She stared at him open-mouthed and he rose to bow to Mrs. Gardiner then Jane. "I wish you a pleasant evening."

Harwick winked at him and Mr. Gardiner chuckled as Darcy raised his brow at Elizabeth. "Will you see me out, Miss Elizabeth?"

"You are so anxious to go, why do you need me?" She huffed.

"Lizzy!" Mrs. Gardiner spoke softly.

"I will do it for you, Aunt." Elizabeth stood and walked past Darcy to the door and out into the hallway. Darcy bowed again and left the room.

Jane looked at everyone. "They are fighting! But I thought they were in love!"

The Gardiners sighed and Harwick looked sadly away from the doorway, and back to Jane and smiled slightly. "I am sure that a cross word will never pass between us, Miss Bennet." Jane smiled happily with his words, and he looked back to the door.

In the hall Darcy stood by the front door, his hat in his hands, and glanced out of the window when his coach appeared. "Well then Miss Elizabeth, I thank you for the very pleasant evening. I am happy that our wedding day has been set, and I wish you a goodnight." He bowed and started to open the door.

"That is all?" Elizabeth cried.

"What else do you wish for? I was under the impression that you were unhappy with me?"

She waved her arms at him. "So this is the man I am marrying? One who runs away from a discussion?"

Darcy stepped away from the door and looked down at her. "What do you suggest?"

"Well at least kiss me and tell me everything is well between us." Her voice still held a hint of exasperation, but he also heard her worry. In a flash she was wrapped in his arms and kissed fiercely. Darcy's one hand supported her neck, the other stole down to rest over her bottom and lifted her up to press tightly against his ever-present arousal. "Ohhhh." She gasped when he tore his mouth away and spoke in pants in her ear.

"When we marry, my Elizabeth, my love, a discussion of this sort will not end by us separating, I assure you. I leave now only because if I do not, you uncle will have me standing before the altar at gunpoint in the morning." He broke away from her, stared intently into her eyes, lifted his fingers to touch her love swollen lips, then left the house.

Elizabeth swallowed hard and leaned heavily against the doorframe. Her hand was on her chest, and she could feel her heart pounding under her palm as he drove away. "Oh my."

26 MAY 1809

Harwick confessed to me today that he is not at all offended by Elizabeth but is actually attracted to her. My good sense tells me she is purely a bittersweet reminder of his lost wife, although my jealous soul cannot ever forget his words. I am a fool. I cannot begin to imagine losing Elizabeth and being forced to find a woman to bear me a son. I would rather leave Pemberley to Georgiana than face that fate. We have decided to write to Mr. Bennet and suggest, strongly, that he come to London and meet Harwick. If Harwick travelled to Longbourn, I know that any possibility of marriage with Miss Bennet would be eliminated before he crossed the threshold. Hopefully this sanctimonious patriarch will deign to appear. Otherwise I am certain that Harwick will very nicely but firmly end his courtship and move on to find another willing woman.

I dread telling Elizabeth about her father coming; I hate to cast any pall over our joy. She was delightful today, so happy and playful. She makes me smile and laugh, she is a pleasure to battle, she brings out boyishness in me that I thought was long dead, and I love her for it. Her kiss in the study, if only she knew how exciting it is to have her kiss me! My desire for her is painful; I can barely believe that I was capable of walking from the house with any dignity at all. I crave the day that I will at last make her mine and relieve for a moment this unending ache, before I must have her again. Fifty-two days, why on earth did I choose a date so long away!

Darcy set down his pen and closed his eyes tightly as his body inevitably reacted to his thoughts. *Again, dearest? What you do to me!* He drew a deep breath and attempted to control the yearning; and giving up, retired for the evening.

26 May 1809
I can think of no better occupation than kissing Fitzwilliam Darcy. Each time he seems to show me a little more, and when it ends, frustratingly soon, I am left wanting desperately for him to continue. He pulls away and I wish to grab his lapels and bring him back! I have discovered that he seems to lose all resolve when I kiss him first, he becomes very still and sways like a tall tree in the breeze and then he wraps me up so tightly in his arms. Oh I could stay there forever!

Elizabeth looked up when Mrs. Gardiner leaned in the doorway. "Are you well, Lizzy? We grew concerned when you did not return."

"Oh, yes Aunt, I wished to record my thoughts while they were fresh." She blushed and closed her journal.

"I see." Mrs. Gardiner walked in and touched her shoulder. "You must be experiencing a great many new emotions. I think that you and I need to have some conversation soon. In only seven weeks you will be a married woman."

"It seems so long." Elizabeth said unhappily.

Laughing softly, her aunt kissed her forehead and gave her a hug. "It will be here before you know it."

"ALL IN." The men threw their cards down and Wickham groaned.

"That's it for you, I think." The grinning man scooped up the coins on the table and drew them back to his chest. He tossed Wickham a shilling. "Here, for your drink."

"Very amusing, Scott." Wickham grabbed the coin and pocketed it. "One more round. I feel lucky."

"And what will you play with? I've got all your cash."

He drew out a pocket watch. "Here, this is worth a hundred pounds, a gift upon graduation from my godfather."

Scott picked it up and studied it, saw that it was not running and tossed it on the table. "Five."

Wickham snatched it back. "Are you out of your mind?"

He shrugged and started counting the money before him, turning the pile into neat columns. Wickham eyed it enviously. "I'll sell it and return to win my money back."

"As you like. I think you should find a new source of income. Cards are not your talent. What happened to that widow you were entertaining?"

"Hmm? Oh, she found a husband." He rubbed his jaw and picked up a paper that was abandoned nearby. "I suppose a new widow would be easy to find." He ignored the war news and turned to the society page, and began searching the gossip for likely victims when a thought struck him. "Darcy."

"Who?"

Wickham looked up and folded the paper under his arm. "Nothing." He stood and lunging forward, knocked over the stacks of coins and disappeared in a second, leaving Scott standing and shaking his fist in his wake.

Chapter 17

"Do not slouch, Georgiana." Lady Matlock watched her niece with a critical eye. "It is an honour to be at the table with the adults, and you must behave as one."

"But I have always sat with Fitzwilliam at dinner." She pointed out.

"He wanted the company. When you are married, your children will eat separately until they are at least fifteen." She glanced at her son. "As Layton can support."

"Yes Cousin, I was relegated to the nursery for a long time, and once allowed to eat with my parents, I found myself wishing to return." He laughed and Georgiana giggled.

"How was your afternoon with Darcy and Miss Elizabeth?" Alicia asked.

"Oh, it was wonderful! Fitzwilliam is so happy! He smiled and laughed. Miss Elizabeth is so good for him." She saw that everyone was listening, and looked down. "He bought her a beautiful locket, and then gave the jeweller a curl of her hair to be made into a ring. He had cut more than was necessary, so he had the rest bound with a gold clip, and purchased a little box made of mother-of-pearl. He said it will fit nicely in the pocket for his watch fob." She sighed happily.

"Who knew that Darcy could be such a sentimental fool?" Layton laughed.

"I think that it is wonderful." Alicia said softly, causing her husband to turn his eyes to her.

"So you approve of the match now? I thought that you were in agreement that Miss Elizabeth is wholly unsuitable."

"If you look beyond her status, there is nothing that is wrong with her." She saw Lady Matlock's raised brows. "Oh, well yes she certainly requires refinement and a great deal of instruction for moving in society, but in essentials, she is a precisely what our cousin needs. No doubt she will quickly pick up what she needs to know, I understand that she is very quick witted. The important point is that our unhappy cousin is at last happy." She smiled to see Georgiana nod.

"I am surprised at you." Layton studied her. "I have never known you to tolerate anyone below our circle."

"No, that is you, Husband." She glanced at him. "I allow room for individual achievement without dismissing the entire population."

"So you are saying that if you had met Miss Elizabeth on her own, without her attachment to Darcy, you would have befriended her?" Lord Matlock asked with a small smile.

Alicia flushed. "No, I suppose not, I would have passed her over."

"So you are a hypocrite!" Layton said triumphantly.

She spoke coldly. "At least I am willing to accept a family member's choice. Audrey likes her and she has spent hours in her company. Do you not trust your own sister?"

"Audrey has stars in her eyes from what she perceives as love." Lady Matlock said quietly.

"Is it not love?" Georgiana asked. The table grew silent and each member contemplated their own marriage and thought of what Darcy had found.

"It may very well be." Lord Matlock said softly and looked at his wife. "Only time will tell." Clearing his throat he added, "I saw the notice in the paper about the engagement. I expect that we will be hearing from Catherine soon."

"Oh, that is right, well that should be interesting!" Layton rubbed his hands together. "I lay down odds she will arrive here within a week, breathing fire!"

"No doubt." Lord Matlock said slowly. "She may cause trouble."

"Darcy told her in no uncertain terms that marriage to Anne was not a possibility. Richard said that she was shocked and disappointed but seemed to accept that fact."

"But did Anne? She has heard that she was to marry her cousin since birth, and has had no opportunity to meet anyone else. She is a bit old to be entering the marriage fray as a novice now."

"I think that it is terrible that a woman be considered old at the age of three and twenty!" Georgiana cried. All eyes turned to her and she flushed and looked back at her plate.

"Have you ever thought that Anne was a little unbalanced?" Lady Matlock asked.

"No more so than her mother." Layton laughed.

"I often wondered if the reason that my sister kept her at Rosings had nothing to do with her delicate health." Lord Matlock chewed thoughtfully. "But then again, she is such a shadow of her mother; it is difficult to say what exactly the problem is there. Well at least Darcy is safe from her now."

"OH DEAR." Elizabeth folded Charlotte's letter and sighed.

"What is it Lizzy?" Mrs. Gardiner looked up from her sewing and smiled at her.

"Mama has been crowing about my engagement and Jane's courtship to the neighbourhood, claiming that it was all her doing. She has been speaking freely of Mr. Darcy's and Mr. Harwick's assets."

"That is not surprising; however in Jane's case it is very premature. Mr. Harwick has made no decision on their future. He is courting her."

Elizabeth nodded and sighed. "Mr. Darcy explained about the invitation to Papa." She thought of the emotional conversation they had in her uncle's study the day previous and closed her eyes for a moment before glancing again at the letter. "At last I am Mama's favourite, and all because of Mr. Darcy's ten thousand a year."

Mr. Gardiner cleared his throat. "That figure is not accurate."

She turned to him with surprise. "What do you mean?"

"Although it could be said that his income from Pemberley alone is that amount, he has many other investments and properties." He saw her confusion and continued. "Mr. Darcy felt that to expose his true income would actually make him an even greater target for women and parents conspiring to capture his attention. So he chooses to tell those who he does not completely trust that his income is not less than ten thousand."

"Not less . . . It is more?" Elizabeth asked with wide eyes.

"Significantly." He tilted his head and smiled. "Would you care to hear?"

"No." She said emphatically. "If there is reason to know he will tell me, but to hear of anything greater will likely frighten me further. As long as the roof over my head does not leak, I am content." Mr. Gardiner chuckled and she laughed.

"I do not believe that will be a problem, dear." He stood and kissed her forehead. "If you think about it, your mother feels the same about Longbourn, and the news of your engagement, as poorly displayed as it is and for as much as she has made you feel insignificant for all of your life, is a very important event for her. Try to keep that in mind."

"I do Uncle, but I also find it difficult to forget so many other things." She glanced out of the window and saw Jane and Mr. Harwick just entering the park, the nanny following with the two eldest children. "Jane was the one who was to save the family. I do hope that he will love her." Mr. and Mrs. Gardiner glanced at each other.

"Lizzy, will you come upstairs with me?" She set down her sewing and they walked up to the nursery, and sent the maid away. She picked up baby Paul and set him on a changing table, and cooed at him while he smiled and reached for her hair. "Lizzy, I have noticed that you and Mr. Darcy express affection for each other." Elizabeth blushed deeply, and Mrs. Gardiner smiled, still tickling her son. "I am not going to chastise you. You are engaged now, and although I would prefer that you follow the dictates of propriety and never kiss him or touch each other before marriage, I will allow reality its due."

"Thank you, Aunt." She whispered.

"Mr. Darcy is a passionate man, I would think, and like any passionate man, he undoubtedly looks forward to the marriage bed." Elizabeth's hands twisted together and she stared at the baby, watching Mrs. Gardiner untie the string around his waist to remove the wet napkin, and hang it on the screen of the unlit fireplace. She picked up a dried cloth, but paused. "Lizzy, when Mr. Darcy has embraced you, have you ever felt something hard pressing against you?" Elizabeth nodded, but said nothing. Mrs. Gardiner placed the napkin around her son and indicated his genitals. "This is what you felt. Of course, for a man it is significantly larger, and when he feels . . .desire, it will grow and become hard. This is what the marriage bed is about, Lizzy." She finished diapering the baby and returned him to his bed, then looked at her niece. "When in the Bible you read that a man knows a woman, it means that part of his body enters her. He will move within her and become increasingly excited until he spills his seed. The purpose of this is to create a baby." She smiled at Paul and back to her unusually silent niece. "Now I see that I have frightened you. Please ask your questions."

"Does it hurt?" She said quietly.

"No, it does not, perhaps the first time it will be uncomfortable, but Mr. Darcy deeply loves you, and I am certain he will try to make it as pleasant an experience as he can, and as you become accustomed to it and relax, you will find that it is very pleasurable. You see, it is not simply lying still and receiving him. Lovemaking is the most intimate way that you can share your feelings with Mr. Darcy, and he with you. It will be a way for you to celebrate the happiest moments in your life, as well as the means to provide comfort in the saddest. It is also simply the way that you will reaffirm your marriage vows on an ordinary day."

"Mama speaks to her friends of it being something to be avoided, and I have heard them laugh about closing their eyes and hoping that their husband would be done with their duty quickly and leave them."

"So you have heard something of this?" Mrs. Gardiner nodded. "I am not surprised that your mother did not curb the volume of her voice. Your uncle mentioned Lydia's behaviour. Well, keep in mind the nature of her marriage." She took Elizabeth's hand and they sat on the bed shared by the elder children. "When Mr. Darcy kisses you, what do you feel?"

"I never want it to end." She whispered. "If anything I . . .I feel that I wish to make him feel as wonderful as I do."

"That is because you love each other. You have nothing to fear, Lizzy. Your marriage bed will be a very happy place. I am so overjoyed for you, it is a rare thing to have a marriage such as you will experience." Mrs. Gardiner hugged her tightly. "I know that Mr. Darcy will care for you, just as your uncle has always cared for me." She held Elizabeth and they rocked together while she cried quietly. "You are relieved?"

"Yes." She sniffed and wiped her eyes. "May I talk with you about this again, when I am able to think clearly?"

Mrs. Gardiner laughed and saw Elizabeth's fear fading a little as she smiled. "Of course dear, anytime. Now, we are to visit Darcy House this afternoon, so I suggest that you wash your face and fix your hair. His coach will be here soon."

"How am I to face him after this conversation?" Elizabeth sighed and her aunt laughed. By the time she came downstairs; Jane and Harwick had returned and were talking to Mr. Gardiner. "Did you enjoy your stroll?" She asked cheerily.

Harwick smiled warmly to her and nodded. "Yes, walking with the children made me miss my girls a little less. I look forward to them being old enough to take such walks."

"Are they at your estate?" She took a seat nearby and glanced at Jane.

"Yes, there was no point in bringing them to town. My sister is looking after them right now, but she will be joining me here in a week or so."

"Your sister lives with you?" Jane asked curiously.

"Yes. Her husband died about three years ago. His estate obviously had to stay in the family, but she was left with a monetary settlement and the use of a home in London. However, she decided to live with us at first, and when my wife died, she was a great help with the children. Now that both of us have ended our mourning, she is considering remarrying and having her own family. She and her husband, Mr. Carter, had no children."

"She is young?" Mrs. Gardiner asked.

"Yes, well, not as young as you two ladies," he smiled at the sisters. "But she is five and twenty."

"May I ask how her husband died?"

"Ah, Miss Elizabeth, it is a not a tale that I like to relate. Let us say that Mr. Carter was rather adept at hiding his dissolute ways during their courtship and disappointed my sister and my parents when they emerged after the wedding. He is not regretted." He saw the wide eyes of the ladies and the curious tilt of Mr. Gardiner's head.

"I imagine that such an unhappy result will encourage great caution when she considers marriage again." Elizabeth said thoughtfully.

"As any person considering such a momentous decision should." Harwick smiled at her, then realized that she was thinking of him and her family. "Have you spoken to Mr. Darcy since your battle of wills the other night?"

The family laughed and Elizabeth blushed but met his slightly raised brow. "Yes, and it was amicably resolved, sir." She noticed a coach arriving and looked at her aunt as she stood. "And we are now to go visit him."

"Well, let us not keep Mr. Darcy waiting." Mrs. Gardiner laughed and followed Elizabeth to the doorway where they said their goodbyes. Harwick watched them boarding the coach with a small smile and turned back to see Jane watching him.

"I should take my leave as well, Miss Bennet. I have trespassed on your company for too long. I enjoyed our walk today, and I look forward to our evening at Vauxhall. I will come with Darcy tomorrow night." He rose and bowed to her and Mr. Gardiner.

"Let me see you to the door, sir." Jane walked ahead of him and watched as he put his hat on and adjusted his gloves. He smiled and bowed again, then departed. Jane watched him through the window and returned to the sitting room. "He did not stay very long."

"He was here two hours, Jane."

"Yes, I guess that he was. He is a very civil man." She sat down and looked at her hands. "This is difficult Uncle; it is not what I expected."

"What do you mean?"

"Marrying for duty and to save the family sounds very noble and romantic until you are faced with a stranger by your side." She stared at the empty sofa where she had watched Darcy and Elizabeth smiling at each other, then shaking her head looked back to her uncle. "But this is what I was raised to do." Mr. Gardiner smiled at her and she straightened her shoulders. "I did not know he has a sister living with him. I wonder what she is like."

"You will meet her soon, it seems. And I am certain that you will get along very well, he certainly seems to think so." He said encouragingly.

"How do you know?" She asked worriedly.

"Because he would not continue with you otherwise." Mr. Gardiner winked and went back to his paper. Jane picked up her sewing and lost herself in thought.

"LOUISA!" Bingley called to his sister when she passed the study door. "May I have a word with you?"

"What is it, Charles?" She came in and followed his silent request to close the door. "Do you have a secret?"

"Well not exactly. How is Caroline doing in her search for a husband?"

Louisa snorted and held up her hand. "Forgive me. It goes poorly. She just is not trying. She has it in her head that you will somehow convince Mr. Darcy that she is the best choice for his wife." Bingley groaned. "I played along at first because frankly it was amusing, but I know as well as you that he would never marry her. He has no reason to take a woman of our status. Her dowry is nothing to what he could easily find with a woman of the first circles. Only love would make him so blind, and clearly he avoids her company so that is not likely."

"No, not at all." Bingley sighed and handed her the morning's *Times*. He pointed to the particular notice and Louisa gasped then started laughing. "This is amusing?"

"I should think so! Caroline wasted this entire season conspiring to be with Mr. Darcy, and here he found an heiress to marry right under her nose." She handed back the paper. "Do you know her?"

"Yes I do, and you have met her as well, do you not remember her from that ball at the beginning of the Season?"

"That daughter of a gentleman from Hertfordshire? With the small estate?" Louisa sat forward in her astonishment.

"She is a delightful girl. Beautiful, engaging, a delight in every way, he is a very lucky man."

"Charles, if I am not mistaken, I would say that you are in love with her yourself, but then you do have a habit of loving every pretty face that walks by." To her surprise Bingley flushed as she spoke. "Do you care for her?"

"No, we are friends!" He glared.

"Does Mr. Darcy agree? You cannot risk losing your friendship with him."

"Louisa enough. Darcy is deeply in love with her, and she with him. Now then, what do we do with Caroline?" He took the engagement announcement and set it aside.

She sighed and shrugged. "Nothing. She will scream and gnash her teeth like the spoiled child she is, but in the end she is meaningless to him. We simply have to convince her that it was never to be and point her in some other man's direction."

Somewhere in the house a screech rent the air. "I think that she knows." Bingley said softly. Louisa heard the pounding of feet in the hallway and stood wearily. "You go and speak to her, and I will attempt to think of a man who would want her. Maybe Hurst . . .?"

"You know that he sleeps to avoid her." Louisa smiled. "He will be so glad to marry her off."

"Then he is not alone in motivation." Bingley raised his brows and watched her go, then looked at the paper again and began to laugh. "You played matchmaker for Darcy and Miss Elizabeth, and were a great success. Now, let us see what you can do with your sister."

DARCY WAS WAITING AT THE DOOR when the coach pulled up to his home. He strode out and handed down Mrs. Gardiner, then smiled warmly at Elizabeth as she stepped to the curb, kissed her hand and tucked it onto his arm. "It is so good to see you come home." He whispered before he greeted them formally. "I am sorry that I did not escort you myself, but my aunt decided to join the tour and arrived just as the coach was ready to depart." He smiled at Elizabeth and noticed that she could not meet his eye. "Dearest?" He whispered.

"I am just nervous about the house." She smiled a little and looked down at his arm.

"There is nothing to fear, trust me. You have already seen the principal rooms; this is simply your opportunity to decide on how you will redecorate your private rooms. Mrs. Mercer is the one in charge." They entered the hallway and he turned to study her face. "What is wrong?"

"Nothing that I can speak about here." She whispered, and his brow creased.

"Ah, there you are." Lady Matlock appeared and looked expectantly at Darcy. "I will conduct the tour, it would be improper for you to see Miss Elizabeth in the mistress's chambers."

Darcy gaped at her in disbelief. "Aunt, I am in your company, surely it will not be inappropriate!"

"We ladies have things to discuss." Lady Matlock nodded at the women and started up the stairs. "We will return before too long, Nephew." Darcy was left standing on the landing, staring up at Elizabeth's retreating form and crestfallen, walked away to his study.

"I do not believe that Mr. Darcy was pleased with your plan, my lady." Mrs. Gardiner smiled.

"Of course not, he has been imagining Miss Elizabeth within these rooms for quite some time." She opened the door to the Mistress's chambers and entered. "I think that it will do him some good to keep on imagining." She smiled and closed the door behind them and noticed Elizabeth's wide eyes and frightened expression. "Well, this is obviously the bedchamber. My sister decorated it upon her marriage, but it has not been changed in six and twenty years, so it is certainly time that it was." She opened a door to show the empty dressing room and another to show the bath. Leading on she indicated a door that opened to the nursery. "Of course you will have a wet nurse so it will not be necessary to have the baby in here; this is a relic of a different time." Elizabeth glanced at Mrs. Gardiner who had raised her brows with hearing Lady Matlock's presumption. The woman walked back across the room and touched another door. "This leads to your private sitting room, and this," she opened one more door, "leads directly to Darcy's bedchamber." She stood aside and looked at Elizabeth expectantly.

Cautiously stepping forward, she peeked in, glimpsed the enormous canopied bed and deep burgundy velvet curtains that surrounded it, and backed out quickly. Lady Matlock proceeded in a businesslike manner. "Now then, I do not know the arrangements that your parents adhered to in your home estate, but marriages in our circle are conducted in an expected fashion. You have your bedchamber, and your husband has his. You will, of course, be expected to accommodate him at his pleasure as is his right by law. He will avoid you during your monthly courses, on Sundays and other church days, and naturally when you are ill and with child. It is disrespectful to claim a false physical ailment to discourage his company." She walked over to the bed and waved her arm. "He will, because he is considerate, come to your chamber. He will knock and enter and join you in the bed. He will raise your night gown and then raise his, unite with you for however long is necessary, thank you for the pleasure, and of course, depart for his rooms. My nephew seems fond of you, so he may wish to kiss you and touch you before he does his duty, but he just as likely may not. He will make faces and grunt as he moves. Do not be alarmed, he is not in pain. I suggest that you keep a linen towel nearby to clean yourself afterwards." She paused for a few moments as she thought then her eyes opened. "Oh, and early in your marriage he may wish to stay with you for convenience sake because he will wish to repeat the act several times before retiring. This will wane with time. Of course you will be willing and compliant with each coupling; the goal is to provide Pemberley with its heir. Do you have any questions?"

Elizabeth stared in horror at Lady Matlock then turned to Mrs. Gardiner who was shaking her head with closed eyes. "I . . . You did not indicate what I am to do . . . when he comes to me."

"Do? Nothing, you lie still." Lady Matlock replied and saw that Elizabeth was close to tears. "Now, now, my dear, this is what we women are made for."

"This is not what you told me, Aunt!" Elizabeth cried.

"No, it is not. And while there may be grains of similarities in our tales, I firmly believe that Mr. Darcy loves you deeply and will not wish to treat you with such indifference. As I told you at home, your mother's experience clouded what you heard her say, just as Lady Matlock's experience affects hers. I think that you and Mr. Darcy will have what I do with your uncle. What do you think?" She took her hand and smiled. Elizabeth looked from one woman to the other and putting her hand to her mouth, ran from the room.

Lady Matlock sank onto the bed. "I frightened her."

Mrs. Gardiner turned and glared at her. "You certainly did. I wish I had known your purpose; I would have made sure that Mr. Darcy came with us. How dare you presume to teach this lesson to my niece? This is my place, not yours! I am thankful that I spoke to her first, and can only hope that my lessons are the ones that she remembers. Is your marriage so cold?" The Lady stared at Mrs. Gardiner for her audacity then sighed.

"No, but my daughter's is, I gave her the speech that you must have delivered to Elizabeth earlier, and she was so terribly hurt when her wedding night was as I just described. I thought it would be better to prepare Elizabeth for the possibility, rather than live with the disappointment."

"Surely you cannot believe that Mr. Darcy would do anything but love her in the kindest way? Have you not seen them together? The man is besotted!"

"MR. DARCY, MR. WICKHAM IS HERE TO SEE YOU."

Darcy looked up from where he sat staring at his hands. "Wickham? Did he state his business?"

"No sir." Foster said tonelessly. "Shall I tell him you are unavailable?"

"No, send him in." Darcy sat back down and glanced at his father's portrait, then turned his eyes back to the doorway.

"Darcy!" Wickham came in amiably and offered his hand, which was ignored. He took a seat and smiled. "You look well. The past years have agreed with you."

"What do you want, Wickham?"

"What, no inquiry after my health?"

"You appear to be breathing. What do you want?"

"I thought that I would pay a call on my old friend, is that so wrong?" He grinned and crossed his legs, then looked around the room. "Ah, I missed this room, I have not seen the like anywhere, except perhaps at Pemberley. I see that you have not changed a thing, why I could imagine your father stepping through . . ."

Darcy sat forward. "State your purpose or be gone."

Wickham laughed uncomfortably seeing that Darcy was not going to play along. "Well . . . I suppose that your time is valuable so I will get to the point." He cleared his throat. "As you know I have been studying the law . . ."

"No, I do not know that, I would not be surprised to learn that you have spent the last two years as you have every other year of your adult life, drunk, dissolute, and let me guess, now destitute?" He spoke softly, "Tell me Wickham, have you run through my father's money and now come to me begging for more?"

Wickham's charm disappeared. "You know that I did not get what I deserved, Darcy! That living was worth far more than three thousand!"

"You had four. You have no estate, no dependants, there is no reason for you to have gone through that sum in two years unless you wasted it on gambling and whores. I doubt that you set foot in a classroom since you left Pemberley."

"I want five thousand more." Wickham declared.

Darcy's voice remained steady and cold beneath his growing fury. "And I want my parents alive by my side. Unfortunately we cannot always get what we want."

Wickham's mouth opened to reply when Elizabeth appeared at the door. "Fitzwilliam, I . . ." She saw Wickham and blushed. "Forgive me Mr. Darcy; I did not know that you were entertaining." She saw the anger in Darcy's eyes just as he saw the distress in hers. He stood immediately and strode across the room.

"It is fine, he was just leaving." Darcy took her arm and led her into the hallway and whispered as they entered the music room. "Please wait here, Elizabeth. You should not be in this man's presence." He returned to the study. "Put that down, Wickham." He snarled. "And stand up. You are leaving now."

"Who was that? It was rude not to introduce me." Wickham replaced the silver letter opener on the desk. "She seemed to be quite familiar with you . . .Fitzwilliam." He smirked.

"Do not presume to lecture me on behaviour. Get out, Wickham. I told you never to come near me, my homes, or my family again. You signed the agreement; you have no business with me." Two burley footmen appeared silently. Foster hovered in the background.

Wickham noticed the reinforcements and stood up to bow. He walked past Darcy then paused and murmured, "She is beautiful, Darcy. Send word when you are through. I do not mind sharing." Darcy grabbed him and threw him into the arms of his men. They hustled him out and onto the street. His hat was thrown at his feet. Darcy stood in the hallway attempting to regain control, and Elizabeth appeared from where she had been listening with her hand to her mouth.

She flew to his side. "Fitzwilliam, who was that? Are you well?" Darcy looked down into her worried eyes and kissed her hand.

"I am fine, dearest. He is an old thorn in my side who came back to demand more blood."

"I do not understand." Elizabeth reached up to caress his face.

"Elizabeth . . ." He took her hand and pulled her into the study, closing the door behind them. He held her face and searched her eyes. "What is wrong? You were crying when you came to me."

She held his face the same way. "Who was he?"

"Nobody. Dearest what happened? You were distressed when you arrived and now you are in tears. Did something happen upstairs?"

"I am well now; please tell me what that man . . ." Her questions were silenced with Darcy's kiss. He drew away and was gratified to find her eyes closed, and her face relaxed. Gently caressing her cheek with the back of his fingers he tenderly kissed her again, then moulded her body to his, nestling his mouth against her ear.

"Tell me what is wrong, my love." His lips touched her throat and he rested his cheek in her hair, unconsciously swaying as they stood embraced. It was exactly the reassurance she needed, and she gave in to his desire to help her first.

"My aunt . . . spoke to me of . . . marriage today." She whispered. Darcy's eyes opened and he drew an unsteady breath. "She told me what will happen between us and . . . how."

"How?" He said shakily. "What do you mean?" In response, Elizabeth shyly pressed herself against his body and he sighed when he understood. "Oh my love." His lips found hers again. "Did it frighten you?"

"No . . .Yes . . . I . . .I was embarrassed, but her assurance that it was something to be shared and enjoyed for both of us made me . . .made my thoughts wander in unseemly ways." She opened her eyes when she heard his delighted chuckle. "Fitzwilliam!"

"Forgive me my love, I was only imagining what you might have imagined, and I am eternally grateful for your aunt's preparation. Her vision of our marriage is the same as mine." He kissed her gently on her brow, then her jaw, and back to her lips. "But that does not explain why you arrived here in tears."

"Your aunt also decided to speak to me of the marriage bed." She hid her face back against his chest. "It was all about submission and duty." She looked up when he swore under his breath, "You will come to me, take your pleasure, and leave."

"No, I will not." Suddenly he let her go then taking her hand, opened the study door, quickly moved into the hallway and started up the stairs. "Come."

"Where are we going?"

"To show you OUR rooms." He walked determinedly and came to the door to the mistress' chambers. Inside he found the two aunts. "Ladies, please leave us."

"Darcy, you know that we cannot do that!" Lady Matlock cried.

"I need to undo the damage that you have wrought, Aunt. Submit to me? Who are you to know my mind or my marriage?" He growled. "We will be along soon enough. Please leave us."

"Five minutes, Mr. Darcy." Mrs. Gardiner said softly and met his eye. He nodded and the women departed. Mrs. Gardiner squeezed Elizabeth's free hand as she walked past.

Darcy turned to her after shutting the door. "Now then, I will show you these rooms as I intended. This is your dressing room, which will very soon be filled with the most-envied gowns in all of London." He took her to the bath and pointed at the tub. "This is where you will soak in scented water, and enjoy the finest soaps and wrap yourself in silk robes." Feeling the time passing, he pulled her from the room and hurried her along with him to enter the sitting room, and touched a beautifully bound book and set of pens, a silver box containing a bottle of ink alongside it. "This is where you can record your thoughts in this journal that waits for your memories to fill its pages." Elizabeth looked up to smile at him and laughed as he pulled her out and across to the nursery. "This is the place where our child will sleep." At last his frenzied tour stopped. He stepped behind her and wrapped his arms around her waist, resting his hands over her womb. "Someday." He whispered in her ear. They stood silently looking at the empty room for a few moments while his lips gently caressed her throat, then found her mouth when she looked up and back to him and whispered, "Someday."

Breathing heavily he took her hand and slowly led her from her chambers and into his. He again stood behind her, and embraced her waist, placing his hands over hers as they looked over the vast empty bed. Feeling her tremble, he kissed her hair and closing his eyes, nudged some tendrils away from her ear. Tenderly he suckled her soft lobe and he spoke huskily, sending frissons of desire through her body. "And this, my love, my Elizabeth, is where I wish to sleep with you in my arms, every night for the rest of my life." He turned her around, again holding her face in his hands and looked into her eyes as his mouth hovered over hers. "If you wish."

"Oh yes, Fitzwilliam, I do."

Elizabeth opened her arms and he gratefully fell into them while simultaneously encasing her body in his embrace. They kissed slowly and he groaned when her hands ran down his back. "Elizabeth . . ." His kiss instantly grew deeper and his hands just started to move down her shoulders when a loud insistent knock sounded from the mistress's chambers. Startled he jumped, then swallowing hard; he gazed at her. "You cannot know how beautiful you are, or how dearly I want our wedding day to come. Please Elizabeth, do not fear me. I cannot bear it."

"I will not." She kissed him lovingly and touched his mouth. "Thank you for your reassurance."

"I am sorry that it was needed." He stepped away and lifted her hand to his lips. Elizabeth's gaze moved to his breeches and her hand went to her mouth as she gasped. Darcy looked down then back to her face. She met his eyes and understood the desire that she saw there. He smiled slightly and kissed her. "Go to your aunts, dearest. I will be along soon, when I am presentable again."

Elizabeth nodded and could not help but steal another look at the prominent display. She bit her lip and startled when she heard his soft chuckle. He kissed her hand then placed it over the arousal, letting her feel the length and hardness, then hearing another knock, kissed his stunned bride and sent her from the room.

"Lizzy?" Mrs. Gardiner asked when she opened the door. "Are you well?"

"Oh, oh, yes Aunt. Mr. Darcy made his . . .wishes for . . .everything quite clear." She drew a deep breath and glanced back in the room, the feel of his desire was very clearly impressed on her mind. The older women exchanged glances and Mrs. Gardiner took Elizabeth's hand.

"Come my dear, we shall await Mr. Darcy downstairs."

Lady Matlock led the way through the house and by the time they arrived in a sitting room, Elizabeth had regained her equilibrium. "I . . . I seem to have had an unexpectedly thorough education today." She said quietly and the ladies laughed. "Well, it is probably far more than most girls receive!"

"I have no doubt of that, Miss Elizabeth." Lady Matlock sighed. "Please accept my apology for frightening you so. I did not mean any harm, and I am delighted to see my nephew's response, although I question his method of reassuring you."

"Why would you do that? Surely his method should affirm exactly how he intends to conduct his marriage. If it were a heartless coupling he would have dismissed Elizabeth's fears out of hand and called for tea." Mrs. Gardiner raised her brows and Lady Matlock raised hers.

"Well, perhaps he would not be quite that dismissive, but I see your point." She smiled. "I am happy for you, dear. This is rare in our world."

"Yes, and Lizzy, when and if the time comes for Jane, leave me to do the talking. If she does marry Mr. Harwick, it will be much more like the description that you heard from Lady Matlock than the one you heard from me."

"Oh how sad!" She cried. "But he is such a kind man!"

"He is, very kind, and I do not see him harming her, but I also do not see him loving her."

"Harwick? Jeffery Harwick? His wife died in childbirth?" Lady Matlock asked. "Oh, yes, that was a great love affair. He looked upon her with the same adoration that Darcy has for you, my dear." She smiled with the memory. "I remember how they danced together at our home several times, the tongues of the room wagged with gossip. He was devastated when he lost her. Yes, my husband said that he is courting your sister. It can never be a love match for him again, I am sure."

"He has made it clear that he needs an heir and that is his purpose in remarrying." Mrs. Gardiner explained.

"Mmm, so he does. It will be a very advantageous match. It is a very good family, although there is a great deal of tragedy. His sister's marriage was a disaster. They were hoodwinked into accepting a man who enjoyed his gambling and cards a great deal. One evening he did not come home, and the next morning his body was found in Hyde Park, the result of a drunken duel. We never heard the exact detail of how it came to be. The man who shot him naturally fled the country to avoid prosecution. Mr. Harwick senior had died just after her wedding so at least he never witnessed this sadness. She is a good girl though." She mused thoughtfully. "I understand there is a plan afoot to bring your father to town?"

Darcy's voice answered her as he joined them, taking a seat next to Elizabeth and smiling at her suddenly blushing face. "Yes, we intend to show him precisely what his daughters will receive as our wives, and thought that an introduction to Uncle would not hurt."

"Ah, scare the breeches off of him with a peer?" Lady Matlock smiled. "You are wicked, Darcy."

"I am prudent, Aunt." He smiled and tilted his head to Elizabeth. "And you agreed, Elizabeth."

She startled when he addressed her so informally then smiled warmly. "Yes, Fitzwilliam, I believe that it will do him a great deal of good."

Lady Matlock looked between the two and glanced at Mrs. Gardiner's raised brows before returning her gaze to Darcy. "Perhaps we can have a family dinner one night at Matlock House?"

"I would not wish to put you out."

"You have no hostess yet." He immediately took Elizabeth's hand and kissed it. "No, I will be glad to host it. It can be the Bennets, Gardiners, Harwick and the houses of Matlock, and Singleton." Lady Matlock nodded. "Richard will undoubtedly welcome a good meal, so we can bring him home for the evening, and you, Miss Elizabeth, will help me to do all of the planning, from the menus to the flowers. This will be an excellent opportunity to expand your education."

"Oh, thank you, I . . . I hope to learn a great deal." She felt Darcy squeeze her hand and smiled playfully. "And I hope that I will learn your favourite dishes to include in the menu."

"You sound like your mother."

"Does that frighten you?"

"It does." He laughed to see her brows rise in mock indignation.

"Just wait until I begin having fits of nerves!" Elizabeth threatened him and he groaned.

"What else do I have to look forward to?"

"Hmm, perhaps I should leave that as a surprise." Elizabeth's eyes sparkled and he drew a long breath while he smiled.

"I believe that we have been forgotten." Mrs. Gardiner said to Lady Matlock.

"I am delighted to see it." She then cleared her throat. "Now then Miss Elizabeth, we shall discuss redecorating your rooms and walk through the house making note of other changes that are necessary. I am afraid that my brother rather neglected things after my sister's death, and Darcy has not really had the time or interest to address decorations." She looked at her nephew. "I am certain that you have work to do?"

His eyes narrowed as his aunt presumed to take charge again. "Yes, it is walking with Elizabeth."

"Do you really wish to talk about fabrics and wallpaper?" Her eyebrow lifted in amusement. "Even if it is in our company?"

Elizabeth saw his hesitation and laughed. "It is fine, Fitzwilliam, I will find you when we finish." He nodded and they all stood. She took his hand in hers and while the aunts spoke she whispered up to him. "And my dear love, I have not forgotten your unhappiness when I came into your study. I have learned that you will tell me in your good time, and when the moment is right. Am I correct?"

Darcy's face reflected his surprise then changed to a warm smile. "Yes, my love, you are correct. It seems that we are beginning to know each other well." He brushed her forehead with his lips, and laid his cheek on her hair for a slight embrace, looked down at their entwined fingers for a moment, then let go.

As he walked from the room, he heard Elizabeth's voice suggesting a little loudly, "Now then I have always been fond of a particular shade of orange . . ." He groaned loud enough for her to hear and was rewarded with her answering giggle. Smilingly, he continued on his way.

"THIS CANNOT BE!" Lady Catherine read the letter through for the fourth time. "It cannot be true! He was serious?"

"What is it Mama?" Anne looked up from the cloth she was sewing.

"Darcy writes that he is engaged to be married!" She dropped the letter and found Anne staring at her.

"He is engaged? To whom? He is promised to me!" Anne stood and picked the letter up from the floor to read Darcy's words. "You told me he would come around!" A note of hysteria began to creep into her voice. Lady Catherine sent a sharp look to Mrs. Jenkinson who hurriedly ran to a sideboard and returned with a glass, stirring a liquid with a spoon.

"Take your medicine, Anne. You heard the physician, it must be taken regularly."

"I do not want my medicine!! I want Darcy! You promised me!!" She clutched the letter and waved it in the air.

"TAKE YOUR ELIXIR!" Lady Catherine demanded. Anne shrunk down and swallowed the liquid. Within minutes she transformed back into her colourless, passive persona. Her mother sighed and looked at her companion. "I expect you to administer this on time Jenkinson or you will find a new situation, do you hear me?"

"Yes, madam." The nervous woman said, and replacing the glass on the side board, took a seat next to her silent charge.

A man's throat cleared. "Pardon me, madam, Mr. Collins has arrived."

Lady Catherine looked around the room, picked up the fallen letter, saw that her daughter was staring at her hands then turned to the butler. "Send him in."

Her prospective pastor bobbed his way into the room. "Ah, Lady Catherine, Miss de Bourgh, what a delight to see you this beautiful day!"

"What brings you to visit, Mr. Collins?" She said icily and shot a glance at Anne, who was blinking slowly.

"I received some wonderful, unexpected news!" He beamed and bounced. "I have been identified as the heir to an estate, well after my father passes that is, it is called Longbourn and is located in Hertfordshire . . ."

Chapter 18

"Come along Darcy pay up, it will be an expensive evening so you may as well keep your purse at hand." Singleton laughed as Darcy provided the admission fee for the party of six.

"You are not destitute, Cousin, I suspect you can buy us dinner."

"He will need a king's ransom for that, I am afraid." Harwick laughed. "The prices are criminal, but it is our fault for not bringing a picnic."

"I hear that the ham is sliced so thinly you can read through it!" Elizabeth said excitedly as she clutched Darcy's arm and looked around her with wide eyes. "Look at all of the people!"

"It is fairly sparse tonight." Audrey observed.

"Sparse?" Jane asked in disbelief.

"Oh yes, we nearly lost Laura Stewart one time." She smiled at Elizabeth, "Lord Moreland's youngest daughter? They are frequent visitors at Matlock. I remember so well playing with her brother, Daniel." She bit her lip and looked away for a moment. Elizabeth startled when she heard the name then studied Audrey's blush, and could not help but wonder if her Mr. Stewart was Audrey's denied love. She recovered and continued, "You will have to meet her, she is just come of age and I think that you two would get along famously. When we all came for the masked ball there were over sixteen thousand people here!" Audrey laughed to see their mouths fall open and then glanced at Darcy whose face was the picture of discomfort. "Come Cousin, relax; this is where everyone comes to play!"

"Well, I have not been amongst them." He said stiffly. Elizabeth looked up and saw his face become expressionless except for his eyes, which registered contempt for everything he observed. "Everyone indeed."

"Come along; let us try the Grand Walk." Singleton called. "Even you cannot protest this avenue amongst the elms Darcy, it is the place to see and be seen." The group stepped onto the gravelled path, and joined the fashionable crowd as they paraded towards the Grove.

Elizabeth was doing her best to imitate the behaviour of the well-dressed women around her, and Darcy's quiet stateliness certainly helped her to maintain her dignity when everything inside of her wished to run and gawk at the wonders that she saw. She glanced up to his stone-like countenance and hearing the sounds of an orchestra ahead, softly began humming the tune. She felt his arm relax a little and looked back up to see his eyes were fixed on her face. "Ah, there you are, Mr. Darcy. I was afraid that you had taken leave of me tonight."

He managed a little smile. "What do you mean, I am right here. Why are you humming?"

"Because I thought that it would embarrass you if I sang." She smiled and started humming again.

"But why sing at all? I love your voice, but I would prefer to hear your thoughts of this place. I have avoided it because I have heard stories from others that did not appeal to me. I would like to hear the judgement of someone so innocent."

Elizabeth blushed and then tilted her head to study him. "I was under the impression that you disapproved."

"No, I am very uncomfortable; I suppose that comes across as haughtiness." He heard his name and he nodded to some passerby, then looked back to her. "I am on display, and you are the object of speculation."

"Why?" She gasped.

"These people are very fond of the society pages, Elizabeth. Our engagement is ripe for gossip. Everyone knows of you, and after the ball at Matlock, I know that our behaviour was discussed." She flushed and looked away. "Dearest, do not be embarrassed, by the end of the evening the speculation was of our attachment, not your origins. It was jealousy that fuelled much of the talk. Everyone wonders what on earth you did to capture me." He smiled when she peeked back up at him and he saw a smile spreading over her face, and then she laughed. "Ah and that sound *is* what captured me, I dreamed of a laughing girl named Lizzy until I finally learned your name." Darcy kissed her hand and put it back on his arm.

"That is the first time you have called me Lizzy." She said as she dealt with the feelings his kiss and confession inspired.

"No dearest, it must be the millionth time I have spoken that name." Drawing a deep breath, he looked quickly about. He heard of the paths that existed in this garden meant for young couples to escape their chaperones, and returned to find her gazing at him, "What are you thinking?"

"Do you know how many times I whispered Fitzwilliam Darcy? And talked to you? So many conversations I had with this phantom man. I conjured so many things. I admit that I almost feared meeting you to have all of my imaginings disappear like smoke."

"And have I lived up to the dream, my love?" he asked hopefully and felt his heart sink when she shook her head.

"No, you have surpassed it."

"If I do not kiss you this instant I will surely die." He gripped her hand on his arm and leaned forward towards her mouth.

"Darcy!" Singleton called and started laughing. "I see that you truly do need a chaperone!" He looked at Harwick for his approval and instead saw a deep frown. "I was just having some fun."

"I am sorry that you derive enjoyment at the expense of others." Harwick said coldly. Audrey glanced at him and smiled with a slight nod. Harwick raised his brows and then nodded to her in understanding. He saw her shoulders square as she looked forward and walked on her husband's arm, then he looked down at Jane. "Are you enjoying the evening, Miss Bennet?"

"Oh yes, I am afraid that the atmosphere is quite beyond anything I have ever experienced before. Travelling performers do come through the county, but I have not seen anything such as this." She smiled at him and he nodded, smiling in return.

"Then I am glad that you are happy here."

"Have you come frequently?"

"I did, Ellen . . . forgive me, Mrs. Harwick was fond of the music and exhibitions." He looked off in the distance to blink hard, then dropped his gaze to rest on Elizabeth who was looking raptly at a tightrope walker and laughing as Darcy bent to say something to her. She turned to smile at him and clearly blushed when he spoke again. Harwick took a breath and looked back to the ground, then noticed Jane's silence. She was staring at her sister as well. "Miss Elizabeth will undoubtedly demand that Darcy bring her back, despite his reticence."

"Yes. She should be careful of her behaviour, everyone is looking at her."

"She is behaving no differently than the other visitors, Miss Bennet. This is a place for frivolity; there is no shame in enjoying a laugh. I notice that you are fond of smiling."

Jane blushed. "I smile where my sister laughs; it has always been that way."

"There are great variations among siblings, Miss Bennet. It does not make one better than another, only different." He gave her a small smile and looked back to Elizabeth and his smile grew wider. Jane looked from him to her sister who was gesturing ahead to the Rotunda and was speaking animatedly to Audrey about the wonders within. The two women laughed together and Darcy was shaking his head, being stuck in the middle of the conversation while Singleton stared off to the side, seeing who was passing by and tilting his head to Darcy and exchanging knowing winks with the curious onlookers.

Darcy heard his name called and was forced to stop, his smile disappeared and his body stiffened when introducing Elizabeth to a group of six people. She performed perfectly, as Lady Matlock and Audrey had worked with her for just such a possibility. They moved on and she smiled as she felt him relax. "See, it was not so very bad."

"Please do not laugh at me." He said softly.

"I was not, dear."

"Forgive me, you were wonderful and I should have said so immediately." He smiled to see her look to the ground. "I think that we both are shy about some things."

She squeezed his arm, then cried out when suddenly the pathways were ablaze with light as thousands of lanterns hanging from the trees all lit simultaneously. "Oh my!" She turned to see Jane's mouth open and even Darcy looking around with wonder. "That was spectacular!"

"I have never seen the like." He laughed. "I have seen well lit gardens, but this was as if some magician waved his wand over the park and the sun appeared!" Darcy looked down to see Elizabeth's face. "Oh darling, your eyes are sparkling like a thousand stars."

"And your smile takes my breath away." She whispered.

"Darcy! Imagine my surprise to see you here. You hate such places." Darcy's head snapped up and instantly his eyes narrowed. "Will you not introduce me to your . . .well, this must be your betrothed. I read the notice in the papers." Bowing low he raked his eyes over Elizabeth then back up again to smile with appreciation. "Just lovely, but of course Darcy, you only prefer the best." He leaned close to Elizabeth and whispered loudly and winked. "I should know; I shared rooms with him for years."

Elizabeth felt great discomfort with this strange yet familiar man, and confusion with the implications of his words. She felt the tension in Darcy's arm and saw that his face was red with anger. "Wickham, I believe that I told you to stay away from my family."

"But she is not family yet, is she?" He bowed again. "Well clearly Darcy has forgotten his manners. I am George Wickham, and I presume that you are Miss Bennet? You do not remember me? I was visiting Darcy House when you were there recently. I do hope that you have recovered from your upset?"

Elizabeth nodded coldly. "I do remember you, sir. And as I recall, manners were being taught to you at the time."

"Ouch, feisty!" He laughed then looked back at Darcy. "I hope that you have rethought our discussion?"

"Why would I do that?"

Wickham shrugged. "I do not know, I could let the news slip about your previous engagement to Miss de Bourgh?" He saw Elizabeth's eyes widen. "Oh, did I say that?"

"Wickham, whatever your game is, drop it. Attempting to disconcert Miss Elizabeth is a waste of time. Leave us alone." He growled in a dangerously low voice. Wickham smiled and bowed as he moved aside.

"Singleton!" Wickham held out his hand. "It has been months, how is your play, man?"

Audrey looked at her husband who was greeting this man like a long-lost brother and back to Darcy whose barely repressed anger was clear. Harwick stepped forward and spoke in Darcy's ear. "You obviously have an unpleasant history with this man. Why do you not take another path and I will remain to look after Mrs. Singleton. We can meet up in the Grove?"

"Thank you Harwick, that is tempting, but I will not allow a pandering profligate to ruin my evening." Darcy said softly. Harwick's brow rose and he looked at Wickham with new eyes. Darcy cleared his throat. "Singleton. I did not know that you had met Wickham."

"Ah yes, we have played many games together!" Singleton chortled and Wickham winked knowingly.

"I am surprised that you made an exception to your rules for him, given your disdain for my friend Bingley."

"What do you mean? Bingley is new money from trade."

"And Wickham is the son of my father's steward. Which man is more worthy of your company now?" Darcy looked at him inquiringly as Singleton startled and turned to Wickham.

"You are what?"

"I see other friends, good evening." Wickham ran off into the crowd and Singleton gaped first at his cousin then his wife, who looked at him with disgust.

"What games do you play with this man, Mr. Singleton? Is this the company you keep instead of coming home?" She said coldly.

"It is none of your concern." He said in a low tone. "You are making a scene."

"What has happened to you? I once respected you . . .and now . . . ."

"Forgive me Audrey; you know that I am trying to do better." He said softly, and placed his hand over hers. Audrey sighed and looked down at the ground. Jane watched the couple, knowing that there was a disagreement but not hearing the words. Harwick shook his head.

"What a fool, she is a good woman and he throws it away."

"Oh, I am sure that all will be well. He seemed to be good friends with Mr. Wickham." Jane smiled and Harwick's brow creased. "Mr. Darcy was a friend as well."

"Did you not hear, or at least see Mr. Darcy's anger?"

"I imagine that Mr. Darcy was just playacting with him, after all, his friend interrupted his behaviour with my sister." She looked at Elizabeth who was holding Darcy's hand and listening intently as he spoke earnestly to her. "I notice that you were watching them."

Harwick took a good look at Jane, and saw what could only be described as envy. He wondered if she would be satisfied with the marriage he might offer. He felt no stirrings of passion for her, if anything, walking with her was pleasant but no more pleasant than walking with his sister's hand on his arm. Returning his attention to the Singletons, he noticed that he was paying her closer attention now, and she seemed to be resigned to accept it as his apology. *Is this the cold marriage that I will have with Miss Bennet? I would not be out at night like Singleton, but there will certainly not be love.*

"Fitzwilliam please tell me who that man is."

"This is not where I wished to have this conversation, Elizabeth."

"I assure you that I have no wish to conduct it here either, but I will not be put off any longer. I cannot bear to allow my imagination to wander any farther than it already has. Who is this man? What does the son of your steward hold over you? And what of this engagement and . . ."

"His other implications?" Darcy sighed and recognized so many conflicting emotions registering in her eyes. "You are so young to hear of these things."

Her eyes flashed at him. "If I am old enough to marry, I am old enough to . . . oh Fitzwilliam, please relieve my fears!"

"Dearest . . ." He looked around and bent his head as close to her as he could, placed his hand over hers and held it tightly. "First . . .Wickham was a favourite of my father's, he is charming, very charming, and my father after Mother's death was very susceptible to it. He also felt an obligation to . . .educate a good servant's child. He sent him to university with me and we roomed together. He was a drunk, a gambler and often I found . . .visitors of questionable worth in our rooms." Darcy looked at her intently to see if she understood.

Elizabeth studied his eyes, trying to appreciate his implicit explanation, and she gasped when she took his meaning. "Women?" He nodded. "Did . . .did you?"

"No dearest, never." He sighed and closed his eyes. "He was disciplined on campus, but it did not stop him from roaming the countryside. I . . .often paid his debts of honour because he was considered my father's ward. It was an error, I should have exposed him. Well, when my father died, he left him a bequest and a living, he agreed to accept four thousand pounds immediately in its stead."

"But . . .that is nearly half of your yearly income!" She cried.

Darcy could not help but smile at her reaction, and lifted her hand to his lips. "It upset me as well, but it was significantly less than what he demanded. When you saw him in our home, he came to request more, saying I had cheated him. I refused."

"I should hope so!" Elizabeth said angrily. "The nerve of that man! Why, four thousand pounds! A man could live for ten years on that if he is prudent!"

"That is the crux of it, my love, this man is not. You saw how he approached Singleton, he is a gambler."

"As is Mr. Singleton. Oh poor Audrey." She whispered and felt Darcy's hand squeeze hers. "Did nobody know when they married?" He shook his head sadly, and Elizabeth looked down. "And . . . this engagement?"

"My aunt spoke loudly and frequently of her desire that I marry my cousin. My father assured me that it was my decision, and I made my feelings clear to her this Easter when I visited, even before I at last found you." Darcy tried to understand what she was feeling and decided that the most upsetting subject was the most intimate. "I have never and will never take a mistress, Elizabeth. The only woman I wish to love is you."

That he had chosen correctly was immediately clear when tears shone from her eyes. "I . . .truly did not even consider that happening between us, but I cannot deny my relief in hearing it from your lips, Fitzwilliam. Thank you. I love you."

Looking again to Darcy and Elizabeth, Harwick saw that the conversation had ended and the couple was leaning into each other. If they could find privacy, he had no doubt that passion would quickly arise. *Will I ever feel passion for Miss Bennet? Would Ellen want me to live the marriage I would have with her, or would she wish me to be happy at the least?* His mind turned over with thoughts and the quiet group finally arrived at the Grove where they secured a supper box and ordered the famous ham and chickens, cakes, cheese and wine. Gradually relaxed conversation as a group was re-established as they took in the sights and sounds of the people passing by.

"The prices are indeed outrageous." Darcy commented as he tossed Harwick some coins that he swiftly pushed back.

"They are, but the arrack is worth it." Harwick laughed as he took a sip then turned to Jane. "Would you care for a taste? It is rather potent, be warned."

"No sir, I will just have this wine."

Darcy cocked a brow at Elizabeth. "And you?"

"Well, I suppose a little would not hurt me." She took the offered glass and sipped the rum punch, and gasped. The men laughed and Audrey hurried to hand her a glass of wine. Darcy looked at her apologetically. She found her voice again and glared at him. "You knew what that would do!"

"I also knew that you would not take much. It is just another first experience for you tonight, something to remember and chastise me about for all of our lives." His eyes twinkled and she leaned against his shoulder, and he whispered huskily in her ear, "Do not fall asleep here, dearest. I might take advantage."

"Before this crowd?" She lifted her head to see his intense stare.

"I can imagine, can I not?"

"Hmm."

Below the table their fingers entwined, and he brought her hand to rest on his thigh. Elizabeth looked up to him, and his eyes stayed with hers as he moved her hand higher to rest briefly over his hardened groin, then moved them back to rest on his thigh. He felt her body tense then relax, saw her eyes widen and heard her breathing change. He nodded and whispered softly in her ear. "I love you."

The night was punctuated by an explosion and suddenly the air was filled with sparks as fireworks burst forth over the Chinese Pavilion. Elizabeth gasped and hid her face against Darcy's chest. He immediately wrapped his arms around her. "Do not be afraid, have you never seen fireworks? Look, Elizabeth, look!" He turned her around in her chair, keeping his arms around her waist, and softly kissed her ear. "Are they not beautiful?"

"I have read about these." She whispered and leaned back against his chest while the crowd *ooohed* and *ahhed* over the dazzling display. Harwick glanced back at the darkened corner of the box where he could barely make out the embraced couple. They were safe from prying eyes. He noticed Jane looking back at them then jumping with the next burst of noise and light.

"Is this your first time seeing fireworks, Miss Bennet?"

"No, I saw them once before on a visit to London, sir. I am not as disconcerted as my sister. I do not require comfort."

"Then it is well as only Miss Elizabeth or Mrs. Singleton are able to provide it for you." He smiled politely and looked up to the sky. His face was illuminated with the next flash and Jane saw none of the longing that was evident in Darcy's every look at Elizabeth.

In front of Darcy, Singleton sat with Audrey. Their disagreement and his apology were past, he had behaved well since meeting Wickham, so when he took her hand and kissed it, she did not pull away. "May I come to you tonight, Audrey?" He said softly.

"Of course you may." She said quietly in return, their eyes met and he whispered. "I am doing better, am I not?"

"Yes, you are much improved." She sighed and closed her eyes. Before long the fireworks ended and the couples decided it was time to begin the journey home, which could take hours. It was good to return to the barges that would transport them across the river to their waiting carriages before the rest of the crowd had the same thoughts. The Singletons departed for their home and the Darcy carriage left for Gracechurch Street. Harwick bid Jane a formal farewell, bowing over her hand and stepping away as she entered the house. Darcy kissed Elizabeth's hand lingeringly and looked into her eyes. She leaned forward to tenderly brush his mouth with her lips then quickly ducked into the house before either could act on their desire for more. When the door shut, Darcy remained standing still on the stoop. Harwick laughed and called for him to come to the coach and embarrassed, he climbed in.

"You are a lost soul."

Darcy smiled and shrugged. "I make no apologies. How was your night, I am afraid that I did not pay much attention . . ."

"If you had I would have been very disappointed in you." Harwick smiled and sat back against the cushions. "I do not know. She smiles, she is nice, she occasionally speaks and displays some talent for brief conversations . . .but I do not know. She seemed jealous of her sister."

"She is engaged."

"No, I think it is the attention. If she is hoping for what you have with Miss Elizabeth, she will be disappointed."

"I wonder Harwick, are you certain that you want such an . . .emotionless existence? Your first wife died early, but you can potentially have decades with Miss Bennet."

"It has crossed my mind. Are you discouraging me? This is your sister, well almost."

"I only want you to be happy with your ultimate choice, and I feel the same for her. She will feel obligated to accept you no matter what her feelings. You will have to decide for both of you. I will be sure that she is cared for if it is needed."

"Thank you for that, Darcy. You have given me some freedom to be honest with myself. But I have made no decisions yet."

"There is no hurry, is there?" Darcy smiled and Harwick shrugged.

"Well, since I am not proposing any time soon, tell me the story with this Wickham character." Darcy groaned, and for the second time that night, he told the tale of his life with George Wickham.

"DID YOU ENJOY YOURSELF, JANE?" Elizabeth asked after they had assured their sleepy uncle that they were well and saw him off to bed. She closed the chamber door and helped Jane with the buttons on her gown.

"Yes, it was pleasant. Mr. Harwick is certainly a perfect gentleman."

"He is, he seems so sad, though. I hope that you will be able to coax a few more smiles out of him. I did notice him smiling more this evening." She said encouragingly.

"I believe that his smiles were for reasons other than me." Jane said quietly.

"What do you mean? The amusements were certainly entertaining enough."

"On Lizzy, surely you saw that his smiles were for you!"

Elizabeth stared. "Do not be ridiculous!"

"You and Mrs. Singleton were getting along and laughing enough to attract any man's eye." She said petulantly.

"Audrey will soon be my cousin, and she needed to laugh after being humiliated by her husband with that man Wickham! I was trying to make her feel better! I would do the same for you; I *have* done the same for you. Are you jealous that I have made friends with her? I am sorry Jane, but I know enough that I need her help to survive this new world I am entering. Fitzwilliam can teach me much, but I need women to help me. And I like her, she is a lovely girl." Elizabeth took Jane's hands. "Truly Jane, what is troubling you? Mr. Harwick is trying to get to know you, but I noticed that you did not speak often. He needs to hear your voice."

"It is a wonder that you notice anything at all with Mr. Darcy's behaviour."

Elizabeth dropped her hands and moved away. "Mr. Darcy behaved with great restraint, as did I. If he occasionally crossed the lines of propriety, it was done in as discreet a manner as possible, and certainly the darkness of the supper box kept his . . . I will not discuss this further. My behaviour with the man I will marry has nothing to do with your courtship with Mr. Harwick. He is a fine man, and if you do not give him some encouragement, you might find yourself in the same position I was with Mr. Stewart. Abandoned." She turned and left for her own room, shutting the door and continuing the argument with her sister in her head as she struggled to unbutton Lady Matlock's remade gown by herself. She finally managed to remove it and dropped onto the bed. She was too tired to write in her journal, but too wound up to sleep. It would be a night for reliving everything.

RICHARD LAUGHED and propped his feet up on the hassock, took a sip of port, and settled back in the deep leather chair in Darcy's library when he came to visit the following afternoon. "Tell me a story, Papa."

"Very amusing, Richard." Darcy set down his glass and mirrored his cousin's position.

"Come on, you still have a ridiculous grin on your perpetually sour face, I want to know what happened on this unprecedented night of frivolity. I am sorry that I missed it."

"I am as well; I could have used your sword." Darcy grimaced. "Well, perhaps you would have been better with it. Your uniform would have saved you from the noose."

"Good Lord, what happened?"

"Wickham arrived out of the blue. I told you of his demands for more money."

"Yes, where did he arrive at five thousand?"

"I am sure that he was expecting to have to lower that through negotiation." Darcy shook his head. "If I had given in to that, I would have found him at my door with his hand out for my lifetime."

"You were wise to see that, now what happened at the Gardens?"

"He suggested I had vast experience with the ladies and was engaged to Anne. Elizabeth handled it well before him, but demanded an explanation immediately. I found myself walking in the midst of the population of London, speaking of the most intimate details of my life with the innocent woman I prayed would still accept me as my wife when I was through. I tell you, I experienced every level of emotion, from anger to . . . well, joy." He glanced at Fitzwilliam and away, but did not miss his raised brows at Darcy's blush.

"You told Miss Elizabeth that you are experienced?"

"No, I assured her that I am a man who does not dally with mistresses. She fortunately found me credible."

"Hmm. What happened with Wickham?"

"Did you know that he seems to have a relationship with Singleton?"

"No." Fitzwilliam sat up, putting his feet on the floor. "He has quite a reputation around town, will lay a bet on anything. My parents had no idea of his behaviour when they arranged Audrey's marriage."

"She seems to be quietly resigned to it. I can understand how a married woman might be tempted away from her husband. He apologized and she took him back. I do not remember him being so bad when they married, either."

"No, he had his interests. I do not know. He is another example of a first son in waiting with nothing better to occupy himself. I think that Audrey's dowry was just too much of a temptation for him. Before that he was on his father's leash, suddenly he had money and has used it. This is the reason for entailments, his estate will not be gambled away, and the reason for trusts placed on the dowry." Fitzwilliam saw Darcy's nod and continued. "He has his life and Audrey has hers. Perhaps if they have children she will finally be happy. She seems happy with Elizabeth's friendship."

"Yes, Elizabeth's entry into my life has seemed to touch a great many members of this family." Darcy sighed and smiled.

"It is a great thing to see such contentment on your miserable face, Darcy." Fitzwilliam smiled and sat back again to raise his glass in toast. "Georgiana is animated in a way I have not seen since Uncle died, although, I think that she is getting a taste of what school will be like with Mother. There is no indulgence in Matlock House."

Darcy smiled and looked at his feet. "I suppose that I was a little too indulgent, but at times I thought I was too hard. I did not know what I was doing; too many things were occupying my mind in the past two years. Perhaps now, with Elizabeth, Georgiana would be better at home . . ."

"No, as her other guardian I must step in here. She needs the experience of school and meeting other girls her age. She is sheltered and shy. And Darcy, you really do want this time alone with Miss Elizabeth, do you not?" He laughed to see Darcy's wistful smile. "No, do not answer."

"Sir, this express has just arrived." Foster stood in the doorway and announced. Darcy waved him over and he took the letter from the salver.

"It is from Rosings." Darcy frowned and sat up straight to open it.

"Congratulations?" Fitzwilliam cocked his head as he watched his cousin read.

"No, she expresses dismay and . . . good Lord she is coming here to talk to me before it is too late!" Darcy looked up in horror. "She says they plan to stay one night, and as it would be too much trouble to open up her house, they will arrive this afternoon and stay here. Besides the fact that I do not want her, I have plans this evening; I am hosting a large party at the theatre. I cannot, will not, change my plans to satisfy the whims of our aunt!"

"Of course not, she will have to entertain herself and Anne here. She should understand that." Richard took the letter and read. "She forbids you this marriage? Who does she think she is?"

"My closest relative, apparently." Darcy rubbed his hand over his face. "Well, the announcement is published; she can do nothing to prevent it. I thought that Wickham trying to upset Elizabeth with the presumption of my marrying Anne was the worst of this, but now . . ."

"Darcy, your announcement to her at Easter was clear; she has nothing to claim against you. Perhaps she is merely upset about the connection with Elizabeth's family."

"I have no doubt of that," Darcy grimaced, "However, she mentions Anne's feelings. No, she is not through with me and her plans." He glanced at the clock. "I must begin to prepare for the evening soon, and she should be arriving within the hour."

"I will stay with you, Darcy. I am certain that my Father will be interested in this."

"Thank you." He pulled the bell cord and gave Mrs. Mercer orders to prepare two guest rooms and places for the servants. "What am I to say to her?"

"See what she says to you first." He looked up, hearing the sound of the knocker on the front door. "It seems that she left immediately behind her rider. Well, twenty minutes notice, how considerate of her." He stood along with Darcy and the men straightened their clothes, and walked to the front door where the grande dame was already sweeping through.

"Aunt Catherine, I just received your letter, this is a surprise."

"I apologize for the short notice, but I felt that I could not delay." She looked at Fitzwilliam. "You are not needed here."

He smiled. "Oh, but I am! Darcy has invited me to stay, and I will be happy to entertain you and my cousin when he departs in an hour's time."

"Where are you going? We have business to discuss!"

"I have long arranged plans Aunt, and as I am the host of the evening at the theatre and you have just arrived, I am afraid that our business will have to wait until the morning. Please let me see that you are comfortably settled. I hope that you will understand that no meal was ordered tonight, so the kitchen will have to do their best to accommodate you." He turned to smile at Anne. "Forgive me Anne for not greeting you sooner."

"I am willing to wait for you, Darcy. I know that you would not forget me. I am patient." She held out her hand to him and he bowed, but did not kiss the thin fingers. Richard bent and did the same, but Anne only had eyes for Darcy. Her possessive glance encouraged him to step quickly away.

"Will you come with me to the blue sitting room? I am afraid that your chambers are being prepared as we speak."

"I thought that your staff was more efficient, Darcy." Lady Catherine sniffed as they moved along.

"They are very efficient; however a half-hour is hardly enough time to accomplish all that you ask." He bowed to them and led the way into the sitting room. "If you can give me some idea as to your concerns?"

Lady Catherine glanced at Anne and Fitzwilliam. "I prefer to do this privately."

"Do this?" Darcy's brow rose. Fitzwilliam shrugged and glanced at the door. "Very well, please come with me to my study." They entered the room and he closed the door, looking at his parents' portrait for strength before turning to face his aunt. "You have your wish."

She did not hesitate. "This marriage cannot happen! Do you know who this girl is?"

"Of course, she is Elizabeth Bennet of Longbourn in Hertfordshire, daughter of a gentleman."

"She has nothing, Darcy! Her father is a gentleman but one of such little consequence that his estate is laughable, and he has no sons!"

"You have researched the family?" Darcy asked incredulously.

"My pastor's intended successor, Mr. Collins, came to me four days ago, telling me that his father has been identified as the future heir of this Longbourn. The entailment gives it to the cousin of this Mr. Bennet, and it will devolve to my pastor. My pastor Darcy! My nephew, Fitzwilliam Darcy of Pemberley will marry the cousin of my pastor! It cannot be borne, Darcy. You are bound for far better things! You must marry Anne!"

"First of all Aunt, I see no correlation between your future pastor eventually inheriting Longbourn, other than incredible coincidence, and my marrying Miss Elizabeth. He is seeking this situation, I presume, because he is the younger son of a gentleman and must earn a living. What is so different between him and Richard? Secondly, I already clearly told you this Easter that I would not marry Anne."

"She will accept no other but you."

"That is perhaps gratifying Aunt, but I do not accept that. There are undoubtedly hundreds of suitors who would gladly accept her hand. Her dowry and Rosings are extremely attractive. You have held her back. I sincerely hope that it was not in the hope that I would agree to marry her."

"Yes and no." Lady Catherine said tiredly. She saw him glancing at the clock. "You must dress for your evening and go, I suppose."

"Yes." He said steadily.

"Will you hear me out in the morning?"

"I will, but I maintain that I will not marry Anne." Lady Catherine pursed her lips and they returned to the silent sitting room. Fitzwilliam rose and looked at Darcy, who met his eye and shook his head. "I will leave you to entertain yourselves, and will ask Mrs. Mercer to show you to your rooms when they are prepared. I apologize for leaving you."

"I will remain . . ." Fitzwilliam began.

"Go Nephew, we are accustomed to our own company." Lady Catherine said tersely. The men bowed and left together.

"Well?"

"I do not know. She expressed unhappiness with Elizabeth's origins and made it clear that marriage to Anne was the reason for her journey. We will discuss it in the morning."

"She just cannot take no for an answer can she?" Fitzwilliam shook his hand and donned his hat before walking to the door. "Lock your chamber door tonight, Cousin, if you know what I mean."

Darcy laughed and saw him out, then went on upstairs to prepare for his evening with Elizabeth. "The woman I *will* be marrying."

Chapter 19

"*T*he girls should be along soon." Mr. Gardiner smiled. Harwick crossed his arms and watched as Darcy paced. "You look like a caged animal!"

"Why did I choose such a ridiculously distant wedding date?" He growled and looked up to hear his companions laughing. "That did sound pathetic, did it not? But it is not without cause. I have relative problems."

"I thought that the Matlocks were welcoming." Mr. Gardiner said with concern.

"They are; it is the House of de Bourgh." He sighed and waved them off. "I will know in the morning. I will not allow my aunt to spoil this . . ." He stopped in mid-sentence when Elizabeth appeared dressed in a dark blue gown made of some translucent, magically light, beautifully embroidered, enticingly fashioned fabric. Her skin glowed, her hair, held up with bejewelled combs, shone, and her eyes while sparkling at him, immediately cast down shyly when she noticed his transfixed gaze. "Oh, Elizabeth." He said softly and moved forward to take both of her hands, and applied kisses before looking up. "You are a vision that would soothe any man's soul."

"Thank you Fitzwilliam." She whispered and watched as his eyes fixed on her blush as it travelled from her breasts to her eyes. His breath hitched and they both swallowed. He tucked her arm securely in his then tore his eyes away in time to see Harwick rise from bowing over Jane's hand and complimenting her.

Gathering his wits he nodded his head. "You are lovely tonight, Miss Bennet."

"Thank you, Mr. Darcy." She smiled and looked back to Harwick, "It is so nice to spend a second evening with you, sir."

He raised his brows and inclined his head. "The feeling is shared, Miss Bennet."

"I expected more members in your party?" Mrs. Gardiner asked.

"We will meet Bingley at the theatre madam, and our chaperones are coming together as well."

"Who are our chaperones?" Harwick smiled. "The Singletons again?"

"I am afraid so." Darcy shrugged. "They were willing."

Elizabeth and Jane kissed their aunt and uncle goodbye, climbed into the carriage, and were followed by the men who took their places opposite. Darcy's gaze stayed fixed on Elizabeth's face as she nervously clasped her hands, and remembered the soft slope of her bare shoulders and arms beneath the unnecessary shawl. Harwick watched his companion and smiled to himself, remembering the longing of days past. He turned to smile at Jane, and found that she was serenely watching the scenery pass by. They arrived at the theatre and stepped carefully out, dancing around the evidence of horses and gripping their escorts' arms tightly to keep balance.

"This is certainly a challenge." Elizabeth laughed when she hopped and fell against Darcy.

"I do not mind." He slipped his hand onto her waist to steady her, catching her eye in the process, and too soon they gained the entrance to the theatre. Reluctantly he let go and assumed the more acceptable position with her hand on his arm. In the intimate confines of the theatre lobby they were on display to all, and Darcy made it clear how proud he was to have Elizabeth by his side. He walked purposely across the floor to approach the steps leading to the private boxes.

"Darcy!" A man called and he groaned softly then turned. "Good evening Miss Elizabeth, it is a great pleasure to see you again, and looking so lovely."

"Thank you, Mr. Stewart, you are very kind." She blushed and looked down.

"Stewart." Darcy could not help feeling uncomfortable and placed his free hand possessively over Elizabeth's on his arm, then smiled a little when he felt her fingers mesh with his. "This is a pleasant surprise." He noticed a young woman on Stewart's arm and saw Elizabeth studying her curiously. "Elizabeth, have you met Miss Stewart?"

"No, I have not." She smiled warmly at the woman. "I remember Mr. Stewart speaking of you."

"He has spoken of you as well." She laughed. "He said that you were the best part of visiting our cousin. I wish that I had accompanied him to Hertfordshire, it would have been so much more fun than being at home with Mama."

"Laura." Stewart warned and saw her brow lift slightly then he shrugged. "Very well, I cannot deny the relief I felt leaving home behind."

"Neither of you paint a pleasant picture of your mother." Elizabeth admonished gently.

"Oh she is a dear woman, she sadly though thinks of us as perpetually five years old; and distinctly resembles a mother hen."

"Particularly when wearing feathers." Laura pointed out.

"But of course." Stewart laughed and the group joined in.

Darcy heard Harwick and turned. "Forgive me, Stewart, Miss Stewart, have you met Jeffrey Harwick? I know that you have met Miss Bennet, Stewart."

"Yes, Miss Bennet, you are lovely tonight, my sister Laura."

"It is a pleasure, Miss Stewart." Jane smiled.

"Harwick, I believe that I know your estate, Meadowbrook?"

"Yes sir." Harwick smiled. "Have you been?"

"No, but my father, Lord Moreland, purchased a few mares from your father about . . . oh six years ago?" He nodded to himself, "Yes, do you still breed them?"

"Yes, I enjoy the hobby of searching out new horseflesh at the auctions, and seeing what I can make of it. I have had some great success." He saw Miss Stewart nodding and smiling. "Do you enjoy horses?"

"Oh yes, I could ride all day, and often do enjoy morning rides in Hyde Park with my brother, and I love joining the hunts on the estate. Father takes me along to the auctions from time to time and I cannot wait to go to the Derby this Saturday."

"Do you study the lineage of the entries?" He asked with interest and looked up when Stewart started laughing and received an elbow to his side.

He rubbed the spot and smiled. "Forgive me, but my sister chooses her winners by seeing which name catches her fancy."

"Well there is nothing wrong with that!" Elizabeth declared as the men laughed. "I chose Pan last year at the Derby and won twenty pounds."

"Well done, Elizabeth! You will have to pick our winner on Saturday." Darcy smiled and kissed her hand before glancing at Stewart who was watching closely. "I hope that we see each other there."

"Why not travel together?" Stewart asked soberly, "Or do you have a party formed already?"

"Unfortunately we do, but perhaps we will spot each other." Darcy looked up when he heard a gong. "Speaking of which we should probably join the rest of our friends."

"Enjoy the performance." Laura called as they departed. She smiled at Harwick and he returned it easily.

Looking down to Jane he realized that she had not joined the conversation. "Forgive me, Miss Bennet, I did not ask your thoughts on horses. Do you ride?"

"Rarely sir, we have the plough horses which also serve as our carriage horses, and Father has his mare."

"Do you enjoy riding when you have the opportunity?" He continued as they walked along.

Jane flushed, "No sir, I do not, I ride only as necessary." Harwick nodded, and looked ahead to Darcy and Elizabeth, and wondered to himself what he and Jane could do together besides sit silently in a drawing room or meeting occasionally in her bed chamber. He wondered if she enjoyed reading and thought that was a topic he had not tried as yet. Hearing Darcy ask Elizabeth the same question about riding, he listened to her answer.

"Oh I am a far better walker than rider." She smiled.

"But you can see so much more when on horseback, and the exercise is significant to both rider and animal." He tilted his head. "I am surprised that your father did not require you to learn."

"Are you really?" Elizabeth raised her brows. "Well, truth be told he did make an attempt with me, but I fell off twice and never got back up."

"That sounds very unlike you." Darcy said disbelievingly. "You are not one to give up on anything. Look at us."

"I could say the same of you." She said softly as they walked.

"I tried so hard to forget you." He whispered sorrowfully.

Elizabeth stiffened. "While honesty is an admirable quality, there are times when too much knowledge is unwelcome."

"But that is the point, do you not understand? I am being honest when I say that I never gave up on loving you. I could not; I hoped from the moment I heard your laughter that someday we would be man and wife." They reached the door to their box, and he let Harwick and Jane enter first then pausing, spoke quietly, "*Like music on the waters is thy sweet voice to me.*"[3]

Elizabeth leaned on him and whispered, "Lord Byron?"

"Yes, dearest. I love your knowing that." His lips brushed her hair and his warm breath caressed her ear. "I think that you must learn to ride."

Her voice shook a little to match the shivers spreading down her back. "Why?"

"So that I can take you to the private places of Pemberley and we can explore all of your admirable qualities." He smiled to see the blush spread over her shoulders and stepped into the box.

Jane and Harwick were greeting Bingley and the Singletons. Audrey gasped over Elizabeth's gown, one of her new purchases, and had her turn around in the confined space as she admired it. "Oh it is perfect!" She cried and clapped her hands together. "Just lovely! And how did my cousin look when he spied you?"

"Dumbstruck." Elizabeth whispered.

"She did that on purpose, you know." Singleton nodded at the women. "Everyone is staring at this box. Your choice is the talk of the theatre tonight."

"And why is that? Who knew that we were coming?" Darcy asked unhappily. "I really do not need your help satisfying the gossips, Singleton."

"Do not be too hard on him Darcy, the gossips were approaching him." Bingley said. "I even had a few come to me; apparently your approval is gaining me some respectability." He winked and puffed his chest a bit.

Darcy relaxed and Harwick touched his shoulder. "After the wedding you will be old news, just ride it out for a few more months."

"Where is your sister, Mr. Bingley? I thought that Miss Bingley was to join us." Jane asked.

Bingley grimaced at Darcy then smiled brilliantly at Jane. "I am afraid that she found better company than her brother tonight. She is accompanying my sister Louisa and her husband to a ball. I decided that I could not let down my

---

[3] George Gordon Noel Byron, Lord Byron, "Stanzas for Music, <u>Poems</u>, 1816.

friend and chose to stay with our original plans." He saw her nod with understanding. "May I say Miss Bennet, you look particularly lovely tonight, blue is a beautiful choice for you. I wish that my sister would choose so well."

Jane lit up and Harwick noticed. "Oh Mr. Bingley, thank you. But you should not comment on your sister's choices if she is not here to defend herself."

"No, it is the best time; I prefer not to receive a lecture in my bad manners from her." He laughed and moved over to visit Elizabeth. Jane smiled at his back as he bowed and had his hand grasped happily in greeting. Darcy's focus was on his friend and Harwick showed Jane to a chair and sat beside her.

"You must be a great defender of your sisters if you stand up for Mr. Bingley's. Do you know her well?"

"No sir, we have never met." She said softly. "I remembered Mr. Darcy mentioned that she might come."

Harwick studied her as everyone else took their places. *And now she withdraws from me. Is it because she knows the importance of making the match that she is trying not to do anything that offends? She was different with Bingley. Does she not like me?*

Before the lights were lowered he looked across the theatre to spot the box where Stewart sat with his parents and sister. Harwick noticed immediately that Laura was watching their box, and when he realized that her gaze was fixed on him, he felt a tiny lurch in his chest. He took a breath and looked down, he had not felt anything remotely resembling such a sensation since Ellen had died and it frankly frightened him. Slowly he raised his eyes to catch hers again. This time she realized that he had noticed her watching, and when she spotted his mouth lifting in a shy smile, Laura blushed and hid her face behind her fan, peeking over the top to see his smile grow.

Elizabeth noticed that Audrey had grown very quiet and was looking across the theatre as well. She leaned over and whispered. "We met Miss Stewart before we came up here, she is very nice."

"Oh, oh yes she is." Audrey startled, then fell back into silence. Darcy took Elizabeth's hand and drew her closer to his side. She smiled at him then looking back to Audrey saw that again she was staring at someone in particular. Elizabeth finally realized that it was Stewart and felt such sadness for her when Singleton, who was speaking animatedly to their neighbours in the next box, took his place at her side but continued his conversation. Darcy leaned down to her ear.

"Are you well? You are too quiet."

Elizabeth looked up to him as the theatre became dark, and felt his lips caress hers for several breathtaking moments before withdrawing. Elizabeth sighed and leaned onto his shoulder. Darcy stroked her cheek with the back of his fingers and lifted her chin for a second lingering kiss, then slipping his arm around her waist, drew her securely to his side.

Stewart had been watching the couple the entire time, confirming their attachment in his own mind, and saw Darcy leaning in for the kiss just as the light disappeared. He resignedly accepted his mistake, then just caught Audrey's focussed gaze, and was left for the rest of the first act to contemplate what his childhood friend was thinking.

When the lamps were relit, Elizabeth was sitting up in her chair, Darcy's face was smooth, the only hint to the observant that anything questionable had occurred was Elizabeth's rosy blush, and Darcy's crossed legs. He remained seated while the other occupants of the box stood. His eyes met Harwick's who smiled broadly and moved to sit next to him, crossing his arms. "Care to go for a drink?"

"No, thank you." He said with a determined look and shifted when Harwick patted his shoulder and stood with a laugh.

Elizabeth had gone to speak to Jane and returned to Darcy, standing by his side and unfortunately for him, leaving her beautifully displayed décolletage directly in front of his mouth. He bit his lip and taking her hand, gently pulled her down to sit. "Are you well?" She asked with concern.

"No dearest, I am not. You are driving me to distraction. Please speak of something . . .anything." He looked at her beseechingly and moaned when she lifted her hand to her mouth and giggled. "That is decidedly *not* what I had in mind."

"Forgive me Fitzwilliam." She bit her lip and he stared at her expressively. "Is there nothing I can do that does not . . .inspire . . .your . . ."

"No. There is not." He sighed and looked over to the opposite side of the theatre and saw Stewart studying someone in their box. Angering, he looked to see if it was Elizabeth and realized that it was a different woman entirely. Seeing Audrey staring, he quickly returned his attention to Stewart who had an expression of confusion on his face. Again he looked at Audrey who looked down and wiped the tear that escaped her eye. "My God." He whispered.

"Fitzwilliam?" Elizabeth saw his expression and noticing Audrey's distress; rose quickly and handed her a handkerchief from her reticule. "I know, it is such an emotional story, is it not? It took everything I had not to burst into tears." Audrey started and Elizabeth smiled.

"Oh, oh yes, I am quite overcome." She clutched the handkerchief and Elizabeth squeezed her hand.

Darcy was now standing and watching the door for Singleton's return and glancing back to Stewart's box, where he saw the man still watching Audrey. Next he noticed Stewart's sister, also staring . . . at Harwick? *Good heavens what is happening tonight?* Harwick seemed to be making an especially earnest attempt to encourage conversation out of Jane.

Bingley ambled over and spoke softly. "Caroline took the news of your engagement rather poorly, so I asked Louisa to take her off of my hands tonight. I did not think you would mind."

Darcy stared at him blankly. "She what?"

"She was set on marrying you."

"Pardon? I have seen her perhaps five times?"

"Yes, her theory is that if I had invited you more often . . ."

"Bingley the reason I did not come more often was to avoid her!" He said heatedly.

"Yes, I . . . um, considered mentioning that, but decided to be a little more tactful."

"How?"

"I said that your heart was already engaged and I did not feel it was fair to tempt you with another pretty face unless you were free . . ."

"No doubt that set her to thinking of how to disengage me." Darcy's fingers itched to grab Elizabeth and either hold her or take her out of this opera and home. *No, what is waiting for me at home? Aunt Catherine and Anne.* Darcy groaned and closed his eyes, only to reopen them when he heard Singleton stumble into the booth. "This is a disaster."

Elizabeth saw him grimace and reached her hand out for his, they entwined their fingers and squeezed. "Fitzwilliam, something has upset Audrey."

"I noticed dearest, but I am sure she will be well." Further conversation was curtailed when visitors began to appear, claiming a desire to give their good wishes to Elizabeth and Darcy, but in truth it was to get a good look at the unknown woman who stole one of their own.

"Elizabeth, this is Lord and Lady Creary."

She curtsied and smiled, but inwardly she was cringing, waiting for the tall man to recognize her. "I am happy to meet you."

Lady Creary looked her up and down and raised her brows. "And we are pleased to meet you. I was telling my husband that we must come and see the girl who won Darcy. We had heard so many whispers of you around town, and of course you know that gossip should never be trusted."

"Gossip tends to inflate small facts into outrageous fable, inspiring equally spectacular conjecture, particularly if it is born with a malicious intent." Elizabeth said without flinching. "Please allow me to correct any misunderstandings you may have heard of me."

The woman's brows rose. "You speak rather decidedly for one so young."

"I have learned that not to speak is to invite confusion. I prefer to live in the light." She smiled and laughed. "Of course, the truth rather curtails everyone else's enjoyment."

Darcy took her hand in his and kissed it before placing it on his arm. "I prefer honesty to entertainment." He smiled into her eyes and looked up to Creary.

"Well you are known to be a stick in the mud amongst the younger set, Darcy." He sniffed and looked Elizabeth over. "You seem to have done a good job on Darcy."

"I have charmed him as much as he has charmed me, sir."

Creary barked out a laugh. "She has a wit, Darcy. That should last over the years."

"Do you mean when her beauty fades, Husband?" Lady Creary asked acidly. He flushed and rubbed his chin.

"I meant no offence, my dear."

"Hmm. Miss Bennet, your dress is particularly beautiful, your modiste?"

"Thank you; I visited Madame Dupree, on Lady Matlock's recommendation." The woman smiled and nodded her approval, and the couple was soon replaced with several more, all making subtly intrusive inquiries over Elizabeth's home, opinions, interests, challenging her thoughts and Darcy's patience. When the last of the visitors left, she practically shrank away when the weight of performing was lifted. Darcy was smiling at her with pride and leaned to whisper his admiration to her. When she looked up her eyes were bright with tears of appreciation and he did not attempt to hide his feelings. She noticed Audrey clapping silently and nodding at her, Harwick tilting his head and smiling, and creased her brow when she noticed Jane watching Harwick's smile unhappily.

Bingley approached and took her hand. "Miss Elizabeth, please, you must give me some lessons on tact and speech. You were magnificent!"

"I hardly know what I said. Look, my hands are still shaking." Darcy enveloped them in his clasp and she smiled up to him. "As long as I did not embarrass Mr. Darcy . . ."

"Nonsense! I am convinced that you are incapable of such a thing."

The gong sounded and everyone returned to their seats. As lights were extinguished the couple stared at each other. Again they kissed as soon it was dark, this time there was a sense of urgency in the caress, and again it was over far too soon.

When the second act ended, Darcy was on his feet quickly. "Come, shall we get something to drink?"

"Oh yes, that would be nice." Elizabeth took his hand and looking over at Stewart, noticed that he was speaking to his parents. Audrey was doing the same with her husband, and was succeeding in engaging him in an apparently easy conversation. Harwick stood after trying several subjects with Jane, and fell into conversation with Bingley. When they gained the hallway and approached the table selling lemonade, Elizabeth felt that the eyes of the crowd were a relief compared to the tension in the box. "What is happening in there?"

Darcy sighed. "I have no idea, and I have no desire to interfere. It seems though that whatever happened at the beginning is being ignored now." He stared distractedly out of a window to the street below.

"Fitzwilliam." Elizabeth said quietly. "Fitzwilliam." She touched his arm. "Something is bothering you, and it is more than the behaviour of our companions."

"You are too good at reading me."

"You are too obvious in your discomfort. Please tell me what it is, do not force me to drag it from you."

He smiled a little. "I can just imagine us having countless talks like this someday."

"Someday is now. Please tell me." Elizabeth's brows rose and she folded her arms.

A steady stream of people approached and they both had to adjust their behaviour and go through the motions of introductions and meaningless conversation. When at last they were alone again, Darcy saw that Elizabeth's smile had disappeared and an increasingly familiar insistent gaze met his eye.

"Do you realize that you were so preoccupied with continuing our conversation that you forgot to be nervous while meeting a Duke?" She was not to be distracted, and he could not help but admire the quality. "Very well." He sighed and closed his eyes while he gathered his thoughts. "Waiting for me at home are my Aunt Catherine and Cousin Anne. They are there to protest our engagement, and I am sure, press my marriage to Anne." Elizabeth's mouth fell open and she hugged herself. "They arrived just before I came to collect you, and I have only the barest idea of what my aunt has planned. I will hear her out in the morning."

"They are staying with you?"

"They invited themselves." He said bitterly. "I could not very well refuse them."

"Why must you listen to her? Can you not feed them breakfast and send them away?"

Darcy heard the fear in her voice, pried her arms from her chest, and placing her hand on his arm, rubbed some warmth into it. "As tempting as that is, I cannot treat them that way, not unless there is cause. So far it has been tense, but civil. I have no desire to cut ties with my family unless it is necessary."

"I understand, I do not like it but I understand. You are tolerating my connections, after all." Elizabeth swallowed and tried to control her emotions when so many eyes were upon them. Darcy presented her with a glass and she gratefully concentrated on the drink. When the cup was empty, she felt him take it away, and then touch her hands gently.

"You have nothing to fear, Elizabeth."

"Would it help if I . . .met them? You thought that I might battle your aunt well."

He laughed quietly. "I know that you would, but I think that I must have this meeting on my own. Thank you for offering, though. You will meet them before too long." The gong sounded and they looked up. "Well, what awaits us within our box, do you think?"

"I hope that everyone is back to normal." They started walking slowly and Elizabeth stopped before they entered. "Jane is not doing well with Mr. Harwick, is she?"

"He is undecided as yet." Darcy said honestly. "He is trying to imagine them living together."

"And she is making little effort to display her assets." Elizabeth sighed.

"Forgive me Elizabeth, but beyond her looks and kindness, what are they?" Her eyes flashed and she started to open her mouth to protest when she was struck dumb. "You can understand Harwick's hesitation then." He smiled sadly and they were almost to the box when Stewart and his sister emerged. Darcy looked between the siblings and caught Elizabeth's confused expression. "Stewart . . ."

"I am sorry Darcy, but we really must dash if we are to return to our seats in time. Laura wished to greet Audrey, Mrs. Singleton."

"We will see you at the Derby!" Laura called as they hurried away.

Darcy looked at Elizabeth. She seemed just as confused as he was. "We should go in." He kissed her hand and they entered the box to find everyone in their places. Harwick was talking with Singleton seriously and the man was listening. Audrey's head was down, but she was listening to the conversation. Bingley was speaking happily to Jane and she was smiling gently at him. Darcy sighed with relief and felt Elizabeth's tense clutch relax a little. "One more act."

"When the lights go down . . ."

He smiled as they sat down and leaned close to her shoulder. "Do not worry sweetheart, I have not forgotten kissing you for an instant. What do you think has been buoying me through this evening?"

Elizabeth laughed as the lamps were extinguished, and when the box once again became pitch black and the musicians began to play; she was silenced with his lips covering hers, and his hands drawing her hard to his chest. He did not withdraw quickly this time, but allowed a hand to slide up from her waist to cup and fondle her breast, and continue to slide up her throat to support the back of her head with his palm while exploring her mouth deeply with his tongue. The kiss ended gently as she daringly nibbled his lower lip. They rested their foreheads together and tried to contain their ragged breathing. He moved his mouth to her ear, "I pray that you are feeling what I am, if we were alone, I would make sure that the fire racing through me was shared by you."

She pressed her lips to his ear and kissed him, and felt his shudder and tightened embrace. "I cannot describe what I feel when you touch me, but if you call it fire, I can only anticipate you fanning the flames."

Darcy contained his moan by pressing his mouth against the pulse rapidly beating on her throat, and when he gradually regained some control, he settled her into his arms. As the actors' singing filled the hall he whispered, "Knowing that your desire matches mine . . . I can face anything now, my love."

ANNE WOKE AND BLINKED. The moonlight filtered through the gap in the curtains when the breeze blew them apart and she realized that she was not in her room. As always when she woke at night, her mind was not slow or fuzzy from her elixir and it did not take long for her to sit up and remember that she was in her new home. "I am in Darcy House!" She said softly. Climbing from the bed she stood and looked around; then lit a candle, and frowned. "I do not remember our wedding." Shaking her head and swearing to never take that elixir again, she explored the room. It was lovely but it did not seem quite right. "Surely this is not the mistress' chambers! Why am I not in my proper place? And why has my husband not come to me, surely I would remember that!" Becoming agitated, she opened the door to the hallway, and carrying her candle she walked along, and spotted a door she remembered from childhood. "The master's chambers!" She turned the handle and found it was locked and frowned again. "That cannot be correct." Continuing along she came to the door she remembered belonging to her namesake, and now knew was her own. She entered and was suddenly assailed by the scents of fresh paint and saw drop cloths everywhere. Her frown disappeared and a smile spread. "Oh, of course, he is redecorating for me; I knew that he loved me!" She held her candle up and examined the chamber. "I will have to chastise him for doing this without seeking my opinion. Gently of course, but I must make my feelings known."

Looking about she saw so many doors, but quickly calculating the position of Darcy's room, she unerringly selected the one that opened into his chambers. The handle turned silently and she slipped inside. Standing at the bedside, she saw her husband stretched out, the covers disturbed around him, and his broad back gloriously bare. He lay with his arms embracing a pillow, deeply asleep. Giddy with delight, Anne untied the top of her nightdress and let it drop to the floor, and whispering words of passion excitedly, she climbed in, wrapping her thin body against him and pressing kisses against his slightly parted lips. Darcy groaned and muttered in his sleep.

"Wake up, Husband!" Anne whispered, touching him and rubbing his back as she kept kissing. "Wake up!" She said louder. When Darcy did not wake she became angry. "WAKE!" She cried. At last he stirred, but still not awake he blinked and closed his eyes again, drifting back to sleep. Anne kissed him determinedly, and in his exhausted haze, he thought he was dreaming.

"Elizabeth?" He murmured, and returned the kiss. When he felt a response he kissed again. "Elizabeth." He sighed, and without thinking drew Anne's body to his. "Oh Elizabeth, I need you, how did you come to be here?" His lips found hers again. As he awakened further, his eyes opened. "Elizabeth?"

He received a sharp slap across his face. "MY NAME IS ANNE!!!" Again he felt the sting of her hand as he stared in horror at his nude cousin in his arms. "I am your wife!!! HOW DARE YOU cry another woman's name!!" Darcy jumped up and away, snatched his nightshirt from the foot of the bed and quickly donned it.

"ANNE!" He bellowed. "What the devil are you doing in here?"

"I am coming to consummate our marriage, Husband." She said sweetly and crawled towards him slowly, a soft smile on her face. "I have dreamed of this night." Darcy stepped further away from the bed and she leapt off and lunged forward to wrap her arms around his waist. "Love me darling."

"Good God." He whispered and fought to find an acceptable location to place his hands and push her away, and giving up, grabbed her shoulders to force her back. His eyes darted around the room and he spotted her gown. *She is delusional!* Forcing calm he moved swiftly away to grab the gown and noticed that she was standing still and looking very angry.

"Why did you push me?" She screeched.

"I was . . . being playful, Anne." He said steadily. "You do not know the ways of the . . . marriage bed."

"ohhh." Immediately she brightened and a happy lilt came to her voice. "But you will teach me now, will you not, Husband?" In a heartbeat she was back and clutching him. "Why did you dress?" Beginning to pull at his nightshirt she felt resistance, and then reached down to lift the shirt up to his waist. "Ahhh!" She smiled happily to find his decidedly flaccid member. She grabbed at him and he quickly moved his hips away.

"Do not touch me there!"

"Why?" She looked at him. "That is what you want, is it not? I watched the footman with the maid."

"You what?" He said in disbelief and realized she was still nude. "Put this on, Anne. Please."

"The maid was naked." Anne shook her head stubbornly. "Am I not pleasing for you?" She spread her arms out and he closed his eyes to the sight.

"I . . .I prefer that you be modest . . .I find it . . .enticing." He held out the gown and again a soft smile appeared on her face.

"ohhhhhh." She slipped the gown over her head and he breathed in relief then looked around the room. *What can I do?* Anne stood before him and smiled. "Is this better, Fitzwilliam?" Darcy's head snapped up. "Oh, you like me calling your name? Fitzwilliam?"

"No . . .no please call me Darcy."

"Oh, no that is not what a wife calls her husband!" She slid back to him. "Fitzwilliam, you may love me now."

"No, no Anne, I . . . it has been a tiring day, I would like you to return to your chambers and we will . . .talk in the morning."

"I will sleep with you!" She ran to jump in his bed and he grabbed her arm.

"NO!" She stopped and turned. Her eyes were angry again.

"What did you say? I am the mistress of Pemberley. I am the mistress of Rosings. NOBODY TELLS ME NO!!"

"I DO!" He bellowed. "YOU BELIEVE ME TO BE YOUR HUSBAND? FINE, I WILL BEHAVE AS ONE. YOU HAVE NO AUTHORITY OVER

ANY ESTATE ANY MORE. YOU GIVE THAT UP WITH MARRIAGE. YOU HAVE NO CHOICE BUT TO DO AS I SAY. GO TO YOUR ROOM!!"

Anne smiled obediently. "Of course Fitzwilliam, will you escort me?"

Darcy returned her to the guest chamber, allowed a peck on his cheek, and closed the door. A footman was standing in the hallway staring fearfully at him. Darcy pulled himself together and met his eye. "Miss de Bourgh is ill. Please locate Mrs. Jenkinson and have her come here immediately. After that I want you to remain stationed here for the rest of the night. Under *NO* circumstances is Miss de Bourgh to exit these chambers. Am I clear?"

"Yes sir!" The man ran down the steps to the servants' quarters in the basement. Darcy drew a deep breath and leaned against the wall, trying to take in what had just occurred.

"She is insane, is that it?" He tried to put it all together. "Thank heaven I did not . . . how could I possibly think that she was . . .oh my Elizabeth, I am so very sorry." He closed his eyes and felt guilt overtaking him. It did not matter that he had been asleep. He had not touched a woman since the day he learned his father was dying, the day he met Elizabeth. Until tonight. His silent agony ended when footsteps pounding on the stairs entered his consciousness. Mrs. Jenkinson appeared, a bottle clutched in her hand.

"Mr. Darcy, did she harm you?" She was examining his face. He touched his cheek and remembered the slaps.

"No, nothing damaging. Is that some medication for her?"

"Yes, may I give it . . .?"

"Yes, by all means and when she is calm, I would like to speak with you, if you can leave. The footman will tell you where to find me." The woman nodded and he could see her steady herself before entering the room. He could hear Anne's happy voice become angry when Mrs. Jenkinson offered her the drug, but after a protracted conversation, Anne seemed to calm, and there was silence. Darcy slowly returned to his chambers and found a pair of breeches and a shirt, and went to wait in his sitting room, a quarter-hour later Mrs. Jenkinson knocked. He invited her to sit down.

"Mrs. Jenkinson . . .what ails my cousin?"

"Sir, I have been forbidden to speak of it by Lady Catherine. I value my employment, sir."

"If what I suspect is wrong is true, I sincerely doubt that my aunt would be in any hurry to replace you with another. She is quite renowned for her sharp address to servants, but you are valuable to her." He relaxed his grim expression slightly, "I will be sure to remind her of that if necessary."

"Thank you, sir." The older woman whispered.

"Now, what can you tell me?"

"Miss Anne is a very good girl most of the time, sir. She suffers so." She said earnestly, his raised brows encouraged her to continue. "She had scarlet fever as a girl, a mild case, and was nearly recovered when it became rheumatic. I understand that the fever was terrible, and it was touch and go for a long time." Darcy nodded, but had no memory of the event. "The fever, they think, addled her a little."

"A little?"

"Well sir, she was confused for a good long time, but she began to feel herself again, but the disease took its toll on her. It affects the joints and heart, you know." She saw his agreement. "Well sir, the disease also comes back from time to time, flare-ups, and well, each time is worse, and the patient recovers but they are weaker, in the heart, you see."

"That does not explain her delusions."

"No sir, Lady Catherine has not spoken to me of that. She is afraid that word would get around and she might be sent to an asylum. She could not abide that, sir."

"For many reasons, I am certain." Darcy mused. "Tonight my cousin was very alert, despite her delusions. Can you explain that?"

"Yes sir, she usually only receives her elixir when she is to see you. It wears off during the night. She must have awakened . . ."

"Why does she only receive it . . .?" He stopped and saw the woman's face grow fearful. "Never mind, I will speak to her mother. May I ask; what does she take?"

"It is a mild dose of laudanum, sir, just enough to make her compliant, but still able to function. We also use it to keep her calm when she becomes agitated." She looked at her hands nervously. "I begged her Ladyship not to take Miss Anne on this trip."

Darcy sighed and stood, then handed a guinea to the amazed woman who rose with him. "I believe that you were correct in your feelings. Thank you. You will remain with her tonight?"

"Yes sir, thank you, sir."

He showed her out and wearily returned to the sitting room where he scratched out two notes. He called the footman, and asked that the first be given to Lady Catherine's maid to be delivered when her mistress woke, and the second was to be delivered at first light to Matlock House. Glancing at the time when he returned to his chamber he saw that it was nearly four o'clock. He stood still and took in the view of his bed, the bedclothes spread over the floor from his hasty escape. He closed his eyes against the vision of Anne standing naked before him and shuddered with the memory of her hands under his nightshirt and grasping at him . . . *Never again can I sleep here!* Instead he left the room for his study to sit and try to drink the disturbing assault away, and wonder what damage the fevers had done to his cousin's mind, why she needed to be sedated to tolerate his presence, and why, in heaven's name, would his aunt demand that he marry her?

Chapter 20

After a sleepless night, Elizabeth decided that she needed to repair the rift that had developed with Jane. She knocked on the open chamber door and smiled. "Did you enjoy yourself?" She entered and sat on the bed. "I was so dismayed with the attention."

"Were you?" Jane said quietly after glancing up. "It certainly seemed that you rather enjoyed it."

She laughed and groaned. "Oh, no those interviews by the so-called friends of Mr. Darcy's family were not enjoyable. I was trying so hard to not make a fool of myself in front of him. I kept trying to remember Lady Matlock's instructions, stand straight, look them in the eye, breathe, smile, disarm, charm . . .be intelligent but not a bluestocking . . .oh it was so difficult! But Fitzwilliam by my side made it bearable. He said that he was proud of me." She smiled happily and blushed a little. "I wish that he would speak more, but I think that his stoic presence was really all that was necessary." Her words were met with silence as Jane moved about the room. "Jane?"

"Oh, were you finished?"

"What has happened to you?" Her tenuous good humour evaporated. "I tell you Jane; I am tired of your . . .what is wrong? Have I done something to upset you?"

"No, you do not upset anyone Lizzy; you are perfect in nearly every way. You are witty and accomplished."

Elizabeth watched her with narrowed eyes. "And where am I lacking?" Jane shrugged. "How do you feel that you are doing with Mr. Harwick? He seemed to try very hard to engage you in conversation."

"He did, but he also spent a great deal of time looking your way."

"If you spent more time endeavouring to capture his attention yourself, he would not be distracted by someone else!"

"Are you implying that I am dull?"

"I am saying that you are making no effort! Jane, I am marrying Fitzwilliam Darcy, this silly jealousy over men looking at me is ridiculous! Can you not see that it makes you look unattractive?"

"Mr. Bingley smiled and spoke to me."

"Mr. Bingley smiles and speaks to everyone!" Elizabeth cried in exasperation. "And may I ask; why were you paying so much more attention to him than Mr. Harwick?"

"I was not!"

"Jane, I know that Mr. Bingley is a very comfortable man to talk with, but *he* is not courting you! He is in no position to marry yet, and he *knows* that! I am sure that you may be flattered by his easy ways, but do not mistake them for anything other than that of a man who is young and has not learned to curb himself. You laughed and talked to him more readily than you ever did to Mr. Harwick, and he *noticed*, Jane! He saw the difference! What do you think that tells him?"

Jane's face grew red and she stammered her excuses. "I . . .I am behaving as I should with him. I am being demure, I am not exposing my interest before he shows me his, I am doing as I should!"

"Did it ever occur to you that Mr. Harwick did expose his interest by calling on you to begin with? Why do you think he is here? Because he is indifferent? You are the one behaving in that manner. Why on earth would he be so frustrated with trying to talk to you that he would instead fall into a deep discussion with Mr. Singleton instead?"

"Mr. Singleton was intoxicated. Mr. Harwick was keeping him occupied." Jane looked away.

"I grant that Mr. Harwick is a good man and very well might have been driven to protect Audrey from embarrassment by her husband, but if you recall, he was doing that while you were clearly enjoying speaking with Mr. Bingley. Why would Mr. Harwick choose to compete with that? He does not have to compete! Jane, do you not understand? Mama was incorrect; to attract a man you must do more than smile! You must promote yourself! Mr. Harwick has a whole city full of women to court. He chose you for a reason, but that does not mean that he will offer for you."

"I will not remake myself for some man. Mama said . . ."

Elizabeth jumped up. "I cannot listen to more of this. Mama did us and our sisters no favours, Jane. You know it is true. She drove Mr. Stewart away as surely as Papa hurt us with our nonexistent education and poor dowries." She left the room to go down for breakfast. Finding Mrs. Gardiner alone at the table, she sat down heavily, and tried to hide the tears of frustration.

"What is wrong, Lizzy?"

"I do not understand, Aunt. I . . . I am so happy with Mr. Darcy, but Jane, Jane is so different ever since we found each other. We used to be so close and now . . .I cannot seem to do anything right!" She wiped her face and looked up. "I apologized for my behaviour with Mr. Harwick at first, and I have come to like him very much. I think that he and Mr. Darcy will surely become good friends. But I am afraid that if Jane does not at least try to . . ."

"Is Mr. Harwick rethinking his courtship to Jane?" Mrs. Gardiner asked quietly.

"I asked Fitzwilliam last night, and he said that he was discouraged. All Jane can focus on is the way that men respond to me. I do not know what to do. I have dealt with her being the centre of men's attention for years and while I wished it for myself, I certainly did not hold it against her!" Elizabeth twisted a napkin then tossed it on the table and clasped her hands together. "Forgive me, Aunt. I do not know what to do. I know how important this match is for Jane, but she just seems to take it for granted that it will happen without any effort on her part, and I am afraid that if it does not, she will lay the blame on me."

"I see." Mrs. Gardiner squeezed her hand and smiled. "It seems that I need to step in between you girls. How was the night otherwise?"

Elizabeth managed to smile. "Overwhelming, but wonderful."

"Good. I look forward to hearing every detail. Mr. Darcy is very happy with you, Lizzy." She left the table and walked upstairs to where Jane sat at the writing table. "Writing home?"

"Yes, I owed Mama a letter." She set down the pen as Mrs. Gardiner closed the door, then sat on the bed.

"Your sister is very upset."

Jane cast her eyes down and spoke softly. "I do not mean to upset her."

"Then why do you continue to pour cold water over her happiness? I have heard enough mean comments from you to think I was speaking to Lydia. This is not your nature, Jane. What is bothering you?"

Jane stared back at her letter and spoke quietly. "She seems to have every man looking at her."

"You are not used to that. Do you know why they look? She is lovely, just as you are, despite your mother's opinion." Mrs. Gardiner noted Jane's confusion. "Lizzy simply needed to grow into her features, although Mr. Darcy apparently knew when he saw her at fifteen."

"Yes."

Mrs. Gardiner heard the bitterness in her tone and understood. "Did that upset you, knowing that he was not at all attracted to you then? Is that why you slight him and his attentions towards Lizzy? He is deeply in love, Jane. Even the most well-behaved man will display his feelings eventually if he feels as strongly as Mr. Darcy does, and as long as he is discreet, your uncle and I will not chastise him. The question is; why do you?"

"I should be the first married. I was the one to save the family and do my duty." She said petulantly. "Mama told me that I am so beautiful for a reason."

Mrs. Gardiner held back her thoughts that they should be grateful if any of them married. "Well, you have an outstanding suitor paying you court, but I wonder if he will continue much longer. He seems undecided to me, and this is before meeting your father. Mr. Stewart left when the family became too much, and Mr. Darcy stayed because he loves Lizzy enough to ignore them. Mr. Harwick is no young lover with stars in his eyes. He is a father, a widower, and a master. He has no reason to fight his feelings if you have given him no encouragement."

"How can I give him encouragement when he smiles at Lizzy all of the time?" She cried out.

"Oh, is that it?" Mrs. Gardiner shook her head at her naive niece. "Jane, Mr. Harwick is still mourning his wife. Did it ever occur to you that Lizzy reminds him of her? Looking at Lizzy smile and laugh gives him some comfort."

"It does?" She whispered.

"I have seen the man watch Lizzy and Mr. Darcy. A sad smile appears, and I have no doubt at all that he is remembering his days with his deceased wife. He chose you because you are different from her, I am positive, but even that resolve to marry someone opposite of his first love will not be enough to settle his decision on you. What can you offer him besides a wan smile? I tell you, if he sees your jealous behaviour towards your sister, he will not think that you would be a good example for his daughters." Mrs. Gardiner stood up and looked her in the eye. "Your sister loves you and has been doing her best to encourage you, and you reward her with envy and spite. It is not attractive. Your mother was incorrect. You do need more than a smile to win a man. You have done nothing to educate yourself, but you can sing if you choose, you can sew, you can provide pleasant company if you would speak. I suggest that you apologize to Lizzy and ask her for help before it is too late."

"WHAT IS THIS?" Lord Matlock took the note from his valet and with a groan, settled in his shaving chair. He opened it and sat up just as the blade was about to sweep his face. "Good Lord!" He leapt up and ran to his wife's room, and into her bath. "Helen!"

"What has gotten into you Henry!" She cried. He shooed out the maid and slammed the door shut.

"This was waiting for me. From Darcy!" He tried to give her the note and she glared at him. He stayed still long enough to hold the letter over her bath water so she could read, at least until the shaving soap began to drip off of his face and onto the page. Her mouth dropped open as Lord Matlock waved the ruined letter. "I suspected she was addled in some way, but I thought it was the weakness from the illnesses, Catherine never let on about this, this, condition!"

"Well, we need to go over there right away. Go get shaved and dressed, he asks us to come for breakfast. We can be there in an hour if we hurry."

"We will be there sooner than that!" He stood up and threw the door of the bath room open with a bang. "Good Lord!"

A few streets away, Darcy blinked his eyes. He had found no peace; he could not sleep in that bed again, ever. He intended to have the room scoured from floor to ceiling and as soon as the staff was awake to boil water, he had his valet scrub him raw. He felt violated and sick, and spent the remainder of the night drinking, resisting the urge to drag his aunt from her bed and demand an explanation before throwing her into her carriage and out of his home. What stopped him was realizing that seeing one female de Bourgh in her nightdress was all he could stomach for one evening.

Mrs. Mercer found him when she began her duties, and had already been informed of the predawn activities by Darcy's valet, who was summoned by the footman to aid his distraught master. The housekeeper plied him with strong coffee, and informed him that the staff had been warned not to speak a word, and she even took the unprecedented step of reassuring him that the staff felt that he had done nothing untoward. Darcy took that news in silently and thanked her, and then told her to destroy the bed linens in his room and that he would replace the mattress, draperies, everything associated with the bed, and spoke of replacing the furniture as well. Then he informed her that he would be sleeping in the mistress's room until further notice and asked not to be disturbed until his relatives arrived. Mrs. Mercer took it all in without a flinch.

After his bath, when Darcy first returned to the study, he composed a short note to Elizabeth, telling her that he would be unable to call that afternoon, and apologized, begging for her forgiveness. He sent the note off with a servant, and stared down at his hands, knowing that the forgiveness he sought was not for breaking their appointment, but for holding another woman in their bed.

His exhausted mind punished him again. "I must confess this to her, but will she reject me? She was so certain that I would leave her behind after meeting her family. I had to convince her I would allow nothing to come between us. Will she stay by me through this? Will she believe me?" He sank into his thoughts and barely registered the knock when it came. Cautiously Foster opened the door but it was pushed hard when Lord Matlock impatiently entered.

"Darcy, what the devil happened?" He demanded.

"Uncle, Aunt, thank you for coming." Darcy rose and approached them.

Lady Matlock brushed the hair from his bloodshot and drooping eyes. "You look terrible dear, come and sit down." She led him willingly to a sofa and pulling up a chair; Lord Matlock sat and leaned his elbows on his knees.

"Well?"

Darcy told them the events of the night, beginning with the barely announced arrival and Lady Catherine's objections to Elizabeth. He indicated that Anne had made advances upon his person but did not speak of her state of dress. He did tell of her fluctuation in mood and what Mrs. Jenkinson had said of her illness. "Did you know of this?"

Lord Matlock studied him, knowing that he was holding back, the man was incapable of deceit, and his sorrow was evident. "We certainly knew of the fevers and the recurring illness. We know that the rheumatic fever will make her heart weaker each time and that it will likely take her life one day, but as to the other . . .I suspected something was hidden from us, but she has never been in this drug-induced state when we visited, has she Helen?"

"No, but I remember that Catherine was careful to keep conversation about you to times when Anne was not present. Where is Catherine? Does she know of this?"

"I wrote a note, she should have received it by now." Darcy said tiredly. "Anne is still asleep, I believe. I want them gone from my home as soon as possible." His relatives exchanged glances.

"I cannot disagree with that at all. I will go up to Catherine." Lady Matlock stood and kissed Darcy's cheek. "You did everything properly."

When she left Lord Matlock saw Darcy staring at his hands. "What are you not saying, Son? Get it off of your chest before it eats you alive. Did you and your cousin . . ."

"No sir, we did not, but in my sleep I imagined it was Elizabeth in my arms. I woke from a beautiful dream to find myself in a nightmare." He closed his eyes and fought back his emotion. "I have betrayed her."

Lord Matlock gripped his arm. "No, I will not accept that. You had no idea, and you escaped as soon as you had your faculties, did you not?"

"Yes." He whispered and swallowed hard. "Elizabeth asked me about my behaviour with women . . . I assured her I had never taken a mistress, but I dodged telling her I was not without experience."

"Darcy, the girl is not naive, of course she expects you to be experienced! You have kissed her have you not?"

"Yes." He said wistfully.

"And you were not a bumbling fool?"

"I hope not." He looked away and tried to hide the tear that escaped and ran down his cheek. Lord Matlock sat back and looked at him with amazement. He could compare the emotion his nephew was feeling to nothing he had ever experienced.

"And I thought that I loved Helen." He said softly. Darcy did not hear him. "Son. I realize that it is useless to tell you to lock this up in your breast forever. You will tell her, but if she feels for you half of what you display for her, I know that she will understand. Would you not do the same for her?"

He thought of how many times he imagined Stewart with her, even though he knew that man had never done any more than kiss her hand. "Yes, but the man would be dead."

Lady Matlock reappeared. "Catherine is with Anne. I told her that you wanted to speak with her before she leaves. She asked that you meet in a half-hour. Perhaps we can go eat a little something before then, you look as if you could use some solid food." She gently stroked his brow and smiled. "You need your strength."

"She feels no remorse, does she?" Lord Matlock asked.

"She expressed no emotion." She took Darcy's hand. "Come dear."

"I could not hold anything down." He whispered. "You go ahead."

"No. Up you go." Lord Matlock stuck his hand under his arm and dragged him upright. "I will not have you fainting when you need to vent your anger." They walked off to the dining room, and under the unrelenting attention of his relatives, Darcy forced down a small meal. Foster appeared and bowed.

"Sir, Lady Catherine awaits your pleasure in the blue room."

"My pleasure." Darcy stood and threw his napkin down. "That is laughable." He was up and on his way, the others scrambled to follow. They entered the drawing room and Lady Matlock closed the door. Lady Catherine was ensconced in the largest chair, her hands folded and her chin up, prepared for battle. Darcy did not hesitate. "What was in your mind, Aunt? Bringing your deranged daughter into my home? Clearly you have known of her delusions for years, and hid them from the family. Are you as ill as she? Must we find an asylum to hold you both?"

"How dare you address me this way!" She snapped.

"I will address you any way I wish. I want an explanation, and I want it now!" Darcy bellowed.

"He is not alone, Catherine. What has happened to your daughter, and why would you try to foist her onto Darcy? What was your plan in bringing her here?" Lord Matlock glowered down at his sister. "And none of this imperious manner, Catherine. I will not have it."

Catherine looked from one face to another. "I understand that Mrs. Jenkinson has betrayed my trust."

"Mrs. Jenkinson is a loyal servant and if she finds herself without a position by your hand, I will be sure that all she has said of Anne is broadcast throughout society." Lord Matlock declared.

"You would not!"

"No, but nor would you dismiss her because she knows too much. I told you to drop the posturing!"

"Enough of this dancing!" Darcy began to pace. "What is wrong with her?"

Lady Catherine shot a look at her glowering brother and backed down. "Anne suffered from very high fevers as a girl, and nearly died. She contracted rheumatic fever, and was bled many times to relieve her temperature, and eventually the treatment worked. She recovered, but it seems that the days she spent in that state affected her mind somehow. At first her physician thought that her fanciful thoughts would disappear as she continued to recover, and they did somewhat. She had to relearn some skills, but was never able to play the pianoforte again. The fever reappeared from time to time, making her weaker and weaker." She sighed and glanced at Darcy. "Then my sister died. I had mentioned to her what a fine thing it would be to see you cousins marry, and she said that she would not force such a thing on you. She had an arranged marriage, but had been fortunate to fall in love with her husband, and hoped for the same for her children. I waited a few years after she died and brought the subject up with your father. You see by then I knew that Anne was too weak to marry and be a wife to any man, and suspected she would not survive childbirth."

"Then why would you wish to foist her on me? Why would you encourage her to believe such a thing?"

"Anne looked forward to coming out and attending the balls, all of the things a young girl wants. I knew that I could not hold her back from those thoughts, but also knew that I could not put her out either. I told her that she would not do those things because she was promised to you." She spoke stiffly and Darcy went to stand and stare into the fireplace. "She had another fever and when she recovered, she seemed fine most of the time, except when the subject of her marriage to you came up. She began to speak of how you were deeply in love with her, and asked why you did not come to her. I explained that you were both too young, which satisfied for a while, but then you came of age, and her demands became more impatient, but she would rationalize that you were on your tour, and then that you were preparing Pemberley for her. I had other physicians examine her and was told that she was suffering from Old Maid's Insanity, and was told to give her the laudanum whenever you would visit, to prevent her from pursuing or harassing you."

"That gambit failed." Lord Matlock glanced at Darcy who remained at the mantle. "So am I to understand that you were incapable of convincing her that Darcy would not marry her, or did you placate her to good behaviour by encouraging the delusion to grow?"

"I thought he would agree." Lady Catherine cringed when Darcy's furious countenance appeared inches before her face.

"YOU THOUGHT I WOULD AGREE TO MARRY AN INSANE WOMAN?" He growled. "I would give up my life, my heritage, have no heir, destroy my name . . . for what reason, Madam?"

She drew herself up in the face of his fury. "My plan was that you would marry her. No other man would marry her, she cannot provide a child, but I did not wish to put her away in an asylum, and certainly I did not wish for the family name to be sullied . . ."

"WHAT OF MY FAMILY?" He demanded. "I need an heir, I need . . .a wife." He stalked away before his hands closed around her neck.

"My plan was for you to marry, and she would remain at Rosings. You could take a mistress and raise her children as your heirs."

"YOUR PLAN?" He spun around. "And what of my plans? Children of a mistress are illegitimate, Aunt. What of that? And what of my desires for marriage? What exactly is my motivation for accepting YOUR delusion?"

"You would have Rosings." She said simply.

"I do not want it." He spat. "I never have, and I assure you, I would sooner see it burned than ever set foot in there again."

"All I wished for was to protect my daughter, do you not understand?" Lady Catherine pled. "When I am gone, who will look after her? If she married someone else, he would have her locked away somewhere before the ink on the marriage contracts was dry. The estate would stay in the family, Darcy! Surely that is worthwhile? Marry her and take up this Bennet girl as your mistress. You will grow tired of her one day and you will be free to take up another . . ."

"HOW DARE YOU SPEAK OF HER SO CALLOUSLY?" He returned to stand over her.

"You have already compromised Anne. She was in your bed." Lady Catherine said quietly.

Lord Matlock had been watching the volley in silence, but this he could not ignore. "I hope very much that you did not tinker with Anne's medication so that she would awaken and act upon her delusion, Catherine." He saw her catch his eye and look away. "You did, you brought her here specifically to attack Darcy."

"I wondered why you did not rise when you heard the commotion." Darcy said softly. "The rest of the house knew. Thank God Georgiana is staying at Matlock House."

"I had no control over her." Lady Catherine sniffed and looked at her rings.

"Then why did you insist that Mrs. Jenkinson sleep in the servant's quarters instead of in the room adjacent to Anne?" He asked. "Why did you mention loudly when I took my leave of you that I had assumed residence in the master's chambers? Why me, Aunt?" Darcy continued. "Why not promote Richard? He could keep a family secret, he has no estate, why me?"

"Because he still has both parents alive to battle." Lord Matlock said as he watched his sister stare at him blankly. "She thought that you were weak, Darcy."

"Well she is wrong." Darcy returned to stand before her. "I want you out of my home immediately. I cut all ties with the House of de Bourgh."

"You cannot do that!"

"And what is to stop me?"

"I will inform your lover of your behaviour with Anne." She said triumphantly.

Darcy laughed hollowly. "No Aunt, I will do that myself, and if Miss Elizabeth Bennet is the woman I believe her to be, she will give me the benefit of her forgiveness." He began to leave and returned. "You sneer at my love for Miss Elizabeth. That tells me that you did all of this for your benefit, and not out of love for your daughter. You were protecting yourself, not her. I did not believe that I could feel any more disgust for you, but somehow I managed. Goodbye, Aunt." He glanced at his uncle and left the room.

Lord Matlock watched his unmoving sister for a few moments. "What will become of Rosings if Anne dies without marrying?"

"It will go to the next male in the de Bourgh line. A cousin of my husband's." She spoke stiffly.

"Richard may have entertained the idea. He has really no expectations to marry, which has always brought me great sorrow. He is so hardened about life; he might have been willing to be husband in name only, something that Darcy could never have entertained. You chose the wrong nephew to promote, but then you started this long ago, before she was so ill. You did this so you could keep Rosings for yourself, not for love of your daughter." Lord Matlock turned and left, leaving the women alone.

"How could you hurt Darcy this way?" Lady Matlock seethed. "His engagement is public knowledge; it will not be broken without justifiable legal action by her family. You expected Miss Elizabeth to give up the respect of being a married woman to become his mistress? You know full well that a woman coming to a man's bed is not compromised, just a fool. Darcy has been happy for the first time in years . . . I have nothing else to say to you." She rose and walked out to find her husband.

Foster appeared in the doorway. "Your carriage is prepared madam, and Miss de Bourgh is waiting for you within." He stood aside and waited expectantly.

Lady Catherine looked to him then noticed the two large footmen standing by his side. She rose and adjusted her shawl, and without a word, exited Darcy House forever.

"SHE IS GONE, DARCY." Lady Matlock reported from the doorway. "The coach is on its way somewhere."

"Well then, I will be on my way as well." He stood and held out his hand to his uncle. "I thank you for all that you have done today; I appreciate it more than I can say."

Lord Matlock took his hand and held it. "Where are you going?"

"To Elizabeth." He said simply. "I need to . . .learn my fate."

"We will come with you." Lady Matlock walked over to embrace him. "You should not face this alone, and I think that Miss Elizabeth will need to hear what I have to say."

"And what is that?" He swallowed hard.

"That is between women." She smiled and taking his arm, led him out to the waiting carriage.

Elizabeth had received Darcy's note that he would be unable to visit, and while she chastised herself for worrying, she could not shake the feeling of foreboding, and the surety that it was somehow related to the visit by his relatives. Jane had not spoken to her since their argument, and her aunt was clearly unhappy with her niece for her behaviour. The walls of the small house seemed to be closing in, and Elizabeth begged for permission to walk alone in the park. Mrs. Gardiner refused that, but allowed her to take a maid along. It was while she was gone that the Darcy carriage arrived.

"This is quite a surprise, sir. We had not expected to see you today." Mrs. Gardiner welcomed him, but she did not miss the signs of exhaustion and distress. The serious expressions of his relatives confirmed that something terrible had happened.

"I am surprised to find myself here as well madam, however my business ended abruptly and I need to discuss something of great importance with Miss

Elizabeth. May I see her, please?" He shifted back and forth, and clenched his hands in an effort to stop from ripping off his strangling cravat.

"She felt a need to walk, sir. She is in the park with the maid." Darcy's eyes shot to the front window. "She only just left."

"Is your husband at home, madam?" Lord Matlock asked.

"Yes, he is working in his study, shall I call for him?"

"No, I would like to speak to him there, if I may. Darcy, will you join us?" He looked at his nephew staring through the window with raised brows. "I think that this is the proper course, Son."

Lady Matlock touched his arm. "I will speak to Mrs. Gardiner, and then perhaps she will join me for a stroll in the park."

"You will speak to her first?" Darcy whispered.

"I think it would be best, do you not?" She smiled and squeezed his hand.

"I do not know anymore, I just want to be sure that she still . . .accepts me."

"When we return, I am sure that Mr. and Mrs. Gardiner will grant you permission to speak with her for as long as is necessary." She looked at Mrs. Gardiner and the women exchanged information with a look.

"I do not know what this concerns as yet, but I gather it is of some distressing subject. If conversation is needed for you to resolve the situation, I am certain that my husband will approve." She saw Darcy's relief and led him and his uncle to her husband's study, announced them, and returned to the drawing room. Dropping formality she took a seat. "What is this all about?"

"It is a tale of deceit and tragedy, Mrs. Gardiner, and two young people in love are caught in the middle." She glanced at the open door. Mrs. Gardiner noticed and went to close it immediately. The ladies sat down and in a very quiet voice, Lady Matlock delivered the news.

In the study, Mr. Gardiner sat behind his desk, his fingers templed beneath his chin as he listened to Lord Matlock first tell of Anne's illness and history, and then Darcy spoke of what happened the night before. His eyes widened when Darcy left out no detail, baring his torture to the man who could end his engagement without cause. Lord Matlock listened in stunned fascination and noticed Mr. Gardiner had seen his reaction.

"I assume this is the first time you have heard the particulars, sir?"

"Yes, and I understand why my nephew held them back at first. No wonder you are so distressed, Darcy. This is far worse than I imagined."

"You showed a great deal of level-headedness, talking your way through her delusion. I am impressed with you. I wonder if I could have done it with such finesse."

"There was no finesse, sir. I was scared witless." Darcy sighed. "I will understand if you feel I am unworthy of . . ." He could not continue.

"Do not be ridiculous. This is not your fault. If anything it shows your love for my niece."

Darcy raised his eyes to ask silently for an explanation. "Well Son, you were speaking her name when you were holding your cousin. Who was in your thoughts all that time? Who has been your primary concern since the incident happened? Who could you not wait to see and confess this to?" He smiled and nodded. "You love her so much that you would risk losing her to tell the truth. You trust her to love you just as deeply. I believe that she does."

Drawing a deep breath he squeezed his eyes shut. "Thank you, sir."

"Indeed, I could not have said it better." Lord Matlock let out his own breath. "I could have said that no man in his right mind would turn you away as the husband for his niece, but I have a feeling Gardiner, that you would not hesitate if you were convinced of his unworthiness."

He smiled. "That is true."

The elder men laughed as Darcy remained silent. Lord Matlock cocked a brow at Darcy. "I believe that the detail you just delivered is not necessary to impart to Miss Elizabeth."

"I agree. Keep in mind that my niece remains innocent, despite your regular attempts to expand her education, sir. She does not need to know everything. She will be hurt enough by the essentials."

"Then what do I tell her?"

"Give her the version you told your aunt, that is shocking enough," Lord Matlock advised. "See how that goes over, but one of you having nightmares about the event is enough. She does not need to have the vision of the man she loves . . .well, you know."

"And when it is over Darcy, you may comfort her however she allows . . .within reason." He smiled but saw that this young man was incapable of frivolity, which made his respect for him grow. "She is a stubborn girl, Darcy. You may have to work at this."

"May I go to her now?" He stood. "I cannot bear to delay longer."

"Of course." Darcy was up and gone from the room before another word could be said. "He is quite a young man." Mr. Gardiner said as he poured Lord Matlock some port. "I can think of few who would be upset at such an event, or who would not have taken advantage."

"It makes me see daily where I failed my sons." Lord Matlock said thoughtfully. "I doubt that my eldest would have done so well at that age if I had died."

"Is it too late to teach him?" Mr. Gardiner asked. His companion sipped the very fine wine and raised his brow, then sat comfortably in his chair.

"Tell me about this business of yours."

"Thinking of investing?" Mr. Gardiner smiled. "Mr. Darcy already has." The men laughed and settled in to wait for whatever came next.

Darcy passed the drawing room on his way to the door and Lady Matlock, hearing his boots, rushed to call him back. He looked at her impatiently. "I am going to see her."

"In the park?" She shook her head and took his arm. "No, she does not want this news from you in so public a place. You wait here and Mrs. Gardiner and I will fetch her."

"Aunt, I know what I want to say."

"Good for you. So do we." She kissed his cheek and smiled. "Let us do this for you, dear."

Mrs. Gardiner took his hand. "I am so sorry for this to have happened, but I will not allow your aunt or your cousin to ruin what has so much promise." The women departed and he was left alone, watching them make their way down the street and finally disappear through the park's gate. He sat down to continue his vigil and startled when he heard a soft "oh."

"Miss Bennet." He stood and bowed.

She looked at his back, not the straight broad stance of a strong man, but bowed and old. Noticing the dark circles and his reddened eyes, she guessed that something terrible had occurred. "Mr. Darcy, may I find Lizzy for you?"

"She is in the park; her aunts have gone to find her." He returned to the window.

Jane was confused, but continued to be his hostess. "May I get you some wine, sir? You seem in need of relief."

"I will be relieved when I speak to your sister." He said shortly then stopped. "Forgive me, it has been a difficult day, you do not deserve my ire."

"I understand, sir." She sat down and bit her lip, and thought to distract him from his misery. "My sister spoke of you this morning."

He turned to regard her, and she gathered her courage to talk. "She was telling me that Mr. Harwick is unsure of my suitability to be his wife and that I need to make more of an effort." He continued to stare, not refuting her statement. "She said that unlike you, who she knows loves her so deeply," He blinked as his eyes became bright; "Mr. Harwick is not blinded by emotion, and will not hesitate to reject me if I or my family does not meet his needs." She took a breath. "Would you agree with that, sir?"

"I cannot disagree with it, Miss Bennet." He said honestly.

"Does a man want to see his object display sentiment?"

"A man would like to know how he fares."

"And what if the woman does not feel any?"

"Then the couple must decide if they wish for a partnership of convenience without regret." He said simply. "Is it duty and security that drives them or are they willing to sacrifice in the hope of finding more?"

"What are you sacrificing to accept my sister, Mr. Darcy?"

"In my eyes, I only gain. In society's eyes, I am a fool."

Darcy noticed movement outside of the window and saw Elizabeth approaching the house at great speed, far outstripping the ladies. He was up and on his feet and at the front door when it flew open. She stopped and stared up at him, saying nothing at all while she took in every detail of his face. She noted his eyes, bleary from lack of sleep and puffy from tears, the black circles below stood out shockingly dark against his pale skin. His lips were dry and bitten, undoubtedly in agitation, and his hands were twisting nervously together, making his bowed shoulders bend deeper with the burden of his worry. She remembered this man. She had seen him before. At that time she had no idea what weighed him down, only knowing that she wished to relieve his suffering and make him laugh, and as she grew to understand what her instincts meant, to love him.

Darcy drew a deep breath, looking into the red eyes of the woman he adored, read the pain and anger that was there, saw her fear, and drew his courage together to offer her his hand. He kept it extended for what felt like an eternity, while she continued her silent examination. His eyes focussed on hers, but finally when he felt that his prayers would be refused, they dropped, along with his hand. Elizabeth caught it before it went to his side, and she was instantly in his arms, tight to his chest, her ear pressed against his pounding heart and her neck pillowing his face while they both sobbed with relief.

"Forgive me." He spoke softly and kissed her neck. "Please Elizabeth, I did not mean to hurt you, I did not know, I truly did not know. I would never betray us."

"I know that Fitzwilliam, I do." Elizabeth looked up to him and kissed his wet cheeks while he caressed away her tears. "I . . .am glad that my aunt told me first."

He nodded. "What did she say?"

Elizabeth let go and held his hand in hers. "Let us go and be private, and you can tell me what you were going to say."

"But . . . what if I . . ."

"Say something different?" She smiled a little and leaned into him while he kissed her hand. "I am the only one who will ever know, and I love you for telling me at all. You did not have to ever say a word, my love. I asked you for respect. This is what I have received from you today."

Darcy drew a shaky breath and holding her waist, walked down the narrow hallway to the sitting room in the back of the house. He escorted her to a sofa then turned to close the door, meeting the eyes of his aunt as he did. He mouthed, "Thank you," then let the latch click. Elizabeth moved on the seat, showing him that he was welcome at her side and he sat, holding her hand and staring at how small it was within his palm. He swallowed and began. "I woke when my face was slapped. I discovered that the woman I dreamed I was kissing was in fact my cousin."

"She slapped you? Why?" Elizabeth asked with an edge to her voice.

"I was calling your name and she objected." He continued in a soft voice. "I immediately left the bed and she followed, continuing to press herself to me, and that is when I came to understand that she thought we were married and about to . . . consummate." He was greeted with silence. "I tried everything I could to discourage her, and pushed her away. She continued to press me and I . . . eventually convinced her to retire to her room." He stopped and felt his hand squeezed. "I had a footman guard the door and spent the night in my study. I have ordered that the bedclothes be discarded and the room cleaned. I . . .I thought that if you still wish to marry me, we could go and select some new furnishings. I will not sleep there again without you."

Elizabeth remained silent for several very long minutes until he finally looked up to her eyes. She lifted her hand and caressed his face. "Where did she strike you?"

He moved her hand over his cheek and she touched him gently. "Do you have any questions?"

"I understand that you have cut your ties to them."

"Yes. I will never welcome them to my home again."

"Is that fair to your cousin? She is ill."

"She has the potential to be violent, and I fear what she might do to you. I will not risk that, and my aunt does not deserve my notice after her deceit." Darcy kissed her palm and held it in his hands. "Surely you do not want them in our home, if you will still have me."

"No, but it is a serious decision to make. I want you to have no regrets." She saw his nod and smiled a little. "And before you ask again, yes Fitzwilliam, I will still have you. I love you."

"Thank you dearest, I love you." He let go of her hand and drew her to his chest, kissed her forehead and rested his cheek in her hair. "May I ask you a favour?"

"Another? Besides my generous forgiveness?"

Darcy kissed her again and smiled a little to hear her tease. "I think that I would like you to think of a new name to call me." Elizabeth had been rubbing his back soothingly and her hand stilled.

"She ruined that for us?" She said angrily when he nodded. "Any feelings of sympathy I had for her are gone." Darcy held her tighter as she sighed, drew her legs up and curled into his arms. "Let me think about this."

"Take all the time in the world." He whispered.

Lord Matlock consulted his watch and glanced around the room. "It has been a half hour, should we at least see if they are alive?"

Mr. Gardiner stood and moved to the doorway. "Well, I suppose this is my duty." Walking across the house he reached the closed door. He paused to listen and heard nothing within. Knocking, he turned the handle and looked inside to see Darcy's eyes closed, his cheek resting on Elizabeth's shoulder and her body encapsulated in his arms, and deeply asleep. Meeting Elizabeth's gaze for a moment, her eyes closed and she snuggled against his chest. Mr. Gardiner hesitated, unsure what to do, then leaving the door cracked open, left them alone.

Chapter 21

The squalling sound of a baby and children's laughter filtered into Darcy's consciousness as he slowly began to wake from the deep exhaustion that seemed to permeate every part of his body. He blinked open his eyes to find that he was in the familiar confines of the Gardiner's back sitting room, and Mr. Gardiner himself was dozing in a chair, an open book resting over his stomach. Movement caught his eye and he just saw Jane's blonde hair disappearing from the partially opened door. Looking down to the woman in his arms, he tightened his embrace, and kissed her forehead whispering, "I love you, Elizabeth."

She took a deep breath and smiled, then looked up to the blue eyes regarding her so seriously. She touched his cheek and gladly welcomed the gentle caress of his lips, then feeling his need for more, encouraged his loving kiss as his tongue tenderly fondled hers. "I love you, Fitzwilliam." Seeing him cringe with the sound of his name, she shook her head, stroking back the hair that fell over his brow as he looked down at her. "I will not allow the memory of your nightmare to take your name from me. Fitzwilliam, Fitzwilliam, I will say it over and over until the only voice you hear is mine. Fitzwilliam, it rolls off of my tongue, it is music to me. It comforts me. Fitzwilliam, I love you, my Fitzwilliam."

"Dearest Elizabeth." He sighed and hugged her to him. "Thank you."

They stayed silently embraced until Mr. Gardiner snored himself awake. He blinked and looked up to see that they were smiling at him. "Well," He cleared his throat and sat up, "Good afternoon."

Elizabeth laughed from her nest in Darcy's arms. "Where has the day gone?"

"Indeed." Mr. Gardiner raised his brows and looked at Darcy pointedly. "Sir, while under the circumstances we were willing to overlook the incredible breach in propriety . . ."

"Uncle, please let him hold me."

"No, I understand." Darcy let her go reluctantly and sat up, only to find his hands immediately held. He smiled at her a little. "I think that we have more to discuss, I believe that my exhaustion interrupted our conversation."

"Perhaps you might take a meal first? Your aunt and uncle departed for their home a few hours ago, and were going to send your coach back for you this evening." Mr. Gardiner stood and stretched. "You may have time afterwards to speak privately again." He noticed the couple exchanging glances and laughed. "Do not deny that your limbs could use some movement."

Darcy nodded when Elizabeth's eyes sparkled at him, and said softly, "Very well, I cannot lie." She extracted herself from his side and awkwardly stood, then held out her hands to help him to his feet. Darcy groaned while she laughed and hugged her again when Mr. Gardiner left. "A sofa is not the ideal resting place."

"No, it is not, but it did well in a pinch."

"Hmm, yes." He played with the tendrils of hair around her face. "Will you help me purchase our new furnishings?"

"I have never purchased furniture; I think it would be a great adventure." Elizabeth smiled to see his amusement. "Do you not realize that everything you do with me is an adventure?"

"I can only echo that sentiment, my love." He squeezed her tight. "Thank you for not rejecting me today. I know that it would not be difficult to believe that I had encouraged what happened."

"Fitzwilliam, would it also not be difficult to believe the worst of me, that I would have accepted you regardless because of your wealth?" His brow knit and she ran her hand over it, smoothing the skin. "You see, you are as incapable as I to believe such mercenary tendencies. I do not want you for your income any more than you want the opportunity to take advantage of an uninvited visitor to your bed."

"We are trusting souls."

"With each other, anyway." She smiled and watched as his gaze drifted from her eyes to her mouth, then felt her heart start to pound when his kiss touched her lips gently. Soon they gave in to their need for reassurance.

"I am having such a hard time holding back from you, Elizabeth." He murmured before kissing her again. Moving his mouth to her ear, he ran his hands down her back to touch her bottom and back up to encircle her body. "You are forever on my mind."

Elizabeth rested her head on his shoulder and pressed against him as his kisses down her throat electrified her senses. "I spent the last hours resisting sleep because I could not stop thinking of how much I love being in my Fitzwilliam's arms."

"I love how that sounds on your tongue. Thank you for ignoring my plea, and most of all, thank you for accepting me." He kissed her mouth again before hearing a throat clearing in the hallway, then pressed his lips to her ear. "I think that your uncle's patience is at an end."

"July seems much too far away."

"Perhaps we should reevaluate our wedding date, my love." He saw her eyes light up with the idea and felt his sadness lift a little. "I think that some decisions must be made."

2 JUNE 1809

Now that a few days have passed, Fitzwilliam has recovered his humour somewhat. He remains deeply hurt by what happened, but will not speak more of it. He unburdened his soul, was reassured of my devotion, and he wishes to move ahead. I think that he has a tendency to bury sadness and thrust himself into activity to distract his mind. We are alike in that, so visiting the Chippendale showroom and selecting fabrics for the master suite was our main occupation. I imagine that it will only be when we are alone, truly alone and married that he will reveal secrets that he keeps hidden. It is not just the violation that disturbs him, I think that it is the callous treatment he received from his aunt, and to be manipulated by a person he trusted as family to achieve her own ends.

I see a parallel with Mama in that behaviour. She wished for Jane and me to be out years before we should have been, and that was to rescue her in the event of Papa's death. The element of good in her behaviour was superseded by the callous way that her desires were carried out. Jane, my dear sister, has become jealous and spiteful because Mama told her repeatedly that her beauty was all that was needed to do her duty to save the family by her marriage, and has found that all Mama told her was wrong. Now I, the supposedly ugly girl who wasted her time in self-education will marry a rich man for love, and will automatically save the family that day. Everything that Jane has been raised to do is dashed, and I wonder if she is confused over just what she is supposed to be now.

Mr. Harwick called yesterday afternoon, and said he would be unable to join us at the Derby, citing the excuse that his sister would be arriving. I hope that is truly the case, and that he is not becoming discouraged. He is a good kind man, and I think that they might do well together if Jane would be the sweet girl I knew, and he would open his heart again. But with no encouragement from her, why should he try further? In the end it is between them. I know that she is unhappy with me for not telling her exactly why Fitzwilliam was so upset, and why our aunt and uncle allowed us to sleep in each other's arms. She seems to be lost in thought quite often, but says nothing to me of it. I wish that I felt I could trust her, I miss going to her to talk, but I cannot, I do not know this girl. How did I become the elder sister and she the petulant youth?

"SO." FITZWILLIAM APPEARED at the study door and leaned against the frame for a moment before entering and shutting it behind him.

Darcy looked up from where he was writing in his journal, and leaned back in his chair. "So." He sighed and closed his eyes for a moment, and opened them to see his cousin smiling at him with his head cocked.

"Scribbling away in that blasted book again, I see?" He noted and saw Darcy's little smile as he looked down. "Does it mend your soul?"

"It helps me to see things clearly, or perhaps lets me look back and see how I have grown as a result." He shrugged and indicated a chair to his cousin. "I am endlessly grateful to your parents."

"They do have their uses." Fitzwilliam laughed and then sobered. "Father told me the unedited version of the evening. I hope that you do not mind."

"No, I expected he would share it with you. Layton as well, this was family." Darcy's hands twisted and Fitzwilliam's eyes did not miss the nervous reaction.

"Interesting." He stood and went to pour them each a glass of port. "A woman is treated as you were and she is compromised, barely escaping from a terrible fate, violated, perhaps forced to marry her attacker . . .a man on the other hand is viewed as a fool to miss the opportunity." Turning around he handed Darcy his portion and sat down. "Are you sleeping?"

"No, not well. Only that afternoon at the Gardiners, and I am afraid that was over far too soon."

"Well you did have an irreplaceable comforter. How is she?"

Darcy swirled the untouched liquid in his glass. "She is angry and hurt, but fortunately it is not directed at me. If I had spoken to her first, I do not know if that would be the case." He sighed and took a sip. "I have told her of my . . .past experience."

"And how on earth, no strike that, *why* on earth did you broach that subject?" Fitzwilliam leaned forward to try and read his expression.

"It was a compelling need to be completely honest with her. I know, you think that I am an idiot." Darcy stared into his glass.

"I do, what was your past has no bearing on what you live now, and for an innocent girl, who has no true knowledge of what happens . . ."

"So I hurt her by telling my truth?" Darcy closed his eyes and ran his hand over his face. "We were in the mistress's chambers, Georgiana and Audrey were downstairs, I was showing Elizabeth the redecoration that I had ordered, and it just happened."

"Without provocation?" Richard asked with a smile. "You just blurted out the news that you spent time visiting the highest quality brothels in London and the continent?"

"You make it sound as if I was there nightly, and you know full well that is not true." Darcy said bitterly. "Do not make me feel worse than she did when she asked if it was servants or women she would someday be forced to meet. That questioning made me feel like the lowest scum."

"It is common enough, Darcy." Richard laughed to see his guilt and delighted to hear of Elizabeth's interrogation. "You simply do not think to take advantage of the privilege of your sex and wealth."

"I told her that I have not been with a woman since the day we met." Darcy saw Richard's wonder and looked down to his hands. "It was dissatisfying and felt wrong. You knew this of me, we have spoken of it."

"I admit that I found it implausible, I should have known better, you never colour the truth. However, I am stunned that you told her *that*. What did she say?"

"Details were not necessary." He looked up again. "But I wanted no secrets between us; not after this experience with Anne, and it seems that her aunt had prepared her for such knowledge during one of their . . .enlightening discussions. Elizabeth hated the confirmation but said that she suspected that I . . .”

"Displayed experience? Good for her, she took a horribly embarrassing conversation and turned it back on you." Fitzwilliam smiled. "I wish all girls were taught what is what, it makes it all so much less embarrassing." Darcy rolled his eyes and Fitzwilliam laughed. "Well, I have heard that our aunt and cousin are back at Rosings."

"I do not care."

"Ah, but you should. She is likely not finished with you."

"And what could she do to me? As if I would marry Anne now." Darcy laughed shortly. "Never."

"Perhaps I will."

Darcy stopped the glass rising to his lips. "Are you out of your mind?"

"Probably, so how appropriate to marry a woman who is as well?" He smiled and saw that Darcy was not amused, and spoke seriously. "It is the only way for me to have an estate. Who wants a second son?"

"But you would be tied for life to . . .you could never have children!"

"Or kill her in the process, but her life will be short I imagine, even without the rigours of childbirth. It is a calculation on my part, I know. The thought of consummation is impossible. What you saw is far more than I ever would want to experience, but there is a compassionate aspect to it as well, she would be protected until her death; and for my sacrifice, I would be a landowner." He met Darcy's insistent gaze. "I cannot see Anne being sent to Bedlam Darcy. That is hell on earth."

"I know. There is that place in the North, the York Retreat run by the Quakers, they take a humanitarian approach and do not treat the patients like freaks or animals." Fitzwilliam looked down at his hands and Darcy watched him steadily. "No, Richard, please do not do this. You are hardened from your experience at war, and making such a match would make it worse. You need . . .you deserve so much more. If Aunt Catherine dies or becomes incapable of her care, you know the family will step in."

"Thank you for reminding me of that. It is a shame to lose Rosings, but it was Uncle Lewis' decision that it be returned to the de Bourghs if Anne died before marriage." Fitzwilliam spoke thoughtfully, "I suppose seeing both of my siblings making unhappy matches just puts me in the mood for feeling undeserving of anything for myself." He sighed. "You have ruined me, you know."

Darcy shrugged with a small smile then became serious. "Speaking of your siblings, Audrey was crying in the theatre."

"What did he do to her?" Fitzwilliam demanded.

"He was drunk. And Richard, she was looking to someone . . .I hope that he can be convinced to reform, I fear that Audrey may look for comfort elsewhere, and that would be a tragedy."

"My duties have kept me from confronting him about Wickham, now I have more ammunition to fire." He stood up. "Nobody hurts my sister."

"Do not make her a widow, Cousin." Darcy said seriously.

"No, but I do believe I will make him soil his breeches with anticipation." Fitzwilliam said grimly. "Derby tomorrow?"

"Yes, are you going?"

"No, have Elizabeth place a bet for me. Lady's luck."

Darcy smiled as he caught the guinea flying his way. "I will give her the message."

"And I will claim the victory kiss!" Fitzwilliam laughed and ducked out the door as Darcy's curse assailed him.

"WICKHAM?" Layton paced the room and returned to stare at his brother. "Are you sure?"

"I believe that Darcy would recognize him." Fitzwilliam said dryly. "I wonder how you did not know of this association. You and Singleton are thick as thieves, practically twins. It is a wonder that Alicia puts up with your shenanigans."

"See here, Richard, I may be a . . . I may be fond of society and all that, but I am not a reckless gambler. I enjoy a game as much as any man, but I would not gamble away the estate even if I could! Father's teachings did make some impact on me."

"Did they? Then why did he recently take you into his study for a thorough tongue-lashing about your lack of pride in the family and your lack of industry in learning the estate?"

"How did you . . .What do you mean?"

Fitzwilliam laughed and leaned against a bookshelf. "Just because I do not live here most of the time does not mean that I am without information. I hear that he is embarrassed for failing you. I disagree; you have never taken the initiative to do more than was absolutely necessary. What happens when Father dies? You will get his seat in the House of Lords and take over Matlock. Do you really know what that all entails?"

Layton looked up and sighed. "Not as much as I should. I actually have been taking steps to change myself." He walked away and played with a shepherdess on the mantle. "It is all Darcy's fault, you know. If he weren't such a damned good example . . ."

"Yes, I had a discussion with him about that recently." Fitzwilliam looked down at his boots and placing his hands behind his back paced a little. "We have failed another as well."

"Who?"

"Our sister."

"What is wrong . . .oh. Singleton."

"I have not been here to protect her from this idiot. He gambles away her dowry, he drinks, what else does he do? Do you two go whoring together? What disease is he bringing home to our sister?"

"You are one to talk, Brother."

"I am not married Brother, and it is from your body that the heir must come."

"It is hardly a . . ." Layton met his glare and sighed. "You do hang about Darcy too much." He caught his brother's raised brow and sighed again. "Forget I said that, Darcy's had enough, especially after Aunt Catherine's scheming, I will give him no trouble over his choice for wife." Layton closed his eyes when he saw Fitzwilliam incline his head with an ironic smile then continued, "Did it occur to you that some women welcome the opportunity to *not* be perpetually with child?"

"Yes, but that would be so if she had ever *been* with child." Fitzwilliam pointed out. "My guess is that Alicia knows of your behaviour and has refused your bed, and although it is your right to force your will, you either are afraid to or . . .you care about her too much to do such a vile thing."

"I have not been out," he met his brother's eye significantly, "in that way since Morris was found with the French disease. I wanted to be sure that I would not infect Alicia, and have stayed away."

Richard was dumbfounded. "Your unprecedented consideration honestly surprises me; may we blame this on Darcy, too?" Layton glanced at him and away. "Does she mind?"

"She does not know why!" He said with frustration.

"If you are not infected, will you return to your previous activities?"

"That depends on my wife. Perhaps after the heir is born she would wish to lead separate lives. I am hoping not." He said quietly. "I truly do care for her, you know."

"It is about time. I know that it was an arranged affair, but she is a wonderful woman. No mistress could replace that. I might actually come to respect you if you follow through with this transformation." Fitzwilliam looked his brother over and their gazes met and held. "I intend to confront Singleton. He made our sister cry in public with his behaviour." Layton's eyes grew angry and focussed. "I see that you agree with me that nobody hurts our little sister? I would like to frighten this fool into seeing the light before he finds himself at the losing end of a duel or Audrey decides to find comfort in the arms of a lover." Layton's head tipped in question. "She would not be the first, Brother. Singleton must secure an heir as well; I do not wish to see our sister endure her husband's doubt of her child's paternity."

"Where is he?"

"At the club, most likely."

Layton opened the door, and held out his arm. "After you, Colonel."

Richard's brow rose as a hint of his childhood playmate reappeared in his brother's demeanour. "Oh no, after you, Viscount."

"I insist."

"By your pleasure." Fitzwilliam smiled. "Together?" Layton nodded in agreement, and yelled when his brother dashed out first.

Arriving at their preferred club, Layton led the way to Singleton's likely haunt. As expected, he was at the card tables, surrounded by many others, and this time, winning. He looked up at his brothers with a smile. "Excellent! Come to join my success?"

Fitzwilliam came around to look at his cards and whistled. Immediately everyone else at the table folded their hands and Singleton glared at him. "I was bluffing."

"Hmm. Well, we want a word." He looked up and across the room. "Wickham!" He called.

Wickham startled and seeing Fitzwilliam's steely gaze, flinched before he smiled. "Fitzwilliam, a pleasure."

"How goes your family?" Fitzwilliam asked loudly, then striding across the room to Wickham's table, he clapped Lord Creary on the back. "Sir, I see that you are welcoming all comers to your play. I am surprised."

"What are you speaking of Fitzwilliam?" He blustered and looked at Wickham. "He is a fine player."

"Of course, all gamesters are." He pointed and nodded. "Where did you learn your craft? Certainly not at your father's knee, he was too busy working as steward at Pemberley." He smiled and bent to Creary, "You know; Darcy's estate?"

"What?" Creary stood while Wickham cringed, drawing his coins into his hands hurriedly. "You are not even a gentleman? Who sponsored you? How dare you enter this club! Begone from here!" Several footmen appeared on the scene and Wickham was grabbed by the arms to be dragged out.

"Damn you Fitzwilliam!"

"You should not have come back after seeing Darcy, you fool!" Fitzwilliam laughed after him. Creary touched his shoulder.

"Darcy recognized him here?"

"No, Darcy saw him at Vauxhall, but his engagement has kept him from the club, otherwise I imagine he would have spotted him here and raised the warning. You have seen his betrothed, have you not?" Fitzwilliam raised his brow. "You can see why he would be preoccupied?"

A small smile appeared on Creary's lips. "Ah, yes. Quite well-formed." He chuckled and then his face grew serious. "I will speak to the serjeant-at-arms about Wickham."

"I leave it to you, sir." Fitzwilliam nodded to the rest and joined his brothers. "Now why is it that I had to identify Wickham? You knew who he was."

Singleton looked down. "I sponsored him here, if I had said who he was, I would have been a laughingstock."

Layton looked at him with disgust. "Come on, we are going to talk about a few more of your failings." They moved off to take a private room, usually meant for very high stakes card games, and locked the door.

"What is this about?" Singleton straightened his coat when Layton let him go, and noted Fitzwilliam leaning against the door with his arms folded.

"You Brother; have disappointed the family."

"What do you mean?" He demanded.

"I mean, our sister was moved to tears in public over your behaviour."

"Did Harwick put you up to this?" Singleton said angrily. "He said he was giving me friendly advice, I did not realize he was going behind my back."

Fitzwilliam and Layton exchanged glances and Layton shrugged. "Obviously his advice fell on deaf ears if we found you here."

"He warned me to cut my ties with Wickham, and pay attention to my wife, that I might regret my behaviour deeply if she were to die unexpectedly or my actions might lead to my premature death and leave her alone." Singleton's voice dwindled away as he spoke.

"Spoken as a man who has lost a great deal. I see that you have repaid his thoughtfulness by continuing as you have?"

"It is a difficult habit to break and besides, I was in my cups and did not really catch all that he said."

"It sounds to me that you caught a great deal," Fitzwilliam said softly, "but chose to ignore it." Advancing to his brother he looked down at him, and put his hand on the hilt of his sabre. Singleton swallowed and watched in fascination as the shining metal was caressed, almost lovingly. "I will say this to you once. You make some changes to your habits and amends to our sister, or we will have more than just words in a closed room in a private club."

"You threaten me?" Singleton's voice shook.

"I promise you." Fitzwilliam spoke softly. "I am very adept with the art of persuasion . . .Brother."

"I have the scars to prove that." Layton added.

"Scars?"

"Hmm." Layton nodded.

"What gives you the right to question my behaviour? You are no better!"

"I take great exception to that. I may play cards, but I have never touched my wife's dowry. I may be a social snob, but that is the right of my position. I have come to see the ways that I have failed myself and my family and have begun to make changes. I am not perfect, but at least I am not you. My wife does not cry." Fitzwilliam unlocked the door and opened it. "I believe that you need to read your marriage contract and make sure that Audrey's assets remain intact. If you have gambled them away, I suggest that you find a way to replace them, and if I catch you doing anything beyond being a good husband to our sister and learning your role for your estate, I . . . will not hold back the Colonel." He smiled and Fitzwilliam nodded.

"We will be watching you, Brother." He touched his blade again and glanced at Singleton's breeches. "Spill something?" He smiled and left. Layton glanced at the fall and laughed, and followed Fitzwilliam out. Singleton looked at himself and sank down on a chair at the table, and sat alone to contemplate their words while he waited for his breeches to dry.

"I HATE TO SAY THIS UNCLE, but this year our trip to Epsom is far more comfortable than the last." Elizabeth smiled across to where Mr. Gardiner sat with Darcy and Bingley.

"You mean that riding on a stagecoach with a group of merrymakers was not enjoyable? Why I am insulted!" He chuckled to see her head shaking.

"You rode a stagecoach?" Darcy said unhappily.

"We did." Elizabeth smiled. "It was better than trying to find somewhere to leave Uncle's coach. We simply paid our fares and agreed to meet at an inn at the appointed time. Our companions were a friendly, if drunken lot."

"I am surprised that you noticed them at all, Lizzy. The ride home you were decidedly in a world of your own." He smiled at her then back at Darcy.

His mouth dropped open when he saw her blushing, then he sat up a little straighter and smiled. "If I might relieve your discomfort Elizabeth, I will own that I spent the ride home wondering where in the convoy a certain girl's carriage was located."

"Oh." She bit her lip and blushed brighter.

Mrs. Gardiner patted her hand and smiled. "I will tell you Mr. Darcy, she did not lose that dreamy countenance for days afterwards."

"Is this embarrass Elizabeth day?" She demanded fiercely as her face grew increasingly red, and Darcy's chest puffed with pride

"May I ask what finally brought you back to earth, Miss Elizabeth?" Bingley asked with a grin.

"Oh, well it was nothing to be remembered, sir." She said quietly and looked down at her hands. "I . . .I met a man in Hyde Park who did not think much of me and I am afraid that effectively burst my bubble of happiness for quite some time." She glanced at Jane who opened her mouth in surprise then at her aunt who nodded with the memory.

"Yes, but he was rather rude, you will recall."

Elizabeth saw Darcy's smile had disappeared as he remembered that moment when he had decided to let her go. "Fitzwilliam?"

"I do not like hearing of anyone who brings you unhappiness, Elizabeth." He said softly.

"Well, I had my revenge, of a sort. We met him at the theatre, and he found me . . . handsome enough, I think." She smiled at him, but saw that the sadness in his eyes remained. It was not the place to question him, and the company prevented any more conversation on that subject.

"Have you chosen your horse yet, Miss Bennet?" Bingley asked, noticing how she had fallen into her own thoughts.

"No sir, I would like to see them first." She smiled a little and his eyes lit up.

"You need to assess their build?"

"No, Mr. Bingley, she likes to look at their eyes." Elizabeth teased and saw Jane blush. "If they have pretty eyes then they will assuredly run well."

The men laughed. "Lizzy!" She said angrily.

"I go by name, and Aunt looks at their colours, what is the difference? We are silly, but may I point out, I did win last year."

"A fluke, I am certain." Mr. Gardiner declared.

"So you will not split your purse with me again this year?" Elizabeth demanded. "And which will you follow? Eyes or colour?"

"I had better follow my wife, I think. Besides, you have Mr. Darcy's funds to play with this year, do you not?"

"And Fitzwilliam's." He added, slowly regaining his humour. "So who is our choice, Elizabeth?"

She studied the list of names that Jane held up, and scanning them she picked one. "Pope."

"Why? You are not Catholic." His lips twitched.

"I doubt that his owner is either, but Papa is coming to visit on Tuesday, so I thought it would be good luck." She saw Jane's confusion. "Pope is from the Latin, Papa."

Darcy looked at her in admiration. "You know Latin as well?"

"I know that women should not learn it but I own to knowing a little." She said shyly. "Enough to make terrible errors in translations."

"We will have to test you sometime." Darcy smiled, and she relaxed to see him happy again.

"I would prefer a good game of chess."

"Oh that would be interesting to watch, Miss Elizabeth. Darcy is the club champion." Bingley grinned to see Darcy shrug. "He routed me countless times at Pemberley."

"What is your impression of the estate, Mr. Bingley?" Mrs. Gardiner asked.

"Oh, it is indescribable. The house is the finest I have ever seen, but truth be told, it is the scenery and sport that gets me. Excellent game, fishing, hunting, very well managed. I rather fancy finding a home in the Peaks someday, but I suppose I will have to settle for whatever estate presents itself to me."

"There is an estate adjacent to Longbourn that is for sale, Mr. Bingley. The owner leases it, but he would prefer to sell. Mr. Stewart's family took it for a while but they are gone now." Jane said quietly.

"Is that so?" Bingley raised his brows and looked at Darcy. "Should I look at it?"

"I think you need another year in town first. And I would like to know why it has not sold. Land is at a premium. There must be something that the owner has not addressed that keeps it on the market, whether the house needs to be repaired or the fields are poor producers, there is a reason. I would look into it before committing and furthermore, take a lease before purchase."

"I will not make a move without you Darcy." Bingley laughed and sat back to smile at them all.

An hour later the carriage arrived in Epsom. The rendezvous point was agreed upon, and the group of six made their way with the crowd to the stands. Darcy and Elizabeth led the procession, and they were ushered to their places. Darcy performed the duty of introducing them to their neighbours and enduring several inane conversations, and the exceptionally calculating examination that Elizabeth received from everyone who learned her identity. When at last it was over, Elizabeth took her seat beside him and smiled up to meet his admiring gaze. "This is such a better spot than last year. I will actually see the race as opposed to a series of backs."

"And not be trampled."

"Oh, if Uncle had not held my shoulders, I surely would have drowned in the stampede for the rail." She laughed as he frowned. "What is it?"

Darcy took her hand. "I should have gone to your side."

"You tried, but you made a good friend who needs you instead."

"You are a good friend who I hope needs me as well." He lifted her hand to his lips and she blushed. "Is it my imagination, or have you become shy with me, Elizabeth?"

"I . . . I do not know." He bent his head to peek up under her new hat. "I spent several hours watching you sleep Fitzwilliam, and I believe that made me feel closer to you than anything. I . . . I imagined that we were at home and I thought of how much I wished to . . ." She grew silent.

"Kiss me?" He whispered.

"Touch you." She whispered back and glanced up to see his delight and looked quickly down. "I . . .I wish to see your neck." Elizabeth murmured to her lap. Darcy laughed softly and she bristled. "What did I say?"

"Oh dearest, you cannot possibly know how much seeing your neck entices me." He smiled at her wide eyes and laughed again. "So you were dreaming of us at home." He sighed happily. "I so like the sound of that."

"I do too. I am sorry that Uncle would not allow us to change our wedding date."

"I can understand his hesitation, I suppose, but it only tries my patience." Darcy saw her renewed blush. "What has gotten into you, my love?"

"Oh leave me be!" She whispered and went back to chewing her lip. "I have to go to Longbourn soon."

Immediately he stiffened. "Why?"

"Fitzwilliam, I have a closet full of clothes to sort through!"

"Have you not just spent a scandalous sum on new ones?" He said with a glint in his eye.

"And who demanded that?"

"My aunt, as I recall."

"I seem to remember you had some say in the process, sir."

"Sir?"

"SIR!"

"Lizzy!" Mrs. Gardiner admonished.

She glanced at her aunt and was greeted by Darcy's raised brow. "I would also like to say goodbye to my sisters, and I imagine that Mama . . ."

"No parties Elizabeth; please."

"I was not expecting you to come." She looked away.

"Pardon me?" He looked at her in great surprise, then realized she sought to spare him her family. Instead of embarrassing her further he chose a different subject. "Do you seriously think that I would allow you to travel alone?"

"Well, I thought you would be busy and we would take the post, and . . ."

"Miss Elizabeth . . ." He said sternly, "MY wife does not take the post!"

"I am not your wife, SIR." She said cheekily.

"*Yet.*" He said huskily and bent back down to whisper. "And I assure you, my dearest, beautiful, challenging love, that when you are, your neck, and every other part of you will be blushing for quite some time." Nodding with satisfaction he watched the colour rising from her breasts to her chin and lost the rest under the brim of her hat. Hearing his name called, he turned and greeted Stewart and his sister.

"Miss Elizabeth." Laura called over to her. "Miss Elizabeth? Are you well?" She saw the blush when Elizabeth looked up. "Oh, you must be overly warm!"

"I am fine, Miss Stewart." She glanced at Darcy's little smile and stepped on his boot. "Mr. Stewart, it is a great pleasure to see you again." Darcy's smile disappeared.

"Thank you Miss Elizabeth. You are lovely today." They took their seats just behind them and Stewart leaned down to Darcy. "It seems all of London made the trip. Is your family in attendance?"

"They should be, but I have not spotted them." He transferred his frown to Stewart. "Are you looking for anyone in particular?"

"Hmm? Oh no, just curious." He scanned the crowd and smiled back at him.

"I am surprised not to see Mr. Harwick with you, Miss Bennet." Laura said with a smile.

Jane startled from her survey of the fashionable crowd. "Oh, his sister was arriving today, and he could not come."

"Oh what a shame, he seemed so interested in the horses." She looked around with barely hidden disappointment and Jane felt strangely defensive.

"Mr. Harwick feels strongly about his family, so of course his sister's arrival is more important than attending a race."

Mrs. Gardiner glanced at her husband in surprise and turned to regard Jane carefully. She was flushed and looked somewhat defiant. "Well that was interesting." Mr. Gardiner murmured.

"What brought that about?" Mrs. Gardiner said softly.

"I do not know, but it is about time." He glanced over to Darcy and Elizabeth and chuckled. "Now these two are lost."

"Your eyes are dancing." Darcy smiled.

"This is exciting; can you not feel the pulse of the crowd?" She looked around to see the milling people, but focussed her attention to the open area where they stood last year.

"I find myself in the odd position of wishing we were down there." Darcy spoke softly.

"With the unwashed hoard?" Elizabeth laughed and turned to smile at him. "I know enough of you Fitzwilliam that you are far happier here. If you must be in a crowd, you prefer one of your peers."

"That shows my disdain for those below me. Are you trying to shame me?"

"No, I am simply being honest. I cannot expect you to disregard who you were raised to be anymore than you can expect me to ever leave my upbringing completely behind." She looked down to her hands and he reached out to hold them.

"But you discount the attraction of anonymity that standing in that crowd gives us. I would love to see how a girl with proper country manners reacts to a race." His comment, instead of making her smile, brought a frown. The first of many races began and while everyone else watched the horses, he watched her, and noticed that her attention was on the ladies in the crowd. He saw her mirroring their movements, and realized that his statement on her country manners had made her self-conscious. When she reined in her natural enthusiasm and applauded politely at the race's conclusion, he stood. "Come."

"Where?"

He bent to Mr. Gardiner. "Sir, I am going to take Elizabeth to place our bets for the Derby, do you mind?"

Seeing the determination in the man's eye, and knowing full well that there was nowhere they could possibly be alone, he smiled and sent them on their way. Darcy offered Elizabeth his arm, nodded to Stewart as he watched them pass and took her out of the stands and through the milling crowds, past the men selling refreshments, placed their bets, and instead of returning to their seats, turned in the opposite direction.

"What are we doing?"

"You will see." He said cryptically and continuing on, stopped short when he saw his uncle and cousin approaching.

"I was wondering if we would see you today." Lord Matlock smiled and bowed to Elizabeth. "Our carriage was delayed with the traffic. We should have come with you, Darcy. You made good time, I suppose."

"We did, but there was no room for you, Elizabeth's family and Bingley joined us." He noticed Layton's raised brows, but appreciated that he made no comment, and was at least behaving politely to Elizabeth. "Did Singleton come with you?"

Layton smiled. "No, he . . .was persuaded to remain home with Audrey and Georgiana." Darcy cocked his head and his cousin continued, "Richard and I persuaded him."

"I am sorry to have missed that."

"I have no doubt that you will hear the details." Layton laughed and saw Elizabeth's curious gaze. "Ahem. In any case, I hope that it was effective. We are on our way back to the ladies, and you?"

"Are taking the air." Darcy smiled and they moved on. "Curious."

"What was that about?" Elizabeth asked as they moved on. "Is Audrey well?"

Darcy looked down at her to see the concern for his cousin, and brought his hand up to cover hers. "I hope that her brothers have inspired her husband to change his ways."

"I know how upset she was at the theatre; I suppose that he behaves that way frequently." She saw Darcy's nod. "And the Colonel and Viscount . . ."

"Spoke up for their sister." He smiled to see her satisfaction. "You are pleased."

"I want her to be happy. I know that Mr. Singleton was not her choice but her parents'. I seem to have the knowledge of how unfathomably fortunate our relationship is driven home to me at every turn. Thank you again for risking so much to marry someone like me."

"I do not know what has made you feel so low about yourself today Elizabeth, but I wish that you would stop. Did my comments about your manners start you thinking this way? Truly dearest, I find nothing at all wanting in you." He leaned down to try and see her eyes. "Why are you so shy with me?"

"I suppose that I have had a great deal to think about of late." She said softly, in great contrast with the roar of the crowd during the second race.

Darcy strained to hear her as she continued. "I have thought much of your cousin, Miss de Bourgh."

"Elizabeth, even if I wanted such a match, marrying a delusional woman is impossible."

"I wonder what she looks like." She said softly. "Is she beautiful?"

"She is sickly, Elizabeth." He heard her sigh and stopped walking. "Please tell me what is wrong."

She said nothing until his insistent gaze drove the thoughts from her; and in a burst it tumbled out. "All around me I see marriages, and the common theme is the wealth of the couples. What one can bring to the other, and the sacrifice they make to secure the funds for another generation. I see it with Audrey and Mr. Singleton, and the Viscount and Lady Layton. I know that it is the reason my parents married and yours. It is the only reason Jane would consider Mr. Harwick, and he is merely looking for a woman to secure his heir. I bring nothing to you, if anything I take away. My lack of dowry takes funds from your wealth to create a settlement, my lack of connection and instruction takes away from my ability to be a good hostess and example to Georgiana, my lack of beauty . . ."

"Enough of this!" Darcy said fiercely. "Enough I say!" She looked up to him with wide eyes, and saw that he was battling hard to restrain his reaction. "Sometimes Elizabeth, you can say the most ridiculous things!"

"What did I say that was incorrect?" She demanded.

He stared into her frightened, angry, beautiful eyes, falling deeper under her spell with each passing moment, and reminded himself that despite her strength, his Elizabeth was not yet eighteen. "Everything you said was true." Her eyes cast down, and he touched her chin to raise it back up to his gaze, "Except what you say of yourself. Your manners are lovely, your care for my sister is invaluable, and your beauty is incomparable, and those qualities barely touch the reasons for my wanting you. You my love, are recovering from my cousin's attack still, just as I am, and I think you are nervous of your father coming to visit and how that might somehow make me reconsider our engagement." She bit her lip and looked back down. "Dearest if I could, I would be kissing you senseless right now to clear your mind of such foolishness." He glanced down to his breeches and she followed his eyes, raising her hand to her mouth in surprise. "Do you see what you do to me?" He whispered heatedly to her ear.

"Fitzwilliam, what can we do? Hide that!" She ordered.

Darcy started to laugh, loudly, happily, and watched as she positioned herself in front of him. He saw that his mirth was attracting attention and did not care. "Come my love; let us go somewhere that I can express my feelings in relative obscurity." He took her hand, placing it back on his arm, still chuckling as she attempted to shield his groin with her skirts, and made their way down the path that led to the spot where they had watched each other one year ago.

3 June 1809

Such an exceptional day I spent with my Elizabeth! I have attended the Derby five times and three were memorable, the first with Father, obviously last year when I saw my love and made a friend of Bingley, and this year, with my endearingly frightened and confusingly shy Elizabeth. I hope that I have managed to reassure her that nothing will send me away. She will be my wife, no matter what her father does, and although I did not express it then, I will have to tell her how much comfort she brings me to see her distress over Anne. It is not right for a man to express excess emotion, but to see her clearly struggling with hers brings me relief in some way from the memory of that horrible night. I was so happy to bring her to the public viewing area and steal a kiss while the crowd pressed forward to the rail. That short embrace and exchange of affection seemed to return my Elizabeth's confidence and humour. She needed my touch, it seems. I cannot express in any way how gratifying that is to me. My kiss returned a wilting rose to full bloom.

Next year when I escort my wife to the Derby, and she undoubtedly wins once again, I will disregard all of propriety and kiss that woman before all of polite society. Never have I seen anything as breathtaking and enticing as my Elizabeth trembling with the joy of her triumph. But I will not wait a full year for this. I am determined to achieve that expression of elation by my hand. Be prepared to blush my love. There will be no chaperones on our honeymoon.

Darcy set down his pen, blew out his candle, and walked from his sitting room, through his empty bedchamber and into the freshly redecorated mistress's chambers. He settled into the bed, closing his eyes, imagining Elizabeth touching him as she whispered all she wished to do . . .then groaned and fell soundly, securely, to sleep.

Chapter 22

"Mmmm." Anne murmured.

"Miss Anne, how do you feel?" Mrs. Jenkinson was at her side, pressing a cold compress to her head. A fever had come not long after their return from the trip to London. The companion kept her views to herself, but she knew that the excitement and the turmoil of the journey was the likely cause. For anyone else, this would have been a simple illness, and easily battled. For Anne, it was just another step closer to death.

"Where am I?" She said as her eyes blinked open.

"You are in your chambers at Rosings, do you not recognize it?"

"Rosings?" She sat up and ripped the cloth from her head, then stared at Mrs. Jenkinson. "Why do you address me as Miss Anne? I am Mrs. Darcy! Why am I not at Pemberley?"

Mrs. Jenkinson gasped; the delusion did not disappear when she was removed from Darcy's company. "Miss Anne, you are not married. Rosings is your home."

"No, I married my cousin! I am Mrs. Fitzwilliam Darcy!" She said stubbornly. "Why are you teasing me? Where is my husband? Why am I here? He is the master of Rosings; we should be in the master's chambers! Mama must move out! Is that what is wrong? Will Mama not leave?" She threw the covers aside and stood, then collapsed on the bed, too weak to walk. "Tell Fitzwilliam, tell him . . ." She closed her eyes.

Mrs. Jenkinson took the opportunity to lift her head and put a glass to her lips. "Come now Miss Anne, drink your medicine." Anne murmured but obediently swallowed the laudanum. Mrs. Jenkinson managed to move her back into place, covered her, and called for a maid to sit by her side while she went in search of her mother.

"Lady de Bourgh." She said quietly from the doorway.

Lady Catherine immediately looked up from where she had been lecturing Mr. Collins on his mentor's choice of sermon topics. "Well?"

"I have some news." She glanced at Mr. Collins.

"Is it about my daughter? Is her fever worse?"

"It is the same, madam; however I need to speak to you." Mrs. Jenkinson tried to impart as much as she could into her look and Lady Catherine nodded.

"Is Miss de Bourgh ill? Shall I go and pray with her, and give her the comfort that she surely will feel with the words of our Lord?" Mr. Collins said eagerly.

It was a convenient excuse to remove him from the room and Mr. Collins was soon on his way with a maid to visit Anne. "What is it, Mrs. Jenkinson?"

"Madam, I hesitate to inform you of this, but Miss Anne awakened from her sleep and firmly believed that she was Mrs. Darcy. She demanded to know why she was not in the mistresses' chambers, and assumed that you had not moved out of them since the wedding. Madam, her delusion grows! She expects Mr. Darcy to come to her. I gave her some elixir and she fell to sleep so she is safe with Mr. Collins, but she cannot go about speaking of such things!"

"She believes herself married to my nephew?" Lady Catherine said with interest, "Even now?"

"Yes, madam. I am certain that with Mr. Darcy's pending wedding he would not appreciate such a story spreading,"

"No, he would not like that at all. It would hurt his reputation, not to mention Anne's . . ." Lady Catherine began thinking quickly when Mr. Collins reappeared.

"My Lady! Imagine my surprise to learn that Miss de Bourgh, pardon me, Mrs. Darcy . . .that your daughter had married! Why it is great news indeed! I regret that I, I mean Reverend Mousely, was not chosen to perform the ceremony; however the description she gave me of the fine service performed by the Bishop himself in London certainly explains why my . . .his poor service was not necessary. Shall I toll the bells in celebration, madam? All the countryside should know that Rosings has a master and I do hope, will soon have an heir? Of course, pending Mrs. Darcy's recovery." He added sorrowfully.

Mrs. Jenkinson stared at him with her mouth open then turned to look at Lady Catherine. A small smile of triumph played over her mouth. "Mr. Collins, I thank you for your congratulations, however Mr. Darcy is not presently at Rosings, and my daughter's illness has made her confused of his location. When he arrives, you may celebrate as is appropriate for such a great occasion, however, until he arrives we will only rejoice in our halls." She quickly ran through the possibilities in her mind. Darcy would not let his cousin be labelled mentally ill by denying their marriage as a delusion. It would hurt the family. He would marry her to protect their name, and to save his reputation. After all, how could he pretend to marry this country upstart if he was already married to Anne?

"Lady de Bourgh!" Mrs. Jenkinson said urgently.

Lady Catherine turned to Mr. Collins. "I have much to do with my daughter. You have the orders for the sermons. Good day, sir."

Bobbing and bowing, and with a shower of congratulations, the little man departed. She turned to Mrs. Jenkinson. "You will say nothing of this to Mr. Darcy."

"Madam, Miss Anne cannot make such claims publicly! Her dosage must not be strong enough now, we must call the physician!"

"You are in no position to question me, Jenkinson! Now go see to your duties!" She watched the woman flee the room and went to her writing desk to compose her nephew an important letter.

"MISS BINGLEY?" The master of ceremonies caught her attention. "Miss Bingley, may I present Mr. Wickham." The ball's host bowed away and left the couple alone. Wickham bowed and smiled at her, looking over her thin, but well-formed body as he did. Caroline felt his eyes raking over her and could not suppress the thrill it gave her. Nonetheless, she was not going to be too welcoming until she knew who he was.

"Miss Bingley, I am very pleased to meet you. When I entered the ballroom tonight and spotted you, I just had to be introduced. I hope that I am welcome? You are not attached to any gentleman here?"

"Mr. Wickham, the pleasure is mine, and no, I have no particular attachments here other than family. I rarely attend balls of this nature." She lifted her chin and gave the room a disdainful look, then turned back to see him nodding with understanding. "You feel the same?"

"Ah yes, I am much more familiar with St. James', however, it is often enjoyable to see how others live." He smirked and saw that he had chosen well. This was a woman who wanted to better herself. Her gown, clearly a poorer version of what he had seen all Season amongst the ladies of the first circles, and her fondness for wearing excessive jewellery, identified her as one who was reaching, not one who had arrived. Nonetheless, she had jewels, and did have access to a modiste. She must then have money.

Caroline's eyes lit up. "St. James's, oh yes, I plan to attend there again soon with my brother. He goes often with his good friend Mr. Darcy."

"Darcy?" Wickham started, then recognized the ploy of a name-dropper, and smiled. "Fitzwilliam Darcy of Pemberley?"

"Yes! Do you know him?"

"Of course, I lived with his family at Pemberley most of my life. We know each other very well. Are you good friends with him as your brother is?"

"I had hoped to be." She said with obvious bitterness. "Unfortunately he has recently become engaged."

Wickham nodded and smiled at her ambition, and inwardly cursed Darcy's easy access to women. "Miss Elizabeth Bennet, yes shocking. I know all about her, she comes from a small estate with little dowry. I met her recently when I spoke with Darcy at Vauxhall Gardens."

"What do you think of her? I have not run across her yet." Caroline lied. She was dying to hear something disparaging.

"She is pretty, that is undeniable, but I can assume that you have so much more to offer a man." Wickham smiled and saw her blush. "There is nothing to be done. If Darcy has chosen a lowly maid as his wife it is his loss. I imagine there is undoubtedly a fascinating story behind it, but the engagement is announced so he is gone. Whatever is a fine woman like you to do?"

"Well, I will certainly not pine for such a fool." Caroline huffed.

"Of course not, I should hope that instead you might dance with me?" Wickham bowed and held out his arm.

Caroline looked over the charming handsome man and smiled. "Yes, I would like that Mr. Wickham. And you can tell me all about living at Pemberley; do not leave out a single detail."

"I would not think of it, Miss Bingley." He smiled and led her away.

ELIZABETH CLOSED HER EYES, trying to block out the undeniable truth that her mother sat next to her in the carriage on the way to Darcy House. She could not decide if Fitzwilliam sending the carriage empty to retrieve them was good or bad. She listened to her mother's chatter and looked up briefly to notice her father's amused smile. Making only noncommittal responses to the insistent questions about Darcy House, at last Mrs. Bennet turned her attention to Jane.

"Now, what progress have you made with Mr. Harwick?"

"I have done all that you taught me, Mama. I have smiled and been demure." Mrs. Bennet nodded happily. "But I do not feel that is enough. He seemed to enjoy my singing when Lizzy asked me to accompany her yesterday." Jane smiled at Elizabeth who nodded, pleased to see some semblance of the sister she knew from Hertfordshire making an appearance.

"Singing?" Mrs. Bennet asked incredulously. "Well, I suppose. How did he react?"

"He smiled Mama, and sat closer to me."

"And did you lean forward to display . . ." Mrs. Bennet glanced at her sister's wide eyes and how she was looking across to the men. Jane's hand went to her mouth in shock; never before had her mother suggested showing herself off in such a manner.

"Well, did he notice your beauty?"

"Mama, Mr. Harwick wants to see if Jane is a fit mother for his girls!" Elizabeth cried.

"And he wants a son!" Mrs. Bennet snapped back. Elizabeth looked to her father who had become interested in the passing scenery and did not say a word. Mr. Gardiner stared expressively at his wife and closed his eyes.

Jane watched the argument play out and began to think of what she might do when she saw Mr. Harwick. Her sister's, her aunt's, and especially Mr.

Darcy's words had begun to sink in, and then hearing Miss Stewart inquire after Mr. Harwick at the Derby made her realize that her position was tenuous indeed.

Mrs. Gardiner slipped her hand over Elizabeth's and squeezed. "We are approaching the park Lizzy; it certainly looks different at this time of day." She smiled to see her niece look out the window. "Just think; you will soon be able to walk here anytime that you wish."

"Fitzwilliam told me that he enjoys looking from the windows to see the sun setting over the trees. It reminds him of being at Pemberley."

"Fitzwilliam? That is a very informal way of referring to him, Lizzy."

"We are engaged Papa, and I am amongst family." Mr. Bennet's brows rose in surprise at her sharp address. Clearly his daughter was very displeased with him.

"Which home is Darcy House?" Mrs. Bennet asked eagerly, scanning the passing townhouses as they drove down Park Lane towards Grosvenor Square.

Elizabeth looked away from her father to touch the window. "It is the grey one there, do you see? Far down the street?"

"All of that is one house?" Mrs. Bennet stared then turned in her seat, leaning over Elizabeth to gawk out of the window as they approached. Mr. Bennet's eyes widened, seeing at last the concrete evidence of Darcy's wealth. "Oh how very rich he is! And his home in Derbyshire; is it similar to this?" She eagerly looked between Elizabeth and Mrs. Gardiner.

"No Mama, Pemberley is quite different. The only similarity is the colour of the stone. There is a landscape of it in his study that he can show you when we tour the rooms."

"Why the townhouse is as large as Longbourn, even larger, I should imagine! What is the size of Pemberley? He has ten thousand a year; it must be a very great home!"

"Mama, please do not embarrass Mr. Darcy by speaking of his wealth." Elizabeth said in a low voice.

"Embarrass? Surely he is not embarrassed to be rich? You should be speaking of it to the entire world! I know I have certainly made sure that all of our neighbours are aware of the fine match my Lizzy has made!"

"Suddenly I am *her* Lizzy." Elizabeth said softly and Jane heard her.

"She is proud of the match you have made." Jane whispered. Elizabeth looked at her and sighed as she nodded resignedly. The sisters squeezed hands and the carriage came to a stop.

"*This* is a palace!" Mrs. Bennet gasped.

"Perhaps you should ask about its size compared to St. James'." Mr. Bennet smiled when she turned to him and nodded vigorously.

"Why do you encourage her?" Mr. Gardiner spoke angrily. "Do you *want* your daughters to be rejected?"

"I doubt that they would be upset to be told how rich they are by a silly fawning woman." Mr. Bennet replied.

Inside of the foyer, Darcy stood with Harwick, watching out the windows for the carriage to arrive. From the background they heard the sound of Fitzwilliam's jovial voice and a woman's amusement. Glancing over to his companion, Darcy saw his head turned to look at the stairs. "He is harmless."

"A colonel in His Majesty's army is harmless?"

Darcy shrugged. "Well, unless your sister is in Napoleon's army . . ."

"I say again, an officer in the army is harmless?"

"She was married, Harwick, I imagine that she knows how to handle herself."

"Hmm." He glanced back again and relaxed. "It is good to hear her laugh. Why is he here again?"

"He is performing reconnaissance for my aunt, he claims. I think that he is just as curious himself."

The men resumed their vigil until Darcy broke the silence. "Are you sure of this?"

"I am sure that I need to meet her father." He said stiffly. "I am sure that my daughters need a mother, and I am sure that I need to try for a son."

"But are you sure . . . Forgive me, it is not my business." He cleared his throat.

Harwick looked at his hands. "She seems different, more welcoming, more interested in me. I did enjoy the ladies singing to us last night. Perhaps she realizes that the end game has come."

"Was she discouraging before?"

Harwick saw his blank expression and smiled slightly. "Surely you noticed her reticence, Darcy. At first I chalked it up to the behaviour of a demure woman, proper behaviour, not showing her interest too soon . . . but I have not been blind to the discomfort between the sisters. I have to admit that her lack of enthusiasm was off-putting and intriguing."

"Intriguing?"

"We are both the subject of interest by women in search of husbands; it was just interesting that a woman with such terrible prospects was not putting more of an effort into the match. I have been forced to search for reasons to accept her, and that is unexpected."

"I understand that she has always been told that her looks would capture the man and nothing more was necessary."

"Her mother?"

"Yes."

"What an odd notion. I mean beyond the initial capture of his attention, the girl does need to keep his interest going. I admit I am a bit at a loss what Miss Bennet and I would do with each other if I brought her home, well besides the obvious, but there are many hours to the day, and one cannot always be at sport or business." He smiled to see Darcy look down. "Forgive me for sounding so crass."

"No sir, you have been married, and know better than I what the life is like. You have made it clear that you are marrying to produce an heir, not to fall in love. I am also aware that your decision is hardly made. You bring up valid points. Naturally I hope that Miss Bennet marries, I also recognize that it may not be to you, and will hold no grudge either way."

"I appreciate that, I hope that her family feels the same way; my decision will be made based upon what will be best for my daughters and any future children."

"I believe that may be part of the conflict in Miss Bennet's behaviour. While she knows she would marry you for duty, she cannot help but wish for . . ."

"Her sister's match. Yes, Darcy, I do understand that very well, which is why I did not give up on this idea of Miss Bennet sooner when my doubts began to surface."

"Sir, may I make one observation, and I will not speak of it again. I think that you are a very good and sincere man, and that you truly believe that you wish to marry entirely without emotion so you will not be hurt again, but every time I see you remembering your wife, I cannot help but see that you must marry with some feeling or not at all. I would hope that you are happy. I would hope for the same for Miss Bennet." Darcy met Harwick's eyes and said quietly. "Forgive me if you feel that I have stepped beyond my place, I am thinking of my future sister and of a man who I have come to regard highly."

"I appreciate that Darcy, sometimes it takes an impartial judge to point out the obvious." Harwick nodded and turned his eyes to the window when a carriage arrived in front of the house.

The door opened and a footman was there to hand them down. Darcy saw them arrive and was on his way through the gate when Elizabeth stepped out first. He had a smile ready for her but it disappeared as soon as she looked up to him. Her beautiful eyes were the picture of distress. "Dearest, whatever is the matter?"

"Oh Fitzwilliam!" Elizabeth took his hand and held it tightly. "Papa brought Mama with him!"

"He *what?*" Darcy looked quickly to the carriage as if he could see through the walls and back to Elizabeth. "We arranged this meeting specifically so that Harwick would *not* be exposed to . . .Dearest, I fear that your mother's presence will give your father reason to be amused at her antics instead of determined to make the match with Harwick as we had planned."

"I have already been witness to it."

Darcy saw her struggle for composure and quickly guided her into the front hall, past Harwick who glanced at them with concern, and back to an alcove where they stood tightly embraced. "Why is she here?" He demanded.

"Papa could not endure listening to her complaints any longer, and decided that the surest way to peace was to allow her to come." Elizabeth's frustration with her parent was obvious and he could feel her anger rising.

Kissing the top of her head, he rested his cheek in her curls before forcing himself to speak calmly. "How has she been so far?"

"She is very excited, but nothing too mortifying."

Darcy could not hold back his laugh. "Forgive me, dearest. But your definition of mortifying behaviour by your mother is likely far different from that of my relatives'."

She gasped. "Must you be so honest?"

"I find it better than living in denial." He looked down to see the flash of anger in her eyes fade. "We both know the truth. Let us hope that the atmosphere will be sufficient to awe and silence."

"Awe yes, silence . . ." Elizabeth was silenced herself by Darcy's mouth being applied convincingly to hers. "oh."

He hugged her and spoke quietly. "I know that you are afraid, Elizabeth. Do not doubt my commitment, no matter what happens here."

Stepping away from her he masked his expression, took her hand tightly in his and emerged from the alcove to the foyer where the carriage occupants had at last arrived and were handing their hats over to the servants. Jane introduced Harwick to her parents, but it was another man who had Mrs. Bennet's heart at that moment and her voice was clear. "Where did Lizzy go? I am certain that I saw Mr. Darcy."

"Good afternoon." He said, then before she could respond, he turned to his cousin, who had come down to greet the guests. "Colonel Richard Fitzwilliam, may I present Elizabeth's parents? Mr. and Mrs. Thomas Bennet."

"I am delighted to meet you and look forward to you joining our family for dinner tomorrow." Fitzwilliam looked at Elizabeth with a question in his eyes.

"Colonel, my mother unexpectedly made the trip with my father. I only learned of her presence an hour ago. I hope that your mother will be able to fit everyone comfortably. I did not have the opportunity to write her a note; would you please tell her the news for me?"

"Oh it is just one more mouth to feed, I am certain there is room at an Earl's table? I imagine that if your uncle's home is half the size of this, the table must be great indeed!" Mrs. Bennet beamed at Darcy.

"Yes, it is." He said shortly.

Mrs. Gardiner spoke up. "Elizabeth designed a very extensive menu, so an extra guest should be no problem, as you say."

"Lizzy designed the menu? Oh, well I did pay particular attention to teaching my girls the proper way to entertain, although I wonder if she paid heed to a thing I said."

"Elizabeth designed every aspect of the evening." Mrs. Gardiner said and smiled to her niece. "She chose the menu, place settings, flowers, and even chose the parlour games should they be necessary. Lady Matlock is very pleased with her work."

"Well that just shows how well I instructed her!" Elizabeth blushed deeply at her mother's words and bit her lip to keep from speaking her mind.

"What was that you said about mortification?" Darcy said softly as he squeezed Elizabeth's hand hard. She looked up to see his loving gaze waiting for her, and leaned against his shoulder. He smiled a little and the two seemed to take a collective breath. Mr. Bennet did not miss Darcy's skill with relieving Elizabeth's distress.

The air was soon pierced again with the sound of Mrs. Bennet's voice. "Oh, Mr. Darcy!" She came forward to grasp his hand. "What a great pleasure it is to see you again, and looking so very handsome, does he not, Mr. Bennet? Why Mr. Bennet would think of coming to town and seeing your home without me I will never understand. After all those years without a woman in the house you will need my experience to advise you on its redecoration. Surely he should have known that! Oh leave it to a man to think that these things take care of themselves! Now I know that Lizzy has been shopping for wedding clothes, but she surely has not visited the proper warehouses. I am fond of my sister, but only a mother who has made a great study of the subject in the ladies' magazines would know where to take her, and she must have the very best to be married to a man such as you. Lizzy knows very little of fashion, poor thing, she just has never filled out a gown properly . . ." She paused to notice that Elizabeth was looking down at the new gown from Madame Dupree that alone cost more than five from the dressmaker in Meryton. "Well perhaps her taste has improved slightly . . .but I cannot see her knowing at all what is necessary to be a good wife. I was going to propose to you today that I be the chaperone on your honeymoon, then live with you for several months, to teach her precisely how to be mistress of your estate." She beamed up at him, expecting his immediate agreement and praise.

Darcy took the breath that apparently Mrs. Bennet did not require, noticed that all eyes except Elizabeth's were on him, then felt the herculean strength of her hand gripping his. Speaking with his most authoritative voice, the one he had recently acquired since becoming master of Pemberley; he addressed his future mother-in-law. "Madam, there is nothing wanting in Elizabeth. I think it is time that you recognized the fact." He lifted Elizabeth's hand and kissing it, met her furious countenance. "And no, a chaperone will be unnecessary, thank you."

"Oh." Mrs. Bennet stared up at him. He held Elizabeth's gaze until he felt her grip relax and saw her take a breath, then Darcy turned to acknowledge Mr. Bennet.

"Sir, I am pleased to see that you have arrived safely and I look forward to showing you your daughter's future home."

"I am interested to see it. However I am also happy to provide my wife's assistance as your chaperone for as many months as is necessary." Mr. Bennet smiled and noticed Mrs. Bennet nodding vigorously.

"I know that it is common to have a woman travel with a new bride sir, however our only plans are to return to Pemberley, so while I understand the sentiment behind your offer, I respectfully decline." Darcy's eyes were cold and he took no enjoyment from Mr. Bennet's amusement. Instead he looked around the room and bowed to Mr. and Mrs. Gardiner.

Elizabeth cleared her throat when an uncomfortable silence descended. Darcy made an effort to be cordial. "Will you please come upstairs? We thought that we would start with tea in the drawing room before taking the tour." Richard led the way and the group began to follow him upstairs, passing Darcy and Elizabeth who remained, still clasping hands.

Mr. Bennet paused, glancing down at their hands then back up to Darcy. "I see that you have not changed your behaviour."

"Mine? I am the same as I ever was. I wonder sir, have you changed yours? I am not the man with four more daughters to marry off. I cannot stress enough how important this meeting is for Miss Bennet. Do you understand me, sir?"

Mr. Bennet glanced at Harwick at the top of the stairs with Jane. "I understand that a man has decided to court her but cannot decide if she is good enough for his purposes."

"And what reasoning did you use when choosing Mrs. Bennet, sir?" Darcy said coldly.

Elizabeth let go of his hand and walked ahead to catch up with Mrs. Gardiner. Mr. Bennet watched his favourite daughter walk away and smiled. "Lizzy is displeased with you."

"Sir, I know well enough by now that if Elizabeth is displeased with me, she will let me know in no uncertain terms. I believe that any displeasure she displays is directed at you, and her silence is due to her respect for you." He held out his hand and indicated that Mr. Bennet precede him. "The family awaits us. We should move forward."

"Just one moment sir. What do you mean that she is displeased with me?"

"Mr. Bennet, Elizabeth has over the past week gradually changed from a joyous woman to one who is shy and reserved. When I told her of my observations, she admitted her fear over your visit. She is terrified that you will do something that will turn me against her. Surely that knowledge alone should influence you. I cannot imagine a child of mine living in fear of embarrassment from me or my wife."

Mr. Bennet's discomfiture was displayed in his weak reply, "What do you know of parenthood?"

Darcy turned to look at him incredulously. "I am the father for my thirteen-year-old sister."

"Where is she? If you are so proficient why is she not here?"

"My sister is visiting her aunt and uncle, however unlike some parents; I have not abdicated my responsibilities to her." He nodded at the silenced man and at last they walked up the stairs to join the rest of the family.

Mr. Bennet remained behind in the hallway and turned slowly, taking in the atmosphere of the stately home. "Mr. Darcy, you fail to remember that had I not sent Lizzy to London, you would never have met her. My deficient parenting has worked to your advantage."

Harwick led Jane across the drawing room and over to his sister. "Mrs. Evangeline Carter, may I present Miss Jane Bennet."

Evangeline made a quick study of her brother's demeanour and voice, then smiled and bowed her head as Jane curtseyed, taking her time to record the young woman's behaviour. "It is a pleasure to meet you Miss Bennet. My brother wrote to me and said that he had met a lovely woman, but his words did not do you justice."

"Thank you Mrs. Carter, that is very kind of both of you." Jane said softly and thought hard of something to say. "I hope that your trip was pleasant?"

"It was, I have not been in town for several years, and I look forward to visiting friends and of course, doing some shopping. Is that a pastime that you enjoy?"

"I have not had a great deal of opportunity in the past, but since my sister's engagement, it seems to be a constant occupation." Jane looked to the doorway where Elizabeth had just entered the room, and her brow creased when she saw her pained expression. Mrs. Carter noted it as well.

"Perhaps you should speak with her." She urged and smiling slightly at her brother's raised brows, rolled her eyes and shook her head. He smiled and shrugged, then started across the room to approach Elizabeth, only to find that she was already occupied.

Fitzwilliam, who had been standing at the head of the stairs listening to the conversation, advanced upon her as soon as she appeared. "Miss Elizabeth!" He bowed gallantly and took possession of her hand, smiling warmly at her until he saw the distress in her eyes replaced by a hint of amusement. "I knew that you were Lady Luck. I thank you for enchanting my poor offering to Poseidon."

"Poseidon, Colonel?" She laughed to see his eyes twinkle as his lips hovered over her hand.

Looking up his smile grew, "The god of horses!"

"I thought it was the sea." Elizabeth laughed again when he sighed dramatically. "I see that I must expand my reading."

"Hmm, do not read too closely, Miss Elizabeth, those Greek gods were a terrible lot." Fitzwilliam bent and at last bestowed a kiss to her hand. "I thank you for my winnings."

"That is quite enough, Richard." Darcy said sternly. "Please unhand my betrothed."

Fitzwilliam made a face at him and tucked Elizabeth's hand onto his arm. "Come my dear; let me introduce you to Mrs. Carter."

"Richard . . ." Darcy said menacingly.

"Just ignore him. He has been on pins and needles all day." Fitzwilliam winked. "I think the poor man was pining for you."

"Then why do you keep me from him?" Elizabeth laughed when Darcy arrived to place her other hand on his arm.

"My dear near-cousin, I know very well that nothing could keep him from you. You really must start taking advantage of that, you know. Ah, Mrs. Carter! May I introduce Miss Elizabeth Bennet?" He smiled and his voice became softer. "Miss Elizabeth, Evangeline Carter is Harwick's sister. It seems that this home is filled with lovely ladies this evening." Mrs. Carter looked quickly from Elizabeth to Fitzwilliam and saw that his warm smile was given entirely to her.

"You are far too kind, sir. I am afraid that the bloom is long gone from this rose."

"No, no, madam, I will hear none of that, and to prove it, I demand that I escort you on this tour and allow me to regale you with poems that will encourage your faith in yourself."

"Mrs. Carter, please accept my cousin's compliment, lest we all request wool to stuff in our ears for the duration of the visit." Darcy pled. He realized very quickly that dragging Elizabeth over to meet Mrs. Carter was just an excuse for Richard to show off to the lovely young widow.

"Your cousin is no orator?" Evangeline said as she returned Fitzwilliam's smile. "I beg to disagree; I find his conversation quite amusing."

"Aha!" Fitzwilliam turned to them in triumph. "I knew that I spotted a unique woman entering the room, she is as wise as she is lovely."

"Colonel." Elizabeth whispered loudly so all could hear. "Sir, I appreciate that you are doing your best to be charming, but an intelligent woman can tell when it is being delivered too lavishly."

"I am trying too hard?" He whispered just as loudly, leaning back and considering his blushing subject. "What do you suggest then? What did my silent cousin do to capture your heart?"

"I will give away none of his secrets, sir."

"Thank you, Elizabeth." Darcy stepped away, moving her from his cousin's side. "Mrs. Carter, it has been a pleasure to meet you, and I hope to see more of you as the afternoon progresses, unfortunately Elizabeth and I must greet the rest of the family. If you can bear it, I leave you to my cousin." He nodded and smiled to see Fitzwilliam's enchanted expression.

Evangeline tilted her head at the colonel. "I believe that I can bear it very nicely, sir."

Elizabeth laughed and looked up to Darcy as they walked away. "Something is brewing there, do you think?"

"I have never seen him in such a state before." He looked back and laughed to see Richard falling over himself with the woman. "This has great possibilities."

"Marriage?"

Darcy chuckled. "Always marriage with the ladies, why is that?"

"Because there are not enough gentlemen to go around." She poked his side and he groaned softly. "So what did you have in mind?"

"I was going to enlist his brother to tease him mercilessly." He felt poked again. "What happened to my sweet Elizabeth?"

"Your sweet Elizabeth is in desperate need of her sweet Fitzwilliam's kiss."

Her words brought him to a dead stop. "Do you have any idea what you said to me? What kind of an effect that has on me?" Looking around the crowded room, he growled in her ear. "Innocence is no longer an excuse my love. You do know what I want; you have had too many talks with your aunt and too many moments alone with me not to know."

"What do you want, Fitzwilliam?" She said affectionately.

"Do not tempt me further, Elizabeth. Please." He closed his eyes and drank in the scent of her perfume, felt the warmth of her bare arm under his hand, and looked longingly at the maddeningly soft breasts that peeked teasingly from her gown. His fingers itched to touch her, just as his tongue longed to taste her.

"Forgive me." He heard her say softly. "I have learned many things, but I do not truly understand."

"You will, I promise, and it is nothing to fear." Darcy sighed and moved them to stand by the window, and waited as the insistent desire gradually subsided. He saw Mrs. Bennet staring around the room in the reflection. "I wonder if your father said something to your mother, she is silent. Perhaps she will remain that way?"

"Wishful thinking, Mr. Darcy." They exchanged glances and he rested his hand on her waist for a moment in a slight embrace.

Elizabeth walked away to serve as hostess for the tea. Darcy stood and quietly admired her skill, and became lost in the thoughts of their life together. "So, this is your father-in-law." Fitzwilliam broke into his reverie.

"Soon."

"He laughs at us." Fitzwilliam observed. "I do not believe that he is awed at all."

Darcy listened to Mr. Gardiner's intelligent conversation and Mr. Bennet's comments. "Perhaps his remarks are meant to inflate his feeling of self-worth in a room where he is very low."

"Could be, a braggart is generally a weak man." Fitzwilliam listened some more. "Do you like him?"

"Not particularly, no." Darcy cocked his head at his cousin.

"The mother is a terror. I wonder if she will be examining the silver to see if it is plate. Mother will not enjoy my report and will be decidedly unhappy. She will not like hosting them for dinner at all."

The two men eyed each other and laughed softly. "I assume that you will not be inviting them to Pemberley frequently?" Darcy said nothing and Fitzwilliam laughed when he looked back to Elizabeth wistfully. "Soon enough Cousin, soon enough."

"How is Audrey? Elizabeth says that she seemed happier. I imagine that she has seen more of her than you."

"Singleton has improved, I think. I understand that he sat alone in that room for nearly an hour." They laughed. "Nothing like a threat of death to convince one to stop gambling. We will see if it continues."

Mrs. Bennet looked around the room, took a bite of a delicate cake and licking the sugar from her fingers cornered Harwick. "Mr. Harwick, I understand that you have two girls?"

"Yes, Mrs. Bennet. Margaret is four and Ella is two."

"I see, and your intention is to remarry and produce a son?"

"My desire is to provide a proper home for my children, madam. If additional children result, then it will be a blessing."

"And what took your wife?"

Harwick hesitated, and felt Evangeline approach to take his hand. "My sister died in childbed, Mrs. Bennet."

"I see, and what of the children with this second marriage, will they be considered lesser or greater than the existing ones? Which wife will take precedence?" She demanded and Harwick looked at Mr. Bennet, expecting him to step in to control the questions, but he did nothing.

"Mrs. Bennet, I will treat all of my children, regardless of their mother's identity, equally."

"And what of this estate?"

"What of it madam?" He said with growing irritation. "It seems to me that these are questions to be asked by Miss Bennet's father."

"I only wish to know of your income, sir. And of course the size of your home and property. How many carriages do you own?"

"Why? So that you can gossip to your friends?" He contained his desire to leave the room immediately. "Forgive me madam, but I assure you that I am quite capable of caring for my family, and that is all you need to know." He walked away and approached Mr. Bennet. "Do you exert any control over your wife, sir? Or do you simply not wish to see your daughters wed?" Looking around the room, he spotted an open door. "Sir, I wish to speak to you privately." Not waiting for an answer he waved off his sister and stalked away. Mr. Gardiner had been listening and stepped up to his brother's side. "Come on, Bennet." He gave him a push. Darcy heard the confrontation and excusing himself from Elizabeth, followed the men into the adjoining room.

Jane stood with her hand to her mouth; saw her aunt's closed eyes, and the sure signs that her mother was going to burst forth with proclamations of her indignation. At last the truth of her parents' failings and her own behaviour sank in, and she went immediately to where Elizabeth was staring in absolute mortification at the closed door. Before she could speak, Mrs. Bennet cried out her unfiltered opinion.

"Well, I have never met a man so rude before! Where did they all go?"

"Mama!" Elizabeth hissed and looked as Evangeline turned to listen. "Mr. Harwick had every right to be unhappy with your questions."

"He made me feel that I was prying!" She huffed. "I was merely inquiring after his estate, is that so wrong? I would want my daughter to be kept properly. It is bad enough that she would be raising another woman's children, I want to be sure that she would not be forgotten when Mr. Harwick dies."

"Papa will certainly be sure that Jane is cared for in the event of Mr. Harwick's death. It is his place to approve the settlement, not yours. And as for the children," She glanced at Evangeline who was watching her, "they are dear to Mr. Harwick, and are a part of him. He would not choose a woman to marry who did not care for them." She turned to face Evangeline. "I am sorry, Mrs. Carter."

"Thank you, Miss Elizabeth." Her gaze shifted to take in Jane, who was clutching a handkerchief and staring down at her feet.

"Lizzy," Mrs. Gardiner said softly, "I will speak to your mother." Elizabeth nodded, and close to tears, walked back over to Jane and flushed again with shame to realize that Colonel Fitzwilliam was still in the room. She turned away from his piercing eyes and did not notice when he walked away to speak quietly with Evangeline. Jane pressed her hand on Elizabeth's arm.

"Oh Lizzy, I am so sorry, how can you be so supportive of me when I have behaved so poorly?"

Elizabeth awakened from her thoughts to face her sister. "What are you saying?"

Jane said tearfully, "I was so happy for you when you first became engaged, and then I allowed my jealousy over your joy to turn me into someone I do not know. I told you that day I would be happy to marry for security, but I begrudged you the love you found with Mr. Darcy."

"Why did you? I have been so hurt Jane, I thought that I was living with my youngest sister, not my eldest."

"But you see, Mama told me that marrying was my duty, that I was the only hope. When you became engaged, I . . . I lost my way, and I think that I feared losing Mama's love. Now I understand how much she has hurt you." She took Elizabeth's hand. "Can you forgive me?"

Relieved to finally see the sister she knew return, Elizabeth gladly embraced her. "Yes, but oh Jane, what of Mr. Harwick? You can see how much his opinion must be hurt after meeting our parents."

"I will accept whatever decision he makes." Jane drew away and steadied herself. "I have hardly done anything to make myself appealing to him."

Harwick was standing in a far corner of the room, examining the portrait of a young woman with dark hair and warm, smiling eyes. When the door shut he turned to find the three men facing him.

"Who is this, Darcy?"

Looking at the portrait, he said slowly, "That was my grandmother, on my father's side, Rebecca Darcy."

"She resembles Miss Elizabeth." He observed. Unsaid, Darcy knew, was that the portrait resembled Ellen Harwick. Addressing Mr. Bennet, Harwick left no doubt of his displeasure. "Sir. You may or may not be aware that this meeting between us was done by design. It was recommended that I meet the father of Miss Bennet without being exposed to her family. Although at the time I felt it was rather unnecessary, how could the family of such a pleasant woman be a problem? I now understand thoroughly the reasoning in my friend Darcy's mind. Your wife has, in a matter of moments, insulted the memory of my beloved wife, questioned my honour, and pried into my business, while you sir, stood silently by, allowing her to continue. I can only assume that you have no desire to see your daughter make, frankly, an extraordinary match. Perhaps you are blinded by Mr. Darcy's devotion to Miss Elizabeth? I have no such sentiment to sway me, sir. I can walk away from this courtship without a heavy heart, and after meeting Miss Bennet's parents I am inclined to do so. What have you to say about this?"

Mr. Bennet took a moment before speaking. "It seems that I journeyed to London to be the subject of chastisement by two rich men today, have you both become tired of society and wished for some sport at the expense of my daughters?"

"Bennet!" Mr. Gardiner exclaimed. "Do not be a fool! This is not a game."

"Mr. Bennet, you knew what was likely to happen if Mrs. Bennet accompanied you here. You cannot feign indignation with our reactions." Darcy spoke quietly. "You created this situation, not we."

"You are ending the courtship with Jane?" He asked Harwick.

"I have made no decision on that particular subject, although I have made decisions on others." Harwick's cold gaze met Mr. Bennet's eyes.

He sighed and nodded. "Very well, I apologize for what occurred, and I will speak to my wife. Your decision for Jane should be based on her behaviour, not her parents'."

"I can accept that." Harwick glanced at the portrait again then caught Darcy's eye, nodding to him when he recognized that he understood, and departed the room to stand pensively by the fireplace. The other men followed.

Darcy went immediately to Elizabeth's side, and did not hesitate to tell her what had just occurred.

"Mr. Harwick, I would like to speak with you privately, if you do not mind." Jane requested quietly. "We could take a seat over in the corner?" He nodded and they walked across the room. She sat down and looked at her family talking and drinking their tea.

He sat beside her and waited. "Miss Bennet?"

She sighed and continued looking down. "Mr. Harwick, please accept my apology."

"What have you done?"

"I . . .I have for the entirety of our friendship displayed little of myself, and further, I have discovered a side of me that I never knew and I hope will be banished forever now that I recognize its existence." She looked up to see his brows knit, but no other expression. "When my sister announced her engagement, I was so happy for her. She had been through a terrible rejection and faced the wrath of our mother in very cruel ways, and Mr. Darcy is the ideal partner for her. However, as I saw her love blooming and how Mr. Darcy displayed his affection for her, I am afraid that I became, shamefully, resentful."

"I noticed some tension between you."

"Yes." She twisted her hands again, and looked over to where Elizabeth stood talking to Darcy.

Harwick followed her gaze and asked gently, "What is the purpose of this conversation, Miss Bennet?"

"Mr. Harwick, I know how poorly I have shown myself to you, and I know that I am wanting in many areas, but now that Lizzy has relieved me of the requirements of duty, I hope that I can . . . learn to be myself."

"I appreciate that you have had to work through these feelings, and admire the conclusions you have drawn. Your parents' decision to put you out at such a young age astounds me, and I must also remind myself that you are still quite young, although you are the eldest." He smiled and touched her hand. "Your words remind me that you are not the only person in this room who has some barriers to overcome."

"You, sir?"

"Me as well. Darcy was kind enough to speak to me earlier about this."

"Sir, you witnessed my parents, I suppose that your private conference was in reference to their behaviour and I fear that it will only grow worse as the tour continues."

"Thank you for the warning, although I hope that it is at an end." He stood up and offered her his hand. "I promise to keep an open mind. Is that what you were asking of me?"

"I suppose that it was, but also I . . . I will understand if you choose against me, and not just based on my parents' behaviour but on mine."

Harwick studied her silently. "I have made no decision, Miss Bennet, however, I will soon." Jane smiled a little and looked back over to Darcy and Elizabeth, who were in turn watching them.

More than anything, Darcy wished to be holding Elizabeth after their quiet emotional discussion, but that was certainly not permissible with a roomful of guests. Instead he took her hand in his and locked their fingers together. "So, she has apologized to you and to him." Darcy said thoughtfully. "That is interesting." He saw her brows rise and smiled. "It fascinates me how you are so shy about our love, but so feisty about your sister's, despite your frustration with her. Well it is up to them now." He touched her cheek. "How did we become matchmakers?"

"I would prefer to just worry about our own match for a change."

Darcy bent near her ear. "We have nothing to worry about, except my pending demise from wanting you."

"What does that mean?" Elizabeth whispered as her shoulder brushed against his chest.

He thought of how they could possibly touch, and moved to stand behind her. Drawing her back so she lightly rested against him, he whispered so nobody else could hear. "It means, my love, my darling Elizabeth, that I want to feel our bodies join together, as man and woman were created to do."

"Ohhhhhh."

"Was that too plain?" He asked as he gently caressed her wrist with his thumb.

"No, it was . . .oh Fitzwilliam. I think that I will die if I do not touch you soon."

His voice shook. "Are you serious, Elizabeth? You would wish to . . .."

"Is that wanton?" She asked and leaned further against him.

"Oh no, dearest, it is everything I have hoped for."

Mrs. Gardiner approached and spoke softly. "I think that it is time to continue the tour."

Darcy flushed and was grateful for Elizabeth's position in front of him. She looked back at him then smiled to her aunt. "Must we? It is at last calm in here."

"Lizzy, your mother will not rest until she sees every corner of this house."

"I doubt that Harwick will welcome her into his." Darcy said as he regained his composure. He drew a deep breath and managed to smile again. "*You* are a problem."

"Why?"

"Because you are so close, but I dare not touch you." Steeling himself, he offered her his arm and raised his voice. "For any who wish to continue the tour, please follow us." Everyone joined them and they moved through the house, visiting the music room, the many sitting rooms, then on to see several bedchambers.

"Where are the masters' and mistress' chambers?" Mrs. Bennet asked. "They must be fine indeed; I must see where my Lizzy will sleep!"

"Mama, they are in the process of being redecorated, so there is nothing to see there right now. We just ordered new furnishings . . ."

"You chose furniture without me?" She huffed. "And what did you purchase? Which warehouse did you visit? Lizzy knows nothing of what is fashionable. I cannot begin to imagine what mistakes she has made . . ."

"Mr. Chippendale came here personally, Mrs. Bennet." Darcy's expression was challenging. "Does that suit?"

"Oh . . .yes of course."

"Do you find any of the rooms of this home in need of improvement?"

"No, no sir, everything is very fine."

"Very well, then perhaps comments should instead be directed to Elizabeth on what an excellent mistress she will be, and not on opinions of her lack of experience. I have found that she has excellent taste, and I trust her to choose well. Furthermore madam, you speak of how pleased you are with our engagement, and yet you continue to disparage Elizabeth with your comments. Which is it madam? Is her discernment only applicable in finding a husband or may it be applied to all aspects of her many talents?"

"Oh, well, I . . . I think that Lizzy is a clever girl . . ."

"And beautiful." He stated and stared at her.

Mrs. Bennet remained silent and all conversation around them had stopped as well. "And . . . beautiful."

"And you will not criticize her before company again."

"I . . . No, why would I do that?"

"Why indeed, madam." Darcy looked to Elizabeth who was gripping his hand tightly and studying the floor. He glanced at Mr. Bennet, saw Richard and Harwick both smiling widely, and caught the Gardiners nodding. Raising Elizabeth's hand to his lips, he kissed it and waited for her look back to him. "Let us show your father our library, Elizabeth."

Chapter 23

10 June 1809
I had hopes that upon this meeting between Papa, Fitzwilliam, and Mr. Harwick, all of our differences of station, opinion, even behaviour would be easily resolved. After Fitzwilliam met Papa at Longbourn and they discussed our engagement, and agreed that Papa's desire to manipulate people and laugh at their reactions or worse, sit back and exert no control over Mama and my sisters was not admired at all, I cannot imagine why he decided that it would be amusing to bring Mama with him to London. Although I can appreciate that she probably did complain loudly about not coming with him, I know that if it was any other circumstance, he probably would have been glad to leave her at home. But no, he chose to see what havoc she could wreak. Stupid, foolish man!! It was all I could do to hold my tongue in the carriage, but both Aunt and Uncle took me aside before we boarded and told me that it was for them to address. I was a floor above them, and still I could easily hear my uncle telling Papa in no uncertain terms that his behaviour that day had likely precluded any hope of establishing a tolerant welcome of the Bennets at Pemberley, and he would not be in the least surprised to see Mr. Harwick coming in the morning to end his courtship with Jane. I will not be surprised either and I know that Jane will accept it as well. How different it might have been if Mama had stayed at home!

She heard a quiet knock on the door and it opened a little to reveal Jane's worried face. "May I come in, Lizzy?"

"Of course." She smiled and closed her journal, and joined Jane on the bed. The sisters held hands and after some silence Jane asked, "Did you hear them?"

"Yes. I do not think I have ever heard Uncle so angry."

"Nor Papa."

"Papa was defensive, not angry. He realizes that he has erred terribly. Did you hear uncle telling him to go to Mr. Harwick first thing in the morning and beg his pardon?"

"Yes, and somehow I do not think it will help."

"He would be marrying you, Jane. Not the family." Elizabeth sighed. "I believe though that he would be justified in not welcoming them into his home."

"I can see that." Jane whispered. "I can also see him rejecting me on my own behaviour."

"But you *did* apologize."

"Yes, but . . ."

"Would you be so very hurt if he did withdraw?"

"Were you hurt when Mr. Stewart left?"

"I knew it was because of our dowry and family . . ."

"I know that part of it is because of me." Jane said sadly. "I do not love him, Lizzy, so I do have that."

"Do you like him?"

"Oh yes, how could I not? He is very gentlemanly and although he is very formal with me at all times, he clearly is an amiable man. I imagine that if he was in a comfortable situation, he might be much more open. He makes me think of your Mr. Darcy sometimes."

"Yes, I think they are cut of the same cloth." Elizabeth mused, then went back to holding Jane's hand. "Whatever happens, Jane, please know that I am with you."

"Thank you, Lizzy, you are too good."

"WELL THAT SOUNDS LIKE AN UTTER NIGHTMARE." Bingley declared the following morning.

"It was, trust me." Darcy glanced at the clock and sighed, he was determined to call on Elizabeth, but he would wait a little longer before appearing in Gracechurch Street. He was grateful that Bingley chose to visit and distract him for a while.

"And you have the dinner with them tonight at Matlock House?"

"Yes." Darcy rubbed his face and looked over to the pile of correspondence he needed to address, then back up to his friend. "This was supposed to be a straightforward event. Show Mr. Bennet my home, introduce him to the Earl, show him Harwick's home . . . well, the best laid plans are not necessarily effective."

"It seems that in the end you made your point; did you not? I mean, he certainly saw what Miss Elizabeth would be gaining as your wife, and meeting Harwick would certainly show him that he had similar prospects?"

"But the problem there is that Harwick . . . well, I will not speculate about his thinking." He looked up to see Bingley's knit brow. "It seems that I will soon be in a position similar to yours, looking for husbands for my sisters. At least Georgiana has many years before I have to face that torment." Hearing a chuckle he looked at him curiously.

Bingley cleared his throat. "Well, at least the Bennet girls still have parents to address that problem, for Caroline it is just me." He smiled and crossed his legs. "I do think, however, we may have a nibble on the line."

"Really?" Darcy smiled and leaned back in his chair. "Do tell."

He laughed. "Well, let us say that she went to a ball with Louisa and Hurst the other night, and a man actually approached her to dance, and followed through with a call the next morning. I was not at home when he called so I can not speculate on his features or really on anything else, but Caroline described him as handsome and charming, and very well-connected."

"Does this prince have a name?"

"Undoubtedly, but I have not heard it as yet." He saw Darcy's concern. "I should be more inquisitive, you think?"

"Yes." Darcy leaned forward. "Women are not the only fortune hunters, Bingley. If he calls again, despite enjoying the novelty, you should see what the man is about, and what he has to offer her, besides charm, that is."

"You see, that is why I come to you, although I know what you say is common sense." He held up his hand and laughed. "No, and I do not need a lecture on my deplorable lack of the attribute."

"I said nothing." Darcy sighed and glanced at the clock again. "I am sorry, but I really should go to visit Elizabeth."

"It is a fine day; shall I offer to be chaperone with Miss Bennet again so you two might walk? I promise not to cough?" He raised his brow and smiled. "And I promise to keep Miss Bennet from coming between you as well."

"I do not know if Harwick . . ."

"I am not courting her, I am aiding you. Unless you would prefer Mrs. Bennet to join you?"

"Get your hat, Bingley." Darcy growled.

INSIDE OF THE FRONT SITTING ROOM in Gracechurch Street, Elizabeth sat and stared unseeing at the book in her lap. In her right hand, the gold locket containing Darcy's hair was held, and she rubbed it unconsciously as she attempted to ignore her father's presence in the chair opposite. The only sound in the room was his throat clearing as he turned a page in his newspaper, and the steady tick of the mantle clock. Upstairs there was a thump and the sound of little feet.

"Marianne has her hands full with the children. It is good that Jane enjoys helping with them so much."

"It is good that Aunt and Uncle employ a nursemaid and will soon hire a governess to teach them. Jane would make a fine mother to anyone's children," Elizabeth said without emotion, "however I suspect that the children of Mr. Harwick will not be amongst them."

"Do you feel that he will not make an offer?"

She looked up and met his eye. "I believe that what was at one time a viable possibility has been crushed by selfishness and sloth."

Mr. Bennet's paper came down. "Explain yourself, young lady."

"You knew what would happen if Mama accompanied you Papa, and did not think of my engagement or of Jane's future. You thought of your entertainment. Sloth is self explanatory. If we had received the education that we ought, and you had saved in some way to give us a reasonable dowry, we would not be in the positions we are, hoping for someone to take notice of the poor assets we possess."

"It seems to me you have done quite well for yourself."

"That is purely by chance, Papa. If I had never met Mr. Darcy, I might still have met Mr. Stewart, and you know why he rejected me in the end." She turned back to her book. "My good fortune does not erase the reality of the situation."

He responded sharply. "I do not appreciate receiving a reprimand from you, Elizabeth. You still require my consent to marry."

"You would refuse consent?" She stared at him in disbelief.

He deflated and shook his head. "Of course not, Lizzy. I could never deny you this marriage. I am a foolish old man who has spent far too much time alone with his books instead of people. I am afraid that I have forgotten the art of proper discourse, and your mother never knew it. I have not had anyone to reprimand me until now." Standing up he walked over to her. "I had to wait for my little girl to grow up and be disappointed in me. You had to meet a better man to see me for what I am and to lose the adoration that all fathers of daughters enjoy until one day . . ." He heard a carriage outside and looked out of the window to see Darcy and Bingley descending. "Ah."

She heard the coach outside and glanced at the window, then jumped to her feet. "Fitzwilliam!" She ran from the room and Mr. Bennet watched the men climbing the steps to the house. Unwilling to meet them, he ducked out of another doorway and escaped to Mr. Gardiner's study.

Impatiently Elizabeth waited as the maid took their hats then came forward to grasp Darcy's hand. "What a wonderful surprise!" She smiled and he could not hold back his own. "I have been wishing that you would appear!"

"I was waiting for a decent hour; otherwise I would have come at dawn." He kissed her hand and searched her face. "Are you well?"

"Are you?" She asked and touched his cheek. Bingley cleared his throat.

"Does anyone care about me?" He said with a little whine.

Elizabeth peeked around Darcy's shoulder and saw Bingley grinning at her. "Of course I care, Mr. Bingley. Are you well?"

"Tolerable, I suppose." He said with an affected air, and sniffed while examining his nails. Grinning at her he reached around Darcy to take her hand. "You are lovely as ever, Miss Elizabeth."

"And you have not lost any of your charm."

Darcy retrieved her hand from Bingley. "I came to take you for a walk in the park, if you are so inclined." He tilted his head. "I assumed it was the best I would be able to manage today."

"No, a private conference is probably out of the question, and leaving the house is wise." Hearing footsteps she looked up at the top of the stairs. "Jane, Mr. Darcy and Mr. Bingley have come to walk; will you join us as a second chaperone?"

"Oh." Jane bit her lip. "Yes, I would be happy to come. Let me tell Aunt where we are going." She disappeared and returned with Mrs. Gardiner. They came down and greetings were said all around.

"Is your father still in the sitting room, Lizzy?"

"No, I heard Uncle's study door close." She looked at Darcy and he shrugged. "I think that is for the best. Mama is still in her chamber so it is a good time to depart."

"Then what are we waiting for?" He smiled and watched as the ladies found their bonnets and gloves, then soon they stepped out on their way. Both visibly relaxed once they had left the house behind. Darcy noticed the dark circles under her eyes. "How was the night?"

"Papa was thoroughly admonished by Uncle, and Jane and I talked for a very long time." She leaned against his shoulder, and he looked down to see her looking up at him. "He just apologized to me."

"That is heartening." Darcy said softly. "I do not believe that I feel very welcoming towards your parents, Elizabeth. Do you mind if we do not invite them to Pemberley any time in the foreseeable future?"

"No, I do not, and your request is not unexpected, nor will it be a surprise to Papa, I think."

"Your mother may not feel the same way."

"I will leave Papa to deliver the news." They exchanged glances. "I wished so much to be talking to you all night instead of my sister."

"If it had been I in your bed Elizabeth, talking would not have been our occupation." His voice was low and warm.

"Oh, would we have played charades?" She smiled and was surprised when he suddenly leaned down to kiss her.

"Oh."

"That was for impertinence." He said with satisfaction.

"What will I receive for outright brazenness?" She asked cheekily.

"Give me some time alone with you and I will be glad to demonstrate." He growled, then raised her hand to his mouth for a kiss, lowered it, and began lightly tracing his thumb over her wrist. "Eight and thirty days. This is far too long to bear."

"I agree." She whispered and leaned against him as they slowly walked along. "Tell me about my new home."

"What would you care to hear? I would be very happy to indulge your desire . . .would you like an accounting of the silver, or perhaps the number of footmen?" He chuckled when she moved her hand from his and quickly retrieving it; continued his gentle rubbing. "Shall I tell you how clean the air smells? How the hills and valleys are alive with colour in the autumn; and the beauty of the peaks with their cap of snow in the winter?" Hearing her sigh he continued, "I remember as a boy, a house filled with laughter and music. I remember seeing my parents stroll through the gardens, and my mother's hand trailing along, touching the flowers as they passed, and watching them disappear down a path that led to a little bridge over a brook. I spied on them there one time, and saw them kiss." He looked back to her and softly brushed his lips over her cheek before looking forward again. "I cannot wait to bring you home, dearest. I have been away too long, and the next time I walk in the door, I will not be alone with my memories. You will be there to make new ones."

Elizabeth studied his expression. "I have nothing to compare with your memories of seeing your parents together. I hope that I will not disappoint you."

He returned his gaze to hers and his mouth lifted in his little smile. "What are we doing together right now? We are walking and talking, and I assure you, I am relishing the experience. I hope you are as well. Do not doubt yourself, Elizabeth. Do not let anyone tell you that we are not suited. The only way that would be possible is if *you* felt that I was not suited for you. Do you think I am not your perfect match?" He lifted his brow and saw her eyes roll. "Am I not?"

"Fitzwilliam."

"Tell me, love. Tell me I am not your one true match and I will walk away, leaving you to search the world for that perfect man . . ."

"Why are you teasing me?"

"Because you are not answering me." He caressed her wrist some more. "Tell me you find me hateful; tell me I am the last man in the world you would ever marry."

"You sir, are no gentleman!"

"And you love me." Darcy said triumphantly. "Admit it, you do."

"I do not recall saying that I felt otherwise, sir." Elizabeth spoke with a glint in her eye. "Mr. Darcy, sir."

"I love you, too." He whispered, and touched the chain for the locket, then smiled when she lifted his hand to kiss his ring. "Obstinate girl."

"Mulish man." They laughed and he continued answering her questions about Pemberley. Behind them walked Jane and Bingley, entertaining themselves with comments about the couple ahead.

"I promised I would leave them alone, Miss Bennet, and I am a man of my word."

"I promised much of the same, sir. They cannot really behave too badly in such a public setting, although I imagine my aunt might disagree."

"That is the job of an aunt! I have several who find my sense of humour deplorable!" He smiled and shrugged. "But it is mine and I will not allow a disapproving frown to quench my happiness."

"You are a very happy person, Mr. Bingley."

"What have I to be unhappy about? Well, perhaps I am impatient; I should try to do something on that score."

"And what are you anxious to do?"

"Oh, scads of things! I want to purchase an estate, I want to be accepted by the *ton*, I want to marry and have a family, many things, but I have a good friend in Darcy and as the Bible says, *to everything there is a season*, and mine has yet to come." He saw her head tilted as she listened. "I have to grow up, to put it plainly, Miss Bennet."

"But you are one and twenty; Mr. Darcy inherited Pemberley when he was but a year older."

"I am no Darcy." He laughed. "No, maybe in a year or two I will settle down. And you; how goes it with Mr. Harwick?"

"That is a good question." She smiled when she saw his kind eyes and looked down. "I think that I have some growing to do as well."

"There is no shame in that, Miss Bennet." He laughed. "I am reminded of it daily!" Looking ahead he said quietly. "Shall we disturb the lovers?"

"What of your promise?" She asked with a smile.

"Miss Bennet, I have a feeling that once walking those two would be at it all day, and truly, I am no walker. Let us steer them onto the path home."

"I will agree because I am no walker either." Jane smiled and he chuckled. "Mr. Bingley, if I do not have the opportunity later, I want to thank you for your company today."

"Delighted, Miss Bennet, and may you have the best of luck tonight."

MRS. JENKINSON CAREFULLY LIFTED the basin of blood and walked to the chamber door where she handed it off to the waiting maid. She returned and watched the physician wipe his hands and step back from his feverish patient. "She is struggling, but I think this bleeding will do the trick." He nodded and looked back to her companion. "I do not think that we will bleed her again. Keep the compresses on her forehead and I will return tomorrow."

"But what of her delusions, sir?" Mrs. Jenkinson asked anxiously. "She still believes herself to be married."

"What occurs when you correct that thought?"

"She is very violent sir, I wonder if we might increase the strength of her elixir? It will not do to have her making such statements. It could harm both her and her cousin."

"Would it hurt to humour her, though? While she is so ill? Could you simply placate her ranting and tell her that Mr. Darcy would not like his wife to be so demanding?" He raised his brow and patted her arm. "If you do not wish to see her taken to an asylum, she must be controlled in some manner at home."

"Will she die, sir?"

"She is very weak, that is true. It is in the Lord's hands now. I will speak to her mother." He removed a bottle from his bag and handed it to her. "Two spoonfuls with a glass of wine."

He left the room and Mrs. Jenkinson turned back to her charge, and touched her forehead. Anne's eyes opened. "Fitzwilliam?"

"Mr. Darcy is not here, Miss Anne."

"Where is he?" She cried. "Why does he not come?"

"He is travelling."

"Here?" She grabbed Mrs. Jenkinson and the cut the physician made in her arm began bleeding freely again.

Holding her down, she said calmly, "I am sure he will come as soon as he can, Miss Anne."

"Why do you call me that?" She sat up again, defying her weakened condition. "I am the mistress!" She stood and stumbled to the door and pulled it open.

"Miss Anne!"

"Mrs. DARCY!" She lurched across the hallway and into the mistress's chambers, collapsing onto the bed. "My chambers. My husband is the master! Why is my mother still in our home? Out!! I want her out!!" She demanded.

Footmen came running and Mrs. Jenkinson looked at them quickly and had an idea. "Miss de Bourgh wishes for the dowager's house to be opened and her ladyship moved in. Please tell the steward."

The footmen stared at her open mouthed and did not move. Anne rose from the bed, and began taking her mother's belongings and throwing them to the floor. "OUT!"

"You heard your mistress, now move!" Mrs. Jenkinson urged. Returning to Anne's chambers she took up the bottle of laudanum and mixed a new dose, then approached her. "Mrs. Darcy, please drink your medication."

Anne stopped her movement and looked at Mrs. Jenkinson. "Mrs. Darcy?"

"I am sorry for calling you Miss Anne, but you have been my dear Miss Anne for so many years, you will not mind so much if I slip and call you that will you?" Mrs. Jenkinson smiled and Anne relaxed and nodded. "He is very concerned for your health. He does not want you to become upset and delay your recovery, and remember, he likes how sweet and demure you are, you must not let him see you so upset and disappoint him when he comes." She held out the glass and Anne happily drank it down.

"He worries for me." She murmured and sank back onto the pillows. When she was asleep, Mrs. Jenkinson began wiping up the blood that was drying over her arm and night dress. Lady Catherine arrived and looked at the scene.

"What is this?"

"Shhh. My Lady, your daughter has asserted her rights as mistress and has ordered you to the dowager's house."

"She *what?*"

"I believe that even if she did not think herself to be Mrs. Darcy she had that right, is she not the true mistress of Rosings, madam?"

Lady Catherine's eyes narrowed. "What are you about, Jenkinson?"

"This is your daughter's delusion, madam. You have chosen to perpetuate it. I am merely following orders. She demands the mistress's chambers and you . . .out." She watched in satisfaction as Lady Catherine spun and left the room.

She looked back to Anne and murmured, "Well something good is coming of this."

"EXTRAORDINARY." Lady Matlock murmured. "And you say that the man was wholly unrepentant?"

"He undoubtedly did not wish to trouble himself with facing the consequences of his actions." Fitzwilliam crossed the room to poke his finger in a bowl containing sweetmeats, pushed aside the green confetti and grinned in triumph to find a sugared piece of apricot. He licked his fingers and his mother glared at him. Shrugging, he resumed his seat. "His introduction to Darcy's library was fascinating though. A look of unhidden lust appeared simultaneously with the realization that he would never be invited to come and explore the works. Of course, I made a point of discussing the vast collection contained at Pemberley." He began to eye the bowl again and Audrey picked it up and moved it far from his reach. The siblings exchanged meaningful glances.

"So you were toying with him?" Lord Matlock grinned. "I am sorry to have missed this afternoon."

"Well you will surely have your fill of them this evening."

"How was Elizabeth through all of this?" Audrey asked. "She had to have been mortified."

"She clearly wished to speak her mind, and when she forgot I was in the room after the rest of the men left to speak with Mr. Bennet, she did deliver a few words to her mother, but she for the most part left it to Darcy to handle. I must say that I was very pleased with him. We were all concerned that he had changed so much since Uncle George died, becoming so lifeless and intolerant, but underneath that he has grown much stronger. The feelings he has for Elizabeth have changed him for the better, and in time to make a difference before he became too arrogant."

"Well there is no doubt that their engagement will continue, no matter what her parents do. Miss Elizabeth will soon be part of this family. How did her sister fare?" Lord Matlock asked.

"Not as well, I think. Harwick's sister and I had some time to speak on the subject."

"Did you?" Layton raised his brows. "And tell us about that? Mrs. Carter is very charming as I recall."

"Mrs. Carter?" Lady Matlock asked, looking from one flushing son to the other grinning one. "I do not recall her in town."

"Mrs. Carter has recently left mourning. Her husband died three years ago; and of course her sister, Mrs. Harwick, died two years ago." Fitzwilliam said quietly.

"Carter, Carter . . . a duel, was it not? Hyde Park, something about a bet?"

"Yes. Something." Fitzwilliam cleared his throat. "Mrs. Carter suffered terribly and in silence as the wife of a drunken gambler." He glanced up to his sister then fixed his gaze on Singleton. "Fortunately her settlement was substantial. Her husband's family naturally removed her from the home estate, and she went to live with her brother."

"So her brother has supported her?" Lady Matlock said and glanced at her husband.

"Yes Mother, her funds remain almost entirely untouched, fortunately her husband did not manage to gamble them all away. They were married only briefly. She only recently has stopped wearing mourning."

"Surely she does not own property, did he leave a house? Why does she not live . . . oh, to care for Harwick's children, am I correct?"

"Yes, when her brother marries, she will depart to live at the small townhouse here in London that her husband left, she has its use for her lifetime."

"How small?" Layton asked.

"It is large enough to live comfortably." Fitzwilliam met his eye. "She has consented to receive my call, and I intend to do so tomorrow. I like her. Please do not scare her away. She has been through enough." Again his eyes rested on Singleton who looked away to meet the sad expression on Audrey's face.

"Son, if you like this woman and she would have you, I would be overjoyed to see you settled in any home, no matter the size, I would be willing to make a gift to you upon your marriage to help you along." Lord Matlock nodded then addressed the gathered family. "We would all be happy to see you out of that uniform."

"I would be happy to see a genuine smile on your face, Brother." Alicia spoke and all eyes turned to her. "You cannot hide it from everyone."

Fitzwilliam said nothing and stood to go look out of the window, keeping his hands clasped behind his back. Layton studied his wife, thinking again how he really never took the time to know her, and moved to sit by her side. She looked at him in surprise when he took her hand and kissed it, then smiled a little to receive the gesture. The room grew quiet until the sound of running feet in the hallway stopped and were replaced by careful steps. Georgiana appeared at the doorway, looking very ladylike. Richard turned to her and smiled.

"You are not fooling anyone, Georgiana."

"Oh I knew you would hear me!" She looked down at her shoes. "I should have worn the slippers."

"No dear; then you would have fallen and you would have broken your neck, and then what would your brother say?" Fitzwilliam gave her a hug and played with her curls. "Are you excited? They will be here very soon."

"I am always happy to see Elizabeth, and I miss Fitzwilliam, even though I see him almost daily."

"What can you possibly miss in your stodgy brother?"

"*He* does not tease me." Georgiana said and looked squarely at Layton.

"Ah, Georgiana, I think that Elizabeth might teach him how to do just that." Fitzwilliam laughed to see her brows knit and glancing back outside, he turned to his family. "They are here."

Lord Matlock joined him at the window. "Two carriages?"

"Perhaps Harwick and Darcy divided the group amongst them so everyone would travel comfortably."

"Come along, Henry." Lady Matlock walked by. "You will see them soon enough." Together they descended the stairs, and stood to the side while they waited for the footman to open the door. Darcy entered first with Elizabeth on his arm. Both had the appearance of people steeling themselves for an unpleasant evening, and received similar fixed smiles in return. Elizabeth came forward and was surprised to receive Lady Matlock's kiss on her cheek. "Do not worry dear; we have every confidence in you."

"Thank you." Elizabeth whispered and Darcy entwined their fingers. She smiled up to him and he kissed her temple. "Thank you."

"Richard apprised us of yesterday's events." Lord Matlock said as the party began to enter the vast hallway. "Quite a story, I look forward to hearing it all when we can really hash it out. Ah, Gardiner!" He strode forward and shook his hand. "Mrs. Gardiner, a pleasure." He glanced around and bowed, "Miss Bennet, you are looking lovely."

Jane smiled and blushed. "Thank you, sir."

Turning away he spotted Harwick, shaking his hand and noticing the man's stiff posture. "Hang in there, man." Harwick nodded and stepped forward to take Jane up the steps to meet the rest of the family.

Finally all that remained were Mr. and Mrs. Bennet. Elizabeth turned and stood by them. "Lord and Lady Matlock, these are my parents, Mr. and Mrs. Thomas Bennet."

"Welcome to Matlock House." Lady Matlock inclined her head. "I hardly expected that the night of our ball we would not only meet your lovely daughter, but find that she and my nephew became engaged in our garden as well. I have been very pleased with Elizabeth. She is naturally formed for the role she must play, and only needs experience to round out her emerging skills as a proper hostess and mistress for her husband. You should be very proud of her."

"My Lady, I am exceedingly pleased to hear that all of my teachings have proven to be . . ."

"Oh no, Mrs. Bennet, did I imply that she arrived here with the proper skills? No. She knew enough to satisfy a simple household, but to be mixing in our circle; I knew that I must take her in hand." She turned to Elizabeth and smiled. "We have been conducting a finishing school of sorts."

"I appreciate your condescension to teach me, madam."

"Now dear, you know that I wish you to call me Aunt Helen." She patted her hand. "Shall we join the family?"

Lord Matlock's lips twitched and he turned to address the thoroughly ignored Mr. Bennet. "Well sir, I understand that you were impressed with Darcy's library? Have you heard about Pemberley?" Lord Matlock started up the stairs, Mr. Bennet walked alongside him and silently listened to the glowing description of a library so vast, the volumes would fill every room of Longbourn three times over. Mr. and Mrs. Gardiner exchanged smiles and started up the stairs. This couple would not allow anything to get out of hand that evening. Left alone in the front hallway, Darcy caught up Elizabeth's hand and drew her into his uncle's study and shut the door.

"Fitzwilliam, what are you doing? We cannot hide in here, as much as I would like that . . ."

"Hush." Darcy's arms were around her, and he made no secret of his desire, kissing her deeply, then relenting to deliver soft gentle kisses over her face and throat. He drew away to smile at her dazed eyes staring up at him, then brushed his lips tenderly over hers. "Elizabeth."

"hmmm?"

Darcy chuckled and kissed her again and laughed when she cuddled into his chest. Kissing her hair he bent to see her face. "Dearest you are becoming far too comfortable."

"Do you mind?"

"No, I could remain this way forever and a day." He rubbed his hands over her back. "You needed to be kissed, and I needed to kiss you. You look frightened to death, my love."

"After yesterday is there any wonder? Fitzwilliam, it was horrible!"

"I noticed." He whispered and held her tightly. "What happened when you returned home from our walk?"

"Papa and Uncle . . .discussed the situation." He kissed her forehead. "After seeing Mr. Harwick, I fear that he is unconvinced of any possibility for improvement, despite Papa's words of contrition."

"He is not alone." Darcy spoke honestly. Hearing footsteps in the hallway he reluctantly let her go, and smiled as she arranged her gown and touched her hair. "You are perfect."

"Hardly." She peered in a mirror over the fireplace then turned to see his outstretched hand. "Help me through this, Fitzwilliam."

"I promise." Opening the door, he stepped out and they started up the staircase. At the top, Layton stood with his arms folded.

"I was thinking of forming a search party for you."

"I was showing Elizabeth the study."

"It is very handsome," She said and her eyes sparkled when Layton's brows rose, "the contents were most impressive, and certainly bespeak of a . .

.powerful man." Darcy looked down to her and his chin rose before Layton burst out in laughter.

"Powerful, I look forward to telling that to Richard." They walked into the blue drawing room where the group was gathered. "Found them, Father."

"I did not realize they were lost." Lord Matlock said pointedly to his son. "Did Darcy show you the landscape in my study? I know that he was anxious to show you the difference between Matlock and Pemberley."

"Oh . . .I am afraid that I will need to view it in daylight to fully appreciate the estate, sir." Elizabeth blushed and Lord Matlock smiled.

Mr. Gardiner stepped up to Darcy and spoke softly. "Sir, you truly do test a chaperone's nerves."

"A landscape?" Mrs. Bennet cried. "Oh, Mr. Darcy showed us the painting of his estate yesterday, and it was most impressive, most impressive indeed! Why I cannot imagine a finer place, and of course so perfect for my Lizzy. I am sure there is nothing to compare with it anywhere! I am looking forward very much to visiting often!"

Elizabeth felt Darcy's arm tense under her hand. "Mama, I am certain that Matlock and Meadowbrook are equally lovely estates, and yours Mr. Singleton, I do not recall your estate's name?"

"Oh, it is named Ashcroft, Miss Elizabeth." He smiled and looked to see Audrey watching him. "I . . . I am very fond of it."

"Do you have a home in town, sir?" Mrs. Bennet asked Singleton. "Mr. Darcy's home was extraordinary to view, but now here I am in the home of an Earl! Lady Matlock, I must tell you that the decoration of this room is beautiful! It is precisely what I would have recommended Elizabeth do for Darcy House." Lady Matlock's eyes met Elizabeth's and instantly she recalled their conversation about redecorating this particular room. "I cannot imagine why she would not wish to take advantage of her rights as a bride and put her mark on the house, why . . ."

"Mrs. Bennet." Darcy said quietly and sent her a quelling glance. Her mouth snapped shut, and she took a sip of her drink. Mr. Bennet looked between them in disbelief, and the rest of the room's occupants directed admiring smiles in his direction.

"How did you do that?" Elizabeth asked quietly as conversation broke out around them.

"I seem to have a talent for it." He shrugged. "Perhaps she is afraid of me?"

"Brother?" Darcy startled and turned to find Georgiana standing beside him.

"Georgiana! I was hoping you would appear." He let go of Elizabeth's hand to embrace her.

"Aunt will not let me come to dinner." She said sadly. "She is so much stricter than you. May I come home?"

"To avoid your aunt or because you miss me?" He chuckled and kissed her cheek.

"I think it is that she misses your ways and wishes to avoid her aunt." Elizabeth laughed.

"I thought you would support me!" Georgiana cried. "Is that not what sisters do?"

"Support, yes, but completely disregard what is best for you? No." Elizabeth opened up her arms to hug her. "I miss you."

"Thank you." Georgiana whispered. "I miss you, too. I wish that you would marry soon so that I really can come home and be your sister."

"If it was up to your brother, I think that would be tomorrow." Elizabeth whispered back. "Are you truly unhappy with all of these ladies?" Georgiana glanced at Darcy then whispered in Elizabeth's ear. She laughed and smiled at him then whispered back to Georgiana, who startled to giggle.

Darcy knew enough to leave them alone for a little while and walked across the room to see Layton standing to the side, watching his father speak to Mr. Bennet and Mr. Gardiner. "I understand from Richard that yesterday was an utter disaster."

"I lost count of the number of insults that flew through the room. Mr. Bennet knew that he was delivering them, but seemed to find it amusing. Mrs. Bennet however . . .well they seem to flow freely from her unstoppable tongue."

Layton chuckled and nodded his head at the woman. "You stopped her, that is certain. I do not believe that her husband enjoyed you usurping his role, or perhaps he was simply surprised that it was possible?"

"I would be glad to see him display a desire to exercise his authority. He tried to make amends to Elizabeth this morning but avoided me entirely when I visited." Darcy watched Harwick and Jane talking together. "I think that this is the greatest effort I have seen either of them put into their courtship."

"I gather that it is not going well." Layton observed. "Really Darcy, what can you expect? The apple does not fall far from the tree." He received a scathing look. "Forgive me; Miss Elizabeth is certainly an exception."

"It is well that you said that, Cousin."

"I only meant that . . . well I am likely to put my foot in it if I continue. You are a braver man than I to want to attach yourself to such a family when there is so little to compensate you, besides of course, Miss Elizabeth."

"It seems that Mrs. Bennet is not the only one with difficulty mastering proper discourse." Darcy said coldly, and relented when he saw Layton's obvious contrition. "Very well, yes the attraction is Elizabeth, but she is priceless."

"So you will be inviting Mrs. Bennet to come and visit often?" Layton smirked.

"Not without a great deal of persuasion from my wife." Darcy looked over to the window where Elizabeth and Georgiana were now talking with Alicia. "How is your wife?"

Layton startled. "She is well, why do you ask?"

"Richard tells me everything, you know. Are you healthy, Cousin?" Darcy looked at him seriously.

"I believe so." He sighed. "A little more time and I think that I will be assured."

"Alicia is not a fool. Does she know why you have abstained?"

"We have not spoken of it."

"Is it not time?" Darcy raised his brows and smiled. "That is, if you ever want an heir."

"When did you become the oracle of marital relations?" Layton laughed and Darcy looked to Elizabeth. "Or is it wishful thinking from a frustrated groom?"

"It is my desire to be done with this interminable waiting and go home." He sighed and smiled. "Go home with my wife."

"Besotted fool." Layton smiled.

A footman appeared with a salver. "Pardon me sir; this express just arrived from Darcy House. The courier had orders to find you no matter your location." Darcy picked up the letter to examine the return and knit his brow as he broke the seal. Conversation in the room stopped, the expression on Darcy's face exposed that this was a serious situation.

"My God." He whispered as he scanned the page, turning it over quickly to read further.

"Fitzwilliam?" Elizabeth approached and touched his arm. He squeezed her hand before walking away, running his hand through his hair while he began to pace.

"Darcy, what is it?" Fitzwilliam stepped up to take the letter from his hand and read it rapidly, and then looked up to him. "I will go with you."

"Can you get away? You only resumed your duties a few weeks ago."

"What is it, may I help?" Harwick stepped forward.

Lord Matlock joined them and took his turn. Layton stood and read over his shoulder. "Good Lord." He whispered, turning the letter over, as if more information would somehow suddenly appear. "How could this happen?" He shook his head. "Well it has, and it must be addressed. Parliament is still in session, I cannot make this trip. Richard, can you really get away?"

"I would have to ask permission . . ."

Darcy was staring down at his boots, making plans in his head. "I have many appointments to cancel and letters to write." He turned to his cousin. "And I must leave as soon as possible. It is too late to begin now; I will have to go at first light."

"Then I will go with you." Layton said. "It could be tomorrow night before you hear from your superiors, Richard."

"Not if I go immediately."

Not really listening to the conversation, Darcy strode off to the window. "I must have the carriage prepared, I only need to pack enough for the journey . . .I must arrange for the inns and changing the horses . . ."

Lord Matlock interrupted. "I will take care of all those details, Darcy. Just notify your coachman of the journey. I will send my people ahead to prepare for the changes. You will stay at the usual places?"

"Yes, yes, of course, thank you." He said distractedly. "I . . . I am unsure what to do when . . ." He turned to see Elizabeth's and Georgiana's frightened expressions and walked over to take their hands. "I am sorry, but I must go, there is no choice. I will not know the extent of the situation until I arrive, and then I do not know how long I will be away. I will write to you as soon as I arrive, but you will not hear from me for at least six days."

"Six days? Fitzwilliam what is wrong? Please tell me!" Elizabeth cried and threw her arms around his waist. Lady Matlock came over to hold Georgiana.

"There was a fire at Pemberley." Both girls gasped. Georgiana rested against her aunt and began to cry, and Darcy held Elizabeth tightly. "The letter says that it was contained to the kitchens but there is a great deal of damage . . . I do not know if I am being spared the truth, Mrs. Reynolds would not wish me to panic." He drew a deep breath and buried his face in her hair, completely disregarding the roomful of people staring at them, particularly her father. "I do not wish to leave you, but I must." He whispered.

"I understand; this is your duty." She looked up and he wiped her teary eyes. "Now what can I do to make this easier for you?"

"Do?"

"May I write letters and cancel all of your appointments for you? Would that save you some time?"

"You would do that for me?" He smiled in wonder.

"Of course!" She touched his face. "Just leave them on your desk, I will find them."

Lady Matlock approached and placed her hand on Elizabeth's shoulder. "I will help her, Darcy."

"Thank you. I . . ." He looked down at Elizabeth and back up to spot Mr. Gardiner. "May I have some time to say goodbye?"

Mr. Gardiner glanced at Mr. Bennet who was staring at the scene in a state of amazement and nodded. "Go ahead." Darcy took Elizabeth's hand and led her from the room, pausing only to speak to Layton. "I hope to leave by seven. I will have my coach pick you up here."

"I will be ready." Layton nodded, and went to inform his valet to begin packing. Lord Matlock quickly wrote a note to be sent to Darcy House to begin the preparations there, then turned to address his guests. "In light of the circumstances, I suggest that we do away with the formalities and eat. We seem to have many assignments tonight."

Harwick held up his hand. "Sir, I will remove myself from this family crisis, although I would still be willing to accompany Darcy and Layton to Pemberley. I have dealt with fire at my estate."

Singleton walked over to join them. "I . . . I have no experience, but I would also like to be of assistance if I can."

"No, you stay here; if Darcy needs anything taken care of in town he can send us a message and that can be your duty." Lord Matlock noticed Mr. Gardiner standing by his side. "Yes, sir?"

"I think that we will depart, you should not be hosting company when there is a crisis to address." He turned to Harwick. "If you would be so kind as to lend us your coach?"

"Oh, yes of course, I can walk home from here. Come, I will tell the coachman to take you all home, without me inside there will be room enough for everyone."

"We must wait for Lizzy." Jane said softly. "Please do not rush her with Mr. Darcy. They may not see each other again for an extended time."

Mr. Gardiner looked at Mr. Bennet, who remained silent. "Bennet, do you anticipate any problem allowing Elizabeth to return separately? Perhaps Mr. Darcy could see her home before returning to his townhouse?"

"Without a chaperone?" Mrs. Gardiner asked, then seeing the raised brows of the entire Matlock household she smiled. "I suppose they are already flaunting that under our noses."

"I will volunteer to accompany them . . ." Audrey began.

"I will, too." Alicia smiled. "But I am certain we will be declined."

Mr. Gardiner smiled. "Well, I am certain she will find her way back to Gracechurch Street before long." He nodded at the family and they moved to the door. "I am sorry this has happened, sir. I can only hope that it is not as terrible as it sounds."

"Thank you; Gardiner. No doubt Elizabeth will be kept informed as much as we." Lord Matlock turned to Mr. Bennet. "I am sorry that we did not have the opportunity to speak."

"No sir, your family has left me speechless." Mr. Bennet bowed. "Good luck." He nodded to Lady Matlock and went to take Mrs. Bennet's arm.

"But, but what of dinner?" She exclaimed. "We are to have dinner with an Earl!"

"Quiet, Mrs. Bennet." He said as he moved her from the room. Lady Matlock rolled her eyes and followed them downstairs to see them out, and the rest of the family took a collective breath before diving into their preparations for the journey.

"OH." ELIZABETH SWALLOWED and rested her boneless body heavily on Darcy's chest. Darcy kept his arms tightly around her, placing his cheek on her hair, and closing his eyes as they both tried to regain their composure after finding their way into a darkened sitting room. "I am dying for you Elizabeth. I have been reliving your words to me constantly since yesterday. You want to touch me. Please, tell me where." Lifting his head he looked to her eyes and kissed her warm swollen lips. "Please."

"I . . . I am too embarrassed to say." She whispered. He responded with another rapturous kiss, and she answered by slipping her hands beneath his topcoat and up over his chest. Darcy groaned.

"More, darling."

She swept her palms across his body to stroke his back; the waistcoat barely masked the heat that her touch generated. "More; please . . ." He begged, releasing her mouth for a moment. Her hands moved lower, to run over his buttocks, feeling the tight muscle through his well-fitted breeches and after another searing kiss, she brought them over his stomach and, "Oh please, please . . ." down to at last touch the hard shaft that pushed prominently forward. Darcy let go of her shoulders, but still kissing her, placed both of his hands over hers, moving them up and down, forming her fingers so that they stroked and cupped him. He let go and lifted her up in his arms, carried her to a sofa and sat her in his lap, then barely stopping to breathe, delivered without hesitation endless kisses.

"Fitzwill . . ."

"hush." He whispered and finding the edge of her gown, slid one warm hand up her silky leg to her hip, then down between her thighs. Elizabeth jumped when his fingers found the moist warm folds, and moaned in his mouth when at last he began to rub the ache she had felt for years, and grew every time he was near. "Ohhh, please. . ."

"More?" He whispered heatedly.

"More . . .more . . ." His fingers, so long, so clever, knew just what to do. She jumped and arched her back, and then her writhing hips fell into a steady motion over his hardened muscle. "Yes, darling, yes." He whispered, and slowly slid one finger inside of her, while still circling her swollen, sensitive pearl with his thumb. The kisses became scorching, and he profoundly wished to tear off her clothes and devour her breasts, but satisfied himself with touching that precious secret place he had dreamed of for so long. Elizabeth's panting took on a desperate hitch, and she began to keen, unsure what she was feeling. "Let go, dearest, let go."

"oh oh . . . Fitzwilliam." She gasped as his stroking hand at last came to a rest in her soft furred mound. He kissed her, then lifting her relaxed body, deftly unbuttoned his breeches. Elizabeth opened her eyes as he freed his rigid member, and watched his hand stroke over it. Their eyes met and she saw him silently encouraging her to touch. Her trembling fingers grazed him and drew away. "Oh, it is so hot."

"Please . . ." he begged and her hand again rested over the tight silky skin, and naturally shaped around him to stroke slowly. Darcy placed his hand over hers, watching as they glided together, then let go and lay his head back as she continued. It would not be long. He moaned softly and whispered her name.

Elizabeth gazed upon him, his mouth was slightly open and his bottom lip caught between his teeth. She could feel his chest as it rose and fell in unsteady pants, and most of all, she felt his hands caressing her body, still stimulating her desire even as he sought his own release. She needed him to know that the same pleasure was spreading over her, exhilarating her senses. The surprise of her mouth suckling his lips abruptly moved him to rapture, he barely remembered to draw out his handkerchief in time before he pressed his mouth into her shoulder to muffle his cry. Elizabeth watched his face transform when his eyes squeezed shut and as he clutched her, his body shaking far harder than hers had. She knew exactly the glorious miracle he was feeling, and thrilled with the knowledge that he had found it by her hand. At last he relaxed, and they stayed embraced until Darcy looked down to the face resting on his shoulder. "I love you."

"I love you."

"This is just the beginning of all we have to experience together Elizabeth." He kissed her, and then held her face in his hands. "I have never felt anything so powerful before."

"Never?"

Her shy question was answered with another deep kiss. "This . . . this is love dearest. Do you know how few people in the world will ever experience what we just did? And we have not even become one body yet." Darcy clasped her to him. "I am eternally grateful that you love me."

"I feel the same for you, Fitzwilliam." They silently held each other, impressing the details of this moment in their memories.

Darcy's lips caressed her ear before whispering, "I could not have left you without this, Elizabeth. I am facing something that I do not feel at all able to address. I know that this experience together was wrong, but I could not possibly . . ."

His apology was silenced with her mouth over his, and again they were lost in their kiss. Finally pulling away, she held his face in her hands and kissed his temple, his eyes, and once again his lips. "You go and do what you must. No matter what you find, it is still our home, and I want you to bring me there."

He absorbed the strength that flowed through her touch. "I will. As soon as I am able, my love, I will."

Chapter 24

"Alicia?" Layton opened the door between their bedchambers and looked inside. The room was dark except for the hint of sunlight through the window as the breeze moved the draperies. He advanced inside to see her in the bed, and stood for a few moments gazing down at her sleeping form. Drawing a long breath he sat on the edge, and brushed her hair back from her face. "I do not wish to wake you, but I do want to say goodbye. I . . . I want to apologize to you. Our marriage did not begin with love but we did have a good friendship, and I . . . I have squandered that. I am ashamed of my behaviour, not just towards you, but towards my future responsibilities. Seeing Darcy's struggles has made me aware of how lazy I have been, and how neglectful. I have separated myself from you for months, and never told you why. It is because I feared I might be carrying disease from my loathsome habits. I have ended them but I wanted to be sure of my health before coming to you. I do not hold with the belief that a cure is had by lying with one who is not ill, and I believe that all is well now, and I was thankfully never infected." He touched her hand, and said softly, "I hope that when I return from helping Darcy, you and I might begin again." He sighed and leaned down to lightly brush her lips. "Please forgive me." He started to move away and was stopped when Alicia's hands came up to embrace his face and drew him back down for a heartfelt kiss. "Alicia."

She sat up and they embraced. "Why did you not say what kept you from me?"

"Why would I confess to visiting courtesans?"

"I knew that you did. I always knew."

"And you said nothing?" He said as he leaned his forehead onto hers. "Why?"

"I had no choice but to accept it, that is what I was taught. You are my master."

He laughed softly. "Have you not lived with my parents long enough to know who is really the master of this home?" Layton drew away and held her hands. "I was very set in my ways when we married. I have been given a great many lessons recently about how to be a husband and a man. May we start anew when I return?"

"Yes." She met his eye. "No more courtesans?"

"Never again. Only you." The clock chimed the half-hour. "I should go and eat before Darcy arrives. He said seven so it will surely be in ten minutes." He smiled to see her agree. "How was Elizabeth when you took her home?"

"Audrey and I left them alone in the carriage for a few moments. If Darcy had his way I think that he would have ordered it to leave for Pemberley that moment and kidnapped her." Alicia smiled wistfully. "It is sweet to see how they need each other. It seems to be growing stronger each time they meet."

"I am happy for him." Layton said with a slight smile. "I thought he was a fool for a long time, but I cannot discount the riches he reaps from his feelings for her." He kissed Alicia and stood. "I will write to you when we arrive. Perhaps I will stop at Matlock while I am near before we return."

"Safe journey, Husband. Care for our cousin." She smiled when he kissed her hand and left the room, then settled back to think about all that he said.

HARWICK ENTERED THE BREAKFAST ROOM and was pleased to see his sister had already arrived. Catching her eye, he smiled slightly and sank down onto his chair. "It is good to have you with me, Eva. I was growing tired of my own company."

"Is that why you have continued to court Miss Bennet?" She asked and took a sip of her tea.

"How long have you been waiting to say something?" He grew silent as he watched a servant bring him his plate and depart, leaving the siblings alone. "So I was a fool to try?"

"Not at all. Miss Bennet is a sweet girl, of course she was burdened with the horrendous behaviour of her parents so I am sure that I hardly saw her at her best, but I have heard enough descriptions from you to have a fairly good picture of her in my mind." She put down her cup and reached to take her brother's hand. "Jeffrey, if you are not deeply in love with this girl, I think that the time to end this courtship has arrived."

"I never wanted to love her." Harwick looked to the ring he wore in Ellen's memory, so similar to Darcy's symbol of love that he wore for Elizabeth, and thought once again about their conversation at Darcy House.

Evangeline broke into his thoughts. "All right then, I have watched you mourn Ellen for two years, and supported your plan to marry without feeling, as much as I hated it." Harwick looked up at her sharply and she smiled, "You are a warm and passionate man, and you need to be loved, and give it in return. Miss Bennet has no feelings for you in that way. Perhaps with time they would grow, but honestly she is too young to marry. Her mother has done a very poor job of preparing her for what is required. I want you to be happy, and what Miss Bennet would receive from you is a father figure to replace the one she has not had. You want a wife, not another child."

"But Miss Elizabeth is younger and seems very capable . . ."

"Miss Elizabeth is an entirely different woman. She is young, but I sense that she is destined to be a very capable wife and mistress for Pemberley. Mr. Darcy is very young as well, and so burdened. I see these two leaning very heavily on each other as they grow and learn their roles, neither one has had enough time with their parents. You did not see Miss Elizabeth when you left to speak to Mr. Bennet. Her mother began complaining about where you all had gone, and how dare you speak to her that way. Miss Elizabeth let loose her tongue, which I rather imagined she had been barely holding in check that entire time. When she realized that Colonel Fitzwilliam was still in the room she was mortified, but he told me he was dying to do the same." She sighed and saw the wistful expression in his eyes. "Yes, I see shades of Ellen in her, too."

"I miss her so much."

"Miss Bennet will never replace her in your heart."

"I do not wish to replace her!" He declared and worked to control his emotion.

She smiled and spoke firmly "No, but you do not want to live a stoic existence either. I want you to marry again, but I want you to marry a woman, not a young girl who has much growing to do. You deserve to be happy, and your girls deserve a strong role model as their mother. I think that you know what you must do."

He sighed. "I had good intentions, and she seems to be less jealous of her sister now, and if her family had been . . . at all different . . ."

"I know." Evangeline squeezed his hand. "I believe that she does as well."

"Well, I told her that I would take some time to think it over, and I meant that. I told her last night that I would see her tomorrow since I was certain the house would be in an uproar today with Darcy's departure. We both made a great effort to talk last night before everything fell apart, it was apologies at first but we were beginning to talk a little about how amusingly love struck Darcy and Miss Elizabeth were. I believe that we might have had a pleasant evening." He looked up to see his sister's smile. "I do not love her, but that does not make me unfeeling, Eva."

"I know that." She smiled. "Take your day to think it through one more time, Brother."

"HOW ARE YOU, LIZZY?"

She looked up from her untouched breakfast when Mr. Bennet entered the empty dining room. "I am well."

"You cannot fool me." He took a seat and accepted the tea she poured for him. "You came in very late."

"There was much to discuss." She said shortly. "Mr. Darcy's family all had thoughts to contribute, and . . . he needed me."

"I imagine that he did. I have never seen a family rise together and support each other in that manner. I hardly knew what to do with myself." Mr. Bennet saw her look back down at her meal. "I imagine they are on their way by now?" Elizabeth nodded and touched the locket. "Is that a gift from him?"

Startling she dropped her hand. "Yes, he gave me a token."

"I see." Mr. Bennet sighed. "I apologize again, Lizzy. He is an exceptional man and his family overwhelms me. I have not followed through with his recommendation that I educate your sisters. He offered to pay, but I believe that in order to redeem myself in his and your eyes, I should at least make that effort. I cannot really supplement their dowries, but at least I can try to give them some accomplishments and hopefully a chance to attract a suitor with their wit, as you did."

"Thank you, Papa." Elizabeth said softly. "I hope that they do not give you any trouble for the effort."

"No, I imagine that will come from Lydia, but Kitty and Mary may welcome the chance." He smiled. "And then your mother will count on you to put them in the way of rich men when they are properly out."

"I have no doubt." Elizabeth said dryly and Mr. Bennet was glad to see the restoration of her humour.

"I spoke with your uncle while we waited for you to return last night. Jane will remain in town after you marry. I observed Mr. Harwick with her, I fear that his offer will not come, and I do not wish for her to suffer your mother's petulance as you did. I endured enough of it the last two nights, first following her lecture by Marianne, then last night in her worry that Mr. Darcy may never return to marry you."

Elizabeth sighed; she had heard it all through the walls. "Thank you, Papa."

"I apologize for making sport of you for so long." He said softly. "I do not expect to be invited to your homes, but perhaps Mr. Darcy will allow you to visit on your own, or maybe the two of you may visit on your way to and from London."

Elizabeth looked up to see absolute contrition in his eyes. "I will speak to him about that."

"Thank you, Daughter." He patted her hand. "You will be deeply missed, but Mr. Darcy deserves you, and you deserve the life he will provide. Now, your mother and I will return to Longbourn this afternoon. Whenever you have your wedding plans prepared, please tell us, and no matter what happens with Jane, do not fear me impeding your marriage. I hope that I will still have the honour of giving you away to Mr. Darcy. My brother has served in my stead for too long."

"I will, Papa. I hoped that you would give me to him." Elizabeth stood and embraced him, and they held each other until Mrs. Bennet's voice announced the ladies' approach. She resumed her seat. "Perhaps while I wait for his return, I could visit Longbourn and pack up my belongings."

"You are welcome to travel with us today." He offered.

She hesitated when she saw the hope in his expression then shook her head. "No, I . . . I promised to help him with his letters and I do not wish to leave before I have word of his plans. Perhaps next week?"

"Very well then." Mr. Bennet smiled. "But be assured that your mother will wish to show you off to the neighbourhood. It is well that Mr. Darcy will be occupied, eh?"

"Lizzy!" Mrs. Bennet spotted her and immediately took the chair by her side, while Jane and Mrs. Gardiner took their places. "What are you doing to keep Mr. Darcy interested?"

Her eyes grew wide and she saw her aunt's close. "Interested? I . . . I do not understand, Mama."

"He has left you, he may not ever return! He has gone back to his estate and he might get lost in his sport or find a new girl while he is there!"

"Fanny, do not be ridiculous, his home suffered a fire. Mr. Darcy will not be standing in his stream fishing!" Mrs. Gardiner sighed. "He is not going to break his engagement to Lizzy! He is a man of honour. He will be back as soon as he can, and is undoubtedly very anxious to return! Why, he will not even arrive at Pemberley for days!"

"Oh Lizzy! He is so far away! He may die in a carriage accident!"

"Mama!" Elizabeth cried. "How can you say such things?"

"Mrs. Bennet, wailing over these ideas does nothing for our daughter. She misses him enough already, there is no need to make her fear for his safety or constancy." Mr. Bennet spoke decisively. The three women looked at him in surprise.

Mrs. Bennet closed her mouth then turned back to Elizabeth. "Have you written to him?"

"No, not yet . . ."

"You must tell him things that will keep him attracted." She rolled her eyes when Elizabeth looked confused. "Encourage him! Tell him that you find him handsome! Tell him of the night dress you have purchased . . . you *have* purchased something special have you not? OH! I must speak to you of your duties!"

"I believe I will depart now before I become ill." Mr. Bennet stood and rapidly left.

"Mama, please . . ."

"Jane, leave the room." Mrs. Bennet said determinedly then turned to Elizabeth. "Now, on your wedding night, Mr. Darcy . . ."

THE FOLLOWING MORNING, Lady Matlock arrived with Alicia to take Elizabeth to Darcy House. The ladies came into the Gardiner home to pay their respects, and when they prepared to depart, Elizabeth paused to hold Jane's hands. "Are you sure that Mr. Harwick will come today?"

"I am certain of it." Jane said quietly. "I am grateful that Mama and Papa departed yesterday. I do not believe that I could abide Mama's reaction when he ends it."

"You do not know that he will!" Elizabeth said reassuringly.

Jane smiled and shook her head. "Go Lizzy. Take care of your Mr. Darcy." Reluctantly Elizabeth left and Mrs. Gardiner whispered on her way out that she would take care of Jane whatever came. She climbed into the carriage with her future family and they set off.

"Is anything wrong, Elizabeth?" Alicia asked as they rode. "Or do you miss Darcy?"

"Of course she misses him." Lady Matlock observed. "But I suspect this mood has more to do with her sister than Darcy."

Elizabeth looked at her hands. "Your suspicions are correct, Aunt Helen." Knowing when to drop a topic the other ladies filled the carriage with conversation until they reached their destination.

"This way My Lady." Mrs. Mercer led them into Darcy's study. "He left several stacks here. These are letters he has read and had agreed to the meetings proposed within, so they are the ones that need to be cancelled. A great many of these are invitations, he said that he did not much care if they were answered or not since none were from friends, and this is the post that came this morning. He said that if you wished, Miss Elizabeth, you may read the letters and forward anything that looked important to Pemberley, but if it was not, just leave it be and he would look at it when he returns." She glanced around the room. "The girls have not been in to clean here yet, madam, please excuse . . ."

"No, that is fine Mrs. Mercer, I am certain that it was quite chaotic here when you sent him on his way." Lady Matlock nodded and the housekeeper closed the door to the spotless room on her way out. "Now then, let us see what we have here." She took a chair near the desk and looked at Elizabeth, who stood quietly, taking in the room and feeling Darcy's presence all around her. "Elizabeth?"

"Oh, forgive me, I . . . I have never had the opportunity to really look at the decoration in here. Fitzwilliam . . ." She blushed as the memory of his warm caressing hands and his deep kisses washed over her.

"I imagine that he was distracting." She smiled at Alicia who laughed, and pointed to Darcy's chair. "Take a seat."

"His chair?"

"Of course!" She laughed. "And definitely make a point of telling him that you sat there when you write." Seeing another blush she smiled and picked up the first letter.

"When should he arrive?" Elizabeth asked and looked to the landscape of Pemberley, and hoped that this would be the view she would soon enjoy.

"Well, he should probably arrive at about this time the day after tomorrow." She glanced at the clock. "Although knowing Darcy, he is probably pressing his driver to make as much progress as possible. I am actually surprised that he did not go on horseback, but it is a long journey."

Elizabeth sank down in the enormous chair, running her fingers over the worn leather, and laid her hands in the depressions made over long years of occupation. Again she felt herself enclosed within his arms, in his lap, his hand sliding under her skirt . . . shaking off the overwhelming feeling, she tried to focus. "Was this Mr. Darcy's chair?"

"I believe so, Darcy changed very little when he came to be master. I think this chair makes him feel that his father is with him." She watched as Elizabeth settled in and became lost in thought. "Elizabeth."

"Oh." She sat up and blinked, the smooth feel of the solid leather warming under hand brought to mind the sensation of caressing Fitzwilliam's rigid length and the pleasure she gave him. Blushing she whispered. "I am being silly."

"No dear, not at all. It makes me very happy to see how preoccupied you are with him." She looked down at the letter to give Elizabeth a moment to compose herself and nodded. "Very well then, as mistress you will spend a great deal of time with correspondence, of course yours will be of a social nature, but declining invitations will certainly be part of it. I will dictate the response and you will write it out. I will sign the letters on Darcy's behalf." She saw Elizabeth's confusion and smiled. "You my dear; are only his betrothed. I am his aunt, and I can cancel an appointment where you . . ."

"Oh." Elizabeth smiled. "Next month I could but not yet."

"Precisely." Lady Matlock nodded. "I suppose we could have had Henry's secretary do this, but I did not want Darcy's affairs exposed to anyone but family, not that there should be anything scandalous in these letters."

"I wonder why he does not employ a man." Alicia said.

"His father did not, so I imagine that Darcy never considered it for himself. In my opinion my brother took on all the tasks in an effort to remain constantly busy and forget my sister. I can see my nephew doing the same to occupy himself after his father died, not that he was in want of activity." She watched Elizabeth studying the landscape thoughtfully. "He has made us very proud."

"I am proud of him as well." She said softly. "He was very . . .he was trying very hard not to show how . . .worried he was when we were alone, but he held me so desperately." Elizabeth blushed and saw that Alicia was looking at her. "I should not have said that."

"Dear, you would be fooling nobody to say that Darcy was not holding you." Lady Matlock smiled.

"Audrey and I chose to give you a blind eye when you said your goodbyes, Elizabeth. It is only natural that you would wish to express yourselves when you cannot know the extent of your separation. Besides you will be married very soon." Alicia added reassuringly.

Elizabeth relaxed and confessed a little more. "My aunt said that . . . physical expressions of love would come at the happiest and saddest times, not just every day."

Lady Matlock glanced at her daughter-in-law then looked back to Elizabeth. "She is correct, and that is why nobody stopped you from comforting him. I assume that he did not press you . . ."

"No madam." Elizabeth blushed again and sat up to take a pen and drew forward a sheet of paper. "Shall we begin?" Lady Matlock and Alicia regarded each other with raised brows. Elizabeth's sudden desire for activity was telling, but they would not compel her to say more.

Over the next hour, Elizabeth wrote out letters and Lady Matlock signed them, all for appointments Darcy had made over the next fortnight, while Alicia read over the enormous stack of neglected invitations. "Quite a variety of interests." His aunt said as she signed the last letter. "I wonder if Henry's investments are so varied."

"I thought it would be all livestock and crops, but he has railroads, mining, engines . . . and I was pleased to see the letter from my uncle." She smiled and saw Lady Matlock nod.

"I believe that Darcy will do a very admirable job of expanding the wealth of his family."

"So perhaps the loss of a wife with a substantial dowry will not be so painful."

Alicia spoke up. "Why are you beating yourself about that? Darcy has had time to consider what such an alliance would mean. Even if you two did only just come together physically, he has had you in his thoughts for years if I am correct about the clues he has let drop over time. Do not tell me that he has not been far from your thoughts." She saw that Elizabeth was focussed on her. "Just because the rest of the family was taken by surprise by his decision does not mean that he was."

"Elizabeth, Darcy knows what he can afford to do. He will lose thirty thousand pounds when Georgiana marries, but that could be five or even ten years from now. That money is earning interest, and that interest will make up for some of its loss. Do not feel terrible for something that does not concern him." She put the pile together, then looked through the invitations. "Hmmm, he is correct, none of these really require responses, but we will just write a note on each saying no thank you, and return them to the sender. These are all people wanting him present to get a look at you, and none of them are people you need to know." She then turned to the new day's post. "You go ahead and open the letters, and I will return. I would like to have a word with Mrs. Mercer. Oh, and Alicia, I saw the invitation from the Crearys'. If it is possible, Darcy and Elizabeth should attend that ball, it is in three weeks so perhaps he will have returned by then." Alicia nodded and made sure that a note was written to accept that invitation.

Elizabeth picked up the letters that had just arrived while Alicia set to work on the rest of the invitations. Two letters were personal and as soon as she realized that she set them aside. One was a proposal asking for an investment and another was a charitable request. The last looked like it may be another personal letter, but quickly her hand went to her mouth and she gasped. "Fitzwilliam!" She cried out and dissolved into sobs.

"Elizabeth!" Lady Matlock rushed into the room, and seeing the letter crushed in her hand pried it out and began to read.

8 June 1809

Dear Mr. Darcy,
May I offer you my most sincere congratulations for your marriage to the daughter of my sponsor's patron, your aunt, Lady Catherine de Bourgh? I was thrilled and delighted to hear from Mrs. Darcy's lips of your nuptials. While I am of course gravely disappointed that I could not perform the service myself, I can certainly understand why a man as distinguished as you would wish to be married by a bishop. Mrs. Darcy was glowing in the description of the ceremony, as could only be expected. I look forward to serving you and your family for many years, and despite Mrs. Darcy's current delicate health, I am certain that very soon the halls of Rosings and your estate in Derbyshire will contain the happy sounds of your heir's cry.
Have I mentioned that I am soon to take Holy Orders and currently serve as an assistant to Reverend Mousely? He sponsored me as I studied, and Lady Catherine de Bourgh indicated that she would award his living to me when he, regrettably, retires. I do hope that you will continue to follow her wishes? I would be very proud to serve a patron as eminent and powerful as you, sir.
Your servant,
William Collins

"Good heavens!" Lady Matlock said softly and looked to Elizabeth who was weeping and hugging herself.

Alicia hurried over and embraced her. "What happened?"

"Why? Why would he lie? Why would he marry her and . . . go through this charade with me? Why?" She sobbed.

"Elizabeth!" Lady Matlock said sharply. "Darcy did not marry his cousin! Now pull yourself together and stop this caterwauling immediately! How can you say that you love him and be so quick to distrust him! I am ashamed of you!"

Elizabeth gulped and took a breath. The verbal slap had the intended effect, and the initial shock from seeing anyone being called Mrs. Darcy besides herself faded. Lady Matlock handed her a handkerchief and poured her some wine. While returning the carafe to its place she looked at the grate in the fireplace and noticed some letters that Darcy had apparently set alight when he was arranging his desk, and did not burn completely. She recognized familiar handwriting on one and reached down to retrieve it. "This is from Catherine." She turned it over and seeing the seal intact she nodded. "He never looked at it, naturally after he cut his ties with her, why would he?" Walking back over to the desk where Elizabeth sat trembling and wiping her eyes, Lady Matlock sat down and broke open the envelope, and began to read the singed page. "I see." Wordlessly she handed the letter to Elizabeth and watched her take in the statement.

8 June 1809
Rosings

Dear Darcy,
Your cousin's illness has expanded to the point where she believes herself to be your wife at all times, and has demanded that she be addressed as such. She asks why you have not come to Rosings, and has even gone so far as to describe your wedding to our pastor's assistant, Mr. Collins. He would like to announce the news of your wedding to the world; of course. I have asked him to delay until you arrive to take your place at Anne's side. There is no other choice. To protect the word of Anne's delusions from being spread and therefore protect the family name, as well as yours and Georgiana's reputations, you must do your duty and marry her.
She is ill, the fever remains unabated, and I doubt she will live long. It is not such a terrible sacrifice for you, is it? You will have Rosings. I know that you prefer Pemberley so I will remain here to care for the estate in your absence. She will die and you will be free to marry that Bennet woman if you find it so distasteful to simply take her as your mistress.
I expect you to arrive very soon, the servants have heard everything; it is only a matter of time before word of your marriage to Anne spreads.
Sincerely,
Lady Catherine de Bourgh

"That horrid woman!" Elizabeth declared. Her eyes flashed in anger and she looked up to see Lady Matlock nodding her head approvingly. "How *DARE* she foist her unbalanced daughter on my Fitzwilliam! He would not bend to such demands, would he?"

"No dear, Darcy deeply believes in duty and honour, but there are some things that he absolutely will not do, and as much as he loves his family, he dearly loves you. He would not accept Catherine's demand that he marry Anne before this occurred, so I doubt that he would now. If he had read this letter before leaving, I wonder which crisis he would have addressed first." She said thoughtfully and looked at the furious woman glaring at the letter in her hands. "I think that he would have chosen you."

Alicia put a comforting arm around Elizabeth and looked to Lady Matlock. "What do we do? Gossip of this nature will not be contained. I cannot imagine the staff at Rosings being particularly loyal to Lady Catherine."

"I suggest that we go to Matlock House and apprise my husband of his sister's activities. He is the head of the family, and it is he who must control her." Lady Matlock rose and gathered together the letters they had prepared, placed Lady Catherine's and Collins' letters in her reticule and watched Elizabeth stand shakily. She embraced her and smiled. "Come my dear, now that the shock has worn off, I would like to see how the true mistress of Pemberley conducts herself in a crisis."

"I will do whatever is necessary." Elizabeth took a steadying breath and joined her aunt, but paused to look once again at Pemberley before she walked out the door.

"THE POST, SIR." Lord Matlock nodded and returned to the letter he was composing. He was putting his papers in order before leaving for an afternoon session at the House of Lords. His work was interrupted by his wife's voice.

"Henry!" She said angrily. "Your sister is a manipulative hag."

He coughed and smiled. "What brings this on?" Then noticing Elizabeth standing behind her, his smile fell away. "Have you been crying, dear?"

"Yes she has, and with good reason." Lady Matlock placed the letters on his desk. "Go ahead, read them! The first was in Darcy's post this morning the second was in his grate, unopened."

He read the first and his jaw dropped. "Who is this fool?" He looked at the signature. "Collins? Is he as barking mad as Anne?"

"Read on, Husband." Lady Matlock said dryly.

He picked up his sister's letter and stood, "What devil has possessed her? What spawn formed her?" He paced the room vigorously as he thought and fumed. "It is all a ploy to keep her in Rosings; she could give a . . .bloody care if her daughter dies, so long as she was married to Darcy!"

"*That* we know, Henry. Do not point out the obvious, let us address the solution."

"Forgive me Helen, you had your opportunity to react, and I am taking mine." He glared at her and saw Elizabeth's uncertain gaze running between the couple. He sighed. "We are not arguing, dear."

Lady Matlock saw her wide eyes and patted her hand. "Darcy will exasperate you, too."

"Oh."

Lord Matlock dropped into his chair, and scanned over the letters lying before him, his eyes drifted to the day's post and on top he noticed a letter from Rosings, but it was not in his sister's hand. "Ah." He reached for it and broke the paste seal, and checked the signature. "I asked Mrs. Jenkinson to apprise me of any unusual events at Rosings. She has done as I bid." Quickly he scanned the page and put it down as he became lost in thought. Sighing loudly Lady Matlock stood and snatched the letter, and returned to her chair to read, then handed it over to Elizabeth.

8 June, 1809

Dear Lord Matlock,
As you asked, I am writing to tell you of things at Rosings. Miss Anne has fallen very ill, her fever came on when we returned from London, and the physician bled her twice. She is weak at times but her delusions seem to give her the strength of a bull. She is convinced at all times that she is married to Mr. Darcy and demands that she be addressed as his wife. She questions why she is not in the mistress's chambers and why he is not home with her. I have refused to call her Mrs. Darcy and she reacts very violently when I try to set her right. The elixir is not strong enough, but her ladyship will not hear of increasing the dose. I fear for your niece, sir.
Then there is Mr. Collins, he is a reverend in waiting, if you will. He is hoping for the living when Mr. Mousely retires. Sir, Mr. Collins is a flatterer and gossip, and a very little man, if you take my meaning. He likes to make himself important by spreading news. He visited Miss Anne and now wishes to tell the world of this sham marriage. Please sir, could you come and visit? Miss Anne needs a doctor who is not paid by her mother; and Mr. Collins must be stopped, although I fear that good Mr. Darcy will be grievously injured by this rumour.
Sincerely,
Adelaide Jenkinson

Lord Matlock studied Elizabeth shrinking as she took in yet another round of bad news. He turned his gaze to his wife who was watching the young girl as well, and their eyes met. "It is well that I did not go to Pemberley."

"Shall I send for Mr. Clarke?"

"Yes, and I will write a note for Richard. I want him to join me on this trip. It is only a few hours to Rosings, so he will not be away for long."

"What are you thinking, Henry?" Lady Matlock said anxiously.

"I am not sure." He spoke softly. "I am not sure. We will see what our physician can do for Anne, and see if we can find a way to contain this news. It will not be easy. Three days have passed since these letters were penned. It may be too late already if this Collins fool has been loose with his tongue."

"But . . . Does that mean that Fitzwilliam must marry her?" Elizabeth said fearfully. "Surely that cannot be so!"

"It would be the simplest solution." Lord Matlock mused and rubbed his chin.

"NO!" Elizabeth cried and stood.

"Henry! Do not frighten the girl any more than she already is!" Lady Matlock put her arm around Elizabeth. "My husband does not know to curb his thoughts." She glared at him. "Think of something else!"

"Let me get this note off to Richard and I will." He glared back, then stood to pat Elizabeth's shoulder. "No dear, Darcy will most certainly not be marrying his cousin. He is very publicly engaged to you. Your parents would be well within their rights to sue him for breach of promise if he left you now."

"He would not do that." She whispered.

"Well there is no sense continuing this speculation. I will go to Rosings as soon as possible, taking Richard and Mr. Clarke with me. Then we will see what we can do. There is no point in writing to Darcy about this until we see Catherine. He will want information."

Lady Matlock left him to write his notes and sent for the physician with a letter of her own. Elizabeth went to join Alicia. Audrey was with her and had been apprised of the events. The three women were sitting together and discussing the situation in low voices when Georgiana appeared. "Elizabeth! I did not expect to see you today!" She sat down and looked at them in anticipation. "Are you planning a shopping trip together? May I join you?"

Elizabeth looked helplessly at the ladies and was saved an answer by Lady Matlock's voice. "Yes, Georgiana, we will be shopping today. We have many places to visit to expand Elizabeth's new wardrobe. I am afraid that the future Mrs. Darcy's closets remain shockingly bare." She looked at her daughters pointedly. "I want to make it very clear that Darcy's betrothed is shopping with us."

Audrey smiled and looked at Elizabeth. "Oh yes, come Elizabeth, you need to wear something else if we are going shopping for *the future Mrs. Darcy's* clothes. You must have something that would do, Mama?"

"Yes." She nodded. "Come Elizabeth. Let us visit my closet, then spend a great deal of my nephew's money."

12 June 1809

Far too many things have happened in such a short time. I have spent hours in the company of the women of Matlock House, shuttling from one fashionable venue to the next, and being introduced in very clear tones to all who were near as Fitzwilliam's bride. The attention was nearly unbearable, but of course I understood the purpose, if this gossip about Fitzwilliam and his cousin is reported in the papers, many important women will be able to state positively that I was seen in Lady Matlock's company purchasing my trousseau. A preemptive strike, as the colonel called it. He will accompany Lord Matlock to Rosings tomorrow. I wish that I was with them so I could indeed take on this horrid woman and give her the piece of my mind that Fitzwilliam feels I would. I wish that he were here!

And then there was Jane. The predictions came true; Mr. Harwick came and spoke to her, and ended the courtship. He apologized for giving her false hope. I cannot be angry with him; he was honest from the beginning. The fault for this failure is our parents' and Jane's. She knows that her assumption of easy acceptance was due to Mama's teaching, but her jealousy of my love with Mr. Darcy was entirely her own. Mr. Harwick was kind in his rejection, and Jane wished him well, but it is still a bitter truth to swallow. I hope that both he and Jane find what they need.

"THERE IS COLLINS." Fitzwilliam pointed as the carriage swept up the drive to Rosings the next day. "He has an unerring sense of when a visitor is arriving."

"He is probably watching for Darcy to arrive so he can lick his boots." Lord Matlock snorted.

Mr. Clarke looked at him with interest. "Not much to him is there?"

"Just a big mouth." Fitzwilliam muttered.

The carriage stopped and into the house the three men went. The footman at the door saw their angry faces and stuttered out that Lady Catherine was in the process of being moved to the dowager's house per the orders of Mrs. Darcy.

"What?" Lord Matlock exclaimed and turned to his son. "She is entertaining the delusion this far as to be willing to leave?"

"She is not pleased to leave, sir. She states that she will not depart while her daughter is ill." The footman intimated, "But Miss Anne, Mrs. Darcy, is most insistent. Do you know when Mr. Darcy will arrive, sir? She is very anxious to see him." He looked hopefully out to the empty carriage and back to Lord Matlock.

"He will not be here in the foreseeable future." Lord Matlock said dryly. "Now, Mr. Clarke is a physician and is here to examine Miss Anne, Yes, *MISS* Anne. She is *NOT* married. Please take him to her. Where might we find Lady Catherine?"

"She is in the green sitting room, sir." The footman stuttered and led Mr. Clarke upstairs.

"Can you believe her?" Fitzwilliam said angrily as they strode forward. "Perpetuating this myth? And with a staff with lips as loose as that man's it will surely be in the papers before the week is out!"

"I know that my sister has a great deal of gall, but this is beyond the pale." Lord Matlock stopped before they reached their destination, and looking around, pulled his son into an empty room and closed the door. "Would you be willing to marry her?"

"What!" Fitzwilliam stared at his father. "Is that why it was so urgent that I come with you?"

Lord Matlock grabbed his shoulders. "I wanted you with me because you are my son, and this is your family. If Mr. Clarke reports that she is indeed near death, and she can be convinced to accept you, would you be willing?"

"Why? So that Darcy's reputation would be saved? He has done nothing!"

"Yes but word of insanity in the family does none of us good." He sighed and admitted his other thought, "And it would give you Rosings."

"And no hope for a future tied to Anne." Fitzwilliam said bitterly. "I admit to having this conversation with Darcy recently, and he thankfully talked me out of it."

"It would do us all good . . ."

"I would be a vulture."

"That is exactly what Darcy would be if he followed Catherine's plan. It is your best chance for an estate, Son."

Fitzwilliam turned and walked to a window to stare out at the precisely manicured garden. "And what of Mrs. Carter?"

"You have only just met; you have not even paid a call yet."

"You said that you would support me if I tried." Fitzwilliam reminded him.

"How likely is it that she would accept you, Richard?" He met his son's hurt look and sighed. "She may not wish to remarry."

"I will not know that at all if I pursue this plan of yours." He strode to the door and opened it. "Now let us go see the former mistress of Rosings."

Together they continued to the end of the long hallway until they at last arrived in the appropriate sitting room. "Catherine." Lord Matlock barked.

"Henry!" She looked up with a smile and then frowned to see Fitzwilliam. "Where is Darcy?"

"That is no concern of yours. What is the meaning of this? How dare you attempt to force his hand to marry Anne?"

"She has decided that she is his wife, there is nothing I can do about that. Do you wish to see her in shackles in some dungeon of an asylum?"

"Of course not, but being married to Darcy . . ."

"Marrying Darcy will stop any gossip that may get out."

"Thanks to your servants and your idiot parson, it may already be out!" Lord Matlock declared. "You are trying to hurt this family?"

"No, not at all, I am merely securing my daughter's future, as any good mother should."

"You have no more interest in Anne than you do in the content of the scripture you spout with authority. You know that she is dying and you do not wish to lose your home." Lord Matlock bent over her and snarled. "I understand that Anne has ordered you out. I will not stop that from moving forward."

Mr. Clarke appeared at the doorway. "Excuse me, sir. I have completed a cursory examination. I believe that Miss de Bourgh's fever, if it does not break soon, will take her life before too many days pass. She has been bled twice, I cannot advise more."

"Is she coherent?" Lord Matlock asked. "Is she sensible?"

"She demands her husband to come to her. She speaks of their unborn child." He looked to Lady Catherine. "Madam, I am sorry to bring you such disturbing news."

Lord Matlock turned to his son. "Even if you wished it, you could not marry her. She would not be able to give her consent or sign the registry. She would demand Darcy."

"I know that Father." Fitzwilliam said quietly. "I will not take an estate that belongs to the de Bourghs falsely."

"You . . .you would be willing to marry her?" Lady Catherine rose from her chair. "Now?"

"No, Aunt. Not now." He sighed and turned to his father. "Do we know the name of the heir?"

"Yes, I found him recently. He is a naval officer." Richard smiled and Lord Matlock nodded. "His mother will be very happy."

"But . . ." Lady Catherine sputtered.

"You sister, will spend the rest of your days in the dowager's house. I will speak to Captain de Bourgh and make certain of that."

"STEADY DARCY, WE ARE ALMOST THERE." Layton spoke softly as the carriage turned from the muddy rutted public roads onto the solid gravelled drive of Pemberley. At last the pace increased and the interminable journey through three days of rain was nearing an end.

Darcy said nothing, only staring out of the window in silence as he had for most of the trip, twisting incessantly the gold ring containing Elizabeth's braided hair under glass, as if touching it brought him closer to her. The carriage began to climb a steep hill, and both Darcy and Layton sat up, looking intently out of the windows. They gained the rise and suddenly there was a break in the trees, and the vista below revealed . . .Pemberley House.

Darcy murmured, "Thank you, Lord." Layton reached over to grip his arm. The carriage continued and Darcy contained his thoughts that the great stone walls could very well be serving as a shell to devastation inside. They would know soon enough.

"It is stunning, Darcy." Layton spoke softly. Darcy swallowed and nodded, unable to say more.

The carriage at last arrived and servants were waiting for them. Mrs. Reynolds appeared and without hesitation grasped Darcy's arms. "Oh sir, thank you for coming so soon! We were so worried for you!"

"I came the first moment I could, Mrs. Reynolds." He looked up to the house. "It appears to be intact, please tell me what lies within."

"The kitchens took the brunt of it, sir. Fortunately the stone floor and walls contained the fire, but everything that could burn, did, I am afraid. Mr. Nichols can tell you the particulars. He had beams brought in to shore up the supports that suffered the greatest harm." They entered and she led the way, the lingering odour of the fire became more potent as they advanced. "The damage to the rest of the house is the smoke, sir. Most of the house was closed up with you absent; and the doors being shut and the furniture covered helped a great deal, but there is much washing to be done, as you see." She indicated servants up on ladders with cloths, cleaning the blackened ceiling and taking down draperies. "I think that the new mistress might want to consider replacing some of the fabrics and rugs, and perhaps paint in the rooms closest to the kitchens."

"How are the bedchambers?" He asked as they passed more blackened rooms.

"They are remarkably fine. When this rain ends we will open every window to air out the house. That was a stroke of luck there sir, all of the windows were closed to keep out the rain and that kept the smoke from creeping in that way." Darcy nodded and they descended the stone stairs to the kitchen area. The stench of the fire was heaviest here, and Darcy took in the destruction as stoically as he could.

Layton placed a hand on his shoulder. "It is not so bad."

"Really?" Darcy turned to see if he was serious.

"Really. Our neighbours lost a wing about ten years ago when a footman fell asleep and kicked his lantern over." Layton looked around the empty room. "I can see that your home is far stronger than theirs was." He continued, "Pemberley has burned before, has it not?"

"Twice, according to the history I have read."

"I imagine that after the last, significant measures were put in to contain fire to small areas. It is good that your kitchens are almost an outbuilding. You might want to study the history again when you have the opportunity." Layton smiled to see Darcy's incredulous look. "Will *you* be doing the cleaning?"

"I . . .I had not thought of it." He looked around again and watched as men appeared with wheel barrows and filled them with the debris. He noticed that a cart was in place to receive the mess. With so many working, the room would soon be clear. Recognizing his steward outside, he approached.

"Nichols, thank you for your efficient work."

"We jumped on it as soon as the room was cool, sir." He watched another load dump into the cart. "I wrote to the man who redesigned the stables for you last year, I expect to hear from him soon. The staff is using the old kitchens for now."

"And the servant quarters? How were they affected?" Darcy walked along with him as they looked up to the sooty walls.

"The smoke went up, and the door separating their rooms was shut fortunately, other than a residual smell, you would never know there was a problem there."

"Well that is something." Darcy sighed. "I think that we should settle in and then . . . perhaps take a tour of the entire building, and note everything that must be repaired in each room, address the structural damage and rebuilding of the kitchens first, then move on to the cleaning, and finally the replacement of damaged textiles?" He looked at Layton who nodded.

"Sounds like a well-formed plan Darcy." He smiled. "You did not need me after all."

"Oh no, I learned my lesson the hard way when Father died, I tried to do things on my own, and was too bull-headed to accept help. Mr. Nichols can attest to my mistakes." He nodded to his steward who remained impassive.

"So I should simply learn from your errors and turn it all over to the steward when my time comes?" The two men looked to Nichols who had turned his attention to the men removing debris, but could not hide his smile. "I think that I have an answer."

"Well, I am relieved to see that this damage is not nearly as bad as my imagination invented." Darcy managed his first smile in days. "The house is intact, what has been damaged can probably be replaced fairly soon, the cleaning is bothersome but all in all, I am greatly relieved, it could have been so much worse. I must write to Elizabeth immediately and tell her the good news. I look forward to her to returning to her joyful self, and let her concentrate on nothing more challenging than the menu for our wedding breakfast." Darcy sighed with relief. "All is well."

Chapter 25

"Look at this Mr. Wickham!" Caroline giggled and pointed a long nail at the item in the gossip column. "It seems that Mr. Darcy is trying to marry twice!"

"What is that?" Wickham bent over the paper and Caroline raked her eyes over his handsome face while he read, then focussed again when he barked out a laugh. "Well, well, who would have guessed, Darcy wished to be a bigamist?"

"Oh I cannot see that." She reverted back to defending her first prey. "I wonder if he simply realized in time what a mistake he was making to marry that country chit and ran to his cousin." Caroline sighed. "Too late."

Wickham cocked a brow at her. "Too late, Miss Bingley?"

"Too late to save him some trouble. He will have to pay her off, of course."

"Hmm." Wickham laughed to himself. He knew that Darcy was the prize she sought. "Well, now he is tied to that sickly wretch. I imagine he will be shopping for a mistress before long." Noting Caroline's wistful expression he jabbed. "A kept woman, all the finery without the honour."

"Oh yes, nothing more than a courtesan, a disgusting life."

"Mmm hmm. Perhaps that is all he wanted with Miss Elizabeth all along." Wickham returned to the paper after shooting a look at her and inwardly laughed at her wide eyes. "So Darcy is master of Pemberley and Rosings. And no entailment on either, such funds at his fingertips." He said jealously and noticing Caroline's continued interest, he decided to bait her a bit. "Perhaps I should pay a call to congratulate him. Well, knowing his cousin, he surely does not have much honeymooning to do."

"Is she really so ill?" Caroline said eagerly.

"Oh yes, thin as a rail and a miserable countenance. I saw her only a few times when she was a girl. I doubt that she has improved. A sour child, perfect for such a sour man." Wickham laughed. "He is getting what he deserves."

"I thought that you were friends?"

"Of course we are my dear, I was only joking!" Wickham covered quickly. "Surely you have seen that thunderous frown he conjures; it has been a point of amusement between us over the years."

Bingley wandered into the room and smiled to see the couple getting on so well. "Here now, what is all of this levity? I should not have shirked my chaperone duties for so long."

"I assure you sir, your sister is safe in my hands, and nothing could really occur in the ten minutes you were absent." Wickham smiled and winked at Caroline.

She covered her blush by holding out the paper. "We were laughing at this item in the society page. Mr. Darcy married his cousin. It seems that Miss Elizabeth has been jilted."

"What?" Bingley sat down and read the item. "When . . .? This is incorrect."

"What do you mean?" Caroline demanded. "It is in the paper!"

"It is in the gossip column, Caroline." Bingley pointed out. "Darcy's engagement announcement to Miss Elizabeth was in the society page, besides, I walked with them last week and if that was an engagement in trouble, I will eat my hat." He shook his head. "This is impossible. Darcy is at Pemberley. He sent me a note that he was leaving town due to a fire there."

"A fire?" Caroline cried and placed her hand on her breast. "At Pemberley? Is it burned to the ground?"

"No, he thinks it is only a small area, well that is what he said to me. I hope that it was not more than that."

She spun around in her seat. "Oh Mr. Wickham, what horrible news! To hear that your childhood home was damaged!"

Wickham noted Bingley eyeing him curiously and cleared his throat, he was not aware that Bingley was a close friend of Darcy's. "Yes, terrible, but of course I did not actually live in the main house. I visited frequently . . ."

"You lived at Pemberley?" Bingley asked. "You know Darcy?"

"I . . .I . . .yes, I lived on the estate, and received a considerable bequest from his father."

"Extraordinary!" Bingley smiled. "Well you will have to join me sometime when I call on Darcy, he will be pleased to see an old friend. Where did you live on the estate?"

"Oh, in my father's house." Wickham smiled and took Caroline's hand. "I am sorry but I must keep my other appointment. You will forgive my haste? I will see you tomorrow evening?"

"Of course, yes, I look forward to another dance with you, Mr. Wickham." Caroline stood and walked him out to the door. When she returned, she saw Bingley still staring at the notice with his brow creased. "Charles, I will thank you for not scaring Mr. Wickham away in the future."

"What? What did I do? You were talking of Pemberley being his home."

"He had a difficult childhood, I just forgot for a moment. Mr. Darcy's father made it right though with his enormous bequest. Mr. Wickham is quite wealthy."

"That is good to know, but it seems to me you have not forgotten Darcy yet. Well he will be married, and not to this cousin of his." Bingley walked from the room carrying the paper, and calling for his hat, stepped outside to hail a passing cab.

12 JUNE 1809
Pemberley

My Love,
Our home is safe. The kitchen is destroyed and the walls blackened, but all will be well, and when I carry you over the threshold, it should be nearly back to its glory. It will require you, though. You resisted redecorating Darcy House, but I am afraid that you have no choice now. Pemberley has wounds that must be dressed, and I refuse to make such decisions without your opinion. So the wounds will wait for your gentle touch. We will visit the warehouses and choose fabrics for the draperies and new carpets. After seeing your wonder over selecting furniture for our bedchamber, I can but imagine the glee you will feel to have free rein amongst endless diversity.
I cannot describe my fear as we approached the crest of the drive. There is a break in the trees that affords a spectacular view of the house, and my heart was in my throat. I held onto my token for want of your hand. My relief was indescribable, not only was my family's home intact, but I still had a home to give you, and I am delighted to report dearest, the roof does not leak, so I can happily fulfil your ideal desire for marrying me.
I hope though that you desire far more from me than a dry place to slumber. I know that my behaviour in my uncle's house was unforgivable, but I cannot regret the love we shared. I think on it constantly, the feel of your skin under my palm, your thighs, your lips, so firm yet so soft. Dearest, I yearn to taste you and plumb your depths, if I could but have you now in my arms, I would be forever happy. To give you that happiness in return will be my greatest achievement. I long to hear you call me Husband. I long more to call you Wife.
I will return to you very soon, my Elizabeth. Once the plans are set, I will be on my way, within a week. I promise.
Forever yours,
Fitzwilliam

"Fitzwilliam." Elizabeth felt a shiver pass through her, and imagined exactly what he wished to do.

"What does Mr. Darcy have to say, Lizzy?" Mr. Gardiner asked then hid his amusement when she jumped and blushed. "Mr. Darcy?"

"Oh . . .the house is intact and he will leave within a week." She stood and flustered, clutched her letter. "Excuse me."

Mrs. Gardiner watched her flee the room and raised her brow. "I suspect there was much more said in that letter than talk of houses and travel."

"Do you?" Mr. Gardiner winked at her then saw Jane staring out at the passing traffic. "What occupies your thoughts Jane?"

She smiled and shook her head. "Nothing sensible, Uncle." Noticing a carriage stopping, she sat up. "Mr. Bingley is here."

"Mr. Bingley?" Mrs. Gardiner set down her sewing and they prepared to receive him. A maid announced him and he entered the room, not quite as enthusiastically as he had in the past. "Sir, please be seated. What brings you to our neighbourhood today?"

"Well Mrs. Gardiner, I could attempt an elaborate explanation of having business here but in truth, I come because of an item I saw in today's paper." He stood and handed the sheet to Mr. Gardiner. "I was not sure if you were aware of this, and now not seeing Miss Elizabeth here, I can but hope that it is the falsehood I believe it to be."

"So it has begun." Mr. Gardiner said softly.

"Sir?" Bingley asked and watched as the paper was passed to Mrs. Gardiner, who sighed and showed Jane.

"What do you know of Miss de Bourgh, Mr. Bingley?"

"She is weak, and her mother fancied her as a mate for Darcy. He told me that was impossible. Please tell me that this news is not true. Darcy has loved Miss Elizabeth for a very long time, I just could not see . . ."

"No, it is not true. This is a fabrication begun by an ill woman, a questionable staff, and a horrendous mother." He spoke angrily. "And now Lizzy must bear it without Darcy by her side."

"It is hardly his fault that he is absent, Mr. Gardiner." Mrs. Gardiner said sharply. He nodded and stood. "I will go tell her." Taking the paper he left the room.

"I am sorry to have brought this news, madam."

"No, I would prefer to have this come from a friend than to hear gossip in the streets." Mrs. Gardiner sighed. "Darcy will return soon, but we have anticipated this news. His family has taken measures to counteract its impact."

"Is there anything that I can do?"

"Perhaps Mr. Bingley, if you share friends with Mr. Darcy, you might speak of your sure knowledge of his pending marriage to my sister." Jane offered.

"Why yes, I can easily do that! I will stop at the club on my way home! After all it was Darcy's word that rescued me; I can do the same for him! Excellent Miss Bennet!" He smiled warmly to her and she was able to return it. "I saw Harwick yesterday with his sister. He looked serious as ever. You will have to show him that smile to cheer him."

"I . . .I will not likely have that opportunity, sir."

"Mr. Harwick ended his courtship, Mr. Bingley." Mrs. Gardiner said quietly.

"Oh." Bingley's eyes grew wide. "I am so very sorry, Miss Bennet."

"You could not have known, sir." Jane stood and curtseyed. "Excuse me, I will go and check on my sister."

Bingley watched her go and turned his mortified face to Mrs. Gardiner. "I am so sorry madam, I had no idea. Perhaps I can come and call . . ."

"To what purpose, Mr. Bingley? Neither of you are ready to wed. If this was two years in the future I would gladly say yes, but she needs to recover from this and understand why it happened. You simply need to learn your new role." She smiled and he looked at his hands. "You are doing what so many of my friends wish for their children."

"Do you wish it for yours?" He asked. "I am unsure if I would have been better off simply learning my father's trade."

"No sir, I think that you are suited to be a gentleman, but my children will grow up in a different world. Tradesmen will become more accepted as time goes on. Times are changing and you know as well as I do that if a wealthy gentleman will not turn up his nose at the dowry from a tradesman's daughter to save his estate, it will not be long before the tradesman's sons are winning the gentleman's daughters."

"So I was born too soon." Bingley smiled.

"I would say too late." She laughed to see his head cock to the side. "Well, your father was bound and determined to have a gentleman son; your course was set by your grandfather. If you had followed your father, your son might have been raised as mine, to appreciate the possibilities of trade as his living."

"Well, I suppose that I will make the best of it, then." Bingley stood. "In the meantime, I will take advantage of my current standing and go spread the word that my friend Darcy is very much the bachelor and that position will be soon changed by Miss Elizabeth and no other."

Mrs. Gardiner stood and walked him to the door. "Thank you very much for coming here Mr. Bingley; and you are welcome to visit our family at any time." He glanced up the stairs then back to Mrs. Gardiner. "I will. Thank you."

She closed the door after him thoughtfully, then joined her family to see what needed to be done for her other niece. She found Elizabeth in her uncle's arms and sobbing. He looked up helplessly. Mrs. Gardiner came in and they gradually exchanged positions. "Why are you crying, Lizzy? You know that it is not true."

"I wish he were here."

"I know, your friends and future relatives can speak all they wish and show you off around town every hour of the day, but the truth of the matter is that Mr. Darcy is not here, and as long as he is missing, the talk will continue. These people need to see him, with you on his arm. I suspect that the small wedding you wished for will have to be changed."

"What do you mean?" Elizabeth sniffed. "Why can we not be married as we wish in the parlour at Darcy House?"

"I think that you may need to marry at the very least in a church, and I suspect it will have to be Darcy's, and with a general invitation to his society."

"But . . . Aunt, that would mean . . . Mama and Papa and . . ."

"Our sisters presented to society." Jane gasped.

"This is a problem." Mr. Gardiner said quietly.

"Can nothing go well?" Elizabeth moaned and dropped her head in her hands. "Come home Fitzwilliam!"

12 JUNE 1809
Gracechurch Street
London

My dearest Fitzwilliam,
I have so many things to tell you, but the most important is that I miss you, my love. I think that if your lap could bear the weight, I would happily spend my days firmly in your embrace, and receiving your kisses. Oh what a terrible thing you have done, sir! How can you leave me after such a wonderful experience! I can hardly concentrate on any task, every free moment I have sends me instantly back to the memory of your arms. I believe that your aunt was growing quite exasperated with me while we worked in your study. There I was in your desk chair, yes my love; I claimed it for my own and felt surrounded by you, and looking up at the beautiful landscape of Pemberley. Oh, I hope that it is as it ever was. I imagined you approaching and your apprehension, and I dearly wished that I was there holding your hand. Whatever the circumstances, if it is intact or ruined, I do not care, only that you are well. A house can be rebuilt, and we will make new memories to fill the halls.
While looking at the landscape, and yes, I finally had the opportunity to examine it and the study closely since a certain persistent man was not nibbling upon me, I determined that the very first place you must take me when we go riding is to the very spot where the artist sat. I imagine it is not an easy place to find, and since my riding skills are somewhat questionable, I believe that I must make the journey by sharing your mount? Do you think that you would mind that so very much, riding with me sitting behind you, and holding your waist? Or would you prefer that I sit in front? It would make it easier for me to distract you with a kiss or two. Oh listen to me, you must think me wanton, but it is entirely your fault!
Your Aunt Catherine has been a bit bothersome, but your uncle will tell you all about it. I will not waste ink and paper on her nonsense. Just know that I am well. I am sorry to tell you that Jane and Mr. Harwick have ended their courtship. I know that you have found a friend in him, and please know that I hold nothing against him and his decision, and will not behave poorly should he visit our homes. Jane is circumspect. She expected this to happen and when it did, she blamed herself more so than our family or upbringing. She says that if I could overcome the effect of Longbourn then she should have as well. I do not know if I should agree or not, but I am glad to see the return of my sweet Jane. She said that she will behave as I did when I faced my rejection. I am simply grateful that I was rejected by Mr. Stewart, because it left me free for you, my love. Perhaps she will be so grateful someday when some man finds her.
Jane will remain in London to avoid Mama, but I was considering travelling to Longbourn to take care of my belongings before our wedding, and perhaps to distract Mama from Jane by showing me off to her friends. Uncle would send a maid

with me as a companion, but when I voiced my thoughts to Aunt Helen, she quite clearly stated that I was out of my mind and that you would not stand for such an idea. I believe that she fumed for a full hour on the subject, even the offer from Alicia to accompany me in her own coach was denied. It seems that I will never collect my things, but with all of the shopping we have done of late, it is difficult to imagine what I could possibly use from Longbourn anyway. Perhaps we can stop briefly on our way home to Pemberley for our honeymoon.

Oh dearest, I am anticipating that trip so much! I have a very vivid imagination, and between my aunt's instruction and your demonstrations, I must admit that I am all curiosity to begin. Must we wait so long to wed? Can we not simply go directly to the church the moment you return? I have so many more places that I wish to touch now. Your neck is only one spot that I must taste. Oh dear, I hope that this letter does not fall into some stranger's hands, what would they think of me? Well, as long as you think well of me, I will be happy for all of my days. I love you my Fitzwilliam, come to me as soon as you are able.

Yours always,
Elizabeth

Darcy's face was lit by an enormous smile. "Elizabeth, dearest, do you have any idea what you are saying to me? What you are doing to me? You are extraordinary! Women do not speak of these things, certainly not wives!" His imagination was firing with so many images, Elizabeth in his chair, in his lap, bouncing against his ready body as they rode, touching him, kissing him, opening herself to him . . . "Ohhhhh." He moaned as his body responded to the vision of Elizabeth sprawled before him. "Calm Darcy, calm yourself," he said repeatedly. "You must be gentle, no matter how willing she is, be gentle." A thought of them making love in the hills overlooking Pemberley immediately appeared and he groaned. "Perhaps Mrs. Bennet's example was not all bad . . ."

A quarter-hour passed and he was relaxed in the lassitude of his relief. Sleepily he drew out the small box he kept in his waistcoat and removed the long curl of Elizabeth's hair, wrapped it around his finger then kissed it before tenderly returning it to its place. He picked up her letter to drink in her words again, but this time he focussed on her carefully hidden message. Aunt Catherine, return to Longbourn, marry soon, come back. *What had happened?*

He looked back to his desk and found the thick packet that arrived by the same messenger who had brought his and Layton's letters. Naturally he had immediately opened Elizabeth's but now he turned to the letter from his uncle.

12 June 1809
Matlock House

Dear Darcy,

I hardly know how to tell you what has occurred in your absence. So I will take the coward's route and let the enclosed letters tell you the tale. Read them in order. I have another note for you at the end.

Matlock

Darcy knit his brow and setting aside his uncle's cryptic note, turned to the numbered opened letters. He picked up the first, *Collins?* And began to read. He was on his feet instantly and swore loud enough to attract Layton's attention from the library. He came running in time to open the study door and see Darcy throw down Lady Catherine's letter before reaching for the one from Mrs. Jenkinson. Noticing his father's handwriting, Layton began reading the letters as well. Darcy finally came to the second letter from his uncle which described Rosings, Elizabeth's shopping with the ladies, and finally the suspicions that gossip will soon be spreading.

"Elizabeth." He whispered. "My love, what are you feeling?" Darcy fell back into his chair, barely acknowledging Layton's expletives as the vision of Elizabeth reading these letters and the pain she must have felt filled his mind. "And you wrote me a love letter." He murmured.

"Darcy." Layton said again. "DARCY!"

"Forgive me." He sat up and noticed that Layton held a letter in his hands. "I did not see that letter, did I?"

"No, this is mine, from Alicia. I suppose in your haste you forgot to send my post to me?" He said with a slight smile. He had picked up Elizabeth's letter and immediately dropped it when he saw the contents. "She says that Elizabeth is well."

"How can she be well? She had this fool parson telling her I was married! A parson!" He stood and paced. "I should be there." Holding up the singed letter from Lady Catherine he shook it at Layton. "I should have opened this instead of ignoring it. I should have gone to Rosings and . . ."

"And what, Darcy? You appearing at Rosings would have cemented this fabrication in the minds of every person who saw you, not to mention Anne. The servants, this idiot Collins, and especially Aunt Catherine, she would have had you two married; you would have done your duty as you saw it, to protect Anne."

"No, I would not have abandoned Elizabeth." He stated positively.

"I do not know, Darcy. You cannot imagine the pressure of being there in person. It is best that the situation was handled without you." He took a seat and crossed his legs, then noticed that his cousin was focussing an intense glare upon him. "I am sorry if I have angered you by questioning your dedication to Elizabeth. You cannot predict how you would have reacted had you been there anymore than you can fully imagine the panic Elizabeth felt when she was faced with these letters without you nearby. However, without a doubt the gossip will be spreading quickly. Alicia writes that they have been taking Elizabeth out very publicly, and making a great show of their acceptance and her preparations for the wedding."

"Yes, Elizabeth referred to it. She did not elaborate." He said softly, picking up her letter to see her barely mention the events. "I am sure that she hates it. No wonder returning to Longbourn seemed as if it were the best solution."

"Alicia referred to that as well." Layton looked at Darcy who was lost in thought. "Mother is correct, for Elizabeth to leave town now would be seen as confirmation that something is amiss between you."

"Where there is smoke there is fire." He murmured. "Speaking of which, there is nothing more that I can do here. I must return to London."

"Are you certain? There is still much to be accomplished." He smiled at the incredulous expression. "I am here to be your sounding board, Cousin. I do not question your desire to return to her."

"As you pointed out, I am not doing the cleaning, my very capable staff will do that, and I have given Mrs. Reynolds the funds to reward them all handsomely when they are finished. The new roof over the kitchen will be up within a few more days, and that builder Singleton found for us has promised a completely outfitted and modern efficient kitchen to be in place within the month. My presence here might spur the work on, but otherwise, my place is with Elizabeth. Her letter begged me to return, and now I truly understand why." He looked up to see his cousin nodding. "You agree?"

"Yes. When shall we go? Unless you would like me to remain?"

"I appreciate your offer, but as you are at last mending your marriage, I would not wish for my troubles to stand in the way. Return with me. I trust my people." He reached for a sheet and his pen. "I will send an express today stating our intentions, and we will leave in the morning."

"I will notify my valet." Layton rose and watched as Darcy's mask fell into place, and he concentrated on the note. "Darcy, she is well."

"I will believe that only when I see her." He said shortly without looking up, and heard the door latch shut when his cousin departed. Sighing, he sealed the note to his uncle, wrote another letter to Elizabeth, and summoned a footman to engage an express rider immediately. He picked up all of the scattered letters, read them through again, and folded them to place in his desk. Elizabeth's he kept out and reaching behind him, found his old journal. It fell open to that one special page. "Lizzy, Longbourn, Gracechurch Street, Gardiner." He repeated the mantra. Rising to his feet he opened the hidden safe and found the velvet bag that he remembered from the day months ago when he entertained Georgiana by examining the family jewels. At the time he noted this particular piece, and how he wondered it would look upon Elizabeth. He dared not imagine it would ever truly be hers, but now . . . "Elizabeth, Park Lane, Pemberley, Darcy." Clutching it in his hand he closed his eyes. "I will be with you soon, my love."

"COLONEL FITZWILLIAM." The footman announced.

Evangeline stood and smiled, "Please come in sir, and take a seat."

Fitzwilliam advanced, feeling unusually nervous and carefully arranging his sword, accepted the chair. He smiled a little, and seeing her waiting expectantly finally burst out with some nonsense. "This is a very fine room."

"Yes, it is." Taking pity on him she laughed. "Colonel are you this nervous on the battlefield?"

He relaxed and shook his head. "No Mrs. Carter, I am not. In fact I cannot remember feeling this nervous since I received my last reprimand from my father."

"And when was that?"

"Last Tuesday, as I recall." He smiled and she smiled in return. "Forgive me; I am very unaccustomed to this whole courtship ritual."

"Is that what it is?" She tilted her head.

"Mrs. Carter, I have espoused for some time that I truly dislike the dance that men and women must play, talking about the weather instead of getting down to the gist of the matter. Too much question hanging in the air when a simple statement can clear up so much hesitancy and confusion."

"Such as what my brother experienced with Miss Bennet."

"Precisely." Fitzwilliam happily seized the example. "Undoubtedly being a man married, he knows exactly what he wants and needs, but Miss Bennet being a maiden can only play by the rules laid down in the etiquette manuals."

"Or her mother."

"I think that Miss Bennet's manners are most certainly not inspired by her mother's teachings, Mrs. Carter."

"Well, I cannot argue entirely with that. So sir, what does all of this have to do with . . ."

"Us."

"Us, sir?"

"Mrs. Carter, you were married, please do not leave me dangling here. Please acknowledge that you know of what I am speaking!"

"Very well sir, I do. And I also know that no woman in her right mind would wish to remarry having at last achieved financial independence with the death of her husband. She would be seen as quite wanton, would she not? Why would she give up her control to another man, especially after experiencing such a marriage as I have?"

Deflated, Fitzwilliam looked at his hands. "Because she did experience that terrible marriage and the man who is interested now is not the one she knew before. And he has had his share of terrible experiences and hopes that maybe he could try to live a quiet life and make some lady happy for the rest of hers." His confession was met by silence and he looked up to see Evangeline with a handkerchief pressed to her mouth. Not knowing what to do he bent towards her. "Mrs. Carter, forgive me for speaking so plainly, I know that it is wrong of me. I just wished to make my intentions clear from the outset. I . . . I have always known that for me to marry at all, it would have to be to a woman of some means. I have never accepted support from my father, except for taking advantage of his hospitality, and I know that it pains my parents terribly to worry for my future. However, my injuries in the last battle were grave and I have for the most part recovered, but I will never return to war again."

"I am happy to hear that, sir." Evangeline said softly. "We have known each other but hours."

"I am not proposing, Mrs. Carter . . . I am . . . well yes, I am proposing." He drew himself up and looked her square in the eye. "I am proposing that we begin a courtship and . . . now that you know my thoughts and . . . motivation, you might consider them as we grow to know each other and weigh them against your own. I . . . I believe that we might have a very comfortable friendship and perhaps . . . it might be more." He smiled and raised his brows. "What do you think?"

Evangeline smiled at this hopeful bear of a man. "I think that I would like very much to be your friend, colonel. But I am in no hurry to marry; I will have to think long and hard about taking such a step again. I must decide if my wish is to remain a doting aunt or if I wish to take the risk of motherhood."

"Of course, your sister's death is on your mind." Fitzwilliam said softly. "Forgive me for thinking only of life as a couple. Marriage carries many more burdens for a woman than a man."

She studied his downcast eyes. "I read that Mr. Darcy married your cousin."

He stood and stalked to the window. "No, Mrs. Carter, he is not. She is ill and believes that to be so, the tongues of the uninformed have spread that rumour and our family is taking steps to counteract it. One solution was offered to me. I was given the opportunity to marry her to gain her estate, and I refused."

"And why is that?" She watched his shoulders bend.

"I would never feel comfortable there. The marriage may have been legitimate from the standpoint of law and church, but to me . . .it would have been a false ceremony, done for gain and without feeling. My cousin never would have known, she is not cognizant of her environment, but I would have known, and that matters to me."

Evangeline closed her eyes. This man was the absolute opposite of the one she had married, and somewhere in her heart, she felt some of her protective armour fall away. "So, what do we need to do next, Colonel? If we are to be friends . . . or more?"

Richard turned to see her smile, it was different, softer and perhaps a little shy. "I am not sure." He laughed. "Does a widow need a chaperone?"

She laughed with him. "I do not know. I will have to consult an etiquette book!"

SINGLETON KICKED HIS HORSE and picked up the pace a little. "Come on Audrey, keep up."

"This is not a race, Robert."

"That would be difficult with this crowd." He smiled and looked over to see her smile briefly then gaze ahead along the riding path through Hyde Park. Trying again, he chose another safe subject. "Is that a new riding habit? It is very becoming."

"It is the same habit I had last Season, you have just not ridden with me for a long time."

"I am trying Audrey." He said quietly.

She relented from her caution. "I know, I am sorry. Thank you."

"Singleton! Where have you been? We have not seen you at the table in weeks; I want a chance to win my purse back!" Singleton closed his eyes then turned to the man.

"I have been occupied with more pressing matters, and I think that my days at the tables are over."

Glancing at his companion the man laughed loudly. "What, are you afraid that your wife will hear? Come on, you are not changing your ways for her, are you? Be a man!"

"That is precisely what I plan to be." Singleton kicked his horse again and moved ahead, then regaining control of his anger he looked back to where Audrey was following him. "Audrey, I . . ."

"Thank you."

"I do not wish to end as Carter did, dead on a field of honour for no honourable reason." He spoke looking straight ahead. "Your brothers have made it clear that they will hound me forever if I misstep again, and perhaps that is a good thing, to be afraid."

"If that is what is required for you to change, then I am grateful for it. I can only hope that it lasts."

"You are a beautiful girl Audrey, when I see you around nearly anyone else you are joyful and so happy, but when you are near me, you become silent, your resentment is difficult to bear."

"I am trying as well." She blinked back the threatening tears. "I am afraid to give you more should you revert back, that you might drive me away."

"Into the arms of another?" He asked in a strained voice.

"I hope not." She stared ahead the same way he was.

"If your brother can change, so can I. I am not foolish enough to demand that you trust me. I know that it must be earned." He reined in his horse and at last looked her in the eye. "All I ask is that you tell me if I disappoint you, no matter the reason."

"You would care for my opinion?"

"I would."

"Singleton!" He glanced up to see another old gambling partner.

"Shall we return home?" He smiled shyly.

Audrey nodded and smiled in return. "That sounds wonderful to me."

"Singleton!"

"You are popular." She observed.

"Losers always are."

15 JUNE 1809
Pemberley

Dearest Elizabeth,

I received the gift of your letter and the horror of my Uncle's. I will leave at daybreak. All is in hand here, my place is with you. I should arrive the afternoon the day after you receive this. Stay where you are my love, I will have you in my arms very soon.

Yours always,
Fitzwilliam

"Thank you." Elizabeth whispered.

15 June 1809
Pemberley

Dear Uncle,

What the devil has happened? Is it possible that my cousin's addled mind is not a product of her illness but something from her mother? She allowed this delusion to continue? What did she think I would do, fly down to Rosings to marry Anne? I am unconcerned about the reasons; the unmitigated gall of the woman astounds me! I regret that I was not with you to confront her! I know my Elizabeth, she is a strong woman but she is also so afraid of something happening to end our engagement. I will never forgive my aunt for this. At least she is gone from Rosings. I heartily suggest that you speak to our lost cousin de Bourgh and recommend that Collins be sent on his way post-haste, and if Mrs. Jenkinson requires a new position, I will be glad to find her one. I am incensed, Uncle! We leave at daybreak. I know what I must do.

Sincerely,
Darcy

"What does that mean; he knows what he must do? He said that before when he nearly began to court Miss Gannon. I hope that he will not do anything rash." Lady Matlock asked when she took the letter from her husband's grasp.

"I believe that it means the master of Pemberley is not going to play by anyone's rules but his own." He shook his head and smiled. "We have done all that we can now, Helen. It is in his hands."

Chapter 26

"Come inside Darcy, Father will want to speak to you."

"I am going to Elizabeth." Darcy said stubbornly. "I will speak to your father tomorrow."

"It is very possible that she may be inside." Layton stood by the carriage door and watched his cousin struggle with a decision, then heard him swear as he climbed out. "I knew that would work."

"If she is not here, I will be gone in fifteen minutes." Darcy growled then looked up to his driver. "Wait here, I will send out word if I am to stay." The man nodded and watched the cousins enter Matlock House.

"Son!" Lord Matlock stood from behind his desk and embraced Layton. "Darcy! You made excellent time; I did not expect to see you until late this afternoon. You must have driven your horses to the limit."

"I did Uncle, and they will be well-rested before they go out again. Is Elizabeth here?"

"No, she is with the Gardiners, I suppose." He saw Darcy turn to leave. "Where are you going?"

"To my Elizabeth."

"We have much to discuss, please stay, take some refreshment . . ." Lord Matlock's eyes widened to receive a cold hard glare. "Now that is an interesting talent, Son."

"I will see you tomorrow." He began to walk and stopped. "Thank you for all you have done in my absence." In a moment he was gone.

"Harrowing trip home?" Lord Matlock asked Layton.

He sank into a chair and sighed. "Ruthless. He was determined to get to her side. How has it been?"

Lord Matlock resumed his seat and folded his hands. "What you would expect. The gossip is so ripe. Darcy is hardly a renowned public figure, but the idea of an extremely rich young man engaged to a girl with nothing then jilting her for his cousin is just too enticing to die off quickly. We could parade Elizabeth around for weeks and talk until we were blue in the face, but with him absent, the talk was free to grow. Do you know his plans? We discussed a large wedding breakfast to be held here."

"Oh he would love that." Layton said sarcastically.

"Well inviting the world to the church is vulgar, as your mother has proclaimed."

Layton laughed. "Well, he has not divulged his plans. I could barely get a word out of him the entire way back. He just stared out of the window and twisted that ring he has." He stood up and walked to the study door. "Let him see her and be reassured that she is well. There is time to fix this. Any news from Rosings?"

"Anne's fever broke, but the damage is done, I think. She is very weak." Lord Matlock pushed back from his desk and crossed his arms. "Catherine refuses to leave Rosings, claiming that her daughter needs her."

"Darcy wants to throttle her."

"He is not alone in that, your mother and I are furious with her, but we decided to stay by Elizabeth instead of haring down to Kent. Once the rumour left Rosings the place to deal with it was here. We will see what Darcy wishes to do but I will handle Catherine, this is my duty, not Darcy's." Noting his son's expression he smiled slightly. "Yes, I am aware that Darcy will feel that it is his, but I doubt that he would want to be separated from Elizabeth again once he sees her. I have formulated a plan. Captain de Bourgh will be in London tomorrow and will be staying here; fortunately his ship was in Portsmouth. I will escort him to Rosings; I would like you to join us."

"As unappealing as that sounds, I will gladly represent my cousin there."

"How does Pemberley fare?"

"It will be fine. His staff loves that house as much as he does. I paid attention to how he treated them, it was an education."

"I look forward to hearing all about it." Lord Matlock seemed ready to listen then and there and his son smiled.

"Later, I need to change and wash, and greet my wife. Is she home?"

"She is. Stephen." Layton turned in surprise to hear his name. "Alicia seems happier. Keep up the good work."

"I will, sir."

DARCY STEPPED OUT of the carriage in front of his townhouse, and ordered that a horse be saddled and ready in a half hour. He realized after leaving his uncle that his horses and coachmen would not appreciate the hours of waiting that would come with his visit to Gracechurch Street, and also decided that Elizabeth would prefer him in a fresh shirt.

He had barely approached the door when he heard quick steps and felt his shoulder pulled back. "YOU BASTARD!"

Darcy's hand flew up just in time to catch Stewart's fist before it landed on his face. "What the devil are you doing?" He bellowed.

The two tall men struggled until Darcy broke free long enough to strike Stewart's stomach. He doubled over and the footmen who were unloading the carriage arrived to lend whatever support was needed. Stewart stood bent and gasping. "How could you?" He panted. "How could you abandon her like this?"

"Abandon? Who?"

"Elizabeth!" Stewart straightened and ran for Darcy. Grabbing him, the footmen held him steady. "I supported you! I helped you! I stepped away when it could have been so easy to come between you. And now you marry your cousin and leave her to the derision of society! Damn you, Darcy!" He spat. "I never should have walked away."

"I am NOT married to my cousin!" Darcy roared. "I am engaged to Elizabeth Bennet and I am going to marry her. At what point did the ravings of the gossip columns become the truth?" He saw Stewart's confusion then watched his eyes narrow with suspicion.

"Where have you been?"

"Pemberley, there was a fire." Darcy said tiredly. "If I had been here, do you really think that I would have remained passive? I did not know this until three days ago when I received my uncle's letter."

"You left immediately." Stewart deflated, and Darcy nodded to his footmen to release him.

"Yes. How did you come to be here?"

"I saw you at Matlock House, I walked over here." He rubbed at his sore stomach and watched Darcy considering him; at last he spoke, "It was an impulse."

"Come inside so the entire neighbourhood does not listen in." Darcy entered the house, nodding to his anxious staff, and they stepped into the study. He looked at his desk chair and had a sudden vision of Elizabeth settled there and turned to his companion. "I am engaged to Elizabeth, nothing will change that except our wedding."

"I am sorry, Darcy. I should have known better. I . . .care about her."

That knowledge struck Darcy cold, and he asked tightly, "What exactly does that mean, Stewart?" He stepped closer to him and Stewart stepped back, finding himself against the wall. Darcy's eyes were dark with anger and he stared him down, inches from his face. "Explain that statement."

"I care for her as a friend." He said with all of the dignity he could muster. "I feel protective of her."

"Do you fancy that you love her?" Darcy growled. "You declared outside that you stepped away when it would have been so easy to claim her from me. Is that what you wished for when you heard this fabrication of my marriage? Did you rejoice in the idea of Elizabeth suffering my rejection and then turning to you? *You* rejected *her*, sir!"

"And you swept in to claim her!" Stewart said heatedly, pushing Darcy away.

"I already had her." He snarled. "You never had a chance."

"Then where were *you*?"

"I did not know where to find her."

"You knew. You chose not to look." Stewart spat at him. "Do not tell me that all of the resources of Pemberley could not have been employed to scour

Hertfordshire for her. You had enough information, it could have been accomplished. But you did not. Why?"

Darcy turned away and closed his eyes. "Because I was an arrogant fool. Why did you not pursue her after December? You thought you loved her, you knew where she was. What is your excuse?"

"I was a coward." Stewart sighed. "I did not even have pride to blame. No that is wrong. I did not love her, there was no time to fall in love with her, it was over too soon. But I do care for her, as a friend. I care for her well-being. I care that she not be hurt."

Darcy listened and then turned to face his old friend. "If I had married Anne, what would you have done?"

"I would have . . ." He stopped. "It does not matter." Stewart sighed. "Forgive me, Darcy."

He took a few moments to consider his response, dealing with the pain of Elizabeth perhaps accepting the man before him, then let his anger die. "No, there is nothing to forgive, I should be grateful that there is someone who would wish to defend her." Darcy poured them each some port and brought Stewart a glass. "How do you feel?"

"Your fist has not lost its power as you age." Stewart rubbed the spot again and accepted his glass.

"You make me feel ancient; the pugilist classes were not that long ago." Darcy smiled slightly and became serious again. "Your behaviour is exceptionally strong for a man who claims only care for a woman, not love."

"I think what it is . . .I believe that it could be compared to a brotherly care. I suppose that reading that notice and hearing the talk around town raised my protective instincts. Bingley has been going around refuting the claim but his voice is so weak nobody will listen to him. Lord Matlock has been more effective, but again, he is alone. Nobody listens to Singleton; his reputation is not the best." He shook his head and sighed. "Laura told me that she saw Elizabeth out with Lady Matlock and Mrs. Singleton, shopping for wedding clothes. She tried to calm me, but I suppose that I did not listen to sense, I did not know of Pemberley. Could you understand that desire to protect Miss Darcy in such circumstances?"

Darcy studied him for several moments, thinking over his responsibility to always protect Georgiana, remembered Richard and Stephen's care for Audrey, then finally nodded. "Very well, that is a protective instinct that I can accept, however, your services as surrogate brother are no longer needed. I am her caretaker, no other." Stewart bowed his head and Darcy let the tension recede. "I need to change and go to her. If that is acceptable to you?" Darcy raised his brow.

"Of course." Stewart finished his drink and held out his hand. "I apologize."

Darcy took it and nodded. "I am just glad that I did not find you in her parlour on your knee."

"It crossed my mind." Stewart smiled to see him bristle. "Relax Darcy; it was a joke, besides you brought it up. What is this about a fire?"

Waiting a moment to see how sincere Stewart was, he let down again. "The kitchens are destroyed, but the house is fine. Smoke damage, but that is all."

"Just what you needed."

"Yes, now . . .I do not mean to be rude, but . . ."

"I understand, and I will add my voice to your defence."

"You need to find yourself a girl."

"And stop worrying about ones that are already taken?" He said quietly. "It seems to be a habit of mine."

"I noticed." Darcy said just as quietly. "Singleton is attempting to change his ways." Stewart looked at him in surprise. "The theatre."

"Ah. I was as surprised as you, I had no idea." He straightened his shoulders. "Well, I understand that Harwick abandoned Miss Bennet."

"Did you pay him a call, as well?" Darcy smiled as they walked to the door.

"No, actually I did not." Stewart laughed. "I am behind in my outraged visits. Good luck, Darcy." He held out his hand and they shook. "If you need anything . . ."

"Thank you." Darcy saw the door close and wearily walked up the stairs to change his clothes. Soon he was back outside and on his mount, and at last arrived at the Gardiner's door. Tossing a coin to a boy, he saw that his horse was tied off and watched, then climbed the steps. The door was opened before he could drop the knocker twice.

"Mr. Darcy, please come in." The maid curtseyed.

He began to remove his gloves when she took his hat. "Where may I find Miss Elizabeth?"

"She is not home, sir." Darcy's movement stopped and the maid continued. "She has not been herself, and Mrs. Gardiner insisted that they go out. You were not expected for some hours, sir."

Darcy spoke very slowly. "And where did they go?"

"I believe they went to Madame Dupree's shop, sir." Darcy took his hat back from the maid. "If they return without me, please inform Miss Elizabeth that I will be here at five o'clock sharp."

"Yes sir!" She watched him storm down the steps and leap upon his horse. Mr. Gardiner appeared by the open front door.

"Was that Mr. Darcy's voice I heard?"

"Yes sir, he was not pleased to find Miss Elizabeth out."

Mr. Gardiner smiled. "No, I imagine that he was not." He dismissed the girl and went back to his study, and decided to finish his letter to Mr. Bennet after Darcy returned from his wild ride.

An hour later, Darcy stopped his horse before the shop of Madame Dupree. A young man employed by the lady took his horse and was tipped to hold it for him. Before he entered he glanced in the front window and saw a simple sign laid carefully against a display of several very fine gowns. *Wedding clothes designed for Miss Elizabeth Bennet, intended of Mr. Fitzwilliam Darcy.* He stood still and smiled, imagining her in each one. "Is this not evidence enough that we are engaged?"

Entering the shop, his tall form immediately attracted the attention of every woman there. Not seeing his object, he looked inquiringly at the young woman who appeared at his side. "Oui, Monsieur?"

"Is Miss Elizabeth Bennet here?"

"Ah non; she left but moments ago, Monsieur. I believe that I heard them speak of tea and books." She curtseyed and he nodded, containing his disappointment.

He stepped outside and looked around, on one side of the street there was a tea room, on the other, a book shop. Hesitating before making a decision, he looked to the boy with his horse. "Did you see three women leave this shop recently, one young with dark hair, another young and blonde, and an older woman?"

"Aye sir! They went to the tea shop!" He said eagerly and Darcy nodded, tossing him another coin. "I will be back."

Striding purposely forward, he was aware of the glances and fingers pointing in his direction, but ignored them, feeling the end of his search had arrived. Opening the door to the little shop he scanned the room and groaned. "Sir?" The proprietor bustled forward.

"Three ladies, were they here?"

"Yes sir, but the youngest was not happy to stay. Kept pulling at this locket she was wearing, and the older one said they should move around a bit. Paid their bill and crossed the street, sir."

"Thank you." Darcy pressed a coin in his hand and left, crossing the busy street and at last entering the bookshop. Scanning the interior he relaxed, seeing Mrs. Gardiner and Jane in one corner examining picture books for the children. Elizabeth was nowhere to be seen. Mrs. Gardiner saw him and he put his finger to his lips and raised his brow. She smiled and mouthed "poetry" to him and he nodded, following the direction she indicated. He slowly walked around the shelves until he heard a soft sigh, then peeked around the corner to see Elizabeth with her back turned. He crept up quietly and saw what she held in her hand. Smiling, he bit his lip, then reaching into his coat pocket; drew out his copy of Shakespeare's sonnets and laid it on top of the open volume in her hands. "I already have one, my love. Remember?"

Elizabeth gasped and spun around. "Fitzwilliam!" Both books landed on the floor with a thud and she was in his arms and receiving his kiss in a heartbeat. Darcy held her tight against him and kissed her hard, with all of the passion that had kept so carefully in check. He broke away to gasp for breath, pushed her bonnet back from her head, then proceeded to cover her face with more kisses. He held her cheeks with his hands and moved around her skin so rapidly that Elizabeth was soon reduced to helpless laughter. "Dearest, stop, I am being eaten alive!"

Darcy withdrew and smiled at her. "Now that is an occupation I would gladly pursue." He looked at her sparkling eyes and at last felt that he was home. "I missed you desperately, my love." Tenderly he kissed her lips. "Your letter made me so happy, but after I read my uncle's letter, I understood what you tried not to say in yours, and I am overwhelmed by your generosity to write me in love instead of anger. I ache for your suffering. I am so sorry dearest. I am so sorry." Darcy held her to his chest and rested his cheek in her hair, then lifted her head to again cradle her face in his hands. "Are you well?"

"Now I am." She reached up to caress his cheek, and he kissed her gently. "I need more of those." He smiled and cuddled her against him.

"I will be happy to oblige, my love."

"Perhaps we should save this reunion for a place with more privacy?" Mrs. Gardiner suggested when she appeared around the corner. The couple separated with a start but their hands were immediately clasped.

"Mrs. Gardiner, in any other circumstances I might agree, but as much as it goes against my nature to expose my personal life to the world, in this instance I believe that exposure is exactly what is necessary." He smiled down to Elizabeth. "Although, my search for you up and down Bond Street will doubtless have tongues wagging already."

"How did you find me?" She smiled and watched as he bent to retrieve his precious book and place it back in his coat, then kept the one she had been reading in his hand.

"I just followed the clues." He leaned to kiss her again. "And here is my reward. Have you finished your shopping? May I return you to your aunt's home? I would like to discuss something important with you."

"Oh yes, I imagine there are any number of subjects that could be labelled important to us right now."

"Mmm, this is the most important of all."

"How is Pemberley?" She asked as they began to walk together.

"It is as I said, the repairs should be completed within a month, but we will need to shop for some new draperies and rugs." He laughed at her wrinkled nose. "I thought that you would enjoy the exercise."

"Only if you come with me, I have spent entirely too much time shopping with ladies."

"I would not consider any other arrangement." He walked to the desk and paid for the volume, and when it was wrapped he handed it to her. "Now we can read together."

Elizabeth hugged the package, but pursed her lips. "I was hoping you would read to me."

"I would love that dearest, and I would love to hear you return the favour." He raised her hand to his lips. "*Her voice was ever soft, gentle and low, an excellent thing in a woman.*[4]"

"That is Shakespeare!"

"So it is, love."

"Hmm, your voice is far sweeter than mine." She leaned into his shoulder as he wrapped her hand around his arm. Darcy kissed her cheek when she smiled up at him.

"I missed you so much, Elizabeth."

"*My true love hath my heart, and I have his.*[5]" She whispered and he sighed. "I see us playing games of quotations on dreary winter days."

"I will have to begin reading now to prepare for them." He tilted his head, "Sidney?"

"Well done."

Mrs. Gardiner noticed Jane watching the couple closely and moved forward. "Fix your bonnet, Lizzy."

She smiled ruefully and adjusted the hat, and retied the ribbons. Darcy observed in happy admiration. "I have many more fashionable hats coming, but they are apparently on display at Madame Dupree's."

"I saw." He reclaimed her arm. "It made me so proud to see our names linked in such a wonderful way."

"It makes me wonder why people would believe this gossip."

"I thought the same." He became serious again. "Come let us return you home, and we will discuss my plan."

"You have a plan?"

"I do, my love. And I hope very much that you like it."

"MAY I SPEAK WITH YOU, SIR?" Darcy said to Mr. Gardiner after he escorted Elizabeth inside of the house.

"Certainly." He led the way back to his study. Darcy closed the door and they took their seats. "How are you, sir?"

"Very tired." Darcy admitted, then straightening, leaned forward. "Sir, when I left here to search for Elizabeth, I took a detour on the way to Bond Street."

"Yes?"

"I stopped at my parish, St. Georges, and spoke to Reverend Hodgson. He said that he is free to marry us any morning at ten. That is exactly what I wish to do. I wish to marry Elizabeth tomorrow."

---

[4] Sir Philip Sidney, Arcadia, 1590
[5] William Shakespeare, King Lear, at V, iii, 1606

"Tomorrow?" He sat up and stared. "Sir, is that not . . ."

"The best solution to this mess?" Darcy gripped the arms of his chair. "I will be married, yes, to the proper woman. The announcement would be published, the register signed, the gossip would die instantly. Why suffer through weeks of speculation? Even if Elizabeth appeared with me everywhere I go, there would be those who say I am merely walking with my mistress. The speculation that surfaced at my uncle's ball will be touted as the truth. If we are married, it is over, and we can go on with our lives. Sir, it is the one clear solution. I applied for a special license in anticipation of our marrying at my home. I have it in hand; it was waiting on my desk when I returned today. Marrying in the church is not the private ceremony that I hoped for, but I know that the slightly more public venue may prove beneficial. I am ready for this, and after I speak to Elizabeth, I am sure that she will agree that this is the best course."

"Her parents would miss the ceremony." Mr. Gardiner said and rubbed his chin. "Her father was looking forward to giving her away, and I do not mean that to sound . . ."

"That he is glad to be rid of her, no I did not think so." Darcy sighed. "Then send them an express and my carriage, and we will bring them here for the day."

"And the sisters?"

"I leave that to Elizabeth to decide."

"I see the merit in your plan, sir." He paused and thought out his next words. "Are you certain that you are advancing the wedding date purely for reasons to end this gossip, and not merely because Elizabeth would be your wife three weeks earlier?"

"I hear you, sir." Darcy's voice was earnest. "I love her; this separation of days was more painful than the separation of years because now I know her. She is everything that is dear to me, and I want to show her my love in every possible way. This situation is hurtful to both of us, and I want to end it and comfort her as only a husband can. Do you not feel the same for your wife when she needs you?"

"I do." Mr. Gardiner smiled. "I believe that as Lizzy's father is absent and yours is gone, I am trying to fill the role of both for you."

"I hope that you will continue to do so in the future. I undoubtedly will need your advice." Darcy smiled and stood. "May I speak to Elizabeth now?"

"Stay here, I will send her in." Mr. Gardiner left the room and Darcy paced around, looking at the bookshelves and rehearsing the speech he had practiced for the last three days.

"Fitzwilliam? You wished to see me?" Elizabeth asked from the doorway.

"Yes, please come in." He took her hand and smiled, leading her forward and closing the door. Taking both hands in his he drew breath and was struck dumb by the trust and love he saw shining from her eyes.

"Yes?" She asked softly. "It was a plan?" He nodded. "To end the gossip?"

"Yes."

Elizabeth smiled and reached up to caress his sweet face. "And how shall we do that?"

He leaned his cheek into her hand and wordlessly reached into his pocket, then taking her left hand in his pressed something into her palm. "Wear this for me."

She opened her hand to find a beautiful, finely engraved circle of gold. She covered her mouth and cried, "Oh!"

Darcy picked up the ring and held it carefully. "This was my mother's ring. I dared not dream that you would ever wear it, but I . . .I wish you to begin . . .tomorrow."

"Tomorrow!" She gasped.

"If you wish, or . . . I know that you want your father to give you away, we can send for your family to come and . . . marry the day following, please dearest, I know that you wish for it as I do, you said so in your letter. I want you to be my wife, shutting up the noise of the gossips will be a happy coincidence."

"We would still marry at your home?"

"Ours, and no, we would marry at our church, just to be sure that . . . well, it would be more public." Darcy watched her intently. "Dearest?"

"Yes." She nodded and smiled up at him, tears were rolling down her cheeks. "Yes, yes, yes!"

Darcy picked her up and hugged her, spinning her around and laughing. "Thank you!" Setting her down he kissed her and beaming, caressed the long curls that spilled down her back. "I am . . . I am so happy."

"As am I." She hugged him and laid her face against his chest, while he kissed her hair then rested his cheek on her head. "I would like my father to give me away, Fitzwilliam. I know that you do not like my family . . ."

"Shhhh. If it is your wish, then they will be here." He kissed her forehead. "I am certain that for your wedding day, they will be considerate."

"I will write to Papa and . . ."

"I will, too." Darcy whispered. "And I will tell my uncle." There was a knock at the door and Mr. Gardiner opened it. The couple did not break apart with his entry.

"So?"

"In two days, sir." Darcy said with a smile. "In two days we will wed."

ELIZABETH SAT UP IN HER ROOM ALONE, her shoulders drooped with exhaustion. Darcy's return lifted the burden that bravery had forced her to carry. In a matter of hours, they would be married and at last they could begin. She picked up her pen and began to write.

19 June 1809

Fitzwilliam returned, he looked so tired, but so happy to find me. I cannot begin to describe the relief and happiness I felt to at last be in his arms again. All I wanted to do was to stay there and forget everything that was swirling around us. But of course Aunt made us separate and we returned to Gracechurch Street. I was called back to Uncle's study and learned of Fitzwilliam's plan to have us wed in the morning. As dearly as I wished to agree, I knew that I must at the least ask Papa to come. I do not want Mama here, but I cannot outright ask that she not come. I pray that she and my sisters curb their tongues. All that I want is to be married and at last love my husband, he needs me as much as I need him. I will spend tomorrow packing up my things and send them over to Darcy House. I suppose that Madame Dupree will have to take down the display of my wedding clothes. It is a tradition that I did not understand until coming to London, but I was so proud to see my name with Fitzwilliam's there in her window. The solid truth of our engagement was there for all to see, and in two days, the proof of it will be on my finger when he gives me his mother's ring.

20 JUNE 1809

Returning to London was hardly the reunion I expected. After defending myself from Stewart's outrage and searching the fashionable shops for Elizabeth, I was ready to simply bundle her onto my horse and set off for Gretna Green. But then, I was so tired I probably would have fallen off at some point, and there my dear Elizabeth would be, undoubtedly holding her hand over her mouth to contain her laughter at my ridiculous romantic notions. Well, it is done. I wrote a note to Uncle of our decision to wed tomorrow, and I am sure that he will appear very soon. There is no better solution, as far as I am concerned. I wondered if word of the fire at Pemberley might have helped to change the opinions of gossips, at least that would have been a good reason for me to be away. But the more that I think on it, the more I realize that such information would also have been twisted to suit whatever story held the most satisfaction for these fools.

I have forwarded Elizabeth's letter to her father and mine, as well as Mr. Gardiner's, to Mr. Bennet. I specifically requested that Mrs. Bennet stay at Longbourn. I cannot bear to see Elizabeth cry anything but happy tears on our wedding day, and I do not wish to spend my time hoping that someone is guarding her mother's tongue. I believe that Mr. Bennet will control his remarks, but if his wife is present, he may not be able to help himself. The staff is delighted with the news that their new mistress will arrive tomorrow. And I discovered that the new furnishings were delivered so we will indeed have a master suite to enjoy for our wedding night. Our bed, I will not sleep there tonight, I will await my bride.

I know that I should have returned to Matlock House to speak to Georgiana about Pemberley, but Layton will surely have passed on the news. She knows nothing of Aunt Catherine's machinations, so I hope that she accepts whatever explanation Aunt Helen has given her for our advanced wedding date. Undoubtedly that will give rise to speculation of Elizabeth's sure pregnancy, and if we are blessed with a child born of our honeymoon, I have no doubt that the gossips will be counting back the months as well. At least that is one embarrassment we have managed to avoid.

My Elizabeth continues her remarkable brave front. She admitted to being frightened, but I know that she deeply needs this drama to end. I felt her cling to me, and I dearly wanted to reassure her. Tomorrow, my love, tomorrow it will be over. No more gossip can touch us, and no other person will drive us apart. Let them talk all they wish, we will be together.

Darcy looked up from his journal when Bingley was announced and set down his pen. He rose to greet him and they both took their seats. "You are about early this morning."

"Forgive the hour, Darcy, but I heard you had returned and was anxious for news."

Darcy smiled grimly. "On what subject, there seem to be a plethora from which to choose."

"Well, I know that the tales of your alleged wedding are false . . .are they not?" Bingley asked worriedly.

"They are, and I thank you for your efforts to dispel them."

He smiled and shrugged. "Well I tried. I think that far too many of them found it far too amusing to drop though. Is it true that you were brawling with Stewart on your front step?"

"I knew that would not go without observation." Darcy sighed. "And I suppose that nobody mentioned that I invited him inside?"

"No . . .No, they spoke only of the blood and teeth flying." Bingley laughed to see Darcy's eyes roll. "Yours seem intact and your face is undeniably handsome . . ." Darcy fixed him with his steely glare and Bingley's amusement grew. "So it was vastly inflated, what was it about?"

"My supposed bad behaviour towards a worthy woman."

"What does Stewart have to do with that?" Bingley asked curiously. "I mean the sentiment is admirable . . ."

"He was a neighbour of the Bennets, actually at that estate Miss Bennet mentioned once, Netherfield. You might approach him for an opinion sometime."

"I will, I will." Bingley's brow furrowed as Darcy seemingly skirted the subject. "Well, onto the issue of the worthy woman, what of these rumours, what can you do? They are rampant, I am afraid."

"Which is why I will marry Elizabeth tomorrow. I hope that you will attend? I was just about to send you a note."

"Tomorrow?" Bingley sat forward. "Is another . . . what is it, three weeks, not soon enough?"

"No."

"Oh." He cleared his throat and smiled. "Well then, where and when?"

"St. Georges, at ten."

"I will be there in my Sunday best." Bingley laughed. "Have you a new coat for the occasion? I understand the blue is the colour for grooms." Seeing the raised brows he laughed. "Caroline. Speaking of which, she seems to have caught herself a serious suitor. He visits nearly daily, and they seem to get on well. In fact, he just may have achieved the impossible and finally distracted her from wishes for you."

"I have enough women in my life wishing to be my wife, I am happy to have lost your sister." Darcy said dryly.

"I am not sure though, they were laughing rather cruelly over your marriage to your cousin, but when I mentioned Pemberley's fire; you would have thought that it was her home that burned." Bingley grinned to see Darcy's confusion. "I know, I wonder if her initial reaction was just jealousy that she lost you, but her second was seemingly genuine, after all her suitor . . . that is right! Her suitor knows you! He says that he grew up at Pemberley!"

"He grew up there?" Darcy's confusion grew. "He claims to have lived in the house?"

"No . . .he said that he grew up in his father's house. Hmm."

"Well what is his name?" Darcy demanded. "If he is using mine to forge a connection, I should like to know who . . ."

"Lord and Lady Matlock, sir." Foster announced. Both men rose to their feet.

"Darcy!" Lady Matlock bustled into the room then stopped. "Mr. Bingley, good morning."

"Good morning, madam, sir." He bowed and smiled. "I am sure that you have family matters to discuss. I will see you tomorrow, Darcy, ten o'clock."

"Thank you, Bingley." The three stood and listened until Bingley's steps faded and the front door closed. Lord Matlock closed the study door and his wife sat down and stared at her nephew. "A wedding tomorrow!" Lady Matlock cried.

"Yes Aunt, I wish to put an end to Aunt Catherine's machinations immediately. The only way to do that is to be married to Elizabeth as soon as possible. If she did not wish for her father's presence we would be marrying in two hours instead of six and twenty. I do not see the problem."

"And when was the last time that you planned a wedding breakfast, nephew?" She fumed.

"Why does it have to be anything more than a simple affair for our family and friends? A cake, some punch, what else is needed?"

"Darcy, you are entering dangerous territory. Do not question a woman on the subject of weddings." Lord Matlock laughed then continued. "I think that we should listen to Georgiana's suggestion."

"Georgiana? What did she have to say?"

"She suggested a small breakfast for the family and then hold a larger reception for all of your friends in a few days when there has been time to prepare. I thought it was very sensible." He looked at his wife then winked at Darcy.

Darcy smiled and nodded. "I think that is a brilliant solution. Aunt?"

"It has its merits." She said grudgingly. "Certain guests would not be present. Are the Bennets invited?"

"Elizabeth wishes for her father to give her away." Darcy said quietly. "I will not refuse her desire."

"It would have hurt me forever to have been denied that for Audrey, although, perhaps she has yet to forgive me for allowing the wedding at all." The parents exchanged glances and sighed. "We did not know."

Lady Matlock squeezed his hand. "He is improving."

Darcy studied them. "I am glad to hear that."

A shroud of silence fell over the room until Lady Matlock suddenly broke it. "Do you have a maid for Elizabeth, Darcy?"

He looked at her with a blank expression. "She does not have a lady's maid?"

"Darcy! Of course not! She shared one maid with her sisters, and her aunt's maid has been serving her and Miss Bennet since they came to London. I sent my girl over to help her the night of the ball."

"Oh. I . . . it never occurred to me . . ."

"You are from vastly different worlds." Lord Matlock reminded him.

"I think that is good for me." Darcy smiled and turned to his aunt. "Will you help?"

She sighed. "Well, the sister of my maid has been following her duties as a training exercise . . ."

He leaned forward and fixed his warm eyes on hers. "Thank you, Aunt. What would I do without you?"

"Your life would be in an uproar." She harumphed but pursed her lips to hide her smile. "Now then, we will have a small wedding breakfast here, I will go speak to your housekeeper, then we will hold a dinner for you . . ." she paused. "No. The wedding breakfast will be at Matlock House tomorrow. The Creary Ball will do for your general introduction as a wedded couple. That is in two weeks, you will have your week of honeymooning, here I assume?" She looked at him inquiringly to see his startled nod, "Fine, then you will have a week of callers, then the ball. After that you are free to return to Pemberley and hopefully peace."

Darcy turned to his uncle. "And what of Aunt Catherine? I would be happy to confront her."

Lord Matlock coughed. "I have no doubt of that, Son. Well, it seems that the heir to Rosings will be at your wedding tomorrow, and then the next day I will take him there. Mrs. Jenkinson has kept me abreast of the news. Anne is unchanged, and medicated enough to keep her tongue under control. If anything new comes from that quarter it is solely at the invention of my sister. She is staying in the mansion because Anne is there, and she has been warned to keep her mouth shut."

"You heard of the supposed pregnancy?" Lady Matlock asked delicately.

"Yes." Darcy said quietly. "Nothing happened between us that night. If she is with child, it is not mine."

"I think that is as much a phantom as the marriage is, Darcy." Lord Matlock said grimly.

"Well, tomorrow at least, it will be over."

"SCHOOL?" Lydia cried. "I do not want to go to school!"

"Mr. Bennet, how could you think of such a thing? Taking my precious girl away?" Mrs. Bennet huffed and settled back in her chair. "I will not have it!"

"Mrs. Bennet, I do not care what you will or will not have. Your daughters will be schooled. I have witnessed the detriment that no schooling has been to our two eldest girls, and I will not see the youngest suffer as they did."

"Suffer?" Mrs. Bennet demanded. "My Jane was used very ill by Mr. Harwick! He promised to marry her!"

"Mr Harwick promised to court her, which he did. He hoped that she would be a suitable mother for his children, and decided to continue his search."

"What is wrong with Jane? She is beautiful!"

"She is, but was not his choice."

"Lizzy caught Mr. Darcy!" She cried triumphantly.

"I doubt that either one of them would appreciate the term *caught* being used in conjunction with their engagement."

"Well at last she has done her duty, she failed with Mr. Stewart." Mrs. Bennet picked up her shawl and adjusted it over her shoulders then glared at the empty chair that was once her second daughter's.

Mr. Bennet glanced at the chair and looked at his foolish wife. "You would prefer her married to a barrister instead of a landowner?"

"Well no, of course not . . . she was clever to drive him away. And Mr. Darcy will save the family when you are dead!" Mrs. Bennet crowed. Mr. Bennet closed his eyes as she continued. "I expect to hear very soon from her, asking me to come and arrange her wedding. Really Mr. Bennet, how could you agree to a wedding in Mr. Darcy's parlour? How am I to show him off to our neighbours?"

"I understand that a parlour wedding is the height of fashion, Mama." Kitty said. "I saw it in *The Ladies' Magazine*. Only a wedding by special license can be in a parlour."

"Well, yes I know that, but nobody here will see him! I have had no opportunity to show him around to the neighbours!"

"I believe that Mr. Darcy would prefer to keep it that way." Mr. Bennet stood and put down his napkin. "Mary, would you come with me to the bookroom, please."

Mary followed him in nervously; this was a very rare invitation. "Yes, Papa?"

"Please close the door, and take a seat." He took up the letters that had arrived from London and watched his daughter sit ramrod straight in the chair that was formerly Elizabeth's domain. "I have some news. Your sister Elizabeth will be married tomorrow morning."

"Tomorrow! But why?"

"Call it an anxious groom." He laughed and saw that she did not understand and cleared his throat. "Mr. Darcy would like to enjoy the rest of the Season with a wife by his side, then take her home to his estate."

"Oh, I suppose that would be better, then Lizzy can be introduced to his friends this year."

"Exactly." He paused and continued. "I will be making the trip to town, and I would like you to come with me."

"Me?" She said with surprise, "But what of Mama?"

"No, she . . .I have my reasons for leaving her at home. However, the reason that I ask you to come with me is because your uncle has arranged a tour of a girl's school, and I would like to hear your opinion."

Mary's mouth gaped. "A school, you really do mean to send us to school?"

"Yes, I was not joking when I mentioned that at dinner. I regret very much not sending your elder sisters to school, or employing a governess for all of you. I can only afford to send you at first, but by the time you return, I will be able to send both Kitty and Lydia as well. What do you think of this?"

"I . . .I would like to go, very much." Mary said quietly. "Would I be near Aunt Gardiner?"

"They would welcome your visits, and Jane will remain in town for the foreseeable future. She does not need to hear your mother's opinions of Mr. Harwick."

"No, we hear enough of them as it is." Mary covered her mouth. "I am sorry!"

Mr. Bennet chuckled. "No, no, I agree. Very well then, Mr. Darcy's carriage will be here very early tomorrow, so be dressed and ready to go two hours past sunrise." She was at the door when he called out to her. "And Mary, you are to leave Mr. Fordyce's sermons behind."

"Why?"

"Orders from your sister, and as she is the bride, we cannot deny her pleasure."

"But what will I read?" She asked as her eyes scanned the shelves worriedly.

"Lizzy suggests that you expand your imagination with a novel." Amused to see her shock, he handed her a book of sonnets. "She also highly recommended Mr. Shakespeare."

"Lizzy always has to have her joke." Mary said with a fond smile. "I hope to hear her laugh, I miss it so. The house seems empty without it." Mr. Bennet watched the door close behind her then looked back to the empty chair across from his desk. Picking up the note that she had sent to him that morning, he read her message once again.

Fitzwilliam wishes to marry tomorrow, but I asked him to delay one more day. I wish for you to be with me. Please come.

He wiped his eyes and chastised himself. "Foolish old man." He carefully folded the letter and placed it in his desk. "Thank you, Lizzy."

Chapter 27

"Well, I suppose that is everything." Elizabeth looked around the small room and smiled at Jane. "I have left out what I need for today and tomorrow morning. Aunt will have a servant deliver the trunks to Darcy House so it will all be unpacked and ready for me when I arrive. She wrote to Madame Dupree as well."

"You are so calm, Lizzy. I admire it so much; you have been so strong through all of this!" Jane sat on the bed and held out her hands to pull her sister down. "Are you not frightened?"

She laughed. "Of course I am! I am not eighteen and I will be the mistress of two enormous homes! I cannot possibly imagine what Pemberley is like, despite all of Georgiana's enthusiastic descriptions. I am terribly afraid of disappointing him." Elizabeth bit her lip and looked down at her hands. "I fear the day when he wakes and wonders what on earth he was thinking to take on this simple country girl."

"Lizzy, I saw the joy in his eyes and the concern in his face when he found you yesterday. When he entered the bookshop and spotted Aunt and me, his expression was of such relief. I have seldom seen him so open with his emotions. You may see it regularly, but it is rarely displayed to anyone else."

"I know." Elizabeth smiled. "It is a special gift for me."

"He loves you." She said quietly to her shoes.

"He does, that is the greatest gift of all." She tilted her head, trying to see Jane's eyes. "Did you love Mr. Harwick? Now that you have had some time to think about it?"

"No." Jane looked back up and smiled. "No, he would have been the marriage I was raised to expect. I was told to marry a man to save the family, and that is precisely what marrying him would have been. When I heard him speak of his children, I knew that he was a man capable of great feeling, not unlike Mr. Darcy, but I knew that if another woman was ever to coax that feeling from him again, it would not be me."

"I am glad that you feel that way, Jane. It leaves you free to fall in love someday without regret, as I did when Mr. Stewart left."

"No Lizzy, you marrying Mr. Darcy is what will give me the freedom to fall in love should it come. He has accepted the burden of our family by accepting you." Jane hugged her. "He is such a dear man, Lizzy! How could I ever be jealous that you found him? How could I deny him the love he has found in you with my pettiness?"

"I hate to admit this Jane, but as I was influenced by Papa, you were influenced by Mama. Both of us have learned that our favourite parents are not infallible." She smiled and saw Jane nod sadly, then look back down to her hands.

"Lizzy," Jane paused then closed her eyes as a blush crept up her face. "I could not help but overhear Mama's talk to you about your duties to Mr. Darcy. It sounds absolutely mortifying. Did she tell you anything of the pain? I cannot imagine being forced to lie still; and . . ."

"Jane, stop!" Elizabeth squeezed her hands. "Mama's description was horrible I know, but Aunt has taken the time to talk to me very openly and honestly about what to expect. Even Lady Matlock's talk, while not as comforting as Aunt's, was not the drama that Mama described. I am not concerned, well, I am; but I am not so frightened as to wish to hide under the bed when Fitzwilliam approaches. We . . . we have shared some intimacies, and . . . I believe . . . I believe that Aunt's teachings will be correct."

"Are you just being brave?" Jane asked worriedly.

"No, I honestly believe that all will be well. I . . . I actually am looking forward to it." She laughed to hear Jane's gasp. "I promise to tell you the truth of it when we can talk privately again."

"Lizzy, a package has come for you." Mrs. Gardiner announced from the doorway.

"Oh, my wedding dress? You just sent the note to Madame Dupree!"

"No, it is not your dress." She winked at Jane and led the way down the stairs to the front sitting room where Darcy stood staring out of the window with his hands clasped behind his back.

"Fitzwilliam, what brings you here?" Elizabeth ran into the room and grasped his hands, and he turned with a smile.

"I may not visit the bride?" He laughed to see her happy eyes, and bent to kiss her hand. "I know that we both have much to accomplish today, but I have to tell you the events of the morning." He led her to a sofa and they sat with their fingers entwined while Mrs. Gardiner shook her head at the couples' complete oblivion. "My aunt will give us a small wedding breakfast tomorrow at Matlock House." At last he turned to Mrs. Gardiner. "No offence, madam, but the church is not so far from Grosvenor Square . . ."

"I understand, sir. Go on."

"Richard has agreed to stand up with me; he replied to my note and said that he was delighted."

"Jane will be my witness." Elizabeth smiled over to her. "What of guests?"

"Well, my coach will leave at dawn for Longbourn."

"Your poor horses!"

"I am borrowing my uncle's." He smiled at her care. "We have enough carriages in the family to take care of everyone handily." He drew breath and continued. "Stewart came over yesterday and . . . very publicly berated me for my horrible treatment of you by marrying Anne. I imagine that he would have offered for you." Elizabeth's hand flew to her mouth when she gasped. "He tried to . . . Well; he tried to strike me in the face. Bingley heard that we both lost teeth, which clearly is not true. I just want you to be prepared for any comments . . ."

"You fought?"

"Briefly, yes."

"Who won?" She tilted her head to see his satisfied smile. "I see. And what is the preferred explanation for his impetuous behaviour?"

"I told Bingley that you had been neighbours in Hertfordshire and he felt concern towards you." He saw her brow lift and sighed. "I thought that was not too far from the truth without confessing all."

"No, I like your choice, but will that satisfy the world?"

"I have decided that the world does not deserve further explanation, however, I have invited him to the wedding as a sign that all is well between us. Does that make you uncomfortable?"

"No, I think he will feel more than I." She smiled to see his nod and took both of his hands again. "Anything else?"

He looked at her steadily. "Georgiana is asking why our wedding date was moved up. It occurred to me that she will not be alone in that curiosity, and that it may very well be assumed that we anticipated our vows."

"Fitzwilliam!"

"Forgive me, but I am sure that the thought struck Mrs. Gardiner, did it not, madam?" Darcy turned to assess her reaction.

"I am afraid that it did, but the benefit to you marrying now is far greater than a birth that will not come when anticipated." She smiled and shrugged. "It is certainly not an unknown phenomenon." Jane gasped and Mrs. Gardiner patted her hand. "What have you told your sister?"

"That the fire is driving my desire to return to Pemberley sooner than expected and we thought we would be married a little earlier to enjoy some of the Season as a wedded couple before departing." He looked to Elizabeth and smiled, "Which is also not false."

"I think that you are becoming more creative with your confessions. I will have to keep that in mind for future reference." Her eyes danced and he shrugged a little. "And?"

"That is all I know of . . . except . . ." He reached into his pocket and handed her a velvet bag. "Please wear this tomorrow with your gown." She began to open it and he stopped her. "I begged Georgiana to give it to you, and she was glad to do so. I traded her a piece that I found in her jewels at Pemberley."

"I think that I know what this is." Elizabeth opened the bag and into her hand spilled the pearl named Richard. "Ohhh."

"Once I saw this on you, I could not imagine any other ever wearing it." He touched it, then smiled up to her. "I know that this means that your locket will have to be abandoned for the day, but . . ."

"I will have the real man by my side." She carefully put the pearl back in the bag and smiled up at him. "Thank you, and Georgiana." Darcy leaned forward and kissed her, then drew back.

"I must go." He stood and she rose with him. "I have to prepare our home for you."

"Do you not have a staff for that?"

"I have correspondence to answer."

"I think that you are trying to avoid me." Elizabeth laughed.

Darcy bowed to the ladies and taking her hand walked to the door, and set his hat down on the steps. "Dearest," he drew her into his arms and kissed her upturned mouth, "it is taking every ounce of my strength not to carry you to some convenient room and teach you the lesson of how dangerous it is to tease a desperate man."

"What did I say?" She asked innocently.

He groaned and traced his hands down her back to rest on her bottom, rubbing his groin against her until her eyes closed, then moved to tenderly suckle her earlobe. Withdrawing, he was satisfied to note her disappointment. "A taste my love, a taste." Darcy kissed her gently. "I will see you tomorrow at the altar." She nodded mutely and gladly returned the soft kiss. "I love you." In a breath he was gone.

"I AM SO SORRY, ELIZABETH." Darcy took her hands in his and pled with her to understand. "I had no choice, my family . . ."

"What of *our* family!!" She cried.

"Too many people are counting on me. Anne . . . it was the only way to stop the ruin of our names, I had to stop the rumours, I had to marry her!"

Elizabeth tore away from him and drawing back, struck him forcefully across the face. A bright red imprint of her small hand glowed from his cheek. She drew back again, and with tears rolling down his face, he stood still and accepted the strike. Again and again Elizabeth beat him, her body shook with sobs, and her touch became weaker as she lost strength. When at last she collapsed to the ground, he fell to his knees. "Wait for me. She will not survive for long. Wait for me."

"How?" She sat up and demanded. "How can I wait? I am the poor girl jilted by the rich man! I am already called your mistress! *You* have ruined *me!* What of my name? What of my sisters? I have no choice but to resolve myself to a life alone. I will never marry."

"Please Elizabeth, I will take care of you, I will give you a home, and when it is over . . ."

"You will be in mourning for two years afterwards! I could be waiting years for you! And what am I in the meantime? I *would* be your mistress! You do not love me, you never loved me!" She climbed to her feet and stood looking down at the devastated man, then reaching to her neck she tore the locket from her throat and threw it on the ground. "I want no part of you."

"Please . . ."

"Give them to me." She stood with her palm extended.

"No, please, leave me with at least this." He begged.

"No, you have rejected me, you have rejected our future, you have rejected our children. I want you to think every day for the rest of your life what your pride has given you. NOTHING!"

Slowly, Darcy removed the box containing her hair from his waistcoat and looking down to his finger, removed the ring, and placed them in her hand. It remained extended, and he reached inside of his coat to remove his book of sonnets. "Please . . ."

"This is your decision, Mr. Darcy."

"Elizabeth . . ."

"Miss Bennet, sir."

"Mrs. Stewart." They both looked up and Stewart was by her side. "I will marry you. I never should have left you. I love you."

Elizabeth looked from the man at her feet to the man offering his hand. She hesitated then nodded. "Yes, I will marry you."

"NO!"

"Darcy! Come! Anne is asking for you!" Lady Catherine called.

"Go Mr. Darcy, your wife wants you." Elizabeth said coldly.

"You are my wife." He whispered. "You, only you. I love you, please . . ."

"Darcy!"

"Please do not marry Stewart, please wait for me, forgive me . . ."

"Darcy, wake up!" Fitzwilliam shook his shoulder.

"Go ahead, strike me again, I deserve it."

Fitzwilliam stood back and considered his cousin, the bed coverings were twisted around his body from thrashing, his face was wet with tears, and he was still very deeply in this obvious nightmare.

"NO!" He screamed. "Get away!"

"Well, we have to put a stop to this now." He looked around for a pitcher of water and spotting the ewer, strode across the room, grabbed it, and returned to his suffering cousin. Judging the best spot, he began pouring water over his face, it filled his nose and open mouth, and instantly Darcy coughed and spluttered, then at last awoke.

"What . . . What the devil!" Darcy sat up and wiped his face then stared at Fitzwilliam. "What . . .why?"

"You are a devil to waken, I sincerely hope that Pemberley does not catch fire while you are asleep or Elizabeth will surely be a widow."

"Elizabeth!" Darcy cried. "Where is she?"

"I imagine she is in her bedchamber dressing for her wedding." Fitzwilliam smiled. "To you."

Darcy sighed and rested his head in his hands. "Thank you, God."

Fitzwilliam sat on the bed and watched his cousin try to wipe away the tears without giving his activity away. "I take it that was a nightmare about Elizabeth marrying Stewart."

"And me marrying Anne."

"Definitely a horrifying experience." He clapped Darcy's back. "What brought that on?"

"I . . . I spent some time reading my journals last night, and I read where I realized that Stewart had been courting her, and then I thought about him storming over here to defend her when he thought I had married Anne . . .and . . ."

"And you had wedding eve fears. I knew that I should have spent the night here. Any other man who marries for convenience would be steady as a rock this morning. You are a lover. What a lucky man you are to have nightmares on your wedding day." He smiled but Darcy was still lost in his memories.

"Layton thought that I would have married her if I had gone to Rosings." Darcy looked up to see Fitzwilliam's expression grow serious. "You were there, what do you think?"

"I am not you, though we share a penchant for duty and honour." Fitzwilliam sighed. "I could have married her, Aunt Catherine was all for it. Father even spoke of it. I just could not do it, and I did not have a beautiful woman waiting for me a carriage ride away. And I had much more to lose than you. Come Darcy, what are you beating yourself over for? Surely you do not regret this decision?"

"No, no not at all. I suppose that I . . . I realized how unlikely it is that this day has come. You are correct; I am a very fortunate man."

"Marrying Elizabeth today *is* protecting the family. It is continuing the Darcy name, is it not?"

"I hope so."

"Well it will if you do not scare the poor girl away by your screams in the night." He chuckled and stood.

Darcy shot him a glance and smiled ruefully. "How loud was I?"

"Your valet was vastly relieved to hear of my arrival. I do not think that he would have opted for the ewer." He crossed his arms while Darcy got to his feet. "What brings you to the mistress' chambers?"

"I did not want to sleep in the new bed . . . yet." He looked away when Fitzwilliam smiled knowingly. "What time is it?"

"Seven. You have plenty of time. Come on, let us eat and get you bathed and dressed for your bride." He eyed him carefully. "Perhaps a nap?"

"Very funny, Richard."

"Do you have these dreams often? Nightmares I mean?"

"Why?"

He shrugged. "I do. Just curious."

Two hours later, Darcy stood in his dressing room with his eyes closed as his valet fussed over his neck cloth. Fitzwilliam was sprawled unceremoniously in the shaving chair while he watched the proceedings. "You will amaze her with your beauty."

"Quiet Richard."

"Overwhelm her with your scent." He picked up a bottle of cologne and sniffed.

"Richard."

"Besiege her with your hooded seductive glance." His lips twitched.

"Are you through?"

"Ah, and she will faint at the suggestion of the night to come." He placed his hand over his breast and sighed.

"I think that I will ask Bingley to stand up with me. You are mocking me far too much."

Fitzwilliam chuckled and waved the thought away. "Oh, you do not want a puppy on this day! You want someone who will distract you from your nerves!"

"What nerves?" Darcy felt Adams move away and twisted his neck around to adjust to the knot. "I am perfectly relaxed."

"Then why are your nails driving into your palm, and your eyes shadowed from lack of sleep?" Fitzwilliam asked softly. Darcy looked down to see that his hands were balled up so tightly that his knuckles were white.

"Fine, I am nervous."

"Would you like a drink?"

"I wish to remember this day, Cousin."

"I am suggesting a drink, not a bottle." A glass was waved under his nose and Darcy grabbed it to take a healthy swallow. He coughed and Fitzwilliam clucked. "It is well that you were a first son. You were not cut out to be a soldier."

"You were not cut out to be a first son!" Darcy glared and took another, more moderated swallow, then drained the glass. Adams held out his new blue coat and he slipped it on, then admired his reflection while the man brushed him off. "What do you think?"

"Hmm? Well it is not red, but I suppose it will do."

"Where is he?" A booming voice called, then was immediately followed by Lord Matlock and Layton. "There you are, Son." He came in and looked him over. "You do look a sight."

"What?" Darcy turned to the glass. "What is amiss?"

"Nothing that a wife cannot cure." Layton smiled. Darcy looked at his cousin's reflection and raised his brow to see a slight nod. Darcy smiled and nodded back.

"Well, the bride is at Matlock so we were unceremoniously removed." Lord Matlock announced. "Georgiana is so excited I was tempted to hand her a glass of wine to calm her down."

"Uncle!"

"No, I did not!" He snorted. "They were all giggles, a gaggle of birds in their pretty feathers." The men all turned to regard him. "What? I can appreciate the beauty of my ladies, can I not? Of course the bride outshined them all."

"Naturally." Fitzwilliam nodded.

"She does." Layton admitted. "She is glowing Darcy, much as you are."

"Men do not glow." He said defensively. "We . . ."

"Smoulder." Fitzwilliam suggested.

The collective gaze turned to him. "I had a long recovery gentlemen, I read many novels." He saw the rolling eyes. "Ah but I know what the ladies expect now, do you?"

"Darcy, the carriage is in position." Singleton announced. "Mr. Bennet is waiting downstairs."

Now all eyes looked upon him and he smiled. "He tells me that he was accompanied by Miss Mary Bennet, but she was left off with the ladies."

Darcy closed his eyes in relief. "Thank you."

Fitzwilliam sat up. "Ah, Miss Mary? And tell us of this one?"

"She is sixteen, I believe. Very fond of Fordyce." He smiled to see the faces fall.

"Well then, shall we be off?" Lord Matlock cleared his throat. "Let us see this young man married!"

"THERE, YOU ARE LOVELY LIZZY." Mrs. Gardiner kissed her cheek, and fixed the lace covering her hair. "A beautiful bride."

"Thank you, Aunt." Elizabeth clasped her hands nervously, and Mrs. Gardiner laid hers over top. "I have felt for so long that you are my mother, I am happy that you are with me today."

"Oh my dear." They embraced and sniffed. "Thank you. You will always be my first daughter." The carriage came to a halt before the church, and passersby stopped to see who exited the bridal coach. While waiting for the women from the other coaches to be handed down, Elizabeth looked again to her clenched hands. Mrs. Gardiner tried to rub some warmth into her icy skin. "I am sorry that your sleep was so poor, dear."

"I do not know why my dreams were so frightening, as if anything could keep me from marrying Fitzwilliam. Why did I dream of him accepting his cousin? And why would I accept Mr. Stewart? It is nonsensical!" She laughed a little and wiped away the tears that had fallen so hard all that night. "I am silly."

"No dear, it is simply you wanting nothing to stand in the way." She smiled and at last the door was opened. Mr. Bennet was there to take Elizabeth's hand.

"Papa." She smiled and stepped out.

"You are beautiful, Daughter." He kissed her cheek and they began walking. Mr. Gardiner was there for his wife. Curious members of society watched the party enter, and one woman asked Jane who was marrying.

"My sister Elizabeth Bennet is marrying Mr. Fitzwilliam Darcy, madam."

"Darcy!" She cried and looking to her friends, followed the family inside of the church and found seats. There were already a small number of people there, all from the most prestigious families. Lady Matlock had tapped her closest friends, and they had all come to witness the event, and of course to report of it to all who were not so privileged to have been invited.

Jane walked ahead to take her place at the altar with Fitzwilliam. The two smiled at each other then simultaneously noted Darcy, standing still and straight, and staring intently to the end of the aisle. Finally, after endless seconds of tortured waiting, his Elizabeth appeared. Fitzwilliam placed his hand on Darcy's forearm, and was surprised that he had to exert a great deal of pressure to keep the groom from striding down the aisle to claim his bride.

Mr. Bennet was not nearly so prepared. When Elizabeth's eyes locked on Darcy's she abandoned her father and began to hasten towards him. Darcy wrested his arm from Fitzwilliam and met her, catching her outstretched hands and gripping them tightly. He fought for control of his emotions and his desire to wrap her securely in his arms. "Dearest, you could not wait to take my hands?" He asked shakily.

"I needed to touch you." Elizabeth blinked back her tears, and failed to stop them from spilling down her cheeks. Darcy stepped closer and bent towards her lips.

"Mr. Darcy." Mr. Bennet spoke softly from behind Elizabeth. "There is something to be accomplished first."

Darcy straightened. "Forgive me." He whispered and kept his eyes with hers. "We do have some vows to take, my love." He glanced at Mr. Bennet. "I will take her from here, thank you."

Mr. Bennet saw the devotion shining from their faces and nodded. He placed his hand over Elizabeth's, still in Darcy's grasp. "Take care of her, sir."

"I will." Darcy drew a deep breath and he lifted her hands to his lips to kiss. "Are you ready to be mine?"

"If you are ready to be mine." She smiled and he chuckled softly.

"That I am."

Turning to the altar, Darcy sedately walked up the aisle. He ignored his cousin's raised brows and the congregation's murmured comments, dropped his eyes appropriately to Reverend Hodgson, then turned to face his radiant bride. Elizabeth gently brushed the tears from his cheeks, and the service at last began.

When the moment arrived to slip the ring on her finger, Darcy's hand was rock steady, and Elizabeth's was warm in his grasp.

"With this ring, I thee wed . . ." Darcy's voice caressed the vow, and when they knelt holding hands to hear the final prayers, her fingers caressed the ring he already wore for her. Through the droning of the endless invocations, the couple closed their eyes, the relief and exhaustion at last overcoming them, and they leaned together, supporting each other. And then it was done.

And they did not rise. The reverend encouraged them to stand. Jane touched Elizabeth's shoulder. Fitzwilliam cleared his throat. Giggles and laughter rippled through the crowd, and finally Fitzwilliam leaned down to Darcy and whispered in his ear. He startled and opened his eyes to find Elizabeth against his shoulder.

"Mrs. Darcy, are you asleep? It is safe to open your eyes now." He whispered and she peeked at him as he helped her to rise. "I love you."

"We are really married?" She saw his brilliant happy smile and returned it. "I love you." She whispered to his bent head. "I was no more asleep than you. I was seeking comfort."

"You are frightened, love?" Darcy's eyes twinkled. "Of me?"

"I was not frightened; I was in need of respite." Her eyes danced. "Marrying you is a trial."

"You suffered for our love." He chuckled as she nodded. "How very brave of you dearest." The two were entirely lost in their banter and each other. The clerk cleared his throat a number of times and finally Fitzwilliam sighed loudly and placing his hand firmly on his cousin's back, gave him a shove towards the registry book.

Elizabeth laughed when they lurched forward, and the family joined in. Darcy flushed to be embarrassed in front of so many, but the laugh that had caught his ear so long ago forced him to smile instead. "You have another promise to make me."

"Have I not made enough for one day?"

"No, oh no, I will extract any number of them this day."

"I shall consider it when I hear your demands." Elizabeth smiled up to him.

"I wish you to promise to laugh once a day before me, for the rest of our lives."

"Just once?"

"No less than once." He kissed her hand and handed her the pen, keeping his palm on the small of her back, and claiming possession of her for all to see.

When they made their way outside again, the guests, invited and not, clapped and cheered their arrival as church bells began to peal. Darcy strode purposely forward, nodding to them, but hurrying along. The door to his coach was opened and he quickly ushered his wife inside. The door instantly closed and the carriage was on its way.

"Are you in a rush to have some cake, Fitzwilliam?" She laughed.

"No." Drawing her to his side, Darcy touched the lace of her veil, then caressed her face with the back of his fingers. "I wish to taste something far sweeter." Tilting up her chin, he kissed her. "More than anything, I want this carriage to take us home right now."

"We must go . . ."

"I know dearest, but as soon as we are able, when we have been toasted and eaten our cake, I want to take you home." He spoke softly, and wound his arm around her to rest her back against his chest. "I need you in our home."

"And what will we do there?" Elizabeth blushed as she felt his lips nibbling her ear, and shivered when his hand gently began to caress her breasts. Darcy felt her trembling and stopped, rested his face against her neck, and held her hands.

"I will endeavour to make you very happy." They closed their eyes and remained embraced for the remainder of the short journey. Further intimacy was impossible, he could not trust himself to stop, and would not risk embarrassing her in any way. When they arrived outside of Matlock House, they were both startled by the halt of the carriage's motion. "Must we go in?" He looked unhappily at the house, then back to the woman in his arms, and drawing his thumb over her moist lips, sighed. "You cannot imagine how alluring you are, Elizabeth."

She touched his mouth and smiled a little. "You are far too kind."

"And you are lovely."

Elizabeth smiled, knowing very well the source of the hard object that had been pressed against her, and what her new husband was thinking. She sat up and touched her hair. "How do I look?"

"Enticing. Utterly bewitching, and," he picked up her hand to kiss her ring, "married."

"To you."

"Thank God." He whispered and sat up straight when the door opened. With some difficulty he managed to exit the carriage and unsuccessfully conjuring any thought other than of her in his bed, offered his hand and walked determinedly inside of his uncle's home. There they remained, chastely standing hand in hand while servants whirled around them, and awaited the rest of the family. Darcy took long calming breaths while Elizabeth watched him with a smile.

"I think that I am going to enjoy keeping you in this state, Mr. Darcy."

"Be careful of what you wish for, Mrs. Darcy. I am not a man to be teased."

"Oh, I disagree. You are a man made to be teased." She laughed to see his head shake. At last the other coaches arrived and they received their formal congratulations. Only family and Darcy's friends were there, the people from the church were not invited to this simple celebration.

Georgiana flew inside and threw her arms around her brother. "You are married!"

Darcy laughed and kissed her cheek. "I know!"

"Oh I am so happy, Brother! Thank you, thank you for giving me a wonderful sister!" She kissed him and turned to hug Elizabeth. "Thank you for marrying him! Now I may pass my father's direction to you." Georgiana stood back and said very seriously, "You are to take care of him."

"I will." She said just as seriously, and entwined her fingers with his outstretched hand. "And I want you to tell me if I am not up to snuff."

"Very well then. He is the dearest of brothers." She then turned to him. "And you must take care of my sister!"

"I have no other plans." He smiled and held out his other hand to her. "We are a family now, we three."

Lord Matlock waited until everyone had gathered together and had a glass of punch in hand. He raised his and called out, "To Elizabeth and Fitzwilliam Darcy, may they live lives of joy and peace, may they have many healthy children, may they prosper, and may the love they share today only grow. May they be an example to us all."

"Here, here!" Fitzwilliam cried.

"To the happy couple." Mr. Bennet toasted them. Everyone drank and conversations burst out all around. Bingley wandered over to Stewart who was watching Darcy talk with Singleton and Lord Matlock, his hand firmly in place on Elizabeth's back, while she carried on a conversation with her new cousins and all of her sisters. Georgiana had moved to her side, and seemingly permanently took possession of her other hand.

Fitzwilliam crossed his arms and nudged his brother. "He is ecstatic."

"How can you tell?" Layton laughed. "He smiles but he still remains inscrutable."

"That is because he is desperately attempting to keep his desire in check." Layton followed Fitzwilliam's gaze and watched Darcy's hand alternately bunching then smoothing the fabric of Elizabeth's gown.

"If he is not careful, he will release the buttons."

They eyed each other and smiled. "And here we were so worried that he had changed into an unfeeling man."

"Oh he is feeling all right." Layton laughed again, and walked over to speak with his cousin de Bourgh.

"Well, so what do you think of your introduction to the family? Can you bear us?"

De Bourgh turned at his salutation. "I think that I can bear you well enough." He smiled and looked over the small crowd. "I had no idea you all even existed, Mother never spoke of Lady Catherine. Your father's first letter was an absolute surprise. He tells me that he has kept track of Lewis de Bourgh's descendents ever since Cousin Anne's health seemed be failing, just in case, but felt that to inform me of a possible inheritance would be cruel if it never came to fruition."

"It would have been." Layton agreed. "Why raise your expectations, unless of course, you prefer the life on a ship?"

"I love the sea, but it is no easy path. I am grateful that my son will not have to choose it." He looked around the room and smiled. "And the bonus in all of this is that I will have the opportunity to marry now, something I never really considered before." He tilted his head and examined Elizabeth. "The bride is jubilant."

"She is; our cousin is very fortunate, and matches her mood."

"And she has sisters?" De Bourgh grinned and Layton laughed as the men examined the ladies in the room. "I know; one thing at a time, I have much to learn."

"And you will be quite a catch, as well. Just wait until the mamas hear of you!" De Bourgh's eyes grew wide and Layton clapped his back. "Do not worry, Darcy and I will teach you how to survive being an heir."

Bingley approached Stewart with a smile, "It is a happy day. He has loved her for a very long time, I am delighted for them."

"Yes, she is very special." Stewart agreed, and listened to Elizabeth's familiar laughter.

"I heard of your dust-up. Darcy said that you were neighbours of the Bennets and became a bit brotherly about the girls."

Stewart started and smiled at Darcy's scant explanation. "Oh, yes . . . I suppose that I did."

Bingley nodded. "I understand; I have a sister to marry off, although she may have found a man, law student."

Stewart turned his attention to Bingley. "Really? I am a barrister myself."

"Yes, I know, Darcy was telling me about you, I am in the market for an estate in the next few years. Miss Bennet mentioned Netherfield as being available, and Darcy recommended that I ask your opinion on it sometime. I understand that your cousin leased it?"

"Yes, but they are gone. You are welcome to come by the inn and I can give you the particulars."

"Excellent!" Bingley smiled. "Yes, it will be good to have a home, although I had figured my sister would serve as hostess, but if she marries, I will have a difficult time arranging events." He mused.

Stewart spoke thoughtfully. "Well, if her husband is studying law, he likely has no estate of his own. He would probably be happy to loan his wife as your hostess if he had the opportunity to enjoy your home." He shrugged, "Younger sons are always guests."

"That is a good point!"

Audrey watched Stewart as he spoke to Bingley, then turned to pay attention to the ladies' conversation. When she next looked up, she realized that Stewart was standing beside her. "Good Morning, Mrs. Singleton." He smiled and bowed. "I did not have the opportunity to greet you in the church. You look lovely today."

"Oh." She said softly, then broke from her thoughts. "Thank you."

"You are very welcome." He smiled warmly, and glanced at Singleton who had looked to him with a concerned expression, and back to her. "I understand that some improvements are being made to your townhouse."

Audrey's brow creased and she looked down. "They are underway, sir."

"I hope for your sake that they are a success." He took her hand, and felt her fingers tighten in his grasp, then let go. "You deserve to be happy with your surroundings." Stewart looked at her to see that she understood and began to walk away.

"Mr. Stewart . . ." Audrey called. "I hope that you are equally successful with your plans."

"I have none, but thank you." He bowed and smiled as Singleton passed him on the way to Audrey's side, and was glad to see her smile and accept his arm. Stewart's progress was stopped by Darcy, who broke away from Elizabeth.

"I need to thank you again."

"For what?" Stewart smiled and saw Elizabeth watching them. "For being a fool and giving her up? Even if I never had a chance, as you said? Well you are very welcome!"

Darcy smiled. "Well there is that, but no, I want to thank you for coming over to beat me."

Surprised, Stewart crossed his arms and regarded his friend. "Very well, go on."

"I realized how destroyed Elizabeth's life would have been had I married my cousin, and what a great gesture it would have been for you to marry her. So, although it would have killed me see her marry anyone besides me, I am grateful that you would have accepted her. She would have been safe."

"But unhappy."

"You are a good man." Darcy said sincerely.

"All right now Darcy, you have had entirely too much punch." Stewart was flushed with embarrassment. "Return to your bride. I think that I will take my leave. Good luck to you both."

"I am not drunk, but I understand. We will see you soon, I hope."

"Not until the knocker is back on your door." Stewart winked, then turned to Elizabeth, who had come to join them. "Take care, Mrs. Darcy." He leaned and kissed her hand. "And take care of your sottish husband."

"Good heavens Mr. Darcy, we are married but moments and you are already in your cups?" She rested her hands on her hips and laughed when Darcy seized and kissed them both.

"If that is what it takes to excuse me from this celebration, then so be it. Yes, Mrs. Darcy, my wife of lo these many minutes, I am drunk with your beauty, and I need to be cared for . . . as my sister charged you . . . immediately. Come, let us leave our friends and family to their merry making and depart for our home." He bowed and smiled, then raised his brow at her inquiringly.

"You sir, are giddy!"

"I am!"

"But what of our guests? You have barely spoken with Captain de Bourgh!"

Darcy sighed and grabbed her hand. They walked over to the tall sandy-haired man. "Cousin de Bourgh?"

"Cousin Darcy, I am delighted to have been invited today, and am pleased to meet you and your lovely bride." De Bourgh smiled at them both. "I hope to know you better in the future."

"I do as well, and I wish you well with your trip tomorrow. If you need assistance understanding Rosings, please do not hesitate to ask me." Darcy smiled down to Elizabeth, "But not for a week or so."

"I understand." He laughed.

"And on that note, I would like to thank you all for our celebration, but Mrs. Darcy and I are exhausted and would like to retire to our home." Darcy shook his uncle's hand and kissed Lady Matlock's cheek. Elizabeth shook her head at his unprecedented silliness and went around the room saying goodbye. She ended with her family.

"Thank you for coming, Papa. What will you tell Mama?"

"The truth, we came to London to visit a school for Mary, and you and Mr. Darcy decided to marry earlier than planned." He shrugged. "She misses out on the planning, but in the end, it is the result that matters. She is saved from the hedgerows."

Jane hugged her and whispered, "I am praying for you to be well, Lizzy."

"I am not afraid." She whispered back.

"Lizzy." Mary held out her arms and hugged her. "I will miss you so much; I hoped you would come home once more before you married. I am so happy that Papa brought me here today. May I come and visit you?"

"Of course!" Elizabeth moved back to look at her. "Perhaps when your school ends, you can come to Pemberley. I am sure that Georgiana would like to have a girl near her age to visit, and then you and I can be free to just be ourselves." She squeezed her hand. "I look forward to that."

"Will you come to Longbourn?"

"I will let you know our plans." They hugged each other and she turned to her aunt and uncle. "Thank you both for everything. You rescued me." She kissed Mr. Gardiner, who was wiping back a tear.

Mrs. Gardiner hugged her tight, and whispered, "Just relax, Lizzy, all will be well." She smiled and patted her cheek. "Remember everything that I told you."

"I will try." She whispered, then turned when she felt Darcy take her hand. She looked up and saw his warm and happy smile. "Are you ready?"

"I am." He squeezed.

She drew a breath and nodded. "So am I."

With one last wave they departed and climbed into their coach, sitting side by side and holding hands. "I shall have to order a new carriage." Darcy said as they were underway. "In honour of our wedding."

"Oh that seems silly, this one is perfectly lovely."

"But not new."

"Does everything have to be new?"

"mmm, not everything." He leaned to kiss her. "I love my new wife."

"As opposed to the old one."

"You are being silly now."

"You have yet to see me be silly, Husband." Elizabeth laughed. "You are in for a rude awakening."

"Oh, and what do you have in mind?"

"That I could not say." She turned to nestle against him. "I shall let whim be my guide."

"That sounds dangerous." Darcy breathed into her ear.

"And that tickles."

"Does it?" He whispered again. Elizabeth rubbed at her ear and he laughed. "I feel so good."

"If I am the cause of this, I am glad." She kissed him and his smile widened. "So Mr. Darcy, we are on our way home, it is the middle of the day, what will we do until nightfall?" Darcy glanced out of the window and saw that they had arrived, and said nothing, only raising her hand to his lips. The door to the carriage opened and without a word, he exited and held out his hand to help her down. "Fitzwilliam? Will you not answer me?"

"Not yet." He said with a small smile, then escorted her inside. The staff was assembled and greeted their new mistress after Darcy made the formal introduction.

"Congratulations to you both." Mrs. Mercer said with a smile. "Is there anything that you would like?"

Darcy looked at Elizabeth and saw her watching him. "No, I . . . We will ring for you if anything is required." Then holding out his arm, he felt her hand take its place and they walked up the stairs. Entering the mistress's chambers, they found Elizabeth's new lady's maid at work. "Millie, Mrs. Darcy will not require your help for some time."

"Oh." She looked from her mistress to her master and disappeared. Darcy laughed and heard his wife's throat clear.

"Yes, my love?" Darcy took her hands in his, and looked at her intently.

Awareness of their location and solitude crept over her. "Fitzwilliam, do you, do you mean for us to . . . to . . ."

He let her splutter a little longer and then took pity. "I cannot pretend to sit through hours of stilted conversation until dark, Elizabeth. I do not want to share a meal that neither of us will taste. I do not wish to tour the house with you, or read to you, or take tea, or hear you play. All of those things we will surely enjoy together, but not now. I need you, I need my wife." Darcy saw her eyes widen and he kept his hands around hers and his voice soft and steady. "Do not fear me, dearest, I love you more than my life. I need to demonstrate that to you in the most intimate way I can."

"I . . .I look forward to it."

"I dreamed that I had lost you last night. I dreamed that I was married to Anne. I begged you to stay with me, but you accepted Stewart. It was horrifying." He looked down at their hands and held them tighter. "I need to make you mine."

"I had the same dream."

"You did?" Darcy lifted his head, "Dearest you dreamed I had abandoned you?" She nodded, and he saw her eyes well up. "How did you wake?"

"Jane came in when I cried out. She stayed with me the rest of the night."

"Richard poured a pitcher of water over my face." Darcy smiled a little and Elizabeth gasped. "It worked, I am a very difficult person to awaken, it seems."

"I suppose that I will discover that soon." She blushed again. "If . . . if you wish for me to sleep with you."

"You know that I do." His head tilted and he looked closely at her, and gently touched her face. "You are exhausted."

"It has been a trying time." She looked down then up to see his face at last exposing the stress of the past weeks. "You are as tired as I."

"I propose, my love, that we discard these wedding clothes for something far more comfortable, and . . . rest together."

"Just rest?"

Darcy smiled and leaned to kiss her. "Yes. Just rest."

"I . . .I would like that."

"Shall I call back your maid?" She nodded and he pulled the bell. "Wear whatever you like, however you feel comfortable."

"What will you choose?"

He looked down and back up. "Breeches and a shirt?" Noting her smile he nodded and started to walk away then stopped. "No neckcloth?"

"Oh, no, I am entitled to see your neck now."

"Of course. What will I be permitted to see?" He asked softly.

"You will find out soon enough." She said with a lift to her chin. Darcy laughed and disappeared. Elizabeth relaxed, he wanted their union, but he was willing to go slowly for her. "I think that I love you even more for this, Fitzwilliam."

When Elizabeth emerged from her dressing room, barefoot and wearing only a silk nightdress, Darcy was standing by the window, leaning on the frame and looking out at the park. He was barefoot and wearing only his breeches and shirt, and did not hear her soft intake of breath when she first saw him.

Although it was afternoon on a bright day his form was shadowed, except for his face which was illuminated by the sun. She stood still and studied his expression. A smile played gently on his lips. His head rested on the glass and she could see that he was looking over the trees of the park, perhaps wishing that they were at Pemberley. Elizabeth sank against the doorframe and took in so many features that she had only imagined before, his neck, seeing it at last exposed made her heart race, her fingers itched to touch that vulnerable skin. His thin shirt, unbuttoned at the collar and cuffs, did not mask the shape of his form the way his coat did. There, easily seen, was the essence of his masculinity, wide shoulders that tapered down to his narrow waist, the coarse hair peeking from the open shirt and more from his exposed forearms. Her gaze travelled downwards, seeing how his breeches hugged his buttocks and legs, again exposing the strength and muscles of an avid horseman. She closed her eyes and pictured his thighs gripping his mount, then blushing, found her view now focussed on his bare calves and feet. An unstoppable need to touch drove her to move from her station and walk quietly to stand behind him. Slipping her arms around his waist, she rested her head on his broad back. Darcy startled then smiled down at the hands exploring his stomach and chest. "I was wondering if I had been abandoned."

"You certainly knew where I was."

"And it was taking every bit of my strength not to rush in and find you." Darcy turned around to find her smiling at him. He combed his fingers through the long unbound curls, then holding her hands made a studied examination of her blushing figure. "Beautiful."

"Blind."

"No, delighted." He closed his eyes when her warm hands traced up his chest to touch his neck.

"You are entirely too tall."

His eyes opened to find her focus on her fingers as they caressed his skin and began wandering into his hair. "I have a solution to that." Bending suddenly, he scooped her up in his arms and laughed when she squealed with surprise. "Come, my love." Darcy carried her through the doorway and into the master's chamber, and from her comfortable position; spun her around as they toured the newly decorated room. "Are you pleased?"

"I cannot believe how quickly this was done." She looked at it all in wonder. "It is overwhelming."

"This is my favourite piece." Darcy walked over to the bed, and lay her down on the pillows, then quickly joined her, lying on his side and slowly tracing his hand down her shoulder. "I cannot tell you how often I have imagined you here."

Elizabeth reached up to his face, and he gladly bent down to kiss her. "I love you, Fitzwilliam."

"I love you." He then settled behind her, spooning their bodies together. His arousal was very evident, but he did not press her. Instead he settled his face onto her shoulder and kissed her ear. "Sleep, dearest." Elizabeth placed her hands over his where they rested on her stomach, and relaxed in the comfort of his arms.

As he felt her slip away into sleep, Darcy watched over her. It was all he could do not to caress every bit of her, his fingers itched to touch and explore, to take possession of the woman who was now forever his, who had been bound to his heart in a moment two years before. Instead he listened to her soft breathing, impressed in his mind the feel of her silky skin under his palm, wondered how he ever managed to lie in a bed before without her in his arms, and slowly his eyes drooped, and he relaxed, and allowed the comfort of his almost-lover to soothe him to rest.

It was the chime of the clock that brought Elizabeth back to awareness. She blinked open her eyes and realized first that it was nearly dusk; and then that she was being kissed. "You are awake." Darcy's lips were wandering over her face and found her mouth. She responded passionately, meeting his deeply stroking lips, accepting and encouraging his exploring tongue, and wrapping her arms around his neck, gladly joined her mouth with his for seemingly endless kisses.

When Darcy moved away to taste her throat, she thrilled with the feel of his hair tickling her face. It was only then that she understood that the warm hand caressing her breasts was touching bare skin. Somehow in her sleep he had removed her gown, and she now saw that he had removed his clothes as well. Darcy paused and smiled into her eyes, seeing them widen as she appreciated their nakedness. He kissed her lips and wordlessly began kissing down her body. Burying his nose in her soft valley, he drank in the heady scent of her perfume, and for the first time tasted her tantalizing breasts. "Elizabeth, I am dying for you." He breathed, and then kissing down her belly, nuzzled his face between her thighs. "I love the scent of you." He licked and savoured her, smiling when she whimpered and remembering what touches elicited moans, kissed upwards to her naval and the sensitive skin below, and delighted in her sighs of discovery.

Darcy rose to his knees to crouch over her, appreciating the beauty of her flushed body, and impossibly became harder with the sight of his wife on the cusp of passion. Elizabeth reached up with both hands to grasp his arousal. Shuddering, he closed his eyes, and revelled in the confidence he felt in her touch as they flowed over and around him. The temptation to lose himself in her caress was enormous, but he had a greater goal to achieve. "I crave this dearest, I dream of this, but we have more to do." Gently he removed her hands, lifting them to his lips to kiss. "Do not forget this touch, love. I want it again."

"I crave the feel of you in my hands." Elizabeth confessed and reached up to touch his face. Darcy's heart nearly stopped. "I know nothing that compares to it."

"Elizabeth . . ." He whispered heatedly, "Let me give you more to desire." Kissing her lips, his hand slid between her thighs to find the sweet evidence of her readiness. Gently, then insistently, relentlessly, he stroked the point of her pleasure. He heard her gasp and felt her fingers in his hair, and continued, licking and kissing her mouth, her tongue, moving to her throat to suckle and down to her shoulder to nip, then back up to her lips. All the while his fingers worked deftly, rubbing and exploring, discovering her secrets, and burying within her wetness until at last she cried out a soft moan of release.

At that moment, Darcy lifted his hips, and with one long stroke, entered his beloved, and claimed his wife and lover forever. Elizabeth was suddenly filled with him, and the sensation was overwhelming. Darcy paused, panting, waiting for her to adjust and hanging on desperately for control as the enveloping warmth and tightness demanded to overcome his last vestiges of restraint. When her eyes opened to look up to him, not with pain as he feared, but with absolute adoration, he gave in at last to his desperate need for her, wrapped his arms around her shoulders, and began to thrust, far, far too fast. He tried to slow but it was hopeless, she had to be his. Their eyes remained locked and he thrilled with her gasping cry each time he buried himself completely within. "Feel it, dearest!" He panted and kissed her open mouth. "Know how I love you! I want all of you!"

Feeling utterly possessed, Elizabeth voiced the exhilaration she was feeling as the rising tide built in the burning spot where their bodies joined again and again, and moaned as she gripped him harder and tighter, She clutched his shoulders as her eyes squeezed shut. "Oh . . .oh Fitzwilliam, I love you!" Darcy experienced every moment of her ecstasy, her muscles tight grip suddenly relaxed and he felt triumph with the achievement of her ultimate release. Her cries were music to him and he kissed her with joy when her eyes opened to meet his again.

Elizabeth stroked his back and the reassuring touch signalled that he could at last let go. She watched his face transform, exulted in his uncontrolled cry of passion and was elated when he pulsed inside of her. Darcy collapsed and turned to cuddle her while remaining buried within. They stayed entwined as they recovered; if anything they were wrapping themselves tighter together.

At last Darcy spoke hoarsely. "Are you well, Elizabeth? I have been thinking so hard of loving you."

"I . . .I am well." She breathed, and nestled against his shoulder. Her shape just naturally fit into his. Darcy's heart was pounding, and he had no desire to let go. Elizabeth closed her eyes, concentrating on the way that their bodies were joined, and remembered every word of instruction that had been uttered to her. Nobody had mentioned this continued connection. "Fitzwilliam?"

"hmmm." He sighed and held her closer. "Yes, my dear love?"

"How long do we remain this way?"

He smiled down at her. "This way? Do you mean unclothed?"

"No . . . I mean . . . joined." She bit her lip and blushed.

Darcy chuckled. "Does it hurt?"

"No, not at all, I rather like being . . ." She paused and Darcy felt ready to burst with pride and kissed her.

"Then do you mind if we stay?"

"No . . . I just was wondering . . ." He caressed her glowing cheeks with his lips, and she hid her face against his chest.

"Do you like what we just experienced?" He asked softly as he stroked her back. "I promise; we will learn how to love each other so it will be better."

"Better? I . . . I am hardly competent, but . . .I am overwhelmed with the feelings you . . ." She jumped when she felt him move within her. "What was that?" Elizabeth whispered.

"That was me, liking very much what you said." Darcy said quietly. "I am no expert either, love. I just know the benefit of edification. I hope you will desire me as much as I want you." Slowly stroking his hand up and over her breasts, he groaned. "Oh darling, they are so soft!" Elizabeth gasped then laughed when he buried his face between them and blew noisily against her skin. Darcy looked up to smile at her. "More?"

"More silliness?" She held his face in her hands and kissed him. "Please."

"Mmm, it is time that you are tasted properly." Elizabeth watched in fascination as he began to suckle her and moaned. "I think that I will happily spend my life nibbling upon you." He raised his chest and rested on his hands, looking over her. His eyes drifted down to her flat belly, wondering if it would someday be swelled with their baby, then down to where his hips rested on hers, and lifting them back to withdraw, watched as he slid back inside of his home. Darcy shuddered and grew hard instantly. "More dearest?"

Elizabeth opened her arms and he contentedly settled into his place. "Teach me." Her hands caressed back the hair that fell around his eyes. "Teach me how to love you."

"Touch me." He whispered. "Please touch me." Drawing his head down she suckled his lips, and as his mouth opened, she did the same for his tongue. Darcy drowned in the pleasure of her attention and hardly felt Elizabeth's nudge so they separated and lay side by side. When she released his mouth he found that she had moved her lips down his chest to kiss then lick his tight nipples. "Oh, Elizabeth . . ." All over his body her hands roamed, and reawakening to his intention, he rolled them over to love her again. Darcy kissed her eyes, her nose, her cheeks, and finally hovered over her softly smiling lips. "I think dearest, that you have much to teach me."

Elizabeth's tongue tenderly touched his. "I have already learned that all I want is you."

Chapter 28

"**G**ood morning." Elizabeth whispered to her sleeping husband. She had managed to extricate herself from his possessive embrace and carefully sliding backwards, her feet found the floor and she stood for the first time since he had carried her to their bed, nearly twelve hours earlier. Sleep was not the main occupation that night. She discovered quickly that Fitzwilliam Darcy was a very passionate man and where in other places in his life he was reticent; here in the privacy of their chambers, he was warm and loving, even silly, and eager to demonstrate his feelings to her. As she slowly straightened, her body acknowledged the fact that she was a maiden no more. "Oh my." She touched her belly; and shaking her head at the man sleeping peacefully, smiled. "You look far too innocent, Fitzwilliam Darcy!"

Elizabeth found her nightdress folded neatly at the end of the bed, then quietly left to enjoy the new luxury of a water closet. Remembering her aunt's instructions, she washed herself and applied the soothing balm that had been packed away with her clothes. When finished, she took up a brush to detangle her much-caressed hair, and at last saw herself clearly in the mirror. "Oh dear!" Elizabeth bent closer and touched her skin. "What have you done to me?" She was covered with red spots all over her throat and shoulders. Pulling her gown away; she examined her breasts, finding small bruises, all perfectly formed in the shape of Darcy's mouth. She closed her eyes with the memory of his kisses and bites of passion. Elizabeth shivered, and hugged herself, and was not at all surprised to feel his hands slipping around her waist, and those same gentle loving lips retracing their way through the path he had forged the long night before.

"I woke and you were gone." He said softly as she leaned into his arms. "I was afraid that this was all a dream."

"What convinced you otherwise?" She smiled up to him.

"Well, there is a great deal of evidence of your presence and our activity in the room." He smiled to see her blush and hugged her. "I rang to have fresh sheets put on, and have called for bath water and breakfast."

"Both sound wonderful, we haven't eaten since the wedding breakfast."

"How do you feel?" Darcy looked at their reflection. "It was a . . .busy night."

"To say the least." Elizabeth laughed to see his face light up. "I am very aware of how busy it was. I am afraid that neither of us have had much sleep."

"Is it painful? I am sorry. If it makes you feel better, I am feeling the effect of the exercise as well." He laughed to see a triumphant gleam in her eye. "And what is that for, Mrs. Darcy?"

"It is only fair that you feel something! Look at what you have done to me!" She touched all of his love bites and glared. "How can I go out looking like this? How can I face my maid?"

"Your maid is well-paid to not say a word, and . . .what makes you think that we have anywhere to go?" Darcy whispered in her ear, "In my experience, the most effective method to relieve the soreness of an overused muscle is to exercise it frequently."

"Oh?" Elizabeth shivered when his hands lowered to rest over her centre and began to rub, "ohhhh."

Darcy nibbled her neck and raised the hem of her night dress to her waist, then slipped his hands between her thighs. "mmmmmm."

"Fitzwill . . ."

Darcy began to lift her gown up over her head, and she clutched it, holding it down. "What is wrong?" He stopped his movement immediately and instead drew her back to rest against his chest. Studying her reflection he saw her eyes were cast down and she was blushing. "Elizabeth?"

"Please do not look at me."

His brow creased and he held her tighter. "Why?"

"I am not . . . please do not look at me."

"Dearest, I spent the better part of the night looking at you, what has changed?"

"That was in the dark, and you were holding me." She whispered and hugged herself.

"Sweetheart, I know that it is hard to believe, but I could see you very well, and I loved everything." He turned her around and resumed holding her, and kissed her forehead. "I know that you grew up hearing how unattractive you are, but remember, I fell in love with you even before you became the breathtaking woman you are now." He tilted his head to see her eyes. "You do not believe me, do you?"

"No."

Darcy remembered Mr. Gardiner once telling him that Elizabeth would want to hear his reassurance but would probably never accept it. Closing his eyes and kissing her hair, he thought about how to help her. "I have an idea." He let her go and untied the robe he had slipped on, and let it fall to the floor. Elizabeth's eyes grew wide to see his completely nude and very aroused body so clearly in the early morning sunshine. "There, look at me, dearest. I am not embarrassed for my wife to see me." Reaching forward, he took her hands and rubbed them over his skin. "I am not embarrassed for you to touch me." He lifted her chin so that she looked up and pointed to his neck. "And I am not at all embarrassed to carry the mark of your love."

"Your clothes cover from head to toe! There is no comparison!" She protested.

Darcy smiled, seeing that he was distracting her from her thoughts. "Of course there is a comparison! Not every one of these marks will be covered by a cravat! My hair is not as long as yours." He ran his fingers through the freshly brushed tresses. "No, your hair . . ."

"Is worn up, if you recall!"

"But you have a new maid who is familiar with the latest styles. I am sure that she will be very creative with you." His lips twitched while she thought it over, and he stepped closer. "Now, shall I don my robe?"

Elizabeth startled from her musings and frowned. "Why?"

"Because you have not joined me." He tugged lightly at her gown, "unless you would care to?" Not hearing a protest he lifted the gown over her head and it fluttered to the floor. "So very beautiful, my love." Turning her around, they faced the mirror and he rested his chin on her shoulder as he embraced her waist. "Look dearest, each one of these marks means something."

"What do you mean?" She sighed as his hands glided over her.

His lips brushed over her silky shoulders. "mmm, I will explain. This on your throat makes you sigh, and this one on your shoulder, makes you moan my name." His caressing fingers moved up to fondle her breasts. "This one makes you shiver." Back up his lips traced to her throat and just below her ear. "And this one, my dearest love, I have learned will make you find heaven if I kiss you just right." Suckling her there, she pressed back against him. "More?" He whispered.

"Please."

He smiled and caressed his hands over her, shoulders to waist, and gently rubbed and tweaked her nipples. "Now, Elizabeth, do you know what I see?"

"What?" She whispered and concentrated her gaze on his hands.

"The only woman in the world I ever want to love me again." He smiled as she blushed. "And do you not think that when making such an important choice, I would want to do so wisely?"

"So you are saying that if I disagree with you, I would be calling you a fool?" Her eyes lit up and he grinned, and rubbed his hips against her.

"I leave it to you. Am I a fool or a wise man? Which do you prefer to call Husband?"

"No woman would admit to loving a fool." Elizabeth stated with conviction.

"Then my logic is proven. If I am a wise man and I chose one woman to be in my embrace for the rest of my life, and you are in fact my wife, then . . . you are lovely."

Elizabeth sighed to feel his lips at work on her throat and his hands smoothly gliding up and over her stomach and breasts. Her voice caught as she tried to maintain her composure. "Mr. Darcy, your theory must be flawed somewhere, but I will not choose to argue with you."

Darcy smiled into her shoulder to see her spirit return, and continued to touch her, tracing his fingers down to wander through her dark curls, and stroking steadily over her tender centre. "Look dearest, look at us. It is beautiful." When Darcy softly suckled beneath her ear, Elizabeth gasped to feel the fire travelling upwards through her body. Withdrawing his moistened fingers, he turned her around to hold her face in his hands and kissed her deeply, then bent to scoop her up in his arms. "Come back to bed with me."

Elizabeth wrapped her arms around his neck and delicately traced her tongue over his lips while he moaned. "What of the baths?"

He laughed and kissed her soundly. "Oh . . . I forgot. I think that a bath for two would be ideal. I cannot wait to experience a wet Elizabeth." He raked his eyes over her flushed form and then stared fixedly at her glistening thighs. "At least, an Elizabeth wet from something other than me."

IT WAS SEVERAL HOURS LATER THAT THE COUPLE, now clean and fed, wandered hand in hand around the house. Darcy was dressed in trousers and a shirt; wearing slippers that Georgiana had bought him but had never worn, having never felt the freedom to be so relaxed outside of his bedchamber before. Elizabeth was wearing a simple morning dress; her stays remained in her dressing room. It was very comfortable to her and a very alluring gift for her husband.

"What do you think? It is only right that you put your mark on the house."

"I have, I helped with the bed chamber."

"But there are your private rooms. You have a sitting room for receiving guests, and your own study." He led the way inside. "You see?"

"Oh." She looked around and he hugged her.

"What is wrong, my love?"

"I know so little of what is to be done." She said quietly. "I am ill-prepared for the position I have accepted."

"No more ill-prepared than I was two years ago when Father died." He said just as softly. "Dearest, I am just barely feeling confident now, and I admit, only to you, that I have moments of great panic." Elizabeth looked up to see his honesty clearly in his expression. "I was so concerned when news of the fire came. I was certain that the house was gone, and grateful that Layton came with me. I wished for you to be there, too."

"I could have done little but hold your hand." She brushed back his hair and he smiled.

"But you see; that is what I needed." Darcy hugged her tightly. "I know so little of the houses. I meant to learn all those things this winter from Mrs. Reynolds. Perhaps we can learn together, but by then, you will be the one teaching me."

"Your confidence is gratifying." Elizabeth rested her head on his chest and listened to his heart. "I . . . I enjoyed answering letters in your study."

"You did?" He looked down. "Would you like to work together there?"

"I would be in your way."

"Only if you were sitting in my chair." He chuckled and kissed her nose. "I will gladly give you a place to work, but . . . I love my chair."

"We will leave it to whoever arrives first." Elizabeth announced. Then with a glint in her eye, she tore away from his embrace and took off down the hallway, "I think it will be me!"

"Elizabeth!" Darcy cried and flew after her. The servants in the surrounding rooms poked their heads out into the hallways. Mr. Foster cleared his throat and they immediately returned to their duties. When the hall was clear, he allowed a smile to cross his lips, and it only grew when he heard the study door shut firmly and the suddenly silenced mistress's laughter.

DARCY SLOWLY OPENED HIS EYES and happily rubbed his face in Elizabeth's hair, then looked down at the sleeping woman in his arms. "I love you so much." He whispered, and sighed as she burrowed closer into his shoulder. Glancing across the room, he noticed the clock, and that two hours had passed since her escape and their torrid loving in his father's chair. He looked around the room, imagining where she could put her things, not even really knowing what her duties would be. She whispered his name in her sleep and he smiled broadly. At last his gaze fell on the invitations and letters that had arrived since he left for Pemberley. Everything had to be rescheduled, but . . . not today. The only invitation that was mandatory to accept was the Creary ball.

"Mr. and Mrs. Fitzwilliam Darcy." He practiced the announcement as he imagined entering the ballroom. "May I introduce my wife, Elizabeth Darcy?" He smiled and hugged her closer. "My wife."

"What are you speaking about, Husband?"

He found her sparkling eyes were open and smiling at him. "I am happy."

"I am as well." She kissed his chin. "Am I too heavy for you? Do you need to change positions?"

"What do you have in mind?" He tightened his hold. "I am not letting go."

"There is a chaise in the library, I noticed." She smiled and looked over at the book on his desk. "Perhaps you could read to me from that handsome volume."

Darcy followed her eyes and his lips pursed. "I brought that back with me from Pemberley."

"What is it?"

He reached for it and it opened automatically to a certain page. "Read."

Elizabeth sat up a little and took the book in her hands. "Your journal." Glancing at the date she looked quickly up at him. "I know this date very well."

"Do you?" He asked quietly. "I visited this page daily for a very long time." Watching her read, he could tell exactly which sentence she was on, he recited it to himself as she took in his words. When she was through, she closed the journal, and set it back on the desk.

"When did I become Elizabeth to you?"

"When we met in the park." He kissed her softly. "When you were no longer a dream."

"When did you stop reading the page?"

"When I left the journal at Pemberley, after I knew that Stewart had courted then abandoned you. I would reach for it here, but . . ." He sighed and hugged her. "I have a confession to make."

"What is it?"

"Do you remember walking in Hyde Park and coming upon a man of about my height, who likely did not like your approach? You were by the Serpentine."

"yes." She whispered. "That was Lord Creary."

"Yes." He sighed. "I came upon him just after you ran away. I . . . I saw you walking with your aunt. I . . .decided not to follow."

"I *knew* you were there!" Elizabeth sat up. "I knew it!"

"I was not ready to . . . I was a fool. I said goodbye to you as you walked away." Darcy's eyes grew bright. "I am so sorry. If I had gone after you then, I could have saved you so much heartache with Stewart and your parents. And I never would have had this experience we are living now with Anne. I . . . I was a different man then. I was full of the wrong ideas about what my duty was to my family." He reached back to his old journal and showed her the special entry again. "On this day I asked my father if I could marry you, and he said to follow my heart as well as my head. I promptly forgot that until the day we met in the park and you became Elizabeth." He kissed her softly. "I remembered him telling me to be proud that I am a Darcy, and I forgot that he meant our history, not our status. I wasted so much time protecting something in his memory that he did not hold dear. I am so grateful that Stewart did not succeed."

"oh."

"Please tell me what you are thinking." He begged. She slipped off of his lap and walked to the door. "Elizabeth!"

"I need to walk. I will go and change my dress."

"You cannot walk alone." He said worriedly.

"I did not say that I would." Elizabeth held out her hand to him and he stood. "I am married now; I need never walk alone again."

"Elizabeth." He took her hand and kissed it.

"I would like to walk around the Serpentine with my husband." She smiled and he visibly relaxed.

"You are not angry?"

"No." She sighed. "Fitzwilliam, the experience with Mr. Stewart forced me to accept many truths about myself and my family, things that I likely would have resisted admitting for years. My opinion of you was never sullied because I did not know the struggle that you faced. I simply thought that fate did not bring us together again."

"But now that you know that I did struggle, that I did stay away, what do you think?"

"I think that time apart matured us both in ways that otherwise may not have come. And the end result is the important fact. When you knew your heart, you did not hesitate. How can I possibly be angry with that? Think only of the past as it gives you pleasure."

Darcy regarded her closely. "You are far too calm."

"Why do you say that?" Elizabeth looked down and clasped her hands and Darcy nodded as he saw the brave front slip.

"I know you, Elizabeth. You say that these experiences matured us, and that is doubtless true, but I cannot help but think that you are feeling fear that my opinion of you might be influenced by outside forces again. You know how close we came to not being married now. Dearest, you do not have to be brave with me."

"What do you want me to say?"

"I do not know. I only want you to know that . . .that you need not fear losing me." Darcy pulled her into his arms and hugged her tightly. "Why you are not berating me for being such a fool is beyond me."

"It would serve no purpose." She buried her face in his shirt. "If I had turned when you saw us walking away and we had seen each other . . ." Darcy's embrace tightened. "You would have come."

"I could not have stayed away." He whispered.

"Things worked as they should." Elizabeth looked up to him and he wiped away the tear that was rolling down her cheek. "Now, come and walk with me."

"But what of the evidence?" He gently touched the mark on her neck and smiled as she regained her composure.

"I have a new lace shawl for my shoulders." She laughed. "And if any of those women speak to us and begin to cluck, I can proudly say that my husband loves me."

"That he does." Darcy hugged her and they started up the stairs.

"However, I beg you to attempt to restrain yourself so that I may heal before this ball. I do want to wear the gown Madame Dupree made for me." Darcy's eyes lit up. "What are you thinking?"

"I am thinking that I will claim every dance."

"Oh, you know that you cannot do that!" She laughed when he slipped his arm around her waist and spun her around the hallway. "Fitzwilliam!"

"We must learn how to waltz together."

"What is that?" She said breathlessly.

"I saw it on the continent. I do not know if it has even reached our shores yet." He laughed. "I do not know really how to do it, but it was scandalous to see."

"Why?" She asked eagerly.

"Dearest, we dance together." He held her the way he had observed in his travels and swayed then turned. "I think that only married couples will be permitted this privilege."

"Then I am grateful to have a husband." She smiled and laughed as he turned her again.

Darcy stopped and kissed her, then brushed her cheek with the back of his fingers. "When was the last time that you had a good long walk?"

"Oh it has been too long. I cannot tell you how I yearn for the countryside. When will we go?"

"Once this ball is through there is no reason to remain here. I am anxious to show you our home." They arrived inside of the mistress's chambers and he looked around, seeing little signals that this space was now occupied. He drew a deep breath. "What is that scent?"

"Lavender. Do you like it? It was a wedding gift from Jane." She entered the dressing room and returned with the bottle. "She said that it was a woman's scent."

"It is, sweet, but seductive." Darcy kissed her. "That is you, my love."

"And what does your scent say of you?" Elizabeth rubbed her cheek on his chest to catch the musky mixture. "It reminds me of the forest after a heavy rain, woodsy."

"Keep this up and we will not be walking." Darcy warned.

"I will not be walking in any case. I feel that I waddle." She walked across the room and back to him. "Does my gait appear as odd as it feels?"

His brow creased. "No, not at all. Why does it feel differently?"

Elizabeth's hands fell on her hips and she stared at him. "Sir, what has been our activity for the past day?"

"Oh." Darcy blushed and grinned. "I did not think of that."

"Selfish, are you not?" She squealed as he grabbed her hand and placed it over his rapidly expanding arousal.

"See, now I will have difficulty walking. Please will we relieve this before we go?" He looked at her hopefully and she smiled, and bent, kissing the hard lump and delighting in his gasp and groan. "Elizabeth!"

She straightened and kissed his mouth softly, then ran her fingers over his shirt, down his stomach, and settling upon his groin where she lightly stroked over him. Darcy's eyes closed as he dropped his head into her hair, and held onto her shoulders. Elizabeth kissed his chest through the open shirt then . . . stepped away. "There, now let us go."

"But . . ." He looked down at his breeches, then to her empty hands and up to her face.

"Yes, dear?" She smiled.

"You cannot leave me like this!"

"Of course I can." She laughed and entered her dressing room. "Fifteen minutes, Mr. Darcy?"

He stood looking after her in disbelief then down at his prominent appendage. He mustered up his dignity and walked awkwardly to his dressing room. "If you think that you have difficulty walking now, my love, just wait until you wake tomorrow!" He growled.

"Did you say something?" She called.

"I certainly did." He replied. The last thing he heard as he closed the door was Elizabeth's laughter.

"WHO WAS THAT MAN?" Captain de Bourgh twisted his neck to catch another glimpse of Mr. Collins as the carriage rolled into the gate at Rosings.

"A candidate for the living at the parsonage. We strongly urge you not to offer it to him."

"Why is that?"

"You are a navy man, do you appreciate sycophants?" Lord Matlock asked. "My son Richard hates them in his own men. He will not grant special consideration to someone who attempts to win his favour without working for it."

"Oh, I understand. Yes, I have experienced a few of those. While it is nice to have someone at your beck and call, that is really the position of my man, not some boy looking for a promotion. Still, there are plenty of officers who rose quickly for just such methods, after all most captains are made through connections, not achievement. I imagine that there is more to it than that though." He turned to regard his new mentor.

"Hmm, yes, he took it upon himself to spread the tales conjured by Anne."

"That I cannot excuse." De Bourgh nodded. "I have a younger brother taking holy orders soon. I shall give the living to him."

"That is good of you."

"Well, we have always got on, and it will be nice to have some family nearby." The carriage rolled around the drive and the house came into view. "My word."

Lord Matlock glanced at Layton and smiled. "It is rather impressive."

"Do you know anything of estate management?" Layton asked.

He laughed at the thought. "Hardly. I was at sea when I was thirteen. The only estates I know are the ones I could spy with a glass from the ship, or perhaps pass to and from London when we were in port." Shaking his head he met Layton's smile. "I am as lost as a frigate in the fog."

Lord Matlock laughed. "The steward is a good man, Darcy's father hired him. We have managed to keep him in place, despite my sister's complaints, and rather close-fisted treatment of her tenants. I am certain that he will be relieved to have you in charge."

"I will do my best." He sighed and looked again at the looming building. "At least we are not far from the sea if I feel a need for some bracing air."

The three men entered the house and were immediately taken in to Lady Catherine. "So this is the heir of Rosings?" She sniffed.

"Catherine, this is your nephew, Captain Peter de Bourgh. He is the son of Lewis' brother, Reginald."

"It is an honour to meet you, Lady Catherine." De Bourgh bowed. "I hope that we will be able to re-establish family ties that I never knew existed. My father died when I was very young, and I am afraid that family tales died with him."

"How did you come to identify this man, Henry?" Lady Catherine looked him over. "How do we know that he is indeed the heir? He might be an imposter."

"Catherine, enough of this, he is the heir."

"Anne may still marry . . ."

"Who?" Layton said angrily. "Who might you try to coerce into that? Oh, some ghoul waiting for her death?"

"Darcy still might, he did leave her with child." She said with her nose in the air. "It is true, and he will do his duty."

Lord Matlock groaned. "If that is true, I will paint my face and join the circus. It is just another fantasy spouted by Anne and encouraged by you, besides none of that matters now. If she is with child and miraculously lives to bear it, it would be a bastard, and the father could be any man. One thing is certain; it is most definitely not Darcy's."

"What do you mean?" Lady Catherine demanded. "Where is Darcy? Why has he not come?"

"Darcy has better things to do with his time." Layton smiled. "Do you not agree, Father?"

"I would. You met Mrs. Darcy, de Bourgh, do you not find her lovely?" Lord Matlock winked at him.

"I do. Charming and lovely." He smiled at Lady Catherine, he had waited to meet her before forming an opinion but now, he knew just what to do. "Your new niece is an asset to the family and will bring much happiness to my cousin, I am certain."

"What is this?" Lady Catherine looked from one man to the next. "What are you saying?"

"Darcy married Miss Elizabeth Bennet yesterday." Lord Matlock smiled. "It is done, Catherine. Irrevocably." He watched her face fall. "And no, Richard will not marry Anne either. Now, I would like to visit my niece. I understand that she is much calmer now that the fever is gone, but that she is very weak. De Bourgh will be resigning his commission and coming to live here. Since Anne is well, you will take your place in the dower's house, as she has demanded, and he will assume the duties of master, and care for her."

"No!"

"Yes." Lord Matlock said sternly. "You have no say in this. She is the mistress of the estate, not you. She has ordered you out, and out you will go."

"You have no control of Rosings! You are not the master!" She screeched.

"Catherine, I said that he would assume the duties, I did not say that he *was* master. As you have proven without a doubt that you are incapable of caring for your daughter, and she clearly wishes you to be gone, it only makes sense that de Bourgh come to stay here, as an invited family member, and help to care for Anne through her final days."

"Invited by Anne?"

"No, by me." Lord Matlock said quietly. "If Anne were to be found incompetent, you know that the court would appoint me as her guardian, not you."

"Because I am a woman." She said bitterly. "How dare Darcy defy me! He was taken in by that fortune hunter. I hope that he regrets his choice and they live for a very long time."

"I almost felt sympathy for you Catherine, but that last statement dashed it away." He turned to de Bourgh. "Well, you now see what you will contend with. Would you prefer to return to the sea?"

He looked between the two siblings then bowed to Lady Catherine. "I should move in within the month, madam." He examined the room. "I will bring my mother and sisters with me, and they will look after Miss de Bourgh. Perhaps they will have some suggestions on the decoration."

Layton contained his smile and looked at his father who did not bother to hide his. "Shall we visit Anne, Cousin?"

"Thank you." The two young men left Lord Matlock with his sister.

"You know, it did not have to be this way. You encouraged Anne's delusions for years. I have no doubt that your whispering about Darcy is what fixated her mind on him. She may have always been weak and likely come to this end, but it is your fault that she is so ill in her mind. Ending in the dower's house is your justice. George Darcy told you to leave his son alone. I am proud of Darcy for making his choice to marry Elizabeth, and not allowing your false claims of duty to sway him. Yes, there are rumours flying through Town, but they will die one by one. And you sister, will end alone."

"Why must I leave Rosings?" She demanded. "My place is with my daughter."

"You gave up your rights as a mother when you began using her to forward your desires. If I had known the extent of her illness and your manipulation of it, I would have become her guardian years ago. I will regret failing Anne to the end of my days." Lord Matlock said quietly. "Within the month, Sister." He bowed and went upstairs to join the others. Lady Catherine was left alone in her throne-like chair, with nothing but the ticking clock to break the oppressive silence.

"You look well, Anne." Layton took her frail hand and smiled. "I am glad to see you feeling better."

"Thank you, Cousin." She whispered, and blinked up at de Bourgh. "Do I know you?"

"No, but I am happy to know you at last. I am your cousin Peter de Bourgh."

"I do not remember hearing of you."

"I am the son of your father's brother Reginald." De Bourgh smiled. "I will be coming to stay here in a few weeks. My mother and sisters will come to keep you company as well."

"Oh . . . I have not hosted guests before. Mother always did."

"That is fine, Cousin Anne. We will be no trouble. You just feel better."

Anne nodded and saw her uncle enter the room. "Uncle Henry." He smiled and kissed her hollow cheek. "Where is my husband?"

"Now you know that you are not married, Anne." He said sternly.

"I am not?" Her brow furrowed. "I was sure that I was." Lord Matlock glanced at the men around him then caught Mrs. Jenkinson's eye. She was smiling. "It was just a dream that you had. Darcy married a very nice young woman yesterday. He is very happy."

"He is?" She asked bemusedly. "But Mama told me that . . ."

"No dear, your mother was incorrect." He kissed her again and patted her hand. "You look tired, take some rest." She nodded and settled back in the pillows. The men left and Mrs. Jenkinson followed them out. "She is much different. The change in treatment is clearly effective."

"That and removing her mother's influence. She never comes to see her anymore."

"She sleeps only two doors away!" Layton cried.

"Anne has served her purpose Son, and it was a failure. Your aunt has no further use for her." Lord Matlock said quietly. He turned to de Bourgh. "Now you might understand why I feel no remorse towards her and have encouraged you to take your place. As you can see, the end is inevitable."

"I do. How long does my cousin have, do you think? She seems on death's doorstep now." They looked to Mrs. Jenkinson and she shrugged.

"It could come at anytime. She could linger this way or simply drift away. She has rallied before, we simply do not know. I am just happy to see that she is not suffering anymore. I know that you told her she is not married to Mr. Darcy, but truly sir, does it do her harm to believe it now?"

"I suppose not. I will be glad to know that her final days will be ones of peace." Lord Matlock said sadly. "I will be glad to reassure Darcy that he did the right thing in marrying Elizabeth, and I hope that Richard is happy with his decision as well." He looked around the halls of the old manor. "He was correct; of course, this place belongs to the de Bourghs. The Fitzwilliam who came to live here did it no favours."

"I disagree sir; you brought it back to my family. I never would have known were it not for your efforts." De Bourgh smiled and drew a deep breath. "Well, I have returned from the sea to live on the land."

"Let us see what you can make of it."

"MR. BENNET, HOW CAN YOU LEAVE here in Mr. Darcy's carriage and return by ours?" Mrs. Bennet demanded. "What have you done?"

"Done, Mrs. Bennet?" He stepped down from the carriage and frowned. "Why should Mr. Darcy bear the cost of transporting us home as well? It was generous of your brother to send us halfway and simple for our man to meet us at the inn." He looked at Mary who nodded and scurried inside. "Come Wife, we have need of conversation."

She followed him into the bookroom. "I suppose that you have found some terrible school for Mary. I disagree with this most vehemently, Mr. Bennet! If Lizzy can catch a man without this schooling, so can the other girls! And what of the funds you will waste? It will leave far less for our girls, and you know that they will all soon be out and will need new wardrobes."

Mr. Bennet closed the door and took his seat. "Mrs. Bennet please sit down."

She sighed and took a seat. "What is this about? I have much too much to accomplish! Lizzy is to be married in a few weeks!"

"No, she is not."

"WHAT! What did she do? I knew that she would ruin it somehow! Could she not at least have married him first before driving him away? You should have brought me with you!" She began fluttering her handkerchief and moaning. "What will become of us?"

"Calm yourself!" He demanded. "Mrs. Bennet, Lizzy married Mr. Darcy three days ago."

Mrs. Bennet's movements stopped. "What did you say?"

"She is married. Mary and I witnessed it. Mr. Darcy needs to return to his estate quickly and they decided to marry as soon as he returned."

"But . . . But she did not come here to get her things, I . . . I did not get to show her off to the neighbours! And Mr. Darcy, nobody has seen him!"

"And they likely will not see him." Mr. Bennet said quietly. "They will stop here on their way to Pemberley next week. Briefly. Mr. Darcy is allowing it purely as a concession to Elizabeth's wishes to say goodbye to her sisters."

"But . . ."

"No Mrs. Bennet. Our daughter is a married woman now, and she will follow her husband's will. He is very unhappy with us. He is angry with our behaviour in his home, and our neglect of our daughters. Most of all he is angry with your berating of Elizabeth and my amusement with it. I was permitted to walk Elizabeth to him in church, but I was treated as a guest at her wedding breakfast. It was a terribly humbling experience, and one that I will never forget. Again, it was Lizzy's desire that I be present that allowed me the honour of giving her away."

"You knew they were to marry before you left?" She cried angrily.

"I did, and I knew that you were not welcome."

"Why? I am her mother!"

"When have you ever done anything but tell her she was unfit?" Mr. Bennet shook his head. "No, it is my fault for allowing it to continue, and allowing you to educate them. You had no education yourself, so you could not prepare our girls for the world they might enter. The Gardiners deserve the credit for that. Mary will begin school in October. Jane will remain in London for as long as she wishes. I have given Gardiner funds for her keep. Our other daughters will not be permitted to come out until they are seventeen."

"That is ridiculous, Mr. Bennet, the girls must be married as soon as possible! If Mr. Darcy dies, who will take care of us? That Mr. Harwick used Jane ill. He promised to marry her!"

"He promised to court her and consider the notion. Our behaviour; and Jane admitted to me, her own, drove him away." He sighed and Mrs. Bennet stared at him with her mouth agape. "Yes, Mrs. Bennet. We seem to have driven away Mr. Stewart and Mr. Harwick. Is it not fortunate that Mr. Darcy met Lizzy outside of our influence?"

"She is Mrs. Darcy?" Mrs. Bennet confirmed.

"She is. She is the mistress of Pemberley at the tender age of seventeen."

"We are saved!" She jumped up and left the room. "Hill! Hill! Where is my bonnet! Call for the carriage! I must visit Mrs. Philips!"

"One moment, madam!" Mr. Bennet called. She returned and stood in the doorway. "Please return to your seat."

"What is it, Mr. Bennet? I must tell my sister of our good fortune!"

"Mrs. Bennet. I have given you freedom to spend the household income as you wished. That will be no more. In order to send the girls to school, we will need to save in other areas. I cannot afford to employ a governess for Lydia and Kitty, so I will expect you to sit down with them and read for at least an hour a day, and we will discuss your assignments at dinner each night. With any luck it might broaden your knowledge as well. Hopefully it is not too late to save them. I am counting on Mrs. Gardiner to help Jane."

"This is ridiculous!" Mrs. Bennet cried. "Reading a book will not help our girls to catch a man!"

"It certainly helped Lizzy." He said quietly. "And she is the daughter who is married." She could not think of an argument to counter that so she left the room, calling for the carriage once again. Mr. Bennet closed his eyes and listened to his wife's voice receding into the background. Nothing he had said made an impact on her. "And now it is up to me, as my brother said." He heard Lydia and Kitty exclaiming over Elizabeth's good fortune and wondering when she would bring them to London. "Never, if her husband has anything to say of it." He said softly. "It will be fortunate enough if he takes care of you when I am gone."

"CAN YOU BELIEVE THIS?" Caroline shook the paper at Wickham. "Mr. Darcy was not married to his cousin! Charles was speaking the truth!"

Wickham took the wedding notice from her hand and narrowed his eyes. "So, he married her. Again, Darcy gets exactly what he wants."

"I do not understand." Caroline said when she grabbed the paper back and stared in disbelief. "Why would he want this girl? She has nothing! His cousin had another estate! If he was not to marry her, you would think that he would at least take an heiress." She huffed and Wickham rolled his eyes.

You mean he would not take you. He thought and wondered what to do next. Caroline was not a woman to be rushed off to Gretna Green, she was much sharper than her brother when it came to marriage. Her anger with Darcy was useful, he might tell her his sad tale of mistreatment one day, but for now his presumed connection to Pemberley and the first circles is what had her interested in him. He could not make her doubt his friendship with Darcy until he had married her, and of course after a suitable honeymoon, disappeared with her dowry. As he pondered the question Bingley appeared and startled him out of his reverie.

"What are you talking about so heatedly, Caroline? You might scare your suitor away!" Bingley laughed and smiled at Wickham as he took his seat. "I do hope that is not the case, sir."

"Oh no, certainly not. We were just noting that you were correct; Darcy did indeed marry Miss Elizabeth."

A wide smile appeared and Bingley chuckled as he sat back and crossed his legs. "It was a joyful ceremony; the two of them were oblivious to all who were asked to bear witness. I was honoured with his invitation."

Caroline's head snapped up. "You were at Mr. Darcy's wedding? Why did you not say something? Mr. Wickham, should you not have been at the nuptials?"

"I have not been in close contact with Darcy since his father died, and I know of his private nature." Wickham soothed her.

Bingley smiled and nodded. "As I said Caroline, only a few were asked to come, and it was even fewer who were invited to Matlock House for the wedding breakfast."

"Of course, the Fitzwilliams." Wickham said softly.

"Why, do you know them as well? I imagine you would know them from their visits to Pemberley! Colonel Fitzwilliam is quite impressive in his uniform;

he did an excellent job moving the groom from his bed to the altar I understand, though I imagine that his sword was not necessary!" Bingley chuckled as Wickham's eyes widened. "I look forward to spending time with the new Darcys, but I think that they will be well out of circulation for quite an extended period, if I can draw anything from the way Darcy hurried his bride out of Matlock House!"

Wickham nodded in agreement and noted Caroline's disappointed expression. He clearly needed to move before the Darcys emerged from their secluded honeymoon, and surely that gave him no more than a month. The time to act was now. Turning to Caroline, he delivered his most charming smile. "All of this talk of weddings and hearing of Darcy's joy has put me in mind to think of my own happiness. Miss Bingley, may I speak to you privately?"

"ELIZABETH, WOULD YOU HELP ME, PLEASE?" Darcy looked across his desk to her and she smiled from behind the pile of invitations she was reading. "I have never done well with reading Bingley's notes. I am always certain that I miss something. Can you decipher this?" He handed her the heavily blotched and nearly illegible sheet and she laughed.

"Did a child of three pen this?" She held it up and turned it, laughing harder and squinting. Looking up she saw her husband's eyes twinkling at her, it had seemingly become a permanent fixture of his expression over the past week of their solitude. "How can a grown man be so careless?"

"I will not begin to try and explain his schooling dearest, I only ask for interpretation." Darcy reached across the corner of the desk to hold her hand while she read.

"I believe . . .my goodness! Miss Bingley is engaged!" She looked up to see his surprise.

"Well does he mention the man's name? He never has managed to reveal his identity."

Elizabeth shook her head and giggled. "It looks like . . . Oh, I cannot say what it looks like. Let us call him Mr. W and hope for a proper introduction on Thursday night."

"What is Thursday night?"

"The engagement dinner." She smiled. "We should go. We will be receiving callers beginning Monday, and it will be safe for you to call at Mr. Bingley's home now. Miss Bingley will have no interest in you."

"That is true. I have avoided Bingley's invitations, and I do feel badly about not going to his home."

Elizabeth squeezed his hand. "He knew why, Fitzwilliam. Perhaps that is why he was so eager to notify you and explains the illegible note." She smiled and Darcy laughed.

"No, that is kind of you to say, but I am afraid it is not the case. He is hopeless." Slowly caressing her hand he sighed. "I do not look forward to next week."

"No, I know that you do not. I cannot say that I anticipate it either." She looked up at him. "Aunt Helen promised to come and help me through the visits."

"I will be with you." He reassured her. "I would not let you face this alone."

"Thank you." She set down Bingley's letter, and responding easily to the tug of his hand, moved to curl up on his lap. "You should probably return to your normal activities as well."

Darcy kissed her and smiled. "What exactly are those?"

"I am not sure." Elizabeth looked at him worriedly. "Surely you must have regular habits?"

"Yes, but . . . I am not terribly social. I would drop by the club briefly but not to spend the day, and generally it was for business." Darcy hugged her. "Are you wishing me gone so that you can begin to enjoy the privileges of married women?"

"What exactly are those?"

"You mean besides the obvious?"

"Are you referring to yourself?" Elizabeth snuggled into him, and listened to his rumbling chuckle. "Oh I love how much you laugh now."

"I do, too." Darcy kissed her forehead, and when she smiled up to him, tasted her lips for a slow, soft exchange. They both sighed and held each other tighter. "Is it not obvious my love, that my preferred companion will always be you?"

"I feel the same way about you." She looked up and they kissed again. Darcy's hand slipped beneath her gown, and he gently stroked her hip and thigh as they spoke. "I just did not want to keep you from your friends."

"I do not have that many, dear. I have you. I have always wanted to have you." He touched her hair and caressed her cheek. "I do not wish to live the life that society expects, do you?"

"I admit that I have no idea what that is." Elizabeth laughed. "Your aunt has not progressed so far in my lessons. Our premature wedding ended them early, I fear."

"I am glad of that. We may forge our own path. Do you mind?"

"No, I like the sound of that very much. So what is our plan? Are you to be the great explorer and I; your trusty companion?"

"That sounds interesting. You have the ebony locks of a mysterious native guide." Darcy wrapped a curl around his finger, "Shall I call you Sacajawea?"

"Are you Lewis or Clark?" Elizabeth giggled, and he smiled, loving that she knew what he had referenced. "Shall we explore Pemberley and map it out together?"

"Now that is something I never did as a boy. Even Richard, the instigator of all adventures, did not suggest such a thing. However, we must begin with your riding lessons."

"Ah, so true."

"Did you know how arousing your letter to me was?" He whispered. "When you wrote of sharing my mount?"

"What did I say?"

"I will demonstrate it for you when we arrive at home." Darcy kissed her. "Frequently."

"Oh." Elizabeth blushed and he hugged her. "It is too bad that we cannot have more time like this, just the two of us. I have read your letters Fitzwilliam, so many want your time."

"I know." Darcy rested his cheek in her hair. "We have two social engagements that we must attend. I must address the meetings I have put off, and then we will depart for home, but when we arrive my love, we will resume what we have begun. Georgiana will not join us for three weeks; she will travel with the Matlock party."

Elizabeth lifted her head. "When was this decided?"

"Uncle mentioned it when he wrote of the trip to Rosings. He said to consider it a honeymoon gift." Darcy laughed to see her blush again. "Georgiana was happy to agree."

"I am looking forward to knowing my new sister, but I admit, I like the idea of knowing my new husband even better." She touched his face and he leaned into her caress. "Fitzwilliam?"

"hmm?" He closed his eyes and kissed her palm, still gently caressing his hand beneath her skirt.

"Do you remember in my letter, I wrote about wanting to taste you?"

Darcy's hand stilled and he said shakily, "yes."

She pressed her lips to his ear and whispered. "I still do."

Chapter 29

"Shoulders back, Elizabeth." Lady Matlock directed. "We are going into battle."

"Yes, Aunt Helen." She bit her lip and met Darcy's eye.

"They will be curious, my love, but not openly rude." He said quietly. "It is a formality of married life."

"And you must then drop your cards off around town. Of course, I will accompany you on that. Not just anybody will receive notice from Mrs. Darcy." Lady Matlock was staring out of the sitting room door, listening to the sounds of the guests arriving, and did not notice Elizabeth's smile. Darcy did and suppressed his chuckle. *That* the grande dame did notice. "Darcy, control yourself."

"Forgive me, Aunt." He straightened and squeezed Elizabeth's hand. "I believe that Elizabeth is still rather unimpressed with her status as my wife."

"I am?" She asked with surprise. "According to whom?"

"You do not attend me with awe."

"No, when you are behaving pompously, I feel that laughter is the best response."

"Elizabeth, wit and laughter are frowned upon strongly in our society." Lady Matlock turned to her and spoke seriously. "Please remember that."

"Why?" She turned to Darcy, "Is it unattractive?"

"No, that is what first drew my attention to you." He looked at his aunt. "Perhaps the absolute absence of it in our society is the reason."

"Proper behaviour for ones of our status is to smile slightly and nod. Great expressions of emotion are seen as crass. Observe and learn." She looked back to the door.

Elizabeth looked worriedly at Darcy and he smiled reassuringly. "Remember how Jane behaves?"

"I am to be like her?"

"Perhaps you should be like me before we married." He kissed her hand. "Dour."

She smiled and he squeezed the hand he still held. "Do not hold her hand, Darcy." Lady Matlock said quietly.

Darcy looked at the hand in his grasp, then up to see fear appear in Elizabeth's eyes. "No, Aunt. They will accept or reject us, but we will be ourselves."

The footman appeared to announce the first visitors and the trio stood. Over the next two hours there was an unending stream, some staying long enough to transmit congratulations and depart, some wished to interview Elizabeth, some wished to observe their behaviour, but mostly it was the curious, the gossip-hungry, and the jealous. When the last guest left, Elizabeth's frozen smile fell away, and Darcy drew her into his arms to kiss her cheek and close his eyes.

"Those were not friends, were they?"

"No, I sent notes around to our friends, telling them that we will see them at the ball." He kissed her again. "I surmised that this day would be exactly as it was."

"You did very well, Elizabeth." Lady Matlock said with an approving nod. "I saw that every eye was drawn to your clasped hands, but your performance was admirable and elegant. You were an excellent hostess. May I ask, who taught you these skills?"

"Because it surely was not my mother?" Lady Matlock did not attempt to disagree and Elizabeth smiled a little as Darcy hugged her. "I watched my aunt."

"I will write her a note of congratulations for her success." Lady Matlock smiled. "Now then, we have the ball in two days. I expect you to spend the day with me and your cousins tomorrow. Darcy, you are to leave us alone."

He laughed. "I am not permitted to visit and observe?"

"No, and you will leave us alone Wednesday morning as well. I am sure that you have neglected business to address. Elizabeth has much to accomplish. You are not welcome."

Darcy sighed and smiled at her sadly. "I am afraid that I must leave you. Will you be well?"

"Of course, I feel completely safe in the bosom of your family."

"Our family." He raised her hand to his lips. "I will miss you."

"Oh Darcy, it is not a week of travel! Both of you have your roles to fulfil and they will not always be together. Most wives would be glad to be rid of their husbands." Lady Matlock declared and stood. "Eleven tomorrow, Elizabeth. Good and early."

"Early?" She stopped her laugh when Lady Matlock looked at her sternly. "Forgive me; I am yet to become accustomed to town hours."

"I am the same, dearest. I assure you, Pemberley does not follow them." He smiled to see her relief. "I will not sleep the day away when my people are working."

"Do you work with them? Do you pull weeds and plough fields?" Elizabeth teased.

"I do not." His lips twitched. "However I do have new seed to plant."

Lady Matlock cleared her throat to gain the attention of the newlyweds before they forgot themselves. "Good afternoon, children."

Elizabeth and Darcy both startled and blushed. "Thank you Aunt." He kissed her cheek. "It would not have been nearly the success it was without you."

"You two have a long way to go before you recover from all of the gossip. You must do well at the ball." She looked at them humourlessly. "Then you may go home and . . .do whatever it is you do with each other."

Elizabeth studied her feet and Darcy smiled happily. "We will."

At last Lady Matlock relaxed and smiled. "I can hardly comprehend your joy, it is clearly beyond me, and I consider myself to be happily married. I hope that my daughters capture a bit of this glow you carry with you, Elizabeth."

"I do as well." Elizabeth looked to Darcy and let go of his hand. "May I see you out?"

"Of course." Lady Matlock waited and followed her to the door. When they arrived, she took Elizabeth's hand and smiled. "You did very well, if you can hold up to such an inquisition at this age, I can only imagine what will happen when you and Darcy have been married a few years."

"As long as he is pleased . . ."

"Dear, I cannot imagine him being otherwise."

5 JULY 1809

I am sitting across from the loveliest, most delightful woman. She is writing studiously in her journal and shooting curious smiles at me. I am endeavouring to keep her guessing my thoughts, however, how she can wonder at them is a mystery. My sweet wife's cheeks still carry the blush of our lovemaking. I am delighted to have so successfully affected her.

She is gaining a little more confidence, she ranges from bold to painfully shy. It surprises me that at times she can tease me mercilessly, and leave me in such a state that I dare not reveal myself to a servant much less step from the house! But then I might simply touch the back of her neck with my lips, and she nearly melts into my arms. I could write of her forever, and I imagine that the pages of my journal will always be filled with the joy of her. I have never been so happy.

Tonight is the Creary Ball. We will meet our equals, be introduced as Mr. and Mrs. Fitzwilliam Darcy, and face the society that likely gossiped eagerly about us over the past months. Some are friends, but most are simply the society we are forced to know. I felt so terrible for Elizabeth, following in Aunt Helen's formidable wake as they paid calls. I am grateful for Aunt's attention; it is in no small part due to her condescension that Elizabeth is being received as well as she is. Alicia has agreed to accompany Elizabeth the rest of the week to make calls following the ball. Audrey will surely come as well. I am very grateful for my family's acceptance.

"Elizabeth!" Darcy cried when a small wad of paper plopped into his inkpot and splashed onto his journal.

She covered her mouth and giggled. "Oh, I am so sorry Fitzwilliam! I missed!"

"Missed?" He checked his cuff to see if it was stained. "A perfect strike, I would say."

"I was aiming for your nose." She laughed to see his surprise. "How I missed amazes me, it is an impressive target!"

"Elizabeth!" She laughed harder and he set down his pen to come around to her chair. "I demand recompense for your insult!"

"I love your nose!" She squealed as his arms closed around her and he began tickling. Elizabeth fought him. "Please, stop!" She gasped.

He relented and growled. "You will not insult my handsome features again?"

"Not in front of you." The tickling resumed. "Will!"

He stopped. "Will?"

"Sometimes I call you Will."

"When?"

"When you are behaving like a little boy." She laughed.

"Very well, little Lizzy. I will keep that in mind." He kissed her, then when she was looking up at him, reached over and snatched up her journal. "Now, what have we here?"

"Fitzwilliam! NO!" She stood and tried to grab it out of his hands, but being far too tall he merely smiled and held it over her head to read. "I will read yours!"

"Go ahead." He offered and watched as she was torn between the two books. Chuckling, he turned back to see what she had written.

5 July 1809

Today is our fifteenth day of marriage. I am so happy; I have never known how good it feels to be completely loved. I hate our time apart, although I certainly understand his need to care for business before we depart, and my need to establish my place in society, I am selfish and want all of my time to be with him. Our reunions can only be described as joyous. I cannot wait to go to Pemberley, be away from the rules and constraints of society and simply love him. He needs to be loved, he clings to me so. I have so many ideas of ways to please him, I am afraid that in the space of fifteen days I have become quite wanton in my thoughts. I find myself sitting in a room full of women, Lady Matlock's approved smile fixed upon my lips, and my mind is in our bedchamber. I imagine that I am looking at my unclothed husband, and drawing my hand down over his glorious body. His skin is so taut and smooth; I become quite undone simply with the sight of him, but the privilege to touch and kiss such beauty is one I will never take for granted. I am overwhelmed that he continues to call me lovely. I am grateful for his wilful blindness. I love him so.

"Elizabeth." Darcy lowered her journal to see her smiling over his. "I please you?"

"Completely."

Darcy stood looking at her with a silly happy smile gracing his lips and Elizabeth became flustered and shy. She looked around his desk and spotted Bingley's miserable excuse for a letter. "Did you confirm our attendance at Mr. Bingley's dinner for tomorrow?"

He blinked and focussed. "No, I do not believe that I did." He picked her up from his chair, dropped her into her own, and resumed his throne with a grin. "I will do that now."

"He would probably appreciate that." She said wryly. "I should go upstairs and begin preparing for tonight."

"Must you? I have some ideas to add to your imagination." He ducked when another little wad of paper was aimed at him. "We will have to practice your aim."

"Does it snow in Derbyshire?"

He chuckled. "Yes, my love, it does." She raised her brows and nodded, then left the room with a swirl of her skirts. Darcy stared at the empty doorway happily, imagining kissing snowflakes from her reddened cheeks, then with a sigh, began a note to Bingley.

"LOUISA." BINGLEY CALLED. "You will need to set two more places for dinner tomorrow. The Darcys have confirmed."

"Well that is a bit late, although, I imagine that they have been preoccupied." She smiled and caught the twinkle in her brother's eye.

"I can well imagine." Bingley said as he read the note and chuckled. "Even in this he gives advice, asking if I have seen a settlement document yet. I admit that it had not crossed my mind until Hurst mentioned it when they became engaged."

"Charles!" Louisa gasped.

"Well what do I know of these things? He must be doing well; he dresses as a gentlemen and attends university. He said he would bring it by today, and that it contains everything that we need to know."

"What else do we know of him? Caroline will not hear of me questioning anything of her *dear Mr. Wickham*." Louisa said quietly. "I know that he is the most charming man of my acquaintance, but Charles, he mentions no family."

"I understand that they are deceased." He mused, looking over Darcy's neatly penned letter.

"Then why does he not own his father's home?"

"He never mentioned one. He grew up on Pemberley in his father's house, perhaps they leased it. His father may have been one of the more prosperous tenants; there are some very wealthy ones at Pemberley. However, I believe his fortune is mainly derived from a bequest by Darcy's father." Bingley's eyes lit up. "I never told Darcy Wickham's first name, I am sure that he does not realize this is the man he knows so well or he would have mentioned it in his note! Let us leave this as a surprise on all sides, Louisa. Do not tell Caroline that the Darcys will attend."

"Charles!"

"It will be a reunion!"

"Caroline is hardly feeling charitable towards Mr. Darcy for rejecting her, not that he ever so much as danced with her. Such a delusion she had over him! Oh the invectives I heard from her mouth when she learned he had married Miss Elizabeth! You would think that she had been jilted herself!" Louisa shook her head, "And yet nearly in the same breath she speaks of him highly."

Bingley listened and became serious. "Maybe that is part of our blindness over Mr. Wickham's prospects, we are grateful that anyone would take her. Why is it that he is her only offer, Louisa? I do not understand. I read letters from lovelorn gentlemen seeking wives in the paper daily, and they seem quite ready to accept a lady with funds as long as she does not resemble the backside of a mare."

"Charles!"

He shrugged. "Go ahead and deny it. I have heard you and Caroline cackling over them."

"Our sister is rather mercenary, but I suppose that should not be a surprise, she was much influenced by our parent's desire to rise far above our roots, more so than I, and even you I suspect." The siblings shared a knowing glance. No man of our circle would meet her desires, no man below is good enough, and she has no opportunity to meet any above. Until Mr. Wickham, who is charming, wealthy, and has a connection to Mr. Darcy."

"I suppose my friendship was not enough for her." Bingley sighed. "I would not promote her to him, and he is happier for it."

"She will not speak of her plans to me, I only know that she is obsessed with the life she envisions having with her infallible Mr. Wickham."

"I suppose that is an admirable way for a wife to view her husband?" Bingley's lips rose in a grin. "Just as you view Hurst?" Louisa rolled her eyes and he laughed. "He will likely return to himself when Caroline is gone, Louisa."

"You have not heard of him discouraging the match, have you?" Louisa smiled and departed the room. Bingley carried Darcy's note over to his desk and furrowed his brow over the perfect penmanship. "How do you do that, man?"

"HOW COULD I POSSIBLY have mistaken him for you?" Elizabeth whispered as she looked out upon the ballroom at the Creary's home. Darcy was standing by her side, his hand laying over hers on his arm. Their fingers were entwined and his thumb was brushing her wrist slowly. Looking down to her, he realized that she was not actually speaking to him. "He has your height, and perhaps his shoulders are as broad, but . . ."

"Elizabeth." He said quietly and she startled. "What are you doing?"

"Oh." She blushed. "I suppose that I am not listening to my own advice."

"We are here now, we are married." He leaned to whisper in her ear, "And if I am not mistaken, Lord Creary was very taken with your looks."

"Old goat." Elizabeth laughed.

"Elizabeth!" His grip tightened, but he was smiling. "So I am in no danger of losing you to him? I need not call him out?"

"The host of the *The* ball of the Season?" She giggled as his eyes rolled. "Why is this ball so important?"

"Because, my love, we are here." He winked and felt her lean against him. "I just know that everybody who is anybody has been invited. Personally, I look forward to leaving."

"I enjoy dancing, but I would rather not be critiqued for it." She watched the people milling about. "Fitzwilliam, look, do you see Mr. Harwick?"

Darcy lifted his chin and tilted his head. "Ah."

"What is it?"

"He is smiling, it is good to see."

"With Miss Stewart." Elizabeth whispered. "I thought that they would do well together."

"What do you mean?" Darcy startled. "When did you think this?"

"It was perfectly obvious that they were drawn to each other at the theatre. Did you not see it?"

"I did, but I thought that it was better not to mention, considering the circumstances."

She sighed. "I know. I had so much hope for Jane, but seeing Mr. Harwick here, I know that Jane is better off without him. No more secure, but, oh I do not know. I want her to be as happy as I am someday, and as dear as Mr. Harwick likely was with his wife, I do not think that Jane would have inspired the smile he is wearing now for Miss Stewart." Darcy was looking at her with a little smile on his lips. "What are you thinking?"

"Your ability to forgive is astounding."

"I have not always been this way." She said softly. "I would nurse wounds to my pride and vanity, rather than try to understand why they were hurt." Darcy followed her eyes and saw that she was staring at Creary. When he looked again, he noticed that her gaze had shifted to Stewart.

"Well Mr. and Mrs. Darcy, it is time to begin the dancing, and as our newlyweds, it is up to you to lead off." Lady Creary directed them forward to the dance floor. The eyes of the room were upon them, the conversation turned to whispers and speculation. Elizabeth tried not to hear but could not help but catch the snippets as they passed.

Darcy leaned down and spoke softly. "Ignore them."

"It is so difficult." She said quietly.

"I know, my love. I am a little more used to it than you, but I hate it. Just look at me. Concentrate on the music and look at me."

They lined up and waited for the others to take their places. Elizabeth heard a woman behind her say loudly that she wondered at Darcy marrying a girl so young and poor, and another asking if she noticed any signs of a pending child. She glanced down at the tightly fitted bodice of her gown and bit her lip. If she were indeed with child, it was certainly not for very long. Another woman said to her companion that Darcy was a fool to give up Rosings for Elizabeth, whatever self-confidence she had when entering the room was beginning to dissipate quickly. Audrey squeezed into the line beside her and grasped her hand.

"Ignore them." She whispered. Elizabeth nodded and kept looking at her shoes. Audrey glanced up to notice Darcy's attention and nudged her. "Look up."

Elizabeth lifted her head to find her husband's unbreakable gaze upon her face. He was smiling in a way that she knew was reserved solely for her. "I love you." He mouthed. The music began and without thinking, Elizabeth stepped forward to take his hand. During the course of the next quarter hour, the Darcys danced to their own tune. Their movements were mimicked by all of the others, but none could match the ebb and flow of their graceful steps, or imagine the feeling that passed between them with each touch, each glance. When the notes drifted away and the participants stopped to clap, different conversations sprang up around Elizabeth. Darcy's eyes remained fixed upon hers; a slight smile lifted his lips. She fell into his deep blue gaze, and only barely registered the new comments of how calf-eyed her husband was, and how well they performed together.

Audrey kept looking between the two, and did not dare break the connection between them. Instead she glanced to her husband and found him gazing wistfully at her. When he noticed her attention he nodded to Darcy and then looked at Elizabeth, and back to her, questioning her. When the next song began and they stepped together, Singleton said softly as they held hands. "I find myself wishing for their happiness."

"That they be happy?"

"No Audrey, that we be happy." He squeezed her hand and they moved apart to change partners. Singleton took Elizabeth's hand and smiled warmly at her. "I believe that any doubts over you will be banished tonight."

"Do you?" She blushed. "I do not want to fail him."

Singleton laughed. "Cousin Elizabeth, he would never notice."

Darcy turned Audrey and smiled at her, speaking softly. "He is improved, I think."

"The debt collectors have all been paid." She whispered as he bent his head. "We are beginning anew."

"Will you allow him to try? You are a lovely woman, Audrey. Holding a grudge against a man who is reforming will not sit well with you." Darcy let her go and passing her back to her husband, reclaimed his wife. "We need to dance much more often, my love."

"Perhaps we can coax Georgiana to play for us at Pemberley so we can dance at home?"

"I am certain that she would enjoy that. We have a musical bird."

"A canary?"

"No, no, a mechanical bird that sings, and I brought home from Geneva a small device that plays a song. I know of a man in Switzerland who is working to make a larger device that plays songs continuously. I wrote to him and have placed an order, whenever he is ready to sell."

"How is this possible?" Elizabeth asked as they spun around.

"I . . .it is difficult to explain on a dance floor, dearest." Darcy laughed. "How on earth did we find this topic?"

"Is it not better than the weather?" She laughed with him.

"I believe that speaking of nearly any topic would be fascinating with you." The song ended and they returned to the side. "That was the most wonderful dance!"

"Better than the waltz we are practicing alone in our rooms?" She whispered and giggled.

"Well, I shall rephrase that; it was the most wonderful country dance." He leaned down to her ear. "Your eyes are sparkling like diamonds, my love."

"When do we dance next?"

"Not until the supper set." He kissed her hand. "I hope that it is slow."

"I would like a slow dance when we return home tonight." She bit her lip and blushed. Darcy squeezed her hand hard and breathed warmly into her ear. "Oh yes, dearest. So would I."

"Who will be your partners tonight, Fitzwilliam?"

"The wives of your partners." He said softly. "No single ladies."

"But you are married now, you are safe." Elizabeth laughed.

"I am, but I have no desire to do otherwise. I prefer to watch you, and wait for my turn." Darcy kissed her hand and then entwined their fingers when he rested it back on his arm. "Have I thanked you yet today for marrying me?"

Elizabeth touched the ruby necklace he had given her before they departed and blushed. "I believe that you did."

Singleton approached the couple and bowed. "Audrey was to dance the next with you Darcy, but she is not feeling well, do you mind if we sit this one out?" He turned to Elizabeth, "Forgive me for giving up our set, I do not wish to leave her."

"I am very happy to sit out a set for such a good purpose. Go ahead, I do not mind." Elizabeth watched him go then found Darcy looking after him as well. "What do you think?"

"I am hopeful." He turned back to take her hand. "Well my love, shall we dance again?"

"Is that not against all of the rules?"

"Probably, but we shall blame it on the joy of our honeymoon, my smitten foolishness, and your bewitching figure." Darcy tilted his head. "I would rather be gossiped about for being a man in love than for anything else the crème of society can determine."

Elizabeth wrapped her hand around his arm and leaned against him. "We have enough gossip to contend with; perhaps some punch would be a better plan." She looked up to his warm eyes and saw his lips twitching. "What are you plotting, Husband?"

"I have not seen you trying the punch yet."

"Do you plan to see me drunk?" She cried.

Darcy whispered so that his warm breath moved the loose strands of hair along her throat. "No, I hope to see you very, very relaxed, and then relax you even further upon returning home." Elizabeth blushed and gasped when his lips brushed lightly over her ear before he straightened. He watched the colour travelling up her breasts to her face and walked her across the room to the punch bowl.

"Your nephew and new niece are keeping too much to themselves!" Lord Creary observed. "They should be making the rounds; everyone should get a good look at them!"

Lord Matlock laughed. "They will be along, Creary. Have no fear; I know how anxious you were to have them as your centrepieces tonight."

"It is quite a catch; they have not been to any other parties." Lady Creary preened. "After all of the gossip! Not a word of it was true?" She asked with disappointment. "Not even that she was his mistress?"

"No, my nephew behaved properly at all times, he courted her, he proposed, they were engaged and married. Everything that spread was the result of overactive imaginations."

"But his cousin!"

"From what I understand, the man who hoped to win the living at Rosings overheard my sister stating the desire that Darcy marry her daughter. This fool assumed it had occurred already. My niece was suffering from a fever and heard the staff rambling on about his ridiculous notion." He shook his head. "You know how servants enjoy gossip."

"Aye, but you must put up with it, once trained; it is too difficult to lose them." Creary nodded. "So your niece is recovered?"

"Yes, quite. She is weakened, but coming along."

"Hmm." Creary watched them depart and looked over to his wife. "What do you think?"

"They are married, it is over." She watched as Darcy set down a cup and laughed while Elizabeth held her hand to her mouth and stared at him. "It is an unusual match."

"She is a beauty." Creary said appreciatively. He saw his wife's disapproval and clearing his throat, wandered across the room, talking up his friends and sipping his drink.

"Elizabeth." Fitzwilliam bowed and held out his arm. "Come, it is our turn."

"I am rescued!" She smiled and gratefully latched onto her cousin's arm. "Please save me from my husband."

"What has the man done to you?" He patted his sword and raised his brow. "Shall I make a widow of you and claim you for myself? After a suitable period of mourning, of course."

"Of course." Darcy said dryly. "Keep this up Richard, and I will see you on the field of honour at dawn."

"You will certainly see the field, as your face will be pressed into it!"

"Gentlemen!" Elizabeth hissed.

The men stopped their banter and both had the grace to look abashed. "Forgive me, dearest."

"I am sorry, Elizabeth." Richard smiled. "I am always happy to defend you from any foe, so what did this lout do?"

"He served me that . . . concoction." She pointed to the punch bowl and Fitzwilliam began to chuckle.

"Was this a first taste for you?"

"No, but . . ." Elizabeth blinked, and slumped upon his shoulder. "Oh my."

"Elizabeth!" Darcy immediately led her to some chairs. "Dearest are you well?" Fitzwilliam sat down beside her and looked at her worriedly.

"This woman is not at all used to drink, Darcy."

"I see that. You have never had trouble with wine, Lizzy."

"I have never had any opportunity to try anything stronger than that or cider." She smiled and leaned on Darcy's shoulder. "I am sorry to embarrass you."

"No, I am sorry for encouraging you. I should have known better, there is nothing to you." Darcy held her hand and Fitzwilliam sat back. "No dance for you."

"May I claim another, perhaps?"

"I will be fine, of course you may." Elizabeth smiled and looked across the room. "Perhaps you might ask Mrs. Carter to dance in my stead?" Fitzwilliam's head shot up and he saw Evangeline looking their way with a concerned expression on her face.

He groaned. "Mother and Father have her!"

Lord Matlock drew her attention back to their conversation. "Mrs. Carter, I am delighted to meet you. Our son told us that he enjoys your company. I must admit I have been anxious to meet anyone who can cheer his mood."

"Thank you My Lord, I am happy to meet you and Lady Matlock, but the colonel seems quite amiable, have I been misled?" She smiled and raised her brow.

"No, my dear, our son is a naturally happy man, but it takes some familiarity before you can read through his expression." Lady Matlock took her hand and gave her an assessing eye. "I understand that you have at last left your mourning behind."

Evangeline's smile faded. "Yes My Lady, it feels good to do so."

"I imagine that it would." She glanced up and spotted Fitzwilliam watching them closely. "Well, please do not let me interrupt your evening further. I see Richard is walking this way." She nodded and Evangeline left to meet him.

"Your parents are most welcoming, Colonel."

"I am pleased and relieved to hear of it. I saw your concern for Elizabeth, and I thought to assure you of her good health."

"I can see that she is well." Evangeline smiled over to where Darcy and Elizabeth were speaking with each other and watching them.

Fitzwilliam nodded and said softly. "May I have the next set, Mrs. Carter?"

"Thank you, yes." She smiled at him, and was pleased to see the usually confident man become shy in her presence.

Darcy laughed and Elizabeth squeezed his hand. "Well, there is no doubt there about his interest, is there?"

"I wonder if she will relent and allow him to court her." She watched as he bowed to Evangeline and gestured their way. "I hope so."

"I hope so for both of them, but it is an unlikely step for her."

"She is so young, she could have a family."

"How do you feel about children?" Darcy asked quietly. "Does it frighten you? Being with child and giving birth?"

"Of course I want children!" Elizabeth said with surprise. "What brought that to mind?"

"I do not know." Darcy kissed her hand and turned his eyes back to watch the dancers. What he did not say was that seeing her for the first time feeling physically weak, even if it was from a too-strong cup of punch, frightened him to the bone.

"Why are you not dancing?" Alicia asked and sat by them. "Are you well?"

"I tried the punch. Do skip it." Elizabeth laughed.

"Oh, I should have warned you. Lord Creary is famous for his concoction. He should be weaving through the crowd before long; and woe to the girl who falls in his clutches."

"What does he do?" Elizabeth asked curiously.

"He kisses them." Alicia wrinkled her nose. "And this man does not appreciate clean breath."

"oh." She glanced at Darcy, who like every other part of his life, was scrupulous with his hygiene, far beyond any dictate she had ever heard before. She had enjoyed more baths since her marriage than she had in the last two months.

"Yes." Darcy returned from his musings and said definitely. "And when your dance with him comes, I will be watching."

"I love you when you are jealous." She whispered. "It makes me feel pretty."

"You are pretty." He stroked his hand over hers. "You are doing very well."

"Darcy, Mrs. Darcy, may I wish you joy?" Harwick bowed.

"Harwick, thank you." Darcy smiled, and looked down to Elizabeth.

"I am sorry that you could not come to our wedding, you were missed." She smiled to him and he nodded.

"That is exceptionally kind of you, Mrs. Darcy. May I enquire after your sister?" He asked quietly.

"She is well, sir. You have no need to berate yourself. It was not meant to be." Elizabeth tilted her head to see him look down. "I know that this is terribly forward of me sir, but I hope that you might do me a favour tonight?"

"Anything, Mrs. Darcy." Harwick smiled at her.

"Will you favour me with one dance?" She smiled. "You see, my husband is very unhappy sharing me and I would prefer to dance with his friends than with strangers."

Harwick laughed and smiled at Darcy. "So the green-eyed monster has entered the room. I understand."

"My wife is far too presumptuous; however, I would consider it a great favour."

"It is my honour." He took Elizabeth's free hand and bowed. "And my great pleasure, thank you."

Over the next hour, Elizabeth danced with Layton, Harwick, and Singleton. At last she was with her husband again, and as they hoped, the pattern was slow. "Fitzwilliam, Mr. Stewart asked me for a dance."

Darcy asked softly. "Do you mind dancing with him?"

"No, I do not. He is your friend, and I would like to think of him as mine, but nothing more. Do you mind?"

"I will not know until I see him touch you." Darcy moved away and looked at the floor. Elizabeth watched his tall slumped figure and already had her answer.

"Perhaps Lord Creary will tread on my foot when we dance after supper?" She whispered when they came together again.

"You would do that for me? Thank you Elizabeth." He sighed. "I am being ridiculous; of course you should accept his offer to dance. I am the man who will take you home tonight."

"And every night." She reminded him. They continued the dance in silence, and when it ended, Darcy escorted her to the supper room where they were kept from eating by the constant attention of the people around them. Elizabeth discovered how withdrawn her husband became in company, and set about the task of addressing the inquiries with as much patience and grace as she could muster, all while feeling his hand tightly grasping hers under the table.

Eventually Elizabeth left Darcy when some school friends of his came to offer their congratulations and took a seat next to Audrey. "How is your evening? I am sorry that I have not had time to speak with you, are you feeling well?"

"I am fine, truly. Besides, you and Darcy are the centre of all attention, I hardly expected you to be bothering with us." She smiled. "We are doing well."

"I am glad to hear of it." She watched Singleton and saw him look up and to his wife, then smile softly. "He seems to be sincere, Audrey."

"I believe that he is." She said quietly. "It is difficult to forget the past, though."

"But what good does it do you to dwell upon it? He is putting forth a good faith effort, but it will not continue without your encouragement." Elizabeth squeezed her hand. "Even my Fitzwilliam needs encouragement."

Audrey turned to her and laughed. "For what? The man is smitten!"

"He is also terribly shy." She whispered and nodded her chin to where Darcy sat alone despite the crowd of men around him, his eyes were down to his plate, and he was only listening to the conversation. "I must return to him." She stood up and looked at Singleton watching them. "Why not do the same?"

Audrey watched Elizabeth walk over to Darcy and resume her seat by his side, and immediately he reanimated. Audrey then moved to sit near Singleton, and tentatively she took his hand under the table. The gratitude that shone from his eyes was heartbreaking, and she squeezed as hard as he did. "Audrey?"

"I have had enough tonight. Could we go home?"

Singleton nodded and took a deep breath. "Yes, anything, yes." He rose to his feet and held out his hand. "Let us go home."

Stewart watched them leave and looked away to find his sister watching him. "Are you well, Daniel?" Laura asked.

"I am." He smiled at her. "Do not worry about me. Go and enjoy your time with Mr. Harwick."

"No, he is not ready for more." She watched him sitting alone and looking her way. She smiled at him warmly and he responded with a small upturn of his lips. "Perhaps next Season."

"I wish that I had an estate to invite him to visit for you." Stewart smiled. "I could play matchmaker."

"I think that I need to become serious about finding a match for you." She laughed and he shrugged. "Give me some time, Brother. I will have you married before long."

Soon the sounds of the musicians beginning to play were heard again. "Mrs. Darcy!" Lord Creary's voice boomed. "Our dance has at last arrived!"

"Oh." She glanced at Darcy and they both stood. "I expected us to meet in the ballroom, sir."

"Nonsense! This is my home, and you are the bride, and I intend to have you on my arm for as long as possible." He laughed at Darcy. "And there is not one thing you can do about it so instead of fuming at me," He scanned the room, and raised his brows, "ah, Victoria, come, Darcy needs a partner!" Elizabeth looked around and saw a young woman about her height and colouring rise and walk over to them. Darcy closed his eyes for a moment and fixed a tight smile on his face. Creary laughed. "There you go!" He turned and led Elizabeth away from the supper room. "Now there is an ironic pairing." He chuckled to himself.

Elizabeth could not look behind her without being obvious, so concentrated on the formidable man by her side. "I thank you for our invitation tonight, sir. We are honoured to be asked."

"Mrs. Darcy, our guest list was made months ago, and of course a man of such consequence as your husband was invited, in fact, our invitation this year had another purpose." They lined up for the dance and Elizabeth glanced at Darcy, who again was staring anywhere but at his partner.

"What was that purpose, sir?"

"Why, it was not so many weeks ago that Darcy started the tongues wagging when he danced with my niece, Miss Victoria Gannon. He had not danced at all this Season, or rarely in any case. I swear; my wife was at her sister's home the next morning with wedding bells ringing in her head! Ah what a match that would have made!" He said nodding thoughtfully; then saw Elizabeth's wide eyes. The music began and he took her hand. "You do resemble her. When did you meet Darcy?"

Elizabeth shot a look at Miss Gannon and did see the resemblance. "Two years ago, sir. In Hyde Park."

"Really?" Lord Creary moved in time to the music. "I remember running into Darcy in the park last summer."

"Do you?" She said quietly. "It is a common enough place for people to walk. Anyone can be found there."

"Yes, I know." He grimaced. "Be sure that you never walk there without an escort, my dear. There are people of questionable worth there."

"Really?" Elizabeth looked down, then moved to change partners and found her hand encapsulated by a very large warm one.

"Are you well, dearest?" Darcy whispered.

She said nothing and the pattern moved her back to Creary.

"So, back to this romance of yours, you met two years ago, that is interesting, why have we never heard of you before you turned up at the Matlock ball? That is when the talk began, you know. Of course the rumours were fascinating but quashed by Lady Matlock." They turned and he glanced at Miss Gannon. "Victoria was crushed, Darcy actually smiled at her. She was sure she was the one." They stepped away from each other and Elizabeth automatically followed the pattern, but her gaze stayed on her husband. "Then you were engaged, and the stories of his cousin came up." He chortled. "It has been delicious. Now the questions lie on the speed of your union."

"What could be wrong about our wedding date?" Elizabeth asked, finally returning her attention to him.

Creary looked at her with a knowing smile. "It was advanced three weeks, my dear."

Elizabeth's eyes narrowed. "Sir, are you aware that Pemberley suffered a fire?"

"No." He frowned. "How devastating was it?"

"Fortunately the damage was limited to the kitchens. My husband travelled there and remained until he was sure that the repairs were underway, then returned to London with the intention that we marry immediately and go back to Pemberley as soon as possible." She glared at him. "Is that acceptable sir?"

"Why certainly, I would wish to be on the spot as well." He considered her carefully. "You are angry with me."

"I am tired of people who have no connection to me judging my or my husband's intentions." She said unhappily. "And furthermore, sir, you should not allow outside appearances to influence your opinions of a person."

"My, you are a feisty little thing." Creary's eyes lit up and raked over her. "A woman like you will quickly become bored with a dull stick like Darcy. I was friends with his father; he is cut from the same cloth." He leaned down. "I know you have to give him his heir, but when that task is complete . . ." He winked. "I would quite enjoy providing you the company you would undoubtedly appreciate, perhaps we would not have to wait so long, eh?" He squeezed her hand and Elizabeth gasped as the music ended. Creary escorted her towards Darcy, but before a word could be said Stewart arrived to claim her hand.

"Sorry old man, it is my turn." He grinned and took Elizabeth back out to the line. "At last, I did not think I would ever get my dance with the bride."

"Pardon?" She whispered and looked back at where Creary was talking to his wife but smiling at her.

"Are you well, Mrs. Darcy?" Stewart asked softly.

"I . . . I do not know." She looked down and back up to see his concern and smiled a little. "I . . . of course, I am fine."

"I suppose that Creary told you about his niece and their hopes for her and Darcy."

"You knew this, too?" Elizabeth met Darcy's burning gaze then looked away.

"Everyone knew." Stewart smiled. "He actually spoke to her. It was the talk of the ballroom that night." They swayed and turned, and Elizabeth stared down at her feet. "Mrs. Darcy, you should know that he left almost immediately afterwards, Bingley said something to him and he was gone like a shot."

"Mr. Bingley?" She whispered.

"Then when you were at the Matlock ball, Miss Gannon stood by Darcy's side for a good quarter-hour and he never acknowledged her. A bit rude, but of course, he knew that to speak to her would just be fanning the flames. My sister tells me that Miss Gannon was sorely disappointed that he did not pay a call the morning after the dance." They advanced up the line and waited for their turn again. Stewart saw a war of emotions playing over Elizabeth, and when they came together, he whispered, "He clearly never was really interested in her, he was hoping for you, the resemblance makes that clear."

"oh." She looked back to see Darcy watching and relaxed a little. "He is so jealous of you dancing with me."

"Only fair do you not think? You are jealous of Miss Gannon." He smiled. "Darcy has nothing to fear from me."

"No." Elizabeth finally smiled. "And I have nothing to fear from her. Perhaps she is the girl for you?"

Stewart laughed. "Perhaps she is; there must have been something to her to attract even the slightest bit of Darcy's attention." The set ended and he escorted her back to his side. "There you go, Darcy. Take care of her." He bowed and walked away to approach Miss Gannon.

"What happened out there?" Darcy kissed her hand. "Lord Creary . . ."

"Is a rude man." She said positively.

"He is powerful."

"He is over-confident."

"What did he say?" Darcy shot a look at his host and back to her. "Elizabeth?"

"It does not matter." She whispered. "May we go home, please?"

"Did he insult you?" He said in a growl and fixed his steely gaze back on Creary. "No man insults my wife." He let go and began to move. Elizabeth caught his arm and he stopped, looking back down to her. "Elizabeth, I will not tolerate discourtesy."

"I am happy to hear that, Fitzwilliam, but it will serve none of us well to start something now. We will be leaving London in a few days, please let it drop."

"So he did insult you." He said angrily.

Fitzwilliam appeared at his elbow. "Your mask is slipping Cousin; the room will soon be seeing your fury. What has happened, did Stewart forget himself?" He chuckled and saw Darcy shoot a look at Elizabeth in inquiry.

"No, he was a wonderful gentleman and told me of Miss Gannon." She watched Darcy's eyes close.

"There is nothing to tell, Elizabeth."

"Ah, the infamous dance." Fitzwilliam smiled. "I am sorry that I was absent that night." Seeing Elizabeth's glare focussing on him he coughed. "Ahem, well, if Stewart is not the problem, I would wager it was Creary? And further was he making an offer of . . . questionable morals?"

She closed her eyes and Darcy's flew back open to study her. "I will kill him!" He growled. Fitzwilliam grabbed his arm.

"Let it go, he does it to every pretty girl."

"Every pretty girl is not my wife." Darcy said through clenched teeth.

Elizabeth put her hand on his chest. "Please Fitzwilliam, take me home. I wish to go home." Darcy stood still, and stared angrily at Creary. "Please Will?" She said softly and his eyes shifted back to hers.

"Listen to your wife, Cousin. Your reserve of good humour is spent for the evening." Fitzwilliam let go of his arm and chuckled. "Nobody should even think of crossing you when it comes to Elizabeth, but a ballroom is not the place for an argument with an arrogant peer."

Darcy nodded and seemed to let down his stance. As soon as his movement was unrestricted though, he quickly turned and began striding across the room to Creary's side. "I would like a word, sir." He said in a low tone, meeting the older man's eye straight on.

Creary's brow creased. "What is it, man?" He glanced back over Darcy's shoulder and saw Fitzwilliam watching closely while Elizabeth stood clutching his arm. "Your wife seems ill."

"My wife is attempting to retain her composure following your offensive behaviour." He snarled in a low tone. "How dare you treat her as anything less than a lady!"

"She is hardly a peer." He sniffed.

"Neither am I, however we are both the children of gentlemen." His voice rose, and heads began to turn.

Creary glanced around, noticing the interest. "Keep your voice down."

"How long has your family held its estate, sir? Mine was a gift from William the Conqueror." Seeing that his point was made, he finished in a low growl. "If you insult my wife again in any fashion I assure you, this matter will not be settled with words in a crowded ballroom. I do not care about your age, and your position is meaningless to me. You treated my wife as a common trollop when earlier you crowed over how pleased you were to have our company. Your ball is the greatest of the Season? Well, not to the Darcys, not anymore." He turned and walked back to Elizabeth. "Come my love, it is time to depart this farce." Creary stared after them, his face colouring after receiving the rare set down.

Lord Matlock stepped by his side and cleared his throat. "Damn fine man my nephew, would you not say, Creary?" He turned and met his eye. "I have no doubt what you suggested to my niece, and you are fortunate that Darcy is not a man of violence. He could take you out in the blink of an eye." Creary started to protest and Lord Matlock held up his hand. "You are too old and frankly unfit for this foolishness, Creary. You deserve his disdain. I look forward to telling my wife this tale, she will get a good laugh out of it, and I love to hear her laugh. I am sure that her friends will as well."

Elizabeth took Darcy's arm and mustering up all of the dignity she had, walked out with her head held high. She remained silent and stiff, just as Darcy did, as they waited on the curb for their carriage. It was not until they climbed inside and the door was firmly shut that she at last collapsed against his chest and began to cry. "I am so sorry."

"You . . .dearest you did nothing wrong. It was he who is at fault." Darcy kissed her and wrapped her up in his arms. "You are wonderful. I love you."

"I love you." She looked up to him.

"Will you tell me what was said?" He asked softly and brushed her cheek with his fingers. "Did he suggest . . ."

"Please Fitzwilliam." She whispered. "Just know that I will never betray you." Darcy closed his eyes, his suspicions were confirmed. "Especially with a man who insults my worthiness as your wife while questioning my devotion and your magnetism in nearly the same breath!" Her spirit began to revive in the safety of Darcy's embrace. "Overbearing old man!"

Darcy's head tilted. "My magnetism?"

"He suggested that you were dull and I would grow bored with you!" She huffed. "Well, I am too much of a lady to declare it in public, but if you are dull, I doubt that any woman could abide the demonstration from a man who he would term passionate! I realize that I am no expert with these things, but my goodness, Fitzwilliam! You arouse feelings in me that make my heart sing! I can barely breathe after . . ." Elizabeth's declaration was silenced by Darcy lifting her up onto his lap and kissing her. When the carriage stopped before their home, the footman wisely did not open the door. Instead he stepped several paces away and turned his back while waiting for his master to appear and hand down his dazed and dishevelled wife.

"Let us finish our discussion inside, my love." He said quietly.

"I . . . I believe that you will make your point most effectively."

"*That* is my intent."

456 LINDA WELLS

Chapter 30

arcy heard the front door closing and the sound of voices in the hallway, one being the soft tones of his wife. He jumped up from his desk and hurried to meet her. The servants disappeared and they were left alone. Darcy took her hands and peered into her eyes, and saw instantly through the attempt she made to smile. "You are exhausted."

"I am relieved to be home." She found herself drawn against his chest and gratefully sank into his embrace. "Oh Fitzwilliam it was awful!"

"I am so sorry, dearest. I thought that Alicia going along would help." He whispered into her hair. "What happened?"

"They were just relentless with questions. Every house that we visited! And it was not cruel or mean; most of them were tolerable in a superior sort of way, but at least accepting of the fact that we were married, but . . . oh Fitzwilliam, they made no bones of hinting that I am wholly unprepared for my position, and although it was not said, clearly they feel that you made a grave error by choosing me." She let the tears she had held in check all day to roll down her cheeks. "I . . . I tried so hard. I smiled and spoke of the subjects Aunt Helen gave me to discuss, but I certainly could offer no opinion about the fashions or the attractions of town, or even of the gossip, especially when gossip about us was a favourite subject, although they all expressed elation at your set down of Lord Creary and surprise with your impressive display of affection towards me. But then there were all of the questions about our courtship and the veiled inquiries about our hopes for children. I feel that I was a failure, and it reflects terribly on you. Perhaps Lord Creary was correct in what he implied last night. I am so sorry Fitzwilliam. I . . . I will understand if you wish to rid yourself of me." She ended softly.

"Rid myself?" He said incredulously, then slanting his head down to find her eyes, eventually resorted to lifting her chin up so she would look into his. "Dearest, I am hardly going to tie a rope around your neck and lead you to the public square and auction you off, no matter how poorly you feel that you performed. You are well and truly my wife until the day we are laid to rest at Pemberley." He gently kissed her lips then kissed away her tears. "I love you for being yourself. Please promise me that you will not ever become like them?" He kissed her again. "Now, I want to hear every detail of your trials. Where shall we go?"

"As long as you are holding me, I do not care." She whispered and returned her head to his chest. Darcy kissed her hair and hugged her, smiling to have her need his love. "Shall we go upstairs? We can rest for a little while before we have to dress for dinner at the Hurst's." He chuckled to hear her groan. "You forgot about the engagement dinner for Miss Bingley and her mysterious Mr. W.?"

"Another woman who wanted you." She said into his waistcoat. "Is there one unmarried woman who wanted someone *other* than you in this town?"

"Ah, is that it?" He chuckled. "You faced the disappointed mothers today? Were they lying in wait at the homes of the women you visited?"

Elizabeth drew back and her eyes flashed. "YES! Fitzwilliam, I know that you were quite the catch, but my goodness, were you at all aware of just how desired you were?"

"Yes I was." He said sheepishly and looked up to see her wide eyes. "I certainly did nothing to encourage them, but first sons are few and far between, and there are more ladies than gentlemen . . ."

"That Miss Gannon . . ."

He interrupted quickly. "Was nobody to me, Lizzy, only a pale likeness to the woman I dearly wished to love. I did not even speak to her during our dance." Tilting his head he was relieved to see her satisfaction with his answer. "Come, upstairs with you." Darcy took her hand and they began to ascend the steps. "So besides unhappy mothers, did they question anything else of you?"

"It seems that some of them are acquainted with Pemberley, they were friends of your parents and had visited when you were a child." He nodded as they walked down the hallway towards their rooms. "Their descriptions of the house are far more fantastic than yours. I know that you are not one given to conceit, but tell me, have you perhaps been a little . . . modest in what I am going to view in a few days? Am I going to faint dead away to see this house appear beyond the trees? I tried to respond by saying that the sight of the estate will be nothing to arriving there as your wife, and that seemed to quiet them." She saw his eyes warm with some unspoken pleasure and grew frustrated. "Please tell me, are their words true?"

He opened the door to his bedchamber and ushered her inside, then turned the lock. "You have seen the landscape in my study."

"Fitzwilliam Darcy! Are you telling me that I am to believe these horrible women over you?" Elizabeth's hands landed on her hips and she stared up at him. "I AM unsuitable! They know it!"

"Elizabeth DARCY!" He said loudly, "Stop this! I would never ever bring a woman who I felt was incapable to Pemberley. You need some confidence in your ability. I have it. Where is yours? Those women are jealous, here you are, not even eighteen, and the mistress of . . . Well, you will see. Keep in mind that many of those ladies are still waiting for their fathers-in-law to die before their husbands inherit. You already have a higher status than they." His lips twitched to see her head tilt and a satisfied smile come to her eyes. Nodding, he pulled her against his chest and began to apply soft kisses over her face, while his busy hands ran down her gown and began to bunch and pull up the skirt.

Elizabeth attempted to quell the rising tension by becoming sensible. "How exactly do you propose to remove this gown? I cannot possibly change out of this without help." Darcy let go and walked from the room while she stood with her arms folded and returned a long minute later, barefooted. She heard a door close in the background and then she watched as he silently removed his topcoat and laid it on a chair. "Fitzwilliam?"

Staring straight at her, he unbuttoned his waist coat and removed it as well, then untied his neck cloth, unwound it, then neatly laid it on top. "Ohhhh." Reaching up, she ran her hands over the bare skin. "Do you know how much I love seeing your neck uncovered?"

"Does it truly please you, dearest?" He whispered and bent his head to nuzzle her throat. She nodded, and barely noticed that his hands were wandering through her hair, working through the carefully arranged curls to methodically remove every comb and pin, until the great swinging mass was at last freed to drop around her shoulders. Stepping back, he admired the sight, then lifting a handful of her heavy tresses; he brought it to his nose for a deep breath. "So lovely." Turning her around, he pushed the curtain of hair aside, and deftly released the row of tiny buttons on her gown.

"How do you do that? Your hands are so large!" She whispered as he reached her waist then lifted his hands to push the gown down her shoulders so that it dropped to the floor. "Piano lessons." He smiled. "They made my fingers very nimble." Gently he caressed his palms over her bare shoulders, and bent to breathe into her ear. "Are you nervous, my love? Surely you are not afraid of me."

"No . . . I do not know why I am trembling . . ."

"Because we are soul mates, do you not feel my body trembling for you?" He turned her back to face him, and lovingly kissed her lips while simultaneously reaching behind to untie her stays. She closed her eyes and drew a deep breath. "Is this uncomfortable?"

"Today it was." She smiled to see his curiosity. "I am used to something softer."

"Why the change, then?"

"I have an insistent modiste, now." Elizabeth laughed and he smiled, dropping the offensive garment to the floor. He stood back and considered her. All that was left were her chemise and stockings. It was extraordinarily arousing to see her so nearly bare, and he noticed that when he stopped his undressing, she began to tremble again. Understanding, he set back to work.

"It is my turn now, I think." Taking her hand, he lifted it to his chest. "Will you help me?"

"Oh." She released the button at the top of his shirt, and watched it fall open, then caressing her hands along his wrists, opened the cuffs. He raised his arms over his head, and she slowly pulled his shirt from his breeches, then helped him to lift it up and off, so that he stood bare-chested before her. "I do not think I will ever grow tired of this view." Her fingers glided up his tightly muscled torso, becoming lost in the thick black nest of hair. Darcy closed his eyes, and then opened them with surprise when he felt her lips press against his skin and felt a bolt of electricity when she licked his nipple; it was his turn to fight nerves, and moving quickly he reasserted control.

"Dearest . . . Come." Holding her hand, he led the way to the bed, pulled back the counterpane, and guided her onto the sheets. Darcy remained standing and she watched with fascination as he lifted her leg and unrolled one stocking, then moved to the other. Holding the leg high in the air, he caressed both hands over it, and then bent to kiss her calf. He lowered it gently, and taking her hand, rested it over his arousal. Her fingers caressed the hard shape then moved to free the buttons of the fall, and reached inside to draw him out. Darcy's eyes closed when her touch found his burning skin and in a flash his breeches were gone, and he was nude before her.

"I love seeing your desire for me." Elizabeth whispered. Caressing his pride with both hands, she sat up to fondle him, and he instantly was on the bed, by her side, and wrapping her safe within his arms.

"Your trembling has stopped." He spoke softly as he kissed her face, her throat, then her lips.

"So has yours."

Darcy whispered, "I become undone when you touch me, Elizabeth. I hardly know what to do with myself."

"We are both shy, then." She smiled and he nodded. "I think that makes me feel even more secure with you."

"I cannot imagine being so open with anyone else, nor do I want to." He nibbled on her neck and she sighed, then opened her eyes suddenly to find his twinkling at her. "I did not leave a mark, love." She sighed again as he smiled to himself. *This time.*

They lay together, kissing and touching. Elizabeth's hands explored his back; Darcy's caressed her breasts through the transparent chemise, then lifted it up and away before he settled over her, finally joining their bodies. As they kissed, his hand explored lower, down over her hip, and then he surprised her by rolling them to their sides. They lay together, slowly rocking and kissing. "Oh Elizabeth, this feels so good." He moaned, then separating a little, he watched their movement and touched her cheek. "Look dearest." Elizabeth gazed down to see his length slide into her.

"Ohhh." She sighed as he filled her and withdrew, filled her and withdrew.

"See how wet you are?" He whispered as he slipped inside again. "See how I am covered with you? I love to watch this. I love to see us together." She reached down to rub his base and he moaned. "More darling, more." Slowly her hand caressed over his heavy curls and he moaned louder, and reciprocated by stroking her pearl. Elizabeth gasped and closed her eyes. "Does this feel good?" He asked softly. "Please tell me."

"Please keep touching me." She sighed and moaned. "Please, come into me." Elated, Darcy did just as she asked, thrusting and stroking steadily while their mutual fondling heightened their anticipation. "Oh, oh, more!" She let him go and embraced his shoulders. Now enveloping her tight in his arms, he began thrusting harder, and could feel the tension growing within her. His excitement grew as he willed her to come with him, and he plunged into her, giving all that he had. Their mouths met and their tongues fought with fervour equal to the motion of their pounding hips. Darcy revelled in the feel of her legs gripping his body and urging him to drive deeper, while Elizabeth drowned in the glory of his possession. When she suddenly relaxed and cried out, Darcy gratefully let go.

"Ohhhhh!" He gasped and swallowed. "Oh, Elizabeth, it was so long, it lasted so long!" Another spasm shook his body and she gripped him tighter as he voiced his pleasure. One more great shiver travelled through him and he rested his face on her shoulder and panted.

"We need to remember this." She sighed and kissed his hair while rubbing his back. "This was glorious."

He pulled himself together and looked up to smile at her in wonder. "What a gift your love is for me! I never imagined . . . Oh dearest, you are correct, we must remember this." They remained lying side by side, and clung together, whispering endearments between kisses. Eventually Darcy turned onto his back and she cuddled against his chest.

"I feel so much better." Elizabeth sighed and hugged his waist.

Darcy chuckled and lifted his head from where it rested on her hair. "I do, too."

"What did you have to be worried about?" She smiled and kissed his nose.

"I had to sit here through countless meetings while worrying about how you fared." He turned and nuzzled his face across her breasts and laughed. "I would wager that you did not spare a thought of me."

"How much?"

"Oh, you thought of me? Let me guess, it was wishing that I was with you?" She lifted her chin. "Perhaps it was cursing you for marrying me?"

"Impossible." He returned his face to her shoulder, and closed his eyes. "You love me too much."

"I do." Elizabeth sighed and hugged him. "I cannot imagine settling for less than what I have with you, grand estate or not."

"So you will not let it frighten you anymore?"

"Oh, I will worry, but . . . you are correct, I should not let the words of those so wholly unconnected to me harm my feelings of worthiness. My sole concern should be your opinion, not theirs."

"And my opinion is irrevocable." He whispered. "Now my love, sleep, we have one more dinner and we can go home."

An hour later, Elizabeth woke, and after a bit of a struggle escaped Darcy's protective embrace. She gathered her discarded clothes and after donning a robe, settled at the writing desk in their sitting room.

6 July, 1809
Today Alicia thankfully joined me while I left the house to pay calls. Fitzwilliam saw us off, whispering apologies to me the whole way to the carriage. I found myself reassuring him more than being worried of the visits to come. When we were at last on our way, Alicia could not stop laughing, and told me that she had no memory of seeing Fitzwilliam so open with his feelings. I have to claim some satisfaction with that knowledge. There is so much of him that I have yet to learn.

We called on four ladies, ones who were specially selected by Aunt Helen. We met Mrs. Kendall, whose husband owns an estate near Rosings and is apparently a great confidant of Lady Catherine's. Then we moved on to Lady Monroe, who advises the Almack's board. Next were Lady Grafton and finally Mrs. Smythe. Alicia kept the conversation to approved topics, and I followed her lead, trying to remember all that I have been taught to do. I felt the women examining everything about me. At least my gown was admired by them all, and I hope that my manners were acceptable. Mrs. Kendall was rather direct with her desire to learn every detail of my courtship with Fitzwilliam; and I believe that Aunt Helen would have been pleased with my ability to skirt the topic. Mrs. Smythe was interested in delving into our plans for children, as if she was hoping for me to make some announcement there and then. She seemed rather disappointed with my absolute ignorance over the signs of pending motherhood. Alicia told me later that the woman was well known as a great gossip; and I understood that her word of my innocence would go far to dispel rumours. Lady Grafton was simply a kind woman. What the ulterior motive was in our visit to her parlour escaped me.

The difficulty with the visits was not these four women, but the others who were also there paying calls. I was questioned and prodded, reminded of my unworthiness and the enormity of the position I had accepted, and it seems, how many women were unhappy that my husband was lost to them all. When we at last returned, Fitzwilliam reassured me of my merit with his words and his touch. I cannot know what the future will bring me, but I do know that I will live in a house filled with love. I am so grateful to have married him. Millie just came into the room and set a bouquet of roses on my dressing table and a little note expressing his feelings was tucked amongst them. When did he prepare this? I thought that I left him asleep! I believe that I can bear anything with such a dear man by my side.

She set down her pen to smell the flowers and looked up to see Darcy standing beside her. "When did you do this?"

"Now, I cannot tell you all of my secrets." He leaned down and kissed her, then read over her entry, his lips set in an unhappy line until he came to the end when he smiled again. "I think that I might have to steal this journal from time to time to learn your secrets."

"I will lock it away." Elizabeth laughed and closed the book before he could page back through it.

"Now that is hardly fair. I know that you read mine." He laughed softly as she blushed with her guilt. "Perhaps someday I will write something in there to gain your attention."

"Such as?" She turned and stood up to embrace him.

"Mmmmm, Let me consider that." He kissed her, and before he became too lost drew reluctantly away. "We should prepare for dinner. Do you have something suitable for the evening?"

"Suitable appropriate or suitable to inspire envy?" She raised her brow and he laughed again. "Both, I think."

"Excellent." He snatched a rose from the vase and handed it to her. "I look forward to it." An hour later he leaned on the doorframe to her dressing room and watched with satisfaction as Millie put the finishing touches on Elizabeth's hair. She spotted him and stood.

"What do you think?" Elizabeth asked when they were alone. "I do not wish to outshine the bride."

"You still are a bride, my love. Miss Bingley is just engaged." Darcy smiled as she stood before him and touched the lovely blue gown. "You are stunning Elizabeth." She looked down and he took her hand. "You have met Miss Bingley before."

"Yes."

"She criticized you."

"Yes." Elizabeth sighed. "Am I really so transparent?"

Darcy slipped his arms around her waist and hugged her. "Yes, to me you are, have you forgotten your resolve not to let other's opinions affect you?"

"This is different. She was interested in me as a wife for her brother until she heard that Longbourn was small. I did not understand her concern; it was not as if Mr. Bingley would receive the estate as part of the marriage settlement."

"He would not have received a large dowry or prestige either." Darcy said softly. "Miss Bingley is always looking for things that would increase her value." He kissed her throat and rested his cheek on her head. "Besides, you were not interested in Bingley anyway." Elizabeth squeezed his waist to reassure him and he squeezed back before continuing. "I am very curious about this man she has accepted. The last person I would have expected her to marry would be an apparently younger son who is studying law. He seems to be a younger version of Stewart."

"But Mr. Stewart has excellent prospects!" She said into his chest. "This man of Miss Bingley's could be the same."

"He could, but Miss Bingley wanted me, or my ilk. This is a spectacular step down from her machinations. I honestly could not understand why there were no other men asking for her. She has an excellent dowry, and she is not without wit or accomplishments. There are any number of gentlemen who would welcome her as their wife. I always thought that she wished to outdo her sister's choice of Mr. Hurst. The only thing that I can consider as problematic is her tie to trade."

"Did you ever consider her?" Elizabeth waited and after a long silence she finally peeked up at him. Darcy was looking down at her with his brows raised. "Was that a foolish question?"

"I was in love with you when I met her, was I not?"

"But you had no hope of me . . ."

"Dearest, I always had hope of you." He kissed her forehead and let her go. "Come, let us go and meet this lucky man."

"Why do I think that you are speaking with your tongue firmly in your cheek?" She laughed and took his hand as they walked down the stairs.

"I do hope for her happiness, Elizabeth. And his." He caught her raised brow and let his lips twitch.

WICKHAM STEPPED FROM HIS CAB and eyed the facade of the Hurst's townhouse. *It is not Grosvenor Square, but it will do for a honeymoon. Damn that Bingley, I was almost certain I would avoid a settlement, not that I have anything to back up those papers I signed.* He laughed, thinking of his friend who worked at the bank and provided the false statements of his account. *Well, soon enough it will be mine, I will disappear, and Caroline will return to mooning over Darcy. It will be good to get away from such a miserable woman.* Raising the knocker he waited for the door to open. *Too bad Georgiana is too young, I am certain I could have talked her into eloping; it would have been so much easier with a little girl. Thirty thousand would have been so much better too, especially if I could have hurt that insufferable bastard in the process. 'Stay off of my land and away from my family!' You do not alarm me, Darcy! Prig!* The door opened and Wickham stepped inside, and was ushered upstairs to join the family.

"Dear Mr. Wickham!" Caroline purred. "Oh, how handsome you are in your blue coat! Do you not agree, Louisa?"

"You look very fine, sir." She said quietly and met her husband's eyes which immediately rolled upwards. She nodded at him and he coughed.

"Wickham, have you determined a date yet?"

"The sooner the better, I say." Wickham laughed and winked at Caroline. "Do you not agree my dear? I have the license; shall we go in the morning?"

"Oh Mr. Wickham, you make me blush!" She gushed.

"I am serious, my dear." He raised her hand and kissed it. "I am more than ready to be your husband, why should we wait a moment longer? I long to introduce you as Mrs. Wickham." He stared into her eyes and watched the flush spread up Caroline's neck to her hair. "Shall we, my dear?"

Hurst cleared his throat. "I assume that you will acquire new apartments as befit a married couple, sir? You can hardly expect to keep your rooms at the boarding house now."

Wickham startled from his quarry. "Oh . . . I had not thought of it. I wished for my wife to join me as we looked at properties." He smiled at her. "I would not think of purchasing our home without her." Caroline giggled.

Hurst nodded and spoke again, "Mrs. Hurst and I will be leaving town, and then we are expecting a great many guests for the little Season and beyond, you see."

Wickham took the hint. "And of course, you will need the rooms . . ." He glanced at Bingley. "Are you being sent away as well, sir?"

"I suppose that I will, but I expect to be visiting Pemberley this autumn, and I have an open invitation to stay at Darcy House, but of course would not dream of imposing during the honeymoon." He laughed. "I can well imagine that my presence would be most adamantly unwanted. The Darcys will leave in a matter of days, I understand." He smiled at Wickham. "Your thought that they had travelled for their honeymoon was incorrect. Mrs. Darcy was making the rounds this morning paying calls. I spotted her carriage twice in Mayfair today."

"Mrs. Darcy." Wickham laughed uncomfortably. The Darcys in town and worse, in public, was not part of his plans, and in his discomfort, he slipped. "I have heard enough of her that I can only offer condolences to him, he could have done so much better." Bingley frowned and looked at Louisa who stared at Wickham, who covered quickly, "Forgive me, Bingley, he is your friend."

"I was under the impression that he was yours as well."

"Of course he is! And like the rest of society I suppose we will have to tolerate his wife." Wickham said solemnly and was pleased to see Caroline's head nodding. "It is only that I know his father's expectations for him; we spent a great deal of time together, talking about his desires for both of us. He was my surrogate father after mine died, and took good care of me. His loss has been devastating."

"I am so sorry to hear of your pain." Bingley said sincerely. "I know how highly Darcy values his father's memory."

"Oh yes, I am sure that he does, but the estate is not the same without Mr. Darcy there." He sighed sadly and looked at Caroline. "You know my feelings about losing his presence, my dear."

"Would you turn down an invitation to Pemberley should it come, I hope that you and Mr. Darcy can share your memories of his father? I do not wish you to reject your friendship with Mr. Darcy simply because of his choice for wife." Caroline asked worriedly then looked to her brother. "Surely you could suggest it, Charles?"

Bingley shook his head adamantly. "I will not Caroline; the Darcys' guests are their own business, I am grateful to have received his card after the date of his wedding. I have heard of a great many men who have been dropped from his acquaintance."

Wickham snorted. "That is no great surprise."

"I dropped a good many from my acquaintance when I married, Wickham. It is a good opportunity to clean the slate." Hurst noted.

"Of course, of course, I meant no offence. I will assuredly do the same very soon." Wickham bowed to Caroline and moved to look out of the window, and noting Caroline's worried expression in the glass' reflection, tried to repair the damage. "If invited I would certainly enjoy returning to my boyhood home. I hold a great many memories of the place." He watched as a carriage pulled up to the door. "I believe that your guests are arriving."

"Our guests, Mr. Wickham." Caroline took his arm. "Come, we must not stand by the window."

"Certainly not."

The Darcys arrived and were met at the front door by the Hursts. Bingley waited for them at the top of the stairs and beamed at them both. "Excellent, you were able to come."

"I responded in the affirmative, did I not?" Darcy smiled. "I would have informed you otherwise."

"Yes, yes, but after last night . . ."

"You heard about that?" Elizabeth gasped.

"Heard? What happened? I just meant that you were probably tired of socializing." Bingley laughed to see her relief. "I have the impression that I should not delve into the subject?" He saw Darcy stiffen and Elizabeth's eyes close. "Do you remember when we first met and we talked about how we were trying to fit into our new circumstances here in London? I would say that you have very handily, a ball with the peers one night, and dinner with the rabble the next."

"I do not share your excitement. And besides, you are hardly rabble. I consider you to be a very dear friend." She looked up at Darcy. "Do you agree?"

"I do, and we are happy to come and celebrate this occasion with you."

"Well come and meet Caroline's betrothed." Bingley led the way. "I must say Darcy, you and Mrs. Darcy are the making of this evening, you have the highest rank."

Darcy sighed. "I suppose that should not come as a surprise."

"No, and I have another surprise for you." Bingley laughed. "Remember I said that Caroline's suitor grew up at Pemberley?"

"In all honesty, Bingley, I had forgotten." Darcy's brow creased as the memory returned.

"Well, he did, and he does not know that you are coming tonight. I thought it would be a reunion for you, he was speaking of his fondness for your father earlier." Bingley entered the drawing room. "Our first guests have arrived. May I introduce Mr. and Mrs. Fitzwilliam Darcy? Darcy, Mrs. Darcy, this is Caroline's betrothed, Mr. George Wickham."

Darcy's eyes widened and his face grew red as he focussed his intense gaze upon the man. Wickham visibly shrank. "Wickham."

"Darcy."

Bingley had been watching eagerly to register their reactions, and his face fell as he sensed the tension between the men. He then looked quickly at Elizabeth when he heard her gasp and saw her hand rise to her mouth. Darcy turned to him. "May I speak to you, please?"

Wickham stepped up beside him and said in a low voice, "See here Darcy, what do you mean to say?"

"The truth. You are welcome to join us."

"Mr. Darcy." Elizabeth said softly and touched his hand. Darcy bent to see her eyes. "Perhaps you should speak after the dinner?"

"I am afraid that I cannot possibly pretend to a good opinion for so long, Mrs. Darcy." He smiled tightly, then turned back to Bingley. "Where shall we go? Your other guests will soon be arriving, and we should not be on display."

"There is another parlour across the hall." He said worriedly and began to move when Caroline swept across the room.

"Mr. Darcy, this is a wonderful surprise! I had no idea that Charles had invited you to come!" She glanced at Elizabeth and forced the smile to remain, "And Mrs. Darcy, may I congratulate you."

"Only if I may offer the same sentiments to you, Miss Bingley." Elizabeth smiled then returned her gaze to Darcy, who was not hiding his disdain for the man before him. "Mr. Darcy." She prodded him.

He broke the gaze and looked at Caroline. "I was happy to hear of your engagement, Miss Bingley."

"I am glad to know of it." She looked worriedly between Darcy and Wickham.

Glancing meaningfully at Bingley, they moved across the hallway. Wickham hesitated. He had worked very hard for this and was too close to concluding the game to concede now, especially to Darcy. He lifted his chin and followed with Caroline trailing behind. Elizabeth, finding herself alone, joined the party. When the door was shut, Darcy looked at Wickham then to Caroline, and spoke without emotion. "I understand that Mr. Wickham claims a connection to me."

"Yes, he grew up at Pemberley." Caroline took his arm. "Surely you have not forgotten him?"

"Did you ever ask in what capacity he lived on my father's land? Miss Bingley, I would have expected you to confirm his background before agreeing to a courtship. Mr. Wickham is the son of my estate's former steward."

"He . . .he is *what?*" She turned to look at Wickham, aghast. "But . . .you attend Cambridge!"

Darcy spoke softly and fixed his gaze directly on Wickham, who did not hide his glare. "He did, with me. What he does now is anybody's guess. He did until recently spend a great deal of time at my club until he was identified as an interloper and was sent off. I see that you simply changed circles and went in search of another sort of pigeon."

"Did it occur to you that I may have changed?" Wickham said through clenched teeth. "Is not a man allowed a second chance?"

Crossing his arms across his chest, Darcy leaned against a table, then gestured with his hand, waving him on. "Certainly, tell me all about school, Wickham. Tell me how you can afford a wife? You are just starting out in law. I know men who have come to the bar who cannot expect to marry for years. Are your successes at cards that spectacular? Did you cheat there as you did in the club and before at Cambridge?"

"Gambling!" Caroline cried and looked between the men. "But . . .he told me of his youth at Pemberley, and how he earned your father's favour and how he was remembered in his will. He is very wealthy because of your father. That is why he can marry! He will be a barrister and is a gentleman! You know this! Your father made him wealthy!"

Darcy shook his head and smiled grimly. "You are still spreading that lie? I thought that you had learned your lesson at the club when you claimed to be rich and one of us. I am surprised that you did not spread the lie that I had refused you the living as well, or would that have harmed your plans? I imagine that the claimed connection to me was useful in this case." He glanced over at Caroline then met Bingley's eye.

"It is no lie!" Wickham growled. "I did receive his bequest and you did cheat me of the living!"

"Oh, and why did you come to me weeks ago asking for more money? Was not the four thousand I gave you quite enough? Just how much did you claim you had inherited?" Bingley groaned and moved to stand by his sister. The door opened and Hurst entered. Seeing the tension, he quietly closed it behind him in time to see Darcy's already angry eyes take on a furious glare. "I will not have my father's good name used by the likes of you, Wickham. I will not allow the faintest rumour of our connection to exist. Nor will I see the sister of my good friend hurt by your schemes. I am positive that your presence in this room is solely to gain her dowry."

"No!" Caroline gasped.

"You cannot make such accusations without proof!" Wickham declared. "Besides, what is the difference if she gives it to me or some . . .so-called gentleman for his use?"

"The difference is that the gentleman's settlement is not a tissue of lies." He turned to Bingley. "If there is one?"

"Yes, yes there is, I have not signed it yet, but . . . he had documents to back up his claims . . ." Bingley's voice trailed off.

"Forged, do you think?" Hurst asked and saw Darcy's raised brow. "I should have caught this, I was too anxious to . . ." He glanced at Caroline then to his brother, "Well, I am grateful for your timely appearance."

"He is making these claims . . . Caroline, surely you believe me! He was always jealous of his father's attention to me!" Wickham declared as he saw his prize slipping away.

"You LIED to me!" She screeched. "I listened to your compliments and tales!"

The prize was not slipping away, it was long gone and Wickham knew it, and turned ugly. Pointing to Elizabeth, he snarled at Caroline. "You heard what you wished! You are angry that Darcy chose a penniless country chit over you! You are a hypocrite, believing what I said and hoping for a connection to him through me and your brother."

"Of course I want to maintain the connection! Without Mr. Darcy my brother would not be accepted into the first circles! He is our only way in! I want that life! I deserve that life!" She looked up at Darcy. "You are rescuing me."

Darcy was disgusted to hear her confession, then recoiled a little, seeing a new light of adoration appearing in Caroline's eyes. "No I am merely giving your family the facts to save it from shame. It is up to you to decide if you believe me or Wickham. I only suggest that you not announce this engagement publicly until you are certain." He looked back to Elizabeth and she slipped her hand around his arm, while his came up to cover hers. "And you Wickham; do not dare to insult my wife again!"

"You cannot tell me what I can say or do, Darcy!"

"He is a thousand times the man you are!" Caroline declared and moved towards Darcy. "He is everything that a man should be!"

"Yes, and he did not want you!" Wickham snorted. "You wanted his life so badly that you were willing to believe me on the chance you might get near it. And your family wanted you gone so badly that they were willing to accept me." He sneered at Bingley. "It was so easy."

"I did not sign the settlement Wickham." Bingley informed him. "At least I waited for that."

"And what sort of fantasy do those papers describe, I wonder?" Darcy said softly.

Caroline's eyes widened. "The settlement was false?" She gasped and her hand went to her mouth. "What were you planning to do with me?"

"What do you think a man does with his wife?" He leered at her. "He owns her."

Bingley stepped forward and drove his fist into Wickham's stomach. Taken unprepared, he gasped and opened his eyes to see Caroline coming at him with her nails ready to strike, and a screech on her lips. Darcy smiled. "I think that this interview is finished, Wickham. I suggest that you run."

"I . . . Damn you, Darcy! I will not forget this!" He turned and threw open the door. They could hear the sound of his boots on the stairs along with a constant barrage of curses. A guest at the window in the drawing room called out that he was striding down the street, gesturing and clearly talking loudly. Hurst held back Caroline from going after him.

"I am such a fool." Bingley turned to his sister who shook off Hurst. "Caroline, I am sorry that I did not protect you as I should."

"I am not a child, Charles." She looked pointedly at Elizabeth. Closing her eyes, she willed herself to calm, then stared up at Darcy and stepped closer. "I was charmed by him and saw what I wished. Thank you for this Mr. Darcy, I will forever be grateful for your timely assistance, if there is any way that I might repay your kindness . . ."

He spoke stiffly and stepped back. "I was merely exposing his character, Miss Bingley, it is not the first time, he has hurt others, and it is my fault for not exposing him long ago when we were in school or at Pemberley. If I had known his identity sooner, I would have informed your brother immediately and you would not have suffered for his actions. Thankfully the settlement was unsigned so there is no contract between you, and this situation is dissolved without further incident. I am sorry to see you disappointed."

"I am sorry to be disappointed as well." Caroline's gaze moved from his eyes to Elizabeth's wedding ring. "I had such hopes."

Darcy shifted uncomfortably, feeling the same sense of foreboding he experienced when in the presence of Anne. He turned to Elizabeth. "Forgive me dearest, but I think that we should return home."

"Darcy . . ." Bingley called. Darcy stopped his movement and turned back to his friend.

"I apologize, Bingley, I should have inquired more when you first mentioned the suitor and his claim to a connection with me. No doubt that claim helped to assure you of his worthiness."

"I admit that it did, but I also knew how you were burdened with your own concerns, and did not pursue the matter as I should." He watched as Caroline walked across the hallway to the drawing room and began whispering to Louisa, then heard Hurst announcing to the other guests that Wickham was called away unexpectedly and no announcement would be made. "I doubt that Wickham will be welcome in any other circles after this gossip makes the rounds. I am certain that Caroline will speak of his betrayal loudly and often. I know her, she will be the picture of propriety until the guests leave and then she will turn ugly. She is humiliated as are we all. We will be laughingstocks." He glanced around the room at the curious and murmuring guests and then back to his friend. "Please stay."

"No, I . . ."

"Mr. Darcy." Elizabeth said softly. "We should stay."

"Elizabeth . . ."

Elizabeth took his hand and squeezed. "Your continued presence will lend credence to your friendship with Mr. Bingley, and show that your offence remains where it should, with Mr. Wickham. I am so proud of you, Fitzwilliam, you knew this was wrong and stopped it from going further. Not speaking immediately would have allowed the farce to continue, and we know how hard it is to live down rumours. In the past two days I have seen you reject my pleas to step away from a confrontation. Clearly I have learned that my husband will protect anyone who he feels resides under his care. I will not question it again."

Darcy raised her hand to his lips and kissed it. "No dearest, I am not infallible. I rely on you to check me. After all, I was about to walk from this house, was I not?"

"We will stay, then?" She smiled and caressed his temple.

He nodded but glanced at Caroline then back to his wife. Elizabeth knew that she needed to relieve his concern if he was to stay and leaned forward to whisper to Bingley. "Do you see how your sister stares at my husband? I do not wish to start a fight with her, now do I? Imagine the gossip! I hope that you will repay the favour of our remaining by keeping her occupied?" She felt Darcy's hand grip hers hard and she laughed to see his expression relax.

Bingley smiled with relief and gladly joined Elizabeth. "I will be happy to do so. I am relieved that I decided to show Darcy the settlement before signing it, as well. At least I managed to do one thing right. I am ashamed of how gullible I have been. Whatever Caroline is thinking, I promise I will make it clear that her future will not in any way be connected to you. We are all aware now that her desire for Wickham was really her desire for Pemberley." Darcy closed his eyes and groaned. "That is what she stated, was it not? That is what was behind her accepting Wickham? It certainly was not his level of society; it was the hope of blending into yours."

"She will never be welcomed there." Darcy said quietly. "Forgive me, Bingley, but I will not be swayed from that."

"I understand, I only hope that I am still welcome."

Darcy felt Elizabeth lean on his shoulder, and he met her gaze. His lips lifted in a little smile and he squeezed her hand. "I think that we can tolerate you. You struck Wickham, that is worth a great deal in my book." His smile fell away. "I apologize for failing you."

"Hardly. I failed my sister, and that is my responsibility. I cannot imagine you being so oblivious that a man could make such an attempt on Miss Darcy." Noting the look of horror on Darcy's face, he nodded. "No man will ever win her hand solely for her dowry; you will make sure of that, Darcy. Your sister will be treasured just as Mrs. Darcy is treasured by you."

"I hope so." He looked back to Elizabeth.

"Will Mr. Wickham seek revenge upon you?" She asked worriedly. "He did narrowly lose a fortune because of your interference."

"I will not lose sleep over him." Darcy kissed her hand.

"Miss Bingley seems to be taking the news surprisingly well." They looked at her and collectively shuddered at the fixed smile on her face.

"As I said, the storm will come after everyone departs. Look how disappointed my brother is." Bingley nodded to Hurst. "He thought he was at last going to be rid of her."

"After this embarrassment, perhaps she will be willing to look at the genuine gentlemen who would not mind marrying her." Darcy said thoughtfully.

"It would have been a good match for her if he was genuine; there is no shame in marrying a gentleman who has studied the law." Elizabeth observed then felt Darcy's finger tracing over her wedding ring and looked up to his face. "Of course, I prefer farmers myself."

At last Darcy's eyes lit up and he smiled and laughed. "And I prefer the farmer's daughter."

8 JULY 1809
There was a small item in the paper this morning about Miss Caroline Bingley withdrawing her affections from George Wickham, Esq. and announcing that any rumours of an engagement were to be ignored. I had to laugh at the speed with which Miss Bingley moved to announce her availability to the world again. I suppose with only a month left in the Season, she needs to act quickly before the available suitors disappear to the countryside, at least the ones that interest her. I remain amazed at the entire situation. I would say that under other circumstances, Wickham and Miss Bingley were actually well-suited for each other. If money had been no object, they would have got on quite well, but each was using the other for their own means. I wonder if he would have abandoned her after marriage. At least this way she still has her dowry and may look again, otherwise she would be Hurst and Bingley's responsibility forever. Elizabeth assures me that an invitation to Miss Bingley to visit Pemberley is not forthcoming from her, and as she is the mistress, I will of course bow to her will. It does not at all pain me to do so.

Tomorrow we will visit the Gardiners and say our farewells. We have not seen them since the wedding and it will be a novelty to sit in their parlour and not be distracted with thoughts of how to steal a moment alone with Elizabeth. Instead I imagine I will be distracted with thoughts of our last encounter. Even now my beautiful bride sleeps only feet away from me, exhausted by our long night of lovemaking. I cannot get enough of her, the feeling of surrounding her body with mine and the sensation of her heart pounding against my own thrills me to the bone. She is still shy at the most unexpected times, I wonder if I will see her that way forever, I cannot help but say that I enjoy it, but I am also enjoying her beginning to take the lead in instigating our play, and each new touch of hers makes me want her more. I suppose that I am simply lost to her no matter how she comes to me, shy or bold. I cannot imagine living with a woman and calling her wife without such desire. It would be a farce. I read the vows we took last night as she slept and it occurred to me that those who marry for security also lie when they marry. We vow to love each other. No love exists in a marriage of convenience. If I am grateful for anything my ancestors have given me it is the freedom to marry honestly. I am desperately anxious to bring my dearest friend home. I dearly wish to hear her opinions and see her happiness. I cannot wait to invite her to work by my side and learn with me. I am still so lost there; I cannot imagine the loneliness I would have felt to return without her.

Elizabeth closed his journal and returned it to its place next to hers on their shared writing desk, and contemplated his words. "You overwhelm me, Fitzwilliam. One moment you are so strong, defending your family and friends from any who would hurt them; and the next you are so gentle and vulnerable." She passed her hand over the cover, then pulling several ribbons from her hair, created an intricate and colourful lover's knot. She reopened his book and placed the token on the last page, so he would know that she had been there to visit. Smiling at the gift that peeked from the pages she stood and looked into their bedchamber, where he lay in his immovable slumber. "I think that when we are home at Pemberley, I will have to experiment with ways to awaken you, my love." She happily considered his uncovered form, remembering which touches aroused his ardour and stealing over to his side for a moment, kissed his bottom. A little sigh escaped from his chest. She giggled and stole away. "I think that I know where to begin!"

"YOU CANNOT BE SERIOUS about Miss Gannon, can you?" Laura asked her brother after he told her about their dancing at another ball the night before. "Surely you will not call on her?"

"Why not?" He smiled at her rolling eyes. "Oh come on, you are the one who told me to start looking around at others!"

"Yes, but a twin of Elizabeth Darcy is not what I had in mind. She is a weak imitation of the woman! If she was so wonderful, do you really think that Mr. Darcy would have abandoned her so quickly at the vaguest suggestion that Elizabeth was in town and thinking of him?" She laughed. "Please Daniel. Victoria Gannon is just as conniving as her mother and as the niece of Lord Creary; I have no doubt that she is not going to entertain any thoughts of marrying a second son, no matter how successful you are. Her nose is so far in the air I wonder that she does not trip when she walks!"

"I think that you are exaggerating a bit. Although after Lord Creary's humiliation spread around town, I imagine that none of their noses are too far off of the ground. Father has certainly been enjoying bringing the subject up to all the other Lords." He chuckled and laughed to see her shaking head. "What do you want of me? Perhaps I am simply meant to be a bachelor; it is certainly fashionable for men not to marry these days. Wives and families are expensive."

"They are, but you are doing well, and I am certain that one day you will be a judge. And besides, you need to be loved."

"That is a sweet sentiment, but very rare. You know that from your experiences. What about you, by the way, you seem to have withdrawn from society."

"I have decided to take care of you. You deserve a good woman who truly cares for you, only you, and I am going to find her for you." She said determinedly.

"You did not answer my question, dear."

"I . . . I am going to wait for Mr. Harwick." She said softly. "I think that he just needs a little more time, but that his experience this Season taught him to hope that . . . That he might marry for affection again." She looked up at Stewart. "Perhaps I am foolish to do so, but I care for him."

"I admire your sentiments, Laura. I hope that you are not disappointed if his decision goes elsewhere." He squeezed her hand and saw her smile softly. "What do you know that I do not?"

"It is just a feeling." She shrugged. "I think that he is waiting, too."

"I do not understand."

"That is because you truly have not been in love before." Laura smiled. "No, not with Elizabeth, and not with Audrey Singleton." She raised her brows at him. "Ah, so I was right about that?"

"I do hope that my rivals in court cannot read me so well." He sighed. "So, I really never loved before?"

"I think that Audrey was a childhood friend to you, and a crush for her, maybe someone to think fondly about when things were so difficult with her husband. Elizabeth would have been a delightful partner for you under different circumstances, and you could have had a wonderful marriage. However, her heart was taken before you met, and you were not really prepared to accept her under any circumstances . . . That is over; it is time to move on. Agreed?"

"No Miss Gannon, then?"

"Absolutely not!" She declared.

"Very well then Sister, guide your hopeless brother." He stood and gave her a hug before leaving the room. "I am counting on you."

Chapter 31

arcy was seated at his desk sorting through papers to take to Pemberley when Foster appeared at the door. "Sir, Mr. Bingley and Mr. Hurst have arrived, shall I tell them you are on your way out?"

He closed his eyes; the visit was not entirely unexpected. "No, no, please show them in." Rising to his feet, he waited for them to enter, glancing down at the papers in the process, and trying to remember his intentions before his friend drove them from his mind.

"Darcy, good morning." Bingley said quietly.

"Thank you for this, Mr. Darcy." Hurst added.

"You are welcome." Looking over the unusually subdued and sober miens of the gentlemen he indicated the chairs before his desk. "Should I assume that this will be a lengthy interview?"

"We need advice regarding Caroline; she is determined to ruin herself with vindictiveness towards Wickham."

Darcy sighed. "Very well, we were about to visit the Gardiners. I will send Elizabeth ahead and join her there later."

"I am sorry Darcy. We are interrupting your plans." Bingley began to rise and Darcy stopped him.

"No, I understand very well the need to act swiftly and of course, we are leaving for Pemberley in two days. If you want my advice it must be now. Excuse me." He left the room and walked upstairs to where Elizabeth was talking to Mrs. Mercer and attempting to stop her itching fingers from helping Millie to pack. "Mrs. Darcy." He said quietly. The women looked up and instantly Mrs. Mercer gave Millie a glance and they disappeared. Elizabeth laughed when the door closed.

"What on earth have you said to them?" She put her hands on her hips. "Do you notice that the servants seem to evaporate whenever you and I are alone?"

Darcy smiled and walking forward, claimed her hands. "I asked Mrs. Mercer to inform them that we value our privacy, to always knock, and when the winter comes, to be mindful of our activity before entering to tend the fires." He kissed her rising brow and chuckled. "I believe that Mrs. Mercer has determined that we do not want any servants separating us at any time."

"I believe that Mrs. Mercer is delighted to see you smile." She rose up on her toes and kissed his nose. "Now what brings you here? We are not to leave for a half hour."

He smiled at her for a few moments before he continued. "Bingley and Hurst have arrived and need advice. It will probably take some time, and rather than delay our visit to the Gardiners, I suggest that you go on ahead, and I will join you as soon as I can. Just send the carriage back when you arrive."

"Oh but Fitzwilliam, it takes so long to get there and back, you would not arrive for three hours that way!"

"I doubt that it will take quite that long." He laughed to see her doubtful expression. "Well, maybe. We were just going to spend the afternoon with them. You will have time to talk with your aunt and sister without worrying over neglecting me." His eyes twinkled and she pursed her lips. "Admit it, love. You would. Go on and enjoy your time, I will be along as soon as I can. I will send a maid and footman with you and . . ."

"I think that I can ride in a carriage alone, Fitzwilliam." She smiled and laughed at his slowly shaking head. "No?"

"No." He leaned forward and kissed her lips. "No." Caressing a tendril of hair from her cheek he smiled and kissed her again. "I will see you later."

"Very well." She watched him depart and sighed. "Good luck." He smiled back at her and disappeared. Almost immediately Mrs. Mercer and Millie reentered the room and resumed their work; leaving Elizabeth to marvel in wonder at the household she had been given.

Darcy returned to the study and closed the door. "Thank you for your patience; now then, what can I do for you?"

"Caroline is, what is that term they use in America? The one for the tribes? Oh, the warpath!" Bingley exclaimed. "She is furious with Wickham's deceit!"

"I should think that she would be grateful to find it out in time."

"Oh she is, believe me, the praise she heaps on you is frightening in its volume." Hurst said wearily. "And I do not mean in pitch. She was interested in you before Darcy, but I would say she is quite fixated now. You should have heard her after everyone left. *Mr. Darcy was so kind, so admirable, so intelligent, so . . . well, it was nauseating.*"

"I presume that you have reminded her of my marriage?" He said coldly and began to twist the ring on his finger.

"Of course." Hurst smiled. "I believe that Bingley made that point very clear to her; did you not?"

Bingley shrugged. "I told her that if she causes you any trouble, including implying some nonexistent fond connection with you or your family, I would send her back north to live with our maiden aunt so she would have a good taste of her future."

"Well done." Darcy said with admiration. "What moved you to be so clear with her?"

"I remembered your tale of telling your aunt to leave you alone regarding your cousin."

"A lot of good that did." Darcy rubbed his hand over his face.

"Louisa gave her a tongue-lashing that I think frightened Hurst, here." Bingley smiled when his brother rolled his eyes. "You did not know she had it in her, did you?"

"What was said?"

"Caroline was praising you and Louisa told her to stop it immediately. She told her that there were countless men who would accept her if she would accept that she was not a peeress. Wickham exposed her motivation as much as she did. My sister is not delusional, she knows that you would never marry her, but that surely did not stop her wishing for the association."

"Has she failed to realize that with you being part of my world she could simply graft onto your success in a few years?"

"I suppose that was not fast enough for her satisfaction." Bingley said softly. "I know I am barely accepted now."

Darcy studied him for a moment. "But the point is, Bingley, that you are being accepted." Bingley smiled gratefully and Darcy nodded. "Well, in any case, you seem to have her handled as far as her . . .whatever her thoughts are towards me. What is your trouble now? I saw the notice in the paper; it seemed unnecessary but relatively harmless. I suppose it confused more people than anything since the engagement had not been announced. I can only presume that she has done more. She is the one who placed it?"

"She did. But now she is determined to go around town describing what a scoundrel Wickham is." Bingley sat forward and glanced at Hurst then at Darcy. "Although he undoubtedly is, I think, well Louisa warned me, that it would not do our family any favours to hear how we were hoodwinked, new money and naiveté, and all that. We would be seen as, what word did she use?"

Hurst snorted. "Simpletons, country bumpkins, fools with money and no sense, taken in by . . ."

Darcy held up his hand. "I understand the gist of her feelings. You are just making headway in the *ton* and this could set you back some, at least you Bingley, not so much Hurst, your place is assured."

"Well, I suppose, but then I never aimed to be more than I already am. I have no grand illusions." He smiled. "Besides, I think that my friends have heard my desires to have a Caroline-free home enough to understand my desire to accept any likely suitor."

Darcy said nothing and looked down to his hands, feeling the intense gaze of the two men upon him as he thought. "Are there, were there, any men interested in her before Wickham appeared?"

"Yes, one."

"Is he still available?"

"I believe so." Bingley saw Hurst nodding.

"Honestly Bingley, as long as you still have my support, you will be fine. I have it on good authority that the rumours and innuendo that followed me have been very well quashed by our marriage, our friends and relatives, the news of the fire, and by the exceptional performance of my wife in every public situation this week. Your association with me is your safety. I will gladly ask my family to inform any who care to hear of our friendship, as well as telling of your invitation to Pemberley. Your sister, however, needs to control herself; I have never known Wickham to purposely hurt someone. His method has always been to charm and cheat his way to profit, and he has always chosen his marks carefully, but ruining his name in your circle may make him vengeful. It would be wise to calm Miss Bingley from her humiliation and redirect her attention to another, more permanent solution."

"Marry this former suitor?"

"If he can be persuaded. He might want you to sweeten the dowry a bit. Her unseemly behaviour would be seen as a liability."

"More than the twenty thousand?" Bingley gaped. "How much?"

"No more than three, I would say." Darcy said softly. "I talked Wickham down to three."

"IT IS VERY GOOD OF MR. DARCY to stay behind with Mr. Bingley." Jane said quietly. "I can only imagine the horror they feel with being so taken in by Mr. Wickham. Do you truly believe that he meant to do wrong by Miss Bingley?"

"Jane, I assure you, Fitzwilliam has told me enough of his dealings with Mr. Wickham that I cannot see this man ever doing anything that would not derive a benefit solely to himself. No, he was not deeply in love with Miss Bingley, and her love, if it existed, was not going to turn his life around." Elizabeth patted Jane's hand. "We have been introduced to some very good men, but I am afraid that Mr. Wickham is not amongst them."

"And he is not alone." Mrs. Gardiner added. "One must be very careful who you accept as your friend."

"A wolf in sheep's clothes." Jane murmured. "How do you know who is good, and how do you know when to let a man know what you are feeling?" Elizabeth and Mrs. Gardiner exchanged glances. Jane did not notice but spoke on. "Charlotte always said to help him along, but then she has never been attached to a man. How would she know? Perhaps her philosophy has scared them away?"

"I let Fitzwilliam know, the best way I could whenever we met, even if it was just a look." Elizabeth smiled. "Is there someone you like?"

Jane startled and looked up to her sister. "Oh, oh no, I was just . . . thinking. I remember that Mr. Darcy did say something about a gentleman wishing to know the lady's feelings." She rose to her feet. "I am sure that you would like to say goodbye to Aunt privately, so I will just go upstairs for a while."

They watched her go and Elizabeth moved to sit next to Mrs. Gardiner. "Is she well? Is she regretting Mr. Harwick?"

"She is regretting her behaviour and wondering over her tendency to be complacent at all times."

"I am surprised that she wants to return to Longbourn with us. She knows what I experienced after Mr. Stewart's rejection, of course I am married, and Mama likes her." Elizabeth looked at her ring and turned it on her finger. "Perhaps she will like me now."

"Whatever the reasons behind her approval, will it not be better than never having received it at all?" Mrs. Gardiner took her hand and looked at the ring. "It is beautiful."

"It is." Elizabeth blinked back her emotion then threw her arms around her aunt. "How can I ever thank you for all you have done for me? How can I ever repay you? You taught me how to be a lady; and what marriage should and could be. You rescued me. Without you and Uncle, I never would have met Fitzwilliam; I would probably not even have been attractive to Mr. Stewart. Thank you so much! I love you."

The two women hugged tightly. "Your uncle and I love you and did nothing that you did not want. You always had the ability to become such a lovely woman. Bringing you to town would have made no difference if you were not determined to make something of yourself." She drew away and smiled. "And look at what all of your hard work has given you! Fitzwilliam is a wonderful man. I wish I could be with you when you at last see Pemberley. It is the perfect place for you. I look forward to the news of your first pregnancy, and can already imagine the joy Fitzwilliam will feel to fill that empty house with children."

"Thank you Aunt." Elizabeth hugged her again. "For everything."

"WELL THEN, I HAVE RECEIVED a message from de Bourgh." Lord Matlock picked up the letter from his desk as the men gathered in his study after dinner the following day. "He asks for remedies for a tired posterior."

All four of the men laughed. "That is the navy for you, all walking and rope climbing, no practical experience on the land." Fitzwilliam raised his glass. "To the cavalry!" They drank and he grinned. "Any other news?"

"He reports that Collins appeared at the house to visit Anne and lick his boots." A collective groan filled the room. "Of course de Bourgh has no power to send him off now, but when he is master and Mousely is retired, Collins will go with him. Until then he will continue to shake him off his leg. He described the encounter as uncomfortably similar to being humped by a mongrel."

Again they laughed, and Fitzwilliam cheered. "I think that I am going to like this cousin of ours!"

"You may have your opinions of Collins, but he is a tenacious little beast." Layton smiled.

"Perhaps you could offer him Kympton when it comes up, Darcy." Lord Matlock's lips twitched.

"I have enough problems, thank you. Collins inherits Longbourn when Elizabeth's father dies." All eyes turned to him and he shrugged. "Well, his father has to die first."

"And which lucky Bennet daughter will win his hand?" Fitzwilliam asked. "And further, can you not anticipate the joy of their visits to Pemberley?"

"Do not even attempt to entertain such a possibility." Darcy threatened him, then looked back at his uncle. "Is there more news?"

"He asks about Catherine's methods. It seems that she would squeeze the tenants for increasingly ridiculous rents and larger portions of their yields. She even limited their cider supply." He looked at Darcy and raised his brow. "I had no idea, did you?"

"I know that she was hard on them, but it seemed that she did these things at harvest time, and of course I did not see the books until the past two springs, Father handled it before then. Her steward did as she bid to keep his position."

"De Bourgh disapproves." Lord Matlock consulted the letter. "He said that he may have spent the past fourteen years on the sea, but his experience leading men tells him enough to know how to care for these tenants. He begs for advice on a number of subjects. Of course I will be happy to help him. Perhaps we might pay a visit there before returning to Matlock." He looked at Layton who nodded his head.

"Yes, we should at least look in on Anne. Aunt Catherine is established in the dowager's house?"

"Yes, she is out of Rosings." Lord Matlock smiled. "Helen heard from the ladies selected for Elizabeth's calls. Catherine's friend Mrs. Kendall came by yesterday, complimenting her for sending Elizabeth to visit. She knew the reason was the hope that she would be persuaded to give her public approval. Helen knew that she was inclined to support Catherine, and winning her opinion was important." He laughed. "Of course she was correct. She called Helen a brilliant strategist, and noted that when Elizabeth at last realizes her power as Mrs. Darcy, she wanted to be on her good side. She suggested that Catherine attempt to reconcile with you Darcy, if she ever wishes to leave the dowager's house again."

Darcy stared down into his glass. He was, after two years, finally becoming fully aware, but not at all confident with the power he held, and was not entirely sure how he felt with the acknowledgement of Elizabeth's potential to be a force in society. "I am glad to hear of her support." He said finally.

"Catherine lost the townhouse did she not?"

"Yes, it is de Bourgh's now, well Anne's." Lord Matlock was watching Darcy, and trying to puzzle out his silence. "Son." Darcy looked up. "I doubt that Elizabeth could ever become like the ladies of society." He smiled at the astonishment on his nephew's face. "I cannot read most of your expressions Darcy, but when it comes to your wife, no mask can cover your feelings."

Layton looked at Singleton and asked for a refill of his port. Fitzwilliam busied himself with the snuff box. Darcy nodded to his uncle and looked back into his glass. Lord Matlock cleared his throat. "I also heard from Mrs. Jenkinson on Anne's welfare."

"She is well?" Darcy asked.

"She is very weak; however she is seemingly thriving under the care of our physician."

Fitzwilliam looked over to his cousin then asked his father, "Does Anne still believe herself to be wed to Darcy?"

"Yes, she lives under the impression that she is preparing Rosings for him. I understand that when she speaks of him she is immediately corrected and is assured that his feelings for her are familial only." Noticing Darcy's stony expression he added, "However, she does not listen and it has been determined that if she were to actually see him, she would likely become physical."

"So Darcy, you will never visit Rosings again."

"Not as long as she lives." He said softly. "I am sorry that it must be this way."

"I certainly hope that you are not regretting marrying Elizabeth instead of Anne." Layton smiled and nudged him, offering a refill of his port.

A small curve appeared on Darcy's lips. "No, no, I am not regretting that decision at all." The room filled with laughter at that understatement and Darcy's smile grew a little as he looked down to his boots.

"Well, we have let him alone long enough. Come on, give us the details!" Fitzwilliam grinned.

"You do not seriously expect me to speak of . . .what are you asking?" Darcy peered at him suspiciously. "You are trying to get me to . . ."

Lord Matlock interrupted. "My son's years in the army have eroded his manners."

"I only wished to ask after Elizabeth's well being after that old snake's imposition at the ball." Fitzwilliam said innocently.

"She is fine." Darcy glared.

"She was much admired there." Singleton added and winked at Layton. "At least by the men."

Layton grinned when Darcy's fiery gaze moved to a new target. "Yes; and the same men were sure you would not have the least idea how to . . ."

"Well they are mistaken." Darcy interrupted with a growl.

"Stick in the mud." Fitzwilliam offered.

"Dullard." Layton agreed.

"I heard many offers to take care of the poor girl." Singleton raised his glass to his lips, and stepped out of range of Darcy's fist.

"Then again, I heard the ladies remarking on his handsome face, particularly when it was glaring so at Creary. Rather similar to what is displayed before us now." Lord Matlock laughed. "Watch yourself Son, you may be married, but there are plenty of bored wives and widows who will willingly take you on. Not to mention the courtesans who will gladly pick your pockets."

"Is that your experience, sir?" Darcy said through clenched teeth.

"Years ago." He said thoughtfully. "I never said yes, of course."

Singleton's smile fell away and he looked down to the floor, as did Layton. Fitzwilliam's eyes travelled between his brothers then met Darcy's. "Seems that the joke has backfired."

"I have had enough of it." Darcy said quietly.

"I am to be a father." Singleton said softly and looked up to Lord Matlock. "Audrey told me this morning."

"My . . . my little girl is . . ." A beaming smile lit up Lord Matlock's face. "Grandfather!" He laughed and shook Singleton's hand. "I knew it! I knew she was with child! Helen was sure ages ago! When?"

Singleton laughed and flexed his crushed fingers. "January, she predicts." He turned to meet the smiles and handshakes of the men of his family. "I thank you all for what you have done for me, Layton and Fitzwilliam for scaring me sober, and you Darcy, for the example of felicity. I realize that Audrey became with child before I began to change, which is a credit to her allowing me . . . But if I had not changed, instead of a wife filled with joy of our pending family, she would likely be cursing me, and I probably would be too drunk to notice."

"If you were still alive."

"Yes, my creditors were becoming impatient with me." He said softly. "The thought of walking in front of a carriage had crossed my mind."

"I had no idea it was so bad." Darcy said with his brow knit. "Audrey never spoke of it."

"She would not." He shook his head and blinked. "I will spend the rest of my life apologizing to her."

"No, spend your life being a dedicated husband and father." Lord Matlock clapped his back. "I am proud of you, Son."

"Perhaps you could mention that to my father." Singleton said softly, "Although a son would likely do just as well."

"I will speak to him before you and Audrey return to the estate." Lord Matlock assured him and smiled.

"It seems that I had better get to work on an heir." Layton smiled. "I can hear Mother now congratulating her daughter and then offering advice to my wife."

"Well, it is certainly about time, Stephen. Perhaps the stories are incorrect; you are the one who needs advice, not Darcy." Fitzwilliam winked. "You are the hopeless dullard."

"Richard." Layton said with a warning in his voice. "Enough."

"You can dish it out but not take it?" Fitzwilliam laughed. "Come big brother; let me whisper some advice to you."

"You give advice?" Darcy smiled. "This I should like to hear." He crossed his arms and leaned against a table. "Speak on!"

"Well, one must, first and foremost, be handsome." He drew himself up. "And intriguing."

"Ha!" Layton laughed. "You certainly do not qualify! Those scars are hardly appealing!"

"But they are intriguing." He raised his brow. "Besides, by the time the scars are visible, I believe that the lady is quite committed to the evening."

Darcy groaned along with the other men. "Enough of this. Perhaps we should return to the ladies before this conversation deteriorates further into the bragging of the schoolyard."

"At least I have stories worth bragging about." Fitzwilliam grinned, and felt his father's arm around his shoulder.

"Another time, Son. Perhaps we might even believe some of them." The men laughed and toasted the father-to-be.

ELIZABETH LIFTED HER HEAD to the sound of laughter floating down the hallway, and felt great satisfaction when she recognized the low rumble of her husband's voice. She caught Georgiana's smile and walked to her side. "He is happy."

"Oh Elizabeth, he is so very happy! I cannot remember him so joyous; it has to be years, even before he went away on his Grand Tour! It is because of you." She threw her arms around her sister and squeezed. "I cannot thank you enough for bringing him back."

"He was never really gone." She hugged her. "Just like you, I think."

"But if it were not for you, we would both be still so sad." Georgiana let go and beamed.

"I believe that your time here with your aunt and uncle has been very important to your improvement." Elizabeth saw Lady Matlock standing nearby and listening. "I am afraid that I will not be nearly as instructive as Aunt Helen."

"I think that Georgiana will welcome simply being a sister for awhile." Lady Matlock patted her shoulder and walked away.

"Is that so?" Elizabeth whispered and squeezed her hand.

"Yes." She sighed. "I am tired of lessons."

"Do you truly wish to go away to school? I know that you were unhappy when Fitzwilliam first spoke to you about it."

"I was." Georgiana looked down at her sister still holding her hand. "I was frightened that if I left something would happen to him and I would be alone, or . . . he would realize that he did not need me anymore and would not want me to come back. I guess that was silly."

"Not at all. I would have felt the same way. You just have to remember that he loves you very much, no matter where you are." Elizabeth smiled as Georgiana's face brightened.

"He cannot wait to take you home. He told me some of his plans! I am jealous!"

"Well you are coming home as well; perhaps he will ask you to join us?" Elizabeth laughed to see a mischievous smile appear. "What is that for?"

"I told Fitzwilliam that I wish to return with our Aunt and Uncle. Mrs. Somers will leave me at the end of the month and it would be silly to have her travel to Pemberley for a few weeks then back here to collect her things and go to her father. I will remain here, and we will see her off properly, and . . .you and Fitzwilliam may follow his plans." She giggled and took her hands. "Oh, he is so excited!"

"How can you tell?" Audrey asked when she joined them. "Your brother has a talent for not letting on his feelings, good or bad."

"Oh, I can tell, can you not, Elizabeth?"

"I can." She sighed. "There is a twinkle to his eye that appears when he is especially pleased."

"So subtle." Audrey shook her head.

"Speaking of which, when are you going to announce?" Lady Matlock and Alicia joined them and patted her daughter's belly. "Have you told him?"

"Told who what?" Georgiana asked.

Elizabeth gasped. "Audrey! Are you . . ."

"Yes." She blushed. "Near New Year we will have our baby."

"And when were you planning to tell us!" Alicia cried and hugged her.

"I just wanted to be sure, and . . . yes, Robert knows." She smiled and tears began to flow. "He is so grateful that he has made the many changes to his life. He . . . He is being so good to me." Elizabeth took out her handkerchief and wiped Audrey's cheeks, then wiped her own. "I never could have imagined us being this way a year ago."

"Oh Audrey, I am so happy for you!" Elizabeth cried.

"It is because of you and Darcy, you know." Audrey took her hands and looked at her sincerely. "Your example has been such a great influence to us."

"How? We have only been married weeks and . . . Well; honestly only together for a few months, you have been with child at least that long." She looked down and blushed. "At least if your time of confinement is correct."

"I never stopped my duty to him, but . . . trust me, your influence is great. I thank you."

"Audrey is correct, Elizabeth. Darcy's behaviour has been influencing Stephen for quite some time. He suspected that Darcy was in love years ago, and he watched how he approached Pemberley as well, the combination moved him to gradually make changes in our marriage. It took time but it is greatly improved. I hope that we will be crying happily over a future heir sometime." She smiled and squeezed Audrey's hand.

"And you will surely be with child soon, Elizabeth." Lady Matlock smiled as she instantly blushed. "Darcy himself was born exactly nine months after his parents' married."

Alicia saw her discomfort and turned to her mother-in-law. "How long did you wait before Stephen was born?"

"Oh, he came within the first year." She laughed. "I remember Henry sitting at the piano trying to pick out the songs his governess sang to him in the nursery while we waited those long months."

Elizabeth walked over to the pianoforte and sat down. She started to play with the keys as she remembered songs from childhood and softly sang, "Lavender's blue, diddle diddle, lavender's green. When I am king, diddle diddle, you shall be queen. Lavender's green, diddle diddle, lavender's blue. You must love me, diddle diddle, 'cause I love you."[6] Elizabeth looked up to see the ladies had gathered around the instrument, but beyond their shoulders she saw Darcy in the doorway, his eyes alive and happy, and fixed on her. She became shy and studied the keys as he walked over. The crowd moved away, and he took a seat beside her on the bench.

"You have not sung for so long, dearest." He kissed her cheek. "Sing to me again."

"What would you like to hear?"

"Do you know any of Robert Burns' songs?"

"I am afraid that I will torture the words with my poor Scottish accent." She laughed and looked back up from her hands. Darcy took advantage of her raised face and softly kissed her lips. Elizabeth blushed as the ladies of the family looked on and began whispering amongst themselves. "Fitzwilliam!"

His twinkling eyes smiled at her and he ignored the conversation as he bent to whisper against her ear. "Nothing could be tortured coming from your lips, my love." Darcy's fingers entwined with hers and Elizabeth leaned against him, then he let go and began to stroke the keys, and sing softly in her ear. "O my Luve's like a red, red rose that's newly sprung in June. O my Luve's like the melodie, that's sweetly play'd in tune."

Elizabeth sighed and he continued on, "As fair art thou, my bonnie lass, so deep in luve am I: and I will luve thee still, my dear, till a' the seas gang dry." Darcy noticed Fitzwilliam mouthing the words, and smiling he sang, "Till a' the seas gang dry, my dear, and the rocks melt wi' the sun; I will love thee still, my

---

[6] *Diddle Diddle*, or *The Kind Country Lovers, 1685*, I. Opie and P. Opie, The Oxford Dictionary of Nursery Rhymes (Oxford University Press, 1951, 2nd edn., 1997), pp. 265-7.

dear, while the sands o' life shall run. And fare thee weel, my only Luve, and fare thee weel, a while! And I will come again, my Luve, tho' it were ten thousand mile."[7]

He ended with another gentle kiss to her lips and the applause of the ladies and groans of the men. Looking up, he noticed Layton's shaking head and smiled. Elizabeth blushed again as he slipped his arm around her waist. "Where did you learn that accent?"

"Father used to take me fishing in Scotland when I was a boy." He smiled with the memory and noticed her considering him.

"Will you sing to me at home, where I can express my admiration freely?"

He chuckled and hugged her to him. "Oh dearest, that would be my great pleasure."

"Besides, we must keep your fingers nimble." She said quietly and glancing up to him was delighted to see his blue eyes darken and his tongue appear to moisten his lips. "I have been considering a number of activities."

"Elizabeth . . ." Darcy's breath hitched and his grip on her waist tightened.

"Another!" Fitzwilliam cried. "Come now, you cannot just stop entertaining us!" Nudging Georgiana he grinned, "Your turn Cousin, dislodge these lovebirds and give us a tune suitable for dancing!"

"Go away, Richard." Darcy said under his breath.

"Why would I do that?" He laughed. "Oh, am I disturbing you?" Leaning down he spoke softly to Darcy's shoulder, "Difficulty in rising?" He snorted and took Georgiana's arm. "Come my dear, he is immovable; therefore it is Elizabeth's turn to perform."

"Your cousin enjoys amusing himself at other's expense." Elizabeth said quietly.

"He does." Darcy glared. "Dearest, please appease him and play. If I try to stand now I will never hear the end of it."

She looked down at his lap and behind the cover of the instrument, she caressed gently over his breeches. He groaned and she giggled. "Oh, so many ideas I have."

"Be careful Wife, I have a long memory for the offences against me."

"I sincerely doubt that you would find my ideas offensive, sir." She began to stand, embarrassed with his response to her attempt to be bold.

Darcy grabbed her hand and drew her back to his side. "Where are you going?"

"I am disturbing you so I will leave." She fixed her glare on his face. "Unless you apologize."

"For what?" His voice rose an octave and she raised her brow. Darcy blushed with the attention he had garnered from the family scattered around the room. Clearing his throat, he tried again. "For what?"

---

[7] Robert Burns, "My Love is Like a Red, Red Rose," 1794.

"For never singing to me before."

Darcy leaned to her ear and whispered warmly. "I believe that I have sung my passion every time that you allow me into your embrace, my love." Elizabeth blushed. "Perhaps I should sing louder?"

"You are hardly quiet, now." She whispered back.

"Neither are you." He kissed her and they smiled at each other. "I did not realize that I was . . ."

"I did not either." Elizabeth giggled to see him blushing just as fiercely. "I cannot wait to hear you sing to me tonight."

"Shall you join us now? We are going to drink a toast to Audrey and Robert." Lady Matlock asked and held back the laugh that threatened to see the startled couple's flushed faces grow brighter. "Come, you will be alone for several weeks. I am surprised that your sister is not accompanying you back to Pemberley, Elizabeth." Pursing her lips to see how both of them seemed dismayed, she added, "How is she?"

Elizabeth felt her hand being squeezed and she pulled herself together. "She is well, I wish that she had sat with me this week to receive the visitors, but she insists that she was a liability and reminder of my past. I tried to convince her otherwise but she would not hear of it."

"I believe that your sister is trying to make up for all of the trouble she caused, and before you become angry and defend her, I will change the subject. Will she remain in town? I would be happy to have her visit us while we remain."

"That is very kind of you, but she will be riding back to Longbourn with us." Elizabeth glanced at Darcy, who had become very quiet and was looking down at their hands. "She has decided that she has been away long enough. Perhaps she will return to Pemberley with us when we bring Georgiana here for school."

"Your sister Mary will be attending school as well?"

"Yes, but a different one. Papa has refused Fitzwilliam's offer to pay." She squeezed his hand and he looked back up. "It was very generous of you."

"I . . . I just wished to be sure that she could go." He kissed her fingers and stood. "Excuse me."

"Is everything well?" Lady Matlock asked and took the seat he had vacated.

"I believe so. He does not like praise." Elizabeth said slowly as he walked to stand alone by the window.

Lady Matlock looked between them and said in the barest of whispers, "I have not had the opportunity to ask, Elizabeth . . . Is everything well between you? Is Darcy kind?"

It took her a few moments to realize what was being asked and said quietly, "Fitzwilliam is wonderful; he is the dearest man." Elizabeth turned her head and found Darcy's eyes were on her. Her cheeks grew pink, remembering what he had written in his journal, and her mind was filled with the image of him walking into the library, her token of ribbon dangling from his fingertips, and how he wordlessly took her in his arms and left her breathless with his kiss. Darcy's cheeks coloured as well and a small smile appeared when he heard her soft laugh.

"I am happy to see my new niece so delighted." Lord Matlock chuckled and joined him.

"As am I. I look forward to our departure."

"Will you stop at Longbourn?" The men moved across the room and sat down.

"Elizabeth received a letter from Mr. Bennet hoping that he would see us. Mrs. Bennet is anxious to invite the neighbourhood to show us off. That is something I will not allow." Darcy said positively. "Elizabeth sent a letter this morning telling Mr. Bennet of our plans, but she asks that her mother not be aware of our expected arrival time. We have no desire to be put on display."

"You do not. But Elizabeth will miss saying farewell to her friends. Make sure that your wishes are not the only ones that are pursued."

"Sir, Elizabeth had very few friends in Hertfordshire." He looked back over to his wife. "She had many acquaintances, but other than her sisters, the only other woman she speaks of with any fondness is Miss Charlotte Lucas. If she wishes, we will pay them a call. This is her decision. She does not wish to stay longer than it will take her to collect a few mementos and properly farewell her family. I believe that she has felt that her home was in London more so than Longbourn. The parents she will regret are the Gardiners." Darcy turned his gaze back to Lord Matlock. "I told Mr. Gardiner yesterday how I am indebted to him for bringing her here."

"I understand that you have known of her address for some time."

"Not specifically, but . . . yes, I could have found it out if I had tried. In all honesty I am rather ashamed that I did not hire a man to do just that. It was rather spineless of me not to do so, especially after I knew of Stewart and his rejection."

"Hmm. I think that you might have done so eventually."

Darcy smiled a little. "Why do you have such confidence in that?"

"I think that you were waiting for her to be a little older, were you not?" Lord Matlock smiled. "Richard told me how surprised you were to learn her age when you first spied her."

"I suppose that he told every secret."

"No, but I think that your worry over her youth has a great deal to do with your fear of childbirth."

Darcy's eyes widened and Lord Matlock laughed. "I saw apprehension appear in your eyes when Robert announced their news, and just now I saw your expression change when Helen said we were to drink a toast. You cannot compare your mother's experience to Elizabeth. She is a good strong girl."

"Sir, I . . ." Darcy looked at his hands. "I anticipate fatherhood greatly, it was one of the first things I thought about when we became engaged, but sir since we married, the worry, how do you address that? I look at Audrey and Singleton, and I feel their joy, but I . . .”

“Pray, and acquire the best care you can.” He looked at his daughter then back to the young man before him. “I know that you have fears, Son. I know the graves at Pemberley. When the time comes, I will be happy to be your confidant, should you need one.”

He said nothing for several moments then said to his hands, “I am fortunate to have you and Mr. Gardiner as surrogate fathers.”

“That is a great compliment, thank you, and I am pleased to share that title with Gardiner.” Servants arrived bearing bottles of champagne and glasses. Everyone stood and Darcy handed Elizabeth a glass and bent to kiss her.

“Are you well?” She whispered.

“As long as you are, dearest, I am too.” He lifted his glass and drank a toast to the baby Singleton, then another to his wife.

THE CARRIAGE WAS NEARING MERYTON and Darcy could feel the tension within growing by the mile, glancing at Elizabeth’s encouraging smile, he addressed his sister. “When we return to London to bring Georgiana to school, we hope that you will travel back home with us. We were planning to invite my cousins to visit, and perhaps a few other friends as well.”

“Mr. Bingley?”

Darcy noted Elizabeth’s interest before looking back to Jane. “Naturally.”

“Have you heard anything more about Miss Bingley?”

“No, nothing new, but her behaviour is not helping anyone.”

Jane’s brow furrowed. “Will she travel to Pemberley with her brother?”

“No.” Elizabeth said shortly and offered nothing more. “However Jane, I do want you to come.”

“It is far too expensive, Lizzy.”

“You would be travelling with us. And no matter how serene your appearance, you know that you will be more than ready to escape Mama by then. Although she may not be as unhappy with you since Fitzwilliam will save the family from the hedgerows.” She laughed when he sighed. “So be prepared to venture north at Michaelmas. Then you will be with us for the Harvest Home. Please Jane! I do not know the first thing about hosting a dance!”

“And I do?”

“Please!” Elizabeth turned to Darcy. “Persuade her, Fitzwilliam!”

“You will come.” Darcy said quietly.

“Well that was simple.” Elizabeth laughed. “He will brook no opposition, and Jane, please do not make him put on his *Master of Pemberley* face. It is quite a sight.”

“Is that so, Mrs. Darcy?” He touched his boot to hers from across the carriage. “I do not know if I like that description.”

"Did I say that it was an awful sight?" Elizabeth tilted her head and he smiled.

"Well, if it is no trouble . . ."

Elizabeth groaned. "Would we beg you to come if it were?" The coach lurched to a stop and the occupants looked up in surprise. "How did that happen? We are here."

The Bennet family streamed from the front door, first in line was Mrs. Bennet, waving her handkerchief and crying out for her salts. Jane looked from the sight of her family back to her sister and brother. "Yes, I will come."

The carriage door opened and Darcy closed his eyes for a moment and stepped out. His expression was inscrutable. "Oh Mr. Darcy!" Mrs. Bennet cried. "We had no idea you were coming!"

"We wished to surprise you, madam." He bowed and turned to the carriage, first handing down Jane, and then smiling to Elizabeth. She made a little face that only he saw and stepped down.

"*MRS. DARCY!*" Mrs. Bennet screeched. "OH how well that sounds! Let me see your ring!" She grabbed Elizabeth's hand and paused to examine the fine crocheted glove she wore. "Oh." Elizabeth carefully removed it and then presented the prized hand to her mother. "It is true." Mrs. Bennet whispered; and promptly fainted dead away.

"THANK YOU, MR. DARCY. I am afraid that I could not have lifted my wife from the ground."

"It was no trouble, sir."

The men sat in silence. Upstairs the floor creaked and they could hear the sound of female voices. Mr. Bennet shifted in his chair, Darcy crossed his legs. "I appreciate your breaking the journey here. I despaired of seeing my daughters again."

"Miss Bennet wished to return to Longbourn. I could not allow her to travel by post, and there was no reason for Mr. Gardiner to foot the expense of her transportation when we could easily modify our path home."

"Did Lizzy wish to come?" He asked quietly.

"Elizabeth was apprehensive, but yes it was her wish to come." Darcy saw a flash of relief appear in his eyes, and decided to relent slightly. "She is happy to see you carry through with your promise to educate your daughters." Mr. Bennet nodded. "My offer to aid you stands."

"I would prefer to do this myself."

"My sister begins school at the same time as Miss Mary."

"Yes, I know. Elizabeth told me."

"It would be a great comfort to me if Georgiana was not alone at this unfamiliar place. She enjoyed meeting Miss Mary at our wedding."

"I noticed that the girls took to each other."

"I believe it was out of relief to find someone of a similar age in that room full of adults." Darcy said tonelessly. "However, they did get along. I would consider it a favour if Miss Mary attended school with Georgiana. I would of course make up the difference in tuition."

"Do you always get your way, Mr. Darcy?"

"No." He said quietly. "If I had, Elizabeth and I would be marrying next week. Or rather, if I had, I would have found my way to the Gardiner's home the very day that I first saw her. My father would have met her, and would have given me his blessing because he would have been as charmed as I." Darcy stared out the window and saw a young woman arrive accompanied by a young man. "Miss Lucas?"

Mr. Bennet nodded. "I sent a note to her, and asked that she come alone without a word to her family, but it seems that her brother escorted her."

"As he should." He watched as Miss Lucas entered and the man remained outside, looking up at the house. "Thank you, Elizabeth will be pleased." His gaze returned to Mr. Bennet. "Do you accept my offer?"

"Your command." Mr. Bennet suggested and felt the flick of Darcy's eyes over him. "Of course, I would be a fool not to."

"Fine. I will pay both tuitions and you may simply send me whatever you were to send the other school, or perhaps it would be better spent purchasing her a new wardrobe." Darcy stood. "I will be walking." He took out his watch and checked it against the mantle clock. "I will return in one hour. I intend to depart a quarter hour later. We need to make the inn before dusk."

"An hour." Mr. Bennet said softly. "Very well. Enjoy your exercise, sir." Darcy nodded and left the room. Mr. Bennet watched him stride out of the house and walk in the direction that Robert Lucas took, then disappeared quickly from view. His eyes lifted to the ceiling and he wondered of the conversations upstairs.

"PLEASE, LIZZY! MAY I HAVE THAT GOWN?" Lydia grabbed at the frock and succeeding; held it up to her. "Will it fit?"

"It should, but it really is not suitable for you." Elizabeth took it back and watched as a bonnet was taken in its stead. "Mary, you should take all of these things. You are out now, and they do not have much wear."

"Oh, but the colours are so bright."

"You will need a great many new things before you go to school." Elizabeth smiled. "Perhaps we can take you to my modiste in town and I can buy you some new things. We will be ordering gowns for Georgiana. I think that you will need to wear some finer dresses than I can give you from my closet."

"Why?" Kitty demanded. "Why does she get new dresses?"

"Because she must have all of the advantages. Georgiana is very excited to have you join her."

"If Papa allows it." Mary said nervously. "He may say no."

"If it is a request of Lizzy's he will say yes." Lydia grabbed another bonnet and tried it on. "I want this one, too."

"I wanted that one! Lizzy! Tell her!" Kitty grabbed at the hat and the two girls ran from the room.

Jane stood up from where she was placing Elizabeth's lifetime of journals in a trunk on the floor and looked at her with a smile. "I know what you are thinking, but I needed to come home. I need to see clearly what you acknowledged long ago, and perhaps do some good with the knowledge I have."

Elizabeth nodded and held her hand. "Uncle will send his carriage if you need to leave. We will be back very soon." The sisters hugged and Charlotte knocked on the open door.

"Eliza." She opened her arms and they embraced. Charlotte held her face in her hands. "Your father sent a servant with a note. Thank you for wishing to say goodbye to me."

"I could not leave without seeing you." Elizabeth smiled and Charlotte took her hand to look at her ring.

"You give hope to all of us spinsters, you know. If you happen to find any lonely rich men in search of a bride, my family would be much obliged."

"I imagine that Mama will not let me marry off the neighbours before her own daughters, but if I find a gentleman for you I will surely point him this way."

"Thank you." Charlotte laughed. "Where is your mother, I thought that she would be here overseeing your packing."

"Mama saw the proof of my marriage on my hand and Fitzwilliam's presence; she does not need more from me." Elizabeth looked up when Mary hugged her. "It is just as well; perhaps the knowledge that Fitzwilliam will not let the family starve will help her to improve."

"I hope so Lizzy." Jane came to add her arms to the hug. "I will do my best to remind her of that. Perhaps when you return she will be a new woman!" The girls laughed and wiped their eyes, it was not long before Elizabeth was summoned to her father's bookroom.

"Oh Lizzy, must you go already?" Mary sighed.

Elizabeth squeezed her hand. "Write to me, please. I want to hear everything that you are learning, and we will see you very soon."

"I fear that we will see no more of you until you depart. I will continue your packing." Jane hugged her once more. "Go on; make your peace with him."

"I will." She took one last look around the room and smiling at the small empty bed, walked away.

10 JULY 1809

My husband sleeps at last, and I still cannot. I have never slept at an inn before, and although this is certainly a very fine establishment, I do not feel comfortable. Fitzwilliam clearly does not either, and he did not even suggest that we love each other here. Perhaps our conversation at Matlock House discouraged him, but I certainly do not appreciate hearing our neighbour's cough, and I definitely would not wish for him to overhear the sounds of our marriage bed. Although as I write this, I hear the steady creaking of a bed on the other side of the hall, and I am no longer ignorant to the meaning.

Papa and I talked, and he apologized for many things. I enjoyed sitting in my old chair again, but already I felt that I was a visitor to that room. He asked me if I saw improvement in my sisters. I was sorry to say that I only noticed a change in Mary, who had been forced to give up her sermons. Kitty and Lydia are still influenced by Mama. She at last recovered from her fit of nerves in time to wave goodbye to us. She is perhaps a little less silly, now that her future is secured by our marriage, but maybe that is only what I hoped to see. It was very refreshing to be treated so kindly by her at the end. I never thought I would see the day that she thought I had done well with anything, but I could not forget a lifetime of disdain in one visit, and honestly, I have no desire for more than seeing her again in autumn.

Papa remarked on Fitzwilliam, how powerful he was. I admit that I laughed. I suppose that I see the side of him that nobody else ever will; he is passionate and playful, and shy, and so very dear to me. Papa is clearly trying to make amends with him, but I do not know if he realizes that the only way to make amends to Fitzwilliam is by doing well by his family. That is what will earn my husband's respect.

"Come to bed, Lizzy." Darcy murmured from his pillow. She looked up in surprise, and saw that he was deeply asleep. Elizabeth closed her journal and blew out the candle, then slipped into the bed beside him. "I love you." He whispered in his dream.

"I love you." She whispered back and stroked his hair. "My sleepy Will." "Kiss me."

Elizabeth smiled, seeing his lips pucker and touch the pillow. She leaned to his ear and kissed the lobe. He sighed and she moved close to give his lips her own to caress, then cuddled her giant of a husband to her, laying her cheek on his head as he burrowed into her embrace and rested his face on her shoulder. "Take me home." She whispered and felt him stir. Darcy lifted his head to look at her sleepily and gave her a slow soft kiss.

"That is where you are now." He smiled and kissed her again before cuddling back into her arms and hugging her. "Sleep Mrs. Darcy, sleep."

Chapter 32

"*E*lizabeth." Darcy whispered urgently. "Dearest please . . ." He slipped his arms around her sleeping form and moaned. "Oh Lizzy my love, you are so soft!" He rested his forehead on the back of her neck and pressed himself against her. It was the third day of their travels, it was long past midnight, the moon was new, and at last the inn was silent. The only sound was the hearty snoring coming from a room down the hall. Darcy had resisted the exceptional temptation that sleeping with Elizabeth presented over the last two nights, being sure to chastely kiss her and lie by her side; and eventually fall asleep, aching and miserable, determined not to give up their privacy by allowing anyone else to hear their lovemaking, only to awaken to find them entwined yet separated by far too much fabric. But Elizabeth had taken a bath when they arrived, and her hair was scented with rosewater, and her warm body was curled against his, and her nightdress lifted away so easily, and . . . and . . . and . . . "Lizzy, please!"

She blinked open her eyes to sense Darcy hovering above, feeling him more than seeing in the pitch black room. His erratic breaths washed over her. "Fitz . . ." Her mouth was engulfed by his, and she was surrounded by his body before another tick of the clock passed. Her fingers ran up into his hair and his kisses devoured her.

"Off. Lizzy this must come off!" He grabbed the night dress, lifting it up and over her head. He groaned, "I cannot see you!" His hands slid up over her form, and holding her breasts, he lowered his head, hungrily suckling one, then moving this head to lick and nip the other.

"Oh Will!" She moaned and he moved back up to her mouth.

"I cannot spend another night this way!" He sighed into her ear. "Please my love, please, if we are very slow and . . ."

"Yes." She tugged at his night shirt and he threw it off, and already forgetting his rules groaned loudly with the feel of their skin meeting once again. "shhhh!" She whispered urgently.

"I cannot help it. You feel so good!" Immediately he started kissing below her ear and she gasped, then moaned. "Shhhhhhh, dearest!"

"Ohhhhh, Will . . . Fitzwill . . ."

"Shhh!" He commanded then suckled her ear, tracing his tongue over the lobe and licking her throat. Elizabeth responded by rubbing her hands up his back and down over his bottom, slipping between them to fondle his manhood then when he begged her for more, she let go and their bed was soon creaking and groaning to the steady and desperate movement of their joined bodies. Their hands and mouths were in constant motion, their moans grew increasingly louder. Darcy lifted his chest up, still thrusting his hips vigorously, and pressed his forehead to hers. "Quiet!"

"Are you insane?" Elizabeth laughed.

Darcy laughed when the bed thumped against the wall. "Yes I am." He closed his eyes as Elizabeth's moans brought him to the edge. When she cried his name, he bellowed hers and collapsed onto her. They lay panting in each other's arms until Elizabeth gulped and began to giggle. Darcy moved off of her and wiped his dripping brow, then hers. He laughed and gathered her up to his chest to bury his face in her damp, sweet hair. Someone pounded on their door to be quiet and they both gasped and felt warm blushes of embarrassment spreading over each other. They lay silently clasped, barely breathing, and listening for the sounds of the footsteps and voices to go away. "We can never stay here again." He said positively.

"No, never." She agreed, and burrowed even closer into the absolute safety of his arms. "I am so embarrassed."

"So am I." He squeezed her tight, and then sighed as they relaxed their grips slightly. "We are such fools."

"But we are happy fools."

"That we are." He kissed her. "I love you."

"I love you."

"I could never be this way with any other person."

"Mortified?"

He smiled and kissed her gently, then closed his eyes. "Yes. Only with you."

She smiled, hearing his deep steady breathing had already begun, and rested her head over his heart. "Only with you could I be so embarrassed and feel so good."

TWELVE HOURS LATER, Darcy took Elizabeth's hand and lifted it to his mouth. "Here we are." The carriage turned onto the gravelled drive and he nodded to the man standing by the gate at the lodge. Feeling her stiffen he slipped his arms around her waist. "Please do not be afraid."

"I cannot help it." She looked away from the endless trees and back to him. "Suddenly this is real."

"What was it before?"

Elizabeth smiled to see the warmth in his eyes. "I suppose that it was a dreamlike state."

"So all of our experiences in London were so very pleasant that you would describe them as fantasy?" Now his lips twitched and she laughed.

"Well, perhaps certain experiences were fantastic." She caressed his cheek and his smile grew. "Please be patient with me."

"I am learning with you, dearest. I know nothing of the houses, not really, I barely know the estate. I rather like the idea that we are on similar footing. I like us learning together." Darcy kissed her then turned so that she was facing the window. He rested his chin on her shoulder. "Now, watch. When we come to the top of the rise, you will see our home." Elizabeth nodded and gripped the hands that rested over her waist. Darcy passed the time pressing light kisses to her cheek and throat, then hearing the changing stride of the horses, he stopped and hugged her. "Look upon your world, my love."

"Oh!" She gasped softly and leaned forward to gaze out of the open window, resting her hands on the frame. Darcy leaned with her, and pointed as they rolled along.

"There, do you see where the stone is blackened in the rear of the house? That is where the fire raged. I can see the new roof there, do you? They have made great progress." Elizabeth began to feel overwhelmed and looked back at him to see that his focus was sharp and his eyes were moving everywhere at once, assessing and examining the view below, and for the first time she saw her husband slip into his role as master. It took him a few moments before he realized that the view Elizabeth was watching was not the valley below, but his face. Darcy's expression became very shy. "Why do you stare at me so? Do you not care for Pemberley?"

"I do very much." She kissed him. "Could we stop the carriage and walk to the house?"

"Walk?" He started to laugh. "It is not a simple stroll through the meadow to arrive there, my love."

"But I can see paths cut through the trees!" She turned back around and pointed. "Look!"

"Yes, those are for hunting, not for . . . Elizabeth; a moment ago you were frightened!"

"I know, it is the strangest thing, but I saw you looking over your land, and you look so proud, and not at all intimidated, even though you just confessed to me how little you know. Well if you can find the courage to be master then I shall find the same to be mistress." She smiled at the passing scenery. "We shall do very well together."

Darcy's embrace grew tighter and he kissed her cheek. "My father would have loved you."

"As long as his son does, I will be fine." She turned back and kissed his chin. "Now, about this walk?"

"No, there will be plenty of time for walking, but I will not bring the mistress home on foot." He moved back and drew her along so that she was turned to face him. "And you promised to learn to ride, remember?"

"Oh yes, when shall you teach me?"

He chuckled as she came alive with excitement. "Is tomorrow too soon?"

"Will you have time? Since you have been away, I am sure that your steward will demand your attention."

"He will, but as far as I am concerned, we are on our honeymoon until Georgiana returns. I will work but only as necessary. This time is a precious gift for us, my love. I shall not waste it." He kissed her slowly and delighted in her response. "Oh, such plans I have for you!"

"Well what are they?" She demanded. "You have given me no inkling of these plans, even Georgiana knows more than I!"

"Jealous?" He chuckled.

"Fitzwilliam!"

"Hush." He kissed her. "Look, the staff is assembled to meet you."

"Oh no." She whispered and sunk back into his arms.

"Courage, my love. They are here for your service. You are the mistress of this home. They work for you now." He raised his brow at her. "The house is yours, Elizabeth, for as long as you live."

"You are not helping me, Mr. Darcy." She sighed and closed her eyes, summoning all of the advice her aunts had heaped upon her before leaving London. The carriage stopped and she made no attempt to move.

"Elizabeth." He said softly. "It is time."

The carriage door opened. Darcy let her go and stepped down, nodding to the staff then offering his hand, Elizabeth stepped out and met his slight smile with a brilliant one of her own. His eyes lit up and she laughed. "Well, one thing is certain, if I make a mistake, I shall not be dismissed from the position."

"I could lock you up in the attic." He suggested as she stepped down.

"Oh that would be far too inconvenient for you." She disagreed and took his arm.

"True, I do so enjoy admiring your figure." Darcy smiled and she laughed. "What would I do without your laugh as well?"

"Are you flirting with me?" Elizabeth tilted her head. "I like it."

"I am not very good at it."

"You are doing just fine." She whispered.

"Keep telling me that." He whispered back, then turning, performed the official introduction of the mistress to the staff. Mrs. Reynolds nodded her head and they all returned to their duties. Darcy then took Elizabeth's hand and led her forward. "Mrs. Darcy, this is Mrs. Reynolds, Pemberley's housekeeper. She has looked after me in one capacity or another since I was a boy of four."

Elizabeth smiled and was pleased to see her smile in return. "Mrs. Mercer told me how you cared for Mr. Darcy and Miss Darcy after their father's death, and Miss Darcy told me of her fondness for you. I am fortunate to have such a dedicated woman to teach me all that I need to know here."

"That was very kind of her, thank you madam." Mrs. Reynolds flushed with pride. "I will be glad to help you. The staff is very pleased indeed to see the master happy."

"Mrs. Reynolds, please." Darcy said quietly.

"Yes sir." Elizabeth saw how his expression changed, and wondered what was behind it. "Pemberley is not too unlike what Mrs. Mercer has told you of Darcy House, madam."

"Only vastly larger." She looked at the enormous house and again felt Darcy's grip on her hand.

"Shall we look it over?" He said softly, "Or would you like to rest?"

"I believe a walk would feel good after so many hours confined in the carriage."

"Then let us change out of these things and I will gladly begin your education." He kissed her hand. "Mrs. Reynolds, I am disappointed that Mr. Nichols is not present. Is there a problem on the estate?"

"No sir, he asked me to inform you that he would leave you alone today, but would like a meeting tomorrow afternoon. He assumed that you would not be interested in business upon arriving with Mrs. Darcy." She smiled as his eyes crinkled.

"He is correct." He nodded and she left them alone in front of the house. Darcy turned and took both of her hands in his. "That was not so bad, was it?"

"Why did you stop Mrs. Reynolds? Was I wrong to speak of Mrs. Mercer to her?"

"No, not at all." He sighed. "Mrs. Reynolds fancies herself as a bit of a mother to me and Georgiana, and she is rather effusive in her praise when she speaks of us. We often have visitors who apply to see the house and grounds, and of course she leads the tours. Some acquaintances of mine did just that last year when I was in London, and when I saw them, well, they were quite amused with how wonderful she described me to be. It was very embarrassing."

"It is clearly not without reason." Elizabeth reached up to caress his cheek. "I think that I will have to hear this speech of Mrs. Reynolds' myself."

"Do not encourage her, Elizabeth." He said seriously. She just smiled and stood on her toes to kiss him, and he sighed. "Very well then, do not tell me about it."

"Agreed." She looped her hand onto his arm and looked towards the house. "I am ready." She squared her shoulders and said determinedly. "Show me our home."

13 JULY 1809

My dearest Elizabeth sleeps now. She is a wonder. We arrived and the moment we had changed clothes, she had me by the hand and demanded her tour. I do not believe I have ever fielded so many questions, laughed so hard, or run so quickly in my life. And I know that I have never been kissed and embraced so often. She was overwhelmed and awed, it was clear, but she did not give in to intimidation by all that she now has. My wife expressed delight, insisted that not one thing be changed, and amazed me with her ability to bring smiles to the faces of every staff member we encountered. I know already that she will be a beloved mistress, but I also know enough of her that she will run her household with efficiency and fairness. Any maid who thinks that she can shirk her duty under the sharp eyes of my young wife will be in for a surprise, I think.

My happiest moment in a day full of them was when we retired last night. Darcy House is a beautiful and important part of our lives, but Pemberley is home, and when I took her into the master's chambers and loved her, I at last felt that Pemberley was mine. Before I felt that I was merely the caretaker for my absent father. The two of us in that most private of rooms, lost in our love and embrace established absolutely that we are the master and mistress, and I pray that it shall remain that way for us, together, until we are very, very old.

When my love wakes, I will begin my plans. I hope that she is pleased; I have spent so many hours imagining her here with no hope of it ever coming to fruition. Today many dreams will be fulfilled.

Elizabeth's lip caught in her teeth, and she took the ribbon from where he kept it in the front cover and placed it back over the page she had just read. It had become a signal between them that she had been reading his journal. Hearing him clearly dismissing his valet, she dashed out of their private sitting room and back to her chambers to finish dressing. Darcy strode into the master's chambers then into the sitting room. Immediately he noticed that the ribbon had moved and a smile spread across his face. He stepped up to the writing desk, fingered the lover's knot then picked up her journal, and casually paged to the last entry.

13 July 1809
Yesterday we arrived and Fitzwilliam introduced me to our home. To say it is breathtaking would be an insult. Words cannot describe it. When I first entered though, the atmosphere was so still, I can hardly express it but to say that the very house seemed to remain in mourning. The splendour in every direction was exceptional, but the veil of sadness was almost smothering. I understand so much of Fitzwilliam now. His personality is stamped throughout the home, even if he has not changed a single thing since his father's death. It is he who preserved it all, which tells me that everything around us is important to him. I will not touch the physical reminders of his family; however, I am determined to change the heartbeat of this place. We explored so much of the house, until it grew far too dark to see more, and I know there are scores of rooms to go. The stories behind the decoration will fill our conversation for a lifetime, I think. What I enjoyed most of all was seeing his face as he told me his memories, they were not sad or painful, and when they became so, I would stop him from dwelling on his losses and instead ask that he tell me how his parents enjoyed this home. I want him to remember his life with pleasure. I want

to make sure that my husband is happy with his past. I firmly believe that will give us the strength to face our future, whatever comes.

I am frightened beyond expression to fail him, but every time I feel myself slipping into despair, I know that all I need to do is look into his eyes. He loves me, and he needs me, just as I do him.

"Oh Elizabeth." Darcy whispered. "When did you become so strong?" He felt her hands sliding around his waist and smiled to feel her head pressing against his back. "You caught me."

"I do not see a thing; your back is far too broad."

"I thought that you liked that." He set down the book and turned around in her embrace to wrap her up in his. "I seem to recall some poetry about the width of my shoulders as well." He chuckled and smiled at her sparkling eyes. "Not quite worthy of publication, but satisfying nonetheless."

"Well if you would like me to work harder on my poetry of your form and send it to the *Times* to be published . . .

"No, no." He laughed.

"Ode to a Lover." Elizabeth grinned. "My lover is . . ."

"Shhh!" Darcy kissed her smile to silence her, and they remained pleasantly engaged for several minutes. "Mmm. Now, my dear, are you prepared for your first adventure?"

"I think so." Elizabeth laughed. "Am I dressed for it?"

He stepped back and looked her over. "It will do. However I suggest riding boots."

"Oh!" She was gone in a flash and returned ten minutes later in a new dress and boots. "There! What do you think?"

"I am flabbergasted with your speed!" Taking her hand he led her down the stairs to the breakfast room, and after enjoying the meal they walked first to the kitchens to inspect the repairs, then examined the rooms that were scrubbed free of smoke, and finally outside to stroll towards the stables.

Elizabeth looked down at their clasped hands and back up to his face. The slight smile was there, but again she could tell that he was lost in thoughts of the estate. "The kitchen is unlike one that I have ever seen before."

Torn from his reverie he looked to her. "It is the newest and most efficient design, I understand. I wonder what our cook thinks of it."

"From what I could see she is delighted. Did you not notice her practically caressing her new things?" She laughed. "I can see her bragging of them to any who would listen."

"I missed that. I suppose that I was more concerned with the structural changes." Darcy smiled. "I am not always so obtuse."

"I suppose I will find that out."

"Hmm. I was just thinking that we need a house steward and a new butler. Both of the positions became available when one man died and the other retired this spring, but I have not been home to interview candidates."

"Would you promote from within? That might encourage a better working environment; the men would be already loyal to Pemberley."

"I thought that as well. I will speak to; we will speak to Mrs. Reynolds and Mr. Nichols about it." He kissed her hand and then swung it back and forth as they walked. "Here we are." They entered the stables and he walked up to a stall holding his black stallion. "This is Onyx." He rubbed the horse's nose and he nickered in recognition of his master. "He is a nervous beast, but fast as the wind." Darcy offered him a carrot and rubbed his forelock before moving along. "This is my favourite gelding, Richard."

Elizabeth giggled. "First a pearl, and now a horse? What is the story this time?"

He laughed softly as he opened the stall and a groom ran up to lead the animal out to be saddled. "When he was a foal Richard stood a little too close and received a rather painful kick in a treasured area of a man's anatomy." Elizabeth blushed but her gaze fell on Darcy's breeches. He cleared his throat and took her hand to walk out to the paddock. "When the horse was castrated, I naturally thought of my cousin."

"Fitzwilliam!" She gasped then covered her mouth with her hand and giggled. "You have a very wicked sense of humour!"

He smiled a little but his eyes were twinkling, then leaning forward he whispered in her ear, "That is a story I never could have told you only a few weeks ago."

"Are there more?"

Darcy shrugged. "I am not given to bawdiness."

"No, but I love to hear you laugh." She smiled at him and he looked down, then led her to the mounting block. "Let us see if I remember what to do." She put her foot in the stirrup, and grabbing a bit of mane, bounced for a moment before pulling herself up.

"Well done!" He said happily. "I thought you were a novice."

"I just prefer walking. I really did fall off twice, but I did have some lessons between the accidents. Besides, our riding horse is very old and tired, and sometimes I felt I was moving faster on foot than Jane was on Nellie." She settled into place. Darcy swung up behind her and gathered the reins. He nodded to the boy who was holding the horse's head and they began to move off and out the gate. "I did not realize that Jane rode."

"Oh yes, but of course with one old horse, that was not a favourite past time."

"She did not tell Harwick, did she? He would have liked to have known that. It may have helped to have some mutual interest."

"I cannot imagine why, unless . . . maybe she was actually trying to give him reasons to reject her?"

"I do not think that he needed much help."

"Fitzwilliam!" Her eyes flashed and he raised his brow and looked at her with his head tilted. "Well . . ." Darcy kissed her and she sighed. "Why are we talking about my sister?"

"Good question." He smiled and hugged her. "I have thought so much of riding together like this." Leaning down to her ear he whispered, "It has been the subject of dreams."

"How so?"

He kicked the horse and they picked up speed, until they were galloping rapidly across the field. They moved together with the horse's gait, and Elizabeth leaned back against him as he kept one arm firmly around her waist while she held onto his with both arms. He pressed his mouth to her ear. "Does this remind you of anything, my love?" Their eyes met as they continued to rise and fall in harmony. "Your letter made me imagine so many things."

"I did not mean to put ideas in your head, truly."

"I know." Darcy kissed her. "I know." He slowed and stopped the horse and put the reins in her hands. "Now, you take control, show me what you remember."

"It is not a great deal. I observed more than I actually rode." She said nervously. Darcy smiled and she drew a deep breath, then slowly urged Richard forward. "Where should we go?"

"Do you see that ridge over there?" He pointed ahead. "Just follow the trace here in the pasture; it will lead you right up." Elizabeth nodded and putting her lip between her teeth, focussed completely on her task. Darcy placed both hands lightly on her waist and gazed from her hands, to the path, to her determined eyes. He did not break her concentration, and only a few times did he involuntarily reach for the reins to resume control, but managed to stop before he wrested them from her. He limited himself to speaking softly and giving her directions to improve her skills. "Perhaps we should have given you your own horse."

"I like this better."

"I do, too." He squeezed her and kissed her cheek. "I do have a new pony for you, just waiting for a name."

"Not Richard."

He chuckled. "No, not Richard."

They gained the top of the ridge and Elizabeth hesitated. "Where do I go now?"

"Nowhere, we have arrived." Jumping down he led the horse to a tree and tied him off, then held up his arms to help her to slide down. When she reached the ground they naturally paused to kiss, then he took her hand. "Come Mrs. Darcy." They walked to the edge of the precipice and he stood behind her, slipping his arms around her waist and kissing her cheek. "What do you see?"

"Oh . . . Fitzwilliam, this is the landscape in your study!" She looked up to his smiling face. "This is where the artist sat?"

"Yes. It is my favourite view. You see the house, and the lake, and even the gardens, there, just around the side of the house."

"It is beautiful."

He held her tighter and whispered. "I had my last conversation with my father here. One of the very last things he said was to remind me that I should marry with my heart. I regret that I forgot that advice until the day we met in the park."

"Stop, Will. Tell me why this is your favourite view." Elizabeth looked around and pulled his hand so they settled down in the grass. Darcy removed his coat and she curled against his chest. "How long have you come up here?"

"Father brought me here for as long as I can remember, and his father brought him." He kissed her smile and rested his head on her hair. "I remember riding here with him and Mother."

"What was she like? I know that Georgiana resembles her in looks, does her personality match as well?"

"Yes, it does, and every so often she will look at me and I have to remember that it is my young sister."

"Is this when she is angry?" Elizabeth laughed.

"No." He chuckled. "No, it is when she is playing." He sighed and looked around them and closed his eyes. "I love you."

"I love you." She caressed over his cheek then holding his jaw kissed him.

Darcy sighed and his eyes reopened. "We need a new memory for this spot." He turned and pressed her down into the grass and stretched out beside her, propping himself onto his elbow. Slowly he traced his fingers down her throat then kissed her tenderly.

"What . . . what do you have in mind?" She said nervously.

"I know what I would like, very much." His gentle fingers continued tracing over her shoulders and he watched them travel slowly lower to draw circles around and around her breast.

"In the open? Fitzwilliam, anyone could come along and hear or . . . or see us!"

Darcy lifted his eyes from her bosom to see her looking so shy, "No one will see."

"How do you know?"

"Look around you dearest, we are surrounded by trees." His hand moved over her gown to slide under the skirt and up her leg, to stroke her thighs. "I have thought of loving you here for so very long. I thought of you kissing me here, and you have. Please kiss me again."

Elizabeth stared up into the sweet blue of his eyes, and read the vulnerability within. He was asking her for reassurance, in this very special place. She sat up to take his shoulders and lay him down on the ground. She smiled at his surprise and leaning over him, gently traced her tongue over his parted lips, then nipped at them lightly. "Like this?"

He moaned, "Oh yes."

"I want to kiss you the way that you kiss me."

"Elizabeth." He swallowed and closed his eyes. "What does that mean?" Again he felt her tongue delicately tasting his lips then slipping inside of his mouth to explore and suckle him. Darcy moaned and his arms rose up to embrace her while Elizabeth's hands held his face and she put all of her feelings into the endless strokes over his lips. She lost herself in her wish to show how deeply she loved him and he lay still, drinking in the sensation and moving far beyond physical desire to become absolutely enveloped in the emotion of her gift. When her sensual soft kisses slowed, and she began to gently kiss the corners of his mouth, then his eyes, he looked up to see her smiling at him. He brushed back the hair that hung loose around her shoulders, dislodged by his caressing hands, then touched his thumb to her lips. They stayed embraced and looking at each other as their hearts beat in tandem until wordlessly, Darcy drew her face back to his, and kissed her, then rolled so that now he hovered above, and proceeded to kiss her exactly as she had done for him, leaving her in no doubt at all of his feelings. When at last he moved away and kissed her nose, he looked down to see her sparkling beautiful eyes smiling at him. He returned the smile and touched her reddened mouth.

Elizabeth brushed his hair back from his forehead. "Now tell me, have we made a memory worthy of this place?"

"I will never forget it." He caressed her cheek with the back of his hand then settling against a tree, drew her up to rest in his arms where they sat silently embraced and looking out over their home. Their quiet reflection was at last interrupted when a grouping of geese announced their arrival and they looked up to watch them fly overhead then on over the house before circling back to land in the lake. Darcy hugged her and she kissed his chin. He looked down and smiled. "What shall we do next?"

"We should have packed a picnic, then we could stay here all day."

"I thought that you would want to be wandering the paths and exploring the park."

"Oh, we have forever for that." She sighed and rested back on his waistcoat. "I am just as happy appreciating the view with you. I never had the opportunity to show you, but there is a place near Longbourn called Oakham Mount, where I would go to sit and contemplate . . . everything. I suspect that is what you do here?"

"Yes." He hugged her. "I am so happy that you understand my need to just be quiet out here. Now I will no longer do it alone. I think that was one thing that spoke to me when I first spied you in the park. I remember you looking around and embracing the trees. I think then was when I first knew how much you would love Pemberley."

"I will." She smiled at the view. "The park is ten miles around?"

"Yes, but the estate covers a great deal more. Many, many acres have been purchased and we have a great many tenants for you to meet. I will come with you, of course."

"Do you have time?" She asked seriously.

He chuckled. "I would certainly not send you alone. I consider tenant relations part of my position. I meet with Mr. Repair, the reverend who has the living here, regularly to discuss their welfare."

"Papa just paid his taxes and grumbled about it." She sighed. "We were not poor, but there never seemed to be much left at the end of the year. Between Mama overspending on clothes and Papa overspending on his books and . . ." She grew quiet then said softly. "I am very aware of how important it is to be careful."

Darcy embraced her and asked quietly, "Did you learn this from observing your parents or the Gardiners?"

She smiled back at him. "Both, the good and the bad examples. I still have the twenty pounds I won last year at the Derby." She gasped and raised her hand to her mouth. "Oh! That is yours now! I should have given it to you!"

Darcy laughed softly. "I do not think that is necessary, my love."

"But I brought so little . . ."

"You brought everything. Now I do not want to hear another word about that." He hugged her tighter, and looked towards the stables. "I see Mr. Nichols has returned."

"How can you tell? They are so far away."

"He always has his two assistants with him, so three riders in the stables, it must be him." He smiled at her. "He is probably there to meet with me."

"Shall we return? There must be so much to talk about; the fire repairs alone should be addressed."

Darcy looked at her for a long moment then nodded. "Yes, duty calls." They rose to their feet and brushed each other off. Elizabeth tried to fix her hair. "You should have worn a bonnet."

"I do not see your hat." She said pointedly.

"It is too hot." He bent to pick up his coat and sighed when he put it back on. "Much too hot." An idea occurred to him and he tilted his head. "Have you ever walked in the moonlight?"

"Only when leaving an evening somewhere. What do you have in mind?" She laughed as he nodded thoughtfully. "Fitzwilliam!"

He shrugged. "You will see." Giving her a leg up, he settled her back onto the horse and swung up behind her. "Now, you are in charge, show me what you know."

"You are a brave man." She nudged Richard backwards then down the path towards home. By the time they arrived, Darcy had taught her how to urge the horse to gallop, and although his hands were hovering ready to take over, and commands were poised to fall from his lips, he bit back his desire to control, and let Elizabeth discover her weaknesses. They walked slowly into the paddock. He leaned around to see her smiling broadly, and was glad to have let her alone.

"What do you think, dearest? Would you like to learn on your own pony next time?"

"I . . . I think so." She tilted her head up and laughed. "I have all the confidence in the world with you sitting behind me."

Darcy chuckled and jumped down. He nodded to a waiting groom, who came to hold the bridle, then held out his arms for her. "I think that you can have just as much confidence if I were riding beside you, Elizabeth."

"How did I do? Really?"

"Satisfactory." He smiled when her eyes narrowed. "You asked."

"I know." She sighed and watched Richard amble away. "I need to practice. Perhaps I can do that while you are out with Mr. Nichols." Darcy's brow creased and she put her hands on her hips. "What are you thinking?"

"Nothing."

"Fitzwilliam, I was not proposing a journey to London, can I not ride around the stables until I know what I am doing? I am sure the boys here will look after me."

Darcy looked up to see several stable hands, all at or very near to Elizabeth's age, looking their way. He spotted the stable master, and strode over to him to have a word before returning. "Mr. Grassel will be glad to supervise you in my absence. However, you are not to ride out alone."

"I had no intention of doing so. I suppose that you wish to assert your husbandly rights and prevent me from doing anything that does not please you, including speaking to the grooms?" She waved over to the young men who were being addressed by Mr. Grassel. "I can take care of myself."

"Lizzy." Darcy said quietly. The name instantly claimed her attention. "I trust my staff with my sister, why would I not trust them with you? As for riding alone, I know how dangerous horses can be for an experienced rider, and frankly if anything ever happens to you, particularly if I could have prevented it, I would never recover." His face had no expression, but his eyes searched hers to see if she understood.

Elizabeth's anger disappeared and she returned to him and took his hand. "Forgive me." He squeezed and nodded, and they began walking towards the house. "I am unused to being protected."

"I am very sorry to learn that, however, it is something that you will have to become accustomed to, Elizabeth. I take your well-being very seriously." His lips were pressed together and he gripped her hand hard. "Very seriously."

"Then I will not jump to conclusions that you are thinking me unworthy or foolish."

"I never would think that in any case."

"I have to grow used to that, as well." She smiled a little. "I apologize."

"You are a challenge." He relaxed and smiled back. "I wonder if you could have caught any man besides me." Elizabeth began to laugh. "Think about it, dearest. You are defensive and ready to take on the man who loves you more than his own life for the tiniest hint of a slight, you are very quick-witted which would frankly frighten most men to feel inadequate, you are . . .

"So if I am so awful, what did I do to deserve you? Please note that I do not mention how proud you must be to think that only you could appreciate me."

Darcy chuckled. "You are intensely loyal, you challenge me, you are deeply vulnerable, exceptionally kind, and so very beautiful." He kissed her hand and watched her blush, "and I love how you make me feel. I am the one who is undeserving."

"Keep speaking like that and I will begin to sound like Mrs. Reynolds in my unending praise of you." She peeked up at him to see his eyes twinkling. "I do not think you would mind it coming from me."

"Not at all. I would cherish it." He closed his eyes when she leaned into him and he slipped his arm around her waist.

Arriving at last inside, Darcy spotted Mr. Nichols working at a table in his study. He turned to Elizabeth and held her hands. "This should not take too long, I was here only a few weeks ago, not too much should have happened."

"I doubt that I would have any trouble occupying myself, but I prefer to continue my tour with your escort alone." Darcy looked down at their hands and she saw him biting his lip. "Fitzwilliam, do you know that I do not think any other woman but I could appreciate you? Thank goodness you did not give in to one of those heiresses, can you imagine any of them lying in the grass with you? Next time I promise not to be so shy." She laughed to see his hopeful smile. "Now go, have your meeting."

"Where will I find you?"

She looked around the vast hallway and laughed. "How on earth should I know?"

The story continues in Volume 2 of the Memory Series, Trials to Bear

Books by Linda Wells:
Chance Encounters

Fate and Consequences

Perfect Fit

Memory

Volume 1: Lasting Impressions
Volume 2: Trials to Bear
Volume 3: How Far We Have Come

Made in the USA
Lexington, KY
13 August 2010